TWELVE
RED HERRINGS
&
FIRST
AMONG
EQUALS

ALSO BY JEFFREY ARCHER

NOVELS

Not a Penny More, Not a Penny Less
Shall We Tell the President?
Kane and Abel
The Prodigal Daughter
A Matter of Honour
As the Crow Flies
Honour Among Thieves
The Fourth Estate
The Eleventh Commandment
Sons of Fortune

SHORT STORIES

A Quiver Full of Arrows
A Twist in the Tale
The Collected Short Stories
To Cut a Long Story Short

PLAYS

Beyond Reasonable Doubt
Exclusive
The Accused

PRISON DIARIES

Volume One – Belmarsh: Hell
Volume Two – Wayland: Purgatory
Volume Three – North Sea Camp: Heaven

Jeffrey Archer is a master storyteller, the author of eleven novels which have all been worldwide bestsellers. *Not a Penny More, Not a Penny Less* was his first book, and it achieved instant success. Next came the tense and terrifying thriller *Shall We Tell the President?*, followed by his triumphant bestseller *Kane and Abel*. His first collection of short stories, *A Quiver Full of Arrows*, came next, and then *The Prodigal Daughter*, the superb sequel to *Kane and Abel*. This was followed by *First Among Equals*, considered by the *Scotsman* to be the finest novel about parliament since Trollope, the thrilling chase story *A Matter of Honour*, his second collection of stories, *A Twist in the Tale*, and the novels *As the Crow Flies* and *Honour Among Thieves*. *Twelve Red Herrings*, his third collection of stories, was followed by the novels *The Fourth Estate* and *The Eleventh Commandment*. A collected edition of his short stories was published in 1997, followed by another collection, *To Cut a Long Story Short*. His latest novel, *Sons of Fortune*, was published by Macmillan in 2002.

Jeffrey Archer was born in 1940 and educated at Wellington School, Somerset, and Brasenose College, Oxford. He represented Great Britain in the 100 metres in the early sixties, and entered the House of Commons when he won the by-election at Louth in 1969. He wrote his first novel, *Not a Penny More, Not a Penny Less*, in 1974. From September 1985 to October 1986 he was Deputy Chairman of the Conservative Party, and he was created a Life Peer in the Queen's Birthday Honours of 1992. In 2001 he was sentenced to four years in prison and was released in July 2003. He is married with two children.

JEFFREY ARCHER

TWELVE RED HERRINGS

&

FIRST AMONG EQUALS

PAN BOOKS

Twelve Red Herrings first published 1994 by HarperCollins Publishers.
First published by Pan Books 2004
First Among Equals first published 1984 by Hodder and Stroughton Publishers Ltd.
First published by Pan Books 2003

This omnibus edition published 2004 by Pan Books
an imprint of Pan Macmillan Ltd
Pan Macmillan, 20 New Wharf Road, London N1 9RR
Basingstoke and Oxford
Associated companies throughout the world
www.panmacmillan.com

ISBN 0 330 43927 8

Printed and bound in Great Britain by
Mackays of Chatham plc, Chatham, Kent

TWELVE
RED HERRINGS

To Chris, Carol . . . and Alyson

Contents

* The stories indicated with an asterisk are based on
known incidents (some of them embellished with
considerable licence). The others are the product of
my own imagination.

J.A.
July 1994

TRIAL AND ERROR

It's HARD TO KNOW EXACTLY WHERE TO begin. But first, let me explain why I'm in jail.

The trial had lasted for eighteen days, and from the moment the judge had entered the courtroom the public benches had been filled to overflowing. The jury at Leeds Crown Court had been out for almost two days, and rumour had it that they were hopelessly divided. On the barristers' bench there was talk of hung juries and retrials, as it had been more than eight hours since Mr Justice Cartwright had told the foreman of the jury that their verdict need no longer be unanimous: a majority of ten to two would be acceptable.

Suddenly there was a buzz in the corridors, and the members of the jury filed quietly into their places. Press and public alike began to stampede back into court. All eyes were on the foreman of the jury, a fat, jolly-looking little man dressed in a double-breasted suit, striped shirt and a colourful bow tie, striving to appear solemn. He seemed the sort of fellow with whom, in normal circumstances, I would have enjoyed a pint at the local. But these were not normal circumstances.

As I climbed back up the steps into the dock, my eyes

3

settled on a pretty blonde who had been seated in the gallery every day of the trial. I wondered if she attended all the sensational murder trials, or if she was just fascinated by this one. She showed absolutely no interest in me, and like everyone else was concentrating her full attention on the foreman of the jury.

The clerk of the court, dressed in a wig and a long black gown, rose and read out from a card the words I suspect he knew by heart.

'Will the foreman of the jury please stand.'

The jolly little fat man rose slowly from his place.

'Please answer my next question yes or no. Members of the jury, have you reached a verdict on which at least ten of you are agreed?'

'Yes, we have.'

'Members of the jury, do you find the prisoner at the bar guilty or not guilty as charged?'

There was total silence in the courtroom.

My eyes were fixed on the foreman with the colourful bow tie. He cleared his throat and said, '. . .

I first met Jeremy Alexander in 1978, at a CBI training seminar in Bristol. Fifty-six British companies who were looking for ways to expand into Europe had come together for a briefing on Community Law. At the time that I signed up for the seminar Cooper's, the company of which I was chairman, ran 127 vehicles of varying weights and sizes, and was fast becoming one of the largest private road haulage companies in Britain.

4

TRIAL AND ERROR

My father had founded the firm in 1931, starting out
with three vehicles – two of them pulled by horses –
and an overdraft limit of ten pounds at his local Martins
bank. By the time we became 'Cooper & Son' in 1967
the company had seventeen vehicles with four wheels
or more, and delivered goods all over the north of England. But the old man still resolutely refused to exceed
his ten-pound overdraft limit.

I once expressed the view, during a downturn in the
market, that we should be looking further afield in search
of new business – perhaps even as far as the Continent.
But my father wouldn't hear of it. 'Not a risk worth
taking,' he declared. He distrusted anyone born south
of the Humber, let alone those who lived on the other
side of the Channel. 'If God put a strip of water between
us, he must have had good reasons for doing so,' were
his final words on the subject. I would have laughed, if
I hadn't realised he meant it.

When he retired in 1977 – reluctantly, at the age of
seventy – I took over as chairman, and began to set in
motion some ideas I'd been working on for the past
decade, though I knew my father didn't approve of them.
Europe was only the beginning of my plans for the company's expansion: within five years I wanted to go public.
By then, I realised, we would require an overdraft facility
of at least a million pounds, and would therefore have to
move our account to a bank which recognised that the
world stretched beyond the county boundaries of Yorkshire.

It was around this time that I heard about the CBI
seminar at Bristol, and applied for a place.

The seminar began on the Friday, with an opening address from the Head of the European Directorate of the CBI. After that the delegates split into eight small working groups, each chaired by an expert on Community Law. My group was headed by Jeremy Alexander. I admired him from the moment he started speaking – in fact, it wouldn't be an exaggeration to say that I was overawed. He was totally self-assured, and as I was to learn, he could effortlessly present a convincing argument on any subject, from the superiority of the Code Napoléon to the inferiority of the English middle-order batting.

He lectured us for an hour on the fundamental differences in practice and procedure between the member states of the Community, then answered all our questions on Commercial and Company Law, even finding time to explain the significance of the Uruguay Round. Like me, the other members of our group never stopped taking notes.

We broke up for lunch a few minutes before one, and I managed to grab a place next to Jeremy. I was already beginning to think that he might be the ideal person to advise me on how to go about achieving my European ambitions.

Listening to him talk about his career over a meal of stargazy pie with red peppers, I kept thinking that, although we were about the same age, we couldn't have come from more different backgrounds. Jeremy's father, a banker by profession, had escaped from Eastern Europe only days before the outbreak of the Second World War.

He had settled in England, anglicised his name, and sent his son to Westminster. From there Jeremy had gone on to King's College, London, where he read Law, graduating with first-class honours.

My own father was a self-made man from the Yorkshire Dales who had insisted I leave school the moment I passed my O levels. 'I'll teach you more about the real world in a month than you'd learn from any of those university types in a lifetime,' he used to say. I accepted this philosophy without question, and left school a few weeks after my sixteenth birthday. The next morning I joined Cooper's as an apprentice, and spent my first three years at the depot under the watchful eye of Buster Jackson, the works manager, who taught me how to take the company's vehicles apart and, more importantly, how to put them back together again.

After graduating from the workshop, I spent two years in the invoicing department, learning how to calculate charges and collect bad debts. A few weeks after my twenty-first birthday I passed the test for my heavy goods vehicles licence, and for the next three years I zig-zagged across the north of England, delivering everything from poultry to pineapples to our far-flung customers. Jeremy spent the same period reading for a master's degree in Napoleonic Law at the Sorbonne.

When Buster Jackson retired I was moved back to the depot in Leeds to take over as works manager. Jeremy was in Hamburg, writing a doctoral thesis on international trade barriers. By the time he had finally left the world of academia and taken up his first real job, as a partner with a large firm of commercial solicitors in the City, I had been earning a working wage for eight years.

Although I was impressed by Jeremy at the seminar, I sensed, behind that surface affability, a powerful combination of ambition and intellectual snobbery that my father would have mistrusted. I felt he'd only agreed to give the lecture on the off-chance that, at some time in the future, we might be responsible for spreading some butter on his bread. I now realise that, even at our first meeting, he suspected that in my case it might be honey.

It didn't help my opinion of the man that he had a couple of inches on me in height, and a couple less around the waist. Not to mention the fact that the most attractive woman on the course that weekend ended up in his bed on the Saturday night.

We met up on the Sunday morning to play squash, when he ran me ragged, without even appearing to raise a sweat. 'We must get together again,' he said as we walked to the showers.' 'If you're really thinking of expanding into Europe, you might find I'm able to help.'

My father had taught me never to make the mistake of imagining that your friends and your colleagues were necessarily the same animals (he often cited the Cabinet as an example). So, although I didn't like him, I made sure that when I left Bristol at the end of the conference I was in possession of Jeremy's numerous telephone and telex numbers.

I drove back to Leeds on the Sunday evening, and when I reached home I ran upstairs and sat on the end of the bed regaling my sleepy wife with an account of why it had turned out to be such a worthwhile weekend.

Rosemary was my second wife. My first, Helen, had been at Leeds High School for Girls at the same time that I had attended the nearby grammar school. The two schools shared a gymnasium, and I fell in love with her at the age of thirteen, while watching her play netball. After that I would find any excuse to hang around the gym, hoping to catch a glimpse of her blue knickers as she leapt to send the ball unerringly into the net. As the schools took part in various joint activities, I began to take an active interest in theatrical productions, even though I couldn't act. I attended joint debates, and never opened my mouth. I enlisted in the combined schools orchestra and ended up playing the triangle. After I had left school and gone to work at the depot, I continued to see Helen, who was studying for her A levels. Despite my passion for her, we didn't make love until we were both eighteen, and even then I wasn't certain that we had consummated anything. Six weeks later she told me, in a flood of tears, that she was pregnant. Against the wishes of her parents, who had hoped that she would go on to university, a hasty wedding was arranged, but as I never wanted to look at another girl for the rest of my life, I was secretly delighted by the outcome of our youthful indiscretion.

Helen died on the night of 14 September 1964, giving birth to our son, Tom, who himself only survived a week. I thought I would never get over it, and I'm not sure I ever have. After her death I didn't so much as glance at another woman for years, putting all my energy into the company.

Following the funeral of my wife and son, my father, not a soft or sentimental man – you won't find many of those in Yorkshire – revealed a gentle side to his character that I had never seen before. He would often phone me in the evening to see how I was getting on, and insisted that I regularly joined him in the directors' box at Elland Road to watch Leeds United on Saturday afternoons. I began to understand, for the first time, why my mother still adored him after more than twenty years of marriage.

I met Rosemary about four years later at a ball given to launch the Leeds Music Festival. Not a natural habitat for me, but as Cooper's had taken a full-page advertisement in the programme, and Brigadier Kershaw, the High Sheriff of the county and Chairman of the Ball Committee, had invited us to join him as his guests, I had no choice but to dress up in my seldom-worn dinner jacket and accompany my parents to the ball.

I was placed on Table 17, next to a Miss Kershaw, who turned out to be the High Sheriff's daughter. She was elegantly dressed in a strapless blue gown that emphasised her comely figure, and had a mop of red hair and a smile that made me feel we had been friends for years. She told me over something described on the menu as 'avocado with dill' that she had just finished reading English at Durham University, and wasn't quite sure what she was going to do with her life.

'I don't want to be a teacher,' she said. 'And I'm

certainly not cut out to be a secretary.' We chatted through the second and third courses, ignoring the people seated on either side of us. After coffee she dragged me onto the dance floor, where she continued to explain the problems of contemplating any form of work while her diary was so packed with social engagements.

I felt rather flattered that the High Sheriff's daughter should show the slightest interest in me, and to be honest I didn't take it seriously when at the end of the evening, she whispered in my ear, 'Let's keep in touch.'

But a couple of days later she rang and invited me to join her and her parents for lunch that Sunday at their house in the country, 'And then perhaps we could play a little tennis afterwards. You do play tennis, I suppose?'

I drove over to Church Fenton on Sunday, and found that the Kershaws' residence was exactly what I would have expected – large and decaying, which, come to think of it, wasn't a bad description of Rosemary's father as well. But he seemed a nice enough chap. Her mother, however, wasn't quite so easy to please. She originated from somewhere in Hampshire, and was unable to mask her feeling that, although I might be good for the occasional charitable donation, I was not quite the sort of person with whom she expected to be sharing her Sunday lunch. Rosemary ignored the odd barbed comment from her, and continued to chat to me about my work.

As it rained all afternoon we never got round to playing tennis, so Rosemary used the time to seduce me in the little pavilion behind the court. At first I was nervous about making love to the High Sheriff's daughter, but I soon got used to the idea. However, as the weeks passed, I began to wonder if I was anything more to her than a 'lorry driver fantasy'. Until, that is, she started to talk about marriage. Mrs Kershaw was unable to hide her disgust at the very idea of someone like me becoming her son-in-law, but her opinion turned out to be irrelevant, as Rosemary remained implacable on the subject. We were married eighteen months later.

Over two hundred guests attended the rather grand county wedding in the parish church of St Mary's. But I confess that when I turned to watch Rosemary progressing up the aisle, my only thoughts were of my first wedding ceremony.

For a couple of years Rosemary made every effort to be a good wife. She took an interest in the company, learned the names of all the employees, even became friendly with the wives of some of the senior executives. But, as I worked all the hours God sent, I fear I may not always have given her as much attention as she needed. You see, Rosemary yearned for a life that was made up of regular visits to the Grand Theatre for Opera North, followed by dinner parties with her county friends that would run into the early hours, while I preferred to work at weekends, and to be tucked up in bed before eleven most nights. For Rosemary I wasn't turning out to be the husband in the title of the Oscar Wilde play she had recently taken me to – and it didn't help that I had fallen asleep during the second act.

After four years without producing any offspring — not that Rosemary wasn't very energetic in bed — we began to drift our separate ways. If she started having affairs (and I certainly did, when I could find the time), she was discreet about them. And then she met Jeremy Alexander.

It must have been about six weeks after the seminar in Bristol that I had occasion to phone Jeremy and seek his advice. I wanted to close a deal with a French cheese company to transport its wares to British supermarkets. The previous year I had made a large loss on a similar enterprise with a German beer company, and I couldn't afford to make the same mistake again.

'Send me all the details,' Jeremy had said. 'I'll look over the paperwork at the weekend and call you on Monday morning.'

He was as good as his word, and when he phoned me he mentioned that he had to be in York that Thursday to brief a client, and suggested we get together the following day to go over the contract. I agreed, and we spent most of that Friday closeted in the Cooper's boardroom checking over every dot and comma of the contract. It was a pleasure to watch such a professional at work, even if Jeremy did occasionally display an irritating habit of drumming his fingers on the table when I hadn't immediately understood what he was getting at.

Jeremy, it turned out, had already talked to the French

company's in-house lawyer in Toulouse about any reservations he might have. He assured me that, although Monsieur Sisley spoke no English, he had made him fully aware of our anxieties. I remember being struck by his use of the word 'our'.

After we had turned the last page of the contract, I realised that everyone else in the building had left for the weekend, so I suggested to Jeremy that he might like to join Rosemary and me for dinner. He checked his watch, considered the offer for a moment, and then said, 'Thank you, that's very kind of you. Could you drop me back at the Queen's Hotel so I can get changed?'

Rosemary, however, was not pleased to be told at the last minute that I had invited a complete stranger to dinner without warning her, even though I assured her that she would like him.

Jeremy rang our front doorbell a few minutes after eight. When I introduced him to Rosemary, he bowed slightly and kissed her hand. After that, they didn't take their eyes off each other all evening. Only a blind man could have missed what was likely to happen next, and although I might not have been blind, I certainly turned a blind eye.

Jeremy was soon finding excuses to spend more and more time in Leeds, and I am bound to admit that his sudden enthusiasm for the north of England enabled me to advance my ambitions for Cooper's far more quickly than I had originally dreamed possible. I had felt for some time that the company needed an in-house lawyer, and within a year of our first meeting I offered Jeremy a place on the board, with the remit to prepare the company for going public.

During that period I spent a great deal of my time in Madrid, Amsterdam and Brussels drumming up new contracts, and Rosemary certainly didn't discourage me. Meanwhile Jeremy skilfully guided the company through a thicket of legal and financial problems caused by our expansion. Thanks to his diligence and expertise, we were able to announce on 12 February 1980 that Cooper's would be applying for a listing on the Stock Exchange later that year. It was then that I made my first mistake: I invited Jeremy to become Deputy Chairman of the company.

Under the terms of the flotation, fifty-one per cent of the shares would be retained by Rosemary and myself. Jeremy explained to me that for tax reasons they should be divided equally between us. My accountants agreed, and at the time I didn't give it a second thought. The remaining 4,900,000 one pound shares were quickly taken up by institutions and the general public, and within days of the company being listed on the Stock Exchange their value had risen to £2.80.

My father, who had died the previous year, would never have accepted that it was possible to become worth several million pounds overnight. In fact I suspect he would have disapproved of the very idea, as he went to his deathbed still believing that a ten-pound overdraft was quite adequate to conduct a well-run business.

During the 1980s the British economy showed continual growth, and by March 1984 Cooper's shares had topped the five-pound mark, following press speculation about a possible takeover. Jeremy had advised me to accept one of the bids, but I told him that I would never allow Cooper's to be let out of the family's control. After that, we had to split the shares on three separate occasions, and by 1989 the *Sunday Times* was estimating that Rosemary and I were together worth around thirty million pounds.

I had never thought of myself as being wealthy – after all, as far as I was concerned the shares were simply pieces of paper held by Joe Ramsbottom, our company solicitor. I still lived in my father's house, drove a five-year-old Jaguar, and worked fourteen hours a day. I had never cared much for holidays, and wasn't by nature extravagant. Wealth seemed somehow irrelevant to me. I would have been happy to continue living much as I was, had I not arrived home unexpectedly one night.

I had caught the last plane back to Heathrow after a particularly long and arduous negotiation in Cologne, and had originally intended to stay overnight in London. But by then I'd had enough of hotels, and simply wanted to get home, despite the long drive. When I arrived back in Leeds a few minutes after one, I found Jeremy's white BMW parked in the driveway.

Had I phoned Rosemary earlier that day, I might never have ended up in jail.

I parked my car next to Jeremy's, and was walking towards the front door when I noticed that there was only one light on in the house – in the front room on the first floor. It wouldn't have taken Sherlock Holmes to deduce what might be taking place in that particular room.

I came to a halt, and stared up at the drawn curtains for some time. Nothing stirred, so clearly they hadn't heard the car, and were unaware of my presence. I retraced my steps and drove quietly off in the direction of the city centre. When I arrived at the Queen's Hotel I asked the duty manager if Mr Jeremy Alexander had booked a room for the night. He checked the register and confirmed that he had.

'Then I'll take his key,' I told him. 'Mr Alexander has booked himself in somewhere else for the night.' My father would have been proud of such thrifty use of the company's resources.

I lay on the hotel bed, quite unable to sleep, my anger rising as each hour passed. Although I no longer had a great deal of feeling for Rosemary, and even accepted that perhaps I never had, I now loathed Jeremy. But it wasn't until the next day that I discovered just how much I loathed him.

The following morning I rang my secretary, and told her I would be driving to the office straight from London. She reminded me that there was a board meeting scheduled for two o'clock, which Mr Alexander was pencilled in to chair. I was glad she couldn't see the smile of satisfaction that spread across my face. A quick glance at the agenda over breakfast and it had become abundantly clear why Jeremy had wanted to chair this particular meeting. But his plans didn't matter any more. I had already decided to let my fellow directors know exactly what he was up to, and to make sure that he was dismissed from the board as soon as was practicable.

I arrived at Cooper's just after 1.30, and parked in the space marked 'Chairman'. By the time the board meeting was scheduled to begin I'd had just enough time to check over my files, and became painfully aware of how many of the company's shares were now controlled by Jeremy, and what he and Rosemary must have been planning for some time.

Jeremy vacated the chairman's place without comment the moment I entered the boardroom, and showed no particular interest in the proceedings until we reached an item concerning a future share issue. It was at this point that he tried to push through a seemingly innocuous motion which could ultimately have resulted in Rosemary and myself losing overall control of the company, and therefore being unable to resist any future takeover bid. I might have fallen for it if I hadn't travelled up to Leeds the previous evening and found his car parked in my driveway, and the bedroom light on. Just when he thought he had succeeded in having the motion agreed without a vote, I asked the company accountants to prepare a full report for the next board meeting before we came to any decision. Jeremy showed no sign of emotion. He simply looked down at his notes and began drumming his fingers on the boardroom table. I was determined that the report would prove to be his downfall. If only it hadn't been for my short temper, I might, given time, have worked out a more sensible way of ridding myself of him.

As no one had 'any other business' to raise, I closed the meeting at 5.40, and suggested to Jeremy that he join Rosemary and me for dinner. I wanted to see them together. Jeremy didn't seem too keen, but after some bluffing from me about not fully understanding his new share proposal, and feeling that my wife ought to be brought in on it at some stage, he agreed. When I rang Rosemary to let her know that Jeremy would be coming to dinner, she seemed even less enthusiastic about the idea than he had been.

'Perhaps the two of you should go off to a restaurant together,' she suggested. 'Then Jeremy can bring you up to date on what's been going on while you've been away.' I tried not to laugh. 'We haven't got much food in at the moment,' she added. I told her that it wasn't the food I was worried about.

Jeremy was uncharacteristically late, but I had his usual whisky and soda ready the moment he walked through the door. I must say he put up a brilliant performance over dinner, though Rosemary was less convincing.

Over coffee in the sitting room, I managed to provoke the confrontation that Jeremy had so skilfully avoided at the board meeting.

'Why are you so keen to rush through this new share allocation?' I asked once he was on his second brandy. 'Surely you realise that it will take control of the company out of the hands of Rosemary and me. Can't you see that we could be taken over in no time?'

He tried a few well-rehearsed phrases. 'In the best

interests of the company, Richard. You must realise how quickly Cooper's is expanding. It's no longer a family firm. In the long term it has to be the most prudent course for both of you, not to mention the shareholders.' I wondered which particular shareholders he had in mind.

I was a little surprised to find Rosemary not only backing him up, but showing a remarkable grasp of the finer details of the share allocation, even after Jeremy had scowled rather too obviously at her. She seemed extremely well-versed in the arguments he had been putting forward, given the fact that she had never shown any interest in the company's transactions in the past. It was when she turned to me and said, 'We must consider our future, darling,' that I finally lost my temper.

Yorkshiremen are well known for being blunt, and my next question lived up to our county's reputation.

'Are you two having an affair, by any chance?'

Rosemary turned scarlet. Jeremy laughed a little too loudly, and then said, 'I think you've had one drink too many, Richard.'

'Not a drop,' I assured him. 'Sober as a judge. As I was when I came home late last night, and found your car parked in the driveway and the light on in the bedroom.'

For the first time since I'd met him, I had completely wrong-footed Jeremy, even if it was only for a moment. He began drumming his fingers on the glass table in front of him.

'I was simply explaining to Rosemary how the new

share issue would affect her,' he said, hardly missing a beat. 'Which is no more than is required under Stock Exchange regulations.'

'And is there a Stock Exchange regulation requiring that such explanations should take place in bed?'

'Oh, don't be absurd,' said Jeremy. 'I spent the night at the Queen's Hotel. Call the manager,' he added, picking up the telephone and offering it to me. 'He'll confirm that I was booked in to my usual room.'

'I'm sure he will,' I said. 'But he'll also confirm that it was I who spent the night in your usual bed.'

In the silence that followed I removed the hotel bedroom key from my jacket pocket, and dangled it in front of him. Jeremy immediately jumped to his feet.

I rose from my chair, rather more slowly, and faced him, wondering what his next line could possibly be.

'It's your own fault, you bloody fool,' he eventually stammered out. 'You should have taken more interest in Rosemary in the first place, and not gone off gallivanting around Europe all the time. It's no wonder you're in danger of losing the company.'

Funny, it wasn't the fact that Jeremy had been sleeping with my wife that caused me to snap, but that he had the arrogance to think he could take over my company as well. I didn't reply, but just took a pace forward and threw a punch at his clean-shaven jaw. I may have been a couple of inches shorter than he was, but after twenty years of hanging around with lorry drivers, I could still land a decent blow. Jeremy staggered first backwards and then forwards, before crumpling in front of me. As he fell, he cracked his right temple on the corner of the glass table, knocking his brandy all over the floor. He lay motionless in front of me, blood dripping onto the carpet.

I must admit I felt rather pleased with myself, especially when Rosemary rushed to his side and started screaming obscenities at me.

'Save your breath for the ex-Deputy Chairman,' I told her. 'And when he comes round, tell him not to bother with the Queen's Hotel, because I'll be sleeping in his bed again tonight.'

I strode out of the house and drove back into the city centre, leaving my Jaguar in the hotel carpark. When I walked into the Queen's the lobby was deserted, and I took the lift straight up to Jeremy's room. I lay on top of the bed, but was far too agitated to sleep.

I was just dozing off when four policemen burst into the room and pulled me off the bed. One of them told me that I was under arrest and read me my rights. Without further explanation I was marched out of the hotel and driven to Millgarth Police Station. A few minutes after five a.m., I was signed in by the custody officer and my personal possessions were taken from me and dropped into a bulky brown envelope. I was told that I had the right to make one telephone call, so I rang Joe Ramsbottom, woke his wife, and asked if Joe could join me at the station as quickly as possible. Then I was locked in a small cell and left alone.

I sat on the wooden bench and tried to fathom out why I had been arrested. I couldn't believe that Jeremy would have been foolish enough to charge me with assault. When Joe arrived about forty minutes later I told him exactly what had taken place earlier in the evening. He listened gravely, but didn't offer an opinion. When I had finished, he said he would try to find out what the police intended to charge me with.

After Joe left, I began to fear that Jeremy might have had a heart attack, or even that the blow to his head from the corner of the table might have killed him. My imagination ran riot as I considered all the worst possibilities, and I was becoming more and more desperate to learn what had happened when the cell door swung open and two plain-clothes detectives walked in. Joe was a pace behind them.

'I'm Chief Inspector Bainbridge,' said the taller of the two. 'And this is my colleague, Sergeant Harris.' Their eyes were tired and their suits crumpled. They looked as if they had been on duty all night, as both of them could have done with a shave. I felt my chin, and realised I needed one as well.

'We'd like to ask you some questions about what took place at your home earlier this evening,' said the Chief Inspector. I looked at Joe, who shook his head. 'It would help our enquiries, Mr Cooper, if you co-operated with us,' the Chief Inspector continued. 'Would you be prepared to give us a statement either in writing or as a tape recording?'

'I'm afraid my client has nothing to say at the moment, Chief Inspector,' said Joe. 'And he will have nothing to say until I have taken further instructions.'

23

I was rather impressed. I'd never seen Joe that firm with anyone other than his children.

'We would simply like to take a statement, Mr Ramsbottom,' Chief Inspector Bainbridge said to Joe, as if I didn't exist. 'We are quite happy for you to be present throughout.'

'No,' said Joe firmly. 'You either charge my client, or you leave us – and leave us immediately.'

The Chief Inspector hesitated for a moment, and then nodded to his colleague. They departed without another word.

'Charge me?' I said, once the cell door had been locked behind them. 'What with, for God's sake?'

'Murder, I suspect,' said Joe. 'After what Rosemary has been telling them.'

'Murder?' I said, almost unable to mouth the word. 'But . . .' I listened in disbelief as Joe told me what he'd been able to discover about the details of the statement my wife had given to the police during the early hours of the morning.

'But that's not what happened,' I protested. 'Surely no one would believe such an outrageous story.'

'They might when they learn the police have found a trail of blood leading from the sitting room to the spot where your car was parked in the drive,' said Joe.

'That's not possible,' I said. 'When I left Jeremy, he was still lying unconscious on the floor.'

'The police also found traces of blood in the boot of your car. They seem quite confident that it will match up with Jeremy's.'

24

'Oh, my God,' I said. 'He's clever. He's very clever. Can't you see what they've been up to?'

'No, to be honest, I can't,' Joe admitted. 'This isn't exactly all in a day's work for a company solicitor like me. But I managed to catch Sir Matthew Roberts QC on the phone before he left home this morning. He's the most eminent criminal silk on the north-eastern circuit. He's appearing in the York Crown Court today, and he's agreed to join us as soon as the court has risen. If you're innocent, Richard,' Joe said, 'with Sir Matthew defending you, there will be nothing to fear. Of that you can be certain.'

Later that afternoon I was charged with the murder of Jeremy Anatole Alexander; the police admitted to my solicitor that they still hadn't found the body, but they were confident that they would do so within a few hours. I knew they wouldn't. Joe told me the following day that they had done more digging in my garden during the past twenty-four hours than I had attempted in the past twenty-four years.

Around seven that evening the door of my cell swung open once again and Joe walked in, accompanied by a heavily-built, distinguished-looking man. Sir Matthew Roberts was about my height, but at least a couple of stone heavier. From his rubicund cheeks and warm smile he looked as if he regularly enjoyed a good bottle of wine and the company of amusing people. He had a full head of dark hair that remained modelled on the old Denis Compton Brylcreem advertisements, and he was attired in the garb of his profession, a dark three-piece suit and a silver-grey tie. I liked him from the moment he introduced himself. His first words were to express the wish that we had met in more pleasant circumstances.

I spent the rest of the evening with Sir Matthew, going over my story again and again. I could tell he didn't believe a word I was saying, but he still seemed quite happy to represent me. He and Joe left a few minutes after eleven, and I settled down to spend my first night behind bars.

I was remanded in custody until the police had processed and submitted all their evidence to the Department of Public Prosecutions. The following day a magistrate committed me to trial at Leeds Crown Court, and despite an eloquent plea from Sir Matthew, I was not granted bail.

Forty minutes later I was transferred to Armley Jail.

The hours turned into days, the days into weeks, and the weeks into months. I almost tired of telling anyone who would listen that they would never find Jeremy's body, because there was no body to find.

When the case finally reached Leeds Crown Court nine months later, the crime reporters turned up in their hordes, and followed every word of the trial with relish. A multi-millionaire, a possible adulterous affair and a missing body were too much for them to resist. The tabloids excelled themselves, describing Jeremy as the

Lord Lucan of Leeds and me as an oversexed lorry driver. I would have enjoyed every last syllable of it, if I hadn't been the accused.

In his opening address, Sir Matthew put up a magnificent fight on my behalf. Without a body, how could his client possibly be charged with murder? And how could I have disposed of the body, when I had spent the entire night in a bedroom at the Queen's Hotel? How I regretted not checking in the second time, but simply going straight up to Jeremy's room. It didn't help that the police had found me lying on the bed fully dressed.

I watched the faces of the jury at the end of the prosecution's opening speech. They were perplexed, and obviously in some doubt about my guilt. That doubt remained, until Rosemary entered the witness box. I couldn't bear to look at her, and diverted my eyes to a striking blonde who had been sitting in the front row of the public gallery on every day of the trial.

For an hour the counsel for the prosecution guided my wife gently through what had taken place that evening, up to the point when I had struck Jeremy. Until that moment, I couldn't have quarrelled with a word she had spoken.

'And then what happened, Mrs Cooper?' prodded counsel for the Crown.

'My husband bent down and checked Mr Alexander's pulse,' Rosemary whispered. 'Then he turned white, and all he said was, "He's dead. I've killed him."'

'And what did Mr Cooper do next?'

'He picked up the body, threw it over his shoulder,

and began walking towards the door. I shouted after him, "What do you think you're doing, Richard?"'

'And how did he respond?'

'He told me he intended to dispose of the body while it was still dark, and that I was to make sure that there was no sign that Jeremy had visited the house. As no one else had been in the office when they left, everyone would assume that Jeremy had returned to London earlier in the evening. "Be certain there are absolutely no traces of blood," were the last words I remember my husband saying as he left the room carrying Jeremy's body over his shoulder. That must have been when I fainted.'

Sir Matthew glanced quizzically up at me in the dock. I shook my head vigorously. He looked grim as counsel for the prosecution resumed his seat.

'Do you wish to question this witness, Sir Matthew?' the judge asked.

Sir Matthew rose slowly to his feet. 'I most certainly do, M'Lud,' he replied. He drew himself up to his full height, tugged at his gown and stared across at his adversary.

'Mrs Cooper, would you describe yourself as a friend of Mr Alexander?'

'Yes, but only in the sense that he was a colleague of my husband's,' replied Rosemary calmly.

'So you didn't ever see each other when your husband was away from Leeds, or even out of the country, on business?'

'Only at social events, when I was accompanied by

my husband, or if I dropped into the office to pick up his mail.'

'Are you certain that those were the only times you saw him, Mrs Cooper? Were there not other occasions when you spent a considerable amount of time alone with Mr Alexander? For example, on the night of 17 September 1989, before your husband returned unexpectedly from a European trip: did Mr Alexander not visit you then for several hours while you were alone in the house?'

'No. He dropped by after work to leave a document for my husband, but he didn't even have time to stay for a drink.'

'But your husband says . . .' began Sir Matthew.

'I know what my husband says,' Rosemary replied, as if she had rehearsed the line a hundred times.

'I see,' said Sir Matthew. 'Let's get to the point, shall we, Mrs Cooper? Were you having an affair with Jeremy Alexander at the time of his disappearance?'

'Is this relevant, Sir Matthew?' interrupted the judge.

'It most assuredly is, M'Lud. It goes to the very core of the case,' replied my QC in a quiet even tone.

Everyone's gaze was now fixed on Rosemary. I willed her to tell the truth.

She didn't hesitate. 'Certainly not,' she replied, 'although it wasn't the first time my husband had accused me unjustly.'

'I see,' said Sir Matthew. He paused. 'Do you love your husband, Mrs Cooper?'

'Really, Sir Matthew!' The judge was unable to

disguise his irritation. 'I must ask once again if this is relevant?'

Sir Matthew exploded. 'Relevant? It's absolutely vital, M'Lud, and I am not being assisted by your lordship's thinly veiled attempts to intervene on behalf of this witness.'

The judge was beginning to splutter with indignation when Rosemary said quietly, 'I have always been a good and faithful wife, but I cannot under any circumstances condone murder.'

The jury turned their eyes on me. Most of them looked as if they would be happy to bring back the death penalty.

'If that is the case, I am bound to ask why you waited two and a half hours to contact the police?' said Sir Matthew. 'Especially if, as you claim, you believed your husband had committed murder, and was about to dispose of the body.'

'As I explained, I fainted soon after he left the room. I phoned the police the moment I came to.'

'How convenient,' said Sir Matthew. 'Or perhaps the truth is that you made use of that time to set a trap for your husband, while allowing your lover to get clean away.' A murmur ran through the courtroom.

'Sir Matthew,' the judge said, jumping in once again. 'You are going too far.'

'Not so, M'Lud, with respect. In fact, not far enough.' He swung back round and faced my wife again.

'I put it to you, Mrs Cooper, that Jeremy Alexander was your lover, and still is, that you are perfectly aware he is alive and well, and that if you wished to, you could tell us exactly where he is now.'

Despite the judge's spluttering and the uproar in the court, Rosemary had her reply ready.

'I only wish he were,' she said, 'so that he could stand in this court and confirm that I am telling the truth.' Her voice was soft and gentle.

'But *you* already know the truth, Mrs Cooper,' said Sir Matthew, his voice gradually rising. 'The truth is that your husband left the house on his own. He then drove to the Queen's Hotel, where he spent the rest of the night, while you and your lover used that time to leave clues across the city of Leeds – clues, I might add, that were intended to incriminate your husband. But the one thing you couldn't leave was a body, because as you well know Mr Jeremy Alexander is still alive, and the two of you have together fabricated this entire bogus story, simply to further your own ends. Isn't that the truth, Mrs Cooper?'

'No, no!' Rosemary shouted, her voice cracking before she finally burst into tears.

'Oh, come, come, Mrs Cooper. Those are counterfeit tears, are they not?' said Sir Matthew quietly. 'Now you've been found out, the jury will decide if your distress is genuine.'

I glanced across at the jury. Not only had they fallen for Rosemary's performance, but they now despised me for allowing my insensitive bully of a counsel to attack such a gentle, long-suffering woman. To every one of Sir Matthew's probing questions, Rosemary proved well capable of delivering a riposte that revealed to me all the hallmarks of Jeremy Alexander's expert tuition.

When it was my turn to enter the witness box, and Sir Matthew began questioning me, I felt my story sounded far less convincing than Rosemary's, despite its being the truth.

The closing speech for the Crown was deadly dull, but nevertheless deadly. Sir Matthew's was subtle and dramatic, but I feared less convincing.

After another night in Armley Jail I returned to the dock for the judge's summing up. It was clear that he was in no doubt as to my guilt. His selection of the evidence he chose to review was unbalanced and unfair, and when he ended by reminding the jury that his opinion of the evidence should ultimately carry no weight, he only added hypocrisy to bias.

After their first full day's deliberations, the jury had to be put up overnight in a hotel – ironically the Queen's – and when the jolly little fat man in the bow tie was finally asked: 'Members of the jury, do you find the prisoner at the bar guilty or not guilty as charged?' I wasn't surprised when he said clearly for all to hear, 'Guilty, my lord.'

In fact I was amazed that the jury had failed to reach a unanimous decision. I have often wondered which two members felt convinced enough to declare my innocence. I would have liked to thank them.

The judge stared down at me. 'Richard Wilfred Cooper, you have been found guilty of the murder of Jeremy Anatole Alexander . . .'

'I did not kill him, my lord,' I interrupted in a calm voice. 'In fact, he is not dead. I can only hope that you will live long enough to realise the truth.' Sir Matthew looked up anxiously as uproar broke out in the court.

The judge called for silence, and his voice became even more harsh as he pronounced, 'You will go to prison for life. That is the sentence prescribed by law. Take him down.'

Two prison officers stepped forward, gripped me firmly by the arms and led me down the steps at the back of the dock into the cell I had occupied every morning for the eighteen days of the trial.

'Sorry, old chum,' said the policeman who had been in charge of my welfare since the case had begun. 'It was that bitch of a wife who tipped the scales against you.' He slammed the cell door closed, and turned the key in the lock before I had a chance to agree with him. A few moments later the door was unlocked again, and Sir Matthew strode in.

He stared at me for some time before uttering a word. 'A terrible injustice has been done, Mr Cooper,' he eventually said, 'and we shall immediately lodge an appeal against your conviction. Be assured, I will not rest until we have found Jeremy Alexander and he has been brought to justice.'

For the first time I realised Sir Matthew knew that I was innocent.

* * *

I was put in a cell with a petty criminal called 'Fingers'
Jenkins. Can you believe, as we approach the twenty-
first century, that anyone could still be called 'Fingers'?
Even so, the name had been well earned. Within
moments of my entering the cell, Fingers was wearing
my watch. He returned it immediately. I noticed it
had disappeared. 'Sorry,' he said. 'Just put it down to
'abit.'

Prison might have turned out to be far worse if it
hadn't been known by my fellow inmates that I was a
millionaire, and was quite happy to pay a little extra for
certain privileges. Every morning the *Financial Times*
was delivered to my bunk, which gave me the chance to
keep up with what was happening in the City. I was
nearly sick when I first read about the takeover bid for
Cooper's. Sick not because of the offer of £12.50 a share,
which made me even wealthier, but because it became
painfully obvious what Jeremy and Rosemary had been
up to. Jeremy's shares would now be worth several million pounds – money he could never have realised had
I been around to prevent a takeover.

I spent hours each day lying on my bunk and scouring
every word of the *Financial Times*. Whenever there was
a mention of Cooper's, I went over the paragraph so
often that I ended up knowing it by heart. The company
was eventually taken over, but not before the share price
had reached £13.43. I continued to follow its activities
with great interest, and I became more and more anxious
about the quality of the new management when they
began to sack some of my most experienced staff,

including Joe Ramsbottom. A week later, I wrote and instructed my stockbrokers to sell my shares as and when the opportunity arose.

It was at the beginning of my fourth month in prison that I asked for some writing paper. I had decided the time had come to keep a record of everything that had happened to me since that night I had returned home unexpectedly. Every day the prison officer on my landing would bring me fresh sheets of blue-lined paper, and I would write out in longhand the chronicle you're now reading. An added bonus was that it helped me to plan my next move.

At my request, Fingers took a straw poll among the prisoners as to who they believed was the best detective they had ever come up against. Three days later he told me the result: Chief Superintendent Donald Hackett, known as the Don, came out top on more than half the lists. More reliable than a Gallup Poll, I told Fingers.

'What puts Hackett ahead of all the others?' I asked him.

''e's honest, 'e's fair, you can't bribe 'im. And once the bastard knows you're a villain, 'e doesn't care 'ow long it takes to get you be'ind bars.'

Hackett, I was informed, hailed from Bradford. Rumour had it among the older cons that he had turned down the job of Assistant Chief Constable for West Yorkshire. Like a barrister who doesn't want to become a judge, he preferred to remain at the coalface.

'Arrestin' criminals is 'ow 'e gets his kicks,' Fingers said, with some feeling.

'Sounds just the man I'm looking for,' I said. 'How old is he?'

Fingers paused to consider. 'Must be past fifty by now,' he replied. 'After all, 'e 'ad me put in borstal for nickin' a toolset, and that was' – he paused again – 'more than twenty years ago.'

When Sir Matthew came to visit me the following Monday, I told him what I had in mind, and asked his opinion of the Don. I wanted a professional's view.

'He's a hell of a witness to cross-examine, that's one thing I can tell you,' replied my barrister.

'Why's that?'

'He doesn't exaggerate, he won't prevaricate, and I've never known him to lie, which makes him awfully hard to trap. No, I've rarely got the better of the Chief Superintendent. I have to say, though, that I doubt if he'd agree to become involved with a convicted criminal, whatever you offered him.'

'But I'm not . . .'

'I know, Mr Cooper,' said Sir Matthew, who still didn't seem able to call me by my first name. 'But Hackett will have to be convinced of that before he even agrees to see you.'

'But how can I convince him of my innocence while I'm stuck in jail?'

'I'll try to influence him on your behalf,' Sir Matthew said after some thought. Then he added, 'Come to think of it, he does owe me a favour.'

After Sir Matthew had left that night, I requested some more lined paper and began to compose a carefully

worded letter to Chief Superintendent Hackett, several
versions of which ended crumpled up on the floor of my
cell. My final effort read as follows:

In replying to this letter, please write on the envelope:

Number A47283   Name COOPER, R.W.

ALL INCOMING MAIL MUST
HAVE SENDERS NAME AND
ADDRESS. ANONYMOUS
MAIL CANNOT BE ACCEPTED
NO NUMBER DELAYS MAIL.

**H.M. PRISON
ARMLEY
LEEDS LS12 2TJ**

Dear Chief Superintendent,

As you can see I am currently detained at
Her Majesty's pleasure. Nevertheless, I wonder
if you would be kind enough to visit me,
as I have a private matter I would
like to discuss with you that could affect
both our futures. I can assure you that my
proposal is both legal and honest, and I am
confident that it will also appeal to your
sense of justice. It has the approval of my
barrister, Sir Matthew Roberts QC, who I understand
you have come across from time to time in your
professional capacity. Naturally I will be happy
to reimburse any expences that this inconvenience
may cause you.

I look forward to hearing from you.

Yours sincerely,

37

I reread the letter, corrected the spelling mistake, and scrawled my signature across the bottom.

At my request, Sir Matthew delivered the letter to Hackett by hand. The first thousand-pound-a-day post-man in the history of the Royal Mail, I told him.

Sir Matthew reported back the following Monday that he had handed the letter to the Chief Superintendent in person. After Hackett had read it through a second time, his only comment was that he would have to speak to his superiors. He had promised he would let Sir Matthew know his decision within a week.

From the moment I had been sentenced, Sir Matthew had been preparing for my appeal, and although he had not at any time raised my hopes, he was unable to hide his delight at what he had discovered after paying a visit to the Probate Office.

It turned out that, in his will, Jeremy had left every-thing to Rosemary. This included over three million pounds' worth of Cooper's shares. But, Sir Matthew explained, the law did not allow her to dispose of them for seven years. 'An English jury may have pronounced on your guilt,' he declared, 'but the hard-headed taxmen are not so easily convinced. They won't hand over Jeremy Alexander's assets until either they have seen his body, or seven years have elapsed.'

'Do they think that Rosemary might have killed him for his money, and then disposed . . .'

'No, no,' said Sir Matthew, almost laughing at my

suggestion. 'It's simply that, as they're entitled to wait for seven years, they're going to sit on his assets and not take the risk that Alexander may still be alive. In any case, if your wife *had* killed him, she wouldn't have had a ready answer to every one of my questions when she was in the witness box, of that I'm sure.'

I smiled. For the first time in my life I was delighted to learn that the taxman had his nose in my affairs.

Sir Matthew promised he would report back if anything new came up. 'Goodnight, Richard,' he said as he left the interview room.

Another first.

It seemed that everyone else in the prison was aware that Chief Superintendent Hackett would be paying me a visit long before I was.

It was Dave Adams, an old lag from an adjoining cell, who explained why the inmates thought Hackett had agreed to see me. 'A good copper is never 'appy about anyone doin' time for somethin' 'e didn't do. 'ackett phoned the Governor last Tuesday, and 'ad a word with 'im on the Q.T., accordin' to Maurice,' Dave added mysteriously.

I would have been interested to learn how the Governor's trusty had managed to hear both sides of the conversation, but decided this was not the time for irrelevant questions.

'Even the 'ardest nuts in this place think you're innocent,' Dave continued. 'They can't wait for the day when Mr Jeremy Alexander takes over your cell. You can be sure the long termers'll give 'im a warm welcome.'

A letter from Bradford arrived the following morning. 'Dear Cooper,' the Chief Superintendent began, and went on to inform me that he intended to pay a visit to the jail at four o'clock the following Sunday. He made it clear that he would stay no longer than half an hour, and insisted on a witness being present throughout.

For the first time since I'd been locked up, I started counting the hours. Hours aren't that important when your room has been booked for a life sentence.

As I was taken from my cell that Sunday afternoon and escorted to the interview room, I received several messages from my fellow inmates to pass on to the Chief Superintendent.

'Give my best regards to the Don,' said Fingers. 'Tell 'im 'ow sorry I am not to bump into 'im this time.'

'When 'e's finished with you, ask 'im if 'e'd like to drop into my cell for a cup of char and a chat about old times.'

'Kick the bastard in the balls, and tell 'im I'll be 'appy to serve the extra time.'

One of the prisoners even suggested a question to which I already knew the answer: 'Ask 'im when 'e's going to retire, 'cause I'm not coming out till the day after.'

When I stepped into the interview room and saw the

Chief Superintendent for the first time, I thought there must have been some mistake. I had never asked Fingers what the Don looked like, and over the past few days I had built up in my mind the image of some sort of superman. But the man who stood before me was a couple of inches shorter than me, and I'm only five foot ten. He was as thin as the proverbial rake and wore pebble-lensed horn-rimmed glasses, which gave the impression that he was half-blind. All he needed was a grubby raincoat and he could have been mistaken for a debt collector.

Sir Matthew stepped forward to introduce us. I shook the policeman firmly by the hand. 'Thank you for coming to visit me, Chief Superintendent,' I began. 'Won't you have a seat?' I added, as if he had dropped into my home for a glass of sherry.

'Sir Matthew is very persuasive,' said Hackett, in a deep, gruff Yorkshire accent that didn't quite seem to go with his body. 'So tell me, Cooper, what do you imagine it is that I can do for you?' he asked as he took the chair opposite me. I detected an edge of cynicism in his voice.

He opened a notepad and placed it on the table as I was about to begin my story. 'For my use only,' he explained, 'should I need to remind myself of any relevant details at some time in the future.' Twenty minutes later, I had finished the abbreviated version of the life and times of Richard Cooper. I had already gone over the story on several occasions in my cell during the past week, to be certain I didn't take too long. I wanted to leave enough time for Hackett to ask any questions.

'If I believe your story,' he said, '– and I only say "if" – you still haven't explained what it is you think I can do for you.'

'You're due to leave the force in five months' time,' I said. 'I wondered if you had any plans once you've retired.'

He hesitated. I had obviously taken him by surprise.

'I've been offered a job with Group 4, as area manager for West Yorkshire.'

'And how much will they be paying you?' I asked bluntly.

'It won't be full time,' he said. 'Three days a week, to start with.' He hesitated again. 'Twenty thousand a year, guaranteed for three years.'

'I'll pay you a hundred thousand a year, but I'll expect you to be on the job seven days a week. I assume you'll be needing a secretary and an assistant – that Inspector Williams who's leaving at the same time as you might well fit the bill – so I'll also supply you with enough money for back-up staff, as well as the rent for an office.'

A flicker of respect appeared on the Chief Superintendent's face for the first time. He made some more notes on his pad.

'And what would you expect of me in return for such a large sum of money?' he asked.

'That's simple. I expect you to find Jeremy Alexander.'

This time he didn't hesitate. 'My God,' he said. 'You

really *are* innocent. Sir Matthew and the Governor both tried to convince me you were.'

'And if you find him within seven years,' I added, ignoring his comment, 'I'll pay a further five hundred thousand into any branch of any bank in the world that you stipulate.'

'The Midland, Bradford will suit me just fine,' he replied. 'It's only criminals who find it necessary to retire abroad. In any case, I have to be in Bradford every other Saturday afternoon, so I can be around to watch City lose.' Hackett rose from his place and looked hard at me for some time. 'One last question, Mr Cooper. Why seven years?'

'Because after that period, my wife can sell Alexander's shares, and he'll become a multi-millionaire overnight.'

The Chief Superintendent nodded his understanding. 'Thank you for asking to see me,' he said. 'It's been a long time since I enjoyed visiting anyone in jail, especially someone convicted of murder. I'll give your offer serious consideration, Mr Cooper, and let you know my decision by the end of the week.' He left without another word.

Hackett wrote to me three days later, accepting my offer.

I didn't have to wait five months for him to start working for me, because he handed in his resignation within a fortnight – though not before I had agreed to continue his pension contributions, and those of the two colleagues he wanted to leave the force and join him.

Having now disposed of all my Cooper's shares, the interest on my deposit account was earning me over four hundred thousand a year, and as I was living rent-free, Hackett's request was a minor consideration.

I would have shared with you in greater detail everything that happened to me over the following months, but during that time I was so preoccupied with briefing Hackett that I filled only three pages of my blue-lined prison paper. I should however mention that I studied several law books, to be sure that I fully understood the meaning of the legal term '*autrefois acquit*'.

The next important date in the diary was my appeal hearing.

Matthew – at his request I had long ago stopped calling him 'Sir' Matthew – tried valiantly not to show that he was becoming more and more confident of the outcome, but I was getting to know him so well that he was no longer able to disguise his true feelings. He told me how delighted he was with the make-up of the reviewing panel. 'Fair and just,' he kept repeating.

Later that night he told me with great sadness that his wife Victoria had died of cancer a few weeks before. 'A long illness and a blessed release,' he called it.

I felt guilty in his presence for the first time. Over the past eighteen months, we had only ever discussed my problems.

*   *   *

I must have been one of the few prisoners at Armley who ever had a bespoke tailor visit him in his cell. Matthew suggested that I should be fitted with a new suit before I faced the appeal tribunal, as I had lost over a stone since I had been in jail. When the tailor had finished measuring me and began rolling up his tape, I insisted that Fingers return his cigarette lighter, although I did allow him to keep the cigarettes.

Ten days later, I was escorted from my cell at five o'clock in the morning. My fellow inmates banged their tin mugs against their locked doors, the traditional way of indicating to the prison staff that they believed the man leaving for trial was innocent. Like some great symphony, it lifted my soul.

I was driven to London in a police car accompanied by two prison officers. We didn't stop once on the entire journey, and arrived in the capital a few minutes after nine; I remember looking out of the window and watching the commuters scurrying to their offices to begin the day's work. Any one of them who'd glanced at me sitting in the back of the car in my new suit, and was unable to spot the handcuffs, might have assumed I was a Chief Inspector at least.

Matthew was waiting for me at the entrance of the Old Bailey, a mountain of papers tucked under each arm. 'I like the suit,' he said, before leading me up some stone steps to the room where my fate would be decided.

Once again I sat impassively in the dock as Sir Matthew rose from his place to address the three appeal judges. His opening statement took him nearly an hour, and by now I felt I could have delivered it quite adequately myself, though not as eloquently, and certainly nowhere near as persuasively. He made great play of how Jeremy had left all his worldly goods to Rosemary, who in turn had sold our family house in Leeds, cashed in all her Cooper's shares within months of the takeover, pushed through a quickie divorce, and then disappeared off the face of the earth with an estimated seven million pounds. I couldn't help wondering just how much of that Jeremy had already got his hands on.

Sir Matthew repeatedly reminded the panel of the police's inability to produce a body, despite the fact they now seemed to have dug up half of Leeds.

I became more hopeful with each new fact Matthew placed before the judges. But after he had finished, I still had to wait another three days to learn the outcome of their deliberations.

Appeal dismissed. Reasons reserved.

Matthew travelled up to Armley on the Friday to tell me why he thought my appeal had been turned down without explanation. He felt that the judges must have been divided, and needed more time to make it appear as if they were not.

'How much time?' I asked.

'My hunch is that they'll let you out on licence within a few months. They were obviously influenced by the police's failure to produce a body, unimpressed by the trial judge's summing up, and impressed by the strength of your case.'

I thanked Matthew, who, for once, left the room with a smile on his face.

You may be wondering what Chief Superintendent Hackett – or rather ex-Chief Superintendent Hackett – had been up to while all this was going on.

He had not been idle. Inspector Williams and Constable Kenwright had left the force on the same day as he had. Within a week they had opened up a small office above the Constitutional Club in Bradford and begun their investigations. The Don reported to me at four o'clock every Sunday afternoon.

Within a month he had compiled a thick file on the case, with detailed dossiers on Rosemary, Jeremy, the company and me. I spent hours reading through the information he had gathered, and was even able to help by filling in a few gaps. I quickly came to appreciate why the Don was so respected by my fellow inmates. He followed up every clue, and went down every side road, however much it looked like a cul-de-sac, because once in a while it turned out to be a highway.

On the first Sunday in October, after Hackett had been working for four months, he told me that he thought he might have located Rosemary. A woman of her description was living on a small estate in the south of France called Villa Fleur.

'How did you manage to track her down?' I asked.

'Letter posted by her mother at her local pillarbox. The postman kindly allowed me to have a look at the

address on the envelope before it proceeded on its way,'
Hackett said. 'Can't tell you how many hours we had
to hang around, how many letters we've had to sift
through, and how many doors we've knocked on in the
past four months, just to get this one lead. Mrs Kershaw
seems to be a compulsive letter writer, but this was the
first time she's sent one to her daughter. By the way,'
he added, 'your wife has reverted to her maiden name.
Calls herself Ms Kershaw now.'

I nodded, not wishing to interrupt him.

'Williams flew out to Cannes on Wednesday, and he's
holed up in the nearest village, posing as a tourist. He's
already been able to tell us that Ms Kershaw's house is
surrounded by a ten-foot stone wall, and she has more
guard dogs than trees. It seems the locals know even
less about her than we do. But at least it's a start.'

I felt for the first time that Jeremy Alexander might
at last have met his match, but it was to be another five
Sundays, and five more interim reports, before a thin
smile appeared on Hackett's usually tight-lipped face.

'Ms Kershaw has placed an advertisement in the local
paper,' he informed me. 'It seems she's in need of a new
butler. At first I thought we should question the old
butler at length as soon as he'd left, but as I couldn't
risk anything getting back to her, I decided Inspector
Williams would have to apply for his job instead.'

'But surely she'll realise within moments that he's
totally unqualified to do the job.'

'Not necessarily,' said Hackett, his smile broadening.
'You see, Williams won't be able to leave his present

employment with the Countess of Rutland until he's served a full month's notice, and in the meantime we've signed him up for a special six-week course at Ivor Spencer's School for Butlers. Williams has always been a quick learner.'

'But what about references?'

'By the time Rosemary Kershaw interviews him, he'll have a set of references that would impress a duchess.'

'I was told you never did anything underhand.'

'That is the case when I'm dealing with honest people, Mr Cooper. Not when I'm up against a couple of crooks like this. I'm going to get those two behind bars, if it's the last thing I do.'

This was not the time to let Hackett know that the final chapter of this story, as I plotted it, did not conclude with Jeremy ending up in jail.

Once Williams had been put on the shortlist for the position of Rosemary's butler, I played my own small part in securing him the job. Rereading over the terms of the proposed contract gave me the idea.

'Tell Williams to ask for 15,000 francs a month, and five weeks' holiday,' I suggested to Hackett when he and Matthew visited me the following Sunday.

'Why?' asked the ex-Chief Superintendent. 'She's only offering 11,000, and three weeks' holiday.'

'She can well afford to pay the difference, and with references like these,' I said, looking back down at my file, 'she might become suspicious if he asked for anything less.'

Matthew smiled and nodded.

49

Rosemary finally offered Williams the job at 13,000 francs a month, with four weeks' holiday a year, which after forty-eight hours' consideration Williams accepted. But he did not join her for another month, by which time he had learnt how to iron newspapers, lay place settings with a ruler, and tell the difference between a port, sherry and liqueur glass.

I suppose that from the moment Williams took up the post as Rosemary's butler, I expected instant results. But as Hackett pointed out to me Sunday after Sunday, this was hardly realistic.

'Williams has to take his time,' explained the Don. 'He needs to gain her confidence, and avoid giving her any reason for the slightest suspicion. It once took me five years to nail a drug smuggler who was only living half a mile up the road from me.'

I wanted to remind him that it was me who was stuck in jail, and that five days was more like what I had in mind, but I knew how hard they were all working on my behalf, and tried not to show my impatience.

Within a month Williams had supplied us with photographs and life histories of all the staff working on the estate, along with descriptions of everyone who visited Rosemary – even the local priest, who came hoping to collect a donation for French aid workers in Somalia.

The cook: Gabrielle Pascal – no English, excellent cuisine, came from Marseilles, family checked out. The gardener: Jacques Reni – stupid and not particularly imaginative with the rosebeds, local and well known. Rosemary's personal maid: Charlotte Merieux – spoke

a little English, crafty, sexy, came from Paris, still checking her out. All the staff had been employed by Rosemary since her arrival in the south of France, and they
appeared to have no connection with each other, or with
her past life.

'Ah,' said Hackett as he studied the picture of Rosemary's personal maid. I raised an eyebrow. 'I was just
thinking about Williams being cooped up with Charlotte
Merieux day in and day out – and more important, night
in and night in,' he explained. 'He would have made
superintendent if he hadn't fooled around so much. Still,
let's hope this time it turns out to our advantage.'

I lay on my bunk studying the pictures of the staff
for hour after hour, but they revealed nothing. I read
and reread the notes on everyone who had ever visited
Villa Fleur, but as the weeks went by, it looked more
and more as if no one from Rosemary's past, other than
her mother, knew where she was – or if they did, they
were making no attempts to contact her. There was certainly no sign of Jeremy Alexander.

I was beginning to fear that she and Jeremy might
have split up, until Williams reported that there was a
picture of a dark, handsome man on a table by the side
of Rosemary's bed. It was inscribed: 'We'll always be
together – J'.

During the weeks following my appeal hearing I was
constantly interviewed by probation officers, social
workers and even the prison psychiatrist. I struggled

to maintain the warm, sincere smile that Matthew had warned me was so necessary to lubricate the wheels of the bureaucracy.

It must have been about eleven weeks after my appeal had been turned down that the cell door was thrown open, and the senior officer on my corridor announced, 'The Governor wants to see you, Cooper.' Fingers looked suspicious. Whenever he heard those words, it inevitably meant a dose of solitary.

I could hear my heart beating as I was led down the long corridor to the Governor's office. The prison officer knocked gently on the door before opening it. The Governor rose from behind his desk, thrust out his hand and said, 'I'm delighted to be the first person to tell you the good news.'

He ushered me into a comfortable chair on the other side of his desk, and went over the terms of my release. While he was doing this I was served coffee, as if we were old friends.

There was a knock on the door, and Matthew walked in, clutching a sheaf of papers that needed to be signed. I rose as he placed them on the desk, and without warning he turned round and gave me a bearhug. Not something I expect he did every day.

After I had signed the final document Matthew asked: 'What's the first thing you'll do once they release you?'

'I'm going to buy a gun,' I told him matter-of-factly.

Matthew and the Governor burst out laughing.

* * *

The great gate of Armley Prison was thrown open for me three days later. I walked away from the building carrying only the small leather suitcase I had arrived with. I didn't look back. I hailed a taxi and asked the driver to take me to the station, as I had no desire to remain in Leeds a moment longer than was necessary. I bought a first-class ticket, phoned Hackett to warn him I was on my way, and boarded the next train for Bradford. I savoured a British Rail breakfast that wasn't served on a tin plate, and read a copy of the *Financial Times* that had been handed to me by a pretty shop assistant and not a petty criminal. No one stared at me – but then, why should they, when I was sitting in a first-class carriage and dressed in my new suit? I glanced at every woman who passed by, however she was dressed, but they had no way of knowing why.

When the train pulled into Bradford, the Don and his secretary Jenny Kenwright were waiting for me on the platform. The Chief Superintendent had rented me a small furnished flat on the outskirts of the city, and after I had unpacked – not a long job – they took me out to lunch. The moment the small talk had been dispensed with and Jenny had poured me a glass of wine, the Don asked me a question I hadn't expected.

'Now that you're free, is it still your wish that we go on looking for Jeremy Alexander?'

'Yes,' I replied, without a moment's hesitation. 'I'm even more determined, now that I can taste the freedom he's enjoyed for the past three years. Never forget, that man stole my freedom from me, along with my wife, my company, and more than half my possessions. Oh yes, Donald, I won't rest until I come face to face with Jeremy Alexander.'

'Good,' said the Don. 'Because Williams thinks Rosemary is beginning to trust him, and might even, given time, start confiding in him. It seems he has made himself indispensable.'

I found a certain irony in the thought of Williams pocketing two wage packets simultaneously, and of my being responsible for one, while Rosemary paid the other. I asked if there was any news of Jeremy.

'Nothing to speak of,' said Donald. 'She certainly never phones him from the house, and we're fairly sure he never attempts to make any direct contact with her. But Williams has told us that every Friday at midday he has to drop her off at the Majestic, the only hotel in the village. She goes inside and doesn't reappear for at least forty minutes. He daren't follow her, because she's given specific instructions that he's to stay with the car. And he can't afford to lose this job by disobeying orders.'

I nodded my agreement.

'But that hasn't stopped him having the occasional drink in the hotel bar on his evening off, and he's managed to pick up a few snippets of information. He's convinced that Rosemary uses the time when she's in the hotel to make a long-distance phone call. She often drops in at the bank before going on to the Majestic, and comes out carrying a small packet of coins. The barman has told Williams that she always uses one of the two phone boxes in the corridor opposite the reception desk. She never allows the call to be put through the hotel switch-board, always dials direct.'

'So how do we discover who she's calling?' I asked.

'We wait for Williams to find an opportunity to use some of those skills he didn't learn at butlers' school.'

'But how long might that take?'

'No way of knowing, but Williams is due for a spot of leave in a couple of weeks, so he'll be able to bring us up to date.'

When Williams arrived back in Bradford at the end of the month I began asking him questions even before he had time to put his suitcase down. He was full of interesting information about Rosemary, and even the smallest detail fascinated me.

She had put on weight. I was pleased. She seemed lonely and depressed. I was delighted. She was spending my money fast. I wasn't exactly ecstatic. But, more to the point, Williams was convinced that if Rosemary had any contact with Jeremy Alexander, it had to be when she visited the hotel every Friday and placed that direct-dial call. But he still hadn't worked out how to discover who, or where, she was phoning.

By the time Williams returned to the south of France a fortnight later I knew more about my ex-wife than I had ever done when we were married.

As happens so often in the real world, the next move came when I least expected it. It must have been about 2.30 on a Monday afternoon when the phone rang.

Donald picked up the receiver, and was surprised to hear Williams's voice on the other end of the line. He switched him on to the squawk box and said, 'All three of us are listening, so you'd better begin by telling us why you're ringing when it's not your day off.'

'I've been sacked,' were Williams's opening words.

'Playing around with the maid, were you?' was Donald's first reaction.

'I only wish, chief, but I'm afraid it's far more stupid than that. I was driving Ms Kershaw into town this morning, when I had to stop at a red light. While I was waiting for the lights to change, a man crossed the road in front of the car. He stopped and stared at me. I recognised him immediately, and prayed the lights would turn to green before he could place me. But he walked back, looked at me again, and smiled. I shook my head at him, but he came over to the driver's side, tapped on the window, and said, "How are you, Inspector Williams?"'

'Who was it?' demanded Donald.

'Neil Case. Remember him, chief?'

'Could I ever forget him? "Never-on-the-Case Neil",' said Donald. 'I might have guessed.'

'I didn't acknowledge him, of course, and as Ms Kershaw said nothing, I thought I might have got away with it. But as soon as we arrived back at the house she told me to come and see her in the study, and without even asking for an explanation she dismissed me. She ordered me to be packed and off the premises within the hour, or she'd call the local police.'

'Damn. Back to square one,' said Donald.

'Not quite,' said Williams.

'What do you mean? If you're no longer in the house, we no longer have a point of contact. Worse, we can't play the butler card again, because she's bound to be on her guard from now on.'

'I know all that, chief,' said Williams, 'but suspecting that I was a policeman caused her to panic, and she went straight to her bedroom and made a phone call. As I wasn't afraid of being found out any longer, I picked up the extension in the corridor and listened in. All I heard was a woman's voice give a Cambridge number, and then the phone went dead. I assumed Rosemary had been expecting someone else to pick up the phone, and hung up when she heard a strange voice.'

'What was the number?' Donald asked.

'6407-something-7.'

'What do you mean, "something-7"?' barked Donald as he scribbled the numbers down.

'I didn't have anything to write with, chief, so I had to rely on my memory.' I was glad Williams couldn't see the expression on the Don's face.

'Then what happened?' he demanded.

'I found a pen in a drawer and wrote what I could remember of the number on my hand. I picked up the phone again a few moments later, and heard a different woman on the line, saying, "The Director's not in at the moment, but I'm expecting him back within the hour." Then I had to hang up quickly, because I could hear someone coming along the corridor. It was Charlotte, Rosemary's maid. She wanted to know why I'd been sacked. I couldn't think of a convincing reply, until she accused me of having made a pass at the mistress. I let her think that was it, and ended up getting a slapped face for my trouble.' I burst out laughing, but the Don and Jenny showed no reaction. Then Williams asked, 'So, what do I do now, chief? Come back to England?'

'No,' said Donald. 'Stay put for the moment. Book yourself into the Majestic and watch her round the clock. Let me know if she does anything out of character. Meanwhile, we're going to Cambridge. As soon as we've booked ourselves into a hotel there I'll call you.'

'Understood, sir,' said Williams, and rang off.

'When do we go?' I asked Donald once he had replaced the receiver.

'Tonight,' he replied. 'But not before I've made a few telephone calls.'

The Don dialled ten Cambridge numbers, using the digits Williams had been able to jot down, and inserting the numbers from nought to nine in the missing slot.

0223 640707 turned out to be a school. 'Sorry, wrong number,' said Donald. 717 was a chemist's shop; 727 was a garage; 737 was answered by an elderly male voice – 'Sorry, wrong number,' Donald repeated; 747 a newsagent; 757 a local policeman's wife (I tried not to laugh, but Donald only grunted); 767 a woman's voice – 'Sorry, wrong number,' yet again; 777 was St Catharine's College; 787 a woman's voice on an answering machine; 797 a hairdresser – 'Did you want a perm, or just a trim?'

Donald checked his list. 'It has to be either 737, 767 or 787. The time has come for me to pull a few strings.'

He dialled a Bradford number, and was told that the new Deputy Chief Constable of Cambridgeshire had been transferred from the West Yorkshire Constabulary the previous year.

'Leeke. Allan Leeke,' said Donald, without needing to be prompted. He turned to me. 'He was a sergeant when I was first made up to inspector.' He thanked his Bradford contact, then rang directory enquiries to find out the number of the Cambridge Police headquarters. He dialled another 0223 number.

'Cambridge Police. How can I help you?' asked a female voice.

'Can you put me through to the Deputy Chief Constable, please?' Donald asked.

'Who shall I say is calling?'

'Donald Hackett.'

The next voice that came on the line said, 'Don, this is a pleasant surprise. Or at least I hope it's a pleasant surprise, because knowing you, it won't be a social call. Are you looking for a job, by any chance? I heard you'd left the force.'

'Yes, it's true. I've resigned, but I'm not looking for a job, Allan. I don't think the Cambridge Constabulary could quite match my present salary.'

'So, what can I do for you, Don?'

'I need a trace done on three numbers in the Cambridge area.'

'Authorised?' asked the Deputy Chief Constable.

'No, but it might well lead to an arrest on your patch,' said Donald.

'That, and the fact that it's you who's asking, is good enough for me.'

Donald read out the three numbers, and Leeke asked him to hang on for a moment. While we waited, Donald told me, 'All they have to do is press a few buttons in the control room, and the numbers will appear on a screen in front of him. Things have changed since I first joined the force. In those days we had to let our legs do the walking.'

The Deputy Chief Constable's voice came back on the line. 'Right, the first number's come up. 640737 is a Wing Commander Danvers-Smith. He's the only person registered as living in the house.' He read out an address in Great Shelford, which he explained was just to the south of Cambridge. Jenny wrote the details down.

'767 is a Professor and Mrs Balcescu, also living in Great Shelford. 787 is Dame Julia Renaud, the opera singer. She lives in Grantchester. We know her quite well. She's hardly ever at home, because of her concert commitments all over the world. Her house has been burgled three times in the last year, always when she was abroad.'

'Thank you,' said Donald. 'You've been most helpful.'

'Anything you want to tell me?' asked the Deputy Chief Constable, sounding hopeful.

'Not at the moment,' replied Donald. 'But as soon as I've finished my investigation, I promise you'll be the first person to be informed.'

'Fair enough,' came back the reply, and the line went dead.

'Right,' Donald said, turning his attention back to us. 'We leave for Cambridge in a couple of hours. That will give us enough time to pack, and for Jenny to book us into a hotel near the city centre. We'll meet back here at' – he checked his watch – 'six o'clock.' He walked out of the room without uttering another word. I remember thinking that my father would have got on well with him.

Just over two hours later, Jenny was driving us at a steady sixty-nine miles per hour down the A1.

'Now the boring part of detective work begins,' said Donald. 'Intense research, followed by hours of surveillance. I think we can safely ignore Dame Julia. Jenny, you get to work on the wing commander. I want details of his career from the day he left school to the day he retired. First thing tomorrow you can begin by contacting RAF College Cranwell, and asking for details of his service record. I'll take the professor, and make a start in the university library.'

'What do I do?' I asked.

'For the time being, Mr Cooper, you keep yourself well out of sight. It's just possible that the wing commander or the professor might lead us to Alexander, so we don't need you trampling over any suspects and frightening them off.'

I reluctantly agreed.

Later that night I settled into a suite at the Garden House Hotel – a more refined sort of prison – but despite feather pillows and a comfortable mattress I was quite unable to sleep. I rose early the next morning and spent most of the day watching endless updates on Sky News, episodes of various Australian soaps, and a 'Film of the Week' every two hours. But my mind was continually switching between RAF Cranwell and the university library.

When we met up in Donald's room that evening, he and Jenny confirmed that their initial research suggested that both men were who they purported to be.

'I was sure one of them would turn out to be Jeremy,' I said, unable to hide my disappointment.

'It would be nice if it was always that easy, Mr Cooper,' said Donald. 'But it doesn't mean that one of them won't lead us to Jeremy.' He turned to Jenny. 'First, let's go over what you found out about the wing commander.'

'Wing Commander Danvers-Smith DFC graduated from Cranwell in 1938, served with Number Two Squadron at Binbrook in Lincolnshire during the Second World War, and flew several missions over Germany and occupied France. He was awarded the DFC for gallantry in 1943. He was grounded in 1958, and became an instructor at RAF Cottesmore in Gloucestershire. His final posting was as Deputy Commanding Officer at RAF Locking in Somerset. He retired in 1977, when he and his wife moved back to Great Shelford, where he had grown up.'

'Why's he living on his own now?' asked Donald.

'Wife died three years ago. He has two children, Sam

and Pamela, both married, but neither living in the area. They visit him occasionally.'

I wanted to ask Jenny how she had been able to find out so much information about the wing commander in such a short time, but said nothing, as I was more interested in hearing what the Don had discovered about Professor Balcescu.

Donald picked up a pile of notes that had been lying on the floor by his feet. 'So, let me tell you the results of my research into a very distinguished professor,' he began. 'Professor Balcescu escaped from Romania in 1989, after Ceausescu had had him placed under house arrest. He was smuggled out of the country by a group of dissident students, via Bulgaria and then on into Greece. His escape was well documented in the newspapers at the time. He applied for asylum in England, and was offered a teaching post at Gonville and Caius College, Cambridge, and three years later the Chair of Eastern European Studies. He advises the government on Romanian matters, and has written a scholarly book on the subject. Last year he was awarded a CBE in the Queen's Birthday Honours.'

'How could either of these men possibly know Rosemary?' I asked. 'Williams must have made a mistake when he wrote down the number.'

'Williams doesn't make mistakes, Mr Cooper,' said the Don. 'Otherwise I wouldn't have employed him. Your wife dialled one of those numbers, and we're just going to have to find out which one. This time we'll need your assistance.'

I mumbled an apology, but remained unconvinced.

Hackett nodded curtly, and turned back to Jenny. 'How long will it take us to get to the wing commander's home?'

'About fifteen minutes, sir. He lives in a cottage in Great Shelford, just south of Cambridge.'

'Right, we'll start with him. I'll see you both in the lobby at five o'clock tomorrow morning.'

I slept fitfully again that night, now convinced that we were embarked on a wild-goose chase. But at least I was going to be allowed to join them the following day, instead of being confined to my room and yet more Australian soaps.

I didn't need my 4.30 alarm call – I was already showering when the phone went. A few minutes after five, the three of us walked out of the hotel, trying not to look as if we were hoping to leave without paying our bill. It was a chilly morning, and I shivered as I climbed into the back of the car.

Jenny drove us out of the city and onto the London road. After a mile or so she turned left and took us into a charming little village with neat, well-kept houses on either side of the road. We passed a garden centre on the left and drove another half mile, then Jenny suddenly swung the car round and reversed into a layby. She switched off the engine and pointed to a small house with an RAF-blue door. 'That's where he lives,' she said. 'Number forty-seven.' Donald focused a tiny pair of binoculars on the house.

Some early-morning risers were already leaving their

homes, cars heading towards the station for the first commuter train to London. The paperboy turned out to be an old lady who pushed her heavily-laden bicycle slowly round the village, dropping off her deliveries. The milkman was next, clattering along in his electric van — two pints here, a pint there, the occasional half-dozen eggs or carton of orange juice left on front door-steps. Lights began to flick on all over the village. 'The wing commander has had one pint of red-top milk and a copy of the *Daily Telegraph* delivered to his front door,' said Donald.

People had emerged from the houses on either side of number forty-seven before a light appeared in an upstairs room of the wing commander's home. Once that light had been switched on Donald sat bolt upright, his eyes never leaving the house.

I became bored, and dozed off in the back at some point. When I woke up, I hoped we might at least be allowed a break for breakfast, but such mundane considerations didn't seem to worry the two professionals in the front. They continued to concentrate on any movement that took place around number forty-seven, and hardly exchanged a word.

At 10.19 a thin, elderly man, dressed in a Harris tweed jacket and grey flannels, emerged from number forty-seven and marched briskly down the path. All I could see at that distance was a huge, bushy white moustache. It looked almost as if his whole body had been designed around it. Donald kept the glasses trained on him.

'Ever seen him before?' he asked, passing the binoculars back to me.

I focused the glasses on the wing commander and studied him carefully. 'Never,' I said as he came to a halt by the side of a battered old Austin Allegro. 'How could anyone forget that moustache?'

'It certainly wasn't grown last week,' said Donald, as Danvers-Smith eased his car out onto the main road.

Jenny cursed. 'I thought that if he used his car, the odds would be on him heading into Cambridge.' She deftly performed a three-point turn and accelerated quickly after the wing commander. Within a few minutes she was only a couple of cars behind him.

Danvers-Smith was not proving to be the sort of fellow who habitually broke the speed limit. 'His days as a test pilot are obviously long behind him,' Donald said, as we trailed the Allegro at a safe distance into the next village. About half a mile later he pulled into a petrol station.

'Stay with him,' said Donald. Jenny followed the Allegro into the forecourt and came to a halt at the pump directly behind Danvers-Smith.

'Keep your head down, Mr Cooper,' said the Don, opening his door. 'We don't want him seeing you.'

'What are you going to do?' I asked, peeping between the front seats.

'Risk an old con's trick,' Donald replied.

He stepped out of the front seat, walked round to the back of the car, and unscrewed the petrol cap just as the wing commander slipped the nozzle of a petrol pump into the tank of his Allegro. Donald began slowly topping up our already full tank, then suddenly turned to face the old man.

'Wing Commander Danvers-Smith?' he asked in a plummy voice.

The wing commander looked up immediately, and a puzzled expression came over his weather-beaten face.

'Baker, sir,' said Donald. 'Flight Lieutenant Baker. You lectured me at RAF Locking. Vulcans, if I remember.'

'Bloody good memory, Baker. Good show,' said Danvers-Smith. 'Delighted to see you, old chap,' he said, taking the nozzle out of his car and replacing it in the pump. 'What are you up to nowadays?'

Jenny stifled a laugh.

'Work for BA, sir. Grounded after I failed my eye test. Bloody desk job, I'm afraid, but it was the only offer I got.'

'Bad luck, old chap,' said the wing commander, as they headed off towards the pay booth, and out of earshot.

When they came back a few minutes later, they were chattering away like old chums, and the wing commander actually had his arm round Donald's shoulder.

When they reached his car they shook hands, and I heard Donald say 'Goodbye, sir,' before Danvers-Smith climbed into his Allegro. The old airman pulled out of the forecourt and headed back towards his home. Donald got in next to Jenny and pulled the passenger door closed.

'I'm afraid *he* won't lead us to Alexander,' the Don

said with a sigh. 'Danvers-Smith is the genuine article – misses his wife, doesn't see his children enough, and feels a bit lonely. Even asked if I'd like to drop in for a bite of lunch.'

'Why didn't you accept?' I asked.

Donald paused. 'I would have done, but when I mentioned that I was from Leeds, he told me he'd only been there once in his life, to watch a test match. No, that man has never heard of Rosemary Cooper or Jeremy Alexander – I'd bet my pension on it. So, now it's the turn of the professor. Let's head back towards Cambridge, Jenny. And drive slowly. I don't want to catch up with the wing commander, or we'll all end up having to join him for lunch.'

Jenny swung the car across the road and into the far lane, then headed back towards the city. After a couple of miles Donald told her to pull into the side of the road just past a sign announcing the Shelford Rugby Club.

'The professor and his wife live behind that hedge,' Donald said, pointing across the road. 'Settle back, Mr Cooper. This might take some time.'

At 12.30 Jenny went off to get some fish and chips from the village. I devoured them hungrily. By three I was bored stiff again, and was beginning to wonder just how long Donald would hang around before we were allowed to return to the hotel. I remembered 'Happy Days' would be on at 6.30.

'We'll sit here all night, if necessary,' Donald said, as if he were reading my thoughts. 'Forty-nine hours is my record without sleep. What's yours, Jenny?' he asked, never taking his eyes off the house.

'Thirty-one, sir,' she replied.

'Then this may be your chance to break that record,' he said. A moment later, a woman in a white BMW nosed out of the driveway leading to the house and stopped at the edge of the pavement. She paused, looked both ways, then turned across the road and swung right, in the direction of Cambridge. As she passed us, I caught a glimpse of a blonde with a pretty face.

'I've seen her before,' I blurted out.

'Follow her, Jenny,' Donald said sharply. 'But keep your distance.' He turned round to face me.

'Where have you seen her?' he asked, passing over the binoculars.

'I can't remember,' I said, trying to focus on the back of a mop of fair, curly hair.

'Think, man. Think. It's our best chance yet,' said Donald, trying not to sound as if he was cross-examining an old lag.

I knew I had come across that face somewhere, though I felt certain we had never met. I had to rack my brains, because it was at least five years since I had seen any woman I recognised, let alone one that striking. But my mind remained blank.

'Keep on thinking,' said the Don, 'while I try to find out something a little more simple. And Jenny – don't get too close to her. Never forget she's got a rear-view mirror. Mr Cooper may not remember her, but she may remember him.'

Donald picked up the carphone and jabbed in ten numbers. 'Let's pray he doesn't realise I've retired,' he mumbled.

'DVLA Swansea. How can I help you?'

'Sergeant Crann, please,' said Donald.

'I'll put you through.'

'Dave Crann.'

'Donald Hackett.'

'Good afternoon, Chief Superintendent. How can I help you?'

'White BMW – K273 SCE,' said Donald, staring at the car in front of him.

'Hold on please, sir, I won't be a moment.'

Donald kept his eye fixed on the BMW while he waited. It was about thirty yards ahead of us, and heading towards a green light. Jenny accelerated to make sure she wouldn't get trapped if the lights changed, and as she shot through an amber light, Sergeant Crann came back on the line,

'We've identified the car, sir,' he said. 'Registered owner Mrs Susan Balcescu, The Kendalls, High Street, Great Shelford, Cambridge. One endorsement for speeding in a built-up area, 1991, a thirty-pound fine. Otherwise nothing known.'

'Thank you, sergeant. That's most helpful.'

'My pleasure, sir.'

'Why should Rosemary want to contact the Balcescus?' Donald said as he clipped the phone back into place. 'And is she contacting just one of them, or both?' Neither of us attempted to answer.

'I think it's time to let her go,' he said a moment later. 'I need to check out several more leads before we risk coming face to face with either of them. Let's head back to the hotel and consider our next move.'

'I know it's only a coincidence,' I ventured, 'but when I knew him, Jeremy had a white BMW.'

'F173 BZK,' said Jenny. 'I remember it from the file.'

Donald swung round. 'Some people can't give up smoking, you know, others drinking. But with some, it's a particular make of car,' he said. 'Although a lot of people must drive white BMWs,' he muttered almost to himself.

Once we were back in Donald's room, he began checking through the file he had put together on Professor Balcescu. The *Times* report of his escape from Romania, he told us, was the most detailed.

P ROFESSOR BALCESCU first came to prominence while still a student at the University of Bucharest, where he called for the overthrow of the elected government. The authorities seemed relieved when he was offered a place at Oxford, and must have hoped that they had seen the last of him. But he returned to Bucharest University three years later, taking up the position of tutor in Politics. The following year he led a student revolt in support of Nicolae Ceausescu, and after he became president, Balcescu was rewarded with a Cabinet post, as Minister of Education. But he soon became disillusioned with the Ceausescu regime, and within eighteen months he had resigned and returned to the university as a humble

tutor. Three years later he was offered the Chair
of Politics and Economics.

Professor Balcescu's growing disillusionment
with the government finally turned to anger, and
in 1986 he began writing a series of pamphlets
denouncing Ceausescu and his puppet regime. A
few weeks after a particularly vitriolic attack on
the establishment, he was dismissed from his post
at the university, and later placed under house
arrest. A group of Oxford historians wrote a letter
of protest to *The Times*, but nothing more was
heard of the great scholar for several years. Then,
late in 1989, he was smuggled out of Romania by
a group of students, finally reaching Britain via
Bulgaria and Greece.

Cambridge won the battle of the universities to
tempt him with a teaching post, and he became a
fellow of Gonville and Caius in September 1990. In
November 1991, after the retirement of Sir Halford
McKay, Balcescu took over the Chair of Eastern
European Studies.

Donald looked up. 'There's a picture of him taken when
he was in Greece, but it's too blurred to be of much use.'

I studied the black-and-white photograph of a bearded
middle-aged man surrounded by students. He wasn't
anything like Jeremy. I frowned. 'Another blind alley,'
I said.

'It's beginning to look like it,' said Donald. 'Especially
after what I found out yesterday. According to his secretary, Balcescu delivers his weekly lecture every Friday
morning, from ten o'clock to eleven.'

'But that wouldn't stop him from taking a call from
Rosemary at midday,' interrupted Jenny.

'If you'll allow me to finish,' said Hackett sharply. Jenny bowed her head, and he continued. 'At twelve o'clock he chairs a full departmental meeting in his office, attended by all members of staff. I'm sure you'll agree, Jenny, that it would be quite difficult for him to take a personal call at that time every Friday, given the circumstances.'

Donald turned to me. 'I'm sorry to say we're back where we started, unless you can remember where you've seen Mrs Balcescu.' I shook my head. 'Perhaps I was mistaken,' I admitted.

Donald and Jenny spent the next few hours going over the files, even checking every one of the ten phone numbers a second time.

'Do you remember Rosemary's second call, sir,' said Jenny, in desperation. '"The Director's not in at the moment." Might that be the clue we're looking for?'

'Possibly,' said Donald. 'If we could find out who the Director is, we might be a step nearer to Jeremy Alexander.'

I remember Jenny's last words before I left for my room. 'I wonder how many directors there are in Britain, chief.'

Over breakfast in Donald's room the following morning, he reviewed all the intelligence that had been gathered to date, but none of us felt we were any nearer to a solution.

'What about Mrs Balcescu?' I said. '*She* may be the

person taking the call every Friday at midday, because that's the one time she knows exactly where her husband is.'

'I agree. But is she simply Rosemary's messenger, or is she a friend of Jeremy's?' asked Donald.

'Perhaps we'll have to tap her phone to find out,' said Jenny.

Donald ignored her comment, and checked his watch. 'It's time to go to Balcescu's lecture.'

'Why are we bothering?' I asked. 'Surely we ought to be concentrating on Mrs Balcescu.'

'You're probably right,' said Donald. 'But we can't afford to leave any stone unturned, and as his next lecture won't be for another week, we may as well get it over with. In any case, we'll be out by eleven, and if we find Mrs Balcescu's phone is engaged between twelve and twelve thirty . . .'

After Donald had asked Jenny to bring the car round to the front of the hotel, I slipped back into my room to pick up something that had been hidden in the bottom of my suitcase for several weeks. A few minutes later I joined them, and Jenny drove us out of the hotel carpark, turning right into the main road. Donald glanced at me suspiciously in the rear-view mirror as I sat silently in the back. Did I look guilty? I wondered.

Jenny spotted a parking meter a couple of hundred yards away from the Department of European Studies, and pulled in. We got out of the car and followed the flow of students along the pavement and up the steps. No one gave us a second look. Once we had entered the building, Donald whipped off his tie and slipped it in his jacket pocket. He looked more like a Marxist revolutionary than most of the people heading towards the lecture.

The lecture theatre was clearly signposted, and we entered it by a door on the ground floor, which turned out to be the only way in or out. Donald immediately walked up the raked auditorium to the back row of seats. Jenny and I followed, and Donald instructed me to sit behind a student who looked as if he spent his Saturday afternoons playing lock forward for his college rugby team.

While we waited for Balcescu to enter the room, I began to look around. The lecture theatre was a large semi-circle, not unlike a miniature Greek amphitheatre, and I estimated that it could hold around three hundred students. By the time the clock on the front wall read 9.55 there was hardly a seat to be found. No further proof was needed of the professor's reputation.

I felt a light sweat forming on my forehead as I waited for Balcescu to make his entrance. As the clock struck ten the door of the lecture theatre opened. I was so disappointed at the sight that greeted me that I groaned aloud. He couldn't have been less like Jeremy. I leaned across to Donald. 'Wrong-coloured hair, wrong-coloured eyes, about thirty pounds too light.' The Don showed no reaction.

'So the connection has to be with Mrs Balcescu,' whispered Jenny.

'Agreed,' said Donald under his breath. 'But we're stuck here for the next hour, because we certainly can't risk drawing attention to ourselves by walking out. We'll just have to make a dash for it as soon as the lecture is over. We'll still have time to see if she's at home to take the twelve o'clock call.' He paused. 'I should have checked the layout of the building earlier.' Jenny reddened slightly, because she knew *I* meant *you*.

And then I suddenly remembered where I had seen Mrs Balcescu. I was about to tell Donald, but the room fell silent as the professor began delivering his opening words.

'This is the sixth of eight lectures,' he began, 'on recent social and economic trends in Eastern Europe.' In a thick Central European accent he launched into a discourse that sounded as if he had given it many times before. The undergraduates began scribbling away on their pads, but I became increasingly irritated by the continual drone of the professor's nasal vowels, as I was impatient to tell Hackett about Mrs Balcescu and to get back to Great Shelford as quickly as possible. I found myself glancing up at the clock on the wall every few minutes. Not unlike my own schooldays, I thought. I touched my jacket pocket. It was still there, even though on this occasion it would serve no useful purpose.

Halfway through the lecture, the lights were dimmed so the professor could illustrate some of his points with slides. I glanced at the first few graphs as they appeared on the screen, showing different income groups across Eastern Europe related to their balance of payments and export figures, but I ended up none the wiser, and not just because I had missed the first five lectures.

The assistant in charge of the projector managed to get one of the slides upside down, showing Germany bottom of the export table and Romania top, which caused a light ripple of laughter throughout the theatre. The professor scowled, and began to deliver his lecture at a faster and faster pace, which only caused the assistant more difficulty in finding the right slides to coincide with the professor's statements.

Once again I became bored, and I was relieved when, at five to eleven, Balcescu called for the final graph. The previous one was replaced by a blank screen. Everyone began looking round at the assistant, who was searching desperately for the slide. The professor became irritable as the minute hand of the clock approached eleven. Still the assistant failed to locate the missing slide. He flicked the shutter back once again, but nothing appeared on the screen, leaving the professor brightly illuminated by a beam of light. Balcescu stepped forward, and began drumming his fingers impatiently on the wooden lectern. Then he turned sideways, and I caught his profile for the first time. There was a small scar above his right eye, which must have faded over the years, but in the bright light of the beam it was clear to see.

'It's him!' I whispered to Donald as the clock struck eleven. The lights came up, and the professor quickly left the lecture theatre without another word.

I leapt over the back of my bench seat, and began charging down the gangway, but my progress was impeded by students who were already sauntering out into the aisle. I pushed my way past them until I had reached ground level, and bolted through the door by which the professor had left so abruptly. I spotted him at the end of the corridor. He was opening another door, and disappeared out of sight. I ran after him, dodging in and out of the chattering students.

When I reached the door that had just been closed behind him I looked up at the sign:

PROFESSOR BALCESCU
Director of European Studies

I threw the door open, to discover a woman sitting behind a desk checking some papers. Another door was closing behind her.

'I need to see Professor Balcescu immediately,' I shouted, knowing that if I didn't get to him before Hackett caught up with me, I might lose my resolve.

The woman stopped what she was doing and looked up at me. 'The Director is expecting an overseas call at any moment, and cannot be disturbed,' she replied. 'I'm sorry, but . . .'

I ran straight past her, pulled open the door and rushed into the room, where I came face to face with Jeremy Alexander for the first time since I had left him lying on the floor of my drawing room. He was talking animatedly on the phone, but he looked up, and recognised me immediately. When I pulled the gun from my pocket, he dropped the receiver. As I took aim, the blood suddenly drained from his face.

'Are you there, Jeremy?' asked an agitated voice on

78

the other end of the line. Despite the passing of time, I had no difficulty in recognising Rosemary's strident tones.

Jeremy was shouting, 'No, Richard, no! I can explain! Believe me, I can explain!' as Donald came running in. He came to an abrupt halt by the professor's desk, but showed no interest in Jeremy.

'Don't do it, Richard,' he pleaded. 'You'll only spend the rest of your life regretting it.' I remember thinking it was the first time he had ever called me Richard.

'Wrong, for a change, Donald,' I told him. 'I won't regret killing Jeremy Alexander. You see, he's already been pronounced dead once. I know, because I was sentenced to life imprisonment for his murder. I'm sure you're aware of the meaning of *"autrefois acquit"*, and will therefore know that I can't be charged a second time with a crime I've already been convicted of and sentenced for. Even though this time they will have a body.'

I moved the gun a few inches to the right, and aimed at Jeremy's heart. I squeezed the trigger just as Jenny came charging into the room. She dived at my legs.

Jeremy and I both hit the ground with a thud.

Well, as I pointed out to you at the beginning of this chronicle, I ought to explain why I'm in jail – or, to be more accurate, why I'm back in jail.

I *was* tried a second time; on this occasion for attempted murder – despite the fact that I had only grazed the bloody man's shoulder. I still blame Jenny for that.

Mind you, it was worth it just to hear Matthew's closing speech, because he certainly understood the meaning of '*autrefois acquit*'. He surpassed himself with his description of Rosemary as a calculating, evil Jezebel, and Jeremy as a man motivated by malice and greed, quite willing to cynically pose as a national hero while his victim was rotting his life away in jail, put there by a wife's perjured testimony of which he had unquestionably been the mastermind. In another four years, a furious Matthew told the jury, they would have been able to pocket several more millions between them. This time the jury looked on me with considerable sympathy.

'Thou shalt not bear false witness against any man,' were Sir Matthew's closing words, his sonorous tones making him sound like an Old Testament prophet.

The tabloids always need a hero and a villain. This time they had got themselves a hero and two villains. They seemed to have forgotten everything they had printed during the previous trial about the oversexed lorry driver, and it would be foolish to suggest that the page after page devoted to every sordid detail of Jeremy and Rosemary's deception didn't influence the jury.

They found me guilty, of course, but only because they weren't given any choice. In his summing up the judge almost ordered them to do so. But the foreman expressed his fellow jurors' hope that, given the circumstances, the judge might consider a lenient sentence. Mr Justice Lampton obviously didn't read the tabloids, because he lectured me for several minutes, and then said I would be sent down for five years.

Matthew was on his feet immediately, appealing for clemency on the grounds that I had already served a long sentence. 'This man looks out on the world through a window of tears,' he told the judge. 'I beseech your lordship not to put bars across that window a second time.' The applause from the gallery was so thunderous that the judge had to instruct the bailiffs to clear the court before he could respond to Sir Matthew's plea.

'His lordship obviously needs a little time to think,' Matthew explained under his breath as he passed me in the dock. After much deliberation in his chambers, Mr Justice Lampton settled on three years. Later that day I was sent to Ford Open Prison.

After considerable press comment during the next few weeks, and what Sir Matthew described to the Court of Appeal as 'my client's unparalleled affliction and exemplary behaviour', I ended up only having to serve nine months.

Meanwhile, Jeremy had been arrested at Addenbrookes Hospital by Allan Leeke, Deputy Chief Constable of Cambridgeshire. After three days in a heavily guarded ward he was charged with conspiracy to pervert the course of public justice, and transferred to Armley Prison to await trial. He comes before the Leeds Crown Court next month, and you can be sure I'll be sitting in the gallery following the proceedings every day. By the way, Fingers and the boys gave him a very handsome welcome. I'm told he's lost even more weight than he did trooping backwards and forwards across Europe fixing up his new identity.

Rosemary has also been arrested and charged with perjury. They didn't grant her bail, and Donald informs me that French prisons, particularly the one in Marseilles, are less comfortable than Armley – one of the few disadvantages of living in the south of France. She's fighting the extradition order, of course, but I'm assured by Matthew that she has absolutely no chance of succeeding, now we've signed the Maastricht Treaty. I knew *something* good must come out of that.

As for Mrs Balcescu – I'm sure you worked out where I'd seen her long before I did.

In the case of Regina v. Alexander and Kershaw, I'm told, she will be giving evidence on behalf of the Crown. Jeremy made such a simple mistake for a normally calculating and shrewd man. In order to protect himself from being identified, he put all his worldly goods in his wife's name. So the striking blonde ended up with everything, and I have a feeling that when it comes to her cross-examination, Rosemary won't turn out to be all that helpful to Jeremy, because it slipped his mind to let her know that in between those weekly phone calls he was living with another woman.

It's been difficult to find out much more about the real Professor Balcescu, because since Ceausescu's downfall no one is quite sure what really happened to the distinguished academic. Even the Romanians believed he had escaped to Britain and begun a new life.

Bradford City have been relegated, so Donald has

bought a cottage in the West Country and settled down to watch Bath play rugby. Jenny has joined a private detective agency in London, but is already complaining about her salary and conditions. Williams has returned to Bradford and decided on an early retirement. It was he who pointed out the painfully obvious fact that when it's twelve o'clock in France, it's only eleven o'clock in Britain.

By the way, I've decided to go back to Leeds after all. Cooper's went into liquidation as I suspected they would, the new management team not proving all that effective when it came to riding out a recession. The official receiver was only too delighted to accept my offer of £250,000 for what remained of the company, because no one else was showing the slightest interest in it. Poor Jeremy will get almost nothing for his shares. Still, you should look up the new stock in the *F.T.* around the middle of next year, and buy yourself a few, because they'll be what my father would have called 'a risk worth taking'.

By the way, Matthew advises me that I've just given you what's termed as 'inside information', so please don't pass it on, as I have no desire to go back to jail for a third time.

CHEAP AT
HALF THE PRICE

WOMEN ARE NATURALLY SUPERIOR TO men, and Mrs Consuela Rosenheim was no exception.

Victor Rosenheim, an American banker, was Consuela's third husband, and the gossip columns on both sides of the Atlantic were suggesting that, like a chain smoker, the former Colombian model was already searching for her next spouse before she had extracted the last gasp from the old one. Her first two husbands – one an Arab, the other a Jew (Consuela showed no racial prejudice when it came to signing marriage contracts) – had not quite left her in a position that would guarantee her financial security once her natural beauty had faded. But two more divorce settlements would sort that out. With this in mind, Consuela estimated that she only had another five years before the final vow must be taken.

The Rosenheims flew into London from their home in New York – or, to be more accurate, from their homes in New York. Consuela had travelled to the airport by chauffeur-driven car from their mansion in the Hamptons, while her husband had been taken from his Wall Street office in a second chauffeur-driven car. They met up in the Concorde lounge at JFK. When they had landed at Heathrow another limousine transported them to the Ritz, where they were escorted to their usual suite without any suggestion of having to sign forms or book in.

The purpose of their trip was twofold. Mr Rosenheim was hoping to take over a small merchant bank that had not benefited from the recession, while Mrs Rosenheim intended to occupy her time looking for a suitable birthday present – for herself. Despite considerable research I have been unable to discover exactly which birthday Consuela would officially be celebrating.

After a sleepless night induced by jetlag, Victor Rosenheim was whisked away to an early-morning meeting in the City, while Consuela remained in bed toying with her breakfast. She managed one piece of thin unbuttered toast and a stab at a boiled egg.

Once the breakfast tray had been removed, Consuela made a couple of phone calls to confirm luncheon dates for the two days she would be in London. She then disappeared into the bathroom.

Fifty minutes later she emerged from her suite dressed in a pink Olaganie suit with a dark blue collar, her fair hair bouncing on her shoulders. Few of the men she passed between the elevator and the revolving doors failed to turn their heads, so Consuela judged that the previous fifty minutes had not been wasted. She stepped out of the hotel and into the morning sun to begin her search for the birthday present.

Consuela began her quest in New Bond Street. As in the past, she had no intention of straying more than a few blocks north, south, east or west from that comforting landmark, while a chauffeur-driven car hovered a few yards behind her.

She spent some time in Asprey's considering the latest slimline watches, a gold statue of a tiger with jade eyes, and a Fabergé egg, before moving on to Cartier, where she dismissed a crested silver salver, a platinum watch and a Louis XIV long-case clock. From there she walked another few yards to Tiffany's, which, despite a determined salesman who showed her almost everything the shop had to offer, she still left empty-handed.

Consuela stood on the pavement and checked her watch. It was 12.52, and she had to accept that it had been a fruitless morning. She instructed her chauffeur to drive her to Harry's Bar, where she found Mrs Stavros Kleanthis waiting for her at their usual table. Consuela greeted her friend with a kiss on both cheeks, and took the seat opposite her.

Mrs Kleanthis, the wife of a not unknown shipowner – the Greeks preferring one wife and several liaisons – had for the last few minutes been concentrating her attention on the menu to be sure that the restaurant served the few dishes that her latest diet would permit. Between them, the two women had read every book that had reached number one on the *New York Times* bestseller list which included the words 'youth', 'orgasm', 'slimming', 'fitness' or 'immortality' in its title.

'How's Victor?' asked Maria, once she and Consuela had ordered their meals.

Consuela paused to consider her response, and decided on the truth.

'Fast reaching his sell-by date,' she replied. 'And Stavros?'

'Well past his, I'm afraid,' said Maria. 'But as I have neither your looks nor your figure, not to mention the fact that I have three teenage children, I don't suppose I'll be returning to the market to select the latest brand.'

Consuela smiled as a salade niçoise was placed in front of her.

'So, what brings you to London – other than to have lunch with an old friend?' asked Maria.

'Victor has his eye on another bank,' replied Consuela, as if she were discussing a child who collected stamps. 'And I'm in search of a suitable birthday present.'

'And what are you expecting Victor to come up with this time?' asked Maria. 'A house in the country? A thoroughbred racehorse? Or perhaps your own Lear jet?'

'None of the above,' said Consuela, placing her fork by the half-finished salad. 'I need something that can't be bargained over at a future date, so my gift must be one that any court, in any state, will acknowledge is unquestionably mine.'

'Have you found anything appropriate yet?' asked Maria.

'Not yet,' admitted Consuela. 'Asprey's yielded nothing of interest, Cartier's cupboard was almost bare, and the only attractive thing in Tiffany's was the salesman, who was undoubtedly penniless. I shall have to continue my search this afternoon.'

The salad plates were deftly removed by a waiter whom Maria considered far too young and far too thin. Another waiter with the same problem poured them both a cup of fresh decaffeinated coffee. Consuela refused the proffered cream and sugar, though her companion was not quite so disciplined.

The two ladies grumbled on about the sacrifices they were having to make because of the recession until they were the only diners left in the room. At this point a fatter waiter presented them with the bill – an extraordinarily long ledger considering that neither of them had ordered a second course, or had requested more than Evian from the wine waiter.

On the pavement of South Audley Street they kissed again on both cheeks before going their separate ways, one to the east and the other to the west.

Consuela climbed into the back of her chauffeur-driven car in order to be returned to New Bond Street, a distance of no more than half a mile.

Once she was back on familiar territory, she began to work her way steadily down the other side of the street, stopping at Bentley's, where it appeared that they hadn't sold anything since last year, and moving rapidly on to Adler, who seemed to be suffering from much the same problem. She cursed the recession once again, and blamed it all on Bill Clinton, who Victor had assured her was the cause of most of the world's current problems.

Consuela was beginning to despair of finding anything worthwhile in Bond Street, and reluctantly began her journey back towards the Ritz, feeling she might even have to consider an expedition to Knightsbridge the following day, when she came to a sudden halt outside the House of Graff. Consuela could not recall the shop from her last visit to London some six months before, and as she knew Bond Street better than she had ever known any of her three husbands, she concluded that it must be a new establishment.

She gazed at the stunning gems in their magnificent settings, heavily protected behind the bulletproof windows. When she reached the third window her mouth opened wide, like a newborn chick demanding to be fed. From that moment she knew that no further excursions would be necessary, for there, hanging round a slender marble neck, was a peerless diamond and ruby necklace. She felt that she had seen the magnificent piece of jewellery somewhere before, but she quickly dismissed the thought from her mind, and continued to study the exquisitely set rubies surrounded by perfectly cut diamonds, making up a necklace of unparalleled beauty. Without giving a moment's thought to how much the object might cost, Consuela walked slowly towards the thick glass door at the entrance to the shop, and pressed a discreet ivory button on the wall. The House of Graff obviously had no interest in passing trade.

The door was unlocked by a security officer who needed no more than a glance at Mrs Rosenheim to know that he should usher her quickly through to the inner portals, where a second door was opened and

Consuela came face to face with a tall, imposing man in a long black coat and pinstriped trousers.

'Good afternoon, madam,' he said, bowing slightly. Consuela noticed that he surreptitiously admired her rings as he did so. 'Can I be of assistance?'

Although the room was full of treasures that might in normal circumstances have deserved hours of her attention, Consuela's mind was focused on only one object.

'Yes. I would like to study more closely the diamond and ruby necklace on display in the third window.'

'Certainly, madam,' the manager replied, pulling back a chair for his customer. He nodded almost imperceptibly to an assistant, who silently walked over to the window, unlocked a little door and extracted the necklace. The manager slipped behind the counter and pressed a concealed button. Four floors above, a slight burr sounded in the private office of Mr Laurence Graff, warning the proprietor that a customer had enquired after a particularly expensive item, and that he might wish to deal with them personally.

Laurence Graff glanced up at the television screen on the wall to his left, which showed him what was taking place on the ground floor.

'Ah,' he said, once he saw the lady in the pink suit seated at the Louis XIV table. 'Mrs Consuela Rosenheim, if I'm not mistaken.' Just as the Speaker of the House of Commons can identify every one of its 650 members, so Laurence Graff recognised the 650 customers who might be able to afford the most extravagant of his treasures. He quickly stepped from behind his desk, walked out of his office and took the waiting lift to the ground floor.

Meanwhile, the manager had laid out a black velvet cloth on the table in front of Mrs Rosenheim, and the assistant placed the necklace delicately on top of it. Consuela stared down at the object of her desire, mesmerised.

'Good afternoon, Mrs Rosenheim,' said Laurence Graff as he stepped out of the lift and walked across the thick pile carpet towards his would-be customer. 'How nice to see you again.'

He had in truth only seen her once before – at a shoulder-to-shoulder cocktail party in Manhattan. But after that, he could have spotted her at a hundred paces on a moving escalator.

'Good afternoon, Mr . . .' Consuela hesitated, feeling unsure of herself for the first time that day.

'Laurence Graff,' he said, offering his hand. 'We met at Sotheby Parke Benett last year – a charity function in aid of the Red Cross, if I remember correctly.'

'Of course,' said Mrs Rosenheim, unable to recall him, or the occasion.

Mr Graff bowed reverently towards the diamond and ruby necklace.

'The Kanemarra heirloom,' he purred, then paused, before taking the manager's place at the table. 'Fashioned in 1936 by Silvio di Larchi,' he continued. 'All the rubies were extracted from a single mine in Burma, over a period of twenty years. The diamonds were purchased from De Beers by an Egyptian merchant who, after the necklace had been made up for him, offered the unique piece to King Farouk – for services rendered. When the monarch married Princess Farida he presented it to her on their wedding day, and she in return bore him four heirs, none of whom, alas, was destined to succeed to the throne.' Graff looked up from one object of beauty, and gazed on another.

'Since then it has passed through several hands before arriving at the House of Graff,' continued the proprietor. 'Its most recent owner was an actress, whose husband's oil wells unfortunately dried up.'

The flicker of a smile crossed the face of Consuela Rosenheim as she finally recalled where she had previously seen the necklace.

'Quite magnificent,' she said, giving it one final look. 'I will be back,' she added as she rose from her chair. Graff accompanied her to the door. Nine out of ten customers who make such a claim have no intention of returning, but he could always sense the tenth.

'May I ask the price?' Consuela asked indifferently as he held the door open for her.

'One million pounds, madam,' Graff replied, as casually as if she had enquired about the cost of a plastic keyring at a seaside gift shop.

Once she had reached the pavement, Consuela dismissed her chauffeur. Her mind was now working at a speed that would have impressed her husband. She slipped across the road, calling first at The White House, then Yves Saint Laurent, and finally at Chanel, emerging some two hours later with all the weapons she required for the battle that lay ahead. She did not arrive back at her suite at the Ritz until a few minutes before six.

Consuela was relieved to find that her husband had not yet returned from the bank. She used the time to take a long bath, and to contemplate how the trap should be set. Once she was dry and powdered, she dabbed a suggestion of a new scent on her neck, then slipped into some of her newly acquired clothes.

She was checking herself once again in the full-length mirror when Victor entered the room. He stopped on the spot, dropping his briefcase on the carpet. Consuela turned to face him.

'You look stunning,' he declared, with the same look of desire she had lavished on the Kanemarra heirloom a few hours before.

'Thank you, darling,' she replied. 'And how did your day go?'

'A triumph. The takeover has been agreed, and at half the price it would have cost me only a year ago.'

Consuela smiled. An unexpected bonus.

'Those of us who are still in possession of cash need have no fear of the recession,' Victor added with satisfaction.

Over a quiet supper in the Ritz's dining room, Victor described to his wife in great detail what had taken place at the bank that day. During the occasional break in this monologue Consuela indulged her husband by remarking 'How clever of you, Victor,' 'How amazing,' 'How you managed it I will never understand.' When he finally ordered a large brandy, lit a cigar and leaned back in his chair, she began to run her elegantly stockinged right foot gently along the inside of his thigh. For the first time that evening, Victor stopped thinking about the takeover.

As they left the dining room and strolled towards the lift, Victor placed an arm around his wife's slim waist. By the time the lift had reached the sixth floor he had already taken off his jacket, and his hand had slipped a few inches further down. Consuela giggled. Long before they had reached the door of their suite he had begun tugging off his tie.

When they entered the room, Consuela placed the 'Do Not Disturb' sign on the outside doorknob. For the next few minutes Victor was transfixed to the spot as he watched his slim wife slowly remove each garment she had purchased that afternoon. He quickly pulled off his own clothes, and wished once again that he had carried out his New Year's resolution.

Forty minutes later, Victor lay exhausted on the bed. After a few moments of sighing, he began to snore. Consuela pulled the sheet over their naked bodies, but her eyes remained wide open. She was already going over the next step in her plan.

Victor awoke the following morning to discover his wife's hand gently stroking the inside of his leg. He rolled over to face her, the memory of the previous night still vivid in his mind. They made love a second time, something they had not done for as long as he could recall.

It was not until he stepped out of the shower that Victor remembered it was his wife's birthday, and that he had promised to spend the morning with her selecting a gift. He only hoped that her eye had already settled on something she wanted, as he needed to spend most of the day closeted in the City with his lawyers, going over the offer document line by line.

'Happy birthday, darling,' he said as he padded back into the bedroom. 'By the way, did you have any luck finding a present?' he added as he scanned the front page of the *Financial Times*, which was already speculating on the possible takeover, describing it as a coup. A smile of satisfaction appeared on Victor's face for the second time that morning.

'Yes, my darling,' Consuela replied. 'I did come across one little bauble that I rather liked. I just hope it isn't too expensive.'

'And how much is this "little bauble"?' Victor asked. Consuela turned to face him. She was wearing only two garments, both of them black, and both of them remarkably skimpy.

Victor started to wonder if he still had the time, but then he remembered the lawyers, who had been up all night and would be waiting patiently for him at the bank.

'I didn't ask the price,' Consuela replied. 'You're so much cleverer than I am at that sort of thing,' she added, as she slipped into a navy silk blouse.

Victor glanced at his watch. 'How far away is it?' he asked.

'Just across the road, in Bond Street, my darling,' Consuela replied. 'I shouldn't have to delay you for too long.' She knew exactly what was going through her husband's mind.

'Good. Then let's go and look at this little bauble without delay,' he said as he did up the buttons on his shirt.

While Victor finished dressing, Consuela, with the help of the *Financial Times*, skilfully guided the conversation back to his triumph of the previous day. She listened once more to the details of the takeover as they left the hotel and strolled up Bond Street together arm in arm.

'Probably saved myself several million,' he told her yet again. Consuela smiled as she led him to the door of the House of Graff.

'Several million?' she gasped. 'How clever you are, Victor.'

The security guard quickly opened the door, and this time Consuela found that Mr Graff was already standing by the table waiting for her. He bowed low, then turned to Victor. 'May I offer my congratulations on your brilliant coup, Mr Rosenheim.' Victor smiled. 'How may I help you?'

'My husband would like to see the Kanemarra heirloom,' said Consuela, before Victor had a chance to reply.

'Of course, madam,' said the proprietor. He stepped behind the table and spread out the black velvet cloth. Once again the assistant removed the magnificent necklace from its stand in the third window, and carefully laid it out on the centre of the velvet cloth to show the jewels to their best advantage. Mr Graff was about to embark on the piece's history, when Victor simply said, 'How much is it?'

Mr Graff raised his head. 'This is no ordinary piece of jewellery. I feel . . .'

'How much?' repeated Victor.

'Its provenance alone warrants . . .'

'How much?'

'The sheer beauty, not to mention the craftsmanship involved . . .'

'How much?' asked Victor, his voice now rising.

'. . . the word unique would not be inappropriate.'

'You may be right, but I still need to know how much it's going to cost me,' said Victor, who was beginning to sound exasperated.

'One million pounds, sir,' Graff said in an even tone, aware that he could not risk another superlative.

'I'll settle at half a million, no more,' came back the immediate reply.

'I am sorry to say, sir,' said Graff, 'that with this particular piece, there is no room for bargaining.'

'There's always room for bargaining, whatever one is selling,' said Victor. 'I repeat my offer. Half a million.'

'I fear that in this case, sir . . .'

'I feel confident that you'll see things my way, given time,' said Victor. 'But I don't have that much time to spare this morning, so I'll write out a cheque for half a million, and leave *you* to decide whether you wish to cash it or not.'

'I fear you are wasting your time, sir,' said Graff. 'I cannot let the Kanemarra heirloom go for less than one million.'

Victor took out a chequebook from his inside pocket, unscrewed the top of his fountain pen, and wrote out the words 'Five Hundred Thousand Pounds Only' below the name of the bank that bore his name. His wife took a discreet pace backwards.

Graff was about to repeat his previous comment, when he glanced up, and observed Mrs Rosenheim silently pleading with him to accept the cheque.

A look of curiosity came over his face as Consuela continued her urgent mime.

Victor tore out the cheque and left it on the table. 'I'll give you twenty-four hours to decide,' he said. 'We return to New York tomorrow morning – with or without the Kanemarra heirloom. It's your decision.'

Graff left the cheque on the table as he accompanied Mr and Mrs Rosenheim to the front door and bowed them out onto Bond Street.

'You were brilliant, my darling,' said Consuela as the chauffeur opened the car door for his master.

'The bank,' Rosenheim instructed as he fell into the back seat. 'You'll have your little bauble, Consuela. He'll cash the cheque before the twenty-four hours are up, of that I'm sure.' The chauffeur closed the back door, and the window purred down as Victor added with a smile, 'Happy birthday, darling.'

Consuela returned his smile, and blew him a kiss as the car pulled out into the traffic and edged its way towards Piccadilly. The morning had not turned out quite as she had planned, because she felt unable to agree with her husband's judgement – but then, she still had twenty-four hours to play with.

Consuela returned to the suite at the Ritz, undressed, took a shower, opened another bottle of perfume, and slowly began to change into the second outfit she had purchased the previous day. Before she left the room she turned to the commodities section of the *Financial Times*, and checked the price of green coffee.

She emerged from the Arlington Street entrance of the Ritz wearing a double-breasted navy blue Yves Saint Laurent suit and a wide-brimmed red and white hat. Ignoring her chauffeur, she hailed a taxi, instructing the driver to take her to a small, discreet hotel in Knightsbridge. Fifteen minutes later she entered the foyer with her head bowed, and after giving the name of her host to the manager, was accompanied to a suite on the fourth floor. Her luncheon companion stood as she entered the room, walked forward, kissed her on both cheeks and wished her a happy birthday.

After an intimate lunch, and an even more intimate hour spent in the adjoining room, Consuela's companion listened to her request and, having first checked his watch, agreed to accompany her to Mayfair. He didn't mention to her that he would have to be back in his office by four o'clock to take an important call from South America. Since the downfall of the Brazilian president, coffee prices had gone through the roof.

As the car travelled down Brompton Road, Consuela's companion telephoned to check the latest spot price of green coffee in New York (only her skill in bed had managed to stop him from calling earlier). He was pleased to learn that it was up another two cents, but not as pleased as she was. Eleven minutes later, the car deposited them outside the House of Graff.

When they entered the shop together arm in arm, Mr Graff didn't so much as raise an eyebrow.

'Good afternoon, Mr Carvalho,' he said. 'I do hope that your estates yielded an abundant crop this year.'

Mr Carvalho smiled and replied, 'I cannot complain.'

'And how may I assist you?' enquired the proprietor.

'We would like to see the diamond necklace in the third window,' said Consuela, without a moment's hesitation.

'Of course, madam,' said Graff, as if he were addressing a complete stranger.

Once again the black velvet cloth was laid out on the table, and once again the assistant placed the Kanemarra heirloom in its centre.

This time Mr Graff was allowed to relate its history, before Carvalho politely enquired after the price.

'One million pounds,' said Graff.

After a moment's hesitation, Carvalho said, 'I'm willing to pay half a million.'

'This is no ordinary piece of jewellery,' replied the proprietor. 'I feel . . .'

'Possibly not, but half a million is my best offer,' said Carvalho.

'The sheer beauty, not to mention the craftsmanship involved . . .'

'Nevertheless, I am not willing to go above half a million.'

'. . . the word unique would not be inappropriate.'

'Half a million, and no more,' insisted Carvalho.

'I am sorry to say, sir,' said Graff, 'that with this particular piece there is no room for bargaining.'

'There's always room for bargaining, whatever one is selling,' the coffee grower insisted.

'I fear that is not true in this case, sir. You see . . .'

'I suspect you will come to your senses in time,' said Carvalho. 'But, regrettably, I do not have any time to spare this afternoon. I will write out a cheque for half a million pounds, and leave *you* to decide whether you wish to cash it.'

Carvalho took a chequebook from his inside pocket, unscrewed the top of his fountain pen, and wrote out the words 'Five Hundred Thousand Pounds Only'. Consuela looked silently on.

Carvalho tore out the cheque, and left it on the counter.

'I'll give you twenty-four hours to decide. I leave for Chicago on the early evening flight tomorrow. If the cheque has not been presented by the time I reach my office . . .'

Graff bowed his head slightly, and left the cheque on

the table. He accompanied them to the door, and bowed again when they stepped out onto the pavement.

'You were brilliant, my darling,' said Consuela as the chauffeur opened the car door for his employer.

'The Exchange,' said Carvalho. Turning back to face his mistress, he added, 'You'll have your necklace before the day is out, of that I'm certain, my darling.'

Consuela smiled and waved as the car disappeared in the direction of Piccadilly, and on this occasion she felt able to agree with her lover's judgement. Once the car had turned the corner, she slipped back into the House of Graff.

The proprietor smiled, and handed over the smartly wrapped gift. He bowed low and simply said, 'Happy birthday, Mrs Rosenheim.'

DOUGIE MORTIMER'S
RIGHT ARM

ROBERT HENRY KEFFORD III, KNOWN TO his friends as Bob, was in bed with a girl called Helen when he first heard about Dougie Mortimer's right arm.

Bob was sorry to be leaving Cambridge. He had spent three glorious years at St John's, and although he hadn't read as many books as he had done for his undergraduate degree at the University of Chicago, he had striven every bit as hard to come head of the river.

It wasn't unusual for an American to win a rowing blue in the early 1970s, but to have stroked a victorious Cambridge eight for three years in a row was acknowledged as a first.

Bob's father, Robert Henry Kefford II, known to his friends as Robert, had travelled over to England to watch his son take part in all three races from Putney to Mortlake. After Bob had stroked Cambridge to victory for the third time, his father told him that he must not return to his native Illinois without having presented a memento to the University Boat Club that they would remember him by.

'And don't forget, my boy,' declared Robert Henry Kefford II, 'the gift must not be ostentatious. Better to show that you have made an effort to present them with an object of historic value than give them something that obviously cost a great deal of money. The British appreciate that sort of thing.'

Bob spent many hours pondering his father's words, but completely failed to come up with any worthwhile ideas. After all, the Cambridge University Boat Club had more silver cups and trophies than they could possibly display.

It was on a Sunday morning that Helen first mentioned the name of Dougie Mortimer. She and Bob were lying in each other's arms, when she started prodding his biceps.

'Is this some form of ancient British foreplay that I ought to know about?' Bob asked, placing his free arm around Helen's shoulder.

'Certainly not,' Helen replied. 'I was simply trying to discover if your biceps are as big as Dougie Mortimer's.'

As Bob had never known a girl talk about another man while he was in bed with her, he was unable to think of an immediate response.

'And are they?' he eventually enquired, flexing his muscles.

'Hard to tell,' Helen replied. 'I've never actually touched Dougie's arm, only seen it at a distance.'

'And where did you come across this magnificent specimen of manhood?'

'It hangs over the bar at my dad's local, in Hull.'

'Doesn't Dougie Mortimer find that a little painful?' asked Bob, laughing.

'Doubt if he cares that much,' said Helen. 'After all, he's been dead for over sixty years.'

'And his arm still hangs above a bar?' asked Bob in disbelief. 'Hasn't it begun to smell a bit by now?'

This time it was Helen's turn to laugh. 'No, you Yankee fool. It's a bronze cast of his arm. In those days, if you were in the University crew for three years in a row, they made a cast of your arm to hang in the club-house. Not to mention a card with your picture on it in every packet of Player's cigarettes. I've never seen *your* picture in a cigarette packet, come to think of it,' said Helen as she pulled the sheet over his head.

'Did he row for Oxford or Cambridge?' asked Bob.

'No idea.'

'So, what's the name of this pub in Hull?'

'The King William,' Helen replied, as Bob took his arm from around her shoulder.

'Is this American foreplay?' she asked after a few moments.

Later that morning, after Helen had left for Newnham, Bob began searching his shelves for a book with a blue cover. He dug out his much-thumbed *History of the Boat Race* and flicked through the index, to discover that there were seven Mortimers listed. Five had rowed for Oxford, two for Cambridge. He began to pray as he checked their initials. Mortimer, A.J. (Westminster and Wadham, Oxon), Mortimer, C.K. (Uppingham and Oriel, Oxon), Mortimer, D.J.T. (Harrow and

St Catharine's, Cantab), Mortimer, E.L. (Oundle and Magdalen, Oxon). Bob turned his attention to Mortimer, D.J.T., biography page 129, and flicked the pages backwards until he reached the entry he sought. Douglas John Townsend Mortimer (St Catharine's), Cambridge 1907, –08, –09, stroke. He then read the short summary of Mortimer's rowing career.

> DOUGIE MORTIMER stroked the Cambridge boat to victory in 1907, a feat which he repeated in 1908. But in 1909, when the experts considered Cambridge to have one of the finest crews for years, the light blues lost to an Oxford boat that was regarded as the rank outsider. Although many explanations were suggested by the press at the time, the result of the race remains a mystery to this day. Mortimer died in 1914.

Bob closed the book and returned it to the shelf, assuming the great oarsman must have been killed in the First World War. He perched on the end of the bed, considering the information he now possessed. If he could bring Dougie Mortimer's right arm back to Cambridge and present it to the Club at the annual Blues' Dinner, it would surely be a prize that met his father's demanding criterion.

He dressed quickly and went downstairs to the pay phone in the corridor. Once directory enquiries had given him the four numbers he required, he set about trying to remove the next obstacle.

The first calls he made were to the King William – or, to be precise, the King Williams, because the directory had supplied him with the numbers of three pubs in Hull which bore that name. When he was put through to the first, he asked, 'Does Dougie Mortimer's right arm hang above your counter?' He couldn't quite make out every word of the broad northern accent that replied, but he was left in no doubt that it didn't.

The second call was answered by a girl who said, 'Do you mean that thing that's nailed to the wall above the bar?'

'Yes, I guess that will be it,' said Bob.

'Well then, this is the pub you're looking for.'

After Bob had taken down the address and checked the pub's opening hours, he made a third call. 'Yes, that's possible,' he was told. 'You can take the 3.17 to Peterborough, where you'll have to change and catch the 4.09 for Doncaster, then change again. You'll arrive in Hull at 6.32.'

'What about the last train back?' asked Bob.

'8.52, change at Doncaster and Peterborough. You should be back in Cambridge just after midnight.'

'Thank you,' said Bob. He strolled off to his college for lunch and took a place at the large centre table, but proved unusually poor company for those around him.

He boarded the train to Peterborough later that afternoon, still thinking about how he could possibly relieve the pub owners of their prize possession. At Peterborough he jumped out, walked across to a waiting train on platform three and climbed aboard, still deep in thought. When his train pulled into Hull a couple of hours later he was no nearer to solving the problem. He asked the first taxi on the rank to take him to the King William.

'Market Place, Harold's Corner or Percy Street?' asked the cabbie.

'Percy Street, please,' replied Bob.

'They don't open until seven, lad,' the cabbie told him once he had dropped Bob outside the front door.

Bob checked the time. Twenty minutes to kill. He walked down a side street at the back of the pub, and stopped to watch some young lads playing football. They were using the front walls of two houses on either side of the street as goals, and showed amazing accuracy in never hitting any of the windows. Bob wondered if the game would ever catch on in America.

He became so captivated by the youngsters' skill that they stopped to ask him if he wanted to join in. He said, 'No thank you,' confident that if he did play with them, he would be the one person who ended up breaking a window.

He arrived back outside the King William a few minutes after seven, and strolled into the empty pub, hoping that no one would pay much attention to him. But at six feet four inches, and dressed in a double-breasted blue blazer, grey flannels, a blue shirt and college tie, the three people behind the bar might well have wondered if he had dropped in from another planet. He stopped himself from looking above the bar, as a young blonde barmaid stepped forward and asked him what he would like.

'A half a pint of your best bitter,' Bob said, trying to

sound like one of his English friends when they ordered a drink from the college buttery.

The landlord eyed Bob suspiciously as he took his half-pint glass over to a small round table in the corner and sat down quietly on a stool. He was pleased when two other men entered the pub, so that the landlord's attention was distracted.

Bob took a sip of the dark liquid and nearly choked. When he had recovered, he allowed his eyes to glance above the bar. He tried to hide his excitement when he saw the bronze cast of a massive arm embedded in a large piece of varnished wood. He thought the object both dreadful and inspiring at the same time. His eyes moved down to the bold lettering printed in gold beneath it:

D. J. T. MORTIMER
1907–08–09
(St Catharine's, stroke)

Bob kept his eye on the landlord as the pub began to fill up, but he soon became aware that it was his wife – everyone called her Nora – who was not only in charge, but who did most of the serving.

When he had finished his drink, he made his way over to her end of the bar.

'What can I do for you, young man?' Nora asked.

'I'll have another, thank you,' said Bob.

'An American,' she said, as she pulled the pump and began to refill his glass. 'We don't get many of you lot up 'ere, at least not since the bases closed.' She placed his half-pint on the counter in front of him. 'So, what brings you to 'ull?'

'You do,' Bob replied, ignoring his drink.

Nora looked suspiciously at the stranger, who was young enough to be her son.

Bob smiled, 'Or, to be more accurate, Dougie Mortimer does.'

'Now I've figured you out,' said Nora. 'You phoned this morning, didn't you? My Christie told me. I should 'ave guessed.'

Bob nodded. 'How did the arm end up in Hull?' he asked.

'Now, that's a long story,' said Nora. 'It was my grandfather's, wasn't it. Born in Ely 'e was, and 'e used to spend his holidays fishin' the Cam. Said it was the only catch he managed that year, which I suppose is one better than sayin' it fell off the back of a lorry. Still, when 'e died a few years back, my father wanted to throw the bloody thing out with the rest of the rubbish, but I wouldn't 'ear of it, told 'im 'e should 'ang it in the pub, didn't I? I cleaned and polished it, it came up real nice, and then I 'ung it above the bar. Still, it's a long way for you to travel just to 'ave a look at that load of old cobblers.'

Bob looked up and admired the arm once again. He held his breath. 'I didn't come just to look.'

'Then why did you come?' she asked.

'I came to buy.'

'Get a move on, Nora,' said the landlord. 'Can't you see there are customers waitin' to be served?'

116

Nora swung round and said, 'Just 'old your tongue, Cyril Barnsworth. This young man's come all the way up to 'ull just to see Dougie Mortimer's arm, and what's more, 'e wants to buy it.' This caused a ripple of laughter from the regulars standing nearest to the bar, but as Nora didn't join in they quickly fell silent.

'Then it's been a wasted journey, 'asn't it?' said the landlord. 'Because it's not for sale.'

'It's not yours to sell,' said Nora, placing her hands on her hips. 'Mind you, lad, 'e's right,' she said, turning back to face Bob. 'I wouldn't part with it for a 'undred quid,' said Nora. Several others in the room were beginning to show an interest in the proceedings.

'How about two hundred,' said Bob quietly. This time Nora burst out laughing, but Bob didn't even smile.

When Nora had stopped laughing, she stared directly at the strange young man. 'My God, 'e means it,' she said.

'I certainly do,' said Bob. 'I would like to see the arm returned to its rightful home in Cambridge, and I'm willing to pay two hundred pounds for the privilege.'

The landlord looked across at his wife, as if he couldn't believe what he was hearing. 'We could buy that little second-hand car I've had my eye on,' he said.

'Not to mention a summer 'oliday and a new overcoat for next winter,' Nora added, staring at Bob as if she still needed to be convinced that he wasn't from another planet. Suddenly she thrust her hand over the counter and said, 'You've got yourself a deal, young man.'

Bob ended up having to supply several rounds of

drinks for those customers who claimed to have been close personal friends of Nora's grandfather, even if some of them looked rather obviously too young. He also had to stay overnight in a local hotel, because Nora wouldn't part with her grandfather's 'heirloom', as she now kept referring to it, until her bank manager had phoned Cambridge to check that Robert Henry Kefford III was good for two hundred pounds.

Bob clung onto his treasure all the way back to Cambridge that Monday morning, and then lugged the heavy object from the station to his digs in the Grange Road, where he hid it under the bed. The following day he handed it over to a local furniture restorer, who promised to return the arm to its former glory in time for the night of the Blues' Dinner.

When, three weeks later, Bob was allowed to see the results of the restorer's efforts, he immediately felt confident that he now possessed a prize not only worthy of the C.U.B.C., but that also complied with his father's wishes. He resolved not to share his secret with anyone – not even Helen – until the night of the Blues' Dinner, although he did warn the puzzled President that he was going to make a presentation, and that he required two hooks, eighteen inches apart and eight feet from the floor, to be screwed into the wall beforehand.

The University Blues' Dinner is an annual event held in the Boat House overlooking the Cam. Any former or current rowing blue is eligible to attend, and Bob was

delighted to find when he arrived that night that it was
a near-record turnout. He placed the carefully wrapped
brown paper parcel under his chair, and put his camera
on the table in front of him.

Because it was his last Blues' Dinner before returning
to America, Bob had been seated at the top table, between
the Honorary Secretary and the current President of
Boats. Tom Adams, the Honorary Secretary, had gained
his blue some twenty years before, and was recognised
as the club's walking encyclopedia, because he could
name not only everyone in the room, but all the great
oarsmen of the past.

Tom pointed out to Bob three Olympic medallists dot-
ted around the room. 'The oldest is sitting on the left
of the President,' he said. 'Charles Forester. He rowed
at number three for the club in 1908–09, so he must be
over eighty.'

'Can it be possible?' said Bob, recalling Forester's
youthful picture on the clubhouse wall.

'Certainly can,' said the Secretary. 'And what's more,
young man,' he added, laughing, 'you'll look like that
one day too.'

'What about the man at the far end of the table?'
asked Bob. 'He looks even older.'

'He is,' said the Secretary. 'That's Sidney Fisk. He
was boatman from 1912 to 1945, with only a break for
the First World War. Took over from his uncle at short
notice, if I remember correctly.'

'So he would have known Dougie Mortimer,' said Bob
wistfully.

'Now, there's a great name from the past,' said Adams.
'Mortimer, D.J.T., 1907–08–09, St Catharine's, stroke.
Oh, yes, Fisk would certainly have known Mortimer,
that's for sure. Come to think of it, Charles Forester must
have been in the same boat as Mortimer when he was
stroke.'

During the meal, Bob continued to quiz Adams about
Dougie Mortimer, but he was unable to add a great deal
to the entry in Bob's *History of the Boat Race*, other
than to confirm that Cambridge's defeat in 1909 still
remained a mystery, as the light blues demonstrably had
the superior crew.

When the last course had been cleared away, the President rose to welcome his guests and to make a short
speech. Bob enjoyed the parts he was able to hear above
the noise made by the rowdy undergraduates, and even
joined in the frenzy whenever Oxford was mentioned.
The President ended with the words, 'There will be a
special presentation to the club this year, by our colonial
stroke Bob Kefford, which I'm sure we're all going to
appreciate.'

When Bob rose from his place the cheering became
even more raucous, but he spoke so softly that the noise
quickly died away. He told his fellow members how he
had come to discover, and later retrieve, Dougie Mortimer's right arm, leaving out only his exact location when
he first learned of its whereabouts.

With a flourish, he unwrapped the parcel that had
been secreted under his chair, and revealed the newly
restored bronze cast. The assembled members rose to

their feet and cheered. A smile of satisfaction came over Bob's face as he looked around, only wishing his father could have been present to witness their reaction.

As his eyes swept the room, Bob couldn't help noticing that the oldest blue present, Charles Forester, had remained seated, and was not even joining in the applause. Bob's gaze then settled on Sidney Fisk, the only other person who had not risen to his feet. The old boatman's lips remained fixed in a straight line, and his hands didn't move from his knees.

Bob forgot about the two old men when the President, assisted by Tom Adams, hung the bronze arm on the wall, placing it between a blade that had been pulled by one of the Olympic crew of 1908, and a zephyr worn by the only blue ever to row in a Cambridge boat that had beaten Oxford four years in a row. Bob began to take photographs of the ceremony, so that he would have a record to show his father that he had carried out his wishes.

When the hanging was over, many of the members and old blues surrounded Bob to thank and congratulate him, leaving him in no doubt that all the trouble he had taken to track down the arm had been worthwhile.

Bob was among the last to leave that night, because so many members had wanted to wish him good luck for the future. He was strolling along the footpath back to his digs, humming as he went, when he suddenly remembered that he had left his camera on the table. He decided to collect it in the morning, as he was sure that the clubhouse would be locked and deserted by now, but when he turned round to check, he saw a single light coming from the ground floor.

He turned and began walking back towards the club-house, still humming. When he was a few paces away, he glanced through the window, and saw that there were two figures standing in the committee room. He strode over to take a closer look, and was surprised to see the elderly blue, Charles Forester, and Sidney Fisk, the retired boatman, trying to shift a heavy table. He would have gone in to assist them if Fisk hadn't suddenly pointed up towards Dougie Mortimer's arm. Bob remained motionless as he watched the two old men drag the table inch by inch nearer to the wall, until it was directly below the plaque.

Fisk picked up a chair and placed it against the wall, and Forester used it as a step to climb onto the table. Forester then bent down and took the arm of the older man, to help him up.

Once they were both safely on the table, they held a short conversation before reaching up to the bronze cast, easing it off its hooks and slowly lowering it until it rested between their feet. Forester, with the help of the chair, stepped back down onto the floor, then turned round to assist his companion again.

Bob still didn't move, as the two old men carried Dougie Mortimer's arm across the room and out of the boathouse. Having placed it on the ground outside the door, Forester returned to switch off the lights. When he stepped back outside into the cold night air, the boatman quickly padlocked the door.

Once again the two old men held a short conversation before lifting Bob's trophy up and stumbling off with it along the towpath. They had to stop, lower the arm to the ground, rest, and start again several times. Bob followed silently in their wake, using the broad-trunked trees to conceal himself, until the elderly pair suddenly turned and made their way down the bank towards the river. They came to a halt at the water's edge, and lowered their bounty into a small rowing boat.

The old blue untied the rope, and the two men pushed the boat slowly out into the river, until the water was lapping around the knees of their evening dress trousers. Neither seemed at all concerned about the fact that they were getting soaked. Forester managed to clamber up into the little boat quite quickly, but it took Fisk several minutes to join him. Once they were both aboard, Forester took his place at the oars, while the boatman remained in the bow, clutching on to Dougie Mortimer's arm.

Forester began to row steadily towards the middle of the river. His progress was slow, but his easy rhythm revealed that he had rowed many times before. When the two men calculated that they had reached the centre of the Cam, at its deepest point, Forester stopped rowing and joined his companion in the bow. They picked up the bronze arm and, without ceremony, cast it over the side and into the river. Bob heard the splash and saw the boat rock dangerously from side to side. Fisk then took his turn at the oars; his progress back to the riverbank was even slower than Forester's. They eventually reached land, and both men stumbled out and shoved the boat up towards its mooring, the boatman finally securing the rope to a large ring.

Soaked and exhausted, their breath rising visibly in the clear night air, the two old men stood and faced each other. They shook hands like two business tycoons who had closed an important deal, before disappearing into the night.

Tom Adams, the Club's Honorary Secretary, rang Bob the following morning to tell him something he already knew. In fact he had lain awake all night thinking of little else.

Bob listened to Adams's account of the break-in. 'What's surprising is that they only took one thing.' He paused. 'Your arm – or rather, Dougie's arm. It's very strange, especially as someone had left an expensive camera on the top table.'

'Is there anything I can do to help?' asked Bob.

'No, I don't think so, old boy,' said Adams. 'The local police are making enquiries, but my bet is that whoever stole the arm will probably be halfway across the county by now.'

'I expect you're right,' said Bob. 'While you're on the line, Mr Adams, I wonder if I could ask you a question about the history of the club.'

'I'll do my best,' said Adams. 'But you must remember that it's only a hobby for me, old chap.'

'Do you by any chance know who is the oldest living

Oxford rowing blue?' There was a long silence the other end of the line. 'Are you still there?' Bob asked eventually.

'Yes. I was just trying to think if old Harold Deering is still alive. I can't remember seeing his obituary in *The Times*.'

'Deering?' said Bob.

'Yes. Radley and Keble, 1909–10–11. He became a bishop, if I remember correctly, but I'm damned if I can recall where.'

'Thank you,' said Bob, 'that's most helpful.'

'I could be wrong,' Adams pointed out. 'After all, I don't read the obituary columns every day. And I'm a bit rusty when it comes to Oxford.'

Bob thanked him once again before ringing off.

After a college lunch he didn't eat, Bob returned to his digs and rang the porter's lodge at Keble. He was answered by a curmudgeonly voice.

'Do you have any record of a Harold Deering, a former member of the college?' Bob asked.

'Deering . . . Deering . . .' said the voice. 'That's a new one on me. Let me see if he's in the college handbook.' Another long pause, during which Bob really did begin to think he'd been cut off, until the voice said, 'Good heavens, no wonder. It was just a bit before my time. Deering, Harold, 1909–11, BA 1911, MA 1916 (Theology). Became Bishop of Truro. Is that the one?'

'Yes, that's the man,' said Bob. 'Do you by any chance have an address for him?'

'I do,' said the voice. 'The Rt Revd Harold Deering,

The Stone House, Mill Road, Tewkesbury, Gloucestershire.'

'Thank you,' said Bob. 'You've been very helpful.'

Bob spent the rest of the afternoon composing a letter to the former bishop, in the hope that the old blue might agree to see him.

He was surprised to receive a call at his digs three days later from a Mrs Elliot, who turned out to be Mr Deering's daughter, with whom he was now living.

'The poor old chap can't see much beyond his nose these days,' she explained, 'so I had to read your letter out to him. But he'd be delighted to meet you, and wonders if you could call on him this Sunday at 11.30, after Matins – assuming that's not inconvenient for you.'

'That's fine,' said Bob. 'Please tell your father to expect me around 11.30.'

'It has to be in the morning,' Mrs Elliot went on to explain, 'because, you see, he has a tendency to fall asleep after lunch. I'm sure you understand. By the way, I'll send directions to your college.'

On the Sunday morning, Bob was up long before the sun rose, and started out on his journey to Tewkesbury in a car he had hired the previous day. He would have gone by train, but British Rail didn't seem willing to rise quite early enough for him to reach his destination on time. As he journeyed across the Cotswolds, he tried to remember to keep the car on the left, and couldn't help wondering how long it would be before the British started to build some highways with more than one lane.

He drove into Tewkesbury a few minutes after eleven, and thanks to Mrs Elliot's clear directions, quickly found The Stone House. He parked the car outside a little wicket gate.

A woman had opened the door of the house even before Bob was halfway up the scrub-covered path. 'It must be Mr Kefford,' she declared. 'I'm Susan Elliot.' Bob smiled and shook her hand. 'I should warn you,' Mrs Elliot explained as she led him towards the front door, 'that you'll have to speak up. Father's become rather deaf lately, and I'm afraid his memory isn't what it used to be. He can recall everything that happened to him at your age, but not even the most simple things that I told him yesterday. I've had to remind him what time you would be coming this morning,' she said as they walked through the open door. 'Three times.'

'I'm sorry to have put you to so much trouble, Mrs Elliot,' said Bob.

'No trouble at all,' said Mrs Elliot as she led him down the corridor. 'The truth is, my father's been rather excited by the thought of an American blue from Cambridge coming to visit him after all these years. He hasn't stopped talking about it for the past two days. He's also curious about why you wanted to see him in the first place,' she added conspiratorially.

She led Bob into the drawing room, where he immediately came face to face with an old man seated in a winged leather chair, wrapped in a warm plaid dressing gown and propped up on several cushions, his legs covered by a tartan blanket. Bob found it hard to believe that this frail figure had once been an Olympic oarsman.

'Is it him?' the old man asked in a loud voice.

'Yes, Father,' Mrs Elliot replied, equally loudly. 'It's Mr Kefford. He's driven over from Cambridge especially to see you.'

Bob walked forward and shook the old man's bony outstretched hand.

'Good of you to come all this way, Kefford,' said the former bishop, pulling his blanket up a little higher.

'I appreciate your seeing me, sir,' said Bob, as Mrs Elliot directed him to a comfortable chair opposite her father.

'Would you care for a cup of tea, Kefford?'

'No, thank you, sir,' said Bob. 'I really don't want anything.'

'As you wish,' said the old man. 'Now, I must warn you, Kefford, that my concentration span isn't quite what it used to be, so you'd better tell me straight away why you've come to see me.'

Bob attempted to marshal his thoughts. 'I'm doing a little research on a Cambridge blue who must have rowed around the same time as you, sir.'

'What's his name?' asked Deering. 'I can't remember them all, you know.'

Bob looked at him, fearing that this was going to turn out to be a wasted journey.

'Mortimer. Dougie Mortimer,' he said.

'D.J.T. Mortimer,' the old man responded without

hesitation. 'Now, there's someone you couldn't easily forget. One of the finest strokes Cambridge ever produced – as Oxford found out, to their cost.' The old man paused. 'You're not a journalist, by any chance?'

'No, sir. It's just a personal whim. I wanted to find out one or two things about him before I return to America.'

'Then I will certainly try to help if I can,' said the old man in a piping voice.

'Thank you,' said Bob. 'I'd actually like to begin at the end, if I may, by asking if you knew the circumstances of his death.'

There was no response for several moments. The old cleric's eyelids closed, and Bob began to wonder if he had fallen asleep.

'Not the sort of thing chaps talked about in my day,' he eventually replied. 'Especially with its being against the law at the time, don't you know.'

'Against the law?' said Bob, puzzled.

'Suicide. A bit silly, when you think about it,' the old priest continued, 'even if it is a mortal sin. Because you can't put someone in jail who's already dead, now can you? Not that it was ever confirmed, you understand.'

'Do you think it might have been connected with Cambridge losing the Boat Race in 1909, when they were such clear favourites?'

'It's possible, I suppose,' said Deering, hesitating once again. 'I must admit, the thought had crossed my mind. I took part in that race, as you may know.' He paused again, breathing heavily. 'Cambridge were the clear favourites, and we didn't give ourselves a chance. The result was never properly explained, I must admit. There were a lot of rumours doing the rounds at the time, but no proof – no proof, you understand.'

'What wasn't proved?' asked Bob. There was another long silence, during which Bob began to fear that the old man might have thought he'd gone too far.

'My turn to ask you a few questions, Kefford,' he said eventually.

'Of course, sir.'

'My daughter tells me that you've stroked the winning boat for Cambridge three years in a row.'

'That's correct, sir.'

'Congratulations, my boy. But tell me: if you had wanted to lose one of those races, could you have done so, without the rest of the crew being aware of it?'

It was Bob's turn to ponder. He realised for the first time since he had entered the room that he shouldn't assume that a frail body necessarily indicates a frail mind.

'Yes, I guess so,' he eventually said. 'You could always change the stroke rate without warning, or even catch a crab as you took the Surrey bend. Heaven knows, there's always enough flotsam on the river to make it appear unavoidable.' Bob looked the old man straight in the eye. 'But it would never have crossed my mind that anyone might do so deliberately.'

'Nor mine,' said the priest, 'had their cox not taken holy orders.'

'I'm not sure I understand, sir,' said Bob.

'No reason you should, young man. I find nowadays

that I think in non sequiturs. I'll try to be less obscure. The cox of the 1909 Cambridge boat was a chap called Bertie Partridge. He went on to become a parish priest in some outpost called Chersfield in Rutland. Probably the only place that would have him,' he chuckled. 'But when I became Bishop of Truro, he wrote and invited me to address his flock. It was such an arduous journey from Cornwall to Rutland in those days, that I could easily have made my excuses, but like you, I wanted the mystery of the 1909 race solved, and I thought this might be my only chance.'

Bob made no attempt to interrupt, fearing he might stop the old man's flow.

'Partridge was a bachelor, and bachelors get very lonely, don't you know. If you give them half a chance, they love to gossip. I stayed overnight, which gave him every chance. He told me, over a long dinner accompanied by a bottle of non-vintage wine, that it was well known that Mortimer had run up debts all over Cambridge. Not many undergraduates don't, you might say, but in Mortimer's case they far exceeded even his potential income. I think he rather hoped that his fame and popularity would stop his creditors from pressing their claims. Not unlike Disraeli when he was Prime Minister,' he added with another chuckle.

'But in Mortimer's case one particular shopkeeper, who had absolutely no interest in rowing, and even less in undergraduates, threatened to bankrupt him the week before the 1909 Boat Race. A few days after the race had been lost, Mortimer seemed, without explanation, to have cleared all his obligations, and nothing more was heard of the matter.'

Once again the old man paused as if in deep thought. Bob remained silent, still not wishing to distract him.

'The only other thing I can recall is that the bookies made a killing,' Deering said without warning. 'I know that to my personal cost, because my tutor lost a five-pound wager, and never let me forget that I had told him we didn't have a snowball's chance in hell. Mind you, I was always able to offer that as my excuse for not getting a First.' He looked up and smiled at his visitor.

Bob sat on the edge of his seat, mesmerised by the old man's recollections.

'I'm grateful for your candour, sir,' he said. 'And you can be assured of my discretion.'

'Thank you, Kefford,' said the old man, now almost whispering. 'I'm only too delighted to have been able to assist you. Is there anything else I can help you with?'

'No, thank you, sir,' said Bob. 'I think you've covered everything I needed to know.'

Bob rose from his chair, and as he turned to thank Mrs Elliot he noticed for the first time a bronze cast of an arm hanging on the far wall. Below it was printed in gold:

H. R. R. DEERING

1909–10–11

(KEBLE, BOW)

'You must have been a fine oarsman, sir.'

'No, not really,' said the old blue. 'But I was lucky enough to be in the winning boat three years in a row, which wouldn't please a Cambridge man like yourself.'

Bob laughed. 'Perhaps one last question before I leave, sir.'

'Of course, Kefford.'

'Did they ever make a bronze of Dougie Mortimer's arm?'

'They most certainly did,' replied the priest. 'But it mysteriously disappeared from your boathouse in 1912. A few weeks later the boatman was sacked without explanation – caused quite a stir at the time.'

'Was it known why he was sacked?' asked Bob.

'Partridge claimed that when the old boatman got drunk one night, he confessed to having dumped Mortimer's arm in the middle of the Cam.' The old man paused, smiled, and added, 'Best place for it, wouldn't you say, Kefford?'

Bob thought about the question for some time, wondering how his father would have reacted. He then replied simply, 'Yes, sir. Best place for it.'

DO NOT PASS GO

Hamid Zebari smiled at the thought of his wife Shereen driving him to the airport. Neither of them would have believed it possible five years before, when they had first arrived in America as political refugees. But since he had begun a new life in the States, Hamid was beginning to think anything might be possible.

'When will you be coming home, Papa?' asked Nadim, who was strapped safely in the back seat next to his sister May. She was too young to understand why Papa was going away.

'Just a fortnight, I promise. No more,' their father replied. 'And when I get back, we'll all go on holiday.'

'How long is a fortnight?' his son demanded.

'Fourteen days,' Hamid told him with a laugh.

'And fourteen nights,' said his wife as she drew into the kerb below the sign for Turkish Airways. She touched a button on the dashboard and the boot flicked up. Hamid jumped out of the car, grabbed his luggage from the boot, and put it on the pavement before climbing into the back of the car. He hugged his daughter first, and then his son. May was crying – not because he was going away, but because she always cried when the car came to a sudden halt. He allowed her to stroke his bushy moustache, which usually stopped the flow of tears.

'Fourteen days,' repeated his son. Hamid hugged his wife, and felt the small swelling of a third child between them.

'We'll be here waiting to pick you up,' Shereen called out as her husband tipped the skycap on the kerb.

Once his six empty cases had been checked in, Hamid disappeared into the terminal, and made his way to the Turkish Airlines desk. As he took the same flight twice a year, he didn't need to ask the girl at the ticket counter for directions.

After he had checked in and been presented with his boarding pass, Hamid still had an hour to wait before they would call his flight. He began the slow trek to Gate B27. It was always the same – the Turkish Airlines plane would be parked halfway back to Manhattan. As he passed the Pan Am check-in desk on B5 he observed that they would be taking off an hour earlier than him, a privilege for those who were willing to pay an extra sixty-three dollars.

When he reached the check-in area, a Turkish Airlines stewardess was slipping the sign for Flight 014, New York–London–Istanbul, onto a board. Estimated time of departure, 10.10.

The seats were beginning to fill up with the usual

cosmopolitan group of passengers: Turks going home to visit their families, those Americans taking a holiday who cared about saving sixty-three dollars, and businessmen whose bottom line was closely watched by tight-fisted accountants.

Hamid strolled over to the restaurant bar and ordered coffee and two eggs sunnyside up, with a side order of hash browns. It was the little things that reminded him daily of his new-found freedom, and of just how much he owed to America.

'Would those passengers travelling to Istanbul with young children please board the plane now,' said the stewardess over the loudspeaker.

Hamid swallowed the last mouthful of his hash browns – he hadn't yet become accustomed to the American habit of covering everything in ketchup – and took a final swig of the weak, tasteless coffee. He couldn't wait to be reunited with the thick Turkish coffee served in small bone china cups. But that was a tiny sacrifice when weighed against the privilege of living in a free land. He settled his bill and left a dollar in the little tin tray.

'Would those passengers seated in rows 35 to 41 please board the aircraft now.'

Hamid picked up his briefcase and headed for the passageway that led to Flight 014. An official from Turkish Airlines checked his boarding pass and ushered him through.

He had been allocated an aisle seat near the back of economy. Ten more trips, he told himself, and he would fly Pan Am Business Class. By then he would be able to afford it.

Whenever the wheels of his plane left the ground, Hamid would look out of the little window and watch his adopted country as it disappeared out of sight, the same thoughts always going through his mind.

It had been nearly five years since Saddam Hussein had dismissed him from the Iraqi Cabinet, after he had held the post of Minister of Agriculture for only two years. The wheat crops had been poor that autumn, and after the People's Army had taken their share, and the middlemen their cut, the Iraqi people ended up with short rations. Someone had to take the blame, and the obvious scapegoat was the Minister of Agriculture. Hamid's father, a carpet dealer, had always wanted him to join the family business, and had even warned him before he died not to accept Agriculture, the last three holders of that office having first been sacked, and later disappeared – and everyone in Iraq knew what 'disappeared' meant. But Hamid did accept the post. The first year's crop had been abundant, and after all, he convinced himself, Agriculture was only a stepping stone to greater things. In any case, had not Saddam described him in front of the whole Revolutionary Command Council as 'my good and close friend'? At thirty-two you still believe you are immortal.

Hamid's father was proved right, and Hamid's only real friend – friends melted away like snow in the morning sun when this particular president sacked you – helped him to escape.

The only precaution Hamid had taken during his days as a Cabinet Minister was to withdraw from his bank account each week a little more cash than he actually needed. He would then change the extra money into American dollars with a street trader, using a different dealer each time, and never exchanging enough to arouse suspicion. In Iraq everyone is a spy.

The day he was sacked, he checked how much was hidden under his mattress. It amounted to eleven thousand two hundred and twenty-one American dollars.

The following Thursday, the day on which the weekend begins in Baghdad, he and his pregnant wife took the bus to Erbil. He left his Mercedes conspicuously parked in the front drive of his large home in the suburbs, and they carried no luggage with them – just two passports, the roll of dollars secreted in his wife's baggy clothing, and some Iraqi dinars to get them as far as the border.

No one would be looking for them on a bus to Erbil.

Once they arrived in Erbil, Hamid and his wife took a taxi to Sulaimania, using most of the remaining dinars to pay the driver. They spent the night in a small hotel far from the city centre. Neither slept as they waited for the morning sun to come shining through the curtainless window.

Next day, another bus took them high into the hills of Kurdistan, arriving in Zakho in the early evening.

The final part of the journey was the slowest of all. They were taken up through the hills on mules, at a cost of two hundred dollars – the young Kurdish smuggler showed no interest in Iraqi dinars. He delivered the former Cabinet Minister and his wife safely over the border in the early hours of the morning, leaving them to make their way on foot to the nearest village on Turkish soil. They reached Kirmizi Renga that evening, and spent another sleepless night at the local station, waiting for the first train for Istanbul.

Hamid and Shereen slept all the way through the long train journey to the Turkish capital, and woke up the following morning as refugees. The first visit Hamid made in the city was to the Iz Bank, where he deposited ten thousand eight hundred dollars. The next was to the American Embassy, where he produced his diplomatic passport and requested political asylum. His father had once told him that a recently sacked Cabinet Minister from Iraq was always a good catch for the Americans.

The Embassy arranged accommodation for Hamid and his wife in a first-class hotel, and immediately informed Washington of their little coup. They promised Hamid that they would get back to him as quickly as possible, but gave him no clue as to how long that might take. He decided to use the time to visit the carpet bazaars on the south side of the city, so often frequented by his father.

Many of the dealers remembered Hamid's father – an honest man who liked to bargain and drink gallons of coffee, and who had often talked about his son going into politics. They were pleased to make his acquaintance, especially when they learned of what he planned to do once he had settled in the States.

The Zebaris were granted American visas within the week and flown to Washington at the government's expense, which included a charge for excess baggage of twenty-three Turkish carpets.

After five days of intensive questioning by the CIA, Hamid was thanked for his co-operation and the useful information he had supplied. He was then released to begin his new life in America. He, his pregnant wife and the twenty-three carpets boarded a train for New York.

It took Hamid six weeks to find the right shop, on the Lower East Side of Manhattan, from which to sell his carpets. Once he had signed the five-year lease, Shereen immediately set about painting their new Americanised name above the door.

Hamid didn't sell his first carpet for nearly three months, by which time his meagre savings had all but disappeared. But by the end of the first year, sixteen of the twenty-three carpets had been sold, and he realised he would soon have to travel back to Istanbul to buy more stock.

Four years had passed since then, and the Zebaris had recently moved to a larger establishment on the West Side, with a small apartment above the shop. Hamid kept telling his wife that this was only the beginning, that anything was possible in the United States. He now considered himself a fully-fledged American citizen, and not just because of the treasured blue passport that confirmed his status. He accepted that he could never return to his birthplace while Saddam remained its ruler. His home and possessions had long ago been requisitioned

143

by the Iraqi state, and the death sentence had been passed on him in his absence. He doubted if he would ever see Baghdad again.

After the stopover in London, the plane landed at Istanbul's Ataturk Airport a few minutes ahead of schedule. Hamid booked into his usual small hotel, and planned how best to allocate his time over the next two weeks. He was happy to be back among the hustle and bustle of the Turkish capital.

There were thirty-one dealers he wanted to visit, because this time he hoped to return to New York with at least sixty carpets. That would require fourteen days of drinking thick Turkish coffee, and many hours of bargaining, as a dealer's opening price would be three times as much as Hamid was willing to pay – or what the dealer really expected to receive. But there was no short cut in the bartering process, which – like his father – Hamid secretly enjoyed.

By the end of the fortnight, Hamid had purchased fifty-seven carpets, at a cost of a little over twenty-one thousand dollars. He had been careful to select only those carpets that would be sought after by the most discerning New Yorkers, and he was confident that this latest batch would fetch almost a hundred thousand dollars in America. It had been such a successful trip that Hamid felt he would indulge himself by taking the earlier Pan Am flight back to New York. After all, he had undoubtedly earned himself the extra sixty-three dollars many times over in the course of his trip.

He was looking forward to seeing Shereen and the

children even before the plane had taken off, and the American flight attendant with her pronounced New York accent and friendly smile only added to the feeling that he was already home. After lunch had been served, and having decided he didn't want to watch the in-flight movie, Hamid dozed off and dreamt about what he could achieve in America, given time. Perhaps his son would go into politics. Would the United States be ready for an Iraqi President by the year 2025? He smiled at the thought, and fell contentedly into a deep sleep.

'Ladies and gentlemen,' a deep Southern voice boomed out over the intercom, 'this is your captain. I'm sorry to interrupt the movie, or to wake those of you who've been resting, but we've developed a small problem in an engine on our starboard wing. Nothing to worry about, folks, but Federal Aviation Authority rulings insist that we land at the nearest airport and have the problem dealt with before we continue with our journey. It shouldn't take us more than an hour at the most, and then we'll be on our way again. You can be sure that we'll try to make up as much of the lost time as possible, folks.'

Hamid was suddenly wide awake.

'We won't be disembarking from the aircraft at any time, as this is an unscheduled stop. However, you'll be able to tell the folks back home that you've visited Baghdad.'

Hamid felt his whole body go limp, and then his head rocked forward. The flight attendant rushed up to his side.

'Are you feeling all right, sir?' she asked.

He looked up and stared into her eyes. 'I must see the captain immediately. Immediately.'

The flight attendant was in no doubt of the passenger's anxiety, and quickly led him forward, up the spiral staircase into the first-class lounge and onto the flight deck.

She tapped on the door of the cockpit, opened it and said, 'Captain, one of the passengers needs to speak to you urgently.'

'Show him in,' said the Southern voice. The captain turned to face Hamid, who was now trembling uncontrollably. 'How can I be of help, sir?' he asked.

'My name is Hamid Zebari. I am an American citizen,' he began. 'If you land in Baghdad, I will be arrested, tortured and then executed.' The words tumbled out. 'I am a political refugee, and you must understand that the regime will not hesitate to kill me.'

The captain only needed to take one look at Hamid to realise he wasn't exaggerating.

'Take over, Jim,' he said to his co-pilot, 'while I have a word with Mr Zebari. Call me the moment we've been given clearance to land.'

The captain unfastened his seatbelt, and led Hamid to an empty corner of the first-class lounge.

'Take me through it slowly,' he said.

During the next few minutes Hamid explained why he had had to leave Baghdad, and how he came to be living in America. When he had reached the end of his story the captain shook his head and smiled. 'No need to panic, sir,' he assured Hamid. 'No one is going to have to leave the aircraft at any time, so the passengers' passports won't even be checked. Once the engine has been attended to, we'll be back up and on our way immediately. Why don't you just stay here in first class, then you'll be able to speak to me at any time, should you feel at all anxious.'

How anxious can you feel? Hamid wondered, as the captain left him to have a word with the co-pilot. He started to tremble once more.

'It's the captain once again, folks, just bringing you up to date. We've been given clearance by Baghdad, so we've begun our descent and expect to land in about twenty minutes. We'll then be taxiing to the far end of the runway, where we'll await the engineers. Just as soon as they've dealt with our little problem, we'll be back up and on our way again.'

A collective sigh went up, while Hamid gripped the armrest and wished he hadn't eaten any lunch. He didn't stop shaking for the next twenty minutes, and almost fainted when the wheels touched down on the land of his birth.

He stared out of the porthole as the aircraft taxied past the terminal he knew so well. He could see the armed guards stationed on the roof and at the doors leading onto the tarmac. He prayed to Allah, he prayed to Jesus, he even prayed to President Reagan.

For the next fifteen minutes the silence was broken only by the sound of a van driving across the tarmac and coming to a halt under the starboard wing of the aircraft.

Hamid watched as two engineers carrying bulky

toolbags got out of the van, stepped onto a small crane and were hoisted up until they were level with the wing. They began unscrewing the outer plates of one of the engines. Forty minutes later they screwed the plates back on and were lowered to the ground. The van then headed off towards the terminal.

Hamid felt relieved, if not exactly relaxed. He fastened his seatbelt hopefully. His heartbeat fell from 180 a minute to around 110, but he knew it wouldn't return to normal until the plane lifted off and he could be sure they wouldn't turn back. Nothing happened for the next few minutes, and Hamid became anxious again. Then the door of the cockpit opened, and he saw the captain heading towards him, a grim expression on his face.

'You'd better join us on the flight deck,' the captain said in a whisper. Hamid undid his seatbelt and somehow managed to stand. He unsteadily followed the captain into the cockpit, his legs feeling like jelly. The door was closed behind them.

The captain didn't waste any words. 'The engineers can't locate the problem. The chief engineer won't be free for another hour, so we've been ordered to disembark and wait in the transit area until he's completed the job.'

'I'd rather die in a plane crash,' Hamid blurted out.

'Don't worry, Mr Zebari, we've thought of a way round your problem. We're going to put you in a spare uniform. That will make it possible for you to stay with us the whole time, and use the crew's facilities. No one will ask to see your passport.'

'But if someone recognises me . . .' began Hamid.

'Once you've got rid of that moustache, and you're wearing a flight officer's uniform, dark glasses and a peaked hat, your own mother wouldn't know you.'

With the help of scissors, followed by shaving foam, followed by a razor, Hamid removed the bushy moustache that he had been so proud of, to leave an upper lip that looked as pale as a blob of vanilla ice cream. The senior flight attendant applied some of her make-up to his skin, until the white patch blended in with the rest of his face. Hamid still wasn't convinced, but after he had changed into the co-pilot's spare uniform and studied himself in the toilet mirror, he had to admit that it would indeed be remarkable if anyone recognised him.

The passengers were the first to leave the plane, and were ferried by an airport bus to the main terminal. A smart transit van then came out to collect the crew, who left as a group and sheltered Hamid by making sure that he was surrounded at all times. Hamid became more and more nervous with each yard the van travelled towards the terminal.

The security guard showed no particular interest in the air crew as they entered the building, and they were left to find themselves seats on wooden benches in the white-walled hall. The only decoration was a massive portrait of Saddam Hussein in full uniform carrying a kalashnikov rifle. Hamid couldn't bring himself to look at the picture of his 'good and close friend'.

Another crew was also sitting around waiting to board

TWELVE RED HERRINGS

their aircraft, but Hamid was too frightened to start up
a conversation with any of them.

'They're French,' he was informed by the senior flight
attendant. 'I'm about to find out if my night classes were
worth all the expense.' She took the spare place next to
the captain of the French aircraft, and tried a simple
opening question.

The French captain was telling her that they were
bound for Singapore via New Delhi, when Hamid saw
him: Saad al-Takriti, once a member of Saddam's personal guard, marched into the hall. From the insignia
on his shoulder, he now appeared to be in charge of
airport security.

Hamid prayed that he wouldn't look in his direction.
Al-Takriti sauntered through the room, glancing at the
French and American crews, his eyes lingering on the
stewardesses' black-stockinged legs.

The captain touched Hamid on the shoulder, and he
nearly leapt out of his skin.

'It's OK, it's OK. I just thought you'd like to know
that the chief engineer is on his way out to the aircraft,
so it shouldn't be too long now.'

Hamid looked beyond the Air France plane, and
watched a van come to a halt under the starboard wing
of the Pan Am aircraft. A man in blue overalls stepped
out of the vehicle and onto the little crane.

Hamid stood up to take a closer look, and as he did
so Saad al-Takriti walked back into the hall. He came to
a sudden halt, and the two men stared briefly at each
other, before Hamid quickly resumed his place next to

the captain. Al-Takriti disappeared into a side room marked 'Do Not Enter'.

'I think he's spotted me,' said Hamid. The make-up started to run down onto his lips.

The captain leant across to his chief flight attendant and interrupted her parley with the French captain. She listened to her boss's instructions, and then tried a tougher question on the Frenchman.

Saad al-Takriti marched back out of the office and began striding towards the American captain. Hamid thought he would surely faint.

Without even glancing at Hamid, al-Takriti barked, 'Captain, I require you to show me your manifest, the number of crew you are carrying, and their passports.'

'My co-pilot has all the passports,' the captain replied. 'I'll see you get them.'

'Thank you,' said al-Takriti. 'When you have collected them, you will bring them to my office so that I can check each one. Meanwhile, please ask your crew to remain here. They are not, under any circumstances, to leave the building without my permission.'

The captain rose from his place, walked slowly over to the co-pilot, and asked for the passports. Then he issued an order which took him by surprise. The captain took the passports into the security office just as a bus drew up outside the transit area to take the French crew back to their plane.

Saad al-Takriti placed the fourteen passports in front of him on his desk. He seemed to take pleasure in checking each one of them slowly. When he had finished the task, he announced in mock surprise, 'I do believe, captain, that I counted fifteen crew wearing Pan Am uniforms.'

'You must have been mistaken,' said the captain. 'There are only fourteen of us.'

'Then I will have to make a more detailed check, won't I, captain? Please return these documents to their rightful owners. Should there happen to be anyone not in possession of a passport, they will naturally have to report to me.'

'But that is against international regulations,' said the captain, 'as I'm sure you know. We are in transit, and therefore, under UN Resolution 238, not legally in your country.'

'Save your breath, captain. We have no use for UN resolutions in Iraq. And, as you correctly point out, as far as we are concerned, you are not legally even in our country.'

The captain realised he was wasting his time, and could bluff no longer. He gathered up the passports as slowly as he could and allowed al-Takriti to lead him back into the hall. As they entered the room the Pan Am crew members who were scattered around the benches suddenly rose from their places and began walking about, continually changing direction, while at the same time talking at the top of their voices.

'Tell them to sit down,' hissed al-Takriti, as the crew zig-zagged backwards and forwards across the hall.

'What's that you're saying?' asked the captain, cupping his ear.

'Tell them to sit down!' shouted al-Takriti.

The captain gave a half-hearted order, and within a few moments everyone was seated. But they still continued talking at the top of their voices.

'And tell them to shut up!'

The captain moved slowly round the room, asking his crew one by one to lower their voices.

Al-Takriti's eyes raked the benches of the transit hall, as the captain glanced out onto the tarmac and watched the French aircraft taxiing towards the far runway.

Al-Takriti began counting, and was annoyed to discover that there were only fourteen Pan Am crew members in the hall. He stared angrily around the room, and quickly checked once again.

'All fourteen seem to be present,' said the captain after he had finished handing back the passports to his crew.

'Where is the man who was sitting next to you?' al-Takriti demanded, jabbing a finger at the captain.

'You mean my first officer?'

'No. The one who looked like an Arab.'

'There are no Arabs on my crew,' the captain assured him.

Al-Takriti strode over to the senior flight attendant. 'He was sitting next to you. His upper lip had make-up on it that was beginning to run.'

'The captain of the French plane was sitting next to me,' the senior flight attendant said. She immediately realised her mistake.

Saad al-Takriti turned and looked out of the window

to see the Air France plane at the end of the runway preparing for take-off. He jabbed a button on his hand phone as the thrust of the jet engines started up, and barked out some orders in his native tongue. The captain didn't need to speak Arabic to get the gist of what he was saying.

By now the American crew were all staring at the French aircraft, willing it to move, while al-Takriti's voice was rising with every word he uttered.

The Air France 747 eased forward and slowly began to gather momentum. Saad al-Takriti cursed loudly, then ran out of the building and jumped into a waiting jeep. He pointed towards the plane and ordered the driver to chase after it. The jeep shot off, accelerating as it weaved its way in and out of the parked aircraft. By the time it reached the runway it must have been doing ninety miles an hour, and for the next hundred yards it sped along parallel to the French aircraft, with al-Takriti standing on the front seat, clinging onto the windscreen and waving his fist at the cockpit.

The French captain acknowledged him with a crisp salute, and as the 747's wheels lifted off, a loud cheer went up in the transit lounge.

The American captain smiled and turned to his chief flight attendant. 'That only proves my theory that the French will go to any lengths to get an extra passenger.'

Hamid Zebari landed in New Delhi six hours later, and immediately phoned his wife to let her know what had happened. Early the next morning Pan Am flew him back to New York – first class. When Hamid emerged from the airport terminal, his wife jumped out of the car and threw her arms around him.

Nadim wound the window down and declared, 'You were wrong, Papa. A fortnight turns out to be fifteen days.' Hamid grinned at his son, but his daughter burst into tears, and not because their car had come to a sudden halt. It was just that she was horrified to see her mother hugging a strange man.

CHUNNEL VISION

WHENEVER I'M IN NEW YORK, I ALWAYS try to have dinner with an old friend of mine called Duncan McPherson. We are opposites, and so naturally we attract. In fact, Duncan and I have only one thing in common: we are both writers. But even then there's a difference, because Duncan specialises in screenplays, which he writes in the intervals between his occasional articles for *Newsweek* and the *New Yorker*, whereas I prefer novels and short stories.

One of the other differences between us is the fact that I have been married to the same woman for twenty-eight years, while Duncan seems to have a different girlfriend every time I visit New York – not bad going, as I average at least a couple of trips a year. The girls are always attractive, lively and bright, and there are various levels of intensity – depending on what stage the relationship is at. In the past I've been around at the beginning (very physical) and in the middle (starting to cool off), but this trip was to be the first time I experienced an ending.

I phoned Duncan from my hotel on Fifth Avenue to let him know I was in town to promote my new novel, and he immediately asked me over for dinner the following evening. I assumed, as in the past, that it would be at his apartment. Another opposite: unlike me, he's a quite superlative cook.

'I can't wait to see you,' he said. 'I've come up with an idea for a novel at last, and I want to try the plot out on you.'

'Delighted,' I replied. 'Look forward to hearing all about it tomorrow night. And may I ask . . .' I hesitated.

'Christabel,' he said.

'Christabel . . .' I repeated, trying to recall if I had ever met her.

'But there's no need for you to remember anything about her,' he added. 'Because she's about to be given the heave-ho, to use one of your English expressions. I've just met a new one – Karen. She's absolutely sensational. You'll adore her.'

I didn't feel this was the appropriate moment to point out to Duncan that I had adored them all. I merely asked which one was likely to be joining us for dinner.

'Depends if Christabel has finished packing,' Duncan replied. 'If she has, it will be Karen. We haven't slept together yet, and I'd been planning on that for tomorrow night. But as you're in town, it will have to be postponed.'

I laughed. 'I could wait,' I assured him. 'After all, I'm here for at least a week.'

'No, no. In any case, I must tell you about my idea for a novel. That's far more important. So why don't you come to my place tomorrow evening. Shall we say around seven thirty?'

Before I left the hotel, I wrapped up a copy of my latest book, and wrote 'Hope you enjoy it' on the outside.

Duncan lives in one of those apartment blocks on 72nd and Park, and though I've been there many times, it always takes me a few minutes to locate the entrance to the building. And, like Duncan's girlfriends, the doorman seems to change with every trip.

The new doorman grunted when I gave my name, and directed me to the elevator on the far side of the hall. I slid the grille doors across and pressed the button for the fourteenth floor. It was one of those top floors that could not be described as a penthouse even by the most imaginative of estate agents.

I pulled back the doors and stepped out onto the landing, rehearsing the appropriate smiles for Christabel (goodbye) and Karen (hello). As I walked towards Duncan's front door I could hear raised voices – a very British expression, born of understatement; let's be frank and admit that they were screaming at each other at the tops of their voices. I concluded that this had to be the end of Christabel, rather than the beginning of Karen.

I was already a few minutes late, so there was no turning back. I pressed the doorbell, and to my relief the voices immediately fell silent. Duncan opened the door, and although his cheeks were scarlet with rage, he still managed a casual grin. Which reminds me that I forgot to tell you about a few more opposites – the damn man has a mop of boyish dark curly hair, the rugged features of his Irish ancestors, and the build of a champion tennis player.

'Come on in,' he said. 'This is Christabel, by the way – if you hadn't already guessed.'

I'm not by nature a man who likes other people's cast-offs, but I'm bound to confess I would have been happy to make Christabel the exception. She had an oval face, deep blue eyes, and an angelic smile. She was also graced with that fine fair hair that only the Nordic races are born with, and the type of figure that slimming advertisements make their profits out of. She wore a cashmere sweater and tapered white jeans that left little to the imagination.

Christabel shook me by the hand, and apologised for looking a little scruffy. 'I've been packing all afternoon,' she explained.

The proof of her labours was there for all to see – three large suitcases and two cardboard boxes full of books standing by the door. On the top of one of the boxes lay a copy of a Dorothy L. Sayers murder mystery with a torn red dustjacket.

I was becoming acutely aware that I couldn't have chosen a worse evening for a reunion with my old friend. 'I'm afraid we're going to have to eat out for a change,' Duncan said. 'It's been' – he paused – 'a busy day. I haven't had a chance to visit the local store. Good thing, actually,' he added. 'It'll give me more time to take you through the plot of my novel.'

'Congratulations,' Christabel said.

I turned to face her.

'*Your* novel,' she said. 'Number one on the *New York Times* bestseller list, isn't it?'

'Yes, congratulations,' said Duncan. 'I haven't got round to reading it yet, so don't tell me anything about it. It wasn't on sale in Bosnia,' he added with a laugh.

I handed him my little gift.

'Thank you,' he said, and placed it on the hall table. 'I'll look forward to it.'

'I've read it,' said Christabel.

Duncan bit his lip. 'Let's go,' he said, and was about to turn and say goodbye to Christabel when she asked me, 'Would you mind if I joined you? I'm starving, and as Duncan said, there's absolutely nothing in the icebox.'

I could see that Duncan was about to protest, but by then Christabel had passed him, and was already in the corridor and heading for the elevator.

'We can walk to the restaurant,' Duncan said as we trundled down to the ground floor. 'It's only Californians who need a car to take them one block.'

As we strolled west on 72nd Street Duncan told me that he had chosen a fancy new French restaurant to take me to.

I began to protest, not just because I've never really cared for ornate French food, but I was also aware of Duncan's unpredictable pecuniary circumstances. Sometimes he was flush with money, at other times stony broke. I just hoped that he'd had an advance on the novel.

'No, like you, I normally wouldn't bother,' he said. 'But it's only just opened, and the *New York Times* gave it a rave review. In any case, whenever I'm in London, you always entertain me "right royally",' he added, in what he imagined was an English accent.

It was one of those cool evenings that make walking in New York so pleasant, and I enjoyed the stroll, as Duncan began to tell me about his recent trip to Bosnia.

'You were lucky to catch me in New York,' he was saying. 'I've only just got back after being holed up in the damned place for three months.'

'Yes, I know. I read your article in *Newsweek* on the plane coming over,' I said, and went on to tell him how fascinated I had been by his evidence that a group of UN soldiers had set up their own underground network, and felt no scruples about operating an illegal black market in whatever country they were stationed.

'Yes, that's caused quite a stir at the UN,' said Duncan. 'The *New York Times* and the *Washington Post* have both followed the story up with features on the main culprits – but without bothering to give me any credit for the original research, of course.'

I turned round to see if Christabel was still with us. She seemed to be deep in thought, and was lagging a few paces behind. I smiled a smile that I hoped said I think Duncan's a fool and you're fantastic, but I received no response.

After a few more yards I spotted a red and gold awning flapping in the breeze outside something called 'Le Manoir'. My heart sank. I've always preferred simple food, and have long considered pretentious French cuisine to be one of the major cons of the eighties, and one that should have been passé, if not part of culinary history, by the nineties.

Duncan led us down a short crazy-paving path through a heavy oak door and into a brightly lit restaurant. One look around the large, over-decorated room and my worst fears were confirmed. The maître d' stepped forward and said, 'Good evening, monsieur.'

'Good evening,' replied Duncan. 'I have a table reserved in the name of McPherson.'

The maître d' checked down a long list of bookings. 'Ah, yes, a table for two.' Christabel pouted, but looked no less beautiful.

'Can we make it three?' my host asked rather half-heartedly.

'Of course, sir. Allow me to show you to your table.'

We were guided through a crowded room to a little alcove in the corner which had only been set for two.

One look at the tablecloth, the massive flowered plates with 'Le Manoir' painted in crimson all over them, and the arrangement of lilies on the centre of the table, made me feel even more guilty about what I had let Duncan in for. A waiter dressed in a white open-neck shirt, black trousers and black waistcoat with 'Le Manoir' sewn in red on the breast pocket hurriedly supplied Christabel with a chair, while another deftly laid a place for her.

A third waiter appeared at Duncan's side and enquired if we would care for an aperitif. Christabel smiled sweetly and asked if she might have a glass of champagne. I requested some Evian water, and Duncan nodded that he would have the same.

For the next few minutes, while we waited for the menus to appear, we continued to discuss Duncan's trip to Bosnia, and the contrast between scraping one's food out of a billycan in a cold dugout accompanied by the sound of bullets, and dining off china plates in a warm restaurant, with a string quartet playing Schubert in the background.

Another waiter appeared at Duncan's side and handed us three pink menus the size of small posters. As I glanced down the list of dishes, Christabel whispered something to the waiter, who nodded and slipped quietly away.

I began to study the menu more carefully, unhappy to discover that this was one of those restaurants which allows only the host to have the bill of fare with the prices attached. I was trying to work out which would be the cheapest dishes, when another glass of champagne was placed at Christabel's side.

I decided that the clear soup was likely to be the least expensive starter, and that it would also help my feeble efforts to lose weight. The main courses had me more perplexed, and with my limited knowledge of French I finally settled on duck, as I couldn't find any sign of 'poulet'.

When the waiter returned moments later, he immediately spotted Christabel's empty glass, and asked, 'Would you care for another glass of champagne, madame?'

'Yes, please,' she replied sweetly, as the maître d' arrived to take our order. But first we had to suffer an ordeal that nowadays can be expected at every French restaurant in the world.

'Today our specialities are,' he began, in an accent that would not have impressed central casting, 'for hors d'oeuvres *Gelée de saumon sauvage et caviar impérial en aigre doux*, which is wild salmon slivers and imperial caviar in a delicate jelly with sour cream and courgettes soused in dill vinegar. Also we have *Cuisses de grenouilles à la purée d'herbes à soupe, fricassée de chanterelles et racines de persil*, which are pan-fried frogs' legs in a parsley purée, fricassee of chanterelles and parsley roots. For the main course we have *Escalope de turbot*, which is a poached fillet of turbot on a watercress purée, lemon sabayon and a Gewürztraminer sauce. And, of course, everything that is on the menu can be recommended.'

I felt full even before he had finished the descriptions.

Christabel appeared to be studying the menu with due diligence. She pointed to one of the dishes, and the maître d' smiled approvingly.

Duncan leaned across and asked if I had selected anything yet.

'Consommé and the duck will suit me just fine,' I said without hesitation.

'Thank you, sir,' said the maître d'. 'How would you like the duck? Crispy, or perhaps a little underdone?'

'Crispy,' I replied, to his evident disapproval.

'And monsieur?' he asked, turning to Duncan.

'Caesar salad and a rare steak.'

The maître d' retrieved the menus and was turning to go as Duncan said, 'Now, let me tell you all about my idea for a novel.'

'Would you care to order some wine, sir?' asked another waiter, who was carrying a large red leather book with golden grapes embossed on its cover.

'Should I do that for you?' suggested Christabel. 'Then there'll be no need to interrupt your story.'

Duncan nodded his agreement, and the waiter handed the wine list over to Christabel. She opened the red leather cover with as much eagerness as if she was about to begin a bestselling novel.

'You may be surprised,' Duncan was saying, 'that my book is set in Britain. Let me start by explaining that the timing for its publication is absolutely vital. As you know, a British and French consortium is currently building a tunnel between Folkestone and Sangatte, which is scheduled to be opened by Queen Elizabeth on 6 May 1994. In fact, *Chunnel* will be the title of my book.'

I was horrified. Another glass of champagne was placed in front of Christabel.

'The story begins in four separate locations, with four different sets of characters. Although they are all from diverse age groups, social backgrounds and countries, they have one thing in common: they have all booked on the first passenger train to travel from London to Paris via the Channel Tunnel.'

I felt a sudden pang of guilt, and wondered if I should say something, but at this point a waiter returned with a bottle of white wine, the label of which Christabel studied intently. She nodded, and the sommelier extracted the cork and poured a little into her empty glass. A sip brought the smile back to her lips. The waiter then filled our glasses.

Duncan continued: 'There will be an American family – mother, father, two teenage children – on their first visit to England; a young English couple who have just got married that morning and are about to begin their honeymoon; a Greek self-made millionaire and his French wife who booked their tickets a year before, but are now considering a divorce; and three students.'

Duncan paused as a Caesar salad was placed in front of him and a second waiter presented me with a bowl of consommé. I glanced at the dish Christabel had chosen. A plate of thinly cut smoked gravadlax with a blob of caviar in the centre. She was happily squeezing half a lemon, protected by muslin, all over it.

'Now,' said Duncan, 'in the first chapter it's important that the reader doesn't realise that the students are connected in any way, as that later becomes central to the plot. We pick up all four groups in the second chapter as they're preparing for the journey. The reader discovers their motivations for wanting to be on the train, and I build a little on the background of each of the characters involved.'

'What period of time will the plot cover?' I asked anxiously, between spoonfuls of consommé.

'Probably three days,' replied Duncan. 'The day before the journey, the day of the journey, and the day after.

169

But I'm still not certain – by the final draft it might all happen on the same day.'

Christabel grabbed the wine bottle from the ice-bucket and refilled her glass before the wine waiter had a chance to assist her.

'Around chapter three,' continued Duncan, 'we find the various groups arriving at Waterloo station to board "le shuttle". The Greek millionaire and his French wife will be shown to their first-class seats by a black crew member, while the others are directed to second class. Once they are all on board, some sort of ceremony to commemorate the inauguration of the tunnel will take place on the platform. Big band, fireworks, cutting of tape by royalty etc. That should prove quite adequate to cover another chapter at least.'

While I was visualising the scene and sipping my soup – the restaurant may have been pretentious, but the food was excellent – the wine waiter filled my glass and then Duncan's. I don't normally care for white wine, but I had to admit that this one was quite exceptional.

Duncan paused to eat, and I turned my attention to Christabel, who was being served a second dollop of caviar that appeared even bigger than the first.

'Chapter five,' said Duncan, 'opens as the train moves out of the station. Now the real action begins. The American family are enjoying every moment. The young bride and groom make love in the rest room. The millionaire is having another row with his wife about her continual extravagance, and the three students have met up for the first time at the bar. By now you should begin to suspect that they're not ordinary students, and that they may have known each other before they got on the train.' Duncan smiled and continued with his salad. I frowned.

Christabel winked at me, to show she knew exactly what was going on. I felt guilty at being made a part of her conspiracy, and wanted to tell Duncan what she was up to.

'It's certainly a strong plot,' I ventured as the wine waiter filled our glasses for a third time and, having managed to empty the bottle, looked towards Madame. She nodded sweetly.

'Have you started on the research yet?' I asked.

'Yes. Research is going to be the key to this project, and I'm well into it already,' said Duncan. 'I wrote to Sir Alastair Morton, the Chairman of Eurotunnel, on *Newsweek* headed paper, and his office sent me back a caseload of material. I can tell you the length of the rolling stock, the number of carriages, the diameter of the wheels, why the train can go faster on the French side than the British, even why it's necessary for them to have a different-gauge track on either side of the Channel . . .'

The pop of a cork startled me, and the wine waiter began pouring from a second bottle. Should I tell him now?

'During chapter six the plot begins to unfold,' said Duncan, warming to his theme, as one of the waiters whipped away the empty plates and another brushed a few breadcrumbs off the tablecloth into a little silver scoop. 'The trick is to keep the reader interested in all four groups at the same time.'

I nodded.

'Now we come to the point in the story when the reader discovers that the students are not really students, but terrorists, who plan to hijack the train.'

Three dishes topped by domed silver salvers were placed in front of us. On a nod from the maître d', all three domes were lifted in unison by the waiters. It would be churlish of me not to admit that the food looked quite magnificent. I turned to see what Christabel had selected: truffles with foie gras. They reminded me of a Miró painting, until she quickly smudged the canvas.

'What do you think the terrorists' motive for hijacking the train should be?' Duncan asked.

This was surely the moment to tell him – but once again I funked it. I tried to remember what point in the story we had reached. 'That would depend on whether you eventually wanted them to escape,' I suggested. 'Which might prove quite difficult, if they're stuck in the middle of a tunnel, with a police force waiting for them at either end.' The wine waiter presented Christabel with the bottle of claret she had chosen. After no more than a sniff of the cork she indicated that it was acceptable.

'I don't think they should be interested in financial reward,' said Duncan. 'They ought to be IRA, Islamic fundamentalists, Basque separatists, or whatever the latest terrorist group catching the headlines happens to be.'

I sipped the wine. It was like velvet. I had only tasted such a vintage once before, in the home of a friend who possessed a cellar of old wine put down with new money. It was a taste that had remained etched in my memory.

'In chapter seven I've come up against a block,' continued Duncan, intent on his theme. 'One of the terrorists must somehow come into contact with the newly-married couple, or at least with the bridegroom.' He paused. 'I should have told you earlier that in the character-building at the beginning of the book, one of the students turns out to be a loner, while the other two, a man and a woman, have been living together for some time.' He began digging into his steak. 'It's how I bring the loner and the bridegroom together that worries me. Any ideas?'

'That shouldn't be too hard,' I said, 'what with restaurant cars, snack bars, carriages, a corridor, not to mention a black crew member, railway staff and rest rooms.'

'Yes, but it must appear natural,' Duncan said, sounding as if he was in deep thought.

My heart sank as I noticed Christabel's empty plate being whisked away, despite the fact that Duncan and I had hardly begun our main courses.

'The chapter ends with the train suddenly coming to a halt about halfway through the tunnel,' said Duncan, staring into the distance.

'But how? And why?' I asked.

'That's the whole point. It's a false alarm. Quite innocent. The youngest child of the American family – his name's Ben – pulls the communication cord while he's sitting on the lavatory. It's such a hi-tech lavatory that he mistakes it for the chain.'

I was considering if this was plausible when a breast of quail on fondant potatoes with a garnish of smoked bacon was placed in front of Christabel. She wasted no time in attacking the fowl.

Duncan paused to take a sip of wine. Now, I felt, I had to let him know, but before I had a chance to say anything he was off again. 'Right,' he said. 'Chapter eight. The train has come to a halt several miles inside the tunnel, but not quite halfway.'

'Is that significant?' I asked feebly.

'Sure is,' said Duncan. 'The French and British have agreed the exact point inside the tunnel where French jurisdiction begins and British ends. As you'll discover, this becomes relevant later in the plot.'

The waiter began moving round the table, topping up our glasses once again with claret. I placed a hand over mine – not because the wine wasn't pure nectar, but simply because I didn't wish to give Christabel the opportunity to order another bottle. She made no attempt to exercise the same restraint, but drank her wine in generous gulps, while toying with her quail. Duncan continued with his story.

'So, the hold-up,' said Duncan, 'turns out to be nothing more than a diversion, and it's sorted out fairly quickly. Child in tears, family apologises, explanation given by the guard over the train's intercom, which relieves any anxieties the passengers might have had. A few minutes later, the train starts up again, and this time it does cross the halfway point.'

Three waiters removed our empty plates. Christabel touched the side of her lips with a napkin, and gave me a huge grin.

'So then what happens?' I asked, avoiding her eye.

'When the train stopped, the terrorists were afraid that there might be a rival group on board, with the same purpose as them. But as soon as they find out what has actually happened, they take advantage of the commotion caused by young Ben to get themselves into the cabin next to the driver's.'

'Would you care for anything from the dessert trolley, madame?' the maître d' asked Christabel. I looked on aghast as she was helped to what looked like a large spoonful of everything on offer.

'It's gripping, isn't it?' said Duncan, misunderstanding my expression for one of deep concern for those on the train. 'But there's still more to come.'

'Monsieur?'

'I'm full, thank you,' I told the maître d'. 'Perhaps a coffee later.'

'No, nothing, thank you,' said Duncan, trying not to lose his thread. 'By the start of chapter nine the terrorists have got themselves into the driver's cabin. At gunpoint they force the chef de train and his co-driver to bring the engine to a halt for a second time. But what they don't realise is that they are now on French territory. The passengers are told by the loner over the train's intercom that this time it's not a false alarm, but the train has been taken over by whichever gang I settle on, and is going to be blown up in fifteen minutes. He tells them to get themselves off the train, into the tunnel, and as far away as they possibly can before the explosion. Naturally, some of the passengers begin to panic. Several of them leap out into the dimly lit tunnel. Many are looking frantically for their husbands, wives, children, whatever, while others begin running towards the British or French side, according to their nationality.'

I became distracted when the maître d' began wheeling yet another trolley towards our table. He paused, bowed to Christabel, and then lit a small burner. He poured some brandy into a shallow copper-bottomed pan and set about preparing a crêpe suzette.

'This is the point in the story, probably chapter ten, where the father of the American family decides to remain on the train,' said Duncan, becoming more excited than ever. 'He tells the rest of his tribe to jump off and get the hell out of it. The only other passengers who stay on board are the millionaire, his wife, and the young newly-married man. All will have strong personal reasons for wanting to remain behind, which will have been set up earlier in the plot.'

The maître d' struck a match and set light to the crêpe. A blue flame licked around the pan and shot into the air. He scooped his *pièce de résistance* onto a warm platter in one movement, and placed it in front of Christabel.

I feared we had now passed the point at which I could tell Duncan the truth.

'Right, now I have three terrorists in the cab with the chef de train. They've killed the co-driver, and there are just four passengers still left on the train, plus the black ticket collector – who may turn out to be SAS in disguise, I haven't decided yet.'

'Coffee, madame?' the maître d' asked when Duncan paused for a moment.

'Irish,' said Christabel.

'Regular, please,' I said.

'Decaff for me,' said Duncan.

'Any liqueurs or cigars?'

Only Christabel reacted.

'So, at the start of chapter eleven the terrorists open negotiations with the British police. But they say they can't deal with them because the train is no longer under their jurisdiction. This throws the terrorists completely, because none of them speaks French, and in any case their quarrel is with the British government. One of them searches the train for someone who can speak French, and comes across the Greek millionaire's wife.

'Meanwhile, the police on either side of the Channel stop all the trains going in either direction. So, our train is now stranded in the tunnel on its own – there would normally be twenty trains travelling in either direction between London and Paris at any one time.' He paused to sip his coffee.

'Is that so?' I asked, knowing the answer perfectly well.

'It certainly is,' Duncan said. 'I've done my research thoroughly.'

A glass of deep red port was being poured for Christabel. I glanced at the label: Taylor's '55. This was something I had never had the privilege of tasting. Christabel indicated that the bottle should be left on the table. The waiter nodded, and Christabel immediately poured me a glass, without asking if I wanted it. Meanwhile, the maître d' clipped a cigar for Duncan that he hadn't requested.

'In chapter twelve we discover the terrorists' purpose,' continued Duncan. 'Namely, blowing up the train as a publicity stunt, guaranteed to get their cause onto every front page in the world. But the passengers who have remained on the train, led by the American father, are planning a counter-offensive.'

The maître d' lit a match and Duncan automatically picked up the cigar and put it in his mouth. It silenced him . . .

'The self-made millionaire might feel he's the natural leader,' I suggested.

. . . but only for a moment. 'He's a Greek. If I'm going to make any money out of this project, it's the American market I have to aim for. And don't forget the film rights,' Duncan said, jabbing the air with his cigar.

I couldn't fault his logic.

'Can I have the check?' Duncan asked as the maître d' passed by our table.

'Certainly, sir,' he replied, not even breaking his stride.

'Now, my trouble is going to be the ending . . .'

began Duncan as Christabel suddenly, if somewhat unsteadily, rose from her chair.

She turned to face me and said, 'I'm afraid the time has come for me to leave. It's been a pleasure meeting you, although I have a feeling we won't be seeing each other again. I'd just like to say how much I enjoyed your latest novel. Such an original idea. It deserved to be number one.'

I stood, kissed her hand and thanked her, feeling more guilty than ever.

'Goodbye, Duncan,' she said, turning to face her former lover, but he didn't even bother to look up. 'Don't worry yourself,' she added. 'I'll be out of the apartment by the time you get back.'

She proceeded to negotiate a rather wobbly route across the restaurant, eventually reaching the door that led out onto the street. The maître d' held it open for her and bowed low.

'I can't pretend I'm sorry to see her go,' said Duncan, puffing away on his cigar. 'Fantastic body, great between the sheets, but she's totally lacking in imagination.'

The maître d' reappeared by Duncan's side, this time to place a small black leather folder in front of him.

'Well, the critics were certainly right about this place,' I commented. Duncan nodded his agreement.

The maître d' bowed, but not quite as low as before.

'Now, my trouble, as I was trying to explain before Christabel decided to make her exit,' continued Duncan, 'is that I've done the outline, completed the research, but I still don't have an ending. Any ideas?' he asked, as a middle-aged woman rose from a nearby table and began walking determinedly towards us.

Duncan flicked open the leather cover, and stared in disbelief at the bill.

The woman came to a halt beside our table. 'I just wanted to tell you how much I enjoyed your new book,' she said in a loud voice.

Other diners turned round to see what was going on.

'Thank you,' I said somewhat curtly, hoping to prevent her from adding to my discomfort.

Duncan's eyes were still fixed on the bill.

'And the ending,' she said. 'So clever! I would never have guessed how you were going to get the American family out of the tunnel alive . . .'

SHOESHINE BOY

TED BARKER WAS ONE OF THOSE MEMBERS of Parliament who never sought high office. He'd had what was described by his fellow officers as a 'good war' – in which he was awarded the Military Cross and reached the rank of major. After being demobbed in November 1945 he was happy to return to his wife Hazel and their home in Suffolk.

The family engineering business had also had a good war, under the diligent management of Ted's elder brother Ken. As soon as he arrived home, Ted was offered his old place on the board, which he happily accepted. But as the weeks passed by, the distinguished warrior became first bored and then disenchanted. There was no job for him at the factory which even remotely resembled active service.

It was around this time that he was approached by Ethel Thompson, the works convenor and – more important for the advancement of this tale – Chairman of the Wedmore branch of the North Suffolk Conservative Association. The incumbent MP, Sir Dingle Lightfoot, known in the constituency as 'Tiptoe', had made it clear that once the war was over they must look for someone to replace him.

'We don't want some clever clogs from London coming up here and telling us how to run this division,' pronounced Mrs Thompson. 'We need someone who knows the district and understands the problems of the local people.' Ted, she suggested, might be just the ticket.

Ted confessed that he had never given such an idea a moment's thought, but promised Mrs Thompson that he would take her proposal seriously, only asking for a week in which to consider his decision. He discussed the suggestion with his wife, and having received her enthusiastic support, he paid a visit to Mrs Thompson at her home the following Sunday afternoon. She was delighted to hear that Mr Barker would be pleased to allow his name to go forward for consideration as the prospective parliamentary candidate for the division of North Suffolk.

The final shortlist included two clever clogs from London – one of whom later served in a Macmillan Cabinet – and the local boy, Ted Barker. When the chairman announced the committee's decision to the local press, he said that it would be improper to reveal the number of votes each candidate had polled. In fact, Ted had comfortably outscored his two rivals put together.

Six months later the Prime Minister called a general election, and after a lively three-week campaign, Ted was returned as the Member of Parliament for North Suffolk with a majority of over seven thousand. He quickly became respected and popular with colleagues on both sides of the House, though he never pretended to be anything other than, in his own words, 'an amateur politician'.

As the years passed, Ted's popularity with his constituents grew, and he increased his majority with each succeeding general election. After fourteen years of diligent service to the party nationally and locally, the Prime Minister of the day, Harold Macmillan, recommended to the Queen that Ted should receive a knighthood.

By the end of the 1960s, Sir Ted (he was never known as Sir Edward) felt that the time was fast approaching when the division should start looking for a younger candidate, and he made it clear to the local chairman that he did not intend to stand at the next election. He and Hazel quietly prepared for a peaceful retirement in their beloved East Anglia.

Shortly after the election, Ted was surprised to receive a call from 10 Downing Street: 'The Prime Minister would like to see Sir Ted at 11.30 tomorrow morning.'

Ted couldn't imagine why Edward Heath should want to see him. Although he had of course visited Number 10 on several occasions when he was a Member of Parliament, those visits had only been for cocktail parties, receptions, and the occasional dinner for a visiting head of state. He admitted to Hazel that he was a little nervous.

Ted presented himself at the front door of Number 10 at 11.17 the next day. The duty clerk accompanied him down the long corridor on the ground floor, and asked him to take a seat in the small waiting area that adjoins the Cabinet Room. By now Ted's nervousness was turning to apprehension. He felt like an errant schoolboy about to come face to face with his headmaster.

After a few minutes a private secretary appeared. 'Good morning, Sir Ted. The Prime Minister will see you now.' He accompanied Ted into the Cabinet Room, where Mr Heath stood to greet him. 'How kind of you to come at such short notice, Ted.' Ted had to suppress a smile, because he knew the Prime Minister knew that it would have taken the scurvy or a localised hurricane to stop him from answering such a summons.

'I'm hoping you can help me with a delicate matter, Ted,' continued the Prime Minister, a man not known for wasting time on small-talk. 'I'm about to appoint the next Governor of St George's, and I can't think of anyone better qualified for the job than you.'

Ted recalled the day when Mrs Thompson had asked him to think about standing for Parliament. But on this occasion he didn't require a week to consider his reply – even if he couldn't quite bring himself to admit that although he'd heard of St George's, he certainly couldn't have located it on a map. Once he'd caught his breath, he simply said, 'Thank you, Prime Minister. I'd be honoured.'

During the weeks that followed Sir Ted paid several visits to the Foreign and Colonial Office to receive briefings on various aspects of his appointment. Thereafter he assiduously read every book, pamphlet and government paper the mandarins supplied.

After a few weeks of boning up on his new subject, the Governor-in-waiting had discovered that St George's was a tiny group of islands in the middle of the North Atlantic. It had been colonised by the British in 1643, and thereafter had a long history of imperial rule, the islanders having scorned every offer of independence. They were one of Her Majesty's sovereign colonies, and that was how they wished to remain.

Even before he set out on his adventure, Ted had become used to being addressed as 'Your Excellency'. But after being fitted up by Alan Bennett of Savile Row with two different full dress uniforms, Ted feared that he looked – what was that modern expression? – O.T.T. In winter he was expected to wear an outfit of dark blue doeskin with scarlet collar and cuffs embroidered with silver oakleaves, while in the summer he was to be adorned in white cotton drill with a gold-embroidered collar and gold shoulder cords. The sight of him in either uniform caused Hazel to laugh out loud.

Ted didn't laugh when the tailors sent him the bill, especially after he learned that he would be unlikely to wear either uniform more than twice a year. 'Still, think what a hit you'll be at fancy dress parties once you've retired,' was Hazel's only comment.

The newly-appointed Governor and Commander-in-Chief of St George's and his lady flew out to take up their post on 12 January 1971. They were greeted by the Prime Minister, as the colony's first citizen, and the

Chief Justice, as the legal representative of the Queen. After the new Governor had taken the salute from six off-duty policemen standing vaguely to attention, the town band gave a rendering of the national anthem. The Union Jack was raised on the roof of the airport terminal and a light splattering of applause broke out from the assembled gathering of twenty or thirty local dignitaries.

Sir Ted and Lady Barker were then driven to the official residence in a spacious but ageing Rover that had already served the two previous Governors. When they reached Government House, the driver brought the car to a halt and leaped out to open the gates. As they continued up the drive, Ted and Hazel saw their new home for the first time.

The colonial mansion was magnificent by any standards. Obviously built at the height of the British Empire, it was vastly out of proportion to either the importance of the island or Britain's current position in the real world. But size, as the Governor and his wife were quickly to discover, didn't necessarily equate with efficiency or comfort.

The air conditioning didn't work, the plumbing was unreliable, Mrs Rogers, the daily help, was regularly off sick, and the only thing Ted's predecessor had left behind was an elderly black labrador. Worse, the Foreign Office had no funds available to deal with any of these problems, and whenever Ted mentioned them in dispatches, he was met only with suggestions for cutbacks.

After a few weeks, Ted and Hazel began to think of St George's as being rather like a great big parliamentary constituency, split into several islands, the two largest being Suffolk and Edward Island. This heartened Ted, who even wondered if that was what had given the Prime Minister the idea of offering him the post in the first place.

The Governor's duties could hardly have been described as onerous: he and Hazel spent most of their time visiting hospitals, delivering speeches at school prize-givings and judging flower shows. The highlight of the year was undoubtedly the Queen's official birthday in June, when the Governor held a garden party for local dignitaries at Government House and Suffolk played Edward Island at cricket – an opportunity for most of the colony's citizens to spend two days getting thoroughly drunk.

Ted and Hazel accepted the local *realpolitik* and settled down for five years of relaxed diplomacy among delightful people in a heavenly climate, seeing no cloud on the horizon that could disturb their blissful existence.

Until the phone call came.

It was a Thursday morning, and the Governor was in his study with that Monday's *Times*. He was putting off reading a long article on the summit meeting taking place in Washington until he had finished the crossword, and was just about to fill in the answer to 12 across – Erring herd twists to create this diversion (3,7) – when his private secretary, Charles Roberts, came rushing into his office without knocking.

Ted realised it had to be something important, because he had never known Charles to rush anywhere, and certainly he had never known him to enter the study without the courtesy of a knock.

'It's Mountbatten on the line,' Charles blurted out. He could hardly have looked more anxious had he been reporting that the Germans were about to land on the north shore of the island. The Governor raised an eyebrow. 'Admiral of the Fleet Earl Mountbatten of Burma,' said Charles, as if Ted hadn't understood.

'Then put him through,' said Ted quietly, folding up his copy of *The Times* and placing it on the desk in front of him. He had met Mountbatten three times over the past twenty years, but doubted if the great man would recall any of these encounters. Indeed, on the third occasion Ted had found it necessary to slip out of the function the Admiral was addressing, as he was feeling a little queasy. He couldn't imagine what Mountbatten would want to speak to him about, and he had no time to consider the problem, as the phone on his desk was already ringing.

As Ted picked up the receiver he was still wondering whether to call Mountbatten 'My Lord' as he was an Earl, 'Commander-in-Chief', as he was a former Chief of the Defence Staff, or 'Admiral', as Admiral of the Fleet is a life appointment. He settled for 'Good morning, sir.'

'Good morning, Your Excellency. I hope I find you well?'

'Yes, thank you, sir,' replied Ted.

'Because if I remember correctly, when we last met you were suffering from a tummy bug.'

'That's right, sir,' said the surprised Governor. He

was reasonably confident that the purpose of Mount-batten's call wasn't to enquire about his health after all these years.

'Governor, you must be curious to know why I am calling.'

'Yes, sir.'

'I am presently in Washington attending the summit, and I had originally planned to return to London tomorrow morning.'

'I understand, sir,' said Ted, not understanding at all.

'But I thought I might make a slight detour and drop in to see you. I do enjoy visiting our colonies whenever I get the chance. It gives me the opportunity to brief Her Majesty on what's happening. I hope that such a visit would not be inconvenient.'

'Not at all, sir,' said Ted. 'We would be delighted to welcome you.'

'Good,' said Mountbatten. 'Then I would be obliged if you could warn the airport authorities to expect my aircraft around four tomorrow afternoon. I would like to stay overnight, but if I'm to keep to my schedule I will need to leave you fairly early the following morning.'

'Of course, sir. Nothing could be easier. My wife and I will be at the airport to welcome you at four o'clock tomorrow afternoon.'

'That's kind of you, Governor. By the way, I'd rather things were left fairly informal. Please don't put yourself to any trouble.' The line went dead.

Once he had replaced the receiver, it was Ted's turn to run for the first time in several months. He found

Charles striding down the long corridor towards him, having obviously listened in on the extension.

'Find my wife and get yourself a notepad – and then both of you join me in my office immediately. Immediately,' Ted repeated as he scuttled back into his study.

Hazel arrived a few minutes later, clutching a bunch of dahlias, followed by the breathless private secretary.

'Why the rush, Ted? What's the panic?'

'Mountbatten's coming.'

'When?' Hazel asked quietly.

'Tomorrow afternoon. Four o'clock.'

'That *is* a good reason to panic,' Hazel admitted. She dumped the flowers in a vase on the windowsill and took a seat opposite her husband on the other side of his desk. 'Perhaps this isn't the best time to let you know that Mrs Rogers is off sick.'

'You have to admire her timing,' said Ted. 'Right, we'll just have to bluff it.'

'What *do* you mean, "bluff it"?' asked Hazel.

'Well, don't let's forget that Mountbatten's a member of the Royal Family, a former Chief of the Defence Staff and an Admiral of the Fleet. The last colonial post he held was Viceroy of India with three regiments under his command and a personal staff of over a thousand. So I can't imagine what he'll expect to find when he turns up here.'

'Then let's begin by making a list of things that will have to be done,' said Hazel briskly.

Charles removed a pen from his inside pocket, turned

over the cover of his pad, and waited to write down his master's instructions.

'If he's arriving at the airport, the first thing he will expect is a red carpet,' said Hazel.

'But we don't have a red carpet,' said Ted.

'Yes we do. There's the one that leads from the dining room to the drawing room. We'll have to use that, and hope we can get it back in place before he visits that part of the house. Charles, you will have to roll it up and take it to the airport' – she paused – 'and then bring it back.'

Charles scowled, but began writing furiously.

'And Charles, can you also see that it's cleaned by tomorrow?' interjected the Governor. 'I hadn't even realised it was red. Now, what about a guard of honour?'

'We haven't got a guard of honour,' said Hazel. 'If you remember, when we arrived on the island we were met by the Prime Minister, the Chief Justice and six off-duty policemen.'

'True,' said Ted. 'Then we'll just have to rely on the Territorial Army.'

'You mean Colonel Hodges and his band of hopeful warriors? They don't even all have matching uniforms. And as for their rifles . . .'

'Hodges will just have to get them into some sort of shape by four o'clock tomorrow afternoon. Leave that one to me,' said Ted, making a note on his pad. 'I'll phone him later this morning. Now, what about a band?'

'Well there's the town band,' said Charles. 'And, of course, the police band.'

'On this occasion they'll have to combine,' said Hazel, 'so we don't offend either of them.'

'But they only know three tunes between them,' said Ted.

'They only need to know one,' said Hazel. 'The national anthem.'

'Right,' said the Governor. 'As there are sure to be a lot of musical feathers that will need unruffling, I'll leave you to deal with them, Hazel. Our next problem is how we transport him from the airport to Government House.'

'Certainly not in the old Rover,' said Hazel. 'It's broken down three times in the last month, and it smells like a kennel.'

'Henry Bendall has a Rolls-Royce,' said Ted. 'We'll just have to commandeer that.'

'As long as no one tells Mountbatten that it's owned by the local undertaker, and what it was used for the morning before he arrived.'

'Mick Flaherty also has an old Rolls,' piped up Charles. 'A Silver Shadow, if I remember correctly.'

'But he loathes the British,' said Hazel.

'Agreed,' said Ted, 'but he'll still want to have dinner at Government House when he discovers the guest of honour is a member of the Royal Family.'

'Dinner?' said Hazel, her voice rising in horror.

'Of course we will have to give a dinner in his honour,' said Ted. 'And, worse, everyone who is anyone will expect to be invited. How many can the dining room hold?' He and Hazel turned to the private secretary.

'Sixty if pushed,' replied Charles, looking up from his notes.

'We're pushed,' said Ted.

'We certainly are,' said Hazel. 'Because we don't have sixty plates, let alone sixty coffee cups, sixty teaspoons, sixty . . .'

'We still have that Royal Worcester service presented by the late King after his visit in 1947,' said Ted. 'How many pieces of that are fit for use?'

'Enough for about fourteen settings, at the last count,' said Hazel.

'Right, then that's dealt with how many people will be at the top table.'

'What about the menu?' asked Charles.

'And, more important, who is going to cook it?' added Ted.

'We'll have to ask Dotty Cuthbert if she can spare Mrs Travis for the evening,' said Hazel. 'No one on the island is a better cook.'

'And we'll also need her butler, not to mention the rest of her staff,' added Ted.

By now Charles was onto his third page.

'You'd better deal with Lady Cuthbert, my dear,' said Ted. 'I'll try to square Mick Flaherty.'

'Our next problem will be the drink,' said Hazel. 'Don't forget, the last Governor emptied the cellar a few days before he left.'

'And the Foreign Office refuses to restock it,' Ted reminded her. 'Jonathan Fletcher has the best cellar on the island . . .'

'And, God bless him, he won't expect to be at the top table,' said Hazel.

'If we're limited to fourteen places, the top table's looking awfully crowded already,' said Ted.

'Dotty Cuthbert, the Bendalls, the Flahertys, the Hodges,' said Hazel, writing down the names. 'Not to mention the Prime Minister, the Chief Justice, the Mayor, the Chief of Police, plus their wives . . . Let's hope that some of them are indisposed or abroad.' She was beginning to sound desperate.

'Where's he going to sleep?' asked Charles innocently.

'God, I hadn't thought of him sleeping,' said Ted.

'He'll have to take our bedroom. It's the only one with a bed that doesn't sink in the middle,' said Hazel.

'We'll move into the Nelson Room for the night, and suffer those dreadful woodwormed beds and their ancient horsehair mattresses.'

'Agreed,' said Hazel. 'I'll make sure all our things are out of the Queen Victoria Room by this evening.'

'And, Charles,' said the Governor, 'phone the Foreign Office, would you, and find out Mountbatten's likes and dislikes. Food, drink, eccentric habits – anything you can discover. They're sure to have a file on him, and this is one gentleman I don't want to catch me out.'

The private secretary turned over yet another page of his pad, and continued scribbling.

For the next hour, the three of them went over any and every problem that might arise during the visit, and after a self-made sandwich lunch, departed in their different directions to spend the afternoon making begging calls all round the island.

It was Charles's idea that the Governor should appear on the local television station's early-evening news programme, to let the citizens know that a member of the Royal Family would be visiting the island the following day. Sir Ted ended his broadcast by saying that he hoped as many people as possible would be at the airport to welcome 'the great war leader' when his plane touched down at four the following afternoon.

While Hazel spent the evening cleaning every room that the great war leader might conceivably enter, Charles, with the aid of a torch, tended to the flowerbeds that lined the driveway, and Ted supervised the shuttling of plates, cutlery, food and wine from different parts of the island to Government House.

'Now, what have we forgotten?' said Ted, as he climbed into bed at two o'clock that morning.

'Heaven only knows,' Hazel said wearily before turning out the light. 'But whatever it is, let's hope Mountbatten never finds out.'

The Governor, dressed in his summer uniform, with gold piping down the sides of his white trousers, decorations and campaign medals across his chest, and a Wolsey helmet with a plume of red-over-white swan's feathers on his head, walked out onto the landing to join his wife. Hazel was wearing the green summer frock she had bought for the Governor's garden party two years before, and was checking the flowers in the entrance hall.

'Too late for that,' said Ted, as she rearranged a sprig that had strayed half an inch. 'It's time we left for the airport.'

They descended the steps of Government House to find two Rolls-Royces, one black, one white, and their old Rover standing in line. Charles followed closely behind them, carrying the red carpet, which he dropped into the boot of the Rover as his master stepped into the back of the leading Rolls-Royce.

The first thing the Governor needed to check was the chauffeur's name.

'Bill Simmons,' he was informed.

'All you have to remember, Bill, is to look as if you've been doing this job all your life.'

'Right, Guv.'

'No,' said Ted firmly. 'In front of the Admiral, you must address me as "Your Excellency", and Lord Mountbatten as "My Lord". If in any doubt, say nothing.'

'Right, Guv, Your Excellency.'

Bill started up the car and drove towards the gates at what he evidently considered was a stately pace, before turning right and taking the road to the airport. When they reached the terminal fifteen minutes later a policeman ushered the tiny motorcade out onto the tarmac, where the combined bands were playing a medley from *West Side Story* – at least, that was what Ted charitably thought it might be.

As he stepped out of the car Ted came face to face

with three ranks of soldiers from the Territorial Army standing at ease, sixty-one of them, aged from seventeen to seventy. Ted had to admit that although they weren't the Grenadier Guards, they weren't 'Dad's Army' either. And they had two advantages: a real-live Colonel in full dress uniform, and a genuine Sergeant Major, with a voice to match.

Charles had already begun rolling out the red carpet when the Governor turned his attention to the hastily-erected barriers, where he was delighted to see a larger crowd than he had ever witnessed on the island, even at the annual football derby between Suffolk and Edward Island.

Many of the islanders were waving Union Jacks, and some were holding up pictures of the Queen. Ted smiled and checked his watch. The plane was due in seventeen minutes.

The Prime Minister, the local Mayor, the Chief Justice, the Commissioner of Police and their wives were lining up at the end of the red carpet. The sun beat down from a cloudless sky. As Ted turned in a slow circle to take in the scene, he could see for himself that everyone had made a special effort.

Suddenly the sound of engines could be heard, and the crowd began to cheer. Ted looked up, shielded his eyes, and saw an Andover of the Queen's Flight descending towards the airport. It touched down on the far end of the runway at three minutes before the hour, and taxied up to the red carpet as four chimes struck on the clock above the flight control tower.

The door of the plane opened, and there stood Admiral of the Fleet the Earl Mountbatten of Burma, KG, PC, GCB, OM, GCSI, GCIE, GCVO, DSO, FRS, DCL (Hon), LLD (Hon), attired in the full dress uniform of an Admiral of the Fleet (summer wear).

'If that's what he means by "fairly informal", I suppose we should be thankful that he didn't ask us to lay on an official visit,' murmured Hazel as she and Ted walked to the bottom of the steps that had been quickly wheeled into place.

As Mountbatten slowly descended the stairway, the crowd cheered even louder. Once he stepped onto the red carpet the Governor took a pace forward, removed his plumed hat, and bowed. The Admiral saluted, and at that moment the combined bands of town and police struck up the national anthem. The crowd sang 'God Save the Queen' so lustily that the occasional uncertain note was smothered by their exuberance.

When the anthem came to an end the Governor said, 'Welcome to St George's, sir.'

'Thank you, Governor,' replied Mountbatten.

'May I present my wife, Hazel.' The Governor's wife took a pace forward, did a full curtsey, and shook hands with the Admiral.

'How good to see you again, Lady Barker. This is indeed a pleasure.'

The Governor guided his guest to the end of the red carpet and introduced him to the Prime Minister and his wife Sheila, the local mayor and his wife Caroline, the Chief Justice and his wife Janet, and the Commissioner of Police and his latest wife, whose name he couldn't remember.

'Perhaps you'd care to inspect the guard of honour before we leave for Government House,' suggested Ted, steering Mountbatten in the direction of Colonel Hodges and his men.

'Absolutely delighted,' said the Admiral, waving to the crowd as the two of them proceeded across the tarmac towards the waiting guard. When they still had some twenty yards to go, the Colonel sprang to attention, took three paces forward, saluted and said crisply, 'Guard of Honour ready for inspection, sir.'

Mountbatten came to a halt and returned a naval salute, which was a sign for the Sergeant Major, standing at attention six paces behind his Colonel, to bellow out the words, 'Commanding officer on parade! General salute, pre–sent arms!'

The front row, who were in possession of the unit's entire supply of weapons, presented arms, while the second and third rows came rigidly to attention.

Mountbatten marched dutifully up and down the ranks, as gravely as if he were inspecting a full brigade of Life Guards. When he had passed the last soldier in the back row, the Colonel came to attention and saluted once again. Mountbatten returned the salute and said, 'Thank you, Colonel. First-class effort. Well done.'

The Governor then guided Mountbatten towards the white Rolls-Royce, where Bill was standing at what he imagined was attention, while at the same time holding open the back door. Mountbatten stepped in as the Governor hurried round to the other side, opened the door for himself, and joined his guest on the back seat. Hazel and the Admiral's ADC took their places in the black Rolls-Royce, while Charles and the Admiral's secretary had to make do with the Rover. The Governor only hoped that Mountbatten hadn't seen two members of the airport staff rolling up the red carpet and placing it in the Rover's boot. Hazel was only praying that they had enough sheets left over for the bed in the Green Room. If not, the ADC would be wondering about their sleeping habits.

The island's two police motorcycles, with white-uniformed outriders, preceded the three cars as they made their way towards the exit. The crowd waved and cheered lustily as the motorcade began its short journey to Government House. So successful had Ted's television appearance the previous evening been that the ten-mile route was lined with well-wishers.

As they approached the open gates two policemen sprang to attention and saluted as the leading car passed through. In the distance Ted could see a butler, two under-butlers and several maids, all smartly clad, standing on the steps awaiting their arrival. 'Damn it,' he almost said aloud as the car came to a halt at the bottom of the steps. 'I don't know the butler's name.'

The car door was smartly opened by one of the under-butlers while the second supervised the unloading of the luggage from the boot.

The butler took a pace forward as Mountbatten stepped out of the car. 'Carruthers, m'lord,' he said, bowing. 'Welcome to the residence. If you would be kind enough to follow me, I will direct you to your quarters.' The Admiral, accompanied by the Governor and Lady Barker, climbed the steps into Government House and followed Carruthers up the main staircase.

'Magnificent, these old government residences,' said Mountbatten as they reached the top of the stairs. Carruthers opened the door to the Queen Victoria Room and stood to one side, as if he had done so a thousand times before.

'How charming,' said the Admiral, taking in the Governor's private suite. He walked over to the window and looked out onto the newly-mown lawn. 'How very pleasant. It reminds me of Broadlands, my home in Hampshire.'

Lady Barker smiled at the compliment, but didn't allow herself to relax.

'Is there anything you require, m'lord?' asked Carruthers, as an under-butler began to supervise the unpacking of the cases.

Hazel held her breath.

'No, I don't think so,' said Mountbatten. 'Everything looks just perfect.'

'Perhaps you'd care to join Hazel and me for tea in the drawing room when you're ready, sir,' suggested Ted.

'How thoughtful of you,' said the Admiral. 'I'll be down in about thirty minutes, if I may.'

The Governor and his wife left the room, closing the door quietly behind them.

'I think he suspects something,' whispered Hazel as they tiptoed down the staircase.

'You may be right,' said Ted, placing his plumed hat on the stand in the hall, 'but that's all the more reason to check we haven't forgotten anything. I'll start with the dining room. You ought to go and see how Mrs Travis is getting on in the kitchen.'

When Hazel entered the kitchen she found Mrs Travis preparing the vegetables, and one of the maids peeling a mound of potatoes. She thanked Mrs Travis for taking over at such short notice, and admitted she had never seen the kitchen so full of exotic foods, or the surfaces so immaculately clean. Even the floor was spotless. Realising that her presence was superfluous, Hazel joined her husband in the dining room, where she found him admiring the expertise of the second under-butler, who was laying out the place settings for that evening, as a maid folded napkins to look like swans.

'So far, so good,' said Hazel. They left the dining room and entered the drawing room, where Ted paced up and down, trying to think if there was anything he had forgotten while they waited for the great man to join them for tea.

A few minutes later, Mountbatten walked in. He was no longer dressed in his Admiral's uniform, but had changed into a dark grey double-breasted suit.

'Damn it,' thought Ted, immediately aware of what he'd forgotten to do.

Hazel rose to greet her guest, and guided him to a large, comfortable chair.

'I must say, Lady Barker, your butler is a splendid chap,' said Mountbatten. 'He even knew the brand of whisky I prefer. How long have you had him?'

'Not very long,' admitted Hazel.

'Well, if he ever wants a job in England, don't hesitate to let me know – though I'm bound to say, you'd be a fool to part with him,' he added, as a maid came in carrying a beautiful Wedgwood tea service that Hazel had never set eyes on before.

'Earl Grey, if I remember correctly,' said Hazel.

'What a memory you have, Lady Barker,' said the Admiral, as the maid began to pour.

'Thank God for the Foreign Office briefing,' Hazel thought, as she accepted the compliment with a smile.

'And how did the Conference go, sir?' asked Ted, as he dropped a lump of sugar – the one thing he felt might be their own – into his cup of tea.

'For the British, quite well,' said Mountbatten. 'But it would have gone better if the French hadn't been up to their usual tricks. Giscard seems to regard himself as a cross between Charlemagne and Joan of Arc.' His hosts laughed politely. 'No, the real problem we're facing at the moment, Ted, is quite simply . . .'

By the time Mountbatten had dealt with the outcome of the summit, given his undiluted views of James Callaghan and Ted Heath, covered the problem of finding a wife for Prince Charles and mulled over the long-term repercussions of Watergate, it was almost time for him to change.

'Are we dressing for dinner?'

'Yes, sir – if that meets with your approval.'

'Full decorations?' Mountbatten asked, sounding hopeful.

'I thought that would be appropriate, sir,' replied Ted, remembering the Foreign Office's advice about the Admiral's liking for dressing up at the slightest opportunity.

Mountbatten smiled as Carruthers appeared silently at the door. Ted raised an eyebrow.

'I have laid out the full dress uniform, m'lord. I took the liberty of pressing the trousers. The bedroom maid is drawing a bath for you.'

Mountbatten smiled. 'Thank you,' he said as he rose from his chair. 'Such a splendid tea,' he added turning to face his hostess. 'And such wonderful staff. Hazel, I don't know how you do it.'

'Thank you, sir,' said Hazel, trying not to blush.

'What time would you like me to come down for dinner, Ted?' Mountbatten asked.

'The first guests should be arriving for drinks at about 7.30, sir. We were hoping to serve dinner at eight, if that's convenient for you.'

'Couldn't be better,' declared Mountbatten. 'How many are you expecting?'

'Around sixty, sir. You'll find a guest list on your bedside table. Perhaps Hazel and I could come and fetch you at 7.50?'

'You run a tight ship, Ted,' said Mountbatten with approval. 'You'll find me ready the moment you appear,' he added as he followed Carruthers out of the room.

Once the door was closed behind him, Hazel said to the maid, 'Molly, can you clear away the tea things, please?' She hesitated for a moment. 'It is Molly, isn't it?'

'Yes, ma'am,' said the girl.

'I think he knows,' said Ted, looking a little anxious.

'Maybe, but we haven't time to worry about that now,' said Hazel, already on her way to carry out a further inspection of the kitchen.

The mound of potatoes had diminished to a peeled heap. Mrs Travis, who was preparing the sauces, was calling for more pepper and for some spices to be fetched from a shop in town. Aware once again that she wasn't needed in the kitchen, Hazel moved on to the dining room, where she found Ted. The top table was now fully laid with the King's dinner service, three sets of wine glasses, crested linen napkins, and a glorious centrepiece of a silver pheasant, which gave added sparkle.

'Who lent us that?' she asked.

'I have no idea,' replied Ted. 'But one thing's for certain – it will have flown home by the morning.'

'If we keep the lighting low enough,' whispered Hazel, 'he might not notice that the other tables all have different cutlery.'

'Heavens, just look at the time,' said Ted.

They left the dining room and walked quickly up the

stairs. Ted nearly barged straight into Mountbatten's room, but remembered just in time.

The Governor rather liked his dark blue doeskin uniform with the scarlet collar and cuffs. He was admiring the ensemble in the mirror when Hazel entered the room in a pink Hardy Amies outfit, which she had originally thought a waste of money because she never expected it to be given a proper outing.

'Men are so vain,' she remarked as her husband continued to inspect himself in the mirror. 'You do realise you're only meant to wear that in winter.'

'I am well aware of that,' said Ted peevishly, 'but it's the only other uniform I've got. In any case, I bet Mountbatten will outdo us both.' He flicked a piece of fluff from his trousers, which he had just finished pressing.

The Governor and his wife left the Nelson Room and walked down the main staircase just before 7.20, to find yet another under-butler stationed by the front door, and two more maids standing opposite him carrying silver trays laden with glasses of champagne. Hazel introduced herself to the three of them, and again checked the flowers in the entrance hall.

As 7.30 struck on the long-case clock in the lobby the first guest walked in.

'Henry,' said the Governor. 'Lovely to see you. Thank you so much for the use of the Rolls. And Bill, come to that,' he added in a stage whisper.

'My pleasure, Your Excellency,' Henry Bendall replied. 'I must say, I like the uniform.'

Lady Cuthbert came bustling through the front door. 'Can't stop,' she said. 'Ignore me. Just pretend I'm not here.'

'Dotty, I simply don't know what we would have done without you,' Hazel said, chasing after her across the hall.

'Delighted to lend a hand,' said Lady Cuthbert. 'I thought I'd come bang on time, so I could spend a few minutes in the kitchen with Mrs Travis. By the way, Benson is standing out in the drive, ready to rush home if you find you're still short of anything.'

'You are a saint, Dotty. I'll take you through . . .'

'No, don't worry,' said Lady Cuthbert. 'I know my way around. You just carry on greeting your guests.'

'Good evening, Mr Mayor,' said Ted, as Lady Cuthbert disappeared in the direction of the kitchen.

'Good evening, Your Excellency. How kind of you to invite us to such an auspicious occasion.'

'And what a lovely dress, Mrs Janson,' said the Governor.

'Thank you, Your Excellency,' said the Mayor's wife.

'Would you care for a glass of champagne?' said Hazel as she arrived back at her husband's side.

By 7.45 most of the guests had arrived, and Ted was chatting to Mick Flaherty when Hazel touched him on the elbow. He glanced towards her.

'I think we should go and fetch him now,' she whispered.

Ted nodded, and asked the Chief Justice to take over the welcoming of the guests. They wove a path through the chattering throng, and climbed the great staircase. When they reached the door of the Queen Victoria Room, they paused and looked at each other.

Ted checked his watch — 7.50. He leaned forward and gave a gentle tap. Carruthers immediately opened the door to reveal Mountbatten attired in his third outfit of the day: full ceremonial uniform of an Admiral of the Fleet, three stars, a gold and blue sash and eight rows of campaign decorations.

'Good evening, Your Excellency,' said Mountbatten.

'Good evening, sir,' said the Governor, star struck.

The Admiral took three paces forward and came to a halt at the top of the staircase. He stood to attention. Ted and Hazel waited on either side of him. As he didn't move, they didn't.

Carruthers proceeded slowly down the stairs in front of them, stopping on the third step. He cleared his throat and waited for the assembled guests to fall silent.

'Your Excellency, Prime Minister, Mr Mayor, ladies and gentlemen,' he announced. 'The Right Honourable the Earl Mountbatten of Burma.'

Mountbatten descended the stairs slowly as the waiting guests applauded politely. As he passed Carruthers, the butler gave a deep bow. The Governor, with Hazel on his arm, followed two paces behind.

'He must know,' whispered Hazel.

'You may be right. But does he know we know?' said Ted.

Mountbatten moved deftly around the room, as Ted introduced him to each of the guests in turn. They bowed and curtsied, listening attentively to the few words the Admiral had to say to them. The one exception was Mick Flaherty, who didn't stop talking, and remained more upright than Ted had ever seen him before.

At eight o'clock one of the under-butlers banged a gong, which until then neither the Governor nor his wife had even realised existed. As the sound died away, Carruthers announced, 'My Lord, Your Excellency, Prime Minister, Mr Mayor, ladies and gentlemen, dinner is served.'

If there was a better cook on St George's than Mrs Travis, no one at the top table had ever been fed by her, and that evening she had excelled herself.

Mountbatten chatted and smiled, making no secret of how much he was enjoying himself. He spent a long time talking to Lady Cuthbert, whose husband had served under him at Portsmouth, and to Mick Flaherty, to whom he listened with polite interest.

Each course surpassed the one before: soufflé, followed by lamb cutlets, and an apricot hazelnut meringue to complete the feast. Mountbatten remarked on every one of the wines, and even called for a second glass of port.

After dinner, he joined the guests for coffee in the drawing room, and managed to have a word with everyone, even though Colonel Hodges tried to buttonhole him about defence cuts.

The guests began to leave a few minutes before midnight, and Ted was amused to see that when Mick Flaherty bade farewell to the Admiral, he bowed low and said, 'Good night, My Lord. It has been an honour to meet you.'

Dotty was among the last to depart, and she curtsied low to the guest of honour. 'You've helped to make this such a pleasant evening, Lady Cuthbert,' Mountbatten told her.

'If you only knew just how much,' thought Hazel.

After the under-butler had closed the door on the last guest, Mountbatten turned to his hostess and said, 'Hazel, I must thank you for a truly memorable occasion. The head chef at the Savoy couldn't have produced a finer banquet. Perfect in every part.'

'You are very kind, sir. I will pass your thanks on to the staff.' She just stopped herself from saying 'my staff'. 'Is there anything else we can do for you before you retire?'

'No, thank you,' Mountbatten replied. 'It has been a long day, and with your permission, I'll turn in now.'

'And at what time would you like breakfast, sir?' asked the Governor.

'Would 7.30 be convenient?' Mountbatten asked. 'That will give me time to fly out at nine.'

'Certainly,' said Ted. 'I'll see that Carruthers brings a light breakfast up to your room at 7.30 – unless you'd like something cooked.'

'A light breakfast will be just the thing,' Mountbatten said. 'A perfect evening. Your staff could not have done more, Hazel. Good night, and thank you, my dear.'

The Governor bowed and his lady curtsied as the great

man ascended the staircase two paces behind Carruthers. When the butler closed the door of the Queen Victoria Room, Ted put his arm around his wife and said, 'He knows we know.'

'You may be right,' said Hazel. 'But does he know we know he knows?'

'I'll have to think about that,' said Ted.

Arm in arm, they returned to the kitchen, where they found Mrs Travis packing dishes into a crate under the supervision of Lady Cuthbert, the long lace sleeves of whose evening dress were now firmly rolled up.

'How did you get back in, Dotty?' asked Hazel.

'Just walked round to the back yard and came in the servants' entrance,' replied Lady Cuthbert.

'Did you spot anything that went badly wrong?' Hazel asked anxiously.

'I don't think so,' replied Lady Cuthbert. 'Not unless you count Mick Flaherty failing to get a fourth glass of Muscat de Venise.'

'Mrs Travis,' said Ted, 'the head chef at the Savoy couldn't have produced a finer banquet. Perfect in every part. I do no more than repeat Lord Mountbatten's exact words.'

'Thank you, Your Excellency,' said Mrs Travis. 'He's got a big appetite, hasn't he?' she added with a smile.

A moment later, Carruthers entered the kitchen. He checked round the room, which was spotless once again, then turned to Ted and said, 'With your permission, sir, we will take our leave.'

'Of course,' said the Governor. 'And may I thank you, Carruthers, for the role you and your amazing team have played. You all did a superb job. Lord Mountbatten never stopped remarking on it.'

'His Lordship is most kind, sir. At what time would you like us to return in the morning to prepare and serve his breakfast?'

'Well, he asked for a light breakfast in his room at 7.30.'

'Then we will be back by 6.30,' said Carruthers.

Hazel opened the kitchen door to let them all out, and they humped crates full of crockery and baskets full of food to the waiting cars. The last person to leave was Dotty, who was clutching the silver pheasant. Hazel kissed her on both cheeks as she departed.

'I don't know how you feel, but I'm exhausted,' said Ted, bolting the kitchen door.

Hazel checked her watch. It was seventeen minutes past one.

'Shattered,' she admitted. 'So, let's try and grab some sleep, because *we'll* also have to be up by seven to make sure everything is ready before he leaves for the airport.'

Ted put his arm back around his wife's waist. 'A personal triumph for you, my dear.'

They strolled into the hall and wearily began to climb the stairs, but didn't utter another word, for fear of disturbing their guest's repose. When they reached the landing, they came to an abrupt halt, and stared down in horror at the sight that greeted them. Three pairs of black leather shoes had been placed neatly in line outside the Queen Victoria Room.

'Now I'm certain he knows,' said Hazel.

Ted nodded and, turning to his wife, whispered, 'You or me?'

Hazel pointed a finger firmly at her husband. 'Definitely you, my dear,' she said sweetly, before disappearing in the direction of the Nelson Room.

Ted shrugged his shoulders, picked up the Admiral's shoes, and returned downstairs to the kitchen.

His Excellency the Governor and Commander-in-Chief of St George's spent a considerable time polishing those three pairs of shoes, as he realised that not only must they pass inspection by an Admiral of the Fleet, but they must look as if the job had been carried out by Carruthers.

When Mountbatten returned to the Admiralty in Whitehall the following Monday, he made a full written report on his visit to St George's. Copies were sent to the Queen and the Foreign Secretary.

The Admiral told the story of his visit at a family gathering that Saturday evening at Windsor Castle, and once the laughter had died down, the Queen asked him, 'When did you first become suspicious?'

'It was Carruthers who gave it away. He knew everything about Sir Ted, except which regiment he had served in. That's just not possible for an old soldier.'

The Queen had one further question: 'Do you think the Governor knew you knew?'

'I can't be certain, Lillibet,' replied Mountbatten after some thought. 'But I intend to leave him in no doubt that I did.'

The Foreign Secretary laughed uproariously when he read Mountbatten's report, and appended a note to the last sheet asking for clarification on two points:

(a) How can you be certain that the staff who served dinner were not part of the Governor's entourage?

(b) Do you think Sir Ted knew that you knew?

The Admiral replied by return:

(a) After dinner, one of the maids asked Lady Barker if she took sugar in her coffee, but a moment later she gave Lady Cuthbert two lumps, without needing to ask.

(b) Possibly not. But he certainly will on Christmas Day.

Sir Ted was pleased to receive a Christmas card from Lord Mountbatten, signed, 'Best wishes, Dickie. Thank you for a memorable stay.' It was accompanied by a gift.

Hazel unwrapped the little parcel to discover a tin of Cherry Blossom shoe polish (black). Her only comment was, 'So now we know he knew.'

'Agreed,' said Ted with a grin. 'But did he know we knew he knew? That's what I'd like to know.'

YOU'LL NEVER LIVE
TO REGRET IT

AND SO IT WAS AGREED: DAVID WOULD leave everything to Pat. If one of them had to die, at least the other would be financially secure for the rest of their life. David felt it was the least he could do for someone who'd stood by him for so many years, especially as he was the one who had been unfaithful.

They had known each other almost all their lives, because their parents had been close friends for as long as either of them could remember. Both families had hoped David might end up marrying Pat's sister Ruth, and they were unable to hide their surprise – and in Pat's father's case his disapproval – when the two of them started living together, especially as Pat was three years older than David.

For some time David had been putting it off and hoping for a miracle cure, despite a pushy insurance broker from Geneva Life called Marvin Roebuck who had been pressing him to 'take a meeting' for the past nine months. On the first Monday of the tenth month he phoned again, and this time David reluctantly agreed to see him. He chose a date when he knew Pat would be on night duty at the hotel, and asked Roebuck to come round to their apartment – that way, he felt, it would look as if it was the broker who had done the chasing.

David was watering the scarlet *clupea harengus* on the hall table when Marvin Roebuck pressed the buzzer on the front door. Once he had poured his visitor a Budweiser, David told him he had every type of insurance he could possibly need: theft, accident, car, property, health, even holiday.

'But what about life?' asked Marvin, licking his lips.

'That's one I don't need,' said David. 'I earn a good salary, I have more than enough security, and on top of that, my parents will leave everything to me.'

'But wouldn't it be prudent to have a lump sum that comes to you automatically on your sixtieth or sixty-fifth birthday?' asked Marvin, as he continued to push at a door that he had no way of knowing was already wide open. 'After all, you can never be sure what disaster might lie around the corner.'

David knew exactly what disaster lay around the corner, but he still innocently asked, 'What sort of figure are you talking about?'

'Well, that would depend on how much you are currently earning,' said Marvin.

'$120,000 a year,' said David, trying to sound casual, as it was almost double his real income. Marvin was obviously impressed, and David remained silent as he carried out some rapid calculations in his head.

'Well,' said Marvin eventually, 'I'd suggest half a million dollars – as a ballpark figure. After all,' he added, quickly running a finger down a page of actuarial tables he had extracted from his aluminium briefcase, 'you're only twenty-seven, so the payments would be well within your means. In fact, you might even consider a larger sum if you're confident your income will continue to rise over the next few years.'

'It has done every year for the past seven,' said David, this time truthfully.

'What kind of business are you in, my friend?' asked Marvin.

'Stocks and bonds,' replied David, not offering any details of the small firm he worked for, or the junior position he held.

Marvin licked his lips again, even though they had told him not to do so on countless refresher courses, especially when going in for the kill.

'So, what amount do you think I should go for?' asked David, continuing to make sure it was always Marvin who took the lead.

'Well, a million is comfortably within your credit range,' said Marvin, once again checking his little book of tables. 'The monthly payments might seem a bit steep to begin with, but as the years go by, what with inflation and your continual salary increases, you can expect that in time they will become almost insignificant.'

'How much would I have to pay each month to end up getting a million?' asked David, attempting to give the impression he might have been hooked.

'Assuming we select your sixtieth birthday for terminating the contract, a little over a thousand dollars a month,' said Marvin, trying to make it sound a mere pittance. 'And don't forget, sixty per cent of it is tax deductible, so in real terms you'll only be paying around fifteen dollars a day, while you end up getting a million, just at the time when you most need it. And by the way, that one thousand is constant, it never goes up. In fact it's inflation-proof.' He let out a dreadful shrill laugh.

'But would I still receive the full sum, whatever happens to the market?'

'One million dollars on your sixtieth birthday,' confirmed Marvin, 'whatever happens, short of the world coming to an end. Even I can't write a policy for that,' he said, letting out another shrill laugh. 'However, my friend, if unhappily you were to die before your sixtieth birthday – which God forbid – your dependants would receive the full amount immediately.'

'I don't have any dependants,' said David, trying to look bored.

'There must be someone you care about,' said Marvin. 'A good-looking guy like you.'

'Why don't you leave the forms with me, Mr Roebuck, and I'll think about it over the weekend. I promise I'll get back to you.'

Marvin looked disappointed. He didn't need a refresher course to be told that you're supposed to nail the client to the wall at the first meeting, not let them get away, because that only gave them time to think things over. His lips felt dry.

Pat returned from the evening shift in the early hours of the morning, but David had stayed awake so he could go over what had happened at the meeting with Marvin. Pat was apprehensive and uncertain about the plan. David had always taken care of any problems they had had in the past, especially financial ones, and Pat wasn't sure how it would all work out once David was no longer around to give his advice. Thank God it was David who'd had to deal with Marvin – Pat couldn't even say no to a door-to-door brush salesman.

'So, what do we do next?' asked Pat.

'Wait.'

'But you promised Marvin you'd get back to him.'

'I know, but I have absolutely no intention of doing so,' said David, placing his arm round Pat's shoulder. 'I'd bet a hundred dollars on Marvin phoning me first thing on Monday morning. And don't forget, I still need it to look as if he's the one who's doing the pushing.'

As they climbed into bed, Pat felt an attack of asthma coming on, and decided now was not the time to ask David to go over the details again. After all, as David had explained again and again, there would never be any need for Pat to meet Marvin.

Marvin phoned at 8.30 on Monday morning.

'Hoped to catch you before you went off to sell those stocks and bonds,' he said. 'Have you come to a decision?'

'Yes, I have,' said David. 'I discussed the whole idea with my mother over the weekend, and she thinks I should go for the million, because five hundred thousand may not turn out to be such a large sum of money by the time I reach sixty.'

Marvin was glad that David couldn't see him licking his lips. 'Your mother's obviously a shrewd woman,' was his only comment.

'Can I leave you to handle all the paperwork?' asked David, trying to sound as if he didn't want to deal with any of the details.

'You bet,' said Marvin. 'Don't even think about it, my friend. Just leave all that hassle to me. I know you've made the right decision, David. I promise you, you'll never live to regret it.'

The following day, Marvin phoned again to say that the paperwork had been completed, and all that was now required was for David to have a medical – 'routine' was the word he kept repeating. But because of the size of the sum insured, it would have to be with the company's doctor in New York.

David made a fuss about having to travel to New York, adding that perhaps he'd made the wrong decision, but after more pleading from Marvin, mixed with some unctuous persuasion, he finally gave in.

Marvin brought all the forms round to the apartment the following evening after Pat had left for work.

David scribbled his signature on three separate documents between two pencilled crosses. His final act was to print Pat's name in a little box Marvin had indicated with his stubby finger. 'As your sole dependant,' the broker explained, 'should you pass away before 1 September 2027 – God forbid. Are you married to Pat?'

'No, we just live together,' replied David.

After a few more 'my friends' and even more 'you'll

never live to regret it's, Marvin left the apartment, clutching the forms.

'All you have to do now is keep your nerve,' David told Pat once he had confirmed that the paperwork had been completed. 'Just remember, no one knows me as well as you do, and once it's all over, you'll collect a million dollars.'

When they eventually went to bed that night, Pat desperately wanted to make love to David, but they both accepted it was no longer possible.

The two of them travelled down to New York together the following Monday to keep the appointment David had made with Geneva Life's senior medical consultant. They parted a block away from the insurance company's head office, as they didn't want to run the risk of being seen together. They hugged each other once again, but as they parted David was still worried about whether Pat would be able to go through with it.

A couple of minutes before twelve, he arrived at the surgery. A young woman in a long white coat smiled up at him from behind her desk.

'Good morning,' he said. 'My name is David Kravits. I have an appointment with Dr Royston.'

'Oh, yes, Mr Kravits,' said the nurse. 'Dr Royston is expecting you. Please follow me.' She led him down a long, bleak corridor to the last room on the left. A small brass plaque read 'Dr Royston'. She knocked, opened the door and said, 'Mr Kravits, doctor.'

Dr Royston turned out to be a short, elderly man with only a few strands of hair left on his shiny sunburnt

227

head. He wore horn-rimmed spectacles, and had a look on his face which suggested that his own life insurance policy might not be far from reaching maturity. He rose from his chair, shook his patient by the hand and said, 'It's for a life insurance policy, if I remember correctly.'

'Yes, that's right.'

'Shouldn't take us too long, Mr Kravits. Fairly routine, but the company does like to be sure you're fit and well if they're going to be liable for such a large amount of money. Do have a seat,' he said, pointing to the other side of his desk.

'I thought the sum was far too high myself. I would have been happy to settle for half a million, but the broker was very persuasive . . .'

'Any serious illness during the past ten years?' the doctor asked, obviously not interested in the broker's views.

'No. The occasional cold, but nothing I'd describe as serious,' he replied.

'Good. And in your immediate family, any history of heart attacks, cancer, liver complaints?'

'Not that I'm aware of.'

'Father still alive?'

'Very much so.'

'And he's fit and well?'

'Jogs every morning, and pumps weights in the local gym at the weekend.'

'And your mother?'

'Doesn't do either, but I wouldn't be surprised if she outlives him comfortably.'

. The doctor laughed. 'Any of your grandparents still living?'

'All except one. My dad's father died two years ago.'

'Do you know the cause of death?'

'He just passed away, I think. At least, that was how the priest described it at his funeral.'

'And how old was he?' the doctor asked. 'Do you remember?'

'Eighty-one, eighty-two.'

'Good,' repeated Dr Royston, ticking another little box on the form in front of him. 'Have you ever suffered from any of these?' he asked, holding up a clipboard in front of him. The list began with arthritis, and ended eighteen lines later with tuberculosis.

He ran an eye slowly down the long list before replying. 'No, none of them,' was all he said, not admitting to asthma on this occasion.

'Do you smoke?'

'Never.'

'Drink?'

'Socially – I enjoy the occasional glass of wine with dinner, but I never drink spirits.'

'Excellent,' said the doctor and ticked the last of the little boxes. 'Now, let's check your height and weight. Come over here, please, Mr Kravits, and climb onto these scales.'

The doctor had to stand on his toes in order to push the wooden marker up until it was flat across his patient's head. 'Six feet one inch,' he declared, then looked down at the weighing machine, and flicked the little weight across until it just balanced. 'A hundred and seventy-nine pounds. Not bad.' He filled in two more lines of his report. 'Perhaps just a little overweight.

'Now I need a urine sample, Mr Kravits. If you would be kind enough to take this plastic container next door, fill it about halfway up, leave it on the ledge when you've finished, and then come back to me.'

The doctor wrote out some more notes while his patient left the room. He returned a few moments later.

'I've left the container on the ledge,' was all he said.

'Good. The next thing I need is a blood sample. Could you roll up your right sleeve?' The doctor placed a rubber pad around his right bicep and pumped until the veins stood out clearly. 'A tiny prick,' he said. 'You'll hardly feel a thing.' The needle went in, and he turned away as the doctor drew his blood. Dr Royston cleaned the wound and fixed a small circular plaster over the broken skin. The doctor then bent over and placed a cold stethoscope on different parts of the patient's chest, occasionally asking him to breathe in and out.

'Good,' he kept repeating. Finally he said, 'That just about wraps it up, Mr Kravits. You'll need to spend a few minutes down the corridor with Dr Harvey, so she can take a chest x-ray, and have some fun with her electric pads, but after that you'll be through, and you can go home to' – he checked his pad – 'New Jersey. The company will be in touch in a few days, as soon as we've had the results.'

'Thank you, Dr Royston,' he said as he buttoned up his shirt. The doctor pressed a buzzer on his desk and the nurse reappeared and led him to another room, with a plaque on the door that read 'Dr Mary Harvey'. Dr Harvey, a smartly-dressed middle-aged woman with her grey hair cropped short, was waiting for him. She smiled at the tall, handsome man and asked him to take off his shirt again and to step up onto the platform and stand in front of the x-ray unit.

'Place your arms behind your back and breathe in. Thank you.' Next she asked him to lie down on the bed in the corner of the room. She leaned over his chest, smeared blodges of paste on his skin and fixed little pads to them. While he stared up at the white ceiling she flicked a switch and concentrated on a tiny television screen on the corner of her desk. Her expression gave nothing away.

After she had removed the paste with a damp flannel she said, 'You can put your shirt back on, Mr Kravits. You are now free to leave.'

Once he was fully dressed, the young man hurried out of the building and down the steps, and ran all the way to the corner where they had parted. They hugged each other again.

'Everything go all right?'

'I think so,' he said. 'They told me I'd be hearing from them in the next few days, once they've had the results of all their tests.'

'Thank God it hasn't been a problem for you.'

'I only wish it wasn't for you.'

'Don't let's even think about it,' said David, holding tightly onto the one person he loved.

Marvin rang a week later to let David know that Dr Royston had given him a clean bill of health. All he had to do now was send the first instalment of $1100 to the insurance company. David posted a cheque off to Geneva Life the following morning. Thereafter his payments were made by wire transfer on the first day of each month.

Nineteen days after the seventh payment had been cleared, David Kravits died of AIDS.

Pat tried to remember the first thing he was meant to do once the will had been read. He was to contact a Mr Levy, David's lawyer, and leave everything in his hands. David had warned him not to become involved in any way himself. Let Levy, as his executor, make the claim from the insurance company, he had said, and then pass the money on to him. If in any doubt, say nothing, was the last piece of advice David had given Pat before he died.

Ten days later, Pat received a letter from a claims representative at Geneva Life requesting an interview with the beneficiary of the policy. Pat passed the letter straight to David's lawyer. Mr Levy wrote back agreeing to an interview, which would take place, at his client's request, at the offices of Levy, Goldberg and Levy in Manhattan.

'Is there anything you haven't told me, Patrick?' Levy asked him a few minutes before the insurance company's claims representative was due to arrive. 'Because if there is, you'd better tell me now.'

'No, Mr Levy, there's nothing more to tell you,' Pat replied, carrying out David's instructions to the letter.

From the moment the meeting began, the representative of Geneva Life, his eyes continually boring into Pat's bowed head, left Mr Levy in no doubt that he was not happy about paying out on this particular claim. But the lawyer stonewalled every question, strengthened by the knowledge that eight months before, when rigorous tests had been taken, Geneva Life's doctors had found no sign of David's being HIV positive.

Levy kept repeating, 'However much noise you make, your company will have to pay up in the end.' He added for good measure, 'If I have not received the full amount due to my client within thirty days, I will immediately instigate proceedings against Geneva Life.' The claims representative asked Levy if he would consider a deal. Levy glanced at Pat, who bowed his head even lower, and replied, 'Certainly not.'

Pat arrived back at the apartment two hours later, exhausted and depressed, fearing that an attack of asthma might be coming on. He tried to prepare some supper before he went to work, but everything seemed so pointless without David. He was already wondering if he should have agreed to a settlement.

The phone rang only once during the evening. Pat rushed to pick it up, hoping it might be either his mother or his sister Ruth. It turned out to be Marvin, who bleated, 'I'm in real trouble, Pat. I'm probably going to lose my job over that policy I made out for your friend David.'

Pat said how sorry he was, but felt there was nothing he could do to help.

'Yes, there is,' insisted Marvin. 'For a start, you could take out a policy yourself. That might just save my skin.'

'I don't think that would be wise,' said Pat, wondering what David would have advised.

'Surely David wouldn't have wanted to see me fired,' Marvin pleaded. 'Have mercy on me, my friend. I just can't afford another divorce.'

'How much would it cost me?' asked Pat, desperate to find some way of getting Marvin off the line.

'You're going to get a million dollars in cash,' Marvin almost shouted, 'and you're asking me what it's going to cost? What's a thousand dollars a month to someone as rich as you?'

'But I can't be sure that I am going to get the million,' Pat protested.

'That's all been settled,' Marvin told him, his voice falling by several decibels. 'I'm not meant to let you know this, but you'll be receiving the cheque on the thirtieth of the month. The company know that your lawyer's got them by the balls . . . You wouldn't even have to make the first payment until after you'd received the million.'

'All right,' said Pat, desperate to be rid of him. 'I'll do it, but not until I've received the cheque.'

'Thank you, my friend. I'll drop round with the paperwork tomorrow night.'

'No, that's not possible,' said Pat. 'I'm working nights this month. You'd better make it tomorrow afternoon.'

'You won't be working nights once you've received that cheque, my friend,' said Marvin, letting out one of his dreadful shrill laughs. 'Lucky man,' he added before he put the phone down.

By the time Marvin came round to the apartment the following afternoon, Pat was already having second thoughts. If he had to visit Dr Royston again, they would immediately realise the truth. But once Marvin had assured him that the medical could be with any doctor of his choice, and that the first payment would be post-dated, he caved in and signed all the forms between the pencilled crosses, making Ruth his sole beneficiary. He hoped David would have approved of that decision, at least.

'Thank you, my friend. I won't be bothering you again,' promised Marvin. His final words as he closed the door behind him were, 'I promise you, you'll never live to regret it.'

Pat saw his doctor a week later. The examination didn't take long, as Pat had recently had a complete check-up. On that occasion, as the doctor recalled, Pat had appeared quite nervous, and couldn't hide his relief when he'd phoned to give him the all-clear. 'Not much wrong with you, Patrick,' he said, 'apart from the asthma, which doesn't seem to be getting any worse.'

Marvin called a week later to let Pat know that the doctor had given him a clean bill of health, and that he had held on to his job with Geneva Life.

'I'm pleased for you,' said Pat. 'But what about my cheque?'

'It will be paid out on the last day of the month. Only a matter of processing it now. Should be with you twenty-four hours before the first payment is due on your policy. Just like I said, you win both ways.'

Pat rang David's lawyer on the last day of the month to ask if he had received the cheque from Geneva Life.

'There was nothing in this morning's post,' Levy told him, 'but I'll phone the other side right now, in case it's already been issued and is on its way. If not, I'll start proceedings against them immediately.'

Pat wondered if he should tell Levy that he had signed a cheque for $1100 which was due to be cleared the following day, and that he only just had sufficient funds in his account to cover it – certainly not enough to see him through until his next pay packet. All his surplus cash had gone to help with David's monthly payments to Geneva Life. He decided not to mention it. David had repeatedly told him that if he was in any doubt, he should say nothing.

'I'll phone you at close of business tonight and let you know exactly what the position is,' said Levy.

'No, that won't be possible,' said Pat. 'I'm on night duty all this week. In fact I have to leave for work right now. Perhaps you could call me first thing tomorrow morning?'

'Will do,' promised the lawyer.

When Pat returned home from work in the early hours, he couldn't get to sleep. He tossed and turned, worrying how he would survive for the rest of the month if his cheque was presented to the bank that morning, and he still hadn't received the million dollars from Geneva Life.

His phone rang at 9.31. Pat grabbed it, and was relieved to hear Mr Levy's voice on the other end of the line.

'Patrick, I had a call from Geneva Life yesterday evening while you were at work, and I must tell you that you've broken Levy's golden rule.'

'Levy's golden rule?' asked Pat, mystified.

'Yes, Levy's golden rule. It's quite simple really, Patrick. By all means drop anything you like, on anyone you like, but don't *ever* drop it all over your own lawyer.'

'I don't understand,' said Pat.

'Your doctor has supplied Geneva Life with a sample of your blood and urine, and they just happen to be identical to the ones Dr Royston has in his laboratory in the name of David Kravits.'

Pat felt the blood draining from his head as he realised the trick Marvin must have played on him. His heart began beating faster and faster. Suddenly his legs gave way, and he collapsed on the floor, gasping for breath.

'Did you hear me, Patrick?' asked Levy. 'Are you still there?'

A paramedic team broke into the apartment twenty minutes later, but, moments before they reached him, Pat had died of a heart attack brought on by a suffocating bout of asthma.

Mr Levy did nothing until he was able to confirm with

Pat's bankers that his client's cheque for $1100 had been cleared by the insurance company.

Nineteen months later Pat's sister Ruth received a payment of one million dollars from Geneva Life, but not until they had gone through a lengthy court battle with Levy, Goldberg and Levy.

The jury finally accepted that Pat had died of natural causes, and that the insurance policy was in existence at the time of his death.

I promise you, Marvin Roebuck lived to regret it.

NEVER STOP
ON THE MOTORWAY

DIANA HAD BEEN HOPING TO GET AWAY by five, so she could be at the farm in time for dinner. She tried not to show her true feelings when at 4.37 her deputy, Phil Haskins, presented her with a complex twelve-page document that required the signature of a director before it could be sent out to the client. Haskins didn't hesitate to remind her that they had lost two similar contracts that week.

It was always the same on a Friday. The phones would go quiet in the middle of the afternoon and then, just as she thought she could slip away, an authorisation would land on her desk. One glance at this particular document and Diana knew there would be no chance of escaping before six.

The demands of being a single parent as well as a director of a small but thriving City company meant there were few moments left in any day to relax, so when it came to the one weekend in four that James and Caroline spent with her ex-husband, Diana would try to leave the office a little earlier than usual to avoid getting snarled up in the weekend traffic.

She read through the first page slowly and made a

couple of emendations, aware that any mistake made hastily on a Friday night could be regretted in the weeks to come. She glanced at the clock on her desk as she signed the final page of the document. It was just flicking over to 5.51.

Diana gathered up her bag and walked purposefully towards the door, dropping the contract on Phil's desk without bothering to suggest that he have a good weekend. She suspected that the paperwork had been on his desk since nine o'clock that morning, but that holding it until 4.37 was his only means of revenge now that she had been made head of department. Once she was safely in the lift, she pressed the button for the basement carpark, calculating that the delay would probably add an extra hour to her journey.

She stepped out of the lift, walked over to her Audi estate, unlocked the door and threw her bag onto the back seat. When she drove up onto the street the stream of twilight traffic was just about keeping pace with the pinstriped pedestrians who, like worker ants, were hurrying towards the nearest hole in the ground.

She flicked on the six o'clock news. The chimes of Big Ben rang out, before spokesmen from each of the three main political parties gave their views on the European election results. John Major was refusing to comment on his future. The Conservative Party's explanation for its poor showing was that only thirty-six per cent of the country had bothered to go to the polls. Diana felt guilty – she was among the sixty-four per cent who had failed to register their vote.

The newscaster moved on to say that the situation in Bosnia remained desperate, and that the UN was threatening dire consequences if Radovan Karadzik and the Serbs didn't come to an agreement with the other warring parties. Diana's mind began to drift – such a threat was hardly news any longer. She suspected that if she turned on the radio in a year's time they would probably be repeating it word for word.

As her car crawled round Russell Square, she began to think about the weekend ahead. It had been over a year since John had told her that he had met another woman and wanted a divorce. She still wondered why, after seven years of marriage, she hadn't been more shocked – or at least angry – at his betrayal. Since her appointment as a director, she had to admit they had spent less and less time together. And perhaps she had become anaesthetised by the fact that a third of the married couples in Britain were now divorced or separated. Her parents had been unable to hide their disappointment, but then they had been married for forty-two years.

The divorce had been amicable enough, as John, who earned less than she did – one of their problems, perhaps – had given in to most of her demands. She had kept the flat in Putney, the Audi estate and the children, to whom John was allowed access one weekend in four. He would have picked them up from school earlier that afternoon, and, as usual, he'd return them to the flat in Putney around seven on Sunday evening.

Diana would go to almost any lengths to avoid being

left on her own in Putney when they weren't around, and although she regularly grumbled about being landed with the responsibility of bringing up two children without a father, she missed them desperately the moment they were out of sight.

She hadn't taken a lover and she didn't sleep around. None of the senior staff at the office had ever gone further than asking her out to lunch. Perhaps because only three of them were unmarried – and not without reason. The one person she might have considered having a relationship with had made it abundantly clear that he only wanted to spend the night with her, not the days.

In any case, Diana had decided long ago that if she was to be taken seriously as the company's first woman director, an office affair, however casual or short-lived, could only end in tears. Men are so vain, she thought. A woman only had to make one mistake and she was immediately labelled as promiscuous. Then every other man on the premises either smirks behind your back, or treats your thigh as an extension of the arm on his chair.

Diana groaned as she came to a halt at yet another red light. In twenty minutes she hadn't covered more than a couple of miles. She opened the glove box on the passenger side and fumbled in the dark for a cassette. She found one and pressed it into the slot, hoping it would be Pavarotti, only to be greeted by the strident tones of Gloria Gaynor assuring her 'I will survive'. She smiled and thought about Daniel, as the light changed to green.

She and Daniel had read Economics at Bristol University in the early 1980s, friends but never lovers. Then Daniel met Rachael, who had come up a year after them, and from that moment he had never looked at another woman. They married the day he graduated, and after they returned from their honeymoon Daniel took over the management of his father's farm in Bedfordshire. Three children had followed in quick succession, and Diana had been proud when she was asked to be godmother to Sophie, the eldest. Daniel and Rachael had now been married for twelve years, and Diana felt confident that they wouldn't be disappointing *their* parents with any suggestion of a divorce. Although they were convinced she led an exciting and fulfilling life, Diana often envied their gentle and uncomplicated existence.

She was regularly asked to spend the weekend with them in the country, but for every two or three invitations Daniel issued, she only accepted one – not because she wouldn't have liked to join them more often, but because since her divorce she had no desire to take advantage of their hospitality.

Although she enjoyed her work, it had been a bloody week. Two contracts had fallen through, James had been dropped from the school football team, and Caroline had never stopped telling her that her father didn't mind her watching television when she ought to be doing her prep.

Another traffic light changed to red.

It took Diana nearly an hour to travel the seven miles out of the city, and when she reached the first dual carriageway, she glanced up at the A1 sign, more out of habit than to seek guidance, because she knew every yard of the road from her office to the farm. She tried to increase her speed, but it was quite impossible, as both lanes remained obstinately crowded.

'Damn.' She had forgotten to get them a present, even a decent bottle of claret. 'Damn,' she repeated: Daniel and Rachael always did the giving. She began to wonder if she could pick something up on the way, then remembered there was nothing but service stations between here and the farm. She couldn't turn up with yet another box of chocolates they'd never eat. When she reached the roundabout that led onto the A1, she managed to push the car over fifty for the first time. She began to relax, allowing her mind to drift with the music.

There was no warning. Although she immediately slammed her foot on the brakes, it was already too late. There was a dull thump from the front bumper, and a slight shudder rocked the car.

A small black creature had shot across her path, and despite her quick reactions, she hadn't been able to avoid hitting it. Diana swung onto the hard shoulder and screeched to a halt, wondering if the animal could possibly have survived. She reversed slowly back to the spot where she thought she had hit it as the traffic roared past her.

And then she saw it, lying on the grass verge – a cat that had crossed the road for the tenth time. She stepped out of the car, and walked towards the lifeless body. Suddenly Diana felt sick. She had two cats of her own, and she knew she would never be able to tell the children what she had done. She picked up the dead animal and laid it gently in the ditch by the roadside.

'I'm so sorry,' she said, feeling a little silly. She gave it one last look before walking back to her car. Ironically, she had chosen the Audi for its safety features.

She climbed back into the car and switched on the ignition to find Gloria Gaynor was still belting out her opinion of men. She turned her off, and tried to stop thinking about the cat as she waited for a gap in the traffic large enough to allow her to ease her way back into the slow lane. She eventually succeeded, but was still unable to erase the dead cat from her mind.

Diana had accelerated up to fifty again when she suddenly became aware of a pair of headlights shining through her rear windscreen. She put up her arm and waved in her rear-view mirror, but the lights continued to dazzle her. She slowed down to allow the vehicle to pass, but the driver showed no interest in doing so. Diana began to wonder if there was something wrong with her car. Was one of her lights not working? Was the exhaust billowing smoke? Was . . .

She decided to speed up and put some distance between herself and the vehicle behind, but it remained within a few yards of her bumper. She tried to snatch a look at the driver in her rear-view mirror, but it was hard to see much in the harshness of the lights. As her eyes became more accustomed to the glare, she could make out the silhouette of a large black van bearing down on her, and what looked like a young man behind the wheel. He seemed to be waving at her.

Diana slowed down again as she approached the next roundabout, giving him every chance to overtake her on the outside lane, but once again he didn't take the opportunity, and just sat on her bumper, his headlights still undimmed. She waited for a small gap in the traffic coming from her right. When one appeared she slammed her foot on the accelerator, shot across the roundabout and sped on up the A1.

She was rid of him at last. She was just beginning to relax and to think about Sophie, who always waited up so that she could read to her, when suddenly those high-beam headlights were glaring through her rear wind-screen and blinding her once again. If anything, they were even closer to her than before.

She slowed down, he slowed down. She accelerated, he accelerated. She tried to think what she could do next, and began waving frantically at passing motorists as they sped by, but they remained oblivious to her predicament. She tried to think of other ways she might alert some-one, and suddenly recalled that when she had joined the board of the company they had suggested she have a car phone fitted. Diana had decided it could wait until the car went in for its next service, which should have been a fortnight ago.

She brushed her hand across her forehead and removed a film of perspiration, thought for a moment, then manoeuvred her car into the fast lane. The van swung across after her, and hovered so close to her bumper that she became fearful that if she so much as touched her brakes she might unwittingly cause an enormous pile-up.

Diana took the car up to ninety, but the van wouldn't be shaken off. She pushed her foot further down on the accelerator and touched a hundred, but it still remained less than a car's length behind.

She flicked her headlights onto high-beam, turned on her hazard lights and blasted her horn at anyone who dared to remain in her path. She could only hope that the police might see her, wave her onto the hard shoulder and book her for speeding. A fine would be infinitely preferable to a crash with a young tearaway, she thought, as the Audi estate passed a hundred and ten for the first time in its life. But the black van couldn't be shaken off.

Without warning, she swerved back into the middle lane and took her foot off the accelerator, causing the van to draw level with her, which gave her a chance to look at the driver for the first time. He was wearing a black leather jacket and pointing menacingly at her. She shook her fist at him and accelerated away, but he simply swung across behind her like an Olympic runner determined not to allow his rival to break clear.

And then she remembered, and felt sick for a second time that night. 'Oh my God,' she shouted aloud in terror. In a flood, the details of the murder that had taken place on the same road a few months before came rushing back to her. A woman had been raped before having her throat cut with a knife with a serrated edge and dumped in a ditch. For weeks there had been signs posted on the A1 appealing to passing motorists to phone a certain number if they had any information that might assist the police with their enquiries. The signs had now disappeared, but the police were still searching for the killer. Diana began to tremble as she remembered their warning to all woman drivers: 'Never stop on the motorway'.

A few seconds later she saw a road sign she knew well. She had reached it far sooner than she had anticipated. In three miles she would have to leave the motorway for the sliproad that led to the farm. She began to pray that if she took her usual turning, the black-jacketed man would continue on up the A1 and she would finally be rid of him.

Diana decided that the time had come for her to speed him on his way. She swung back into the fast lane and once again put her foot down on the accelerator. She reached a hundred miles per hour for the second time as she sped past the two-mile sign. Her body was now covered in sweat, and the speedometer touched a hundred and ten. She checked her rear-view mirror, but he was still right behind her. She would have to pick the exact moment if she was to execute her plan successfully. With a mile to go, she began to look to her left, so as to be sure her timing would be perfect. She no longer needed to check in her mirror to know that he would still be there.

The next signpost showed three diagonal white lines, warning her that she ought to be on the inside lane if

she intended to leave the motorway at the next junction.
She kept the car in the outside lane at a hundred miles
per hour until she spotted a large enough gap. Two white
lines appeared by the roadside: Diana knew she would
have only one chance to make her escape. As she passed
the sign with a single white line on it she suddenly
swung across the road at ninety miles per hour, causing
cars in the middle and inside lanes to throw on their
brakes and blast out their angry opinions. But Diana
didn't care what they thought of her, because she was
now travelling down the sliproad to safety, and the black
van was speeding on up the A1.

She laughed out loud with relief. To her right, she
could see the steady flow of traffic on the motorway.
But then her laugh turned to a scream as she saw the
black van cut sharply across the motorway in front of a
lorry, mount the grass verge and career onto the sliproad, swinging from side to side. It nearly drove over
the edge and into a ditch, but somehow managed to
steady itself, ending up a few yards behind her, its lights
once again glaring through her rear windscreen.

When she reached the top of the sliproad, Diana
turned left in the direction of the farm, frantically trying
to work out what she should do next. The nearest town
was about twelve miles away on the main road, and the
farm was only seven, but five of those miles were down
a winding, unlit country lane. She checked her petrol
gauge. It was nearing empty, but there should still be
enough in the tank for her to consider either option.
There was less than a mile to go before she reached the

turning, so she had only a minute in which to make up her mind.

With a hundred yards to go, she settled on the farm. Despite the unlit lane, she knew every twist and turn, and she felt confident that her pursuer wouldn't. Once she reached the farm she could be out of the car and inside the house long before he could catch her. In any case, once he saw the farmhouse, surely he would flee.

The minute was up. Diana touched the brakes and skidded into a country road illuminated only by the moon.

Diana banged the palms of her hands on the steering wheel. Had she made the wrong decision? She glanced up at her rear-view mirror. Had he given up? Of course he hadn't. The back of a Land Rover loomed up in front of her. Diana slowed down, waiting for a corner she knew well, where the road widened slightly. She held her breath, crashed into third gear, and overtook. Would a head-on collision be preferable to a cut throat? She rounded the bend and saw an empty road ahead of her. Once again she pressed her foot down, this time managing to put a clear seventy, perhaps even a hundred, yards between her and her pursuer, but this only offered her a few moments' respite. Before long the familiar headlights came bearing down on her once again.

With each bend Diana was able to gain a little time as the van continued to lurch from side to side, unfamiliar with the road, but she never managed a clear break of more than a few seconds. She checked the mileometer. From the turn-off on the main road to the farm it was just over five miles, and she must have covered about two by now. She began to watch each tenth of a mile clicking up, terrified at the thought of the van overtaking her and forcing her into the ditch. She stuck determinedly to the centre of the road.

Another mile passed, and still he clung on to her. Suddenly she saw a car coming towards her. She switched her headlights to full beam and pressed on the horn. The other car retaliated by mimicking her actions, which caused her to slow down and brush against the hedgerow as they shot past each other. She checked the mileometer once again. Only two miles to go.

Diana would slow down and then speed up at each familiar bend in the road, making sure the van was never given enough room to pull level with her. She tried to concentrate on what she should do once the farmhouse came into sight. She reckoned that the drive leading up to the house must be about half a mile long. It was full of potholes and bumps which Daniel had often explained he couldn't afford to have repaired. But at least it was only wide enough for one car.

The gate to the driveway was usually left open for her, though on the odd rare occasion Daniel had forgotten, and she'd had to get out of the car and open it for herself. She couldn't risk that tonight. If the gate was closed, she would have to travel on to the next town and stop outside the Crimson Kipper, which was always crowded at this time on a Friday night, or, if she could find it, on the steps of the local police station. She checked her petrol gauge again. It was now touching red. 'Oh my God,' she said, realising she might not have enough petrol to reach the town.

She could only pray that Daniel had remembered to leave the gate open.

She swerved out of the next bend and speeded up, but once again she managed to gain only a few yards, and she knew that within seconds he would be back in place. He was. For the next few hundred yards they remained within feet of each other, and she felt certain he must run into the back of her. She didn't once dare to touch her brakes – if they crashed in that lane, far from any help, she would have no hope of getting away from him.

She checked her mileometer. A mile to go.

'The gate must be open. It must be open,' she prayed. As she swung round the next bend, she could make out the outline of the farmhouse in the distance. She almost screamed with relief when she saw that the lights were on in the downstairs rooms.

She shouted, 'Thank God!' then remembered the gate again, and changed her plea to 'Dear God, let it be open.' She would know what needed to be done as soon as she came round the last bend. 'Let it be open, just this once,' she pleaded. 'I'll never ask for anything again, ever.' She swung round the final bend only inches ahead of the black van. 'Please, please, please.' And then she saw the gate.

It was open.

Her clothes were now drenched in sweat. She slowed down, wrenched the gearbox into second, and threw the car between the gap and into the bumpy driveway, hitting the gatepost on her right-hand side as she careered on up towards the house. The van didn't hesitate to follow her, and was still only inches behind as she straightened up. Diana kept her hand pressed down on the horn as the car bounced and lurched over the mounds and potholes.

Flocks of startled crows flapped out of overhanging branches, screeching as they shot into the air. Diana began screaming, 'Daniel! Daniel!' Two hundred yards ahead of her, the porch light went on.

Her headlights were now shining onto the front of the house, and her hand was still pressed on the horn. With a hundred yards to go, she spotted Daniel coming out of the front door, but she didn't slow down, and neither did the van behind her. With fifty yards to go she began flashing her lights at Daniel. She could now make out the puzzled, anxious expression on his face.

With thirty yards to go she threw on her brakes. The heavy estate car skidded across the gravel in front of the house, coming to a halt in the flowerbed just below the kitchen window. She heard the screech of brakes behind her. The leather-jacketed man, unfamiliar with the terrain, had been unable to react quickly enough, and as soon as his wheels touched the gravelled forecourt he began to skid out of control. A second later the van came crashing into the back of her car, slamming it against the wall of the house and shattering the glass in the kitchen window.

Diana leapt out of the car, screaming, 'Daniel! Get a gun, get a gun!' She pointed back at the van. 'That bastard's been chasing me for the last twenty miles!'

The man jumped out of the van and began limping towards them. Diana ran into the house. Daniel followed and grabbed a shotgun, normally reserved for rabbits, that was leaning against the wall. He ran back outside to face the unwelcome visitor, who had come to a halt by the back of Diana's Audi.

Daniel raised the shotgun to his shoulder and stared straight at him. 'Don't move or I'll shoot,' he said calmly. And then he remembered the gun wasn't loaded. Diana ducked back out of the house, but remained several yards behind him.

'Not me! Not me!' shouted the leather-jacketed youth, as Rachael appeared in the doorway.

'What's going on?' she asked nervously.

'Ring for the police,' was all Daniel said, and his wife quickly disappeared back into the house.

Daniel advanced towards the terrified-looking young man, the gun aimed squarely at his chest.

'Not me! Not me!' he shouted again, pointing at the Audi. 'He's in the car!' He quickly turned to face Diana. 'I saw him get in when you were parked on the hard shoulder. What else could I have done? You just wouldn't pull over.'

Daniel advanced cautiously towards the rear door of the car and ordered the young man to open it slowly, while he kept the gun aimed at his chest.

The youth opened the door, and quickly took a pace backwards. The three of them stared down at a man crouched on the floor of the car. In his right hand he held a long-bladed knife with a serrated edge. Daniel swung the barrel of the gun down to point at him, but said nothing.

The sound of a police siren could just be heard in the distance.

NOT FOR SALE

SALLY SUMMERS WON HER SCHOOL'S senior art prize at the age of fourteen. In her last four years at St Bride's the only serious competition was for second place. When, in her final year, she was awarded the top scholarship to the Slade School of Fine Art none of her contemporaries was at all surprised. The headmistress told the assembled parents on Speech Day that she was confident Sally had a distinguished career ahead of her, and that her work would soon be exhibited in one of London's major galleries. Sally was flattered by all this unqualified praise, but still wasn't sure if she had any real talent.

By the end of her first year at the Slade, the staff and senior students were already becoming aware of Sally's work. Her drawing technique was regarded as quite exceptional, and her brushwork became bolder with each term. But, above all, it was the originality of her ideas that caused other students to stop and stare at her canvases.

In her final year, Sally won both the Mary Rischgitz Prize for oil painting and the Henry Tonks Prize for drawing: a rare double. They were presented to her by

Sir Roger de Grey, the President of the Royal Academy, and Sally was among that tiny group who were spoken of as 'having a future'. But surely, she told her parents, that could be said of the top student in any year – and most of them ended up working in the creative departments of advertising agencies, or teaching art to bored schoolchildren in far-flung parts of the kingdom.

Once she had graduated, Sally had to decide whether she too would apply for a job with an advertising agency, take up a teaching appointment, or risk everything and try to put together enough original work for a London gallery to consider her for a one-woman show.

Her parents were convinced that their daughter had real talent, but what do parents know when you're their only child? thought Sally. Especially when one of them was a music teacher and the other an accountant who were the first to admit that they didn't know much about art, but they knew what they liked. Still, they seemed quite willing to support her for another year if she wanted (to use an expression of the young) to go for it.

Sally was painfully aware that, although her parents were fairly comfortably off, another year in which she produced no income could only be a burden for them. After much soul-searching she told them, 'One year, and one year only. After that, if the paintings aren't good enough, or if no one shows any interest in exhibiting them, I'll be realistic and look for a proper job.'

For the next six months Sally worked hours that she hadn't realised existed when she'd been a student.

During that time she produced a dozen canvases. She allowed no one to see them, for fear that her parents and friends would not be frank with her. She was determined to finish her portfolio and then listen only to the toughest opinions possible, those of the professional gallery owners, and, tougher still, those of the buying public.

Sally had always been a voracious reader, and she continued to devour books and monographs on artists from Bellini to Hockney. The more she read, the more she became aware that however talented an artist might be, it was industry and dedication that ultimately marked out the few who succeeded from the many who failed. This inspired her to work still harder, and she began to turn down invitations to parties, dances, even weekends with old friends, making use of every spare moment to visit art galleries or to attend lectures on the great masters.

By the eleventh month, Sally had completed twenty-seven works, but she still wasn't sure whether they displayed any real talent. Nevertheless, she felt the time had finally come to allow others to pass judgement on them.

She looked long and hard at each of the twenty-seven paintings, and the following morning she packed six of them in a large canvas folder her parents had given her the previous Christmas, and joined the early-morning commuters on their journey from Sevenoaks into London.

Sally began her quest in Cork Street, where she came across galleries exhibiting works by Bacon, Freud,

Hockney, Dunston and Chadwick. She felt overawed at the prospect of even entering their portals, let alone submitting her own humble work to the appraisal of their proprietors. She humped her canvas folder a couple of blocks north to Conduit Street, and in the windows she recognised the works of Jones, Campbell, Wczenski, Frink and Paolozzi. She became even more discouraged and unwilling to push open any of the galleries' front doors.

Sally returned home that night exhausted, her canvas folder unopened. She understood for the first time how an author must feel after receiving a string of rejection slips. She was unable to sleep that night. But as she lay awake she came to the conclusion that she must know the truth about her work, even if it meant being humiliated.

She joined the commuters again the following morning, and this time headed for Duke Street, St James's. She didn't bother with the galleries exhibiting old masters, Dutch still lifes or English landscapes, and therefore walked straight past Johnny van Haeften and Rafael Valls. Halfway down the street she turned right, and finally came to a halt outside the Simon Bouchier Gallery, which was exhibiting the sculptures of the late Sydney Harpley and the paintings of Muriel Pemberton, whose obituary Sally had read in the *Independent* only a few days before.

It was the thought of death that made Sally settle on the Bouchier Gallery. Perhaps they would be looking for someone young, she tried to convince herself, someone who had a long career ahead of them.

She stepped inside the gallery and found herself in a large, empty room, surrounded by Muriel Pemberton's watercolours. 'Can I help you?' asked a young woman who was sitting behind a desk near the window.

'No, thank you,' Sally replied. 'I was just looking.'

The girl eyed Sally's canvas folder, but said nothing. Sally decided she would do one circuit of the room, and then make good her escape. She began to circle the gallery, studying the pictures carefully. They were good, very good – but Sally believed she could do just as well, given time. She would have liked to see Muriel Pemberton's work when *she* was her age.

When Sally reached the far end of the gallery, she became aware of an office in which a short, balding man, wearing an old tweed jacket and corduroy trousers, was closely examining a picture. He looked about the same age as her father. Also studying the picture was another man, who caused Sally to stop in her tracks. He must have been a little over six foot, with those dark Italian looks that people normally only come across in glossy magazines; and *he* was old enough to be her brother.

Was he Mr Bouchier? she wondered. She hoped so, because if he owned the gallery she might be able to summon up the courage to introduce herself to him, once the little man in the scruffy jacket had left. At that moment the young man looked up and gave her a huge grin. Sally turned quickly away and began to study the pictures on the far wall.

She was wondering if it was worth hanging around any longer when the two men suddenly strolled out of the office and began walking towards the door.

She froze, pretending to concentrate on a portrait of a young girl in pastel blues and yellows, a picture that had a Matisse-like quality about it.

'What's in there?' asked a cheeky voice. Sally turned round and came face to face with the two men. The smaller one was pointing at her canvas bag.

'Just a few pictures,' Sally stammered. 'I'm an artist.'

'Let's have a look,' said the man, 'and perhaps *I* can decide if you're an artist or not.'

Sally hesitated.

'Come on, come on,' he teased. 'I haven't got all day. As you can see, I have an important client to take to lunch,' he added, indicating the tall, well-dressed young man, who still hadn't spoken.

'Oh, are *you* Mr Bouchier?' she asked, unable to hide her disappointment.

'Yes. Now, am I going to be allowed to look at your pictures or not?'

Sally quickly unzipped her canvas bag and laid out the six paintings on the floor. Both of the men bent down and studied them for some time before either offered an opinion.

'Not bad,' said Bouchier eventually. 'Not bad at all. Leave them with me for a few days, and then let's meet again next week.' He paused. 'Say Monday, 11.30. And if you have any more examples of your recent work, bring them with you.' Sally was speechless. 'Can't see you before Monday,' he continued, 'because the RA's Summer Exhibition opens tomorrow. So for the next few days I won't have a moment to spare. Now, if you'll excuse me . . .'

The younger man was still examining Sally's pictures closely. At last he looked up at her. 'I'd like to buy the one of the interior with the black cat on the windowsill. How much is it?'

'Well,' said Sally, 'I'm not sure . . .'

'N.F.S.,' said Mr Bouchier firmly, guiding his client towards the door.

'By the way,' the taller man said, turning back, 'I am Antonio Flavelli. My friends call me Tony.' But Mr Bouchier was already pushing him out onto the street.

Sally returned home that afternoon with an empty canvas folder, and was prepared to admit to her parents that a London dealer had shown an interest in her work. But it was, she insisted, no more than an interest.

The following morning Sally decided to go to the opening day of the Royal Academy Summer Exhibition, which would give her the chance to find out just how good her rivals were. For over an hour she stood in the long queue that stretched from the front door, right across the carpark and out onto the pavement. When she eventually reached the top of the wide staircase, she wished she was six feet six tall, so that she could see over the tops of the heads of the mass of people who were crowding every room. After a couple of hours strolling round the many galleries, Sally was confident that she was already good enough to enter a couple of her pictures for next year's exhibition.

She stopped to admire a Craigie Aitchison of Christ

on the cross, and checked in her little blue catalogue to find out the price: ten thousand pounds, more than she could hope to earn if she were to sell every one of her canvases. Suddenly her concentration was broken, as a soft Italian voice behind her said, 'Hello, Sally.' She swung round to find Tony Flavelli smiling down at her.

'Mr Flavelli,' she said.

'Tony, please. You like Craigie Aitchison?'

'He's superb,' Sally replied. 'I know his work well – I had the privilege of being taught by him when I was at the Slade.'

'I can remember, not so long ago, when you could pick up an Aitchison for two, three hundred pounds at the most. Perhaps the same thing will happen to you one day. Have you seen anything else you think I ought to look at?'

Sally was flattered to have her advice sought by a serious collector, and said, 'Yes, I think the sculpture of "Books on a Chair" by Julie Major is very striking. She has talent, and I'm sure she has a future.'

'So do you,' said Tony.

'Do you think so?' asked Sally.

'It's not important what I think,' said Tony. 'But Simon Bouchier is convinced.'

'Are you teasing me?' asked Sally.

'No, I'm not, as you'll find out for yourself when you see him next Monday. He talked of little else over lunch yesterday – "The daring brushwork, the unusual use of colour, the originality of ideas." I thought he was never going to stop. Still, he's promised I can have "The Sleeping Cat that Never Moved" once you've both settled on a price.'

Sally was speechless.

'Good luck,' Tony said, turning to leave. 'Not that I think you need it.' He hesitated for a moment before swinging back to face her. 'By the way, are you going to the Hockney exhibition?'

'I didn't even know there was one,' Sally confessed.

'There's a private view this evening. Six to eight.' Looking straight into her eyes he said, 'Would you like to join me?'

She hesitated, but only for a moment. 'That would be nice.'

'Good, then why don't we meet in the Ritz Palm Court at 6.30.' Before Sally could tell him that she didn't know where the Ritz was, let alone its Palm Court, the tall, elegant man had disappeared into the crowd.

Sally suddenly felt gauche and scruffy, but then, she hadn't dressed that morning with the Ritz in mind. She looked at her watch – 12.45 – and began to wonder if she had enough time to return home, change, and be back at the Ritz by 6.30. She decided that she didn't have much choice, as she doubted if they would let her into such a grand hotel dressed in jeans and a T-shirt of Munch's 'The Scream'. She ran down the wide staircase, out onto Piccadilly, and all the way to the nearest tube station.

When she arrived back home in Sevenoaks – far earlier than her mother had expected – she rushed into the kitchen and explained that she would be going out again shortly.

'Was the Summer Exhibition any good?' her mother asked.

'Not bad,' Sally replied as she ran upstairs. But once she was out of earshot she muttered under her breath, 'Certainly didn't see a lot that worried me.'

'Will you be in for supper?' asked her mother, sticking her head out from behind the kitchen door.

'I don't think so,' shouted Sally. She disappeared into her bedroom and began flinging off her clothes before heading for the bathroom.

She crept back downstairs an hour later, having tried on and rejected several outfits. She checked her dress in the hall mirror – a little too short, perhaps, but at least it showed her legs to best advantage. She could still remember those art students who during life classes had spent more time staring at her legs than at the model they were supposed to be drawing. She only hoped Tony would be similarly captivated.

' 'Bye, Mum,' she shouted, and quickly closed the door behind her before her mother could see what she was wearing.

Sally took the next train back to Charing Cross. She stepped on to the platform unwilling to admit to any passer-by that she had no idea where the Ritz was, so she hailed a taxi, praying she could get to the hotel for four pounds, because that was all she had on her. Her eyes remained fixed on the meter as it clicked past two pounds, and then three – far too quickly, she thought –

three pounds twenty, forty, sixty, eighty . . . She was just about to ask the cabbie to stop, so she could jump out and walk the rest of the way, when he drew in to the kerb.

The door was immediately opened by a statuesque man dressed in a heavy blue trenchcoat who raised his top hat to her. Sally handed over her four pounds to the cabbie, feeling guilty about the measly twenty pence tip. She ran up the steps, through the revolving door and into the hotel foyer. She checked her watch: 6.10. She decided she had better go back outside, walk slowly around the block, and return a little later. But just as she reached the door, an elegant man in a long black coat approached her and asked, 'Can I help you, madam?'

'I'm meeting Mr Tony Flavelli,' Sally stammered, hoping he would recognise the name.

'Mr Flavelli. Of course, madam. Allow me to show you to his table in the Palm Court.'

She followed the black-coated man down the wide, deeply carpeted corridor, then up three steps to a large open area full of small circular tables, almost all of which were occupied.

Sally was directed to a table at the side, and once she was seated a waiter asked, 'Can I get you something to drink, madam? A glass of champagne, perhaps?'

'Oh, no,' said Sally. 'A coke will be just fine.'

The waiter bowed and left her. Sally gazed nervously around the beautifully furnished room. Everyone seemed so relaxed and sophisticated. The waiter returned a few moments later and placed a fine cut-glass tumbler

with Coca-Cola, ice and lemon in front of her. She
thanked him and began sipping her drink, checking her
watch every few minutes. She pulled her dress down as
far as it would go, wishing she had chosen something
longer. She was becoming anxious about what would
happen if Tony didn't turn up, because she didn't have
any money left to pay for her drink. And then suddenly
she saw him, dressed in a loose double-breasted suit and
an open-neck cream shirt. He had stopped to chat to an
elegant young woman on the steps. After a couple of
minutes he kissed her on the cheek, and made his way
over to Sally.

'I am so sorry,' he said. 'I didn't mean to keep you
waiting. I do hope I'm not late.'

'No, no you're not. I arrived a few minutes early,'
Sally said, flustered, as he bent down and kissed her
hand.

'What did you think of the Summer Exhibition?' he
asked as the waiter appeared by his side.

'Your usual, sir?' he asked.

'Yes, thank you, Michael,' he replied.

'I enjoyed it,' said Sally. 'But . . .'

'But you felt you could have done just as well yourself,' he suggested.

'I didn't mean to imply that,' she said, looking up to
see if he was teasing. But the expression on his face
remained serious. 'I'm sure I will enjoy the Hockney
more,' she added as a glass of champagne was placed on
the table.

'Then I'll have to come clean,' said Tony.

Sally put down her drink and stared at him, not knowing what he meant.

'There isn't a Hockney exhibition on at the moment,' he said. 'Unless you want to fly to Glasgow.'

Sally looked puzzled. 'But you said . . .'

'I just wanted an excuse to see you again.'

Sally felt bemused and flattered, and was uncertain how to respond.

'I'll leave the choice to you,' he said. 'We could have dinner together, or you could simply take the train back to Sevenoaks.'

'How did you know I live in Sevenoaks?'

'It was inscribed in big bold letters on the side of your canvas folder,' said Tony with a smile.

Sally laughed. 'I'll settle for dinner,' she said. Tony paid for the drinks, then guided Sally out of the hotel and a few yards down the road to a restaurant on the corner of Arlington Street.

This time Sally did try a glass of champagne, and allowed Tony to select for her from the menu. He could not have been more attentive, and seemed to know so much about so many things, even if she didn't manage to find out exactly what he did.

After Tony had called for the bill, he asked her if she would like to have coffee at 'my place'.

'I'm afraid I can't,' she said, looking at her watch. 'I'd miss the last train home.'

'Then I'll drive you to the station. We wouldn't want you to miss the last train home, would we?' he said, scrawling his signature across the bill.

This time she knew he was teasing her, and she blushed.

When Tony dropped her off at Charing Cross he asked, 'When can I see you again?'

'I have an appointment with Mr Bouchier at 11.30 . . .'

'. . . next Monday morning, if I remember correctly. So why don't we have a celebration lunch together after he's signed you up? I'll come to the gallery at about 12.30. Goodbye.' He leaned over and kissed her gently on the lips.

Sitting in a cold, smelly carriage on the last train back to Sevenoaks, Sally couldn't help wondering what coffee at Tony's place might have been like.

Sally walked into the gallery a few minutes before 11.30 the following Monday to find Simon Bouchier kneeling on the carpet, head down, studying some paintings. They weren't hers, and she hoped he felt the same way about them as she did.

Simon looked up. 'Good morning, Sally. Dreadful, aren't they? You have to look through an awful lot of rubbish before you come across someone who shows any real talent.' He rose to his feet. 'Mind you, Natasha Krasnoselyodkina does have one advantage over you.'

'What's that?' asked Sally.

'She would draw the crowds for any opening.'

'Why?'

'Because she claims to be a Russian countess. Hints

she's a direct descendant of the last tsar. Frankly, I think the Pearly Queen is about the nearest she's been to royalty, but still, she's the "in" face at the moment – a sort of "Minah Bird" of the nineties. What did Andy Warhol say – "In the future, everyone will be famous for fifteen minutes." By that standard, Natasha looks good for about thirty. I see this morning's tabloids are even hinting she's the new love in Prince Andrew's life. My bet is they've never met. But if he were to turn up at the opening, we'd be packed out, that's for sure. We wouldn't sell a picture, of course, but we'd be packed out.'

'Why wouldn't you sell anything?' asked Sally.

'Because the public are not that stupid when it comes to buying paintings. A picture is a large investment for most people, and they want to believe that they have a good eye, and that they've invested wisely. Natasha's pictures won't satisfy them on either count. With you, though, Sally, I'm beginning to feel they might be convinced on both. But first, let me see the rest of your portfolio.'

Sally unzipped her bulging folder, and laid out twenty-one paintings on the carpet.

Simon dropped to his knees, and didn't speak again for some time. When he eventually did offer an opinion, it was only to repeat the single word 'Consistent.'

'But I'll need even more, and of the same quality,' he said after he had risen to his feet. 'Another dozen canvases at least, and by October. I want you to concentrate on interiors – you're good at interiors. And they'll have to be better than good if you expect me to invest my time, expertise, and a great deal of money in you, young lady. Do you think you can manage another dozen pictures by October, Miss Summers?'

'Yes, of course,' said Sally, giving little thought to the fact that October was only five months away.

'That's good, because if you deliver, and I only say *if*, I'll risk the expense of launching you on an unsuspecting public this autumn.' He walked into his office, flicked through his diary and said, 'October the seventeenth, to be precise.'

Sally was speechless.

'I don't suppose you could manage an affair with Prince Charles lasting, say, from the end of September to the beginning of November? That would knock the Russian Countess from the Mile End Road off the front pages and guarantee us a full house on opening night.'

'I'm afraid not,' said Sally, 'especially if you expect me to produce another dozen canvases by then.'

'Pity,' said Simon, 'because if we can attract the punters to the opening, I'm confident they'll want to buy your work. The problem is always getting them to come for an unknown.' He suddenly looked over Sally's shoulder and said, 'Hello, Tony. I wasn't expecting to see you today.'

'Perhaps that's because you're not seeing me,' Tony replied. 'I've just come to whisk Sally off to what I was rather hoping might be a celebratory lunch.'

'"The Summers Exhibition",' Simon said, grinning

at his little play on words, 'will open not in June at the Royal Academy, but in October at the Bouchier Gallery. October the seventeenth is to be Sally's day of reckoning.'

'Congratulations,' said Tony, turning to Sally. 'I'll bring all my friends.'

'I'm only interested in the rich ones,' said Simon, as someone else entered the Gallery.

'Natasha,' said Simon, turning to face a slim, dark-haired woman. Sally's first reaction was that she should have been an artists' model, not an artist.

'Thanks for coming back so quickly, Natasha. Have a nice lunch, you two,' he added, smiling at Tony, who couldn't take his eyes off the new arrival.

Natasha didn't notice, as her only interest seemed to be in Sally's pictures. She was unable to conceal her envy as Tony and Sally walked out of the gallery.

'Wasn't she stunning?' said Sally.

'Was she?' said Tony. 'I didn't notice.'

'I wouldn't blame Prince Andrew if he was having an affair with her.'

'Damn,' said Tony placing a hand in his inside pocket. 'I forgot to give Simon a cheque I promised him. Don't move, I'll be back in a minute.'

Tony sprinted off in the direction of the gallery, and Sally waited on the corner for what seemed like an awfully long minute before he reappeared back on the street.

'Sorry. Simon was on the phone,' Tony explained. He took Sally's arm and led her across the road to a small Italian restaurant, where once again he seemed to have his own table.

He ordered a bottle of champagne, 'To celebrate your great triumph.' As Sally raised her glass in response, she realised for the first time just how much work she would have to do before October if she was going to keep her promise to Simon.

When Tony poured her a second glass, Sally smiled. 'It's been a memorable day. I ought to phone my parents and let them know, but I don't think they'd believe me.'

When a third glass had been filled and Sally still hadn't finished her salad, Tony took her hand, leaned across and kissed it. 'I've never met anyone as beautiful as you,' he said. 'And certainly no one as talented.'

Sally quickly took a gulp of the champagne, to hide her embarrassment. She still wasn't sure whether to believe him, but a glass of white wine, followed by two glasses of red, helped to convince her that she should.

After Tony had signed the bill, he asked her again if she would like to come back to his place for coffee. Sally had already decided that she wasn't going to be able to do any work that day, so she nodded her agreement. In any case, she felt she had earned an afternoon off.

In the taxi on the way to Chelsea, she rested her head on Tony's shoulder, and he began to kiss her gently.

When they arrived at his town house in Bywater Street, he helped her out of the taxi, up the steps and through the front door. He led her along a dimly lit corridor and into the drawing room. She curled up in a corner of the sofa, as Tony disappeared into another room. Most of the furniture, and the pictures that covered every inch of the walls, were a blur to her. Tony returned a moment later, carrying another bottle of champagne and two glasses. Sally didn't notice that he was no longer wearing his jacket, tie or shoes.

He poured her a drink, which she sipped as he sat down next to her on the sofa. His arm slipped round her shoulder and he drew her close to him. When he kissed her again, she felt a little silly dangling an empty glass in mid-air. He took it from her and placed it on a side table, then held her in his arms and began to kiss her more passionately. As she fell back, his hand slipped onto the inside of her thigh, and began moving slowly up her leg.

Every time Sally was about to stop him going any further, Tony seemed to know exactly what to do next. She had always felt in control in the past whenever an over-enthusiastic art student had started to go a little too far in the back row of a cinema, but she had never experienced anyone as subtle as Tony. When her dress fell off her shoulders, she hadn't even noticed that he had undone the twelve little buttons down the back.

They broke away for a second. Sally felt she ought to make a move to go, before it was too late. Tony smiled, and undid the buttons of his own shirt before taking her back in his arms. She felt the warmth of his chest, and he was so gentle that she did not complain when she realised that the clasp of her bra had come loose. She sank back, enjoying every second, knowing that until that moment she had never experienced what it was like to be properly seduced.

Tony finally lay back and said, 'Yes, it has been a memorable day. But I don't think I'll phone my parents to let them know.' He laughed, and Sally felt slightly ashamed. Tony was only the fourth man who had made love to her, and she had known the other three for months beforehand – in one case, years.

For the next hour they talked about many things, but all Sally really wanted to know was how Tony felt about her. He gave her no clue.

Then, once again, he took her in his arms, but this time he pulled her onto the floor and made love to her with such passion that afterwards Sally wondered if she had ever made love before.

She was just in time to catch the last train home, but she couldn't help wishing she had missed it.

Over the next few months Sally devoted herself to getting her latest ideas onto canvas. When each new painting was finished, she would take it up to London for Simon to comment on. The smile on his face became broader and broader with each new picture he saw, and the word he kept repeating now was 'Original.' Sally would tell him about her ideas for the next one, and he would bring her up to date with his plans for the opening in October.

Tony would often meet her for lunch, and afterwards they would go back to his house, where they would make love until it was time for her to catch the last train home.

Sally often wished she could spend more time with Tony. But she was always conscious of the deadline set by Simon, who warned her that the printers were already proof-reading the catalogue, and that the invitations for the opening were waiting to be sent out. Tony seemed almost as busy as she was, and lately he hadn't always been able to fit in with her expeditions to London. Sally had taken to staying overnight, and catching an early train home the following morning. Tony occasionally hinted that she might consider moving in with him. When she thought about it – and she often did – she reflected that his attic could easily be converted into a studio. But she decided that before such a move could even be contemplated, the exhibition had to be a success. Then, if the hint became an offer, she would have her answer ready.

Just two days before the exhibition was due to open, Sally completed her final canvas and handed it over to Simon. As she pulled it out of the canvas folder he threw his arms in the air, and shouted, 'Hallelujah! It's your best yet. As long as we're sensible about our prices, I think that, with a touch of luck, we should sell at least half of your pictures before the exhibition closes.'

'Only half?' said Sally, unable to hide her disappointment.

'That wouldn't be at all bad for your first attempt, young lady,' said Simon. 'I only sold one Leslie Anne

Ivory at her first exhibition, and now she sells everything in the first week.'

Sally still looked crestfallen, and Simon realised he had perhaps been a little tactless.

'Don't worry. Any unsold ones will be put into stock, and they'll be snapped up the moment you start getting good reviews.'

Sally continued to pout.

'How do you feel about the frames and mounts?' Simon asked, trying to change the subject.

Sally studied the deep golden frames and light-grey mounts. The smile returned to her face.

'They're good, aren't they?' said Simon. 'They bring out the colour in the canvases wonderfully.'

Sally nodded her agreement, but was now beginning to worry about how much they must have cost, and whether she would ever be given a second exhibition if the first one wasn't a success.

'By the way,' Simon said, 'I have a friend at the P.A. called Mike Sallis who . . .'

'P.A.?' said Sally.

'Press Association. Mike's a photographer – always on the lookout for a good story. He says he'll come round and take a picture of you standing next to one of the pictures. Then he'll hawk the photo around Fleet Street, and we'll just have to cross our fingers, and pray that Natasha has taken the day off. I don't want to get your hopes up, but someone just might bite. Our only line at present is that it's your first exhibition since leaving the Slade. Hardly a front-page splash.' Simon paused, as once again Sally looked discouraged. 'It's not too late for you to have a fling with Prince Charles, you know. That would solve all our problems.'

Sally smiled. 'I don't think Tony would like that.'

Simon decided against making another tactless remark.

Sally spent that evening with Tony at his home in Chelsea. He seemed a little distracted, but she blamed herself – she was unable to hide her disappointment at Simon's estimate of how few of her pictures might be sold. After they had made love, Sally tried to raise the topic of what would happen to them once the exhibition was over, but Tony deftly changed the subject back to how much he was looking forward to the opening.

That night Sally went home on the last train from Charing Cross.

The following morning she woke up with a terrible feeling of anti-climax. Her room was bereft of canvases, and all she could do now was wait. Her mood wasn't helped by the fact that Tony had told her he would be out of London on business until the day of her opening. She lay in the bath thinking about him.

'But I'll be your first customer on the night,' he had promised. 'Don't forget, I still want to buy "The Sleeping Cat that Never Moved".'

The phone was ringing, but someone answered it before Sally could get out of the bath.

'It's for you,' shouted her mother from the bottom of the stairs.

Sally wrapped a towel around her and grabbed the phone, hoping it would be Tony.

'Hi, Sally, it's Simon. I've got some good news. Mike Sallis has just called from the P.A. He's coming round to the gallery at midday tomorrow. All the pictures should be framed by then, and he'll be the first person from the press to see them. They all want to be first. I'm trying to think up some wheeze to convince him that it's an exclusive. By the way, the catalogues have arrived, and they look fantastic.'

Sally thanked him, and was about to ring Tony to suggest that she stay overnight with him, so that they could go to the gallery together the following day, when she remembered that he was out of town. She spent the day pacing anxiously around the house, occasionally talking to her most compliant model, the sleeping cat that never moved.

The following morning Sally caught an early commuter train from Sevenoaks, so she could spend a little time checking the pictures against their catalogue entries. When she walked into the gallery, her eyes lit up: half a dozen of the paintings had already been hung, and she actually felt, for the first time, that they really weren't bad. She glanced in the direction of the office, and saw that Simon was occupied on the phone. He smiled and waved to indicate that he would be with her in a moment.

She had another look at the pictures, and then spotted a copy of the catalogue lying on the table. The cover read 'The Summers Exhibition', above a picture of an interior looking from her parents' drawing room through an open window and out onto a garden overgrown with weeds. A black cat lay asleep on the windowsill, ignoring the rain.

Sally opened the catalogue and read the introduction on the first page.

> Sometimes judges feel it necessary to say: It's been hard to pick this year's winner. But from the moment one set eyes on Sally Summers' work, the task was made easy. Real talent is obvious for all to see, and Sally has achieved the rare feat of winning both the Slade's major prizes, for oils and for drawing, in the same year. I much look forward to watching her career develop over the coming years.

It was an extract from Sir Roger de Grey's speech when he had presented Sally with the Mary Rischgitz and the Henry Tonks Prizes at the Slade two years before.

Sally turned the pages, seeing her works reproduced in colour for the first time. Simon's attention to detail and layout was evident on every page.

She looked back towards the office, and saw that Simon was still on the phone. She decided to go downstairs and check on the rest of her pictures, now that they had all been framed. The lower gallery was a mass of colour, and the newly framed paintings were so skilfully hung that even Sally saw them in a new light.

Once she had circled the room Sally suppressed a smile of satisfaction before turning to make her way back upstairs. As she passed a table in the centre of the gallery, she noticed a folder with the initials 'N.K.' printed on it. She idly lifted the cover, to discover a pile of undistinguished watercolours.

As she leafed through her rival's never-to-be-exhibited efforts, Sally had to admit that the nude self-portraits didn't do Natasha justice. She was just about to close the folder and join Simon upstairs when she came to a sudden halt.

Although it was clumsily executed, there was no doubt who the man was that the half-clad Natasha was clinging on to.

Sally felt sick. She slammed the folder shut, walked quickly across the room and back up the stairs to the ground floor. In the corner of the large gallery Simon was chatting to a man who had several cameras slung over his shoulder.

'Sally,' he said, coming towards her, 'this is Mike . . .'

But Sally ignored them both, and started running towards the open door, tears flooding down her cheeks. She turned right into St James's, determined to get as far away from the gallery as possible. But then she came to an abrupt halt. Tony and Natasha were walking towards her, arm in arm.

Sally stepped off the pavement and began to cross the road, hoping to reach the other side before they spotted her.

The screech of tyres and the sudden swerve of the van came just a moment too late, and she was thrown headlong into the middle of the road.

When Sally came to, she felt awful. She blinked her eyes, and thought she could hear voices. She blinked again, but it was several moments before she was able to focus on anything.

She was lying in a bed, but it was not her own. Her right leg was covered in plaster, and was raised high in the air, suspended from a pulley. Her other leg was under the sheet, and it felt all right. She wiggled the toes of her left foot: yes, they were fine. Then she began to try to move her arms. A nurse came up to the side of the bed.

'Welcome back to the world, Sally.'

'How long have I been like this?' she asked.

'A couple of days,' said the nurse, checking Sally's pulse. 'But you're making a remarkably quick recovery. Before you ask, it's only a broken leg, and the black eyes will have gone long before we let you out. By the way,' she added, as she moved on to the next patient, 'I loved that picture of you in the morning papers. And what about those flattering remarks your friend made? So what's it like to be famous?'

Sally wanted to ask what she was talking about, but the nurse was already taking the pulse of the person in the next bed.

'Come back,' Sally wanted to say, but a second nurse

had appeared by her bedside with a mug of orange juice, which she thrust into her hand.

'Let's get you started on this,' she said. Sally obeyed, and tried to suck the liquid through a bent plastic straw.

'You've got a visitor,' the nurse told her once she'd emptied the contents of the mug. 'He's been waiting for some time. Do you think you're up to seeing him?'

'Sure,' said Sally, not particularly wanting to face Tony, but desperate to find out what had happened.

She looked towards the swing doors at the end of the ward, but had to wait for some time before Simon came bouncing through them. He walked straight up to her bed, clutching what might just about have been described as a bunch of flowers. He gave her plaster cast a big kiss.

'I'm so sorry, Simon,' Sally said, before he had even said hello. 'I know just how much trouble and expense you've been to on my behalf. And now I've let you down so badly.'

'You certainly have,' said Simon. 'It's always a let-down when you sell everything off the walls on the first night. Then you haven't got anything left for your old customers, and they start grumbling.'

Sally's mouth opened wide.

'Mind you, it was a rather good photo of Natasha, even if it was an awful one of you.'

'What are you talking about, Simon?'

'Mike Sallis got his exclusive, and you got your break,' he said, patting her suspended leg. 'When Natasha bent over your body in the street, Mike began clicking away for dear life. And I couldn't have scripted her quotes better myself: "The most outstanding young artist of our generation. If the world were to lose such a talent . . ."'

Sally laughed at Simon's wicked imitation of Natasha's Russian accent.

'You hit most of the next morning's front pages,' he continued. '"Brush with Death" in the *Mail*; "Still Life in St James's" in the *Express*. And you even managed "Splat!" in the *Sun*. The punters flocked into the gallery that evening. Natasha was wearing a black see-through dress and proceeded to give the press soundbite after soundbite about your genius. Not that it made any difference. We'd already sold every canvas long before their second editions hit the street. But, more important, the serious critics in the broadsheets are already acknowledging that you might actually have some talent.'

Sally smiled. 'I may have failed to have an affair with Prince Charles, but at least it seems I got something right.'

'Well, not exactly,' said Simon.

'What do you mean?' asked Sally, suddenly anxious. 'You said all the pictures have been sold.'

'True, but if you'd arranged to have the accident a few days earlier, I could have jacked up the prices by at least fifty per cent. Still, there's always next time.'

'Did Tony buy "The Sleeping Cat that Never Moved"?' Sally asked quietly.

'No, he was late as usual, I'm afraid. It was snapped up in the first half hour, by a serious collector. Which reminds me,' Simon added, as Sally's parents came through the swing doors into the ward, 'I'll need another forty canvases if we're going to hold your second show in the spring. So you'd better get back to work right away.'

'But look at me, you silly man,' Sally said, laughing. 'How do you expect me to –'

'Don't be so feeble,' said Simon, tapping her plaster cast. 'It's your leg that's out of action, not your arm.'

Sally grinned and looked up to see her parents standing at the end of the bed.

'Is this Tony?' her mother asked.

'Good heavens no, Mother,' laughed Sally. 'This is Simon. He's far more important. Mind you,' she confessed, 'I made the same mistake the first time I met him.'

TIMEO DANAOS...

ARNOLD BACON WOULD HAVE MADE A fortune if he hadn't taken his father's advice.

Arnold's occupation, as described in his passport, was 'banker'. For those of you who are pedantic about such matters, he was the branch manager of Barclays Bank in St Albans, Hertfordshire, which in banking circles is about the equivalent of being a captain in the Royal Army Pay Corps.

His passport also stated that he was born in 1937, was five feet nine inches tall, with sandy hair and no distinguishing marks – although in fact he had several lines on his forehead, which served only to prove that he frowned a great deal.

He was a member of the local Rotary Club (Hon. Treasurer), the Conservative Party (Branch Vice-Chairman), and was a past Secretary of the St Albans Festival. He had also played rugby for the Old Albanians 2nd XV in the 1960s and cricket for St Albans C.C. in the 1970s. His only exercise for the past two decades, however, had been the occasional round of golf with his opposite number from the National Westminster. Arnold did not boast a handicap.

During these excursions round the golf course Arnold would often browbeat his opponent with his conviction that he should never have been a banker in the first place. After years of handing out loans to customers who wanted to start up their own businesses, he had become painfully aware that he himself was really one of nature's born entrepreneurs. If only he hadn't listened to his father's advice and followed him into the bank, heaven knows what heights he might have reached by now.

His colleague nodded wearily, then holed a seven-foot putt, ensuring that the drinks would not be on him.

'How's Deirdre?' he asked as the two men strolled towards the clubhouse.

'Wants to buy a new dinner service,' said Arnold, which slightly puzzled his companion. 'Not that I can see what's wrong with our old Coronation set.'

When they reached the bar, Arnold checked his watch before ordering half a pint of lager for himself and a gin and tonic for the victor, as Deirdre wouldn't be expecting him back for at least an hour. He stopped pontificating only when another member began telling them the latest rumours about the club captain's wife.

Deirdre Bacon, Arnold's long-suffering wife, had come to accept that her husband was now too set in his ways for her to hope for any improvement. Although she had her own opinions on what would have happened to Arnold if he hadn't followed his father's advice, she no longer voiced them. At the time of their engagement she had considered Arnold Bacon 'quite a catch'. But as the years passed, she had become more realistic about her expectations, and after two children, one of each sex, she had settled into the life of a housewife and mother – not that anything else had ever been seriously contemplated.

The children had now grown up, Justin to become a solicitor's clerk in Chelmsford, and Virginia to marry a local boy whom Arnold described as an official with British Rail. Deirdre, more accurately, told her friends at the hairdresser's that Keith was a train driver.

For the first ten years of their marriage, the Bacons had holidayed in Bournemouth, because Arnold's parents had always done so. They only graduated to the Costa del Sol after Arnold read in the *Daily Telegraph*'s 'Sun Supplement' that that was where most bank managers were to be found during the month of August.

For many years Arnold had promised his wife that they would do 'something special' when it came to celebrating their twenty-fifth wedding anniversary, though he had never actually committed himself to defining what 'special' meant.

It was only when he read in the bank's quarterly staff magazine that Andrew Buxton, the Chairman of Barclays, would be spending his summer sailing around the Greek islands on a private yacht that Arnold began writing off to numerous cruise companies and travel agents, requesting copies of their brochures. After having studied hundreds of glossy pages, he settled on a seven-day cruise aboard the *Princess Corina*, starting out from Piraeus to sail around the Greek islands, ending up at

Mykonos. Deirdre's only contribution to the discussion was that she would rather go back to the Costa del Sol, and spend the money they saved on a new dinner service. She was delighted, however, to read in one of the brochures that the Greeks were famous for their pottery.

By the time they boarded the coach to Heathrow, Arnold's junior staff, fellow members of the Rotary Club, and even a few of his more select customers were becoming tired of being reminded of how Arnold would be spending his summer break. 'I shall be sailing around the Greek islands on a liner,' he would tell them. 'Not unlike the bank's Chairman, Andrew Buxton, you know.' If anyone asked Deirdre what she and Arnold were doing for their holidays, she said that they were going on a seven-day package tour, and that the one thing she hoped to come home with was a new dinner service.

The old 'Coronation' service that had been given to them by Deirdre's parents as a wedding gift some twenty-five years before was now sadly depleted. Several of the plates were chipped or broken, while the pattern of crowns and sceptres on the pieces that were still serviceable had almost faded away.

'I can't see what's wrong with it myself,' said Arnold when his wife raised the subject once more as they waited in the departure lounge at Heathrow. Deirdre made no effort to list its defects again.

Arnold spent most of the flight to Athens complaining that the aircraft was full of Greeks. Deirdre didn't feel it was worth pointing out to him that, if one booked a passage with Olympic Airways, that was likely to be the outcome. She also knew his reply would be, 'But it saved us twenty-four pounds.'

Once they had landed at Hellenikon International Airport, the two holidaymakers climbed aboard a bus. Arnold doubted whether it would have passed its MOT in St Albans, but nevertheless it somehow managed to transport them into the centre of Athens, where Arnold had booked them overnight into a two-star hotel (two Greek stars). Arnold quickly found the local branch of Barclays and cashed one of his travellers' cheques, explaining to his wife that there was no point in changing more, as once they were on board the liner everything had already been paid for. He was sure that was how entrepreneurs conducted themselves.

The Bacons rose early the following morning, mainly because they hadn't been able to get a great deal of sleep. Their bodies had continually rolled to the centre of the lumpy concave mattress, and their ears ached after a night resting on the brick-hard convex pillows. Even before the sun had risen, Arnold jumped out of bed and threw open the little window that looked out onto a back yard. He stretched his arms and declared he had never felt better. Deirdre didn't comment, as she was already busy packing their clothes.

Over breakfast – a meal consisting of a croissant, which Arnold felt was too sticky, and which in any case fell apart in his fingers, feta cheese, which he didn't care for the smell of, and an obstinately empty cup, because the management refused to serve tea – a long debate developed between them as to whether they should hire a taxi or take a bus to the liner. They both came to the conclusion that a taxi would be more sensible, Deirdre because she didn't want to be crammed into a hot bus with a lot of sweaty Athenians, and Arnold because he wanted to be seen arriving at the gangplank in a car.

Once Arnold had settled their bill – having checked the little row of figures presented to him three times before he was willing to part with another travellers' cheque – he hailed a taxi and instructed the driver to take them to the quayside. The longer than expected journey, in an ancient car with no air conditioning, did not put Arnold into a good humour.

When he first set eyes on the *Princess Corina*, Arnold was unable to mask his disappointment. The ship was neither as large nor as modern as it had appeared in the glossy brochure. He had a feeling his Chairman would not be experiencing the same problem.

Mr and Mrs Bacon ascended the gangplank and were escorted to their cabin, which to Arnold's dismay consisted of two bunks, a washbasin, a shower and a porthole, without even enough room between the bunks for both of them to be able to undress at the same time. Arnold pointed out to his wife that this particular cabin had certainly not been illustrated in the brochure, even if it had been described on the tariff by the encomium 'De Luxe'. The brochure must have been put together by an out-of-work estate agent, he concluded.

Arnold set out to take a turn around the deck – not a particularly lengthy excursion. On the way he bumped into a solicitor from Chester who had been innocently strolling with his wife in the opposite direction. After Arnold had established that Malcolm Jackson was a senior partner in his firm, and his wife Joan was a magistrate, he suggested they should join up for lunch.

Once they had selected their meal from the buffet, Arnold lost no time in telling his new-found friends that he was a born entrepreneur, explaining, for example, the immediate changes he would make to improve efficiency on the *Princess Corina* had he been the chairman of this particular shipping line. (The list, I fear, turned out to be far too long to include in a short story.)

The solicitor, who had not had to suffer any of Arnold's opinions before, seemed quite content to listen, while Deirdre chatted away to Joan about how she was hoping to find a new dinner service on one of the islands. 'The Greeks are famous for their pottery, you know,' she kept saying.

The conversation didn't vary a great deal when the two couples reunited over dinner that evening.

Although the Bacons were tired after their first day on board, neither of them slept for more than a few moments that night. But Arnold was unwilling to admit, as they bobbed across the Aegean in their little cabin, that given the choice he would have preferred the two-star hotel (two Greek stars), with its lumpy mattress and brick-hard pillows, to the bunks on which they were now being tossed from side to side.

After two days at sea the ship docked at Rhodes, and by then even Arnold had stopped describing it as a

'liner'. Most of the passengers piled off down the gangway, only too delighted to have the chance of spending
a few hours on land.

Arnold and Malcolm beat a path to the nearest Barclays Bank to cash a travellers' cheque each, while
Deirdre and Joan set off in the opposite direction in
search of a dinner service. At the bank, Arnold immediately informed the manager who he was, ensuring that
both he and Malcolm received a tiny improvement on
the advertised rate of exchange.

Arnold smiled as they stepped out of the bank, and
onto the hot, dusty, cobbled street. 'I should have gone
into futures trading, you know,' he told Malcolm as
they sauntered off down the hill. 'I would have made a
fortune.'

Deirdre's quest for a dinner service didn't turn out to
be quite so straightforward. The shops were numerous
and varied in quality, and she quickly discovered that
Rhodes boasted a great many potters. It was therefore
necessary for her to establish which of them was the
most highly regarded by the locals, and then find the
shop that sold his work. This information was gained
by talking to the old women dressed in black who could
be found sitting silently on the street corners, about one
in ten of whom, she discovered, had some broken English. While her husband was at the bank saving a few
drachmas, Deirdre managed to find out all the inside
information she required.

The four of them met up at a small taverna in the
centre of the town for lunch. Over a plate of souvlakia

Arnold tried to convince Deirdre that as they were visiting five islands in the course of the trip, it might perhaps be wise to wait until their final port of call, so they could purchase the dinner service at the last possible moment.

'Prices will undoubtedly fall,' declared Arnold, 'the closer we get to Athens.' He spoke with the air of a true entrepreneur.

Although Deirdre had already seen a thirty-two-piece set she liked, at a price well within their budget, she reluctantly agreed to Arnold's suggestion. Her acquiescence was largely brought about by the fact that it was her husband who was in possession of all the travellers' cheques.

By the time the ship had docked at Heraklion on Crete, Arnold had vetted all the British nationals on board, and had permitted a Major (Territorial Reserve) and his spouse to join their table for lunch – but only after discovering that the fellow held an account at Barclays. A dinner invitation followed once it had been established that the Major occasionally played bridge with Arnold's area manager.

From that moment Arnold spent many happy hours at the bar explaining to the Major or to Malcolm – neither of whom actually listened any longer – why he should never have taken his father's advice and followed him into the bank, as he was after all one of nature's born entrepreneurs.

By the time the ship had weighed anchor and sailed from Santorini, Deirdre knew exactly the type of dinner service she wanted, and how to establish quickly which potter she should trade with as soon as they set foot in a new port. But Arnold continued to insist that they should wait for the bigger market as they approached Athens – 'More competition, forces prices down,' he explained for the umpteenth time. Deirdre knew there was no point in telling him that prices seemed to be rising with each sea-mile they covered on their journey back towards the Greek capital.

Páros only served as further proof of Deirdre's suspicions – if proof were still needed – as the prices there were noticeably steeper than they had been on Santorini. As the *Princess Corina* steamed on towards Mykonos, Deirdre felt that although their final port of call would probably be able to supply her with a satisfactory dinner service, it would surely no longer be at a price they could afford.

Arnold kept assuring her, with the confidence of a man who knows about such things, that all would be well. He even tapped the side of his nose with his forefinger. The Major and Malcolm had reached the stage of simply nodding at him to indicate that they were still awake.

Deirdre was among the first down the gangplank when they docked at Mykonos that Friday morning. She had told her husband that she would carry out a recce of the pottery shops while he did the same with the banks. Joan and the Major's wife were happy to accompany Deirdre, as by now she had become something of an expert on the subject of Greek pottery.

The three ladies began their search at the north end of the town, and Deirdre was relieved to find that there was a greater variety of shops in Mykonos than there had been on any of the other islands. She was also able to discover, with the help of several black-clad ladies, that the town boasted a potter of genuine fame, whose work could only be purchased from one shop, The House of Pétros.

Once Deirdre had located this establishment, she spent the rest of the morning inspecting all the dinner services they had to offer. After a couple of hours she came to the conclusion that the 'Delphi' set which was prominently displayed in the centre of the shop would be a prized possession for any housewife in St Albans. But as it was double the cost of anything she had seen on any of the other islands, she knew that Arnold would dismiss it as being out of their price range.

As the three ladies finally left the shop to join their husbands for lunch, a good-looking young man in a grubby T-shirt and torn jeans, with a couple of days' stubble on his chin, jumped out in front of them and asked, 'You English?'

Deirdre stopped and stared into his deep blue eyes for a moment, but said nothing. Her companions stepped out into the cobbled road and quickened their pace, pretending it was not them to whom the stranger had spoken. Deirdre smiled at him as he stood to one side, allowing her to continue on her way. Arnold had warned her never to engage in conversation with the natives.

When they reached ρεγγα κοκκινη, the restaurant at

which they'd arranged to meet up for lunch, the three ladies found their husbands drinking imported lager at the bar. Arnold was explaining to the Major and Malcolm why he had refused to pay his subscription to the Conservative Party that year. 'Not a penny will I part with,' he insisted, 'while they can't get their own house in order.' Deirdre suspected that his unwillingness to pay had rather more to do with his recent defeat when he had stood as Chairman of the local branch.

Arnold passed the next hour offering his views on everything from defence cuts to New Age travellers to single-parent families, all of which he was resolutely against. When the bill for lunch was finally presented, he spent some considerable time working out what each of them had eaten, and therefore how much they should contribute towards the total.

Arnold had already resigned himself to the fact that he would have to allocate part of his afternoon to bargaining on Deirdre's behalf, now that she had finally found the dinner service she had set her heart on. Everyone else had agreed to come along and watch the born entrepreneur at work.

When Arnold entered The House of Pétros, he had to admit that Deirdre seemed to have 'located the correct establishment'. He kept repeating this observation, as if to prove that he had been right all along to insist that she wait until their final port of call before the big decision was taken. He seemed blissfully unaware of how the price of pottery had increased from island to island, and Deirdre made no attempt to enlighten him.

She simply guided him over to the 'Delphi' service displayed on a large table in the centre of the room, and prayed. They all agreed it was quite magnificent, but when Arnold was told the price, he shook his head sadly. Deirdre would have protested, but she, like so many of the bank's customers over the years, had seen that look on her husband's face before. She therefore resigned herself to settling for the 'Pharos' set – excellent, but unquestionably second best, and far more expensive than comparable sets had been on any of the other four islands.

The three wives began selecting the pieces they would like to buy, while their husbands gravely reminded them how much they could afford. The choices having been made, Arnold spent a considerable time haggling with the shopkeeper. He finally managed to get a twenty per cent discount on the total. Once the figure had been established, Arnold was dispatched to find an English bank at which he could change the necessary travellers' cheques. With passports and signed cheques in hand, he left the shop to carry out his mission.

As he stepped onto the pavement, the young man who had approached Deirdre leaped into his path and asked, 'You English?'

'Naturally,' replied Arnold, sidestepping him and marching on briskly in order to avoid any further conversation with such a scruffy individual. As he had told the Major over lunch, *'Timeo Danaos et dona ferentis.'* It was the one snippet of Latin he could still recall from his schooldays.

When he had selected a bank, Arnold marched straight into the manager's office and changed everyone's cheques at a minutely better rate than the one displayed on the board in the window. Pleased with his saving of fifty drachmas, he headed back to The House of Pétros.

He was displeased to find the young man was still loitering on the pavement outside the shop. Arnold refused to favour the unshaven ruffian with even a glance, but he did catch the words, 'You want to save money, Englishman?'

Arnold stopped in his tracks, as any born entrepreneur would, and turned to study more closely the loutish youth who had addressed him. He was about to continue on his way when the young man said, 'I know where pottery is everything half price.'

Arnold hesitated once again, and looked through the shop window to see his companions standing around waiting for his return; on the counter stood six large packages, already wrapped up and awaiting payment.

Arnold turned back to take a closer look at the inarticulate foreigner.

'Potter comes from village called Kalafatis,' he said. 'Bus journey only half hour, then everything half price.'

While Arnold was digesting this piece of information, the young Greek's hand shot out hopefully. Arnold extracted a fifty-drachma note from the roll of money he had obtained at the bank, willing to speculate with the profit he had made on that particular transaction in exchange for the information he had just acquired – the act of a true entrepreneur, he thought as he marched triumphantly into the shop.

'I have made an important discovery,' he announced, and beckoned them all into a corner to impart his inside information.

Deirdre did not seem at all convinced, until Arnold suggested, 'Perhaps we might even be able to afford the "Delphi" set you hankered after, my dear. In any case, why pay double, when the only sacrifice you need to make is a half-hour bus journey.'

Malcolm nodded his agreement, as if listening to sage advice from senior counsel, and even the Major, though grumbling a little, finally fell into line.

'As we set sail for Athens early this evening,' declared the Major, 'we ought to take the next bus to Kalafatis.' Arnold nodded, and without another word led his little band out of the shop, not even glancing towards the packages that were left behind on the counter.

When they stepped out onto the street, Arnold was relieved to find that the young man who had given him the tip-off was no longer to be seen.

They came to a halt at the bus stop, where Arnold was a little disappointed to discover several passengers from the ship already standing in the queue, but he persuaded himself that they would not be heading for the same destination. They waited in the hot sun for another forty minutes before a bus eventually pulled up. When Arnold first saw the vehicle, his heart sank. 'Just think of how much money we'll be saving,' he said when he noticed the looks of despair on the faces of his companions.

The journey across the island to the east coast might well have taken thirty minutes had it been in a Range Rover with no reason to slow down. But as the bus driver picked up everybody he saw along the way, without regard to official stops, they eventually arrived in Kalafatis an hour and twenty minutes later. Long before they had clambered off the ancient vehicle Deirdre was exhausted, Joan was exasperated, and the Major's wife was developing a migraine.

'Bus goes no further,' said the driver as Arnold and his companions filed off. 'Leave for return journey to Khóra one hour. Last bus of the day.'

The little band gazed up at the narrow, winding track that led to the potter's workplace.

'The journey was worth it for the view alone,' gasped Arnold, as he came to a halt halfway along the path and gazed out over the Aegean. His companions didn't even bother to stop and look, let alone offer an opinion. It took them another ten minutes of determined walking before they reached their destination, and by then even Arnold had fallen silent.

As the six weary tourists finally entered the pottery, what breath they had left was taken away. They stood mesmerised by shelf after shelf of beautiful objects. Arnold felt a warm glow of triumph.

Deirdre immediately went about her business, and quickly located the 'Delphi' dinner service. It looked even more magnificent than she remembered, but when she checked a little label that hung from a soup tureen's handle she was horrified to discover that the cost was only a little less than it had been at The House of Pétros.

Deirdre came to a decision. She turned to face her husband, who was toying with a pipe stand, and declared in a clarion voice that all could hear, 'As everything is at half price, Arnold, presumably I can go ahead and buy the "Delphi"?'

The other four swung round to see how the great entrepreneur would react. Arnold seemed to hesitate for a moment before he placed the pipe stand back on the shelf and said, 'Of course, my dear. Isn't that why we came all this way in the first place?'

The three women immediately began selecting items from the shelves, finally gathering between them one dinner service, two tea sets, one coffee set, three vases, five ashtrays, two jugs and a toast rack. Arnold abandoned the pipe stand.

When the bill for Deirdre's purchases was presented to her husband he hesitated once again, but he was painfully aware that all five of his shipmates were glaring at him. He reluctantly cashed his remaining travellers' cheques, unwilling to bring himself even to glance at the disadvantageous exchange rate that was displayed in the window. Deirdre made no comment. Malcolm and the Major silently signed away their own travellers' cheques, with little appearance of triumph showing on either of their faces.

The goods having been paid for, the six tourists

emerged from the workshop, laden down with carrier bags. As they began to retrace their steps back down the winding track, the door of the pottery was closed behind them.

'We'll have to get a move on if we're not going to miss the last bus,' shouted Arnold as he stepped into the centre of the path, avoiding a large cream Mercedes that was parked outside the workshop. 'But what a worthwhile excursion,' he added as they trundled off down the track. 'You have to admit, I saved you all a fortune.'

Deirdre was the last to leave the shop. She paused to rearrange her numerous bags, and was surprised to see a number of the pottery's staff forming a queue at a table by the side of the shop. A handsome young man in a grubby T-shirt and torn jeans was presenting each of them in turn with a small brown envelope.

Deirdre couldn't take her eyes off the young man. Where had she seen him before? He looked up, and for a moment she stared into those deep blue eyes. And then she remembered. The young man shrugged his shoulders and smiled. Deirdre returned the smile, picked up her bags and set off down the path after her companions.

As they clambered onto the bus, Deirdre was just in time to hear Arnold declare: 'You know, Major, I should never have taken my father's advice and settled for the life of a banker. You see, I'm one of nature's born entre . . .'

Deirdre smiled again as she looked out of the window

and watched the good-looking young man speed past them in his large cream Mercedes.

He smiled and waved to her as the last bus began its slow journey back to Mykonos.

AN EYE FOR AN EYE

S IR MATTHEW ROBERTS QC CLOSED THE
file and placed it on the desk in front of him. He was
not a happy man. He was quite willing to defend Mary
Banks, but he was not at all confident about her plea of
not guilty.

Sir Matthew leaned back in his deep leather chair to
consider the case while he awaited the arrival of the
instructing solicitor who had briefed him, and the junior
counsel he had selected for the case. As he gazed out
over the Middle Temple courtyard, he only hoped he
had made the right decision.

On the face of it, the case of Regina v. Banks was a
simple one of murder; but after what Bruce Banks
had subjected his wife to during the eleven years of
their marriage, Sir Matthew was confident not only
that he could get the charge reduced to manslaughter,
but that if the jury was packed with women, he might
even secure an acquittal. There was, however, a
complication.

He lit a cigarette and inhaled deeply, something his
wife had always chided him for. He looked at Victoria's
photograph on the desk in front of him. It reminded

him of his youth: but then, Victoria would always be young – death had ensured that.

Reluctantly, he forced his mind back to his client and her plea of mitigation. He reopened the file. Mary Banks was claiming that she couldn't possibly have chopped her husband up with an axe and buried him under the pigsty, because at the time of his death she was not only a patient in the local hospital, but was also blind. As Sir Matthew inhaled deeply once again, there was a knock on the door.

'Come in,' he bellowed – not because he liked the sound of his own voice, but because the doors of his chambers were so thick that if he didn't holler, no one would ever hear him.

Sir Matthew's clerk opened the door and announced Mr Bernard Casson and Mr Hugh Witherington. Two very different men, thought Sir Matthew as they entered the room, but each would serve the purpose he had planned for them in this particular case.

Bernard Casson was a solicitor of the old school – formal, punctilious, and always painstakingly correct. His conservatively tailored herringbone suit never seemed to change from one year to the next; Matthew often wondered if he had purchased half a dozen such suits in a closing-down sale and wore a different one every day of the week. He peered up at Casson over his half-moon spectacles. The solicitor's thin moustache and neatly parted hair gave him an old-fashioned look that had fooled many an opponent into thinking he had a second-class mind. Sir Matthew regularly gave thanks that his friend was no orator, because if Bernard had been a barrister, Matthew would not have relished the prospect of opposing him in court.

A pace behind Casson stood his junior counsel for this brief, Hugh Witherington. The Lord must have been feeling particularly ungenerous on the day Witherington entered the world, as He had given him neither looks nor brains. If He had bestowed any other talents on him, they were yet to be revealed. After several attempts Witherington had finally been called to the Bar, but for the number of briefs he was offered, he would have had a more regular income had he signed on for the dole. Sir Matthew's clerk had raised an eyebrow when the name of Witherington had been mooted as junior counsel in the case, but Sir Matthew just smiled, and had not offered an explanation.

Sir Matthew rose, stubbed out his cigarette, and ushered the two men towards the vacant chairs on the other side of his desk. He waited for both of them to settle before he proceeded.

'Kind of you to attend chambers, Mr Casson,' he said, although they both knew that the solicitor was doing no more than holding with the traditions of the Bar.

'My pleasure, Sir Matthew,' replied the elderly solicitor, bowing slightly to show that he still appreciated the old courtesies.

'I don't think you know Hugh Witherington, my junior in this case,' said Sir Matthew, gesturing towards the undistinguished young barrister.

Witherington nervously touched the silk handkerchief in his breast pocket.

'No, I hadn't had the pleasure of Mr Witherington's acquaintance until we met in the corridor a few moments ago,' said Casson. 'May I say how delighted I am that you have been willing to take on this case, Sir Matthew?'

Matthew smiled at his friend's formality. He knew Bernard would never dream of calling him by his Christian name while junior counsel was present. 'I'm only too happy to be working with you again, Mr Casson. Even if you have presented me on this occasion with something of a challenge.'

The conventional pleasantries over, the elderly solicitor removed a brown file from his battered Gladstone bag. 'I have had a further consultation with my client since I last saw you,' he said as he opened the file, 'and I took the opportunity to pass on your opinion. But I fear Mrs Banks remains determined to plead not guilty.'

'So she is still protesting her innocence?'

'Yes, Sir Matthew. Mrs Banks emphatically claims that she couldn't have committed the murder because she had been blinded by her husband some days before he died, and in any case, at the time of his death she was registered as a patient at the local hospital.'

'The pathologist's report is singularly vague about the time of death,' Sir Matthew reminded his old friend. 'After all, they didn't discover the body for at least a couple of weeks. As I understand it, the police feel the murder could have been committed twenty-four or even forty-eight hours before Mrs Banks was taken to the hospital.'

'I have also read their report, Sir Matthew,' Casson replied, 'and informed Mrs Banks of its contents. But she remains adamant that she is innocent, and that the jury will be persuaded of it. "Especially with Sir Matthew Roberts as my defender," were the exact words she used, if I remember correctly,' he added with a smile.

'I am not seduced, Mr Casson,' said Sir Matthew, lighting another cigarette.

'You did promise Victoria —' interjected the solicitor, lowering his shield, but only for a moment.

'So, I have one last chance to convince her,' said Sir Matthew, ignoring his friend's comment.

'And Mrs Banks has one last chance to convince you,' said Mr Casson.

'Touché,' said Sir Matthew, nodding his appreciation of the solicitor's neat riposte as he stubbed out his almost untouched cigarette. He felt he was losing this fencing match with his old friend, and that the time had come to go on the attack.

He returned to the open file on his desk. 'First,' he said, looking straight at Casson, as if his colleague were in the witness box, 'when the body was dug up, there were traces of your client's blood on the collar of the dead man's shirt.'

'My client accepts that,' said Casson, calmly checking his own notes. 'But . . .'

'Second,' said Sir Matthew before Casson had a chance to reply, 'when the instrument that had been used to chop up the body, an axe, was found the following day, a hair from Mrs Banks's head was discovered lodged in its handle.'

'We won't be denying that,' said Casson.

'We don't have a lot of choice,' said Sir Matthew, rising from his seat and beginning to pace around the room. 'And third, when the spade that was used to dig the victim's grave was finally discovered, your client's fingerprints were found all over it.'

'We can explain that as well,' said Casson.

'But will the jury accept our explanation,' asked Sir Matthew, his voice rising, 'when they learn that the murdered man had a long history of violence, that your client was regularly seen in the local village either bruised, or with a black eye, sometimes bleeding from cuts around the head – once even nursing a broken arm?'

'She has always stated that those injuries were sustained when working on the farm where her husband was manager.'

'That places a strain on my credulity which it's quite unable to withstand,' said Sir Matthew, as he finished circling the room and returned to his chair. 'And we are not helped by the fact that the only person known to have visited the farm regularly was the postman. Apparently everyone else in the village refused to venture beyond the front gate.' He flicked over another page of his notes.

'That might have made it easier for someone to come in and kill Banks,' suggested Witherington.

Sir Matthew was unable to hide his surprise as he

looked across at his junior, having almost forgotten that he was in the room. 'Interesting point,' he said, unwilling to stamp on Witherington while he still had it in his power to play the one trump card in this case.

'The next problem we face,' he went on, 'is that your client claims that she went blind after her husband struck her with a hot frying pan. Rather convenient, Mr Casson, wouldn't you say?'

'The scar can still be seen clearly on the side of my client's face,' said Casson. 'And the doctor remains convinced that she is indeed blind.'

'Doctors are easier to convince than prosecuting counsels and world-weary judges, Mr Casson,' said Sir Matthew, turning another page of his file. 'Next, when samples from the body were examined – and God knows who was willing to carry out that particular task – the quantity of strychnine found in the blood would have felled a bull elephant.'

'That was only the opinion of the Crown's pathologists,' said Mr Casson.

'And one I will find hard to refute in court,' said Sir Matthew, 'because counsel for the prosecution will undoubtedly ask Mrs Banks to explain why she purchased four grams of strychnine from an agricultural supplier in Reading shortly before her husband's death. If I were in his position, I would repeat that question over and over again.'

'Possibly,' said Casson, checking his notes, 'but she has explained that they had been having a problem with rats, which had been killing the chickens, and she feared for the other animals on the farm, not to mention their nine-year-old son.'

'Ah, yes, Rupert. But he was away at boarding school at the time, was he not?' Sir Matthew paused. 'You see, Mr Casson, my problem is a simple one.' He closed his file. 'I don't believe her.'

Casson raised an eyebrow.

'Unlike her husband, Mrs Banks is a very clever woman. Witness the fact that she has already fooled several people into believing this incredible story. But I can tell you, Mr Casson, that she isn't going to fool me.'

'But what can we do, Sir Matthew, if Mrs Banks insists that this is her case, and asks us to defend her accordingly?' asked Casson.

Sir Matthew rose again and paced around the room silently, coming to a halt in front of the solicitor. 'Not a lot, I agree,' he said, reverting to a more conciliatory tone. 'But I do wish I could convince the dear lady to plead guilty to manslaughter. We'd be certain to gain the sympathy of any jury, after what she's been put through. And we can always rely on some women's group or other to picket the court throughout the hearing. Any judge who passed a harsh sentence on Mary Banks would be described as chauvinistic and sexually discriminatory by every newspaper leader writer in the land. I'd have her out of prison in a matter of weeks. No, Mr Casson, we *must* get her to change her plea.'

'But how can we hope to do that, when she remains so adamant that she is innocent?' asked Casson.

A smile flickered across Sir Matthew's face. 'Mr Witherington and I have a plan, don't we, Hugh?' he said, turning to Witherington for a second time.

'Yes, Sir Matthew,' replied the young barrister, sounding pleased to at last have his opinion sought, even in this rudimentary way. As Sir Matthew volunteered no clue as to the plan, Casson did not press the point.

'So, when do I come face to face with our client?' asked Sir Matthew, turning his attention back to the solicitor.

'Would eleven o'clock on Monday morning be convenient?' asked Casson.

'Where is she at the moment?' asked Sir Matthew, thumbing through his diary.

'Holloway,' replied Casson.

'Then we will be at Holloway at eleven on Monday morning,' said Sir Matthew. 'And to be honest with you, I can't wait to meet Mrs Mary Banks. That woman must have real guts, not to mention imagination. Mark my words, Mr Casson, she'll prove a worthy opponent for any counsel.'

When Sir Matthew entered the interviewing room of Holloway Prison and saw Mary Banks for the first time, he was momentarily taken aback. He knew from his file on the case that she was thirty-seven, but the frail, grey-haired woman who sat with her hands resting in her lap looked nearer fifty. Only when he studied her fine cheekbones and slim figure did he see that she might once have been a beautiful woman.

Sir Matthew allowed Casson to take the seat opposite her at a plain formica table in the centre of an otherwise empty, cream-painted brick room. There was a small, barred window halfway up the wall that threw a shaft of light onto their client. Sir Matthew and his junior took their places on either side of the instructing solicitor. Leading counsel noisily poured himself a cup of coffee.

'Good morning, Mrs Banks,' said Casson.

'Good morning, Mr Casson,' she replied, turning slightly to face the direction from which the voice had come. 'You have brought someone with you.'

'Yes, Mrs Banks, I am accompanied by Sir Matthew Roberts QC, who will be acting as your defence counsel.'

She gave a slight bow of the head as Sir Matthew rose from his chair, took a pace forward and said, 'Good morning, Mrs Banks,' then suddenly thrust out his right hand.

'Good morning, Sir Matthew,' she replied, without moving a muscle, still looking in Casson's direction. 'I'm delighted that you will be representing me.'

'Sir Matthew would like to ask you a few questions, Mrs Banks,' said Casson, 'so that he can decide what might be the best approach in your case. He will assume the role of counsel for the prosecution, so that you can get used to what it will be like when you go into the witness box.'

'I understand,' replied Mrs Banks. 'I shall be happy to answer any of Sir Matthew's questions. I'm sure it won't prove difficult for someone of his eminence to show that a frail, blind woman would be incapable of chopping up a vicious sixteen-stone man.'

'Not if that vicious sixteen-stone man was poisoned before he was chopped up,' said Sir Matthew quietly.

'Which would be quite an achievement for someone lying in a hospital bed five miles from where the crime was committed,' replied Mrs Banks.

'If indeed that *was* when the crime was committed,' responded Sir Matthew. 'You claim your blindness was caused by a blow to the side of your head.'

'Yes, Sir Matthew. My husband picked up the frying pan from the stove while I was cooking breakfast, and struck me with it. I ducked, but the edge of the pan caught me on the left side of my face.' She touched a scar above her left eye that looked as if it would remain with her for the rest of her life.

'And then what happened?'

'I passed out and collapsed onto the kitchen floor. When I came to I could sense someone else was in the room. But I had no idea who it was until he spoke, when I recognised the voice of Jack Pembridge, our postman. He carried me to his van and drove me to the local hospital.'

'And it was while you were in hospital that the police discovered your husband's body?'

'That is correct, Sir Matthew. After I had been in Parkmead for nearly two weeks, I asked the vicar, who had been to visit me every day, to try and find out how Bruce was coping without me.'

'Did you not think it surprising that your husband

hadn't been to see you once during the time you were in hospital?' asked Sir Matthew, who began slowly pushing his cup of coffee towards the edge of the table.

'No. I had threatened to leave him on several occasions, and I don't think . . .' The cup fell off the table and shattered noisily on the stone floor. Sir Matthew's eyes never left Mrs Banks.

She jumped nervously, but did not turn to look in the direction of the broken cup.

'Are you all right, Mr Casson?' she asked.

'My fault,' said Sir Matthew. 'How clumsy of me.'

Casson suppressed a smile. Witherington remained unmoved.

'Please continue,' said Sir Matthew as he bent down and began picking up the pieces of china scattered across the floor. 'You were saying, "I don't think . . ."'

'Oh, yes,' said Mrs Banks. 'I don't think Bruce would have cared whether I returned to the farm or not.'

'Quite so,' said Sir Matthew after he had placed the broken pieces on the table. 'But can you explain to me why the police found one of your hairs on the handle of the axe that was used to dismember your husband's body?'

'Yes, Sir Matthew, I can. I was chopping up some wood for the stove before I prepared his breakfast.'

'Then I am bound to ask why there were no finger-prints on the handle of the axe, Mrs Banks.'

'Because I was wearing gloves, Sir Matthew. If you had ever worked on a farm in mid-October, you would know only too well how cold it can be at five in the morning.'

This time Casson did allow himself to smile.

'But what about the blood found on your husband's collar? Blood that was shown by the Crown's forensic scientist to match your own.'

'You will find my blood on many things in that house, should you care to look closely, Sir Matthew.'

'And the spade, the one with your fingerprints all over it? Had you also been doing some digging before breakfast that morning?'

'No, but I would have had cause to use it every day the previous week.'

'I see,' said Sir Matthew. 'Let us now turn our attention to something I suspect you didn't do every day, namely the purchase of strychnine. First, Mrs Banks, why did you need such a large amount? And second, why did you have to travel twenty-seven miles to Reading to purchase it?'

'I shop in Reading every other Thursday,' Mrs Banks explained. 'There isn't an agricultural supplier any nearer.'

Sir Matthew frowned and rose from his chair. He began slowly to circle Mrs Banks, while Casson watched her eyes. They never moved.

When Sir Matthew was directly behind his client, he checked his watch. It was 11.17. He knew his timing had to be exact, because he had become uncomfortably aware that he was dealing not only with a clever woman, but also an extremely cunning one. Mind you, he reflected, anyone who had lived for eleven years with such a man as Bruce Banks would have had to be cunning simply to survive.

'You still haven't explained why you needed such a large amount of strychnine,' he said, remaining behind his client.

'We had been losing a lot of chickens,' Mrs Banks replied, still not moving her head. 'My husband thought it was rats, so he told me to get a large quantity of strychnine to finish them off. "Once and for all" were his exact words.'

'But as it turned out, it was he who was finished off, once and for all – and undoubtedly with the same poison,' said Sir Matthew quietly.

'I also feared for Rupert's safety,' said Mrs Banks, ignoring her counsel's sarcasm.

'But your son was away at school at the time, am I not correct?'

'Yes, you are, Sir Matthew, but he was due back for half term that weekend.'

'Have you ever used that supplier before?'

'Regularly,' said Mrs Banks, as Sir Matthew completed his circle and returned to face her once again. 'I go there at least once a month, as I'm sure the manager will confirm.' She turned her head and faced a foot or so to his right.

Sir Matthew remained silent, resisting the temptation to look at his watch. He knew it could only be a matter of seconds. A few moments later the door on the far side of the interview room swung open and a boy of about nine years of age entered. The three of them watched their client closely as the child walked silently towards her. Rupert Banks came to a halt in front of his mother and smiled, but received no response. He waited for a further ten seconds, then turned and walked back out, exactly as he had been instructed to do. Mrs Banks's eyes remained fixed somewhere between Sir Matthew and Mr Casson.

The smile on Casson's face was now almost one of triumph.

'Is there someone else in the room?' asked Mrs Banks. 'I thought I heard the door open.'

'No,' said Sir Matthew. 'Only Mr Casson and I are in the room.' Witherington still hadn't moved a muscle.

Sir Matthew began to circle Mrs Banks for what he knew had to be the last time. He had almost come to believe that he might have misjudged her. When he was directly behind her once again, he nodded to his junior, who remained seated in front of her.

Witherington removed the silk handkerchief from his breast pocket, slowly unfolded it, and laid it out flat on the table in front of him. Mrs Banks showed no reaction. Witherington stretched out the fingers of his right hand, bowed his head slightly, and paused before placing his right hand over his left eye. Without warning he plucked the eye out of its socket and placed it in the middle of the silk handkerchief. He left it on the table for a full thirty seconds, then began to polish it. Sir Matthew completed his circle, and observed beads of perspiration appearing on Mrs Banks's forehead as he sat down.

When Witherington had finished cleaning the almond-shaped glass object, he slowly raised his head until he was staring directly at her, then eased the eye back into its socket. Mrs Banks momentarily turned away. She quickly tried to compose herself, but it was too late.

Sir Matthew rose from his chair and smiled at his client. She returned the smile.

'I must confess, Mrs Banks,' he said, 'I would feel much more confident about a plea of guilty to manslaughter.'

ONE MAN'S MEAT...

COULD ANYONE BE THAT BEAUTIFUL?

I was driving round the Aldwych on my way to work when I first saw her. She was walking up the steps of the Aldwych Theatre. If I'd stared a moment longer I would have driven into the back of the car in front of me, but before I could confirm my fleeting impression she had disappeared into the throng of theatregoers.

I spotted a parking space on my left-hand side and swung into it at the last possible moment, without indicating, causing the vehicle behind me to let out several appreciative blasts. I leapt out of my car and ran back towards the theatre, realising how unlikely it was that I'd be able to find her in such a mêlée, and that even if I did, she was probably meeting a boyfriend or husband who would turn out to be about six feet tall and closely to resemble Harrison Ford.

Once I reached the foyer I scanned the chattering crowd. I slowly turned 360 degrees, but could see no sign of her. Should I try to buy a ticket? I wondered. But she could be seated anywhere – the stalls, the dress circle, even the upper circle. Perhaps I should walk up and down the aisles until I spotted her. But I realised I wouldn't be allowed into any part of the theatre unless I could produce a ticket.

And then I saw her. She was standing in a queue in front of the window marked 'Tonight's Performance', and was just one away from being attended to. There were two other customers, a young woman and a middle-aged man, waiting in line behind her. I quickly joined the queue, by which time she had reached the front. I leant forward and tried to overhear what she was saying, but I could only catch the box office manager's reply: 'Not much chance with the curtain going up in a few minutes' time, madam,' he was saying. 'But if you leave it with me, I'll see what I can do.'

She thanked him and walked off in the direction of the stalls. My first impression was confirmed. It didn't matter if you looked from the ankles up or from the head down – she was perfection. I couldn't take my eyes off her, and I noticed that she was having exactly the same effect on several other men in the foyer. I wanted to tell them all not to bother. Didn't they realise she was with me? Or rather, that she would be by the end of the evening.

After she had disappeared from view, I craned my neck to look into the booth. Her ticket had been placed to one side. I sighed with relief as the young woman two places ahead of me presented her credit card and picked up four tickets for the dress circle.

I began to pray that the man in front of me wasn't looking for a single.

'Do you have one ticket for tonight's performance?' he asked hopefully, as the three-minute bell sounded. The man in the booth smiled.

I scowled. Should I knife him in the back, kick him in the groin, or simply scream abuse at him?

'Where would you prefer to sit, sir? The dress circle or the stalls?'

'Don't say stalls,' I willed. 'Say Circle . . . Circle . . . Circle . . .'

'Stalls,' he said.

'I have one on the aisle in row H,' said the man in the box, checking the computer screen in front of him. I uttered a silent cheer as I realised that the theatre would be trying to sell off its remaining tickets before it bothered with returns handed in by members of the public. But then, I thought, how would I get around that problem?

By the time the man in front of me had bought the ticket on the end of row H, I had my lines well rehearsed, and just hoped I wouldn't need a prompt.

'Thank goodness. I thought I wasn't going to make it,' I began, trying to sound out of breath. The man in the ticket booth looked up at me, but didn't seem all that impressed by my opening line. 'It was the traffic. And then I couldn't find a parking space. My girlfriend may have given up on me. Did she by any chance hand in my ticket for resale?'

He looked unconvinced. My dialogue obviously wasn't gripping him. 'Can you describe her?' he asked suspiciously.

'Short-cropped dark hair, hazel eyes, wearing a red silk dress that . . .'

'Ah, yes. I remember her,' he said, almost sighing. He picked up the ticket by his side and handed it to me.

'Thank you,' I said, trying not to show my relief that he had come in so neatly on cue with the closing line from my first scene. As I hurried off in the direction of the stalls, I grabbed an envelope from a pile on the ledge beside the booth.

I checked the price of the ticket: twenty pounds. I extracted two ten-pound notes from my wallet, put them in the envelope, licked the flap and stuck it down.

The girl at the entrance to the stalls checked my ticket. 'F-11. Six rows from the front, on the right-hand side.'

I walked slowly down the aisle until I spotted her. She was sitting next to an empty place in the middle of the row. As I made my way over the feet of those who were already seated, she turned and smiled, obviously pleased to see that someone had purchased her spare ticket.

I returned the smile, handed over the envelope containing my twenty pounds, and sat down beside her. 'The man in the box office asked me to give you this.'

'Thank you.' She slipped the envelope into her evening bag. I was about to try the first line of my second scene on her, when the house lights faded and the curtain rose for Act One of the real performance. I suddenly realised that I had no idea what play I was about to see. I glanced across at the programme on her lap and read the words *'An Inspector Calls*, by J.B. Priestley'.

I remembered that the critics had been full of praise for the production when it had originally opened at the National Theatre, and had particularly singled out the performance of Kenneth Cranham. I tried to concentrate on what was taking place on stage.

The eponymous inspector was staring into a house in which an Edwardian family were preparing for a dinner to celebrate their daughter's engagement. 'I was thinking of getting a new car,' the father was saying to his prospective son-in-law as he puffed away on his cigar.

At the mention of the word 'car', I suddenly remembered that I had abandoned mine outside the theatre. Was it on a double yellow line? Or worse? To hell with it. They could have it in part-exchange for the model sitting next to me. The audience laughed, so I joined in, if only to give the impression that I was following the plot. But what about my original plans for the evening? By now everyone would be wondering why I hadn't turned up. I realised that I wouldn't be able to leave the theatre during the interval, either to check on my car or to make a phone call to explain my absence, as that would be my one chance of developing my own plot.

The play had the rest of the audience enthralled, but I had already begun rehearsing the lines from my own script, which would have to be performed during the interval between Acts One and Two. I was painfully aware that I would be restricted to fifteen minutes, and that there would be no second night.

By the time the curtain came down at the end of the first act, I was confident of my draft text. I waited for the applause to die down before I turned towards her.

'What an original production,' I began. 'Quite modernistic.' I vaguely remembered that one of the critics had followed that line. 'I was lucky to get a seat at the last moment.'

'I was just as lucky,' she replied. I felt encouraged. 'I mean, to find someone who was looking for a single ticket at such short notice.'

I nodded. 'My name's Michael Whitaker.'

'Anna Townsend,' she said, giving me a warm smile.

'Would you like a drink?' I asked.

'Thank you,' she replied, 'that would be nice.' I stood up and led her through the packed scrum that was heading towards the stalls bar, occasionally glancing back to make sure she was still following me. I was somehow expecting her no longer to be there, but each time I turned to look she greeted me with the same radiant smile.

'What would you like?' I asked, once I could make out the bar through the crowd.

'A dry martini, please.'

'Stay here, and I'll be back in a moment,' I promised, wondering just how many precious minutes would be wasted while I had to wait at the bar. I took out a five-pound note and held it up conspicuously, in the hope that the prospect of a large tip might influence the barman's sense of direction. He spotted the money, but I still had to wait for another four customers to be served before I managed to secure the dry martini and a Scotch on the rocks for myself. The barman didn't deserve the tip I left him, but I hadn't any more time to waste waiting for the change.

I carried the drinks back to the far corner of the foyer, where Anna stood studying her programme. She was silhouetted against a window, and in that stylish red silk dress, the light emphasised her slim, elegant figure.

I handed her the dry martini, aware that my limited time had almost run out.

'Thank you,' she said, giving me another disarming smile.

'How did you come to have a spare ticket?' I asked as she took a sip from her drink.

'My partner was held up on an emergency case at the last minute,' she explained. 'Just one of the problems of being a doctor.'

'Pity. They missed a quite remarkable production,' I prompted, hoping to tease out of her whether her partner was male or female.

'Yes,' said Anna. 'I tried to book seats when it was still at the National Theatre, but they were sold out for any performances I was able to make, so when a friend offered me two tickets at the last minute, I jumped at them. After all, it's coming off in a few weeks.' She took another sip from her martini. 'What about you?' she asked as the three-minute bell sounded.

There was no such line in my script.

'Me?'

'Yes, Michael,' she said, a hint of teasing in her voice. 'How did you come to be looking for a spare seat at the last moment?'

'Sharon Stone was tied up for the evening, and at the last second Princess Diana told me that she would have loved to have come, but she was trying to keep a low profile.' Anna laughed. 'Actually, I read some of the crits, and I dropped in on the off-chance of picking up a spare ticket.'

'And you picked up a spare woman as well,' said Anna, as the two-minute bell went. I wouldn't have dared to include such a bold line in her script – or was there a hint of mockery in those hazel eyes?

'I certainly did,' I replied lightly. 'So, are you a doctor as well?'

'As well as what?' asked Anna.

'As well as your partner,' I said, not sure if she was still teasing.

'Yes. I'm a GP in Fulham. There are three of us in the practice, but I was the only one who could escape tonight. And what do you do when you're not chatting up Sharon Stone or escorting Princess Diana to the theatre?'

'I'm in the restaurant business,' I told her.

'That must be one of the few jobs with worse hours and tougher working conditions than mine,' Anna said as the one-minute bell sounded.

I looked into those hazel eyes and wanted to say – Anna, let's forget the second act: I realise the play's superb, but all I want to do is spend the rest of the evening alone with you, not jammed into a crowded auditorium with eight hundred other people.

'Wouldn't you agree?'

I tried to recall what she had just said. 'I expect we get more customer complaints than you do,' was the best I could manage.

'I doubt it,' Anna said, quite sharply. 'If you're a woman in the medical profession and you don't cure your patients within a couple of days, they immediately want to know if you're fully qualified.'

I laughed, and finished my drink as a voice boomed over the Tannoy, 'Would the audience please take their seats for the second act. The curtain is about to rise.'

'We ought to be getting back,' Anna said, placing her empty glass on the nearest window ledge.

'I suppose so,' I said reluctantly, and led her in the opposite direction to the one in which I really wanted to take her.

'Thanks for the drink,' she said as we returned to our seats.

'Small recompense,' I replied. She glanced up at me questioningly. 'For such a good ticket,' I explained.

She smiled as we made our way along the row, stepping awkwardly over more toes. I was just about to risk a further remark when the house lights dimmed.

During the second act I turned to smile in Anna's direction whenever there was laughter, and was occasionally rewarded with a warm response. But my supreme moment of triumph came towards the end of the act, when the detective showed the daughter a photograph of the dead woman. She gave a piercing scream, and the stage lights were suddenly switched off.

Anna grabbed my hand, but quickly released it and apologised.

'Not at all,' I whispered. 'I only just stopped myself from doing the same thing.' In the darkened theatre, I couldn't tell how she responded.

A moment later the phone on the stage rang. Everyone in the audience knew it must be the detective on the other end of the line, even if they couldn't be sure what he was going to say. That final scene had the whole house gripped.

After the lights dimmed for the last time, the cast returned to the stage and deservedly received a long ovation, taking several curtain calls.

When the curtain was finally lowered, Anna turned to me and said, 'What a remarkable production. I'm so glad I didn't miss it. And I'm even more pleased that I didn't have to see it alone.'

'Me too,' I told her, ignoring the fact that I'd never planned to spend the evening at the theatre in the first place.

We made our way up the aisle together as the audience flowed out of the theatre like a slow-moving river. I wasted those few precious moments discussing the merits of the cast, the power of the director's interpretation, the originality of the macabre set and even the Edwardian costumes, before we reached the double doors that led back out into the real world.

'Goodbye, Michael,' Anna said. 'Thank you for adding to my enjoyment of the evening.' She shook me by the hand.

'Goodbye,' I said, gazing once again into those hazel eyes.

She turned to go, and I wondered if I would ever see her again.

'Anna,' I said.

She glanced back in my direction.

'If you're not doing anything in particular, would you care to join me for dinner . . .'

Author's Note

At this point in the story, the reader is offered the choice of four different endings.

You might decide to read all four of them, or simply select one, and consider that your own particular ending. If you do choose to read all four, they should be taken in the order in which they have been written:

1   RARE

2   BURNT

3   OVERDONE

4   À POINT

Rare

'Thank you, Michael. I'd like that.'

I smiled, unable to mask my delight. 'Good. I know a little restaurant just down the road that I think you might enjoy.'

'That sounds fun,' Anna said, linking her arm in mine. I guided her through the departing throng.

As we strolled together down the Aldwych, Anna continued to chat about the play, comparing it favourably with a production she had seen at the Haymarket some years before.

When we reached the Strand I pointed to a large grey double door on the other side of the road. 'That's it,' I said. We took advantage of a red light to weave our way through the temporarily stationary traffic, and after we'd reached the far pavement I pushed one of the grey doors open to allow Anna through. It began to rain just as we stepped inside. I led her down a flight of stairs into a basement restaurant buzzing with the talk of people who had just come out of theatres, and waiters dashing, plates in both hands, from table to table.

'I'll be impressed if you can get a table here,' Anna said, eyeing a group of would-be customers who were clustered round the bar, impatiently waiting for someone to leave.

I strolled across to the reservations desk. The head waiter, who until that moment had been taking a customer's order, rushed over. 'Good evening, Mr Whitaker,' he said. 'How many are you?'

'Just the two of us.'

'Follow me, please, sir,' Mario said, leading us to my usual table in the far corner of the room.

'Another dry martini?' I asked her as we sat down.

'No, thank you,' she replied. 'I think I'll just have a glass of wine with the meal.'

I nodded my agreement, as Mario handed us our menus. Anna studied hers for a few moments before I asked if she had spotted anything she fancied.

'Yes,' she said, looking straight at me. 'But for now I think I'll settle for the fettucini, and a glass of red wine.'

'Good idea,' I said. 'I'll join you. But are you sure you won't have a starter?'

'No, thank you, Michael. I've reached that age when I can no longer order everything I'm tempted by.'

'Me too,' I confessed. 'I have to play squash three times a week to keep in shape,' I told her as Mario reappeared.

'Two fettucini,' I began, 'and a bottle of . . .'

'Half a bottle, please,' said Anna. 'I'll only have one glass. I've got an early start tomorrow morning, so I shouldn't overdo things.'

I nodded, and Mario scurried away.

I looked across the table and into Anna's eyes. 'I've always wondered about women doctors,' I said, immediately realising that the line was a bit feeble.

'You mean, you wondered if we're normal?'

'Something like that, I suppose.'

'Yes, we're normal enough, except every day we have to see a lot of men in the nude. I can assure you, Michael, most of them are overweight and fairly unattractive.'

I suddenly wished I were half a stone lighter. 'But are there many men who are brave enough to consider a woman doctor in the first place?'

'Quite a few,' said Anna, 'though most of my patients are female. But there are just about enough intelligent, sensible, uninhibited males around who can accept that a woman doctor might be just as likely to cure them as a man.'

I smiled as two bowls of fettucini were placed in front of us. Mario then showed me the label on the half-bottle he had selected. I nodded my approval. He had chosen a vintage to match Anna's pedigree.

'And what about you?' asked Anna. 'What does being "in the restaurant business" actually mean?'

'I'm on the management side,' I said, before sampling the wine. I nodded again, and Mario poured a glass for Anna and then topped up mine.

'Or at least, that's what I do nowadays. I started life as a waiter,' I said, as Anna began to sip her wine.

'What a magnificent wine,' she remarked. 'It's so good I may end up having a second glass.'

'I'm glad you like it,' I said. 'It's a Barolo.'

'You were saying, Michael? You started life as a waiter . . .'

'Yes, then I moved into the kitchens for about five years, and finally ended up on the management side. How's the fettucini?'

'It's delicious. Almost melts in your mouth.' She took another sip of her wine. 'So, if you're not cooking, and no longer a waiter, what do you do now?'

'Well, at the moment I'm running three restaurants in the West End, which means I never stop dashing from one to the other, depending on which is facing the biggest crisis on that particular day.'

'Sounds a bit like ward duty to me,' said Anna. 'So who turned out to have the biggest crisis today?'

'Today, thank heaven, was not typical,' I told her with feeling.

'That bad?' said Anna.

'Yes, I'm afraid so. We lost a chef this morning who cut off the top of his finger, and won't be back at work for at least a fortnight. My head waiter in our second restaurant is off, claiming he has 'flu, and I've just had to sack the barman in the third for fiddling the books. Barmen always fiddle the books, of course, but in this case even the customers began to notice what he was up to.' I paused. 'But I still wouldn't want to be in any other business.'

'In the circumstances, I'm amazed you were able to take the evening off.'

'I shouldn't have, really, and I wouldn't have,

except . . .' I trailed off as I leaned over and topped up Anna's glass.

'Except what?' she said.

'Do you want to hear the truth?' I asked as I poured the remains of the wine into my own glass.

'I'll try that for starters,' she said.

I placed the empty bottle on the side of the table, and hesitated, but only for a moment. 'I was driving to one of my restaurants earlier this evening, when I spotted you going into the theatre. I stared at you for so long that I nearly crashed into the back of the car in front of me. Then I swerved across the road into the nearest parking space, and the car behind almost crashed into me. I leapt out, ran all the way to the theatre, and searched everywhere until I saw you standing in the queue for the box office. I joined the line and watched you hand over your spare ticket. Once you were safely out of sight, I told the box office manager that you hadn't expected me to make it in time, and that you might have put my ticket up for resale. After I'd described you, which I was able to do in great detail, he handed it over without so much as a murmur.'

Anna put down her glass of wine and stared across at me with a look of incredulity. 'I'm glad he fell for your story,' she said. 'But should I?'

'Yes, you should. Because then I put two ten-pound notes into a theatre envelope and took the place next to you. The rest you already know.' I waited to see how she would react.

She didn't speak for some time. 'I'm flattered,' she

eventually said, and touched my hand. 'I didn't realise there were any old-fashioned romantics left in the world.' She squeezed my fingers and looked me in the eyes. 'Am I allowed to ask what you have planned for the rest of the evening?'

'Nothing has been planned so far,' I admitted. 'Which is why it's all been so refreshing.'

'You make me sound like an After Eight mint,' said Anna with a laugh.

'I can think of at least three replies to that,' I told her as Mario reappeared, looking a little disappointed at the sight of the half-empty plates.

'Was everything all right, sir?' he asked, sounding anxious.

'Couldn't have been better,' said Anna, who hadn't stopped looking at me.

'Would you like some coffee?' I asked.

'Yes,' said Anna. 'But perhaps we could have it somewhere a little less crowded.'

I was so taken by surprise that it was several moments before I recovered. I was beginning to feel that I was no longer in control. Anna rose from her place and said, 'Shall we go?' I nodded to Mario, who just smiled.

Once we were back out on the street, she linked her arm with mine as we retraced our steps along the Aldwych and past the theatre.

'It's been a wonderful evening,' she was saying as we reached the spot where I had left my car. 'Until you arrived on the scene it had been a rather dull day, but you've changed all that.'

'It hasn't actually been the best of days for me either,'
I admitted. 'But I've rarely enjoyed an evening more.
Where would you like to have coffee? Annabels? Or
why don't we try the new Dorchester Club?'

'If you don't have a wife, your place. If you do . . .'

'I don't,' I told her simply.

'Then that's settled,' she said as I opened the door of
my BMW for her. Once she was safely in I walked round
to take my seat behind the wheel, and discovered that I
had left my sidelights on and the keys in the ignition.

I turned the key, and the engine immediately purred
into life. 'This has to be my day,' I said to myself.

'Sorry?' Anna said, turning in my direction.

'We were lucky to miss the rain,' I replied, as a few
drops landed on the windscreen. I flicked on the wipers.

On our way to Pimlico, Anna told me about her childhood in the south of France, where her father had taught
English at a boys' school. Her account of being the only
girl among a couple of hundred teenage French boys
made me laugh again and again. I found myself becoming more and more enchanted with her company.

'Whatever made you come back to England?' I asked.

'An English mother who divorced my French father,
and the chance to study medicine at St Thomas's.'

'But don't you miss the south of France, especially on
nights like this?' I asked as a clap of thunder crackled
above us.

'Oh, I don't know,' she said. I was about to respond
when she added, 'In any case, now the English have
learnt how to cook, the place has become almost

civilised.' I smiled to myself, wondering if she was teasing me again.

I found out immediately. 'By the way,' she said, 'I assume that was one of your restaurants we had dinner at.'

'Yes, it was,' I said sheepishly.

'That explains how you got a table so easily when it was packed out, why the waiter knew it was a Barolo you wanted without your having to ask, and how you could leave without paying the bill.'

I was beginning to wonder if I would always be a yard behind her.

'Was it the missing waiter, the four-and-a-half-fingered chef, or the crooked bartender?'

'The crooked bartender,' I replied, laughing. 'But I sacked him this afternoon, and I'm afraid his deputy didn't look as if he was coping all that well,' I explained as I turned right off Millbank, and began to search for a parking space.

'And I thought you only had eyes for me,' sighed Anna, 'when all the time you were looking over my shoulder and checking on what the deputy barman was up to.'

'Not *all* the time,' I said as I manoeuvred the car into the only space left in the mews where I lived. I got out of the car and walked round to Anna's side, opened the door and guided her to the house.

As I closed the door behind us, Anna put her arms around my neck and looked up into my eyes. I leaned down and kissed her for the first time. When she broke away, all she said was, 'Don't let's bother with coffee, Michael.' I slipped off my jacket, and led her upstairs and into my bedroom, praying that it hadn't been the housekeeper's day off. When I opened the door I was relieved to find that the bed had been made and the room was tidy.

'I'll just be a moment,' I said, and disappeared into the bathroom. As I cleaned my teeth, I began to wonder if it was all a dream. When I returned to the bedroom, would I discover she didn't exist? I dropped the toothbrush into its mug and went back to the bedroom. Where was she? My eyes followed a trail of discarded clothes that led all the way to the bed. Her head was propped up on the pillow. Only a sheet covered her body.

I quickly took off my clothes, dropping them where they fell, and switched off the main lights, so that only the one by the bed remained aglow. I slid under the sheets to join her. I looked at her for several seconds before I took her in my arms. I slowly explored every part of her body, as she began to kiss me again. I couldn't believe that anyone could be that exciting, and at the same time so tender. When we finally made love, I knew I never wanted this woman to leave me.

She lay in my arms for some time before either of us spoke. Then I began talking about anything that came into my head. I confided my hopes, my dreams, even my worst anxieties, with a freedom I had never experienced with anyone before. I wanted to share everything with her.

And then she leaned across and began kissing me once again, first on the lips, then the neck and chest, and as she slowly continued down my body I thought I would explode. The last thing I remember was turning off the light by my bed as the clock on the hall table chimed one.

When I woke the following morning, the first rays of sunlight were already shining through the lace curtains, and the glorious memory of the night before was instantly revived. I turned lazily to take her in my arms, but she was no longer there.

'Anna?' I cried out, sitting bolt upright. There was no reply. I flicked on the light by the side of the bed, and glanced across at the bedside clock. It was 7.29. I was about to jump out of bed and go in search of her when I noticed a scribbled note wedged under a corner of the clock.

I picked it up, read it slowly, and smiled.

'So will I,' I said, and lay back on the pillow, thinking about what I should do next. I decided to send her a dozen roses later that morning, eleven white and one red. Then I would have a red one delivered to her on the hour, every hour, until I saw her again.

After I had showered and dressed, I roamed aimlessly around the house. I wondered how quickly I could persuade Anna to move in, and what changes she would want to make. Heaven knows, I thought as I walked through to the kitchen, clutching her note, the place could do with a woman's touch.

As I ate breakfast I looked up her number in the telephone directory, instead of reading the morning paper. There it was, just as she had said. Dr Townsend, listing a surgery number in Parsons Green Lane where she could be contacted between nine and six. There was a second number, but deep black lettering requested that it should only be used in case of emergencies.

Although I considered my state of health to be an emergency, I dialled the first number, and waited impatiently. All I wanted to say was, 'Good morning, darling. I got your note, and can we make last night the first of many?'

A matronly voice answered the phone. 'Dr Townsend's surgery.'

'Dr Townsend, please,' I said.

'Which one?' she asked. 'There are three Dr Townsends in the practice – Dr Jonathan, Dr Anna and Dr Elizabeth.'

'Dr Anna,' I replied.

'Oh, Mrs Townsend,' she said. 'I'm sorry, but she's not available at the moment. She's just taken the children off to school, and after that she has to go to the airport to pick up her husband, Dr Jonathan, who's returning this morning from a medical conference in Minneapolis. I'm not expecting her back for at least a couple of hours. Would you like to leave a message?'

There was a long silence before the matronly voice asked, 'Are you still there?' I placed the receiver back on the hook without replying, and looked sadly down at the hand-written note by the side of the phone.

Dear Michael,
I will remember tonight for the rest of my life.
Thank you.
Anna

Burnt

'THANK YOU, MICHAEL. I'D LIKE THAT.'
I smiled, unable to mask my delight.

'Hi, Anna. I thought I might have missed you.'

I turned and stared at a tall man with a mop of fair hair, who seemed unaffected by the steady flow of people trying to pass him on either side.

Anna gave him a smile that I hadn't seen until that moment.

'Hello, darling,' she said. 'This is Michael Whitaker. You're lucky – he bought your ticket, and if you hadn't turned up I was just about to accept his kind invitation to dinner. Michael, this is my husband, Jonathan – the one who was held up at the hospital. As you can see, he's now escaped.'

I couldn't think of a suitable reply.

Jonathan shook me warmly by the hand. 'Thank you for keeping my wife company,' he said. 'Won't you join us for dinner?'

'That's very kind of you,' I replied, 'but I've just remembered that I'm meant to be somewhere else right now. I'd better run.'

'That's a pity,' said Anna. 'I was rather looking

forward to finding out all about the restaurant business. Perhaps we'll meet again sometime, whenever my husband next leaves me in the lurch. Goodbye, Michael.'

'Goodbye, Anna.'

I watched them climb into the back of a taxi together, and wished Jonathan would drop dead in front of me. He didn't, so I began to retrace my steps back to the spot where I had abandoned my car. 'You're a lucky man, Jonathan Townsend,' was the only observation I made. But no one was listening.

The next word that came to my lips was 'Damn!' I repeated it several times, as there was a distressingly large space where I was certain I'd left my car.

I walked up and down the street in case I'd forgotten where I'd parked it, cursed again, then marched off in search of a phone box, unsure if my car had been stolen or towed away. There was a pay phone just around the corner in Kingsway. I picked up the handset and jabbed three nines into it.

'Which service do you require? Fire, Police or Ambulance,' a voice asked.

'Police,' I said, and was immediately put through to another voice.

'Charing Cross Police Station. What is the nature of your enquiry?'

'I think my car has been stolen.'

'Can you tell me the make, colour and registration number please, sir.'

'It's a red Ford Fiesta, registration H107 SHV.'

There was a long pause, during which I could hear other voices talking in the background.

'No, it hasn't been stolen, sir,' said the officer when he came back on the line. 'The car was illegally parked on a double yellow line. It's been removed and taken to the Vauxhall Bridge Pound.'

'Can I pick it up now?' I asked sulkily.

'Certainly, sir. How will you be getting there?'

'I'll take a taxi.'

'Then just ask the driver for the Vauxhall Bridge Pound. Once you get there, you'll need some form of identification, and a cheque for £105 with a banker's card – that is if you don't have the full amount in cash.'

'£105?' I repeated in disbelief.

'That's correct, sir.'

I slammed the phone down just as it started to rain. I scurried back to the corner of the Aldwych in search of a taxi, only to find that they were all being commandeered by the hordes of people still hanging around outside the theatre.

I put my collar up and nipped across the road, dodging between the slow-moving traffic. Once I had reached the far side, I continued running until I found an overhanging ledge broad enough to shield me from the blustery rain.

I shivered, and sneezed several times before an empty cab eventually came to my rescue.

'Vauxhall Bridge Pound,' I told the driver as I jumped in.

'Bad luck, mate,' said the cabbie. 'You're my second this evening.'

I frowned.

As the taxi manoeuvred its way slowly through the rainswept post-theatre traffic and across Waterloo Bridge, the driver began chattering away. I just about managed monosyllabic replies to his opinions on the weather, John Major, the England cricket team and foreign tourists. With each new topic, his forecast became ever more gloomy.

When we reached the car pound I passed him a ten-pound note and waited in the rain for my change. Then I dashed off in the direction of a little Portakabin, where I was faced by my second queue that evening. This one was considerably longer than the first, and I knew that when I eventually reached the front of it and paid for my ticket, I wouldn't be rewarded with any memorable entertainment. When my turn finally came, a burly policeman pointed to a form sellotaped to the counter.

I followed its instructions to the letter, first producing my driving licence, then writing out a cheque for £105, payable to the Metropolitan Police. I handed them both over, with my cheque card, to the policeman, who towered over me. The man's sheer bulk was the only reason I didn't suggest that perhaps he ought to have more important things to do with his time, like catching drug dealers. Or even car thieves.

'Your vehicle is in the far corner,' said the officer, pointing into the distance, over row upon row of cars.

'Of course it is,' I replied. I stepped out of the Portakabin and back into the rain, dodging puddles as I ran between the lines of cars. I didn't stop until I reached the farthest corner of the pound. It still took me several more minutes to locate my red Ford Fiesta – one disadvantage, I thought, of owning the most popular car in Britain.

I unlocked the door, squelched down onto the front seat, and sneezed again. I turned the key in the ignition, but the engine barely turned over, letting out only the occasional splutter before giving up altogether. Then I remembered I hadn't switched the sidelights off when I made my unscheduled dash for the theatre. I uttered a string of expletives that only partly expressed my true feelings.

I watched as another figure came running across the pound towards a Range Rover parked in the row in front of me. I quickly wound down my window, but he had driven off before I could shout the magic words 'jump leads'. I got out and retrieved my jump leads from the boot, walked to the front of the car, raised the bonnet, and attached the leads to the battery. I began to shiver once again as I settled down for another wait.

I couldn't get Anna out of my mind, but accepted that the only thing I'd succeeded in picking up that evening was the 'flu.

In the following forty rain-drenched minutes, three people passed by before a young black man asked, 'So what's the trouble, man?' Once I had explained my problem he manoeuvred his old van alongside my car, then raised his bonnet and attached the jump leads to his battery. When he switched on his ignition, my engine began to turn over.

'Thanks,' I shouted, rather inadequately, once I'd revved the engine several times.

'My pleasure, man,' he replied, and disappeared into the night.

As I drove out of the car pound I switched on my radio, to hear Big Ben striking twelve. It reminded me that I hadn't turned up for work that night. The first thing I needed to do, if I wanted to keep my job, was to come up with a good excuse. I sneezed again, and decided on the 'flu. Although they'd probably taken the last orders by now, Gerald wouldn't have closed the kitchens yet.

I peered through the rain, searching the pavements for a pay phone, and eventually spotted a row of three outside a post office. I stopped the car and jumped out, but a cursory inspection revealed that they'd all been vandalised. I climbed back into the car and continued my search. After dashing in and out of the rain several times, I finally spotted a single phone box on the corner of Warwick Way that looked as if it might just be in working order.

I dialled the restaurant, and waited a long time for someone to answer.

'Laguna 50,' said an Italian-sounding young girl.

'Janice, is that you? It's Mike.'

'Yes, it's me, Mike,' she whispered, reverting to her Lambeth accent. 'I'd better warn you that every time your name's been mentioned this evening, Gerald picks up the nearest meat-axe.'

'Why?' I asked. 'You've still got Nick in the kitchen to see you through.'

'Nick chopped the top off one of his fingers earlier this evening, and Gerald had to take him to hospital. I was left in charge. He's not best pleased.'

'Oh, hell,' I said. 'But I've got . . .'

'The sack,' said another voice, and this one wasn't whispering.

'Gerald, I can explain . . .'

'Why you didn't turn up for work this evening?'

I sneezed, then held my nose. 'I've got the 'flu. If I'd come in tonight I would have given it to half the customers.'

'Would you?' said Gerald. 'Well, I suppose that might have been marginally worse than giving it to the girl who was sitting next to you in the theatre.'

'What do you mean?' I asked, letting go of my nose.

'Exactly what I said, Mike. You see, unfortunately for you, a couple of our regulars were two rows behind you at the Aldwych. They enjoyed the show almost as much as you seemed to, and one of them added, for good measure, that he thought your date was "absolutely stunning".'

'He must have mistaken me for someone else,' I said, trying not to sound desperate.

'He may have done, Mike, but I haven't. You're sacked, and don't even think about coming in to collect your pay packet, because there isn't one for a head waiter who'd rather take some bimbo to the theatre than do a night's work.' The line went dead.

I hung up the phone and started muttering obscenities under my breath as I walked slowly back towards my car. I was only a dozen paces away from it when a young lad jumped into the front seat, switched on the ignition, and lurched hesitatingly into the centre of the road in what sounded horribly like third gear. I chased after the retreating car, but once the youth began to accelerate, I knew I had no hope of catching him.

I ran all the way back to the phone box, and dialled 999 once again.

'Fire, Police or Ambulance?' I was asked for a second time that night.

'Police,' I said, and a moment later I was put through to another voice.

'Belgravia Police Station. What is the nature of your enquiry?'

'I've just had my car stolen!' I shouted.

'Make, model and registration number please, sir.'

'It's a red Ford Fiesta, registration H107 SHV.'

I waited impatiently.

'It hasn't been stolen, sir. It was illegally parked on a double . . .'

'No it wasn't!' I shouted even more loudly. 'I paid £105 to get the damn thing out of the Vauxhall Bridge Pound less than half an hour ago, and I've just seen it being driven off by a joyrider while I was making a phone call.'

'Where are you, sir?'

'In a phone box on the corner of Vauxhall Bridge Road and Warwick Way.'

'And in which direction was the car travelling when you last saw it?' asked the voice.

'North up Vauxhall Bridge Road.'

'And what is your home telephone number, sir?'

'081 290 4820.'

'And at work?'

'Like the car, I don't have a job any longer.'

'Right, I'll get straight onto it, sir. We'll be in touch with you the moment we have any news.'

I put the phone down and thought about what I should do next. I hadn't been left with a great deal of choice. I hailed a taxi and asked to be taken to Victoria, and was relieved to find that this driver showed no desire to offer any opinions on anything during the short journey to the station. When he dropped me I passed him my last note, and patiently waited while he handed over every last penny of my change. He also muttered an expletive or two. I bought a ticket for Bromley with my few remaining coins, and went in search of the platform.

'You've just about made it, mate,' the ticket collector told me. 'The last train's due in at any minute.' But I still had to wait for another twenty minutes on the cold, empty platform before the last train eventually pulled into the station. By then I had memorised every advertisement in sight, from Guinness to Mates, while continuing to sneeze at regular intervals.

When the train came to a halt and the doors squelched open I took a seat in a carriage near the front. It was another ten minutes before the engine lurched into action, and another forty before it finally pulled into Bromley station.

I emerged into the Kent night a few minutes before one o'clock, and set off in the direction of my little terraced house.

Twenty-five minutes later, I staggered up the short path to my front door. I began to search for my keys, then remembered that I'd left them in the car ignition. I didn't have the energy even to swear, and began to grovel around in the dark for the spare front-door key that was always hidden under a particular stone. But which one? At last I found it, put it in the lock, turned it and pushed the door open. No sooner had I stepped inside than the phone on the hall table began to ring.

I grabbed the receiver.

'Mr Whitaker?'

'Speaking.'

'This is the Belgravia police. We've located your car, sir, and . . .'

'Thank God for that,' I said, before the officer had a chance to finish the sentence. 'Where is it?'

'At this precise moment, sir, it's on the back of a pick-up lorry somewhere in Chelsea. It seems the lad who nicked it only managed to travel a mile or so before he hit the kerb at seventy, and bounced straight into a wall. I'm sorry to have to inform you, sir, that your car's a total write-off.'

'A total write-off?' I said in disbelief.

'Yes, sir. The garage who towed it away has been given your number, and they'll be in touch with you first thing in the morning.'

I couldn't think of any comment worth making.

'The good news is we've caught the lad who nicked it,' continued the police officer. 'The bad news is that he's only fifteen, doesn't have a driver's licence, and, of course, he isn't insured.'

'That's not a problem,' I said. 'I'm fully insured myself.'

'As a matter of interest, sir, did you leave your keys in the ignition?'

'Yes, I did. I was just making a quick phone call, and thought I'd only be away from the car for a couple of minutes.'

'Then I think it's unlikely you'll be covered by your insurance, sir.'

'Not covered by my insurance? What are you talking about?'

'It's standard policy nowadays not to pay out if you leave your keys in the ignition. You'd better check, sir,' were the officer's final words before ringing off.

I put the phone down and wondered what else could possibly go wrong. I slipped off my jacket and began to climb the stairs, but came to a sudden halt when I saw my wife waiting for me on the landing.

'Maureen . . .' I began.

'You can tell me later why the car is a total write-off,' she said, 'but not until you've explained why you didn't turn up for work this evening, and just who this "classy tart" is that Gerald said you were seen with at the theatre.'

Overdone

'No, I'm not doing anything in particular,' said Anna.

I smiled, unable to mask my delight.

'Good. I know a little restaurant just down the road that I think you might enjoy.'

'That sounds just fine,' said Anna as she made her way through the dense theatre crowd. I quickly followed, having to hurry just to keep up with her.

'Which way?' she asked. I pointed towards the Strand. She began walking at a brisk pace, and we continued to talk about the play.

When we reached the Strand I pointed to a large grey double door on the other side of the road. 'That's it,' I said. I would have taken her hand as she began to cross, but she stepped off the pavement ahead of me, dodged between the stationary traffic, and waited for me on the far side.

She pushed the grey doors open, and once again I followed in her wake. We descended a flight of steps into a basement restaurant buzzing with the talk of people who had just come out of theatres, and waiters dashing, plates in both hands, from table to table.

'I don't expect you'll be able to get a table here if you haven't booked,' said Anna, eyeing a group of would-be customers who were clustered round the bar, impatiently waiting for someone to leave.

'Don't worry about that,' I said with bravado, and strode across to the reservations desk. I waved a hand imperiously at the head waiter, who was taking a customer's order. I only hoped he would recognise me.

I turned round to smile at Anna, but she didn't look too impressed.

After the waiter had taken the order, he walked slowly over to me. 'How may I help you, sir?' he asked.

'Can you manage a table for two, Victor?'

'Victor's off tonight, sir. Have you booked?'

'No, I haven't, but . . .'

The head waiter checked the list of reservations and then looked at his watch. 'I might be able to fit you in around 11.15 – 11.30 at the latest,' he said, not sounding too hopeful.

'No sooner?' I pleaded. 'I don't think we can wait that long.' Anna nodded her agreement.

'I'm afraid not, sir,' said the head waiter. 'We are fully booked until then.'

'As I expected,' said Anna, turning to leave.

Once again I had to hurry to keep up with her. As we stepped out onto the pavement I said, 'There's a little Italian restaurant I know not far from here, where I can always get a table. Shall we risk it?'

'Can't see that we've got a lot of choice,' replied Anna. 'Which direction this time?'

'Just up the road to the right,' I said as a clap of thunder heralded an imminent downpour.

'Damn,' said Anna, placing her handbag over her head for protection.

'I'm sorry,' I said, looking up at the black clouds. 'It's my fault. I should have . . .'

'Stop apologising all the time, Michael. It isn't your fault if it starts to rain.'

I took a deep breath and tried again. 'We'd better make a dash for it,' I said desperately. 'I don't expect we'll be able to pick up a taxi in this weather.'

This at least secured her ringing endorsement. I began running up the road, and Anna followed closely behind. The rain was getting heavier and heavier, and although we couldn't have had more than seventy yards to cover, we were both soaked by the time we reached the restaurant.

I sighed with relief when I opened the door and found the dining room was half-empty, although I suppose I should have been annoyed. I turned and smiled hopefully at Anna, but she was still frowning.

'Everything all right?' I asked.

'Fine. It's just that my father had a theory about restaurants that were half-empty at this time of night.'

I looked quizzically at my guest, but decided not to make any comment about her eye make-up, which was beginning to run, or her hair, which had come loose at the edges.

'I'd better carry out some repair work. I'll only be a

couple of minutes,' she said, heading for a door marked 'Signorinas'.

I waved at Mario, who was serving no one in particular. He hurried over to me.

'There was a call for you earlier, Mr Whitaker,' Mario said as he guided me across the restaurant to my usual table. 'If you came in, I was to ask you to phone Gerald urgently. He sounded pretty desperate.'

'I'm sure it can wait. But if he rings again, let me know immediately.' At that moment Anna walked over to join us. The make-up had been restored, but the hair could have done with further attention.

I rose to greet her.

'You don't have to do that,' she said, taking her seat.

'Would you like a drink?' I asked, once we were both settled.

'No, I don't think so. I have an early start tomorrow morning, so I shouldn't overdo things. I'll just have a glass of wine with my meal.'

Another waiter appeared by her side. 'And what would madam care for this evening?' he asked politely.

'I haven't had time to look at the menu yet,' Anna replied, not even bothering to look up at him.

'I can recommend the fettucini, madam,' the waiter said, pointing to a dish halfway down the list of entrées. 'It's our speciality of the day.'

'Then I suppose I might as well have that,' said Anna, handing him the menu.

I nodded, indicating 'Me too,' and asked for a half-bottle of the house red. The waiter scooped up my menu and left us.

'Do you . . . ?'

'Can I . . . ?'

'You first,' I said, attempting a smile.

'Do you always order half a bottle of the house wine on a first date?' she asked.

'I think you'll find it's pretty good,' I said, rather plaintively.

'I was only teasing, Michael. Don't take yourself so seriously.'

I took a closer look at my companion, and began to wonder if I'd made a terrible mistake. Despite her efforts in the washroom, Anna wasn't quite the same girl I'd first seen – admittedly at a distance – when I'd nearly crashed my car earlier in the evening.

Oh my God, the car. I suddenly remembered where I'd left it, and stole a glance at my watch.

'Am I boring you already, Michael?' Anna asked. 'Or is this table on a time share?'

'Yes. I mean no. I'm sorry, I've just remembered something I should have checked on before we came to dinner. Sorry,' I repeated.

Anna frowned, which stopped me saying sorry yet again.

'Is it too late?' she asked.

'Too late for what?'

'To do something about whatever it is you should have checked on before we came to dinner?'

I looked out of the window, and wasn't pleased to see

that it had stopped raining. Now my only hope was that the late-night traffic wardens might not be too vigilant.

'No, I'm sure it will be all right,' I said, trying to sound relaxed.

'Well, that's a relief,' said Anna, in a tone that bordered on the sarcastic.

'So. What's it like being a doctor?' I asked, trying to change the subject.

'Michael, it's my evening off. I'd rather not talk about my work, if you don't mind.'

For the next few moments neither of us spoke. I tried again. 'Do you have many male patients in your practice?' I asked, as the waiter reappeared with our fettucini.

'I can hardly believe I'm hearing this,' Anna said, unable to disguise the weariness in her voice. 'When are people like you going to accept that one or two of us are capable of a little more than spending our lives waiting hand and foot on the male sex.'

The waiter poured some wine into my glass.

'Yes. Of course. Absolutely. No. I didn't mean it to sound like that . . .' I sipped the wine and nodded to the waiter, who filled Anna's glass.

'Then what did you mean it to sound like?' demanded Anna as she stuck her fork firmly into the fettucini.

'Well, isn't it unusual for a man to go to a woman doctor?' I said, realising the moment I had uttered the words that I was only getting myself into even deeper water.

'Good heavens, no, Michael. We live in an enlightened age. I've probably seen more naked men than you have

– and it's not an attractive sight, I can assure you.' I laughed, in the hope that it would ease the tension. 'In any case,' she added, 'quite a few men are confident enough to accept the existence of women doctors, you know.'

'I'm sure that's true,' I said. 'I just thought . . .'

'You didn't think, Michael. That's the problem with so many men like you. I bet you've never even considered consulting a woman doctor.'

'No, but . . . Yes, but . . .'

' "No but, yes but" – Let's change the subject before I get really angry,' Anna said, putting her fork down. 'What do you do for a living, Michael? It doesn't sound as if you're in a profession where women are treated as equals.'

'I'm in the restaurant business,' I told her, wishing the fettucini was a little lighter.

'Ah, yes, you told me in the interval,' she said. 'But what does being "in the restaurant business" actually mean?'

'I'm on the management side. Or at least, that's what I do nowadays. I started life as a waiter, then I moved into the kitchens for about five years, and finally . . .'

'. . . found you weren't very good at either, so you took up managing everyone else.'

'Something like that,' I said, trying to make light of it. But Anna's words only reminded me that one of my other restaurants was without a chef that night, and that that was where I'd been heading before I'd allowed myself to become infatuated by Anna.

'I've lost you again,' Anna said, beginning to sound exasperated. 'You were going to tell me all about restaurant management.'

'Yes, I was, wasn't I? By the way, how's your fettucini?'

'Not bad, considering.'

'Considering?'

'Considering this place was your second choice.'

I was silenced once again.

'It's not that bad,' she said, taking another reluctant forkful.

'Perhaps you'd like something else instead? I can always . . .'

'No, thank you, Michael. After all, this was the one dish the waiter felt confident enough to recommend.'

I couldn't think of a suitable response, so I remained silent.

'Come on, Michael, you still haven't explained what restaurant management actually involves,' said Anna.

'Well, at the moment I'm running three restaurants in the West End, which means I never stop dashing from one to the other, depending on which is facing the biggest crisis on that particular day.'

'Sounds a bit like ward duty to me,' said Anna. 'So who turned out to have the biggest crisis today?'

'Today, thank heaven, was not typical,' I told her with feeling.

'That bad?' said Anna.

'Yes, I'm afraid so. We lost a chef this morning who cut off the top of his finger, and won't be back at work for at least a fortnight. My head waiter in our second restaurant is off, claiming he has 'flu, and I've just had to sack the barman in the third for fiddling the books. Barmen always fiddle the books, of course, but in this case even the customers began to notice what he was up to.' I paused, wondering if I should risk another mouthful of fettucini. 'But I still wouldn't want to be in any other business.'

'In the circumstances, I'm frankly amazed you were able to take the evening off.'

'I shouldn't have, really, and wouldn't have, except . . .' I trailed off as I leaned over and topped up Anna's wine glass.

'Except what?' she said.

'Do you want to hear the truth?' I asked as I poured the remains of the wine into my own glass.

'I'll try that for starters,' she said.

I placed the empty bottle on the side of the table, and hesitated, but only for a moment. 'I was driving to one of my restaurants earlier this evening, when I spotted you going into the theatre. I stared at you for so long that I nearly crashed into the back of the car in front of me. Then I swerved across the road into the nearest parking space, and the car behind almost crashed into me. I leapt out, ran all the way to the theatre, and searched everywhere until I saw you standing in the queue for the box office. I joined the line and watched you hand over your spare ticket. Once you were safely out of sight, I told the box office manager that you hadn't expected me to make it in time, and that you might have put my ticket up for resale. Once I'd described you, which I was able to do in great detail, he handed it over without so much as a murmur.'

'More fool him,' said Anna, putting down her glass and staring at me as if I'd just been released from a lunatic asylum.

'Then I put two ten-pound notes into a theatre envelope and took the place next to you,' I continued. 'The rest you already know.' I waited, with some trepidation, to see how she would react.

'I suppose I ought to be flattered,' Anna said after a moment's consideration. 'But I don't know whether to laugh or cry. One thing's for certain; the woman I've been living with for the past ten years will think it's highly amusing, especially as you paid for her ticket.'

The waiter returned to remove the half-finished plates. 'Was everything all right, sir?' he asked, sounding anxious.

'Fine, just fine,' I said unconvincingly. Anna grimaced, but made no comment.

'Would you care for coffee, madam?'

'No, I don't think I'll risk it,' she said, looking at her watch. 'In any case, I ought to be getting back. Elizabeth will be wondering where I've got to.'

She stood up and walked towards the door. I followed a yard behind. She was just about to step onto the pavement when she turned to me and asked, 'Don't you think you ought to settle the bill?'

'That won't be necessary.'

'Why?' she asked, laughing. 'Do you own the place?'

'No. But it is one of the three restaurants I manage.'

Anna turned scarlet. 'I'm so sorry, Michael,' she said. 'That was tactless of me.' She paused for a moment before adding, 'But I'm sure you'll agree that the food wasn't exactly memorable.'

'Would you like me to drive you home?' I asked, trying not to sound too enthusiastic.

Anna looked up at the black clouds. 'That would be useful,' she replied, 'if it's not miles out of your way. Where's your car?' she said before I had a chance to ask where she lived.

'I left it just up the road.'

'Oh, yes, I remember,' said Anna. 'When you jumped out of it because you couldn't take your eyes off me. I'm afraid you picked the wrong girl this time.'

At last we had found something on which we could agree, but I made no comment as we walked towards the spot where I had abandoned my car. Anna limited her conversation to whether it was about to rain again, and how good she had thought the wine was. I was relieved to find my Volvo parked exactly where I had left it.

I was searching for my keys when I spotted a large sticker glued to the windscreen. I looked down at the front offside wheel, and saw the yellow clamp.

'It just isn't your night, is it?' said Anna. 'But don't worry about me, I'll just grab a cab.'

She raised her hand and a taxi skidded to a halt. She turned back to face me. 'Thanks for dinner,' she managed, not altogether convincingly, and added, even less convincingly, 'Perhaps we'll meet again.' Before I could respond, she had slammed the taxi door closed.

As I watched her being driven away, it started to rain.

I took one more look at my immovable car, and decided I would deal with the problem in the morning.

I was about to rush for the nearest shelter when another taxi came around the corner, its yellow light indicating that it was for hire. I waved frantically and it drew up beside my clamped car.

'Bad luck, mate,' said the cabbie, looking down at my front wheel. 'My third tonight.'

I attempted a smile.

'So, where to, guv?'

I gave him my address in Lambeth and climbed into the back.

As the taxi manoeuvred its way slowly through the rainswept post-theatre traffic and across Waterloo Bridge, the driver began chattering away. I just about managed monosyllabic replies to his opinions on the weather, John Major, the England cricket team and foreign tourists. With each new topic, his forecast became ever more gloomy.

He only stopped offering his opinions when he came to a halt outside my house in Fentiman Road. I paid him, and smiled ruefully at the thought that this would be the first time in weeks that I'd managed to get home before midnight. I walked slowly up the short path to the front door.

I turned the key in the lock and opened the door quietly, so as not to wake my wife. Once inside I went through my nightly ritual of slipping off my jacket and shoes before creeping quietly up the stairs.

Before I had reached the bedroom I began to get undressed. After years of coming in at one or two in the morning, I was able to take off all my clothes, fold and stack them, and slide under the sheets next to Judy without waking her. But just as I pulled back the cover she said drowsily, 'I didn't think you'd be home so early, with all the problems you were facing tonight.' I wondered if she was talking in her sleep. 'How much damage did the fire do?'

'The fire?' I said, standing in the nude.

'In Davies Street. Gerald phoned a few moments after you'd left to say a fire had started in the kitchen and had spread to the restaurant. He was just checking to make certain you were on your way. He'd cancelled all the bookings for the next two weeks, but he didn't think they'd be able to open again for at least a month. I told him that as you'd left just after six you'd be with him at any minute. So, just how bad is the damage?'

I was already dressed by the time Judy was awake enough to ask why I had never turned up at the restaurant. I shot down the stairs and out onto the street in search of another cab. It had started raining again.

A taxi swung round and came to a halt in front of me.

'Where to this time, guv?'

À Point

'THANK YOU, MICHAEL. I'D LIKE THAT.'

I smiled, unable to mask my delight.

'Hi, Pipsqueak. I thought I might have missed you.'

I turned and stared at a tall man with a mop of fair hair, who seemed unaffected by the steady flow of people trying to pass him on either side.

Anna gave him a smile that I hadn't seen until that moment.

'Hello, Jonathan,' she said. 'This is Michael Whitaker. You're lucky – he bought your ticket, and if you hadn't turned up I was just about to accept his kind invitation to dinner. Michael, this is my brother, Jonathan – the one who was held up at the hospital. As you can see, he's now escaped.'

I couldn't think of a suitable reply.

Jonathan shook me warmly by the hand. 'Thank you for keeping my sister company,' he said. 'Won't you join us for dinner?'

'That's kind of you,' I replied, 'but I've just remembered that I'm meant to be somewhere else right now. I'd better . . .'

'You're not meant to be anywhere else right now,'

interrupted Anna, giving me the same smile. 'Don't be so feeble.' She linked her arm in mine. 'In any case, we'd *both* like you to join us.'

'Thank you,' I said.

'There's a restaurant just down the road that I've been told is rather good,' said Jonathan, as the three of us began walking off in the direction of the Strand.

'Great. I'm famished,' said Anna.

'So, tell me all about the play,' Jonathan said as Anna linked her other arm in his.

'Every bit as good as the critics promised,' said Anna.

'You were unlucky to miss it,' I said.

'But I'm rather glad you did,' said Anna as we reached the corner of the Strand.

'I think that's the place I'm looking for,' said Jonathan, pointing to a large grey double door on the far side of the road. The three of us weaved our way through the temporarily stationary traffic.

Once we reached the other side of the road Jonathan pushed open one of the grey doors to allow us through. It started to rain just as we stepped inside. He led Anna and me down a flight of stairs into a basement restaurant buzzing with the talk of people who had just come out of theatres, and waiters dashing, plates in both hands, from table to table.

'I'll be impressed if you can get a table here,' Anna said to her brother, eyeing a group of would-be customers who were clustered round the bar, impatiently waiting for someone to leave. 'You should have booked,' she added as he began waving at the head waiter, who was fully occupied taking a customer's order.

I remained a yard or two behind them, and as Mario came across, I put a finger to my lips and nodded to him.

'I don't suppose you have a table for three?' asked Jonathan.

'Yes, of course, sir. Please follow me,' said Mario, leading us to a quiet table in the corner of the room.

'That was a bit of luck,' said Jonathan.

'It certainly was,' Anna agreed. Jonathan suggested that I take the far chair, so his sister could sit between us.

Once we had settled, Jonathan asked what I would like to drink.

'How about you?' I said, turning to Anna. 'Another dry martini?'

Jonathan looked surprised. 'You haven't had a dry martini since . . .'

Anna scowled at him and said quickly, 'I'll just have a glass of wine with the meal.'

Since when? I wondered, but only said, 'I'll have the same.'

Mario reappeared, and handed us our menus. Jonathan and Anna studied theirs in silence for some time before Jonathan asked, 'Any ideas?'

'It all looks so tempting,' Anna said. 'But I think I'll settle for the fettucini and a glass of red wine.'

'What about a starter?' asked Jonathan.

'No. I'm on first call tomorrow, if you remember – unless of course you're volunteering to take my place.'

393

'Not after what I've been through this evening, Pipsqueak. I'd rather go without a starter too,' he said. 'How about you, Michael? Don't let our domestic problems get in your way.'

'Fettucini and a glass of red wine would suit me just fine.'

'Three fettucini and a bottle of your best Chianti,' said Jonathan when Mario returned.

Anna leaned over to me and whispered conspiratorially, 'It's the only Italian wine he can pronounce correctly.'

'What would have happened if we'd chosen fish?' I asked her.

'He's also heard of Frascati, but he's never quite sure what he's meant to do when someone orders duck.'

'What are you two whispering about?' asked Jonathan as he handed his menu back to Mario.

'I was asking your sister about the third partner in the practice.'

'Not bad, Michael,' Anna said. 'You should have gone into politics.'

'My wife, Elizabeth, is the third partner,' Jonathan said, unaware of what Anna had been getting at. 'She, poor darling, is on call tonight.'

'You note, two women and one man,' said Anna as the wine waiter appeared by Jonathan's side.

'Yes. There used to be four of us,' said Jonathan, without explanation. He studied the label on the bottle before nodding sagely.

'You're not fooling anyone, Jonathan. Michael has

already worked out that you're no sommelier,' said Anna, sounding as if she was trying to change the subject. The waiter extracted the cork and poured a little wine into Jonathan's glass for him to taste.

'So, what do you do, Michael?' asked Jonathan after he had given a second nod to the wine waiter. 'Don't tell me you're a doctor, because I'm not looking for another man to join the practice.'

'No, he's in the restaurant business,' said Anna, as three bowls of fettucini were placed in front of us.

'I see. You two obviously swapped life histories during the interval,' said Jonathan. 'But what does being "in the restaurant business" actually mean?'

'I'm on the management side,' I explained. 'Or at least, that's what I do nowadays. I started life as a waiter, then I moved into the kitchens for about five years, and finally ended up in management.'

'But what does a restaurant manager actually do?' asked Anna.

'Obviously the interval wasn't long enough for you to go into any great detail,' said Jonathan as he jabbed his fork into some fettucini.

'Well, at the moment I'm running three restaurants in the West End, which means I never stop dashing from one to the other, depending on which is facing the biggest crisis on that particular day.'

'Sounds a bit like ward duty to me,' said Anna. 'So who turned out to have the biggest crisis today?'

'Today, thank heaven, was not typical,' I said with feeling.

'That bad?' said Jonathan.

'Yes, I'm afraid so. We lost a chef this morning who cut off the top of his finger, and won't be back at work for at least a fortnight. My head waiter in our second restaurant is off, claiming he has 'flu, and I've just had to sack the barman in the third for fiddling the books. Barmen always fiddle the books, of course, but in this case even the customers began to notice what he was up to.' I paused. 'But I still wouldn't want to be in any other . . .'

A shrill ring interrupted me. I couldn't tell where the sound was coming from until Jonathan removed a tiny cellular phone from his jacket pocket.

'Sorry about this,' he said. 'Hazard of the job.' He pressed a button and put the phone to his ear. He listened for a few seconds, and a frown appeared on his face. 'Yes, I suppose so. I'll be there as quickly as I can.' He flicked the phone closed and put it back into his pocket.

'Sorry,' he repeated. 'One of my patients has chosen this particular moment to have a relapse. I'm afraid I'm going to have to leave you.' He stood up and turned to his sister. 'How will you get home, Pipsqueak?'

'I'm a big girl now,' said Anna, 'so I'll just look around for one of those black objects on four wheels with a sign on the top that reads T-A-X-I, and then I'll wave at it.'

'Don't worry, Jonathan,' I said. 'I'll drive her home.'

'That's very kind of you,' said Jonathan, 'because if it's still pouring by the time you leave, she may not be able to find one of those black objects to wave at.'

'In any case, it's the least I can do, after I ended up getting your ticket, your dinner and your sister.'

'Fair exchange,' said Jonathan as Mario came rushing up.

'Is everything all right, sir?' he asked.

'No, it isn't. I'm on call, and have to go.' He handed over an American Express card. 'If you'd be kind enough to put this through your machine, I'll sign for it and you can fill in the amount later. And please add fifteen per cent.'

'Thank you, sir,' said Mario, and rushed away.

'Hope to see you again,' said Jonathan. I rose to shake him by the hand.

'I hope so too,' I said.

Jonathan left us, headed for the bar and signed a slip of paper. Mario handed him back his American Express card.

As Anna waved to her brother, I looked towards the bar and shook my head slightly. Mario tore up the little slip of paper and dropped the pieces into a waste-paper basket.

'It hasn't been a wonderful day for Jonathan, either,' said Anna, turning back to face me. 'And what with your problems, I'm amazed you were able to take the evening off.'

'I shouldn't have, really, and wouldn't have, except . . .' I trailed off as I leaned over and topped up Anna's glass.

'Except what?' she asked.

'Do you want to hear the truth?' I asked as I poured the remains of the wine into my own glass.

'I'll try that for starters,' she said.

397

I placed the empty bottle on the side of the table, and hesitated, but only for a moment. 'I was driving to one of my restaurants earlier this evening, when I spotted you going into the theatre. I stared at you for so long that I nearly crashed into the back of the car in front of me. Then I swerved across the road into the nearest parking space, and the car behind almost crashed into me. I leapt out, ran all the way to the theatre, and searched everywhere until I saw you standing in the queue for the box office. I joined the line and watched you hand over your spare ticket. Once you were safely out of sight, I told the box office manager that you hadn't expected me to make it in time, and that you might have put my ticket up for resale. After I'd described you, which I was able to do in great detail, he handed it over without so much as a murmur.'

Anna put down her glass of wine and stared across at me with a look of incredulity. 'I'm glad he fell for your story,' she said. 'But should I?'

'Yes, you should. Because then I put two ten-pound notes into a theatre envelope and took the place next to you,' I continued. 'The rest you already know.' I waited to see how she would react. She didn't speak for some time.

'I'm flattered,' she said eventually. 'I didn't realise there were any old-fashioned romantics left in the world.' She lowered her head slightly. 'Am I allowed to ask what you have planned for the rest of the evening?'

'Nothing has been planned so far,' I admitted. 'Which is why it's all been so refreshing.'

'You make me sound like an After Eight mint,' said Anna with a laugh.

'I can think of at least three replies to that,' I told her as Mario reappeared, looking a little disappointed at the sight of the half-empty plates.

'Is everything all right, sir?' he asked, sounding anxious.

'Couldn't have been better,' said Anna, who hadn't stopped looking at me.

'Would you like a coffee, madam?' Mario asked her.

'No, thank you,' said Anna firmly. 'We have to go in search of a marooned car.'

'Heaven knows if it will still be there after all this time,' I said as she rose from her place.

I took Anna's hand, led her towards the entrance, back up the stairs and out onto the street. Then I began to retrace my steps to the spot where I'd abandoned my car. As we strolled up the Aldwych and chatted away, I felt as if I was with an old friend.

'You don't have to give me a lift, Michael,' Anna was saying. 'It's probably miles out of your way, and in any case it's stopped raining, so I'll just hail a taxi.'

'I want to give you a lift,' I told her. 'That way I'll have your company for a little longer.' She smiled as we reached a distressingly large space where I had left the car.

'Damn,' I said. I quickly checked up and down the road, and returned to find Anna laughing.

'Is this another of your schemes to have more of my company?' she teased. She opened her bag and took out a mobile phone, dialled 999, and passed it over to me.

'Which service do you require? Fire, Police or Ambulance?' a voice asked.

'Police,' I said, and was immediately put through to another voice.

'Charing Cross Police Station. What is the nature of your enquiry?'

'I think my car has been stolen.'

'Can you tell me the make, colour and registration number please, sir.'

'It's a blue Rover 600, registration K857 SHV.'

There was a long pause, during which I could hear other voices talking in the background.

'No, it hasn't been stolen, sir,' said the officer who had been dealing with me when he came back on the line. 'The vehicle was illegally parked on a double yellow line. It's been removed and taken to the Vauxhall Bridge Pound.'

'Can I pick it up now?' I asked.

'Certainly, sir. How will you be getting there?'

'I'll take a taxi.'

'Then just ask the driver for the Vauxhall Bridge Pound. Once you get there, you'll need some form of identification, and a cheque for £105 with a banker's card – that is if you don't have the full amount in cash.'

'£105?' I said quietly.

'That's correct, sir.'

Anna frowned for the first time that evening.

'Worth every penny.'

'I beg your pardon, sir?'

'Nothing, officer. Goodnight.'

I handed the phone back to Anna, and said, 'The next thing I'm going to do is find you a taxi.'

'You certainly are not, Michael, because I'm staying with you. In any case, you promised my brother you'd take me home.'

I took her hand and hailed a taxi, which swung across the road and came to a halt beside us.

'Vauxhall Bridge Pound, please.'

'Bad luck, mate,' said the cabbie. 'You're my fourth this evening.'

I gave him a broad grin.

'I expect the other three also chased you into the theatre, but luckily they were behind me in the queue,' I said to Anna as I joined her on the back seat.

As the taxi manoeuvred its way slowly through the rainswept post-theatre traffic and across Waterloo Bridge, Anna said, 'Don't you think I should have been given the chance to choose between the four of you? After all, one of them might have been driving a Rolls-Royce.'

'Not possible.'

'And why not, pray?' asked Anna.

'Because you couldn't have parked a Rolls-Royce in that space.'

'But if he'd had a chauffeur, that would have solved all my problems.'

'In that case, I would simply have run him over.'

The taxi had travelled some distance before either of us spoke again.

'Can I ask you a personal question?' Anna eventually said.

'If it's what I think it is, I was about to ask you the same thing.'

'Then you go first.'

'No – I'm not married,' I said. 'Nearly, once, but she escaped.' Anna laughed. 'And you?'

'I was married,' she said quietly. 'He was the fourth doctor in the practice. He died three years ago. I spent nine months nursing him, but in the end I failed.'

'I'm so sorry,' I said, feeling a little ashamed. 'That was tactless of me. I shouldn't have raised the subject.'

'I raised it, Michael, not you. It's me who should apologise.'

Neither of us spoke again for several minutes, until Anna said, 'For the past three years, since Andrew's death, I've immersed myself in work, and I seem to spend most of my spare time boring Jonathan and Elizabeth to distraction. They couldn't have been more understanding, but they must be heartily sick of it by now. I wouldn't be surprised if Jonathan hadn't arranged an emergency for tonight, so someone else could take me to the theatre for a change. It might even give me the confidence to go out again. Heaven knows,' she added as we drove into the car pound, 'enough people have been kind enough to ask me.'

I passed the cabbie a ten-pound note and we dashed through the rain in the direction of a little Portakabin.

I walked up to the counter and read the form sellotaped

to it. I took out my wallet, extracted my driving licence, and began counting.

I only had eighty pounds in cash, and I never carry a chequebook.

Anna grinned, and took the envelope I'd presented to her earlier in the evening from her bag. She tore it open and extracted the two ten-pound notes, added a five-pound note of her own, and handed them over to me.

'Thank you,' I said, once again feeling embarrassed.

'Worth every penny,' she replied with a grin.

The policeman counted the notes slowly, placed them in a tin box, and gave me a receipt.

'It's right there, in the front row,' he said, pointing out of the window. 'And if I may say so, sir, it was perhaps unwise of you to leave your keys in the ignition. If the vehicle had been stolen, your insurance company would not have been liable to cover the claim.' He passed me my keys.

'It was my fault, officer,' said Anna. 'I should have sent him back for them, but I didn't realise what he was up to. I'll make sure he doesn't do it again.'

The officer looked up at me. I shrugged my shoulders and led Anna out of the cabin and across to my car. I opened the door to let her in, then nipped round to the driver's side as she leant over and pushed my door open. I took my place behind the wheel and turned to face her. 'I'm sorry,' I said. 'The rain has ruined your dress.' A drop of water fell off the end of her nose. 'But, you know, you're just as beautiful wet or dry.'

'Thank you, Michael,' she smiled. 'But if you don't have any objection, on balance I'd prefer to be dry.'

I laughed. 'So, where shall I take you?' I asked, suddenly aware that I didn't know where she lived.

'Fulham, please. 49 Parsons Green Lane. It's not too far.'

I pushed the key into the ignition, not caring how far it was. I turned the key and took a deep breath. The engine spluttered, but refused to start. Then I realised I had left the sidelights on.

'Don't do this to me,' I begged, as Anna began laughing again. I turned the key a second time, and the motor caught. I let out a sigh of relief.

'That was a close one,' Anna said. 'If it hadn't started, we might have ended up spending the rest of the night together. Or was that all part of your dastardly plan?'

'Nothing's gone to plan so far,' I admitted as I drove out of the pound. I paused before adding, 'Still, I suppose things might have turned out differently.'

'You mean if I hadn't been the sort of girl you were looking for?'

'Something like that.'

'I wonder what those other three men would have thought of me,' said Anna wistfully.

'Who cares? They're not going to have the chance to find out.'

'You sound very sure of yourself, Mr Whitaker.'

'If you only knew,' I said. 'But I would like to see you again, Anna. If you're willing to risk it.'

She seemed to take an eternity to reply. 'Yes, I'd like

that,' she said eventually. 'But only on condition that you pick me up at my place, so I can be certain you park your car legally, and remember to switch your lights off.'

'I accept your terms,' I told her. 'And I won't even add any conditions of my own if we can begin the agreement tomorrow evening.'

Once again Anna didn't reply immediately. 'I'm not sure I know what I'm doing tomorrow evening.'

'Neither do I,' I said. 'But I'll cancel it, whatever it is.'

'Then so will I,' said Anna as I drove into Parsons Green Lane, and began searching for number forty-nine.

'It's about a hundred yards down, on the left,' she said.

I drew up and parked outside her front door.

'Don't let's bother with the theatre this time,' said Anna. 'Come round at about eight, and I'll cook you some supper.' She leant over and kissed me on the cheek before turning back to open the car door. I jumped out and walked quickly round to her side of the car as she stepped onto the pavement.

'So, I'll see you around eight tomorrow evening,' she said.

'I'll look forward to that.' I hesitated, and then took her in my arms. 'Goodnight, Anna.'

'Goodnight, Michael,' she said as I released her. 'And thank you for buying my ticket, not to mention dinner. I'm glad my other three would-be suitors only made it as far as the car pound.'

I smiled as she pushed the key into the lock of her front door.

She turned back. 'By the way, Michael, was that the restaurant with the missing waiter, the four-and-a-half-fingered chef, or the crooked bartender?'

'The crooked bartender,' I replied with a smile.

She closed the door behind her as the clock on a nearby church struck one.

FIRST
AMONG
EQUALS

To Alan and Eddie

Raymond Gould

Simon Kerslake

Charles Seymour

Andrew Fraser

PROLOGUE

WEDNESDAY 10 APRIL 1931

If Charles Gurney Seymour had been born nine minutes earlier he would have become an earl, inherited a castle in Scotland, 22,000 acres in Somerset, and a thriving merchant bank in the City of London.

It was to be several years before young Charles worked out the full significance of coming second in life's first race.

His twin brother, Rupert, only just came through the ordeal, and in the years that followed contracted not only the usual childhood illnesses but managed to add scarlet fever, diphtheria and meningitis, causing his mother, Lady Seymour, to fear for his survival.

Charles, on the other hand, *was* a survivor, and had inherited enough Seymour ambition for both his brother and himself. Only a few years passed before those who came into contact with the brothers for the first time mistakenly assumed Charles was the heir to the earldom.

As the years passed Charles's father tried desperately to discover something at which Rupert might triumph over his brother – and failed. When they were eight the two boys were sent away to Summer Fields where generations of Seymours had been prepared for the rigours of Eton. During his first month at the Oxford prep school Charles was voted form captain and no one hindered his advance *en route* to becoming head boy at the age of twelve, by which time Rupert was looked upon as Seymour Minor. Both boys proceeded to Eton, where in their first half Charles beat

Rupert at every subject in the classroom, outrowed him on the river and nearly killed him in the boxing ring.

When in 1947 their grandfather, the thirteenth Earl of Bridgwater, finally expired, the sixteen-year-old Rupert became Viscount Seymour while Charles inherited a meaningless prefix.

The Hon Charles Seymour felt angry every time he heard his brother deferentially addressed by strangers as 'My Lord'.

At Eton, Charles continued to excel and ended his schooldays as President of Pop before being offered a place at Christ Church, Oxford, to read History. Rupert covered the same years without over-burdening the examiners, internal or external. At the age of eighteen the young viscount returned to the family estate in Somerset to pass the rest of his days as a landowner. No one destined to inherit 22,000 acres could be described as a farmer.

At Oxford, Charles, free of Rupert's shadow, progressed with the air of a man who found the university something of an anticlimax. He would spend his weekdays reading the history of his relations and the weekends at house parties or riding to hounds. As no one had suggested for one moment that Rupert should enter the world of high finance, it was assumed once Charles had left Oxford that he would succeed his father at Seymour's Bank: first as a director and then in time as its chairman: although it would be Rupert who would eventually inherit the family shareholding.

This 'best laid plan' changed, however, when one evening the Hon Charles Seymour was dragged off to the Oxford Union by a nubile undergraduate from Somerville, who demanded he should listen to the Eights Week motion, 'I would rather be a commoner than a lord'. The President of the Union had achieved the unique coup of having the motion proposed by the Prime Minister, Sir Winston Churchill.

Charles sat at the back of a hall packed with eager students mesmerised by the elder statesman's performance. Never once did he take his eyes off the great war leader during his witty and powerful speech, although what kept flashing across his mind was the realisation that, but for an accident of birth, Churchill would have been the ninth Duke of Marlborough. Here was a man who had dominated the world stage for three decades and then turned down every hereditary honour a grateful nation could offer, including the title of Duke of London.

From that moment Charles never allowed himself to be referred to as 'the Hon' again: his ultimate ambition was now above mere titles.

Another undergraduate who listened to Churchill that night was also considering his future. But he did not view proceedings crammed between his fellow students at the back of the crowded hall. The tall young man dressed in white tie and tails sat alone in a large chair on a raised platform, for such was his right as President of the Oxford Union.

Although Simon Kerslake *was* the first-born, he had otherwise few of Charles Seymour's advantages. The only son of a family solicitor, he had come to appreciate how much his father had denied himself to ensure that his son should remain at the local public school. Simon's father had died during his son's last year at Lancing College, leaving his widow a small annuity and a magnificent MacKinley grandfather clock. Simon's mother sold the clock a week after the funeral in order that her son could complete his final year with all the 'extras' the other boys took for granted. She also hoped that it would give Simon a better chance of going on to university.

From the first day he could walk Simon had always wanted to outdistance his rivals. The Americans would have described him as 'an achiever', while many of his contemporaries thought of him as pushy, or even arrogant, according to their aptitude for jealousy. During his last term at Lancing Simon was passed over for head of school and he still found himself unable to forgive the headmaster his lack of foresight. Later that year, some weeks after he had completed his S-levels and been interviewed by Magdalen, a circular letter informed him that he would not be offered a place at Oxford; it was a decision Simon was unwilling to accept.

In the same mail Durham University offered him a
scholarship, which he rejected by return of post. "Future
Prime Ministers aren't educated at Durham," he informed
his mother.

"How about Cambridge?" she enquired, continuing to
wipe the dishes.

"No political tradition," replied Simon.

"But if there is no chance of being offered a place at
Oxford, surely –?"

"That's not what I said, Mother," replied the young man.
"I shall be an undergraduate at Oxford by the first day of
term."

After eighteen years of forty-yard goals Mrs Kerslake had
learned to stop asking her son, "How will you manage that?"

Some fourteen days before the start of the Michaelmas Term
at Oxford Simon booked himself into a small guest house just
off the Iffley Road. On a trestle table in the corner of lodgings
he intended to make permanent he wrote out a list of all the
colleges, then divided them into five columns, planning to
visit three each morning and three each afternoon until his
question had been answered positively by a resident Tutor
for Admissions: "Have you accepted any freshmen for this
year who are now unable to take up their places?"

It was on the fourth afternoon, just as doubt was beginning
to set in and Simon was wondering if after all he would have
to travel to Cambridge the following week, that he received
the first affirmative reply.

The Tutor for Admissions at Worcester College removed
the glasses from the end of his nose and stared at the tall
young man with a mop of dark hair falling over his forehead.
Alan Brown was the twenty-second don Kerslake had visited
in four days.

"Yes," he replied. "It so happens that a young man from
Nottingham High School, who had been offered a place here,
was tragically killed in a motor cycle accident last month."

"What course – what subject was he going to read?"
Simon's words were unusually faltering. He prayed it wasn't
Chemistry, Anthropology or Classics. Alan Brown flicked

through a rotary index on his desk, obviously enjoying the little cross-examination. He peered at the card in front of him. "History," he announced.

Simon's heartbeat reached 120. "I just missed a place at Magdalen to read Politics, Philosophy and Economics," he said. "Would you consider me for the vacancy?"

The older man was unable to hide a smile. He had never in twenty-four years come across such a request.

"Full name?" he said, replacing his glasses as if the serious business of the meeting had now begun.

"Simon John Kerslake."

Dr Brown picked up the telephone by his side and dialled a number. "Nigel?" he said. "It's Alan Brown here. Did you ever consider offering a man called Kerslake a place at Magdalen?"

Mrs Kerslake was not surprised when her son went on to be President of the Oxford Union. After all, she teased, wasn't it just another stepping stone on the path to Prime Minister – Gladstone, Asquith . . . Kerslake?

Ray Gould was born in a tiny, windowless room above his father's butcher's shop in Leeds. For the first nine years of his life he shared that room with his ailing grandmother until she died at the age of sixty-one.

Ray's close proximity to the old woman who had lost her husband in the Great War at first appeared romantic to him. He would listen enraptured as she told him stories of her hero husband in his smart khaki uniform – a uniform now folded neatly in her bottom drawer, but still displayed in the fading sepia photograph at the side of her bed. Soon, however, his grandmother's stories filled Ray with sadness, as he became aware that she had been a widow for nearly thirty years. Finally she seemed a tragic figure as he realised how little she had experienced of the world beyond that cramped room in which she was surrounded by all her possessions and a yellowed envelope containing 500 irredeemable war bonds.

There had been no purpose in Ray's grandmother making a will, for all he inherited was the room. Overnight it became his study – full of ever-changing library and school books, the former often returned late, using up Ray's meagre pocket money in fines. But as each school report was brought home it became increasingly apparent to Ray's father that he would not be extending the sign above the butcher's shop to proclaim 'Gould and Son'.

Shortly after his eleventh birthday Ray won the top scholarship to Roundhay School. Wearing his first pair of long trousers – turned up several inches by his mother – and hornrimmed spectacles that didn't quite fit, he set off for the opening day at his new school. Ray's mother hoped there were other boys as thin and spotty as her son, and that his wavy red hair would not cause him to be continually teased.

By the end of his first term Ray was surprised to find he was far ahead of his classmates, so far in fact that the headmaster considered it prudent to put him up a form – "to stretch the lad a little", as he explained to Ray's parents.

By the end of that year, one spent mainly in the classroom, Ray managed to come third in the form, and top in Latin and English. Only when it came to selecting teams for any sport did Ray find he came bottom in anything. However brilliant his mind might have been, it never seemed to co-ordinate with his body. His single greatest academic achievement during the year, though, was to be the youngest winner of the prize essay competition in the school's history.

Each year the winner of the essay was required to read his entry to the assembled pupils and parents on Speech Day. Even before he handed in his entry Ray rehearsed his efforts out loud several times in the privacy of his study-bedroom, fearing he would not be properly prepared if he waited until the winner was announced.

Ray's form master had told all his pupils that the subject of the essay could be of their own choosing, but that they should try to recall some experience that had been unique to them. Thirty-seven entries arrived on his desk by nine o'clock on the closing date six weeks later. After reading Ray's account of his grandmother's life in the little room above the butcher's shop the form master had no inclination to pick up another script. When he had dutifully struggled through the remainder he did not hesitate in recommending Gould's essay for the prize. The only reservation, he admitted to its author, was the choice of title. Ray thanked him for the advice but the title remained intact.

On the morning of Speech Day the school hall was packed with 700 pupils and their parents. After the headmaster had delivered his speech and the applause had died down, he announced, "I shall now call upon the winner of the prize essay competition to deliver his entry: Ray Gould."

Ray left his place in the hall and marched confidently up on to the stage. He stared down at the 2,000 expectant faces but showed no sign of apprehension, partly because he found it difficult to see beyond the third row. When he announced the title of his essay some of the younger children began to snigger, causing Ray to stumble through his first few lines. But by the time he had reached the last page the packed hall was still, and after he had completed the final paragraph he received the first standing ovation of his career.

Twelve-year-old Ray Gould left the stage to rejoin his parents in the body of the hall. His mother's head was bowed but he could still see tears trickling down her cheeks. His father was trying not to look too proud. Even when Ray was seated the applause continued, so he too lowered his head to stare at the title of his prize-winning essay: 'The first changes I will make when I become Prime Minister'.

Andrew Fraser attended his first political meeting in a pram. True, he was left in the corridor while his parents sat on the stage inside another draughty hall, but he quickly learned that applause signalled his mother would soon be returning. What Andrew did not know was that his father, who had made his name as Scotland's finest scrum-half since the Great War, had delivered yet another speech to the citizens of Edinburgh Carlton in his efforts to capture a marginal seat on the City Council. At that time few believed Duncan Fraser was more than a rugby hero, and consequently he failed to win the seat for the Conservatives, if only by a few hundred votes. Three years later Andrew, a sturdy four-year-old, was allowed to sit at the back of several sparsely filled halls as once again he and his mother trailed round the city to support their candidate. This time Duncan Fraser's speeches were almost as impressive as his long pass, and he won his place on the City Council by 207 votes.

Hard work and consistent results on behalf of his constituents ensured that the marginal seat remained in the hands of Councillor Fraser for the next nine years. By the age of thirteen, Andrew, a stocky wee lad with straight black hair and a grin that no one seemed to be able to remove from his face, had learned enough about local politics to help his father organise a fifth campaign, by which time neither party considered Edinburgh Carlton a marginal seat.

At the Edinburgh Academy it came as no surprise to his fellow pupils that Andrew was chosen to captain the school debating society; however, they were impressed when under his leadership the team went on to win the Scottish Schools debating trophy. Although Andrew was destined to be no taller than five-foot-nine it was also widely accepted that he was the most complete scrum-half the Academy had produced since his father had captained the school side in 1919.

On matriculating from the Academy Andrew took up a place at Edinburgh University to read Politics, and by his third year he had been elected President of the Union and captain of rugby.

When Duncan Fraser became Lord Provost of Edinburgh he made one of his rare visits to London, to receive a knighthood from the Queen. Andrew had just completed his final exams and, along with his mother, attended the investiture at Buckingham Palace. After the ceremony Sir Duncan travelled on to the House of Commons to fulfil an engagement with his local member, Ainslie Munro. Over lunch Munro informed Sir Duncan that he had contested the Edinburgh Carlton seat for the last time, so they had better start looking for a new candidate. Sir Duncan's eyes lit up as he savoured the thought of his son succeeding Munro as his Member of Parliament.

After Andrew had been awarded an honours degree at Edinburgh, he remained at the university to complete a thesis entitled 'The history of the Conservative party in Scotland'. He planned to wait for his father to complete the

statutory three years as Lord Provost before he informed him
of the most significant outcome the research for his doctor-
ate had produced. But when Ainslie Munro announced
officially that he would not be contesting the next election
Andrew knew he could no longer hide his true feelings if he
wanted to be considered for the seat.

'Like father, like son,' read the headline in the centre-page
of the *Edinburgh Evening News*, who considered that Andrew
Fraser was the obvious candidate if the Conservatives hoped
to hold on to the marginal seat. Sir Duncan, fearing the local
burghers would consider Andrew too young, reminded them
at the first selection meeting that eight Scots had been Prime
Ministers and every one had been in the House before the age
of thirty. He was pleased to find members nodding their
agreement. When Sir Duncan returned home that night he
phoned his son and suggested that they should have lunch at
the New Club the following day to discuss a plan of campaign.

"Think of it," said Sir Duncan, after he had ordered a
second whisky. "Father and son representing the same
constituency. It will be a great day for the Edinburgh
Conservative party."

"Not to mention the Labour party," said Andrew, looking
his father in the eye.

"I am not sure I take your meaning," said the Lord
Provost.

"Precisely that, Father. I do not intend to contest the seat
as a Conservative. I hope to be selected as the Labour
candidate – if they'll adopt me."

Sir Duncan looked disbelieving. "But you've been a Conservative all your life," he declared, his voice rising with
every word.

"No, Father," replied Andrew quietly. "It's you who have
been a Conservative all my life."

BOOK ONE
1964·1966
THE BACK BENCHES

CHAPTER
ONE

THURSDAY 10 DECEMBER 1964

Mr Speaker rose and surveyed the Commons. He tugged at his long black silk gown, then nervously tweaked the full-bottomed wig that covered his balding head. The House had almost got out of control during a particularly rowdy session of Prime Minister's questions, and he was delighted to see the clock reach three-thirty. Time to pass on to the next business of the day.

He stood shifting from foot to foot waiting for the 500-odd members present to settle down before he intoned solemnly, "Members desiring to take the oath." The packed assembly switched its gaze from the Speaker to the far end of the Chamber, like a crowd watching a tennis match. There, standing at the bar of the Commons, was the victor of the first by-election since the Labour party had taken office some two months before.

The new member, flanked by his proposer and seconder, took four paces forward. Like well-drilled guardsmen, they stopped and bowed. The stranger stood at six-foot-four. He looked like a man born with the Tory party in mind, his patrician head set on an aristocratic frame, a mane of fair hair combed meticulously into place. Dressed in a dark grey, double-breasted suit and wearing a Guards' tie of maroon and blue, he advanced once again towards the long table that stood in front of the Speaker's chair between the two front benches which faced each other a mere sword's length apart.

Leaving his sponsors in his wake, he passed down the Government side, stepping over the legs of the Prime

Minister and Foreign Secretary before being handed the oath by the Clerk of the House.

He held the little card in his right hand and pronounced the words as firmly as if they had been his marriage vows.

"I, Charles Seymour, do swear that I will be faithful, and bear true allegiance to Her Majesty Queen Elizabeth, her heirs and successors according to law, so help me God."

"Hear, hear," rose from his colleagues on the benches opposite as the new MP leaned over to subscribe the Test Roll, a parchment folded into book-shape. Charles was introduced to the Speaker by the Clerk. The new member then proceeded towards the chair where he stopped and bowed.

"Welcome to the House, Mr Seymour," said the Speaker, shaking his hand. "I hope you will serve this place for many years to come."

"Thank you, Mr Speaker," said Charles, and bowed for a final time before continuing on behind the Speaker's chair. He had carried out the little ceremony exactly as the Tory Chief Whip had rehearsed it with him in the long corridor outside his office.

Waiting for him behind the Speaker's chair and out of sight of the other members was the leader of the Opposition, Sir Alec Douglas-Home, who also shook him warmly by the hand.

"Congratulations on your splendid victory, Charles. I know you have a great deal to offer to our party and indeed your country."

"Thank you," replied the new MP, who after waiting for Sir Alec to return to take his place on the Opposition front bench made his way up the steps of the side gangway to find a place in the back row of the long green benches.

For the next two hours Charles Seymour followed the proceedings of the House with a mixture of awe and excitement. For the first time in his life he had found something that wasn't his by right or by effortless conquest. Glancing up at the Strangers' Gallery he saw his wife Fiona, his father the fourteenth Earl of Bridgwater and his brother, the Viscount Seymour, peering down at him with pride. Charles settled back on the first rung of the ladder. He smiled to himself: only six weeks ago he had feared it would be many more years before he could hope to take a seat in the House of Commons.

At the general election a mere two months before, Charles had contested a South Wales mining seat with an impregnable Labour majority. "Good for the experience, not to mention the soul," the vice-chairman in charge of candidates at Conservative Central Office had assured him. He had proved to be right on both counts, for Charles had relished the contest and brought the Labour majority down from 22,300 to 20,100. His wife had aptly described it as a 'dent', but it had turned out to be enough of a dent for the party to put Charles's name forward for the Sussex Downs seat when Sir Eric Koops had died of a heart attack only a few days after Parliament had assembled. Six weeks later Charles Seymour sat in the Commons with a 20,000 majority of his own.

Charles listened to one more speech before leaving the Chamber. He stood alone in the Members' Lobby not quite certain where to begin. Another young member strode purposefully towards him. "Allow me to introduce myself," the stranger said, sounding to Charles every bit like a fellow Conservative. "My name is Andrew Fraser. I'm the Labour member for Edinburgh Carlton and I was hoping you hadn't yet found yourself a pair." Charles admitted that so far he hadn't found much more than the Chamber. The Tory Chief Whip had already explained to him that most members paired with someone from the opposite party for voting purposes, and that it would be wise for him to select someone of his own age. When there was a debate on less crucial issues a two-line whip came into operation: pairing made it possible for members to miss the vote and return home to their wife and family before midnight. However, no member was allowed to miss the vote when there was a three-line whip.

"I'd be delighted to pair with you," continued Charles. "Am I expected to do anything official?"

"No," said Andrew, looking up at him. "I'll just drop you a line confirming the arrangement. If you'd be kind enough to reply letting me have all the phone numbers where you can be contacted we'll just take it from there. Any time you need to miss a vote just let me know."

"Sounds a sensible arrangement to me," said Charles as a rotund figure wearing a light grey three-piece suit, blue shirt and a pink-spotted bow tie trundled over towards them.

"Welcome to the club, Charles," said Alec Pimkin. "Care to join me for a drink in the smoking room and I'll brief you on how this bloody place works."

"Thank you," said Charles, relieved to see someone he knew. Andrew smiled when he heard Pimkin add, "It's just like being back at school, old chum," as the two Tories retreated in the direction of the smoking room. Andrew suspected that it wouldn't be long before Charles Seymour was showing his 'old school chum' just how the bloody place really worked.

Andrew also left the Members' Lobby but not in search of a drink. He had to attend a meeting of the Parliamentary Labour party at which the following week's business was due to be discussed. He hurried away.

Andrew had been duly selected as the Labour candidate for Edinburgh Carlton and had gone on to capture the seat from the Conservatives by a majority of 3,419 votes. Sir Duncan, having completed his term as Lord Provost, continued to represent the same seat on the City Council. In six weeks Andrew – the baby of the House – had quickly made a name for himself and many of the older members found it hard to believe that it was his first Parliament.

When Andrew arrived at the party meeting on the second floor of the Commons he found an empty seat near the back of the large committee room and settled down to listen to the Government Chief Whip go over the business for the following week. Once again it seemed to consist of nothing but three-line whips. He glanced down at the piece of paper in front of him. The debates scheduled for Tuesday, Wednesday and Thursday all had three thick lines drawn under them: only Monday and Friday had two-liners which at least after his agreement with Charles Seymour he could arrange to miss. The Labour party might have returned to power after thirteen years but, with a majority of only four and a full legislative programme, it was proving almost impossible for members to get to bed much before midnight during the week.

As the Chief Whip sat down the first person to jump to his feet was Tom Carson, the new member for Liverpool Dockside. He launched into a tirade of abuse against the Government, complaining that they were looking more like Tories every day. The under-the-breath remarks and coughing that continued during his speech showed how little support there was for his views. Tom Carson had also made a name for himself in a very short time, for he had openly attacked his own party from the first day he had arrived.

"Enfant terrible," muttered the man sitting on the right of Andrew.

"Those aren't the words I'd use to describe him," muttered Andrew. "Altogether too many letters." The man with wavy red hair smiled as they listened to Carson ranting on.

If Raymond Gould had acquired any reputation during those first six weeks it was as one of the party's intellectuals, and for that reason older members were immediately suspicious of him, although few doubted he would be among the first from the new intake to be promoted to the front bench. Not many of them had really got to know Raymond as the north-countryman appeared remarkably reserved for someone who had chosen a career in public life. But with a majority of over 10,000 in his Leeds constituency he looked destined for a long career.

Leeds North had chosen Raymond to be their candidate from a field of thirty-seven, when he showed himself to be so much better informed than a local trade-union official whom the press had tipped as favourite for the seat. Yorkshire folk like people who stay at home and Raymond had been quick to point out to the selection committee – in an exaggerated Yorkshire accent – that he had been educated at Roundhay School on the fringes of the constituency. But what really tipped the vote in his favour had been Raymond's refusal of an open scholarship to Cambridge. He had preferred to continue his education at Leeds University, he explained.

Raymond took a first-class honours degree in Law at

Leeds before moving to London to complete his studies for the bar at Lincoln's Inn. At the end of his two-year course Raymond joined a fashionable London chambers to become a much sought-after junior counsel. From that moment he rarely mentioned his family background to his carefully cultivated circle of Home Counties friends, and those comrades who addressed him as Ray received a sharp 'Raymond' for their familiarity.

When the last question had been asked, the party meeting broke up, and Raymond and Andrew made their way out of the committee room – Andrew for his tiny office on the second floor to finish off the day's mail, Raymond to return to the Chamber as he hoped to deliver his maiden speech that day. He had waited patiently for the right moment to express his views to the House on the subject of widows' pensions and the redemption of war bonds, and the debate in progress on the economy was an obvious opportunity. The Speaker had dropped Raymond a note earlier in the day saying he expected to call him some time that evening.

Raymond had spent many hours in the Chamber, carefully studying the techniques demanded by the House and noting how they differed from those of the law courts. F. E. Smith had been right in his assessment of his colleagues when he had described the Commons as nothing more than a noisy courtroom with over 600 jurors and absolutely no sign of a judge. Raymond was dreading the ordeal of his maiden speech; the dispassionate logic of his arguments had always proved more appealing to judges than to juries.

As he approached the Chamber an attendant handed him a note from his wife Joyce. She had just arrived at the Commons and had been found a seat in the Strangers' Gallery so that she could be present for his speech. After only a cursory glance Raymond scrunched up the note, dropped it into the nearest waste-paper basket and hurried on towards the Chamber.

The door was held open for him by a Conservative member who was on his way out.

"Thank you," said Raymond. Simon Kerslake smiled back, trying in vain to recall the man's name. Once Simon

was in the Members' Lobby he checked the message board to
see if the light under his name was lit up. It wasn't, so he
continued on through the swing doors to the right of the
lobby on his way down past the cloisters to the Members' Car
Park. Once he had found his car he headed off in the direction
of St Mary's, Paddington, to pick up his wife. They had seen
little of each other during Simon's first six weeks in Parliament which made the thought of tonight even more enjoy-
able. Simon couldn't see any easing of the pressure until
there was another general election and one party had gained
a sensible working majority. But what he feared most –
having won his seat by the slimmest of margins – was that
such a working majority would not include him and he might
end up with one of the shortest political careers on record.
After such a prolonged stretch of Tory rule the new Labour
Government was looking fresh, idealistic and certain to
increase their numbers whenever the Prime Minister chose
to go to the country.

Once Simon had reached Hyde Park Corner he headed on
up towards Marble Arch thinking back over how he had
become a member. On leaving Oxford he had completed
two years' national service with the Sussex Yeomanry,
finishing his military days as a second lieutenant. After a
short holiday he had joined the BBC as a general trainee. He
spent five years moving from drama, to sport, to current
affairs before being appointed a producer on 'Panorama'.
During those early days in London he had rented a small flat
in Earl's Court and continued his interest in politics by
becoming a member of the Tory Bow Group. When he
became the Group's secretary he helped to organise meetings, and had then progressed to writing pamphlets and
speaking at weekend conferences before being invited to
work at Central Office as personal assistant to the chairman
during the 1959 election campaign.

Two years later Simon met Elizabeth Drummond when
'Panorama' carried out an investigation into the National
Health Service and she had been invited to be a participant.
Over drinks before the programme Elizabeth made it per-
fectly clear to Simon that she distrusted media men and

detested politicians. They were married a year later. Elizabeth had since given birth to two sons, and with only a small break on each occasion she had continued her career as a doctor.

Simon had left the BBC somewhat abruptly when, in the summer of 1964, he had been offered the chance to defend the marginal constituency of Coventry Central. He held on to the seat at the general election by a majority of 918.

Simon drove up to the gates of St Mary's and checked his watch. He was a few minutes early. He pushed back the mop of brown hair from his forehead and thought about the evening ahead. He was taking Elizabeth out to celebrate their fourth wedding anniversary, and had prepared one or two surprises for her. Dinner at Mario & Franco, followed by dancing at the Establishment Club, and then home together for the first time in weeks.

"Um," he said, savouring the thought.

"Hi, stranger," said the lady who jumped in beside him and gave him a kiss. Simon stared at the woman with a perfect smile and long fair hair that turned up at the shoulder. He had stared at her when she had first arrived at the 'Panorama' studio that night nearly five years before and he had hardly stopped staring since.

He switched on the ignition. "Want to hear some good news?" he asked, and answered his own question before she could reply. "I'm paired for tonight. That means dinner at Mario & Franco, dancing at the Establishment, home and . . .'

"Do you want to hear the bad news?" asked Elizabeth, also not waiting for a reply. "There's a shortage of staff because of the flu epidemic. I have to be back on duty by ten o'clock."

Simon switched off the ignition. "Well, which would you prefer?" he asked. "Dinner, dancing or straight home?"

Elizabeth laughed. "We've got three hours," she said. "So we might even find time for dinner."

CHAPTER
TWO

Raymond Gould stared down at the invitation. He had never seen the inside of No. 10 Downing Street. During the last thirteen years few Socialists had. He passed the embossed card across the breakfast table to his wife.

"Should I accept or refuse, Ray?" she asked in her broad Yorkshire accent.

She was the only person who still called him Ray, and even her attempts at humour now annoyed him. The Greek tragedians had based their drama on 'the fatal flaw', and he had no doubt what his had been.

He had met Joyce at a dance given by the nurses of Leeds General Infirmary. He hadn't wanted to go but a second-year undergraduate friend from Roundhay convinced him it would make an amusing break. At school he had shown little interest in girls as his mother kept reminding him that there would be occasion enough for that sort of thing once he had taken his degree. By the time he graduated he felt certain that he was the only virgin left at the university.

He had ended up sitting on his own in the corner of a room decorated with wilting balloons and Day-glo orange crêpe paper. He sucked disconsolately at a shandy through a bent straw. Whenever his school friend turned round from the dance floor – each time with a different partner – Raymond would smile broadly back. With his National Health spectacles tucked away in an inside pocket, he couldn't always be certain he was smiling at the right person. He began contemplating at what hour he could possibly leave without having to admit the evening had been a total disaster. He wouldn't even have answered her question if it hadn't been for that familiar accent.

"You at the university as well?"

"As well as what?" he asked, without looking directly at her.

"As well as your friend," she said.

"Yes," he replied, looking up at a girl he guessed was about his age.

"I'm from Bradford."

"I'm from Leeds," he admitted, aware he was going redder by the second.

"My name is Joyce," she volunteered.

"Mine's Ray — Raymond," he said.

"Like to dance?"

He wanted to tell her that he had rarely been on a dance floor before in his life but he didn't have the courage. Like a puppet he found himself standing up and being guided by her towards the jivers. So much for his assumption that he was one of nature's leaders.

Once they were on the dance floor he looked at her properly for the first time. She wasn't half bad, any normal Yorkshire boy might have admitted. She was about five-foot-seven, and her auburn hair was tied up in a pony-tail, matching the dark brown eyes that had a little too much make-up round them. She wore pink lipstick, the same colour as her short skirt from which emerged two very attractive legs. They looked even more attractive when she twirled to the music of the four-piece student band. Raymond discovered that if he twirled Joyce very fast he could see the tops of her stockings, and he remained on the dance floor for longer than he would ever have thought possible. After the quartet had put their instruments away Joyce kissed him goodnight. He walked slowly back to his small room above the butcher's shop.

The following Sunday, in an attempt to gain the upper hand, he took Joyce rowing on the Aire, but his performance was no better than his dancing, and everything on the river overtook him including a hardy swimmer. He watched out of the side of his eyes for a mocking laugh but Joyce only smiled and chatted about missing Bradford and wanting to return home to nurse. After only a few weeks at university Raymond knew he wanted to get away from Leeds, but he didn't admit it to anyone. When he eventually returned the boat Joyce invited him back to her digs for tea. He went scarlet as they passed her landlady. Joyce hustled him up the worn stone staircase to her room.

Raymond sat on the end of the narrow bed while Joyce made two milkless mugs of tea. After they had both pretended to drink she sat beside him, her hands in her lap. He found himself listening intently to an ambulance siren as it faded away in the distance. She leaned over and kissed him, taking one of his hands and placing it on her knee.

She parted his lips and their tongues touched: he found it a peculiar sensation, an arousing one; his eyes remained closed as she gently led him through each new experience, until he was unable to stop himself committing what he felt sure his mother had once described as a mortal sin.

"It will be easier next time," she said shyly, manoeuvring herself from the narrow bed to sort out the crumpled clothes spread across the floor. She was right: he wanted her again in less than an hour, and this time his eyes remained wide open.

It was another six months before Joyce talked about their future and by then Raymond was bored with her and had his sights set on a bright little mathematician in her final year. The mathematician hailed from Surrey.

Just at the time Raymond was summoning up enough courage to let her know the affair was over Joyce told him she was pregnant. His father would have taken a meat axe to him had he suggested an illegal abortion. His mother was only relieved that she was a Yorkshire girl; like the county cricket selection committee, Mrs Gould did not approve of outsiders.

Raymond and Joyce were married at St Mary's in Bradford during the long vacation. When the wedding photos were developed Raymond looked so distressed and Joyce so happy they resembled father and daughter rather than husband and wife. After a reception given at the church hall the newly-married couple travelled down to Dover to catch the night ferry. Their first night as Mr and Mrs Gould was a disaster. Raymond turned out to be a particularly bad sailor. Joyce only hoped that Paris would prove to be memorable – and it was. She had a miscarriage on the second night of their honeymoon.

"Probably caused by all the excitement," his mother said on their return. "Still, you can always have another, can't you? And this time folk won't be able to call it a little . . ." She checked herself.

Raymond showed no interest in having another. Ten years had passed since that memorable honeymoon; he had escaped to London and become a barrister, but had long since accepted that he was tethered to her for life. Although Joyce was only thirty-two she already needed to cover those once-slim legs that had first so attracted him. How could he be so punished for such a pathetic mistake? Raymond wanted to ask the gods. How mature he had thought he was: how immature he had turned out to be. Divorce made sense, but it would have meant the end of his political ambitions: Yorkshire folk would not have considered selecting a divorced man. To be fair, it hadn't all been a disaster: he had to admit that the locals adored her, and his parents seemed every bit as proud of Joyce as they did of their son. She mixed with the trade unionists and their frightful wives far better than he ever managed. He also had to acknowledge that Joyce had been a major factor in his winning the seat by over 10,000 votes. He wondered how she could sound so sincere the whole time: it never occurred to him that it was natural.

"Why don't you buy yourself a new dress for Downing Street?" Raymond said as they rose from the breakfast table. She smiled: he had not volunteered such a suggestion for as long as she could remember. Joyce had been left with no illusions about her husband and his feelings for her, but hoped that eventually he would realise she could help him achieve his unspoken ambition.

On the night of the reception at Downing Street Joyce made every effort to look her best. She had spent the morning at

Harvey Nichols searching for an outfit appropriate for the occasion, finally returning to a suit she had liked the moment she had walked in to the store. It was not the perfect fit but the sales assistant assured Joyce that "Modom looked quite sensational in it". She only hoped that Raymond's remarks would be half as flattering. By the time she reached home she realised she had nothing to match the unusual colour.

Raymond was late returning from the Commons and was pleased to find Joyce ready when he leaped out of the bath. He bit back a remark about the incongruity of her shoes and new suit. As they drove towards Westminster he rehearsed the names of every member of the Cabinet with her, making Joyce repeat them as if she were a child.

The air was cool and crisp that night so Raymond parked his Sunbeam in New Palace Yard and they strolled across Whitehall together to No. 10. A solitary policeman stood guard at the door. Seeing Raymond approach, the officer banged the brass knocker once and the door was opened for the young member and his wife.

Raymond and Joyce stood awkwardly in the hall as if they were waiting outside a headmaster's study. Eventually they were directed to the first floor. They walked slowly up the staircase, which turned out to be less grand than Raymond had anticipated, passing photographs of former Prime Ministers. "Too many Tories," muttered Raymond as he passed Chamberlain, Churchill, Eden, Macmillan and Home, with Attlee the only framed compensation.

At the top of the stairs stood Harold Wilson, pipe in mouth, waiting to welcome his guests. Raymond was about to introduce his wife when the Prime Minister said, "How are you, Joyce? I'm so glad you could make it."

"Make it? I've been looking forward to the occasion all week." Her frankness made Raymond wince; he failed to notice that it made Wilson chuckle.

Raymond chatted to the Prime Minister's wife about the difficulty of getting poetry published until she turned away to greet the next guest. He then moved off into the drawing-room and was soon talking to Cabinet ministers, trade union leaders and their wives, always keeping a wary eye on Joyce, who seemed engrossed in conversation with the General Secretary of the Trades Union Congress.

Raymond moved on to the American Ambassador, who was telling Andrew Fraser how much he had enjoyed the Edinburgh Festival that summer. Raymond envied Fraser his relaxed clubbable manner and had already worked out that the Scotsman would be a formidable rival among his contemporaries.

"Good evening, Raymond," said Andrew. "Do you know David Bruce?" he asked, as if they were old friends.

"No," Raymond replied, rubbing his palm on his trousers before shaking hands. "Good evening, Your Excellency," he said, glad to see Andrew slipping away. "I was interested to read Johnson's latest communiqué on Vietnam and I must confess the escalation . . ."

Andrew had spotted the Minister of State for Scotland arriving and went over to chat to him.

"How are you, Andrew?" Hugh McKenzie asked.

"Never better."

"And your father?"

"In great form."

"I'm sorry to hear that," said the minister, grinning. "He's giving me a lot of trouble over the Highlands and Islands Development Board."

"He's a sound chap basically," said Andrew, "even if his views are a little misguided." They both laughed as a slight, attractive woman with long brown hair came up to the minister's side. She wore a white silk blouse and a McKenzie tartan skirt.

"Do you know my daughter Alison?"

"No," Andrew said, holding out his hand. "I've not had that pleasure."

"I know who you are," she said, in a slight lowland accent, her eyes flashing. "Andrew Fraser, the man who makes Campbells look trustworthy. The Tories' secret mole."

"It can't be much of a secret if the Scottish Office know about it," said Andrew.

A waiter, wearing the smartest dinner-jacket in the room,

approached them carrying a silver tray of thinly-cut sandwiches.

"Would you care for a smoked salmon sandwich?" Alison
asked mockingly.

"No, thank you. I gave them up with my Tory background. But beware – if you eat too many you won't appreciate your dinner tonight."

"I wasn't thinking of having dinner."

"Oh, I thought you might enjoy a bite at Sigie's," teased
Andrew.

Alison hesitated, then said, "It'll be the first time anyone's
picked me up at No. 10."

"I hate to break with tradition," said Andrew. "But why
don't I book a table for eight?"

"Is Sigie's one of your aristocratic haunts?"

"Good heavens no, it's far too good for that lot. Why don't
we leave in about fifteen minutes? I must have a word with
one or two people first."

"I'll bet." She grinned as she watched Fraser comb the
room. His years as a Tory party fellow-traveller had taught
Andrew all he needed to know about how to make the best
use of a cocktail party. His trade union colleagues would
never understand that it was not in pursuit of endless smoked
salmon sandwiches drowned by whisky. When he arrived
back at Alison McKenzie's side she was chatting to
Raymond Gould about Johnson's landslide victory at the
polls.

"Are you trying to pick up my date?" asked Andrew.

Raymond laughed nervously and pushed his spectacles
back up his nose. A moment later Andrew was guiding
Alison towards the door to say their farewells, and Raymond
watching them, wondered if he would ever learn to be that
relaxed. He looked around for Joyce: it might be wise not to
be the last to leave.

Andrew was ushered discreetly to a corner table at Sigie's
Club and it became quickly evident to Alison that he had
been there several times before. The waiters ran around him
as if he were a Tory Cabinet minister, and she had to admit to
herself that she enjoyed the experience. After an excellent

dinner of roast beef that wasn't burnt and a *crème brûlée* that was they strolled over to Annabel's where they danced until the early morning. Andrew drove Alison back to her Chelsea flat a little after two a.m.

"Care for a nightcap?" she asked casually.

"Daren't," he replied. "I'm making my maiden speech tomorrow."

"So this maiden is to be rejected," she said to his retreating back.

The House of Commons was well attended at five o'clock the following afternoon when Andrew rose to address his fellow members. The Speaker had allowed him to follow the front-bench contributions, an honour Andrew would not be granted again for some considerable time. His father and mother looked down over the railings from the Strangers' Gallery as he informed the commoners that the Lord Provost of Edinburgh had spent a lifetime teaching him all he knew about the constituency he was now proud to represent. The Labour party chuckled at the Opposition's obvious discomfort, but they abided by tradition and made no interruption during a maiden speech.

Andrew had chosen as his subject the question of whether Scotland should remain part of the United Kingdom despite the recent oil discoveries. He delivered a well-argued case, assuring members that he saw no future for his country as a tiny independent state. His rhetoric, and his relaxed turn of phrase, had members laughing on both sides of the House. When he came to the end of his argument, never having once referred to a note, he sat down to loud cheers from his own benches and generous acknowledgement from the Tory side. In his moment of glory he glanced up towards the Strangers' Gallery. His father was leaning forward, following every word. To his surprise sitting in front of his mother on the benches reserved for distinguished visitors was Alison McKenzie, her arms folded on the balcony. He smiled.

Andrew's success was considerably enhanced when later that afternoon another member from the Labour benches rose to address the House for the first time. Tom Carson

cared nothing for convention and even less for keeping to
tradition and made no attempt to avoid controversy in his
maiden speech. He began with an attack on what he described as "the Establishment conspiracy", pointing an
accusing finger as much at the ministers on his own front
bench as at those opposite him, describing them all as
"puppets of the capitalist system".

Members present in the Chamber restrained themselves
from interrupting the scowling Liverpudlian, but the
Speaker stirred several times as the accusing finger appeared
to cross his path as well. He was painfully aware that the
member from Liverpool Dockside was going to cause all sorts
of problems if this was the way he intended to conduct
himself in the House.

When Andrew left the Chamber three speeches later he
went to look for Alison, but she had already left; so he took
the members' lift up to the Public Gallery and invited his
parents to join him for tea in the Harcourt Rooms.

"The last time I had tea here was with Ainslie
Munro . . ." Sir Duncan began.

"Then it may be a very long time before you're invited
again," Andrew interrupted.

"That may depend on whom we select as Tory candidate
to oppose you at the next election," retorted his father.

Several members from both sides of the House came up
one by one to congratulate Andrew on his speech. He
thanked them all individually but kept glancing hopefully
over his father's shoulder; but Alison McKenzie did not
appear.

After his parents had finally left to catch the last flight back
to Edinburgh Andrew returned to the Chamber to hear
Alison's father summing up the debate on behalf of the
Government. The Minister of State described Andrew's
contribution as one of the finest maiden speeches the House
had heard in years. "Maiden it may have been but virginal it
was not," concluded Hugh McKenzie.

Once the debate was over and the usual ten o'clock
division had been declared by the tellers Andrew left the
Chamber. One final vote on a prayer detained members for a

further forty-five minutes and Andrew found the tea room – the traditional haunt of the Labour party – as crowded as it had been earlier in the afternoon.

Members jostled for the remains of unappetising-looking lettuce leaves that any self-respecting rabbit would have rejected accompanied by blobs of plastic-covered sweating cheese, described optimistically on the bill board as salad. Andrew contented himself with a cup of Nescafé.

Raymond Gould sat alone, slumped in an armchair in the far corner of the tea room, apparently engrossed in a week-old copy of the *New Statesman*. He stared impassively as several of his colleagues went over to Andrew to congratulate him. His own maiden speech the previous week had not been as well received and he knew it. He believed just as passionately about war widows' pensions as Andrew did about the future of Scotland but reading from a prepared manuscript he had been unable to make members hang on his every word. He consoled himself with the thought that Andrew would have to choose the subject for his next speech very carefully as the Opposition would no longer treat him with kid gloves.

Andrew was not concerning himself with such thoughts as he slipped into one of the many internal telephone booths and after checking in his diary dialled a London number. Alison was at home, washing her hair.

"Will it be dry by the time I arrive?"

"It's very long," she reminded him.

"Then I'll have to drive slowly."

When Andrew appeared on the Chelsea doorstep he was greeted by Alison in a housecoat, her newly-dry hair falling down well below shoulder level.

"The victor come to claim his spoils?"

"No, only last night's coffee," he said.

"But won't that keep you awake?"

"I certainly hope so."

By the time Andrew left Alison's home at eight the next morning he had already decided he wanted to see a lot more of Hugh McKenzie's daughter. He returned to his own flat in

Cheyne Walk, showered and changed before making breakfast for himself and going over his mail. There were several more messages of congratulations including one from the Secretary of State for Scotland, while *The Times* and the *Guardian* carried brief but favourable comments.

Before leaving for the Commons Andrew checked over an amendment he wanted to move in committee that morning. When he had reworded his efforts several times he picked up his papers and headed off towards Westminster.

Arriving a little early for the ten-thirty committee meeting, Andrew found time to collect his mail from the Members' Post Office just off the Central Lobby. He set off, head down, along the corridor towards the library, flicking through the envelopes to see if he recognised any familiar hand or official-looking missive that demanded to be opened immediately.

As he turned the corner he was surprised to find the House ticker-tape machine surrounded by Conservative members, including the man who had agreed to be his 'pair' for voting purposes.

Andrew stared up at the tall figure of Charles Seymour, who, although standing on the fringe of the crowd, still found it possible to read the tapped-out message on the telex machine.

"What's causing so much interest?" he asked, prodding Seymour's elbow.

"Sir Alec has just announced the timetable that'll be followed when we select the new Tory leader."

"We all await with baited breath," said Andrew.

"As well you might," said Charles, ignoring the sarcasm, "since the next announcement will undoubtedly be his resignation. Then the real politics will begin."

"Be sure you back the winner," said Andrew, grinning.

Charles Seymour smiled knowingly but made no comment.

CHAPTER THREE

Charles Seymour drove his Daimler from the Commons to his father's bank in the City. He still thought of Seymour's of Cheapside as his father's bank although for two generations the family had been only minority shareholders, with Charles himself in possession of a mere two per cent of the stock. Nevertheless as his brother Rupert showed no desire in representing the family interests the two per cent guaranteed Charles a place on the board and an income sufficient to ensure that his paltry parliamentary salary of £1,750 a year was adequately supplemented.

From the day Charles had first taken his place on the board of Seymour's he had no doubt that the new chairman, Derek Spencer, considered him a dangerous rival. Spencer had lobbied to have Rupert replace his father on retirement and only because of Charles's insistence had Spencer failed to move the old earl to his way of thinking.

When Charles went on to take his seat in Parliament Spencer at once raised the problem of his burdensome responsibilities at the House preventing him from carrying out his day-to-day duties for the board. However, Charles was able to convince a majority of his fellow directors of the advantages of having someone on the board at Westminster, although he knew that would cease if he was ever invited to be a minister.

As Charles left the Daimler in Seymour's courtyard it amused him to consider that his parking space was worth twenty times the value of the car. The area at the front of Seymour's was a relic of his great-grandfather's day. The twelfth Earl of Bridgwater had insisted on an entrance large enough to allow a complete sweep for his coach and four. That conveyance had long disappeared, to be replaced by twelve car spaces for Seymour directors. The bank's new management-conscious chairman, despite all his grammar school virtues, had never suggested the land be used for any other purpose.

The young girl seated at the reception desk abruptly stopped polishing her nails in time to say "Good morning, Mr Charles," as he came through the revolving doors and disappeared into a waiting lift. A few moments later Charles was seated behind a desk in his small oak-panelled office, a clean white memo pad in front of him. He pressed a button on the intercom and told his secretary that he did not want to be disturbed during the next hour.

Sixty minutes later the white pad had twelve names pencilled on it, but ten already had lines drawn through them. Only the names of Reginald Maudling and Edward Heath remained.

Charles tore off the piece of paper and the indented sheet underneath and put them both through the shredder by the side of his desk. He tried to summon up some interest in the agenda for the bank's weekly board meeting; only one item, item seven, seemed to be of any importance. Just before eleven, he gathered up his papers and headed towards the boardroom. Most of his colleagues were already seated when Derek Spencer called item number one as the boardroom clock chimed the hour.

During the ensuing predictable discussion on bank rates, the movement in metal prices, Eurobonds and client investment policy Charles's mind kept wandering back to the forthcoming leadership election and the importance of backing the winner if he were to be quickly promoted from the back benches.

By the time they reached item seven on the agenda Charles had made up his mind. Derek Spencer opened a discussion on the proposed loans to Mexico and Poland, and most of the board members agreed with him that the bank should participate in one but not risk both.

Charles's thoughts, however, were not in Mexico City or Warsaw. They were far nearer home and when the chairman called for a vote, Charles didn't register.

"Mexico or Poland, Charles. Which of the two do you favour?"

"Heath," he replied.

"I beg your pardon," said Derek Spencer.

Charles snapped back from Westminster to Cheapside to find everyone around the boardroom table staring at him. With the air of a man who had been giving the matter considerable thought Charles said firmly, "Mexico", and added, "The great difference between the two countries can best be gauged by their attitudes to repayment. Mexico might not want to repay, but Poland won't be able to, so why not limit our risks and back Mexico? If it comes to litigation I'd prefer to be against someone who won't pay rather than someone who can't." The older members round the table nodded in agreement; the right son of Bridgwater was sitting on the board.

When the meeting was over Charles joined his colleagues for lunch in the directors' dining-room. On the walls hung two Hogarths, a Brueghel, a Goya and a Rembrandt that could distract even the most indulgent gourmet: just another reminder of his great-grandfather's ability to select winners. Charles did not wait to make a decision between the Cheddar and the Stilton as he wanted to be back in the Commons for question time.

On arrival at the House he immediately made his way to the smoking room, long regarded by the Tories as their preserve. There in the deep leather armchairs and cigar-laden atmosphere the talk was entirely of who would be Sir Alec's successor.

Charles could not avoid overhearing Pimkin's high-pitched voice. "As Edward Heath is Shadow Chancellor while we debate the Finance Bill on the floor of the House, it is he who is bound to be the centre of attention."

Later that afternoon Charles returned to the Commons Chamber. He wanted to observe Heath and his Shadow team deal with the Government's amendments one by one.

He was about to leave the Chamber when Raymond Gould rose to move an amendment. Charles listened with grudging admiration as Raymond's intellectual grasp and force of argument easily compensated for his lack of oratorical skill. Although Gould was a cut above the rest of his intake on the Labour benches he didn't frighten Charles. Twelve generations of shrewd business acumen had kept large parts of Leeds in the hands of the Bridgwater family without the likes of Raymond Gould even being aware of it.

Charles took supper in the Members' Dining-room that night and sat at the large table in the centre of the room frequented by Tory back-benchers. There was only one topic of conversation and as the same two names kept emerging it was obvious that it was going to be a very close run thing.

When Charles arrived back at his Eaton Square home after the ten o'clock division Fiona was already tucked up in bed reading Philip Larkin's *The Whitsun Weddings*.

"They let you out early tonight."

"Not too bad," said Charles, and began regaling her with how he had spent his day, before disappearing into the bathroom.

If Charles imagined he was cunning, his wife, Lady Fiona, only daughter of the Duke of Falkirk, was in a different league. She and Charles had been selected for each other at an early age and neither had questioned or doubted the wisdom of the choice. Although Charles had squired numerous girl-friends before their marriage in between he had always assumed he would return to Fiona. Charles's grandfather always maintained that the aristocracy was becoming far too lax and sentimental about marriage. "Women," he declared, "are for bearing children and ensuring a continuation of the male line." The old earl became even more staid in his convictions when he was made aware that Rupert showed little interest in the opposite sex, and was rarely to be found in the company of women. Fiona would never have dreamed of disagreeing with the old man to his face as she was determined that it would be a son of hers that would inherit the earldom. But despite enthusiastic and then contrived efforts Charles seemed unable to sire an heir. Fiona was later

assured by a Harley Street physician that there was no
reason *she* could not bear children. The specialist had suggested that perhaps her husband pay the clinic a visit. She
shook her head, knowing Charles would dismiss such an idea
out of hand, and never mentioned the subject to anyone
again.

Fiona spent a considerable amount of her spare time in
their Sussex Downs constituency furthering Charles's political career. She had learned to live with the fact that theirs
was not destined to be a romantic marriage and resigned
herself to its other advantages. Although many men confessed covertly and overtly that they found the tall elegant
lady desirable she either ignored their overtures or pretended
not to notice them.

By the time Charles returned from the bathroom in his
blue silk pyjamas Fiona had formed a plan, but first she
needed some questions answered.

"Whom do you favour?"

"I'd like Sir Alec to carry on: after all, the Homes have
been friends of our two families for over 400 years."

"But that's a non-starter," said Fiona. "Everyone knows
Alec is on the way out."

"I agree, and that's exactly why I spent the entire afternoon observing the worthwhile candidates."

"Did you come to any serious conclusions?" Fiona asked.

"Heath and Maudling are out on their own, though to be
honest I've never had a conversation with either of them that
lasted for more than five minutes."

"In that case we must turn a disadvantage into an advantage."

"What do you mean, old girl?" Charles asked as he
climbed into bed beside his wife.

"Think back. When you were President of Pop at Eton,
could you have put a name to any of the first-year boys?"

"Certainly not," said Charles.

"Exactly. And I'd be willing to bet that neither Heath nor
Maudling could put a name to twenty of the new intake on
the Tory benches."

"Where are you leading me, Lady Macbeth?"

"No bloody hands will be needed for this killing. Simply, having chosen your Duncan you volunteer to organise the new intake for him. If he becomes leader, he's bound to feel it would be appropriate to select one or two new faces for his team."

"You could be right."

"Well, let's sleep on it," said Fiona, turning out the light on her side of the bed.

Charles didn't sleep on it but lay restless most of the night turning over in his mind what she had said. When Fiona awoke the next morning she carried on the conversation as if there had been no break in between. "Do you have to be rushed into a decision?"

"No, but if I let it drift I could be accused of jumping on the bandwagon and then I would have lost my chance to be seen as a leader among the new intake."

"Better still," she continued, "before the man you choose announces he is a candidate, demand that he stand on behalf of the new members."

"Clever," said Charles.

"Whom have you decided on?"

"Heath," Charles replied without hesitation.

"I'll back your political judgement," said Fiona. "Just trust me when it comes to tactics. First, we compose a letter."

In dressing-gowns, on the floor at the end of the bed, the two elegant figures drafted and redrafted a note to Edward Heath. At nine-thirty it was finally composed and sent round by hand to his rooms in Albany.

The next morning Charles was invited to the small, bachelor flat for coffee. They talked for over an hour and later, as the two men stood below a Piper landscape in the drawing-room, the deal was struck.

Charles thought Sir Alec would announce his resignation in the late summer which would give him eight to ten weeks to carry out a campaign. Fiona typed out a list of all the new members and during the next eight weeks every one of them was invited to their Eaton Square flat for drinks. Fiona was subtle enough to see that members of the Lower House were

outnumbered by other guests, often from the House of Lords.
Heath managed to escape from his front-bench duties on the
Finance Bill to spend at least an hour with the Seymours once
a week. As the day of Sir Alec Douglas-Home's resignation
drew nearer Charles realised the leadership result could be
almost as important to him as it would be to Heath, but he
also remained confident that he had carried out his plan in a
subtle and discreet way. He would have been willing to place
a wager that no one other than Edward Heath had worked
out how deeply he was involved.

One man who attended the second of Fiona's soirées saw
exactly what was going on. While many of the guests spent
their time admiring the Seymour art collection Simon Kerslake kept a wary eye on his host and hostess. Kerslake was
not convinced that Edward Heath would win the forthcoming election and felt confident that Reginald Maudling
would turn out to be the party's natural choice. Maudling
was, after all, Shadow Foreign Secretary, a former Chancellor and far senior to Heath. More important, he was a
married man. Simon doubted the Tories would ever pick a
bachelor to lead them.

As soon as Kerslake had left the Seymours he jumped into
a taxi and returned immediately to the Commons. He found
Reginald Maudling in the Members' Dining-room seated at
the table frequented only by the Shadow Cabinet. He waited
until Maudling had finished his meal before asking if they
could have a few moments alone. The tall shambling figure –
not altogether certain of the name of the new member –
leaned over and invited Simon to join him for a drink in his
room.

Maudling listened intently to all the enthusiastic young
man had to say and accepted the judgement of the well-
informed member without question. It was agreed that
Simon should try to counter the Seymour campaign and
report back his results twice a week.

While Seymour could call on all the powers and influence
of his Etonian background, Kerslake could rely on the
knowledge and arm-twisting skills gained from his time as

President of the Oxford Union. Simon weighed up the advantages and disadvantages he possessed. He did not own a palatial home in Eaton Square in which Turners, Constables and Holbeins were not to be found in books but on the walls. He also lacked a glamorous society wife. Simon lived in a small house in Beaufort Street in Chelsea and Elizabeth was a gynaecologist at St Mary's Hospital, Paddington. Although Elizabeth gave Simon's political aspirations her full backing she still considered her own career every bit as important, an opinion with which Simon concurred. The local Coventry press had on several occasions recalled in their columns how Elizabeth had left her three-day-old child to help perform a Caesarian section on a mother in the adjoining ward and, two years later, had to be dragged off night duty just as she went into labour with their second child.

This independence of character was one of the reasons Simon had admired Elizabeth when they first met, but he realised she was no match for Lady Fiona Seymour as a hostess and he never wanted her to be. He despised pushy political wives.

Simon spent the following days trying to work out the certain Maudling and certain Heath supporters, although many members claimed they would favour both candidates, according to who asked them. These he listed as doubtfuls. When Enoch Powell threw his cap into the ring Simon could not find a single new member other than Alec Pimkin who openly supported him. That left forty members from the new intake who still had to be followed up. He estimated twelve certain Heath, eleven certain Maudling and one Powell, leaving sixteen undecided. As the day of the election drew nearer it became obvious that few of the remaining sixteen actually knew either candidate well, and were still not sure for whom they should vote.

Simon realised that he could not invite them all round to Beaufort Street between Elizabeth's ward duties, so he would have to go to them. During the last eight weeks he accompanied his chosen leader as he addressed the party faithfuls in twenty-three new members' constituencies. Simon travelled from Bodmin to Glasgow, from Penrith to Great Yarmouth, briefing Maudling studiously before every meeting.

Gradually it became obvious to everyone that Charles Seymour and Simon Kerslake were the chosen lieutenants among the new intake. Some members resented the whispered confidences at the Eaton Square cocktail parties, or the discovery that Simon Kerslake had visited their constituencies under false pretences, while others were simply envious of the reward that would inevitably be heaped on the victor.

"But why do you support Maudling?" Elizabeth had asked him one evening over dinner.

"Reggie has a great deal more experience of Government than Heath – and in any case he's more caring about those around him."

"But Heath appears to be so much more professional," Elizabeth insisted, pouring her husband a glass of wine.

"That may well be the case, but the British have always preferred good amateurs to preside over their affairs."

"If you believe all that stuff about amateurs why become so involved yourself?"

Simon considered her question for some time before answering. "Because I don't come from the type of background that automatically commands the centre of the Tory stage," he admitted.

"Neither does Heath," commented Elizabeth dryly.

Although everyone inside and outside of Parliament knew it could not be long before Sir Alec formally announced his resignation it did not become official until 22 July 1965, when he addressed the 1922 Committee of Tory back-benchers.

The date chosen for the leadership election was just five days later. During that time Simon Kerslake and Charles Seymour worked almost round the clock but, despite many national papers' commissioned polls, columns of newsprint offering statistics and opinions, no one seemed certain of the outcome, other than to predict that Powell would come third.

Charles and Simon began avoiding each other and Fiona started referring to Kerslake, first in private then in public, as "that pushy self-made man". She stopped using the expression when Alec Pimkin asked in all innocence whether she was referring to Edward Heath.

On the morning of the secret ballot Simon and Charles voted early and spent the rest of the day pacing the corridors of the Commons trying to assess the result. By lunchtime they were both outwardly exuberant, while inwardly despondent.

At two-fifteen they were seated in the large committee room to hear the chairman of the 1922 Committee make the historic announcement:

"The result of the first election for leader of the Conservative parliamentary party," said Sir William Anstruther-Gray, "is as follows:

Edward Heath	150 votes
Reginald Maudling	133 votes
Enoch Powell	15 votes."

An hour later Reginald Maudling, who had been lunching in the City, telephoned Heath to say he would be happy to serve under him as the new leader. Charles and Fiona opened a bottle of Krug while Simon took Elizabeth to the Old Vic to see *The Royal Hunt of the Sun*. He slept the entire way through Robert Stephens' brilliant performance, before Elizabeth drove him home.

"How come you didn't fall asleep? After all, you've been just as busy as I have the last few weeks," Simon asked.

Elizabeth smiled. "It was my turn to want to be involved with what was happening on the centre of the stage."

Two weeks later, on 4 August, Edward Heath announced his Shadow team. Reggie Maudling was to be deputy leader. Sir Alec accepted the Foreign Office brief while Powell went to Defence. Charles Seymour received an invitation to join the Housing and Local Government team as its junior spokesman, thus becoming the first of the new intake to be given front-bench responsibilities.

Simon Kerslake received a handwritten letter from Reggie Maudling thanking him for his valiant efforts.

BOOK TWO

1966-1974

JUNIOR OFFICE

CHAPTER
FOUR

When Alison McKenzie moved into Andrew Fraser's Cheyne Walk flat everyone, including her father, the Minister of State for Scotland, assumed they would soon announce their engagement.

For the previous three months Andrew had had his head down in committee helping out with the public bills relating exclusively to Scotland which were referred to the committee from the House itself. He found much of the committee work boring, as so many members repeated the views of their colleagues, less and less articulately, and for some time only his doodling improved. Even so, Andrew's energy and charm made him a popular companion through the long summer months and he quickly gained enough confidence to suggest first minor and later major changes to amendments considered by the committee. The disparity between penalties under English and Scottish law had long worried him, and he pressed hard for changes that would bring the two systems closer together. He soon discovered that the Scottish Labour members were more traditional and clannish than even the most hide-bound of Tories.

When the session came to an end Andrew invited Alison to spend a long weekend with his parents at their country home in Stirling at the end of the recess.

"Do you expect me to sleep under the same roof as a former Conservative Lord Provost of Edinburgh?" she demanded.

"Why not? You've been sleeping with his son for the past six months."

"Well, the same roof perhaps, but there's one weekend we won't be able to sleep in the same bed."

"Why not? The Tories may be snobs but they're not hypocrites."

Alison didn't want to admit that she was actually quite nervous about spending the weekend with Andrew's father, as she had heard him continually maligned at her parents' breakfast table for over twenty years.

When she did meet 'Old Dungheap', as her father referred to the former Lord Provost, Alison liked him immediately. He reminded her so much of her own father, while Lady Fraser was not at all the snobbish little battle-axe her mother had prepared her for.

It was immediately agreed that during the weekend nobody would talk politics. Andrew and Alison spent most of the Friday afternoon walking through the heather-covered hills and discussing in detail how they saw their future. On the Saturday morning the minister telephoned Sir Duncan and invited them over to Bute House – the official residence of the Secretary of State for Scotland – for dinner.

After so many years of opposing each other both families were nervous of the social get-together, but it seemed the children were to bridge the political gap they had failed to build for themselves. The McKenzies had invited two other Edinburgh families to dinner in the hope that it would ease the tension of the occasion, a branch of the Forsyths who owned the departmental store in Princes Street, and the Menzies, who ran the largest chain of newsagents in the country.

Andrew had decided to use the gathering to make an announcement at the end of dinner, and having spent longer shopping than he originally intended was the last to arrive at Bute House.

After they had all found their place cards around the long dining-room table the fourteen guests remained silent as a lone piper played a lament before the chef entered carrying a silver salver which bore on it a large haggis for the minister's inspection. Sir Duncan's opinion was sought: "Warm – reekin rich!" he declared. It was the first occasion the two men had wholeheartedly agreed on anything.

Andrew did not eat as much as the others because he

couldn't take his eyes off the guest who had been placed opposite him. She didn't pay much attention to Andrew, but seemed always to be smiling or laughing, making those around her enjoy her company. When Andrew had last seen Louise Forsyth it had been scoring goals on a hockey pitch. She had been a dumpy little girl with long pigtails and a tendency to go for one's ankles rather than for the ball. Now the jet black hair was short and curly, while the body had become slim and graceful. After dinner Andrew mixed among the guests and it was well after one o'clock when the party broke up: he never managed a moment alone with her. Andrew was relieved to discover that Alison wanted to spend the night with her parents at Bute House while the Frasers travelled back to their home in Stirling.

"You're very silent for a Socialist," his father said, in the car on the way home.

"He's in love," said his mother fondly.

Andrew made no reply.

The next morning he rose early and travelled into Edinburgh to see his agent. The minister had caught the first flight back to London but had left a message asking if Andrew would be kind enough to see him at ten o'clock in Dover House, the London headquarters of the Scottish Office, the following day, 'on an official matter'.

Andrew was delighted but it didn't change his attitude.

Having answered his local post and dealt with some constituents' problems he left his office and made his way over to the New Club to make a private phone call. He was relieved to find her still at home. She reluctantly agreed to join him for lunch. Andrew sat alone for forty minutes, checking the grandfather clock every few moments while pretending to read the *Scotsman*. When she was eventually ushered in by the steward, Andrew knew this was the woman with whom he wanted to spend the rest of his life. He would have laughed, if he had been told – before the previous evening – that he could change his well-ordered plans on what was nothing more than a casual meeting. But then he had never met anyone like Louise before and was already convinced he never would again.

"Miss Forsyth," said the man wearing the green livery uniform of the Club. He inclined his head slightly and left them alone.

Louise smiled and Andrew guided her to a table in the corner.

"It was kind of you to come at such short notice," he said nervously.

"No," she said. "It was very stupid of me."

Over a lunch which he ordered but didn't eat Andrew learned that Louise Forsyth was engaged to an old friend of his from university days and that they planned to be married the following spring. By the end of lunch he had convinced her they should at least meet again.

Andrew caught the five-ten flight back to London and sat alone in his flat and waited. Alison returned a little after nine o'clock and asked why he hadn't travelled down from Scotland with her or at least phoned. Andrew immediately told her the truth. She burst into tears while he stood helplessly by. Within the hour she had moved all her possessions out of Andrew's flat and left.

At ten-thirty he phoned Louise again.

The next morning Andrew dropped into the Commons to collect his mail from the Members' Post Office, and to check with the Whips' office as to what time they were anticipating the votes that day.

"One at six and two at ten," shouted a junior Whip from behind his desk. "And we could lose the second so be certain you're not far away if we need you."

Andrew nodded and turned to leave.

"By the way, congratulations."

"On what?" queried Andrew.

"Oh hell, another indiscretion to start the week on. It's pencilled in on the morning sheet," said the Whip, tapping a piece of paper in front of him.

"What is?" asked Andrew impatiently.

"Your appointment as Parliamentary Private Secretary to Hugh McKenzie. For pity's sake don't let him know I told you."

"I won't," promised Andrew, breathing a sigh of relief. He

checked his watch: perfect timing to stroll over to Dover House and keep his appointment with the minister.

He whistled as he walked down Whitehall and the doorman saluted as he entered the ministry. They had obviously been briefed as well. He tried not to show too much anticipation. He was met at the top of the stone steps by the minister's secretary.

"Good morning," Andrew said, trying to sound as if he had no idea what was in store for him.

"Good morning, Mr Fraser," replied the secretary. "The minister has asked me to apologise for not being available to see you, but he has been called away to a Cabinet committee to discuss the new IMF standby credit."

"I see," said Andrew. "Has the minister rearranged my appointment?"

"Well, no, he hasn't," replied the secretary, sounding a little surprised. "He simply said that it was no longer important, and he was sorry to have wasted your time."

Charles Seymour was enjoying the challenge of his new appointment as a junior Opposition spokesman. Even if he was not actually making decisions on future policy he was listening to them, and at least he felt he was near the centre of affairs. Whenever a debate on housing took place in the Commons he was allowed to sit on the front bench along with the rest of the team. He had already caused the defeat of two amendments on the Town and Country Planning Bill in standing committee, and had added one of his own, relating to the protection of trees, during the report stage of the bill on the floor of the House. "It isn't preventing a world war," he admitted to Fiona, "but in its own way it's quite important because if we win the election I'm confident of being offered junior office and then I'll have a real chance to shape policy."

Fiona continued to play her part, hosting monthly dinner parties at their Eaton Square house. By the end of the year every member of the Shadow Cabinet had dined with the Seymours at least once and Fiona never wore the same dress twice or allowed a menu to be repeated.

When the parliamentary year began again in October

Charles was one of the names continually dropped by the
political pundits. Here was someone to watch. "He makes
things happen," was the sentiment that was expressed again
and again. He could barely cross the Members' Lobby
without a correspondent trying to solicit his views on everything from butter mountains to rape. Fiona cut out of the
papers every mention of her husband and couldn't help
noticing that, if any new member was receiving more press
coverage than Charles, it was a young Socialist from Leeds
called Raymond Gould.

Raymond's name began to disappear from political columns
soon after his success on the budget debate; his colleagues
assumed it was because he was busy building a career at the
bar. Had they passed his room at the Temple they would
have heard the continual tap of a typewriter and been unable
to contact him on his off-the-hook phone.

Each night Raymond could be found in chambers writing
page after page, checking then rechecking his proofs, and
often referring to the piles of books that cluttered his desk.
When his *Full Employment at any Cost? Reflections of a worker
educated after the Thirties* was published it caused an immediate
sensation. The suggestion that the unions would become
impotent and the Labour party would need to be more
radical to capture the young vote was never likely to endear
him to the party activists. Raymond had anticipated that it
would provoke a storm of abuse from union leaders, and even
among some of his more left-wing colleagues. But A. J. P.
Taylor suggested in *The Times* that it was the most profound
and realistic look at the Labour party since Anthony Crosland's *The Future of Socialism*, and had given the country a
politician of rare honesty and courage. Raymond soon became aware that his strategy and hard work was paying
dividends. He found himself a regular topic of conversation
at political dinner-parties in London.

Joyce thought the book a magnificent piece of scholarship
and she spent a considerable time trying to convince trade
unionists who had only read out-of-context quotations from
it in the *Sun* or *Daily Mirror* that it in fact showed a passionate

concern for the trade union movement, while at the same time realistically considering the Labour party's future in the next decade.

The Labour Chief Whip took Raymond on one side and told him, "You've caused a right stir, lad. Now keep your head down for a few months and you'll probably find every Cabinet member quoting you as if it was party policy."

Raymond took the Chief Whip's advice, but he did not have to wait months. Just three weeks after the book's publication the Prime Minister quoted a whole passage at the Durham Miners' Rally. A few weeks later Raymond received a missive from No. 10 requesting him to check over the Prime Minister's speech to the TUC conference and add any suggestions he might have.

Simon Kerslake had sulked for about twenty-four hours after Maudling's defeat for the leadership. He then decided to turn his anger and energy towards the Government benches. It hadn't taken him long to work out that there was a fifteen-minute period twice a week when someone with his skills of oratory could command notice. At the beginning of a new session each week he would carefully study the order paper and in particular the first five questions listed for the Prime Minister on the Tuesday and Thursday. Every Monday morning he would prepare a supplementary for at least three of them. These he worded, then reworded, so that they were biting and witty and always likely to embarrass the Government. Although preparation of such supplementary questions could take several hours Simon would make them sound as though they had been jotted down on the back of the order paper during question time – and in fact would even do so. Elizabeth teased him about how long he took on something she considered trivial. He reminded her of Churchill's comment after being praised for a brilliant rejoinder, "All my best off-the-cuff remarks had been worked on days before."

Even so Simon was surprised at how quickly the House took it for granted that he would be there on the attack, probing, demanding, harrying the Prime Minister's every move. Whenever he rose from his seat the party perked up in anticipation, and many of his interruptions reached the political column of the daily newspapers the following day.

Unemployment was the subject of that day's question. Simon was on his feet leaning forward jabbing a finger in the direction of the Government front bench.

"With the appointment of four extra Secretaries of State this week the Prime Minister can at least claim he has full employment – in the Cabinet."

The Prime Minister sank lower into his seat, looking forward to the recess.

CHAPTER
FIVE

When the Queen opened Parliament the talk was not of the contents of her speech, which traditionally lists the aims of the Government of the day, but of how much of the legislation could possibly be carried out while the Labour party retained a majority of only four. Any contentious legislation was likely to be defeated at the committee stage and everyone knew it. The Conservatives were convinced they could win the forthcoming election whatever date the Prime Minister chose until the by-election held in Hull increased the Labour majority from 1,100 to 5,350. The Prime Minister couldn't believe the result and asked the Queen to dissolve Parliament immediately and to call a general election. The date announced from Buckingham Palace was 31 March.

Simon Kerslake began spending most of his spare time in his Coventry constituency. The local people seemed pleased with the apprenticeship of their new member, but the disinterested statisticians pointed out that a swing of less than one per cent would remove him from the House for another five years. By then his rivals would be on the second rung of the ladder.

The Tory Chief Whip advised Simon to stay put in Coventry and not to participate in any further parliamentary business. "There'll be no more three-line whips between now and the election," he assured him. "The most worthwhile thing you can do is pick up votes in Coventry, not give them in Westminster."

Elizabeth could only manage two weeks' leave of absence from St Mary's, and yet between the two of them they

covered the entire constituency before election day. Simon's
opponent was the former member, Alf Abbott, who became
progressively confident of victory as the national swing to
Labour accelerated during the campaign. The slogan 'You
know Labour Government works' was sounding convincing
after only eighteen months in power. The Liberals fielded a
third candidate, Nigel Bainbridge, but he admitted openly
that he only hoped to save his deposit.

Alf Abbott felt assured enough to challenge Simon to a
public debate. Although it was usual for the sitting member
to refuse to be drawn on such occasions Simon jumped at his
opponent's challenge and prepared for the encounter with
his usual diligence. Seven days before the election Simon and
Elizabeth stood in the wings behind the stage of Coventry
town hall with Alf Abbott, Nigel Bainbridge and their wives.
The three men made stilted conversation while the women
eyed each other's outfits critically. The political correspondent of the *Coventry Evening Telegraph*, acting as chairman,
introduced each of the protagonists as they walked on to the
stage, to whipped-up applause from different sections of the
hall. Simon spoke first and held the attention of the large
audience for over twenty minutes. Those who tried to heckle
him ended up regretting having brought attention to themselves. Without once referring to his notes, he quoted figures
and clauses from Government bills with an ease that impressed even Elizabeth. Abbott followed him and made a
bitter attack on the Tories, accusing them of still wanting to
tread down the workers at any cost, and was greeted by large
cheers from his section of the audience. Bainbridge claimed
that neither understood the real issues and went into an
involved dissertation on the problem of the local sewers.
During the questions that followed Simon once again proved
to be far better informed than Abbott or Bainbridge, but he
was aware that the packed hall only held 700 that cold March
evening while elsewhere in Coventry were 50,000 more
voters, most of them glued to 'Coronation Street'.

Although the local press proclaimed Simon the victor of a
one-sided debate he remained downcast by the national
dailies which were now predicting a landslide for Labour.

On election morning Simon and Elizabeth were up by six and among the first to cast their votes at the local primary school. They spent the rest of the day travelling from polling station to committee room to party checking posts, trying to keep up the morale of their supporters. Everywhere they went the committed believed in his victory but Simon knew that the national swing would be impossible to ignore. A senior Conservative back-bencher had once told him that an outstanding member could be worth a thousand personal votes and a weak opponent might sacrifice another thousand. It wasn't going to be enough.

By nine o'clock the last polling station had been locked and Simon and Elizabeth collapsed into a local pub and ordered two halves of bitter. They sat and watched the television above the bar. The commentator was saying that during the day a straw poll had been taken outside six constituencies in London and from those figures they were predicting a Labour majority of sixty to seventy seats. Up on the screen flashed the seventy seats most vulnerable to siege by Labour. Ninth on the list was Coventry Central: Simon ordered the other half.

"We should be off to watch the count soon," said Elizabeth.

"There's no hurry."

"Don't be such a wimp, Simon. And remember you're still the member," she said, surprisingly sharply. "You owe it to your supporters to remain confident after all the work they've put in."

In the town hall black boxes were being delivered by police vehicles from every ward in the constituency. Their contents were tipped on to trestle tables which made up three sides of a square on the vast cleared floor. The town clerk and his personal staff stood alone in the well made by the tables, while council workers sat around the outside carefully stacking up the votes into little piles of a hundred. These in turn were checked by party scrutineers who hovered over them, hawk-like, often demanding that a particular hundred be rechecked.

The little piles grew into large stacks which were then

placed next to each other, and as the hours passed it became obvious even to a casual observer that the outcome was going to be extremely close.

The tension on the floor mounted as each hundred, then each thousand, was handed over to the clerk. Rumours that began at one end of the room had been puffed up like *soufflés* long before they had reached the waiting crowd standing in a chill wind outside the hall. By midnight, several constituencies' results around the country had been declared. The national swing seemed to be much as predicted, around three per cent to Labour, which would give them the promised majority of seventy or over.

At twelve-twenty-one the Coventry town clerk invited all three candidates to join him in the centre of the room. He told them the result of the count.

A recount was immediately demanded. The town clerk agreed, and each pile of voting slips was returned to the tables and checked over again.

An hour later the town clerk called the three candidates together again and briefed them on the result of the recount; it had changed by only three votes.

Another recount was requested and the town clerk reluctantly acquiesced. By two o'clock in the morning Elizabeth felt she had no nails left. Another hour passed, during which Heath conceded defeat while Wilson gave an extended interview to ITN spelling out his programme for the new Parliament.

At two-twenty-seven the town clerk called the three candidates together for the last time and they all accepted the result. The town clerk walked up on to the stage accompanied by the rivals. He tapped the microphone to check the speaker was working, cleared his throat and said:

"I, the undersigned, being the acting returning officer for the constituency of Coventry Central, hereby announce the total number of votes cast for each candidate to be as follows:

Alf Abbot	19,716
Nigel Bainbridge	7,002
Simon Kerslake	19,731

I therefore declare Simon Kerslake to be the duly elected Member of Parliament for the constituency of Coventry Central."

Even though the Labour party ended up with an overall majority in the House of ninety-seven, Simon had still won by fifteen votes.

Raymond Gould increased his majority to 12,413 in line with the national swing, and Joyce was ready for a week's rest.

Andrew Fraser improved his vote by 2,468 and announced his engagement to Louise Forsyth on the night after the election.

Charles Seymour could never recall accurately the size of his majority because, as Fiona explained to the old earl the following morning, "They don't count the Conservative vote in Sussex Downs, darling, they weigh it."

CHAPTER SIX

In most democratic countries a newly elected leader enjoys a transitional period during which he is able to announce the policies he intends to pursue and whom he has selected to implement them. In Britain MPs sit by their phones and wait for forty-eight hours immediately after the election result has been declared. If a call comes in the first twelve hours they will be asked to join the Cabinet, the second twelve given a position as a Minister of State, the third twelve made an Under-Secretary of State, and the last twelve a Parliamentary Private Secretary to a Cabinet minister. If the phone hasn't rung by then, they remain on the back benches.

Andrew Fraser had not bothered to be anywhere near a phone when the BBC midday news announced that Hugh McKenzie had been promoted from Minister of State to Secretary of State for Scotland, with a seat in the Cabinet. Andrew and Louise Forsyth decided to spend a quiet weekend at Aviemore, he to relax and climb other mountains before returning to the House, she to make plans for their forthcoming wedding.

It had taken Andrew countless trips to Edinburgh to convince Louise what had happened to him at Bute House that night had not been mere infatuation that would soon pass, but held long-term conviction. When the one weekend he couldn't travel to the Scottish capital and she came down to London he knew she no longer doubted his resolve. Andrew had found in the past that once the conquest was achieved interest soon waned. For him, though, his love for 'the wee slip of a thing', as his mother had come to describe Louise, grew and grew.

Although Louise was only five foot three she was so slim she appeared far taller, and her short black hair, blue eyes and laughing smile had many tall men bending down to take a closer look.

"You eat like a pig and look like a rake. I don't know how you manage it," grumbled Andrew over dinner one night. He played regular games of squash and swam three times a week to keep his own heavy frame in trim. He stared in admiration and not a little envy as Louise's eyes twinkled mischievously before she devoured another portion of Black Forest gâteau.

Although she had been brought up in a strict Calvinist household in which politics were never discussed Louise quickly learnt about the machinery of Government and soon found herself debating long into the night with Sir Duncan. At first he scored points off her with ease, but it was not long before he had to answer her demands with more and more reasoned arguments, and sometimes even that was not enough.

By the time the election had taken place Louise had become a total convert to Andrew's views. The squalor in some of the parts of the Edinburgh Carlton constituency, which she had never set foot in before, made her sick at heart. Like all converts, she became zealous and began by trying to reform the entire Forsyth clan. She even paid twelve shillings to join the Scottish Labour party.

"Why did you do that?" asked Andrew, trying not to show his pleasure.

"I'm against mixed marriages," she replied.

Andrew was delighted and surprised by the interest she took, and the local constituency suspicions of 'the wealthy lady' soon turned to affection.

"Your future husband will be Secretary of State for Scotland one day," many of them shouted, as she walked down the narrow cobbled streets.

"It's Downing Street, not Bute House, that I want to live in," he had once confided to her. "And in any case I've still got to become a junior minister."

"That could change in the very near future."

"Not while Hugh McKenzie is Secretary of State," he said, not under his breath.

"To hell with McKenzie," she said. "Surely one of his Cabinet colleagues has the guts to offer you the chance to be his PPS?" But despite Louise's sentiments the phone did not ring that weekend.

Raymond Gould returned from Leeds the moment the count was over, leaving Joyce to carry out the traditional 'thank you' drive around the constituency.

When he wasn't sitting by the phone the following day he was walking around it, nervously pushing his glasses back up his nose. The first call came from his mother who had rung to congratulate him.

"On what?" he asked. "Have you heard something?"

"No, love," she said, "I just rang to say how pleased I was about your increased majority."

"Oh."

"And to add how sorry we were not to see you before you left the constituency, especially as you have to pass the shop on the way to the A1."

Not again, Mother, he wanted to say.

The second call was from a colleague inquiring if Raymond had been offered a job.

"Nothing so far," he said before learning of his contemporary's promotion.

The third call was from one of Joyce's friends.

"When will she be back?" another Yorkshire accent enquired.

"I've no idea," said Raymond, desperate to get the caller off the line.

"I'll call again this afternoon, then."

"Fine," said Raymond, putting the phone down quickly.

He went into the kitchen to make himself a cheese sandwich, but there wasn't any cheese, so he ate stale bread smeared with three-week-old butter. He was half-way through a second slice when the phone rang.

"Raymond?"

He held his breath.

"Noel Brewster."

He exhaled in exasperation as he recognised the vicar's voice.

"Can you read the second lesson when you're next up in Leeds? We had rather hoped you would read it this morning – your dear wife . . ."

"Yes," he promised. "The first weekend I am back in Leeds." The phone rang again as soon as he placed it back on the receiver.

"Raymond Gould?" said an anonymous voice.

"Speaking," he said.

"The Prime Minister will be with you in one moment."

Raymond waited. The front door opened and another voice shouted, "It's only me. I don't suppose you found anything to eat, poor love." Joyce joined Raymond in the drawing-room.

Without looking at his wife he waved his hand at her to keep quiet.

"Ray," said a voice on the other end of the line.

"Good afternoon, Prime Minister," he replied, rather formally in response to the more pronounced Yorkshire accent.

"I was hoping you would feel able to join the new team as Under-Secretary for Employment?"

Raymond breathed a sigh of relief. It was exactly what he'd hoped for. "I'd be delighted, Prime Minister."

"Good, that will give the trade union leaders something new to think about." The phone went dead.

Raymond Gould, Under-Secretary of State at the Department of Employment, sat motionless on the third rung of the ladder.

As Raymond left the house the next morning he was greeted by a driver standing next to a gleaming black Austin Westminster. Unlike his second-hand Sunbeam, it glowed in the morning light. The rear door was opened and Raymond climbed in to be driven off to the department. Thank God he knows where my office is, thought Raymond as he sat alone in the back. By his side on the back seat was a red leather box the size of a very thick briefcase with gold lettering running along the edge: 'Under-Secretary of State for Employment'. Raymond turned the small key, knowing what Alice must have felt like on her way down the rabbit hole. The inside was crammed with buff files. He opened the first to see, 'A five-point plan for discussion by Cabinet on how to keep unemployment under one million'. He immediately started to read the closely-typed documents.

When Charles Seymour returned to the Commons on the Tuesday there was a note from the Whips' office waiting for him on the Members' Letter-board. One of the Housing and Local Government team had lost his seat in the general election and Charles had been promoted to number two on the Opposition bench. "No more preservation of trees. You'll be on to higher things now," chuckled the Chief Whip. "Pollution, water shortage and exhaust fumes . . ."

Charles smiled with pleasure as he walked through the Commons, acknowledging old colleagues and noticing a considerable number of new faces. He didn't stop and talk to any of the newcomers as he could not be certain if they were Labour or Conservative and, given the election result, most of them had to be Socialist. A doorkeeper in white tie and black tail-jacket handed him a message to say that a constituent was waiting to see him in the Central Lobby. He hurried off to find out what the problem was, passing some of his older colleagues who wore forlorn looks on their faces. For some it would be a considerable time before they were offered the chance of office again, while others knew they had served as ministers for the last time. As Macmillan had proclaimed, even the most glittering political career always ends in tears.

But at thirty-five Charles dismissed such thoughts as he marched towards the waiting constituent. He turned out to be a red-faced Master of Hounds who had travelled up to London to grumble about the proposed private member's bill banning hare coursing. Charles listened to a fifteen-minute monologue before assuring his constituent that any such bill was doomed through lack of parliamentary time. The Master of Hounds went away happy and Charles returned to his room to check over the constituency mail.

Fiona had reminded him of the 800 letters of thanks to the party workers that had been franked but still needed topping and tailing after every election. He groaned.

"Mrs Blenkinsop, the chairman of Sussex Ladies' Luncheon Club, wants you to be their guest speaker this year," his secretary told him once he had settled.

"Reply yes – what's the date?" asked Charles, reaching for his diary.

"16 June."

"Stupid woman, that's Ladies Day at Ascot. Tell her that I'm delivering a speech at a Housing Conference, but I'll be certain to make myself free for the function next year."

The secretary looked up anxiously.

"Don't fuss, she'll never know any better."

She moved on to the next letter. "Mr Heath wonders if you can join him for a drink on Thursday, six o'clock?"

Simon Kerslake also knew it was going to be a long slog. He was aware the Tories would not change their leader until Heath had been given a second chance at the polls, and that could take every day of five years with a Government which had a ninety-seven majority.

He began writing articles for the *Spectator* and for the *Sunday Express* centre pages, in the hope of building a reputation outside the House while at the same time supplementing his parliamentary salary of £3,400. Even with Elizabeth's income as a consultant he was finding it difficult to make ends meet, and soon their two young sons would have reached prep school age. He envied the Charles Seymours of this world who did not have to give a second thought about their next pay cheque. Simon wondered if the damn man had any problems at all. He ran a finger down his own bank account: as usual there was a figure around £500 in the right-hand margin, and as usual it was in red. Many of his Oxford contemporaries had already established themselves in the City or at the bar and on a Friday evening could be seen being driven to large houses in the country. Simon laughed whenever he read that people went into politics to make money.

He pressed on with demanding questions to the Prime Minister, and tried not to show how frustrated he was by the expectations of his colleagues whenever he rose each Tuesday and Thursday. Even after it became routine he prepared himself thoroughly, and on one occasion he even elicited praise from his normally taciturn leader. But as the weeks passed he found that his thoughts continually returned to money – or to his lack of it.

That was before he met Ronnie Nethercote.

Andrew Fraser had often read that the anger or jealousy of one man could block the advance of a political career but he still found it hard to accept that it could apply to him. What annoyed him even more was that Hugh McKenzie's tentacles seemed to have spread through every other department.

Andrew's marriage to Louise Forsyth had been expansively covered in the national papers and the absence of the Secretary of State at the wedding did not escape the notice of the *Daily Express*'s William Hickey. They even published an out-of-date photograph of Alison McKenzie looking sorrowful.

Sir Duncan reminded his son that politics was for long-distance runners, not sprinters, and that he still had a few more laps to complete yet. "An unfortunate analogy," considered Andrew as he had been a member of the Edinburgh University 4 × 110 relay team. Nevertheless he prepared himself for the marathon.

"Don't forget, Harold Macmillan spent fourteen years on the back benches before holding office," Sir Duncan added.

Louise accompanied Andrew all over the country for his speeches 'of major importance', usually to an audience of less than twenty; she only stopped travelling to Scotland every week when she discovered she was pregnant.

To Louise's surprise, Andrew turned out to be a keen anticipatory father, determined his son would not think of him only as a politician. Single-handed, he converted one of the upstairs bedrooms in Cheyne Walk into a nursery and sought her approval for a variety of blue decorative schemes.

Louise was anxious that Andrew should extend the same feelings to their unborn child, if they had a daughter.

Raymond Gould quickly gained a reputation at the Department of Employment. He was thought of as extremely bright, demanding, hard working and, not that it was ever reported to him, arrogant. His ability to cut a junior civil servant off in mid-sentence or to correct his principal Private Secretary on matters of detail did not endear him even to his closest staff, who always want to be loyal to their master.

Raymond's work load was prodigious and even the Permanent Secretary experienced Gould's unrelenting 'Don't make excuses' when he tried to trim one of the minister's private schemes. Soon senior civil servants were talking of when, not whether, he would be promoted. His Secretary of State, like all men who were expected to be in six places at once, often asked Raymond to stand in for him, but even Raymond was surprised when he was invited to represent the department as guest of honour at the annual CBI dinner.

Joyce checked to see that her husband's dinner-jacket was well brushed, his shirt spotless and his shoes shining like a guards officer's. His carefully worded speech – a combination of civil-servant draughtsmanship and a few more forceful phrases of his own to prove to the assembled capitalists that not every member of the Labour party was a 'raving commie' – was safely lodged in his inside pocket. His driver ferried him from his Lansdowne Road home towards the West End.

Raymond enjoyed the occasion; although he was nervous when he rose to represent the Government in reply to the toast of the guests. By the time he had resumed his seat he felt it had been one of his better efforts. The ovation that followed was certainly more than polite from what had to be classified as a naturally hostile audience.

"That speech was dryer than the Chablis," one guest whispered in the chairman's ear but he had to agree that, with men like Gould in high office, it was going to be a lot easier to live with the Socialists.

The man on Simon Kerslake's left was far more blunt in

voicing his opinion of Gould. "Bloody man thinks like a Tory, talks like a Tory, so why isn't he a Tory?" he demanded.

Simon grinned at the prematurely balding man who had been expressing his equally vivid views throughout dinner. Corpulent and ruddy-faced, Ronnie Nethercote looked as if he was trying to escape from every part of his bulging dinner-jacket.

"I expect," said Simon in reply, "that Gould would have found it hard to join the Young Conservatives, born in the thirties and living in Leeds."

"Balls," said Ronnie. "I managed it and I was born in the East End of London without any of his advantages. Now tell me, Mr Kerslake, what do you do when you're not wasting your time in the House of Commons?"

Raymond stayed on after dinner and chatted for some time to the captains of industry. A little after eleven he left to return to Lansdowne Road.

As his chauffeur drove slowly away from Grosvenor House down Park Lane, the Under-Secretary waved expansively back to his host. Someone else waved in reply. At first Raymond only glanced across, assuming it was another dinner guest, until he saw her legs. Standing on the corner outside the petrol station on Park Lane stood a young girl smiling at him invitingly, her white leather mini skirt so short it might have been better described as a handkerchief. Her long legs reminded him of Joyce ten years before except that they were black. Her finely curled hair and the set of her hips remained firmly implanted in Raymond's mind all the way home.

When they reached Lansdowne Road Raymond climbed out of the official car and said "Goodnight" to his driver before walking slowly towards his front door, but he did not take out his latch key. He waited until he was sure the driver had turned the corner before looking up and checking the bedroom window. All the lights were out. Joyce must be asleep.

He crept down the path and back on to the pavement, then

looked up and down the road, finally spotting the space where Joyce had parked the Sunbeam. He checked the spare key was on his key-ring and fumbled about, feeling like a car thief. It took three attempts before the car spluttered into life, and Raymond wondered if he would wake up the whole road as he moved off and headed back to Park Lane, not certain what to expect. When he reached Marble Arch he travelled slowly down in the centre stream of traffic. A few dinner guests in evening dress were still spilling out of Grosvenor House. He passed the petrol station: she hadn't moved. She smiled again and he accelerated, nearly running into the car in front of him. Raymond travelled back up to Marble Arch but, instead of turning towards home, he drove down Park Lane again, this time not as quickly and on the inside lane. He took his foot off the accelerator as he approached the petrol station and she waved again. He returned to Marble Arch before repeating his detour down Park Lane, this time even more slowly. As he passed Grosvenor House for a third time he checked to be sure that there were no stragglers still chatting on the pavement. It was clear. He touched the brakes and his car came to a stop just beyond the petrol station. He waited.

The girl looked up and down the street before strolling over to the car, opening the passenger door and taking a seat next to the Under-Secretary of State for Employment.

"Looking for business?"

"What do you mean?" asked Raymond hoarsely.

"Come on, darling. You can't imagine I was standing out there hoping to get a sun tan."

Raymond turned to look at the girl more carefully and wanted to touch her despite the aura of cheap perfume. Her black blouse had three buttons undone; a fourth would have left nothing to the imagination.

"It's ten pounds at my place."

"Where's your place?" he heard himself say.

"I use a hotel in Paddington."

"How do we get there?" he asked, putting his hand nervously through his red hair.

"Just head up to Marble Arch and I'll direct you."

Raymond pulled out and went off towards Hyde Park
Corner, and drove round before travelling on up towards
Marble Arch once again.

"I'm Mandy," she said, "what's your name?"

Raymond hesitated. "Malcolm."

"And what do you do, Malcolm, in these hard times?"

"I . . . I sell second-hand cars."

"Haven't picked out a very good one for yourself, have
you?" She laughed.

Raymond made no comment. It didn't stop Mandy.

"What's a second-hand car salesman doing dressed up like
a toff, then?"

Raymond had quite forgotten he was still in evening dress.

"I've . . . just been to a convention . . . at the . . . Hilton
Hotel."

"Lucky for some," she said, and lit a cigarette. "I've been
standing outside Grosvenor House all night in the hope of
getting some rich feller from that posh party." Raymond's
cheeks nearly turned the colour of his hair. "Slow down and
take the second on the left."

He followed her instructions until they pulled up outside a
small dingy hotel. "I'll get out first, then you," she said.
"Just walk straight through reception and follow me up the
stairs." As she got out of the car he nearly drove off and might
have done so if his eye hadn't caught the sway of her hips as
she walked back towards the hotel.

He obeyed her instructions and climbed several flights of
narrow stairs until he reached the top floor. As he
approached the landing, a large bosomy blonde passed him
on the way down.

"Hi, Mandy," she shouted back at her friend.

"Hi, Sylv. Is the room free?"

"Just," said the blonde sourly.

Mandy pushed open the door and Raymond followed her
in. The room was small and narrow. In one corner stood a
tiny bed and a threadbare carpet. The faded yellow wall-
paper was peeling in several places. There was a wash basin
attached to the wall; a dripping tap had left a brown stain on
the enamel.

Mandy put her hand out, and waited.

"Ah, yes, of course," said Raymond, taking out his wallet to find he only had nine pounds on him.

She scowled. "Not going to get overtime tonight, am I, darling?" she said, tucking the money carefully away in the corner of her bag before matter-of-factly taking off all her clothes.

Although the act of undressing had been totally sexless he was still amazed by the beauty of her body. Raymond felt somehow detached from the real world. He watched, eager to feel the texture of her skin, but made no move. She lay down on the bed.

"Let's get on with it, darling. I've got a living to earn."

The minister undressed quickly, keeping his back to the bed. He folded his clothes in a neat pile on the floor as there was no chair. Then he lay down on top of her. It was all over in a few minutes.

"Come quickly, don't you, darling?" said Mandy, grinning.

Raymond turned away from her and started washing himself as best he could in the little basin. He dressed hurriedly, realising he must get out of the place as rapidly as possible.

"Can you drop me back at the petrol station?" Mandy asked.

"It's exactly the opposite direction for me," he said, trying not to sound anxious as he made a bolt for the door. He passed Sylv on the stairs accompanied by a man. She stared at him more closely the second time. Raymond was back in his car a few moments later. He drove home quickly but not before unwinding the windows in an attempt to get rid of the smell of stale tobacco and cheap perfume.

Back in Lansdowne Road he had a long shower before creeping into bed next to Joyce; she stirred only slightly.

CHAPTER SEVEN

Charles drove his wife down to Ascot early to be sure to avoid the bumper-to-bumper traffic that always developed later in the day. With his height and bearing, Charles Seymour was made for tails and a topper and Fiona wore a hat which on anyone less self-assured would have looked ridiculous. They had been invited to join the McFarlands for the afternoon and when they arrived they found Sir Robert awaiting them in his private box.

"You must have left home early," said Charles.

"About thirty minutes ago," he said, laughing. Fiona looked politely incredulous.

"I always come here by helicopter," he explained.

They lunched on lobster and strawberries accompanied by a fine vintage champagne which the waiter kept pouring and pouring. Charles might not have drunk quite as much had he not picked the winners of the first three races. He spent the fifth race slumped in a chair in the corner of the box and only the noise of the crowd kept him from nodding off.

If they hadn't waited for a farewell drink after the last race Charles might have got away with it. He had forgotten that his host was returning by helicopter.

The long tail of cars across Windsor Great Park all the way back to the M4 made Charles very short-tempered. When he eventually reached the motorway he put his Daimler into fourth gear. He didn't notice the police car until the siren sounded and he was directed to pull over.

"Do be sensible, Charles," whispered Fiona.

"Don't worry, old girl, I know exactly how to deal with the

law," he said, and wound down his window to address the policeman who stood by the car. "Do you realise who I am, officer?"

"No, sir, but I would like you to accompany me —"

"Certainly not, officer, I am a Member of . . ."

"Do be quiet," said Fiona, "and stop making such a fool of yourself."

". . . Parliament and I will not be treated . . ."

"Have you any idea how pompous you sound, Charles?"

"Perhaps you will be kind enough to accompany me to the station, sir?"

"I want to speak to my solicitor."

"Of course, sir. As soon as we reach the station."

When Charles arrived at the constabulary he proved quite incapable of walking in a straight line and refused to provide a blood sample.

"I am the Conservative MP for Sussex Downs."

Which will not help you, Fiona thought, but he was past listening and only demanded that she phone the family solicitor at Speechly, Bircham and Soames.

After Ian Kimmins had spoken first gently, then firmly to Charles his client eventually co-operated with the police.

Once Charles had completed his written statement Fiona drove him home, praying that his stupidity would pass unnoticed by the press the following day.

Andrew even bought a football but hid it from Louise.

As the months passed Louise's slight frame expanded alarmingly. Andrew would rest his head on the bulge and listen for the heartbeat. "It's a scrum-half," he declared.

"Perhaps she's a centre forward," Louise suggested, "and will want to emulate the distaff side of the family."

"If he has to be a centre forward he will play for Hearts," Andrew assured her.

"Male chauvinist pig," she called to his back as he headed off to the Commons that morning. Andrew toyed with the names of Jamie, Robert, Hector and Iain and had settled on Robert before he had reached Westminster. On arrival at

New Palace Yard he hailed the policeman on the gate and was surprised to see the familiar figure immediately rush towards him.

Andrew wound down the window. "What's the problem, officer?"

"Your wife's been taken to St Mary's, Paddington, sir. Emergency wing."

Andrew would have broken the speed limit all the way to Marble Arch if it hadn't been for the traffic. He kept praying he would be there in time, but he couldn't help remembering that Louise was only six months pregnant. When he arrived the doctor on duty would not allow him to see her.

"How is Louise?" were Andrew's first words.

The young doctor hesitated, then said, "Your wife's fine, but I'm afraid she's lost the baby."

Andrew felt his whole body go limp. "Thank God she's all right," he said.

"I'm afraid I can't let you see her until she has come out of sedation."

"Of course, Doctor," said Andrew, glancing at the lapel badge on her white coat.

"But I can see no reason why you shouldn't have more children in the future," she added gently, before he had the chance to ask the quesion.

Andrew smiled with relief and began pacing up and down the corridor, unaware of the passing of time, until the doctor returned and said it would now be all right for him to see his wife.

"I hope you're not too disappointed?" were Louise's first words when eventually he was allowed to see her.

"Don't be silly – we'll have a dozen before we're through," he said, taking her hand.

She tried to laugh. "Do you know my doctor's husband?"

"Not that I'm aware of," said Andrew.

"Simon Kerslake."

"Good heavens, yes. Very capable fellow. Look aye, lass," said Andrew, putting on a deep brogue, "you'll be a new woman after a couple of days' rest, I'll guarantee it."

"And if I'm not?"

"I'll stick with the old one. And I'll tell you what: as soon as they let you out of this place we'll go down to the South of France for the weekend."

"You don't like him because he comes from the East End," said Simon, after she had read the letter.

"That's not true," replied Elizabeth. "I don't like him because I don't trust him."

"But you've only met him twice."

"Once would have been quite enough."

"Well, I can tell you I'm impressed by the not inconsiderable empire he's built up over the last ten years, and frankly it's an offer I can't refuse," said Simon, pocketing the letter.

"I know we could do with a little more money," said Elizabeth, "but surely not at any cost."

"I won't be offered many chances like this," continued Simon, "and frankly we could use the money. The belief people have that every Tory MP has some lucrative sinecure and two or three non-executive directorships is plain baloney and you know it. Not one other serious proposition has been put to me since I've been in the House, and another £2,000 a year for a monthly board meeting would come in very handy."

"And what else?"

"What do you mean, what else?"

"What else does Mr Nethercote expect for his £2,000? Don't be naive, Simon, he's not offering you that kind of money on a plate unless he's hoping to receive some scraps back."

"Well, maybe I have a few contacts and a little influence with one or two people . . ."

"I'll bet."

"You've just taken against him, Elizabeth."

"I'm against anything that might in the long term harm your career, Simon. Struggle on but never sacrifice your integrity, as you're so fond of reminding the people of Coventry."

On Friday morning, two weeks later, Andrew and Louise set
out for London airport with one suitcase between them. As
Andrew locked the front door the phone rang.

"No one's in," he shouted at the door knob, "but we'll be
back on Monday."

He had booked a suite at the Colombe d'Or nestled in the
hills of St Paul in the south of France. He was determined to
prise Louise away from London and see she had some sun
and rest.

The famous old hotel was everything the brochure had
promised. On the walls hung paintings by Picasso, Monet,
Manet, Utrillo – all of which the patroness, Madame Reux,
had accepted many years before in place of payment from
artists who needed lodging and a square meal. On the way up
the winding staircase Louise was nearly knocked out by a
Calder mobile and a Courbet hung above the bed in their
room. But it was the bed itself, a sixteenth-century four-
poster, that they both coveted. They were soon to discover it
possessed a mattress so comfortable that visitors always
overslept.

The food was memorable and they walked through the
green hills each day to be sure they could tackle another full
dinner at night. Three days of no radio, no television, no
papers and no telephone ensured that by Monday morning
they were ready to face London. They swore they would
return again soon.

Once their plane had landed at Heathrow they were made
aware that the holiday was over. Twenty minutes passed
before someone pushed the waiting steps up to the Van-
guard's door. Then a crowded bus to the terminal that
seemed miles away was followed by a route-march to cus-
toms. Despite their first-class tickets their bags were among
the last off. By the time the taxi had crawled through the
morning rush hour to their front door in Cheyne Walk all
Louise could say was, "I need another holiday." As Andrew
put his latch key in the door the telephone started ringing.

"I hope they haven't been trying all weekend," Louise
said.

Andrew put the phone to his ear as it went dead.

"Just missed whoever it was," said Andrew, picking up several brown envelopes from the floor. "France already seems about a week ago." He kissed his wife. "Must get changed and be off to the House," he said, checking his watch.

"How has the nation managed to survive without you?" mocked Louise.

When the phone rang again Andrew was just stepping out of the bath.

"Can you take it, Louise?" he shouted. A moment later he heard her rushing up the stairs.

"Andrew, it's the Prime Minister's office."

He ran dripping and naked to the bedroom phone and picked up the extension.

"Andrew Fraser," he said.

"This is No. 10," said an official-sounding voice, "the Prime Minister has been wanting to contact you since Friday morning."

"I'm sorry, I took my wife to Provence for the weekend."

"Really, sir?" said the voice, not sounding at all interested. "May I tell the Prime Minister you are now free to speak to him?"

"Of course," said Andrew, frowning at his nude reflection in the mirror. He must have put on half a stone; it would have to be four games of squash this week and no more wine at lunch.

"Andrew."

"Good morning, Prime Minister."

"Sad news about Hugh McKenzie."

"Yes, sir," said Andrew, automatically.

"They warned me about his heart before the last election but he insisted he wanted to carry on. I've asked Bruce to be the new Secretary of State and Angus to take his place as minister. They both want you to be the new Under-Secretary – how do you feel about it?"

"I'd be delighted, Prime Minister," Andrew stammered, trying to take in the news.

"Good. And by the way, Andrew, when you open your first red box you won't find any tickets for Colombe d'Or, so I do hope Louise is fully recovered.'' The phone clicked.

They had tracked him down, but the Prime Minister had left him in peace.

The first official function Andrew Fraser attended as Her Majesty's Under-Secretary of State at the Scottish Office was Hugh McKenzie's funeral.

"Think about it, Simon," said Ronnie, as they reached the boardroom door. "Two thousand pounds a year may be helpful but if you take shares in my property company it would give you a chance to make some capital."

"What did you have in mind?" asked Simon, doing up the middle button of his blazer and trying not to sound too excited.

"Well, you've proved damned useful to me. Some of those people who you bring to lunch wouldn't have allowed me past their front doors. I'd let you buy in cheap . . . you could get hold of 50,000 shares at one pound so when we go public you'll make a killing."

"Raising £50,000 won't be that easy, Ronnie."

"When your bank manager has checked over my books he'll be only too happy to lend you the money, you see."

After the Midland Bank had studied the authorised accounts of Nethercote and Company and the area manager had interviewed Simon, they agreed to his request, on the condition that Simon lodge the shares with the bank.

How wrong Elizabeth was proving to be, Simon thought, and when Nethercote and Company went on to double their profits for the year he brought home a copy of the annual report for his wife to study.

"Looks good," she had to admit. "But that still doesn't mean I have to trust Ronnie Nethercote."

When Charles Seymour's drink-driving charge came up in front of the Reading Bench he listed himself as C. G. Seymour – no mention of MP. Under profession he entered 'Banker'.

He came sixth in the list that morning, and on behalf of his absent client Ian Kimmins apologised to the Reading magis-

trates and assured them it would not happen again. Charles
received a fifty-pound fine and was banned from driving for
six months. The whole case was over in four minutes.

When Charles was told the news by telephone later that
day he was appreciative of Kimmins's sensible advice and
felt he had escaped lightly. He couldn't help remembering
how many column inches George Brown, the Labour Foreign Secretary, had endured after a similar incident outside
the Hilton Hotel.

Fiona kept her own counsel.

At the time Fleet Street was in the middle of 'the silly
season', that period in the summer when the press are
desperate for news. There had only been one cub reporter in
the court when Charles's case came up, and even he was
surprised by the interest the nationals took in his little scoop.
The pictures of Charles taken so discreetly outside the
Seymours' country home were now glaring from the pages
the following morning. Headlines ranged from 'Six months'
ban for drink-drive son of earl' to 'MP's Ascot binge ends in
heavy fine'. Even *The Times* mentioned the case on its home
news page.

By lunchtime the same day every Fleet Street newspaper
had tried to contact Charles – and so had the Chief Whip.
When he did track Charles down his advice was short and to
the point. A junior Shadow minister can survive that sort of
publicity once, not twice.

"Whatever you do, don't drive a car during the next six
months and don't ever drink and drive again."

Charles concurred, and after a quiet weekend hoped he
had heard the last of the case. Then he caught the headline on
the front page of the *Sussex Gazette*, 'Member faces no confidence motion': Mrs Blenkinsop, the chairman of the Ladies'
Luncheon Club, was proposing the motion – not for the
drunken driving but for deliberately misleading her about
why he had been unable to fulfil a speaking engagement at
their annual luncheon.

Raymond had become so used to receiving files marked
'Strictly Private', 'Top Secret', or even 'For Your Eyes Only'

in his position as a Government Under-Secretary that he
didn't give a second thought to a letter marked 'Confidential
and Personal' even though it was written in a scrawled hand.
He opened it while Joyce was boiling his eggs.

"Four minutes and forty-five seconds, just the way you like
them," she said as she returned from the kitchen and placed
two eggs in front of him. "Are you all right, dear? You're
white as a sheet."

Raymond recovered quickly, pushing the letter into a
pocket before checking his watch. "Haven't the time for the
other egg," he said. "I'm already late for Cabinet committee,
I must dash."

Strange, thought Joyce, as her husband hurried to the
door. Cabinet committees didn't usually meet until ten and
he hadn't even cracked open his first egg. She sat down and
slowly ate her husband's breakfast, wondering why he had
left all his post behind.

Once he was in the back of his official car Raymond read
the letter again. It didn't take long.

> Dear 'Malcolm',
>   I enjoind our little get together the other evening and five
> hundrud pounds would help me to forget it once and for
> all.
> Love, Mandy.
> PS. I'll be in touch again soon.

He read the letter once more and tried to compose his
thoughts. There was no address on the top of the notebook
paper. Neither letter nor envelope gave any clue as to where
they had come from.

After he had arrived outside the Department of Employment Raymond remained in the back seat for several moments.

"Are you feeling all right, sir?" his driver asked.

"Fine, thank you," he replied, and jumped out of the car
and ran all the way up to his office. As he passed his
secretary's desk he barked at her, "No interruptions."

"You won't forget Cabinet committee at ten o'clock, will
you, Minister?"

"No," replied Raymond sharply and slammed his office door. Once at his desk he tried to calm himself and recall what he would have done had he been approached by a client as a barrister at the bar: first instruct a good solicitor. Raymond considered the two most capable lawyers in England to be Arnold Goodman and Sir Roger Pelham. Goodman was getting too high a profile for Raymond's liking whereas Pelham was just as sound but virtually unknown to the general public. He called Pelham's office and made an appointment to see him that afternoon.

Raymond hardly spoke in Cabinet committee, but as most of his colleagues wanted to express their own views nobody noticed. As soon as the meeting was over Raymond hurried out and took a taxi to High Holborn.

Sir Roger Pelham rose from behind his large Victorian desk to greet the junior minister.

"I know you're a busy man, Gould," Pelham said as he fell back into his black leather chair, "so I shan't waste your time. Tell me what I can do for you."

"It was kind of you to see me at such short notice," Raymond began and without further word handed the letter over.

"Thank you," the solicitor said courteously and, pushing his half-moon spectacles higher up his nose he read the note three times before he made any comment.

"Blackmail is something we all detest," he began, "but it will be necessary for you to tell me the whole truth, and don't miss out any details. Please remember I am on your side. You'll recall only too well from your days at the bar what a disadvantage one labours under when one is in possession of only half the facts."

The tips of Pelham's fingers touched, forming a small roof in front of his nose as he listened intently to Raymond's account of what had happened that night.

"Could anyone else have seen you?" was Pelham's first question.

Raymond thought back and then nodded. "Yes," he said. "Yes, I'm afraid there was another girl who passed me on the stairs."

Pelham read the letter once more. "My immediate advice," he said, looking Raymond in the eye and speaking slowly and deliberately, "and you won't like it, is to do nothing."

"But what do I say if she contacts the press?"

"She will probably get in touch with someone from Fleet Street anyway, even if you pay the £500, or however many other £500s you can afford. Don't imagine you're the first minister to be blackmailed, Mr Gould. Every homosexual in the House lives in daily fear of it. It's a game of hide and seek. Very few people other than saints have nothing to *hide*, and the problem with public life is that a lot of busybodies want to *seek*." Raymond remained silent, trying not to show his anxiety. "Phone me on my private line immediately the next letter arrives," said Pelham, scribbling a number on a piece of paper.

"Thank you," said Raymond, at least relieved that his secret was now shared with someone else. Pelham rose from behind his desk and accompanied Raymond to the door. "You'll be glad to see Yorkshire back as county champions," said the solicitor as he walked down the long passage with the minister. Raymond did not reply. When they reached the outer door they shook hands formally. "I'll wait to hear from you," said Pelham. A pity that the man showed no interest in cricket.

Raymond left the solicitor's office feeling better, but he found it hard to concentrate on his work the rest of that day and slept only in fits and starts during the night. When he read the morning papers he was horrified to see how much space was being given to Charles Seymour's peccadillo. What a field day they would be able to have with him. When the post came, he searched anxiously for the scrawled handwriting. It was hidden under an American Express circular. He tore it open. The same hand was this time demanding that the £500 should be deposited at a newsagent in Pimlico. Sir Roger Pelham saw the minister one hour later.

Despite the renewed demand the solicitor's advice remained the same.

Andrew Fraser never stopped moving from one city to another because the Scottish Office had to show a presence in Edinburgh and Glasgow as well as in London. Louise did not complain; she had never seen her husband so happy. The only moment of light relief during his first three months as a minister came when Andrew found it necessary to send a letter to his father addressed, "Dear Sir Duncan," which went on to explain why he had to reject his offered advice on a Highlands and Islands Board project. Andrew was particularly pleased with the line, "I have for some considerable time listened to both sides of the argument."

Once he had settled in his favourite chair that night with a large whisky in his hand Louise told him she was pregnant again. "When did I find the time?" he asked, taking her in his arms.

"Maybe the half-hour between your meeting with the Norwegian Fishing Minister and the address to the Oil Conference in Aberdeen?"

When the AGM of the Sussex Downs Conservative Association came round in October Charles was pleased to learn that Mrs Blenkinsop's 'no confidence' motion had been withdrawn. The local press tried to build up the story but the nationals were full of the Aberfan coal-tip disaster, in which 116 schoolchildren had lost their lives. No editor could find space for Sussex Downs.

Charles delivered a thoughtful speech to his association which was well received. During question time he was relieved to find no embarrassing questions directed at him.

When the Seymours finally said goodnight, Charles took the chairman to one side and enquired: "How did you manage it?"

"I explained to Mrs Blenkinsop," replied the chairman, "that if her motion of no confidence was discussed at the AGM it would be awfully hard for the member to back my recommendation that she should receive an OBE in the New Year's Honours for service to the party. That shouldn't be too hard for you to pull off, should it, Charles?"

Every time the phone rang Raymond assumed it would be the press asking him if he knew someone called Mandy. Often it was a journalist, but all that was needed was a quotable remark on the latest unemployment figures, or a statement of where the minister stood on devaluation of the pound.

It was Mike Molloy, a reporter from the *Daily Mirror*, who was the first to ask Raymond what he had to say about a statement phoned in to his office by a girl with a West Indian accent called Mandy Page.

"I have nothing to say on the subject. Please speak to my solicitor, Sir Roger Pelham," was the Under-Secretary's succinct reply. The moment he put the phone down he felt queasy.

A few minutes later when the phone rang again Raymond still hadn't moved. He picked up the receiver, his hand still shaking. Pelham confirmed that Molloy had been in touch with him.

"I presume you made no comment," said Raymond.

"On the contrary," replied Pelham. "I told him the truth."

"What?" exploded Raymond.

"Be thankful she hit on a fair journalist because I expect he'll let this one go. Fleet Street are not quite the bunch of shits everyone imagines them to be," Pelham said uncharacteristically, and added, "they also detest two things, bent policemen and blackmailers. I don't think you'll see anything in the press tomorrow."

Sir Roger Pelham was wrong.

Raymond was standing outside his local newsagent the next morning when it opened at five-thirty and he surprised the proprietor by asking for a copy of the *Daily Mirror*. Raymond Gould was plastered all over page five saying, "Devaluation is not a course I can support while the unemployment figures remain so high." The photograph by the side of the article was unusually flattering.

Simon Kerslake read a more detailed account of what the minister had said on devaluation in *The Times*, and noted

Raymond Gould's firm stand against what was beginning to look like inevitable Government policy.

Simon looked up from his paper and started to consider a ploy that might trap Gould. If he could make the minister commit himself again and again on devaluation in front of the whole House he knew that when the inevitable happened Gould would be left with no choice but to resign. Simon pencilled a question on the top of the paper before returning to the political columns.

The devaluation news had caused a Tory lead in the opinion polls of eight per cent, and despite a majority of ninety-five in the Commons the Government had actually lost a vote on the floor of the House the previous day. Nevertheless, Simon still could not envisage a general election for at least another two years.

On the business front Simon had advised Ronnie Nethercote not to allow his company shares to be traded on the Stock Exchange until the Tories returned to power. "The climate," he assured Ronnie, "should be much easier then."

Charles Seymour was glad to be behind the wheel again after his driving ban had been completed, and he had the grace to smile when Fiona showed him the photograph of the happy Mrs Blenkinsop displaying her OBE outside Buckingham Palace to a reporter from the *Sussex Gazette*.

It was six months to the day of his first meeting with Sir Roger Pelham that Raymond Gould received an account from the solicitor for services rendered – £500. He sent the cheque by return of post in a parcel that also contained a copy of the recently published edition of *Wisden*.

CHAPTER
EIGHT

Andrew had been warned by his ministerial colleagues that the first day answering questions at the dispatch box would be an experience he was unlikely to forget.

Questions for the Scottish Office appear on the order paper on a Wednesday once every four or five weeks, and each minister answers on behalf of his own department between two-thirty-five and three-twenty. There are usually four or five ministers of the Crown, not including the law officer available to represent each great department of state. During the forty-minute to one-hour period the ministers would expect to reply to about twenty-five questions, but it is rarely the questions that are the problem; it is the supplementaries.

Any member can place a question through the table office to any minister, and can word it in a seemingly innocuous way. "When does the minister hope next to visit Aberdeen?" to which the minister concerned may reply anything from "next week" to "I have no plans to do so in the foreseeable future" – but when the member who put down the question rises from his seat to ask his supplementary he can change the subject completely. "Does the minister realise that Aberdeen has the highest rate of unemployment in the United Kingdom, and what new ideas does his department have to deal with this problem?" The hapless minister must then come up with a convincing reply on the spot.

In an attempt to see that a minister is adequately briefed, his department will spend the morning scrutinising each tabled question and looking for pitfalls he might encounter. A variety of possible supplementaries will be placed in his brief with appropriate answers. Ministers can, of course, always ask colleagues on their own side what they are hoping to find out from their tabled questions, but Opposition members use question time to test a minister in the hope of discovering some weakness in his armoury, thus making the Government appear incompetent.

Andrew spent a considerable time in preparation for his first encounter at the dispatch box although the more senior and experienced ministers in the Scottish Office had agreed to handle any questions that looked hostile.

He ended up having to respond to only one question from the Opposition benches, while fielding four from his own. Added to which, the timing was such that question number twenty-three from the Opposition member seemed unlikely to be reached by three-twenty, when the Solicitor General for Scotland would have to start answering questions himself.

Andrew's first four answers to questions numbers five, nine, eleven and fourteen, went smoothly enough. He opened his dark blue file and was pleased to confirm the well-prepared briefs to everything that was thrown at him. By three-fifteen, when question number nineteen was being answered, Andrew sat back on the front bench and began to relax for the first time that day.

The Solicitor General for Scotland entered a now packed Commons and, moving alongside the table in the centre of the Chamber, he crouched slightly to be sure he did not obscure the Speaker's view of the Government benches on his right. The Prime Minister had been left a place between the Chancellor and the Foreign Secretary and waited for the clock to reach three-twenty.

The Speaker called question number twenty-one but the member was not present. He called number twenty-two and once again the member was absent. Each had obviously considered that their question had little chance of being reached before three-twenty. At three-eighteen the Speaker called question twenty-three – Andrew's heart sank – which read on the order paper, "Had the minister been invited to visit the Kinross Nursing Home?"

Andrew rose, opened his folder and said, "No, sir."

"No one in the House will be surprised by the minister's reply," said George Younger, the member for Ayr, "because the nursing home has forty-nine occupants, forty-seven of whom have their own television sets and yet the minister demands forty-seven separate licence fees. If they were to congregate in one room, he would expect only one fee. Is this another example of the Labour party's 'Care for the Aged' programme that we hear so much about nowadays?"

Andrew rose to the dispatch box to cries of "Answer, answer," from the Opposition benches. He had checked his crib sheet while sitting on the edge of his seat. Andrew had a prepared answer for medical facilities, old-age pensions, supplementary benefits, food allowances, medical charges – but nothing on TV licences. As he stood stranded at the dispatch box he was aware for the first time of the pitfalls that a minister encounters when he is not fully prepared. Such a system might appear wonderfully democratic to onlookers, he thought, until you are the Christian facing the 300 hungry lions.

A handwritten note was quickly passed along the front bench to him from one of the civil servants who sit in the official box to the left behind the Speaker's chair. With no time to consider its implications Andrew crossed his fingers and read the note out to the House.

"This was a decision taken by the last administration, of which the Honourable Gentleman was a member. We have seen no reason to reverse that decision," he read, thinking how much like a parrot he sounded. He sat down to polite Government murmurs and some considerable relief.

Mr Younger rose again and was allowed a second supplementary.

"Mr Speaker, this is the sort of inaccuracy we have grown to expect from this Government. The decision he refers to was made by his Right Honourable friend, the Secretary of State, only last year, and I think the minister will find, if he does his research more fastidiously, that his party was in power at the time." The Opposition howled their delight.

Andrew rose again and gripped the sides of the dispatch box to avoid anyone seeing that he was shaking in fear.

Several members of the Government front bench had their heads bowed. The Opposition had drawn blood and were baying in triumph. Lord Attlee's words came back to Andrew. "When you are caught out by the House admit it, apologise, and sit down."

Andrew waited for the noise to subside before he replied. "The Secretary of State warned me that a new minister will never forget his first question time and I feel bound to agree with him." Andrew, who knew how the atmosphere in the House can change in a moment, felt such a moment now, and before it could turn back added, "On the question of television licences in the Kinross Nursing Home, I apologise to the Honourable Gentleman for Ayr for my mistake and I will look into the case immediately and send him a written reply within twenty-four hours." "Hear, hears" could now be heard from his own benches and the Opposition benches were quietened. Mr Younger was trying to interrupt again but as Andrew didn't give way he had to resume his seat, knowing the Speaker would not call on him again once the clock had passed three-nineteen. Andrew waited for silence before adding, "And I blame my grandmother for this who, as President of the Kinross Nursing Home and a staunch Conservative, has always believed in increasing old-age pensions rather than looking for false subsidies that can never be fair to everyone." By now the Labour members were laughing and all the heads on the front bench were looking towards the new minister, who remained at the dispatch box until the House was silent again. "My grandmother would be delighted to learn that this administration has raised that old-age pension by fifty per cent in the three years since we have taken office." The Labour back-benchers were now cheering and waving their order papers as Andrew resumed his seat, while the Opposition were silent and glum.

The hands of the clock touched three-twenty and the Speaker said, "The Solicitor General's questions."

Andrew Fraser had made a political reputation, and as the laughter echoed round the House the intense figure sitting on the end of the front bench put a hand through his red hair and wondered if he could ever match Andrew's skill at the dispatch box. On the Opposition back benches Simon Kerslake made a mental note to be cautious if he ever thought of putting a sharp question to Andrew Fraser.

As soon as the Solicitor General's questions were over Simon left the House and drove himself to Whitechapel Road. He arrived a few minutes after the four o'clock board meeting of Nethercote and Company had begun, quietly took his seat and listened to Ronnie Nethercote describing another coup.

Ronnie had signed a contract that morning to take over a major city block at a cost of fifteen million pounds with a guaranteed rental income of over 1.1 million per annum for the first seven years of a twenty-one year lease with seven-year rent reviews.

Simon formally congratulated him and asked if this made any difference to the company's timing for going public.

"Why do you ask?" said Ronnie.

"Because I still feel it might be wise to wait until we know the result of the next general election. If the Conservatives return to power, as the opinion polls forecast, that could change the whole atmosphere for launching a new company."

"If they don't, I shan't hold up going public much longer."

"I wouldn't disagree with that decision either, Mr Chairman," said Simon.

When the meeting was over he joined Nethercote in his office for a drink.

"I want to thank you," Ronnie said, "for that introduction to Harold Samuel and Louis Freedman. It made the deal go through much more smoothly."

"Does that mean you'll allow me to purchase some more shares?"

Ronnie hesitated. "Why not? You've earned them. But only another 10,000. Don't get ahead of yourself, Simon, or the other directors may become jealous."

In the car on the way to pick up Elizabeth Simon decided to take a second mortgage out on the house in Beaufort Street to raise the extra cash needed for the new shares. He thought it might be wise not to trouble her with the details. He savoured the prospect of the Conservatives winning the next election, perhaps being given office in the Government and selling his shares for a sum that would make it possible for him to stop the continual worries of how he would finance his children's education. Perhaps he could even give Elizabeth that holiday in Venice she had talked about so often.

When he drove up to the hospital Elizabeth was waiting outside the gates. "We won't be late, will we?" were her first words.

"No," said Simon, checking the clock on the dashboard as he turned the car round in the direction of Beaufort Street.

They arrived at the hall five minutes before the curtain was due to rise. The occasion was their sons' pantomime, and both Peter and Michael had assured their parents that they had major parts. It was Charles Kingsley's *The Water Babies*, and Michael turned out to be a crab, who although he never left the stage lay on his stomach throughout the entire performance and never uttered a word. Peter, who had spent the week learning his words off by heart, was an unconvincing water baby standing at the end of a row of twelve. His speaking part turned out to be one sentence: "If grown-ups go on eating all the fish in the sea there will be none left for me." King Neptune fixed his imperial eye on Peter and said, "Don't blame us, it's your father who's the MP," upon which Peter bowed his head and blushed, though not as deeply as Elizabeth when the audience in front of them turned round and smiled at Simon, who felt more embarrassed than if he had been in the centre of a raging debate in the Commons.

At coffee afterwards the headmaster admitted that the sentence had been added without the approval of the late Charles Kingsley. When Simon and Elizabeth took the children home that night they insisted on repeating Peter's one line again and again.

"If the Government did an about-turn and devalued the pound, would the Under-Secretary find it possible to remain in office?"

Raymond Gould stiffened when he heard Simon Kerslake's question. His grasp of the law and his background knowledge of the subject made all except the extremely

articulate or highly experienced wary of taking him on.
Nevertheless Raymond had one Achilles' heel arising from
his firmly stated views in *Full Employment at any Cost?*: any
suggestion that the Government would devalue. Time and
again eager back-benchers would seek to tackle him on the
subject but once more it was Simon Kerslake who felled his
opponent.

Andrew, sitting on the front bench, composed in his mind
a sharp reply about his colleagues' collective responsibility,
but Raymond Gould said rather ponderously: "The policy of
Her Majesty's Government is one hundred per cent against
devaluation, and therefore the question does not arise."

"Wait and see," shouted Kerslake.

"Order," said the Speaker, rising from his seat and turning towards Simon as Raymond sat down. "The Honourable
member knows all too well he must not address the House
from a sedentary position. The Under-Secretary of State."

Raymond rose again. "This Government believes in a
strong pound, which still remains our best hope for keeping
unemployment figures down."

"But what would you do if Cabinet does go ahead and
devalue?" Joyce asked him when she read her husband's
reply to Kerslake's question reported in *The Times* the next
morning.

Raymond was already facing the fact that devaluation
looked more likely every day. A strong dollar causing imports
to reach record levels coupled with a run of strikes during the
summer of sixty-seven was causing foreign bankers to ask
when, not if.

"I'd have to resign," he said in reply to Joyce's question.

"Why? No other minister will."

"I'm afraid Kerslake is right. I'm on the record and he's
made sure everybody knows it. Don't worry, Harold will
never devalue. He's assured me of that many times."

"He only has to change his mind once."

Pressure on the pound increased during the following weeks
and Raymond began to fear that Joyce might turn out to be
right.

Andrew Fraser had read *Full Employment at any Cost?* and considered it a succinctly argued case although he did not agree with all the small print. He personally was in favour of devaluation but felt it should have been pushed through in the Labour party's first week in office, so that the blame could be left at the door of the Tories. After three years and a second election victory any such suggestion would rightly be considered outrageous.

As Louise's time of delivery approached she was getting larger by the day. Andrew helped to take pressure off her as much as he could, but this time he did not prepare so obviously for the birth, as he felt his unbridled enthusiasm might have contributed to her previous anxiety. He tried as often as possible to bring the red boxes home each night, but it remained an exception if he returned to Cheyne Walk before eleven o'clock.

"Voting every night at ten o'clock and sometimes on through the night into the next day is one system the rest of the world has *not* considered worth emulating," Andrew had told Louise after one particularly gruelling session. He couldn't even remember what he had been voting on – although he didn't admit that to her. "But as no Government of whatever party has ever seriously considered the idea of limiting the time for ending business 'the troops', as back-benchers are known, go on charging through the lobbies day in and day out. That's why the press refer to us as 'lobby fodder'."

"More like a bunch of unruly children," she chided.

When Louise went into hospital one week early Elizabeth Kerslake assured her there was nothing to be worried about, and two days later Louise gave birth to a beautiful girl.

Andrew was in a departmental meeting discussing Glasgow's high-rise housing programme when the hospital staff nurse rang to congratulate him. He went straight to his fridge and took out the bottle of champagne his father had sent him the day he joined the Scottish Office. He poured a plastic mug of Krug for each of his team of advisers.

"Just better than drinking it out of the bottle," he suggested as he left his civil servants to go to the hospital.

On arrival at St Mary's Andrew was relieved to find Elizabeth Kerslake was on duty. She warned him that his wife was still under sedation after a particularly complicated Caesarian delivery. Elizabeth took him to see his daughter who remained under observation in an isolation unit.

"Nothing to fret about," Elizabeth assured him. "We always take this precaution after any Caesarian birth as there are a number of routine tests we still have to carry out."

She left Andrew to stare at his daughter's large blue eyes. Although he knew it might change in time the soft down on the crown of her head was already dark.

He slipped out an hour later when she had fallen asleep to return to Dover House, where he had a second celebration in the Secretary of State's office, but this time the champagne was served in crystal glasses.

When Andrew climbed into bed that night the champagne helped him fall into a deep sleep with the only problem on his mind being what they should call their daughter. Claire had always been the name Louise favoured.

The phone had rung several times before he answered it and as soon as he had replaced the receiver he dressed and drove to the hospital as quickly as possible. He parked the car and ran to the now-familiar ward. Elizabeth Kerslake was standing waiting by the door. She looked tired and dishevelled, and even with all her training and experience she found it hard to explain to Andrew what had happened.

"Your daughter died forty minutes ago when her heart stopped beating. Believe me, we tried everything."

Andrew collapsed on the bench in the corridor and didn't speak for several moments. "How's Louise?" was all he could eventually manage.

"She hasn't been told yet. She's still under sedation. Be thankful she never saw the baby."

Andrew thumped his leg until it was numb. He stopped suddenly. "I'll tell her myself," he said quietly and remained on the bench, tears coursing down his cheeks. Elizabeth sat down beside him but didn't speak. When she left it was only to check that Mrs Fraser was ready to see her husband.

Louise knew the moment Andrew walked in. It was over an hour before she managed to speak.

"I bet Alison McKenzie would have given you a dozen sons," she said, trying to make him smile.

"No doubt about that," said Andrew, "but they would have all been ugly and stupid."

"I agree with you," said Louise. "But that wouldn't have been her fault."

They both tried to laugh.

Andrew returned to Cheyne Walk a little after four o'clock, but he didn't sleep again that night.

The great orator Iain Macleod once remarked that it was the first two minutes of a speech that decided one's fate. One either grasps the House and commands it or dithers, and loses it, and once the House is lost it can rarely be brought to heel. When Charles Seymour was invited to present the winding-up speech for the Opposition during the Economic debate, he felt he had prepared himself well, and although he knew he could not expect to convert Government back-benchers to his argument he hoped the press would acknowledge the following day that he had won the argument and embarrassed the Government. The Administration was already rocking over daily rumours of devaluation and economic trouble, and Charles was confident that this was the chance to make his name.

Full parliamentary debates usually start at three-thirty, after question time, but can be delayed if there are ministerial statements to be made. The senior minister in the department concerned makes the opening speech for approximately thirty minutes and then the Opposition spokesman addresses the House for the same period of time. Between four-thirty and nine the debate is thrown open to the floor and the Speaker tries to be scrupulously fair in calling a cross-section of back-benchers who have demonstrated an interest in the subject, as well as preserving a party and regional balance. These back-bencher speeches are frowned on if they last for more than fifteen minutes. Some of the most memorable speeches delivered in the House have lasted eight or nine minutes, some of the worst over thirty.

At nine o'clock the Opposition spokesman makes his final comments, and at nine-thirty a Government minister winds up.

When Charles rose and stood at the dispatch box he intended to press home the Tory case on the Government's economic record, the fatal consequences of devaluation, the record inflation, coupled with record borrowing and a lack of confidence in Britain unknown in any member's lifetime.

He stood his full height and stared down belligerently at the Government benches.

"Mr Speaker," he began, "I can't think . . ."

"Then don't bother to speak," someone shouted from the Labour benches. Laughter broke out as Charles tried to compose himself, cursing his initial over-confidence. He began again.

"I can't imagine . . ."

"No imagination either," came another voice. "Typical Tory."

". . . why this motion was ever put before the House."

"Certainly not for you to give us a lesson in public speaking."

"Order," growled the Speaker, but it was too late.

The House was lost and Charles stumbled through thirty minutes of embarrassment until no one but the Speaker was listening to a word he said. Several members of his own front bench had their feet up on the table and their eyes closed. Back-benchers on either side sat chattering amongst themselves waiting for the ten o'clock division: the ultimate humiliation the House affords to its worst debaters. The Speaker had to call for order several times during Charles's speech, once rising to rebuke noisy members, "The House does its reputation no service by behaving in this way." But his plea fell on deaf ears as the conversations continued. At nine-thirty Charles sat down in a cold sweat. A few of his own back-benchers managed to raise an unconvincing "Hear, hear."

When the Government minister opened his speech by

describing Charles's offering as among the most pathetic he
had heard in a long political career he may well have been
exaggerating, but from the expressions on the Tory front
benches not many Opposition members were going to disagree with him.

CHAPTER NINE

The decision was finally made by the inner Cabinet of twelve on Thursday 16 November 1967. By Friday every bank clerk in Tokyo was privy to the inner Cabinet's closest secret, and by the time the Prime Minister made the announcement official on Saturday afternoon the Bank of England had lost 600 million dollars of reserves on the foreign exchange market.

At the time of the Prime Minister's statement Raymond was in Leeds conducting one of his fortnightly constituency 'surgeries'. He was in the process of explaining the new housing bill to a young married couple when Fred Padgett, his agent, burst into the room.

"Raymond, sorry to interrupt you, but I thought you'd want to know immediately. No. 10 have just announced that the pound has been devalued from two dollars eighty to two dollars forty." The sitting member was momentarily stunned, the local housing problem driven from his mind. He stared blankly across the table at the two constituents who had come to seek his advice.

"Will you please excuse me for a moment, Mr Higginbottom," Raymond asked courteously, "but I must make a phone call." The moment turned out to be fifteen minutes, in which time Raymond had made contact with a senior civil servant from the Treasury and had all the details confirmed. He called Joyce and told her not to answer the phone until he arrived back home. It was several minutes before he felt composed enough to put his head round the office door.

"How many people are still waiting to see me, Fred?" he asked.

"After the Higginbottoms there's only the mad major, still convinced that Martians are about to land on the roof of Leeds town hall."

"Why would they want to come to Leeds first?" asked Raymond, trying to hide his anxiety with false humour.

"Once they've captured Yorkshire, the rest would be easy."

"Hard to find fault with that argument. Nevertheless, tell the major I'm deeply concerned but I need to study his claim in more detail and to seek further advice from the Ministry of Defence. Make an appointment for him to see me at the next surgery and by then I should have a strategic plan ready for him."

Fred Padgett grinned. "That will give him something to tell his friends about for at least two weeks."

Raymond returned to Mr and Mrs Higginbottom and assured them he would have their housing problem sorted out within a few days. He made a note on his file to ring the Leeds Council Housing Officer.

"What an afternoon," exclaimed Raymond after the door had closed behind them. "One wife-beating, one electricity turned off by the YEB with four children under ten in the house, one pollution of the Aire river and one appalling housing problem – never forgetting the mad major and his itinerant Martians. And on top of all of that the devaluation news."

"How can you remain so calm?" asked Fred Padgett.

"Because I can't afford to let anyone know how I really feel."

After his surgery Raymond would normally have gone round to the local pub for a pint and an obligatory natter with the locals. This always gave him the chance to catch up on what had been happening in Leeds during the past fortnight. But on this occasion he bypassed the pub and returned quickly to his parents' home.

Joyce told him that the phone had rung so often that she had finally taken it off the hook, without letting his mother know the real reason.

"Very sensible," said Raymond.

"What are you going to do?" she asked.

"I shall resign, of course."

"Why do that, Raymond? It will only harm your career."

"You may turn out to be right, but that won't stop me going."

"But you're only just beginning to get on top of your work."

"Joyce, without trying to sound pompous, I know I have many failings but I'm not a coward and I'm certainly not so self-seeking as totally to desert any principles I might have."

"You know, you just sounded like a man who is destined to become Prime Minister."

"A moment ago you said it would harm my chances. Make up your mind."

"I have," she said.

Raymond smiled wanly before retreating to his study to write a short handwritten letter.

Saturday, 18 November 1967

Dear Prime Minister,

After your announcement this afternoon on devaluation and the stand I have continually taken on the issue I am left with no choice but to resign my position as Under-Secretary of State at the Department of Employment.

I would like to thank you for having given me the opportunity to serve in your administration. Be assured that I shall continue to support the Government on all other issues from the back benches.

Yours,
Raymond Gould.

When the red box arrived at the house that Saturday night Raymond instructed the messenger to deliver the letter to No. 10 immediately. As he opened the box for the last time he reflected that his department was answering questions on employment in the House that Monday. He wondered who would take his place.

Because of the paraphernalia surrounding devaluation, the Prime Minister did not get round to reading Raymond's letter until late Sunday morning. The Goulds' phone was still off the hook when an anxious Fred Padgett was heard knocking on the front door later that day.

"Don't answer it," said Raymond. "It's bound to be another journalist."

"No, it's not, it's only Fred," said Joyce, peeping through an opening in the curtain.

She opened the door. "Where the hell's Raymond?" were Fred's first words.

"Right here," said Raymond, appearing from the kitchen holding the Sunday newspapers.

"The Prime Minister has been trying to contact you all morning." Raymond turned round and replaced the phone on the hook, picked it up a few seconds later and checked the tone before dialling London WHI 4433. The Prime Minister was on the line in moments. He sounded calm enough, thought Raymond.

"Have you issued any statement to the press, Ray?"

"No, I wanted to be sure you had received my letter first."

"Good. Please don't mention your resignation to anyone until we've met. Could you be at Downing Street by eight o'clock?"

"Yes, Prime Minister."

"Remember, not a word to the press."

Raymond heard the phone click.

Within the hour he was on his way to London, and arrived at his house in Lansdowne Road a little after seven. The phone was ringing again. He wanted to ignore the insistent *burr-burr* but thought it might be Downing Street.

He picked the phone up. "Hello."

"Is that Raymond Gould?" said a voice.

"Who's speaking?" asked Raymond.

"Walter Terry, *Daily Mail.*"

"I am not going to say anything," said Raymond.

"Do you feel the Prime Minister was right to devalue?"

"I said nothing, Walter."

"Does that mean you are going to resign?"

"Walter, nothing."

"Is it true you have already handed in your resignation?"

Raymond hesitated.

"I thought so," said Terry.

"I said nothing," spluttered Raymond and slammed down the phone – before lifting it back off the hook.

He quickly washed and changed his shirt before leaving the house. He nearly missed the note that was lying on the doormat, and he wouldn't have stopped to open it had the envelope not been embossed with large black letters across the left-hand corner – 'Prime Minister'. Raymond ripped it open. The handwritten note from a secretary asked him on his arrival to come by the rear entrance of Downing Street and not the front door. A small map was enclosed. Raymond was becoming weary of the whole exercise.

Two more journalists were waiting by the gate and followed him to his car.

"Have you resigned, Minister?" asked the first.

"No comment."

"Are you on your way to see the Prime Minister?"

Raymond did not reply and leaped into his car. He drove off so quickly that the pursuing journalists were left with no chance of catching him.

Twelve minutes later, at five to eight, he was seated in the ante-room of No. 10 Downing Street. As eight struck he was taken through to Harold Wilson's study. He was surprised to find the Secretary of State for Employment seated in the corner of the room.

"Ray," said the Prime Minister. "How are you?"

"I'm well, thank you, Prime Minister."

"I was sorry to receive your letter and thoroughly understand the position you are in, but I hope perhaps we can work something out."

"Work something out?" Raymond repeated, puzzled.

"Well, we all realise devaluation is a problem for you after *Full Employment at any Cost?* but I felt perhaps a move to the Foreign Office as Minister of State might be a palatable way out of the dilemma. It's a promotion you've well earned."

Raymond hesitated. The Prime Minister continued. "It may interest you to know that the Chancellor of the

Exchequer has also resigned, but will be moving to the Home Office."

"I am surprised," said Raymond.

"What with the problems we are about to tackle in Rhodesia and Europe your legal skills would come in very useful."

Raymond remained silent as he listened to the Prime Minister; he knew what decision he must now make.

Monday usually gets off to a quiet start in the Commons. The Whips never plan for any contentious business to be debated, remembering that members are still arriving back from their constituencies all over the country. The House is seldom full before the early evening. But the knowledge that the Chancellor of the Exchequer would be making a statement on devaluation at three-thirty ensured that the Commons would be packed long before that hour.

The green benches, accommodating just 427 members, had deliberately been restored as they were after the Germans had bombed the Palace of Westminster on 10 May 1941. The intimate theatrical atmosphere of the House had remained intact. Sir Giles Gilbert Scott could not resist highlighting some of the Gothic décor of Barry, but he concurred with Churchill's view that to enlarge the Chamber would only destroy the packed atmosphere of great occasions.

The Commons filled up quickly, and by two-forty-five there was not a seat to be found. Members huddled up on the steps by the Speaker's canopied chair and around the legs of the chairs of the clerks at the table. One or two even perched like unfed sparrows on the empty petition bag behind the Speaker's chair. The galleries to the side and above the Chamber, which normally resembled empty benches at the Oval on a rainy day, had taken on the look of a crucial last Test match against Australia.

The chief doorkeeper checked his supply of snuff that it had been his office to keep since those days when 'unpleasant odours' wafted through London.

Raymond Gould rose to answer question number seven on

the order paper, an innocent enough inquiry concerning supplementary benefits for women. As soon as he reached the dispatch box the first cries of "Resign" came from the Tory benches. Raymond couldn't hide his embarrassment. Even those seated on the back benches could see he had gone scarlet. It didn't help that he hadn't slept the previous night following the agreement he had come to with the Prime Minister. He answered the question, but the calls for his resignation did not subside. The Opposition fell silent as he sat down, only waiting for him to rise for a further question. The next question on the order paper for Raymond to answer was from Simon Kerslake; it came a few minutes after three. "What analysis has been made by his department of the special factors contributing to increasing unemployment in the Midlands?"

Raymond checked his brief before replying. "The closure of two large factories in the area, one in the Honourable member's constituency, has exacerbated local unemployment. Both of these factories specialised in car components which have suffered from the Leyland strike."

Simon Kerslake rose slowly from his place to put his supplementary. The Opposition benches waited in eager anticipation. "But surely the minister remembers informing the House, in reply to my adjournment debate last April, that devaluation would drastically increase unemployment in the Midlands, indeed in the whole country. If the Honourable Gentleman's words are to carry any conviction, why hasn't he resigned?" Simon sat down as the Tory benches demanded, "Why, why, why?"

"My speech to the House on that occasion is being quoted out of context, and the circumstances have since changed."

"They certainly have," shouted a number of Conservatives and the benches opposite Raymond exploded with demands that he give up his office.

"Order, order," shouted the Speaker into the tide of noise.

Simon rose again, while everyone on the Conservative benches remained seated to ensure no one else was called. They were now hunting as a pack. Everyone's eyes switched back and forth between the two men, watching the dark, assured figure of Kerslake once again jabbing his forefinger at the bowed head of Raymond Gould who was now only praying for the clock to reach three-thirty.

"Mr Speaker, during the debate, which he now seems happy to orphan, the Honourable Gentleman was only echoing the views he so lucidly expressed in his book *Full Employment at any Cost?* Can those views have altered so radically in three years, or is his desire to remain a minister so great that he now realises that *his* employment can be retained at any cost?"

"This question has nothing to do with what I said to the House on that occasion," retorted Raymond angrily. His last few words were lost in Opposition shouts of "Resign, resign!"

Simon was up in a flash and the Speaker called him for a third time.

"Is the Honourable Gentleman telling the House that he has one set of moral standards when he speaks, and yet another when he writes?"

The House was now in total uproar and few members heard Raymond say, "No, sir, I try to be consistent."

The Speaker rose and the noise subsided slightly. He looked about him with an aggrieved frown. "I realise the House feels strongly on these matters, but I must ask the Honourable member for Coventry Central to withdraw his remark suggesting that the minister has behaved dishonourably."

Simon rose and retracted his statement at once, but the damage had been done. Nor did it stop members from calling "Resign" until Raymond left the Chamber a few minutes later.

Simon sat back smugly as Gould left the Chamber. Conservative members turned to nod their acknowledgement of his professional demolition of the Government's Under-Secretary of State. The Chancellor of the Exchequer rose to deliver his prepared statement on devaluation. Simon felt sick as he listened with horror to the Chancellor's opening words. "The Honourable member for Leeds North handed in his resignation to the Prime Minister on Saturday evening but graciously agreed not to make this public until I had had an opportunity to address the House."

The Chancellor went on to praise Raymond for his work in the Department of Employment, and to wish him well on the back benches.

Andrew visited Raymond in his room immediately after the Chancellor had finished answering questions. He found him slumped at his desk, a vacant look on his face. Andrew had never considered Raymond a natural friend but he wanted to express his admiration for the way he had conducted himself.

"It's kind of you," said Raymond, who was still shaking from the experience. "Particularly as you would have demolished the lot of them."

"Well, they're all demolished now," said Andrew. "Simon Kerslake must feel the biggest shit in town."

"There's no way he could have known," said Raymond. "He'd certainly done his homework and the questions were spot on. I suspect we would have approached the situation in much the same way given the circumstances."

Several other members dropped in to commiserate with Raymond after which he returned to his old department to say farewell to his team before he went home to spend a quiet evening with Joyce. There was a long silence before the Permanent Secretary ventured an opinion: "I hope, sir, it will not be long before you return to Government. You have certainly made our lives hard but for those you ultimately serve you have undoubtedly made life easier." The sincerity of the statement touched Raymond, especially as the civil servant was already serving a new master.

It felt strange to sit down and watch television, read a book, even go for a walk and not be perpetually surrounded by red boxes and ringing phones. Within forty-eight hours he missed it all.

He was to receive over a hundred letters from colleagues in the House but he kept only one.

Monday, 20 November 1967

Dear Gould,

I owe you a profound apology. We all in our political life make monumental mistakes about people and I certainly made one today.

I believe that most members of the House have a genuine desire to serve the country, and there can be no more honourable way of proving it than by resigning when one feels one's party has taken a wrong course.

I envy the respect in which the whole House now holds you.

Yours sincerely,
Simon Kerslake.

When Raymond returned to the Commons that afternoon, he was cheered by the members of both sides from the moment he entered the Chamber. The minister who had been in the middle of addressing the House at the time had no choice but to wait until Raymond had taken his seat on the back benches.

CHAPTER
TEN

Simon had already left when Edward Heath called his home. It was another hour before Elizabeth was able to pass on the message that the party leader wanted to see him at two-thirty.

Charles was at the bank when the Chief Whip called, asking if they could meet at two-thirty that afternoon before Commons business began. Charles felt like a schoolboy who had been told the headmaster expected him to be in his study after lunch. The last time the Chief Whip had phoned was to ask him to make the winding-up speech and they had hardly spoken since. Charles remained apprehensive; he always preferred to be told what a problem was immediately.

He decided to skip lunch at the bank and join his colleagues in the House, to be certain he wouldn't be late for the afternoon appointment.

Charles did not enjoy eating at the House as the food, with the exception of the *hors d'oeuvres* trolley, was only a little better than Paddington station and rather worse than London airport.

He joined some of his colleagues at the large table in the centre of the Members' Dining-room and took the only seat available, next to Simon Kerslake. The two men had not really been on good terms since the Heath–Maudling leadership contest. Charles did not care much for Kerslake: he had once told Fiona that he was one of the new breed of Tories who tried a little too hard and he had not been displeased to see him embarrassed over the Gould resignation. Not that he allowed anyone other than Fiona to know his true feelings.

Simon watched Charles sit down and wondered how much longer the party could go on electing Etonian guardsmen who spent more time making money in the City and spending it at Ascot than they did working in the House – not that it was an opinion he would have expressed to anyone but his closest friend. The discussion over lunch centred on the remarkable run of by-election results the Tories had had at Acton, Meriden and Dudley. It was obvious that most of those around the table could not wait for a general election, although the Prime Minister did not have to call one for at least another three years.

Neither Charles nor Simon ordered coffee.

At two-twenty-five Charles watched the Chief Whip leave his private table in the corner of the room and turn to walk towards his office. Charles checked his watch and waited a moment before leaving his colleagues to begin a heated discussion about entry into the Common Market.

He strolled past the smoking room before turning left at the entrance to the library. Then he continued down the old Ways and Means corridor, passed through the swing doors and entered the Members' Lobby which he crossed to reach the Government Whips' office. He put his head round the secretary's door. Miss Norse OBE, the Chief's invaluable secretary, stopped typing.

"I have an appointment with the Chief Whip," said Charles.

"Yes, Mr Seymour, he is expecting you. Please go through." The typing recommenced immediately.

Charles walked on down the corridor and found the Chief Whip blocking his own doorway.

"Come on in, Charles. Can I offer you a drink?"

"No, thank you," replied Charles, not wanting to delay the news any longer.

The Chief Whip poured himself a gin and tonic before sitting down.

"I hope what I'm about to tell you will be looked upon as good news." The Chief Whip paused and took a gulp of his drink. "The leader thinks you might benefit from a spell in the Whips' office, and I must say I would be delighted if you felt able to join us . . ."

Charles wanted to protest but checked himself. "And give up my Housing and Local Government post?"

"Oh yes, and more of course, because Mr Heath expects all Whips to forgo outside commitments. Working in this office is not a part-time occupation."

Charles needed a moment to compose his thoughts. "And if I turn it down, will I keep my post at Housing and Local Government?"

"That's not for me to decide," said the Chief Whip, "but it is no secret that Ted Heath is planning several changes in the run-up to the election."

"How long do I have to consider the offer?"

"Perhaps you could let me know your decision by question time tomorrow."

"Yes, of course. Thank you," said Charles. He left the Chief Whip's office and drove to Eaton Square.

Simon arrived at two-twenty-five, five minutes before his meeting with the party leader. He had tried not to speculate as to why Heath wanted to see him, in case the meeting only resulted in disappointment. Douglas Hurd, the head of the private office, ushered him straight through to the Conservative leader.

"Simon, how would you like to join the Housing and Local Government team in the run-up to the election?" It was typical of Heath not to waste any time on small talk and the suddenness of the offer stunned Simon. He recovered quickly.

"Thank you very much," he said. "I mean er . . . yes . . . thank you."

"Good, let's see you put your back into it, and be sure the results at the dispatch box are as effective as they have been from the back benches."

The door was opened once again by the private secretary; the interview was clearly over. Simon found himself back in the corridor at two-thirty-three. It was several moments before the offer sank in. Then he suddenly felt elated and made a dash for the nearest phone. He dialled the St Mary's switchboard and asked if he could be put through to Dr Kerslake. As he spoke, his voice was almost drowned by the sound of the division bells, signalling the start of the day's business at two-thirty-five following prayers. A woman's voice came on the line.

"Is that you, darling?" asked Simon above the din.

"No, sir. It's the switchboard operator. Dr Kerslake's in the operating theatre."

"Is there any hope of getting her out?"

"Not unless you're expecting a baby, sir."

"What brings you home so early?" asked Fiona as Charles came charging through the front door.

"I need to talk to someone." Fiona could never be sure if she ought to be flattered, but she didn't express any opinion as it was all too rare these days to have his company at all.

Charles repeated to his wife as nearly verbatim as possible his conversation with the Chief Whip. Fiona remained silent when Charles had come to the end of his monologue. "Well, what's your opinion?" he asked anxiously.

"All because of one bad speech from the dispatch box," Fiona commented wryly.

"I agree," said Charles, "but nothing can be gained by tramping over that ground again."

"We'll miss the salary you earn as a director of the bank," said Fiona. "The tax on my private income has made the amount I now receive derisory."

"I know, but if I turn it down, and we win the next election . . .?"

"You'll be left out in the cold."

"More to the point, stranded on the back benches."

"Charles, politics has always been your first love," said Fiona, touching him gently on the cheek. "So I don't see that you have a choice, and if that means some sacrifices you'll never hear me complain."

Charles rose from his chair saying, "Thank you. I'd better go and see Derek Spencer immediately."

As Charles turned to leave, Fiona added, "And don't

forget, Ted Heath became leader of the party via the Whips' office.''

Charles smiled for the first time that day.

"A quiet dinner at home tonight?" suggested Fiona.

"Can't," said Charles. "I've got a late vote."

Fiona sat alone wondering if she would spend the rest of her life cohabiting with three-line whips.

At last they put him through.

"Let's have a celebration dinner tonight."

"Why?" asked Elizabeth.

"Because I've been invited to join the front-bench team to cover Housing and Local Government."

"Congratulations, darling, but what does Housing and Local Government consist of?"

"Housing, urban land, transport, devolution, water, historic buildings, Stansted or Maplin airport, the Channel tunnel, royal parks . . ."

"Have they left anything for anyone else to do?"

"That's only half of it, if it's out of doors it's mine. I'll tell you the rest over dinner."

"Oh, hell, I don't think I can get away until eight tonight, and we'd still have to get a baby-sitter. Does that come under Housing and Local Government, Simon?"

"Sure does," he said, laughing. "I'll fix it and book a table at the Grange for eight-thirty."

"Have you got a ten o'clock vote?"

"Afraid so."

"I see, coffee with the baby-sitter," she said. She paused. "Simon."

"Yes, darling?"

"I'm very proud of you."

Derek Spencer sat behind his massive partner's desk in Cheapside and listened intently to what Charles had to say.

"You will be a great loss to the bank," were the chairman's first words. "But no one here would want to hold up your political career, least of all me."

Charles noticed that Spencer could not look him in the eye as he spoke.

"Can I assume that I would be invited back on the board if for any reason my situation changed at the Commons?"

"Of course," said Spencer. "There was no need for you to ask such a question."

"That's kind of you," said Charles, genuinely relieved. He stood up, leaned forward and shook hands rather stiffly.

"Good luck, Charles," were Spencer's parting words.

"Does that mean you can no longer remain on the board?" asked Ronnie Nethercote when he heard Simon's news.

"No, not while I'm in Opposition and only a Shadow spokesman. Only the Chief Whip receives a salary and is therefore disqualified, but if we win the next election and I'm offered a job in Government I would have to resign immediately."

"So I've got your services for another three years?"

"Unless the Prime Minister goes earlier, or we lose the next election."

"No fear of the latter," said Ronnie. "I knew I'd picked a winner the day I met you, and I don't think you'll ever regret joining my board."

Over the months that followed Charles was surprised to find how much he enjoyed working in the Whips' office, although he had been unable to hide from Fiona his anger at Kerslake taking over his shadow post at Housing and Local Government. The order, discipline and *camaraderie* of the job brought back memories of his days in the Grenadier Guards. His duties were manifold and ranged from checking that members were all present in their committees to sitting on the front bench in the Commons and picking out the salient points members made in their speeches to the House. He also had to keep an eye out for any signs of dissension or rebellion on his own benches while remaining abreast of what was happening on the other side of the House. In addition he had fifty of his own members from the Midlands area to shepherd, and had to be certain that they never missed a vote unless paired, and only then when the Whips' office had been informed.

As Whips are never called on to make speeches in the House at any time Charles seemed to have discovered a role for which he was best cut out. Fiona reminded him once again that Ted Heath had a spell in the Whips' office on his way to becoming Shadow Chancellor. She was delighted to see how involved her husband had become with Commons life but still hated going to bed alone each night and regularly falling asleep before he had even arrived home.

Simon also enjoyed his new appointment from the first moment. As the junior member of the Housing and Local Government team he was given transport as his special subject. During the first year he read books, studied pamphlets, held meetings with national transport chairmen from air, sea and rail and frequently worked long into the night trying to master his new brief. Simon was one of those rare members who, after only a few weeks, looked as if he had always been on the front bench.

Both parties were surprised by the fourteen per cent swing to the Conservatives at the Louth by-election towards the end of 1969. It began to look as if the Labour party did not have enough time to recover before they had to call an election. But in March 1970 the Labour party had a surprisingly good result in the Ayrshire South by-election; it caused the press to speculate that the Prime Minister might go to the country early. The May local elections in England and Wales showed a further swing to Labour, which was contrary to every other political trend of the previous two years. Talk of a general election was suddenly in the air.

When the following month's opinion polls confirmed the swing to Labour Harold Wilson visited the Queen at Buckingham Palace and asked her to dissolve Parliament. The date of the general election was set for 18 June 1970.

The press were convinced that Wilson had got it right again, and would lead his party to victory for the third time in a row, a feat no man in political history had managed. Every

Conservative knew that would spell the end of Edward
Heath's leadership of his party.

Andrew and Louise returned to Edinburgh as soon as the
Queen had made the announcement. Parliament went into a
limbo period while members dispersed all over the country
only in order to try and return to Westminster.

Andrew found his local committee had been taken by
surprise by the PM's announcement, and realised he only
had a matter of days to prepare himself.

The evening he arrived back in Edinburgh he called his
General Purposes Committee together and over coffee and
sandwiches mapped out a demanding three-week timetable
which would allow him to reach every part of the constituency not once but several times. Street cards were pinned on
to an old trestle table, soon to be filled in with crayon of
various colours according to the canvassing returns: a red
line through a definite Labour vote, a blue line through a
Conservative one, a yellow through a Liberal and a black line
through the growing Scottish Nationalist party.

Andrew began each day of the campaign with a press
conference at which he discussed local matters that affected
his constituents, answered criticisms made by the other
candidates and dealt with any national issues that had arisen
during the previous twenty-four hours. He then spent the rest
of the morning touring the constituency with a loudspeaker
van, entreating people to "Send Fraser back to Westminster". He and Louise would fit in a pub lunch together before
the dreaded door-to-door canvassing began.

"You'll enjoy this," said Andrew as they walked up to the
first door on a cold Monday morning. The street list of names
was on a card in his pocket. Andrew pressed the door bell,
and a little jingle could be heard. A woman still in her
dressing-gown answered it a few moments later.

"Good morning, Mrs Foster," he began. "My name is
Andrew Fraser. I'm your Labour candidate."

"Oh, how nice to meet you. I have so much I need to
discuss with you – won't you come in and have a cup of tea?"

"It's kind of you, Mrs Foster, but I have rather a lot of

ground to cover during the next few days." When the door closed, Andrew put a blue line through her name on his card.

"How can you be sure she's Conservative?" demanded Louise, "she seemed so friendly."

"The Conservatives are trained to ask all the other candidates in for tea and waste their time. Your own side will always say, 'You have my vote, don't spend your time with me,' and let you get on to those who are genuinely uncommitted."

"I always vote for Fraser," said Mrs Foster's next-door neighbour. "Labour for parliament, Tory for the local council."

"But don't you feel Sir Duncan should be removed from the council?" asked Andrew, grinning.

"Certainly not, and that's what I told him when he suggested I shouldn't vote for you."

Andrew put a red line through the name and knocked on the next door.

"My name is Andrew Fraser and I –"

"I know who you are, young man, and I'll have none of your politics, or your father's for that matter."

"May I ask who you will be voting for?" asked Andrew.

"Scottish Nationalist."

"Why?" asked Louise.

"Because the oil belongs to us, not those bloody Sassenachs."

"Surely it's better for the United Kingdom to remain as one body?" suggested Andrew. "At least that way –"

"Never. The Act of 1707 was a disgrace to our nation."

"But –" began Louise enthusiastically. Andrew put a hand on her arm. "Thank you, sir, for your time," and prodded his wife gently down the path.

"Sorry, Louise," said Andrew, when they were back on the pavement. "Once they mention the 1707 Act of Union we have no chance; some Scots have remarkably long memories."

He knocked on the next door. A fat man answered it, a dog lead in his hand.

"My name is Andrew Fraser, I –"

"Get lost, creep," came back the reply.

"Who are you calling creep?" Louise retaliated as the door was slammed in their faces. "Charming man."

"Don't be offended, darling. He was referring to me, not you."

"What will you put by his name?"

"A question mark. No way of telling who he votes for. Probably abstains."

He tried the next door.

"Hello, Andrew," said a lady before he could open his mouth. "Don't waste your time on me, I always vote for you."

"Thank you, Mrs Irvine," said Andrew, checking his house list. "What about your next-door neighbour?" he asked, pointing back.

"Ah, he's an irritable old basket, but I'll see he gets to the polls on the day and puts his cross in the right box. He'd better, or I'll stop keeping an eye on his greyhound for him when he's out."

"Thank you very much, Mrs Irvine," said Andrew, laughing.

"One more red," he told Louise as they returned to the pavement.

"And you might even pick up the greyhound vote."

They covered four streets during the next three hours, and Andrew put red lines through those names he was certain would support him on polling day.

"Why do you have to be so sure?" asked Louise.

"Because when we pick them up to vote on election day we don't want to remind the opposition, let alone arrange a lift for someone who then takes pleasure in voting Tory."

Louise laughed. "Politics is so dishonest."

"Be relieved you're not married to an American senator," said Andrew, putting a red line through the last name in the street. "At least we don't have to be millionaires to stand. Time for a quick bite before the evening meeting," he added, taking his wife's hand. On their way back to their head-quarters they came across their Conservative opponent, but Andrew didn't respond when Hector McGregor tried to engage him in conversation, again holding him up.

Louise never joined her husband again on these sessions, deciding she could be of more use working back in the Committee Rooms.

In the public meetings held each evening, Andrew made the same speech thirty-two times in twenty-four days with only slight variations to account for national developments. Louise sat loyally through every one of them, always laughing at his punch lines and starting the clapping whenever he made a telling point. Somehow she managed to remain fresh and lively even at the end of the day when she drove her husband home.

By the eve of the election all the press were predicting a clear majority for Labour, but Andrew observed the gleam in his father's eye when he passed him in the street canvassing for McGregor.

At five-thirty on the morning of the election Louise woke Andrew with a cup of tea. He didn't see another cup that day. To his relief the sun was shining when he pulled back the curtains after he had had his bath: bad weather invariably helped the Tories with their never-ending pool of cars, ferrying voters to the polling booths. He returned to the bedroom to find his wife pinning to the lapel of his jacket a vast red rosette bearing the exhortation, 'Send Fraser back to Westminster'.

He was strolling through the streets of Edinburgh shaking hands, chatting to well-wishers, trying to convince last-minute 'don't knows' when he spotted his father heading towards him. They ended up facing each other in the middle of the street.

"It's going to be a close-run thing," said Sir Duncan.

"Then I'll know who to blame if I lose by one vote," said Andrew.

Sir Duncan looked conspiratorially about him, then lowered his voice. "If you win by one vote you'll have me to thank, laddie." He marched away entreating the citizens of Edinburgh to remove the turncoat Fraser.

The next time father and son met was at the count that evening. As the little piles of votes began to grow it became obvious that Andrew would be returned to Parliament, and Hector McGregor was soon shaking his head in disappointment.

But when the first result was announced in Guildford and showed a four per cent swing to the Tories all the previous predictions of a strong Labour victory began to look unrealistic. As each return was announced from town hall platforms all over the country it became progressively more obvious that the Tories were going to end up with a large enough majority to govern.

"I would have thought," Sir Duncan said to his son as the trend was confirmed across the nation, "that you'll be in for a wee spell of Opposition."

"Wee is the important word," was all that Andrew replied.

Andrew retained his seat, keeping the swing against him down to one per cent and his majority a safe 4,009. Scotland wasn't as sure about Heath as the rest of the country, which showed an average swing against Labour of 4.7 per cent.

Simon Kerslake managed a four-figure majority for the first time when he won Coventry Central by 2,118.

When Fiona was asked by the old earl how many votes Charles had won by, she said she couldn't be certain but she did recall Charles telling a journalist it was more than the other candidates put together.

Raymond Gould suffered an adverse swing of only two per cent and was returned with a 10,416 majority. The people of Leeds admire independence in a member, especially when it comes to a matter of principle.

The Conservatives captured Parliament with an overall majority of thirty. Her Majesty the Queen called for Edward Heath and asked him to form a Government. He kissed the hands of his sovereign and accepted her commission.

CHAPTER
ELEVEN

When Simon awoke on the morning after the election he felt both exhausted and exhilarated. He lay in bed trying to imagine how those Labour ministers, who only the previous day had assumed they would be returning to their departments, would be feeling now.

Elizabeth stirred, let out a small sleep-filled sigh. Simon stared down at his wife. In the seven years of their marriage she had lost none of her attraction for him, but he still took pleasure in just looking at her sleeping form. Her long fair hair rested on her shoulders and her slim, firm figure curved gently beneath the silk nightgown. He started stroking her back and watched her slowly come out of sleep. When she finally awoke she turned over and he took her in his arms.

"I admire your energy," she said. "If you're still fit after three weeks on the trail I can hardly claim to have a headache."

He smiled, delighted to catch a moment of privacy between the seeming lunacy of electioneering and the anticipation of office. No voter was going to interrupt this rare moment of pleasure.

"Mum," said a voice, and Simon quickly turned over to see Peter standing at the door in his pyjamas. "I'm hungry."

On the way back to London in the car Elizabeth asked, "What do you think he'll offer you?"

"Daren't anticipate anything," said Simon. "But I would hope – Under-Secretary of State for Housing and Local Government."

"But you're still not certain to be offered a post?"

"Not at all. One can never know what permutations and pressures a new Prime Minister has to consider."

"Like what?" asked Elizabeth.

"Left and right wings of the party, north and south of the country – countless debts to be cleared with those people who can claim they played a role in getting him into No. 10." Simon yawned.

"Are you saying he could leave you out?"

"Oh yes. But I'll be livid if he does, and I'd certainly want to know who had been given my job – and why."

"And what could you do about it?"

"Nothing. There is absolutely nothing one can do and every back-bencher knows it. The Prime Minister's power of patronage is absolute."

"It won't matter, if you continue driving on the centre line," she said. "Are you sure you wouldn't like me to take a turn at the wheel?"

Louise let Andrew lie in on the Friday morning. She knew he had been expecting to return to a higher ministerial office and had been shattered by the election result.

By the time Andrew woke it was nearly eleven. He sat in silence in his dressing-gown, unshaven, and tapped a hard-boiled egg that refused to crack. An unopened *Times* lay by his side.

"Thank you for all your hard work," he said once the second cup of coffee had taken effect. She smiled.

An hour later, dressed in sports jacket and grey flannels, he toured the constituency in a loudspeaker van, thanking his supporters for returning him to Westminster. Louise was by his side, often able to jog his memory on names he couldn't recall.

After they had shaken the last hand they spent a quiet weekend with Sir Duncan in Stirling – who found it extremely hard to remove the smirk from his face.

Raymond was astonished by the election result. He couldn't believe that the opinion polls had been so wrong. He didn't confide in Joyce that he had hoped a Labour victory would bring him back into office after languishing on the back benches for what seemed an interminable time.

"There's nothing for it," he told her, "but to rebuild a career at the bar. We may be out of office for years."

"But surely that won't be enough to keep you fully occupied?"

"I have to be realistic about the future," he said slowly. "Although I don't intend to let Heath drag us into Europe without putting up one hell of a fight."

"Perhaps they'll ask you to Shadow someone?"

"No, there are always far fewer jobs available in Opposition, and in any case they always give the orators like Fraser the dispatch box when all you can do is to sit and make noises while we wait for another election."

Raymond wondered how he would broach what was really on his mind and tried to sound casual when he said, "Perhaps it's time we considered having our own home in the constituency."

"That seems an unnecessary expense," said Joyce, "especially as there's nothing wrong with your parents' home. And, in any case, wouldn't they be offended?"

"My first interest should be my duty to the constituents and this would be a chance to prove a long-term commitment to them. Naturally my parents will understand."

"But we can't afford the cost of two houses," said Joyce uncertainly.

"I realise that, but it's you who have always wanted to live in Leeds, and this will give you the chance to stop commuting from London every week. After I've done the rounds why don't you stay up, contact a few local estate agents and see what's on the market?"

"All right, if that's what you really want," said Joyce. "I'll start next week."

Charles and Fiona spent a quiet weekend at their cottage in Sussex. Charles tried to do some gardening while he kept one ear open for the telephone. Fiona began to realise how anxious he was when she looked through the French windows and saw her finest delphinium being taken for a weed.

Charles eventually gave the weeds a reprieve and came in and turned on the television to catch Maudling, Macleod, Thatcher and Carrington enter No. 10 Downing Street looking pensive, only to leave smiling. The senior appointments had been made: the Cabinet was taking shape. The new Prime Minister came out and waved to the crowds before being whisked away in his official car.

Would he remember who had organised the young vote for him before he was even the party leader?

"When do you want to go back to Eaton Square?" Fiona enquired from the kitchen.

"Depends," said Charles.

"On what?"

"On whether the phone rings."

Simon sat staring at the television. All those hours of work on Housing and Local Government, and the PM had offered the portfolio to someone else. He had left the set on all day but didn't learn who it was, only that the rest of the Housing and Local Government team had remained intact.

"Why do I bother?" he said out loud. "The whole thing's a farce."

"What were you saying, darling?" asked Elizabeth as she came into the room.

The phone rang again. It was the newly appointed Home Secretary, Reginald Maudling.

"Simon?"

"Reggie, many congratulations on your appointment – not that it came as a great surprise."

"That's what I'm calling about, Simon. Would you like to join me at the Home Office as Under-Secretary?"

"Like to? I'd be delighted."

"Thank heavens for that," said Maudling. "It took me a dickens of a time to convince Ted Heath that you should be released from the Housing and Local Government team."

When Andrew and Louise arrived back at Cheyne Walk after

the weekend a red box was waiting for him in the drawing-room. 'Under-Secretary of State for Scotland' was printed in gold on the side.

"They'll be round to collect that later today," he told Louise. He turned the key to find the box was empty: and then he saw the small envelope in one corner. It was addressed to 'Andrew Fraser Esquire, MP'. He tore it open. It contained a short handwritten note from the Permanent Secretary, the senior civil servant at the Scottish Office.

"In keeping with a long tradition, ministers are presented with the last red box from which they worked. *Au revoir*. No doubt we will meet again."

"I suppose it could be used as a lunch box," said Louise, standing by the door.

"Or perhaps an overnight case," offered Andrew.

"Or a very small cot," added his wife, trying to make her words casual.

Andrew looked up to see Louise looking radiant.

"I let your parents know last night, but I wasn't going to tell you until dinner this evening."

Andrew threw his arms around her.

"By the way," Louise added, "we've already decided on her name."

When Raymond arrived back at Lincoln's Inn he let his clerk know that he wanted to be flooded with work. Over lunch with Sir Nigel Hartwell, the head of chambers, he explained that he thought it unlikely that the Labour party would be in Government again for some considerable time.

"Age is on your side, Raymond. Another full Parliament and you'll be barely forty, so you can still look forward to many years in the Cabinet."

"I wonder," said Raymond, uncharacteristically hesitant.

"Well, you needn't worry about briefs. Solicitors have been calling constantly since it was known you were back on a more permanent basis."

Raymond began to relax.

Joyce phoned him after lunch with the news that she hadn't found anything suitable, but the estate agent had assured her that they were expecting a lot more on the market in the autumn.

"Well, keep looking," said Raymond.

"Don't worry, I will," said Joyce, sounding as if she was enjoying the whole exercise. "If we find something perhaps we can think of starting a family," she added tentatively.

"Perhaps," said Raymond brusquely.

Charles eventually received a call on the Monday night, not from No. 10 Downing Street but from No. 12, the office of the Chief Whip. Because the Chief Whip's is not an official post, he is paid as the Parliamentary Secretary to the Treasury and he works from No. 12. The Prime Minister and the Chancellor of the Exchequer, being the first and second Lords of the Treasury, live at Nos. 10 and 11 Downing Street respectively.

The Chief Whip had phoned to say he hoped that Charles would be willing to soldier on as a junior Whip. When he heard the disappointment in Charles's voice he added, "For the time being."

"For the time being," repeated Charles and put the phone down.

"At least you're a member of the Government. You haven't been left out in the cold," said Fiona gamely.

"True," he replied.

"People are sure to come and go during the next five years."

Charles had to agree with his wife but it didn't lessen his disappointment. Returning to the Commons as a member of the Government, however, turned out to be far more rewarding than he had expected. This time it was his party that were making the decisions.

The Queen travelled early that July morning to the House of Lords in the Irish State Coach. An escort of the Household Cavalry accompanied her, preceded by a procession of lesser state carriages in which the Imperial State Crown and other royal trappings were transported. Charles could remember watching the ceremony from the streets when he was a boy. Now he was taking part in it. When the Queen arrived at the

Upper House she was accompanied by the Lord Chancellor through the Sovereign's entrance to the robing room, where her ladies-in-waiting began to prepare her for the ceremony.

Charles always considered the State opening of Parliament a special occasion for members of both Houses. As a Whip he watched the members take their seats in the Commons and await the arrival of Black Rod. Once the Queen was seated on the throne the Lord Great Chamberlain commanded the Gentleman Usher of Black Rod to inform the Commons that: "It is Her Majesty's pleasure they attend her immediately in this House." Black Rod, wearing his black topcoat, black waistcoat, black knee-breeches, black stockings and black shoes, resembled the devil's advocate rather than the Queen's messenger. He marched alone across the great tiled floor joining the two Chambers until he reached the doors of the House of Commons which were slammed in his face when he was just two paces away from them.

He struck the door three times with the silver tip of his long thin black rod. In response a little window in the door was flicked back to check on who it was – not unlike a sleazy nightclub, Charles's father had once observed. Black Rod was then allowed admittance to the Lower House. He advanced towards the table and made three obeisances to the chair before saying, "Mr Speaker, the Queen commands this Honourable House to attend Her Majesty immediately in the House of Peers."

With that, the Serjeant-at-Arms, bearing the mace, led Mr Speaker, in full court dress, a gold embroidered gown of black satin damask, back towards the Lords. They were followed by the Clerk of the House and the Speaker's chaplain, behind whom came the Prime Minister, accompanied by the leader of the Opposition, then Government ministers with their opposite numbers, and finally as many backbenchers as could squeeze into the rear of the Lords' Chamber.

The Lords themselves were waiting in the Upper House, dressed in red capes with ermine collars, looking somewhat like benevolent Draculas, accompanied by peeresses glittering in diamond tiaras and wearing long evening dresses. The Queen was seated on the throne, in her full Monarchical robes, the Imperial State Crown on her head originally made for George IV. She waited until the procession had filled the Chamber and all was still.

The Lord Chancellor shuffled forward and, bending down on one knee, presented her with a printed document. It was the speech, written by the Government of the day, and although she had read over a copy of the script earlier that morning she had made no personal contribution to its contents, as her role on this occasion was only ceremonial. She looked up at her subjects and began to read.

Charles stood at the back of the cramped gathering, but with his height he had no trouble in following the entire proceedings. Their lordships were all in their places for the Queen's speech, with the law lords seated in their privileged position in the centre of the Chamber, an honour bestowed upon them by an Act of 1539. The Lord Chancellor stood to one side of the Woolsack, which was stuffed with wool from the days when it was the staple commodity of England. When the Lords are in session he acts much as the Speaker does for the Commons.

Charles could spot his elderly father, the Earl of Bridgwater, nodding off during the Queen's speech, which promised that Britain would make a determined effort to become a full member of the EEC. "My Government also intends to bring in a bill to enact trade union reform," she declared. Charles, along with everyone else from the Commons, was counting the likely number of bills that would be presented during the coming months and soon worked out that the Whips' office were going to be in for a busy session.

As the Queen finished her speech Charles took one more look at his father, now sound asleep. How Charles dreaded the moment when he would be standing there watching his brother Rupert in ermine. The only compensation would be if he could produce a son who would one day inherit the title, as it was now obvious Rupert would never marry.

It was not as if he and Fiona had not tried. He was

beginning to wonder if the time had not come to suggest that she visit a specialist. He dreaded finding out she was unable to bear a child.

The speech delivered, the Sovereign left the Upper House followed by Prince Philip and Prince Charles to a fanfare of trumpets. At the other end of the Chamber the procession of MPs, led again by the Speaker, made their way back in pairs from the red benches of the Lords to the green of the Commons.

The leader of the Opposition, having formed his own team, invited Andrew to cover the Home Office brief as number two. Andrew was delighted by the challenge of this new responsibility, especially when he discovered Simon Kerslake was to be his opposite number in Government.

Louise once again became very large in a short period, but Andrew tried to keep his mind off the pregnancy, as he dreaded her going through that amount of pain and sorrow for a third time. He telephoned Elizabeth Kerslake and they agreed to meet privately.

"That's a hard question to answer without ifs and buts," she told Andrew over coffee in her room the following day.

"But what would your advice be if Louise were to lose the third child?"

Elizabeth took a long time considering her reply. "If that happened I cannot believe it would be wise to put her through the same ordeal again," she said flatly. "The psychological repercussions alone might affect her for the rest of her life."

Andrew sat staring in front of him.

"Enough of this morbid talk," Elizabeth added. "I checked Louise last week and I can see no reason why this shouldn't turn out to be a routine birth."

As the first weeks of the new Tory administration took shape, Simon and Andrew became locked in battle over several issues and were soon known as 'the mongoose and the rattlesnake'. When either of the names 'Kerslake' or 'Fraser' was cranked up on the old-fashioned wall machines indicating one of them had risen to speak, members drifted back into the Chamber. Andrew found himself a constant visitor to the table office, a tiny room in the corridor behind the Speaker's chair where members tabled their questions, usually scribbled on yellow sheets, but still acceptable to the omniscient clerks had they been written on postage stamps.

The clerks often helped Andrew reword a question so that it would be acceptable to the chair, a function they carried out for any member, even Tom Carson, who had once accused them of political bias when they suggested one of his questions was out of order. When Carson was finally referred to the Speaker, he was called for and reprimanded, and his question deposited in one of the mock-Gothic waste-paper baskets in the Order office.

Once behind the Speaker's chair, Simon and Andrew would good-humouredly discuss the issues on which they were crossing swords. The opportunity to be out of sight of the Press Gallery above them was often taken by the two opposing members, but once they had both returned to the dispatch box they would tear into each other, looking for any weakness in the other's argument.

On one subject they found themselves in total accord. Ever since August 1969, when the troops had first been sent in, Parliament had been having another of its periodic bouts of trouble with Northern Ireland. In October 1970 the House devoted a full day's business to listen to members' opinions in the never-ending effort to find a solution to the growing clash between the Protestant extremists and the IRA. The motion before the House was to allow emergency powers to be renewed in the province.

Andrew rose from his seat on the front bench to deliver the opening speech for the Opposition. He said he took no side in this unhappy affair, but he felt sure the House was united in condemning violence. Yet however hard he searched for the answer he found neither faction willing to give an inch. 'Goodwill' and 'trust' were words that might as well have been left out of any dictionary printed in Ulster. It was not long before Andrew came to the conclusion that Gladstone was right when he had said, "Every time I find the solution to the Irish question, they change the question."

When Andrew had finished he surprised members by leaving the Chamber and not returning for several minutes.

Simon had been selected to wind up for the Government and had prepared his speech with meticulous care. Although both sides appeared in agreement on the main issue, the mood as always could change in a moment if an unfortunate view was expressed by a Government minister.

During the debate, much to everyone's surprise, Andrew Fraser kept leaving the Chamber. Simon left only twice between three-thirty and the ten o'clock division, once to take a call from his wife, and then again at seven-thirty for a quick supper.

When Simon came back Andrew was still absent from the Chamber, and he had not returned by the time the Shadow Home Secretary began to sum up. Andrew did eventually take his seat on the front bench but Simon had already begun his speech.

As Andrew entered the Chamber and took his place on the front bench, an elderly Conservative rose from his seat.

"On a point of order, Mr Speaker."

Simon sat down immediately and turned his head to listen to the point his colleague wanted to make.

"Is it not a tradition of this House, sir," began the elder statesman rather ponderously, "for a front-bench spokesman to have the courtesy to remain in his seat during the debate in order that he may ascertain views other than his own?"

"That is not a point of order," replied the Speaker above the cries of "Hear, hear" from the Conservative benches. Andrew scribbled a quick note and hurriedly passed it over to Simon. On it was written a single sentence.

"I accept the point my Right Honourable friend makes," Simon began, "and would have complained myself had I not known that the Honourable Gentleman, the member for Edinburgh Carlton, has spent most of the afternoon in hospital." Simon paused to let the effect sink in. "Where his wife was in labour. I am not given to accepting as necessarily accurate all the Opposition tells me," he continued, "but I am able to confirm this statement because it was my wife who delivered the baby." The House began to laugh. "I can assure my Honourable friend that my wife has spent her entire afternoon indoctrinating the infant in the value of Conservative policies as understood by his grandfather, which is why the Honourable Gentleman has found it necessary to be absent himself from so much of the debate." Simon waited for the laughter to subside. "For those members of the House who thrive on statistics, it's a boy and he weighs four pounds three ounces."

There are times in the House when affection is displayed on both sides, thought Andrew, who considered it was ironic that during an Irish debate an Englishman had demonstrated such affection for a Scotsman.

There was no challenge when the Speaker 'collected the voices' at ten o'clock so the matter was decided 'on the nod' and Simon joined Andrew behind the Speaker's chair.

"Just over four pounds doesn't sound very big to me. I thought I'd take a second opinion from the Minister of Health."

"I agree," said Andrew, "the little blighter is stuck in an incubator, but your wife is doing everything she can to fatten him up. I'm off to watch him now."

"Good luck," said Simon.

Andrew sat by the incubator all night, hating the drip, drip, drip of the little plastic tube that passed up the child's nose and down into his stomach. He feared that when he woke his son would be dead and continually went to the wash basin and put a damp, cold cloth over his eyes to ensure he remained awake. He finally lost the battle and dozed off in a 'dad's bed' in the corner.

When his father woke, Robert Bruce Fraser was very much alive. The crumpled father rose from his bed to admire his crumpled offspring, who was receiving milk down the plastic tube from a night nurse.

Andrew stared down at the crinkly face. The boy had inherited his square jaw, but he had his mother's nose and hair colouring. Andrew chuckled at the time Louise had wasted over girls' names. Robert it would be.

Robert Bruce Fraser travelled to Cheyne Walk with his

mother and father three weeks later, having topped the scales earlier that morning at five pounds ten ounces.

Elizabeth Kerslake had told them to be thankful: the post-natal examination had shown that it would not be possible for Louise to bear another child.

CHAPTER
TWELVE

The Chief Whip looked round at his colleagues, wondering which of them would volunteer for such a thankless task.

A hand went up, and he was pleasantly surprised.

"Thank you, Charles."

Charles had already warned Fiona that he was going to volunteer to be the Whip responsible for the issue that had most dominated the last election: Britain's entry into the EEC. Everyone in that room realised that it would be the most demanding marathon of the entire Parliament, and there was an audible sigh of relief when Charles volunteered.

"Not a job for anyone with a rocky marriage," he heard one Whip whisper. At least that's something I don't have to worry about, thought Charles, but he made a note to take home some flowers that night.

"Why was it the bill everyone wanted to avoid?" asked Fiona as she arranged the daffodils.

"Because many of our side don't necessarily back Edward Heath in his lifelong ambition to take Britain into Europe, while quite a few of the Opposition do," said Charles, accepting a large brandy. "Added to that, we have the problem of presenting a bill to curb the trade unions at the same time which may well influence many members of the Labour party from voting with us on Europe. Because of this problem, the Prime Minister requires a regular 'state of play' assessment on Europe even though legislation may not be presented on the floor of the Commons for at least another year. He'll want to know periodically how many of our side are still against entry, and how many from the Opposition we can rely on to break ranks when the crucial vote is taken."

"Perhaps I should become Member of Parliament and then at least I could spend a little more time with you."

"Especially on the European issue if you were a 'don't know'."

The 'Great Debate' was discussed by the media to the point of boredom. Members were nevertheless conscious that they were playing a part in history. And, because of the unusual spectacle of the Whips not being in absolute control of the voting procedure, the Commons sprang to life, and excitement began to build up over the weeks and months of debate.

Charles retained his normal task of watching over fifty members on all normal Government bills, but because of the priority given to the issue of entry into Europe he had been released from all other duties. He knew that this was his chance to atone for his disastrous winding-up speech on the economy which he sensed his colleagues had still not completely forgotten.

"I'm gambling everything on this one," he told Fiona. "And if we lose the final vote I will be sentenced to the back benches for life."

"And if we win?"

"It will be hard to keep me off the front bench," replied Charles.

Robert Fraser was one of those noisy children who after only a few weeks sounded as if he was on the front bench.

"Perhaps he's going to be a politician after all," concluded Louise, staring down at her son.

"What has changed your mind?" asked Andrew.

"He never stops shouting at everyone, he's totally pre-occupied with himself and he falls asleep as soon as someone else offers an opinion," she replied.

"At last I think I've found it." After Raymond heard the news he took the train up to Leeds the following Friday. Joyce had selected four houses for him to consider, but he had to agree with her that the one in Chapel Allerton was exactly what they were looking for. It was also by far the most expensive.

"Can we afford it?" asked Joyce anxiously.

"Probably not, but one of the problems of seeing four houses is that you end up only wanting the best one."

"I could go on looking."

"No, you've found the right house; now I'll have to work out how we can pay for it, and I think I may have come up with an idea."

Joyce said nothing, waiting for him to continue.

"We could sell our place in Lansdowne Road."

"But where would we live when you're in London?"

"I could rent a small flat somewhere between the law courts and the Commons while you set up our real home in Leeds."

"But wouldn't you get lonely?"

"Of course I will," said Raymond, trying to sound convincing. "But almost every member north of Birmingham is parted from his wife during the week. In any case, you've always wanted to settle in Yorkshire, and this might be our best chance. If my practice continues to grow we can buy a second house in London at a later date."

Joyce looked apprehensive.

"One added bonus," said Raymond, "your being in Leeds will ensure I never lose the seat."

She smiled, as she always felt reassured whenever Raymond showed the slightest sign of needing her.

On Monday morning Raymond put in a bid for the house in Chapel Allerton before returning to London. After a little bargaining over the phone during the week, he and the owner settled on a price. By Thursday Raymond had put his Lansdowne Road house on the market and was surprised by the amount the estate agent thought it would fetch.

All Raymond had to do now was find himself a flat.

Simon sent a note to Ronnie expressing his thanks for keeping him so well informed about what was happening at Nethercote and Company. It had been eight months since he had resigned from the board because of his appointment as a minister, but Ronnie saw that the minutes of each meeting were posted to him to study in his own time. 'His own time': Simon had to laugh at the thought.

His overdraft at the bank now stood at a little over £72,000, but as Ronnie intended the shares should be offered at five pounds each when they went public Simon felt sure there was still a fair leeway, as his personal holding should realise £300,000. Elizabeth warned him not to spend a penny of the profit until the money was safely in the bank. He was thankful she didn't know the full extent of his borrowing.

Over one of their occasional lunches at the Ritz, Ronnie spelt out to Simon his plans for the future of the company.

"Now that the Tories are in I think I'll go public in eighteen months' time. This year's profits are up again and next year's look even better. So 1973 looks a perfect bet."

Simon looked apprehensive and Ronnie responded quickly. "If you're having any problem, Simon, I'll be happy to take the shares off your hands at their market value. At least that way you'd show a small profit."

"No, no," said Simon. "I'll hang in there now that I've waited this long."

"Suit yourself," said Ronnie. "Now tell me – how are you enjoying the Home Office?"

Simon put down his knife and fork. "Of the three great offices of state, it's the one most involved with people, so there's a new challenge at a personal level every day, although it can be depressing too. Locking people up in prisons, banning immigrants and deporting harmless aliens isn't my idea of fun. The Home Office never seems to want anyone to enjoy too much freedom."

"And what about Ireland?"

"What about Ireland?" said Simon, shrugging his shoulders.

"I'd give the north back to Eire," said Ronnie, "or let them go independent and give them a large cash incentive to do so. At the moment the whole exercise is money down the drain."

"We're discussing people," said Simon, "not money."

"Ninety per cent of the voters would back me," said Ronnie, lighting a cigar.

"Everyone imagines ninety per cent of the people support their views, until they stand for election," said Simon. "The issue of Ireland is far too important to be glib about. I repeat, we're discussing people, eight million people, all of whom have the same right to justice as you and I. And as long as I work in the Home Office I intend to see that they get it."

Ronnie remained silent.

"I'm sorry, Ronnie," continued Simon. "Too many people have an easy solution to Ireland. If there *was* an easy solution the problem wouldn't have lasted over two hundred years."

"Don't be sorry," said Ronnie. "I'm so stupid, I've only just worked out for the first time why you're in public office."

"You're a typical self-made Fascist," said Simon, teasing his companion once again.

"You may be right, but you won't change my mind on hanging. Your lot should bring back the rope; the streets aren't safe any longer."

"For property developers like you, hoping for a quick killing?"

Both men laughed.

"Andrew, do you want lunch?"

"In a moment, in a moment."

"That's what you said half an hour ago."

"I know, but he's nearly got it. Just give me a few more minutes." Louise waited and watched, but Robert collapsed in a heap again.

"No doubt you're expecting him to play soccer for England by the time he's two."

"No, certainly not," said Andrew, carrying his son back into the house. "Rugby for Scotland."

Louise was touched by the amount of time Andrew spent with Robert. She told her disbelieving friends that he regularly fed and bathed the baby and even changed his nappy.

"Don't you think he's good-looking?" asked Andrew, strapping his son carefully into his chair.

"Yes," said Louise, laughing.

"That's because he looks like me," said Andrew, putting his arms round his wife.

"He most certainly does not," said Louise firmly.

Crash. A bowlful of porridge had been deposited on the floor, leaving just a lump left in the spoon, which Robert was now smearing across his face and hair.

"He looks as if he has just stepped out of a concrete mixer," said Andrew.

Louise stared at her son. "Perhaps you're right. There *are* times when he looks like you."

"How do you feel about rape?" asked Raymond.

"I can't see that it's relevant," Stephanie Arnold replied.

"I think they'll go for me on it," said Raymond.

"But why?"

"They'll be able to pin me in a corner, damage my character."

"But where does it get them? They can't prove lack of consent."

"Maybe, but they will offer it as background to prove the rest of the case."

"Because you raped someone doesn't prove you murdered them."

Raymond and Stephanie Arnold, who was new to chambers, continued discussing their first case together on the way to the Old Bailey, and she left Raymond in no doubt that she was delighted to be led by him. They were to appear together to defend a labourer accused of the rape and murder of his step-daughter.

"Open and shut case unfortunately," said Raymond, "but we're going to make the Crown prove their argument beyond anyone's doubt."

When the case stretched into a second week Raymond began to believe that the jury were so gullible they might even get their client off. Stephanie was sure they would.

The day before the judge's summing up Raymond invited Stephanie to dinner at the House of Commons. That'll make them turn their heads, he thought to himself. They won't have seen anything in a white shirt and black stockings that looks like that for some time, certainly not Mr Speaker.

Stephanie seemed flattered by the invitation and sat through the stodgy meal served in the Strangers' Dining-room, obviously impressed as former Cabinet ministers flitted in and out, all of them acknowledging him.

"How's the new flat?" asked Stephanie.

"Worked out well," replied Raymond. "The Barbican is so convenient for Parliament and the law courts."

"Does your wife like it?" she asked, lighting a cigarette but not looking at him directly.

"She's not in town that much nowadays. She spends most of her time in Leeds – doesn't care much for London."

The awkward pause that followed was interrupted by a sudden clanging of bells.

"Are we on fire?" said Stephanie, quickly stubbing out her cigarette.

"No," said Raymond laughing. "Just the ten o'clock division. I have to leave you and vote. I'll be back in about fifteen minutes."

"Shall I order coffee?"

"No, don't bother," said Raymond. "It's foul. Perhaps . . . perhaps you'd like to come back to the Barbican? Then you can give a verdict on my flat."

"Maybe it's an open and shut case," she smiled.

Raymond returned the smile before joining his colleagues as they flooded out of the dining-room down the corridor towards the Commons Chamber. He didn't have time to explain to Stephanie that he had only six minutes to get into the right lobby. As Raymond had no idea what they were voting on that night he followed the surge of Labour members into the Noes lobby. The bells stopped and the doors were bolted.

Whenever the vote is called for at the end of the debate the Speaker puts the question and the moment he reaches the words, "I think the Ayes have it," the roar of "No" from those opposed to the motion ensures a vote at ten o'clock. Bells peal out over the Palace of Westminster, and in some nearby restaurants and members' homes in the division-bell area.

Members then scurry into the Ayes or Noes division lobby before the cry of "Lock the doors" is heard. Once the doors have been secured each member then files past two clerks seated at a high desk at the far end of the corridor who tick off his name. As Raymond stepped past the clerks he came towards the exit doors which were angled so as to make a funnel through which only one member at a time could pass. The Whip acting as teller shouted out the mounting vote. "Seventy-three," he called as Raymond passed him. The only particular rule relating to voting was that members could not wear a hat or overcoat while in the lobby. A clerk had once told Raymond that this dated from the days when lazy members sent their driver off in the hansom cab, hats over ears, coat buttoned up to the nose, to march through the corridors and give their masters' names. Some of them would have been a damn sight better MPs then their employers, Raymond had often thought.

While in the corridor he discovered that they were voting on a clause of the Trade Union Bill concerning the validity of closed shops. He was in no doubt that he supported his party on that subject.

When he returned to the Strangers' Dining-room after the vote he found Stephanie checking her face in a compact mirror, a small round face with green eyes and brunette hair. She was replacing the trace of lipstick. He suddenly felt conscious of being a little overweight for a man not yet forty.

"Shall we go?" he suggested, after he had signed the bill.

Once they had reached the flat Raymond put on a Charles Aznavour record and retired to the small kitchen to prepare coffee. He was totally oblivious to the fact that women were beginning to find him attractive. A little extra weight and a few grey hairs had not harmed his appearance, if anything giving him an air of authority.

"There's no doubting this is a bachelor flat," Stephanie remarked as she took in the one comfortable leather chair, the pipe stand, and the Spy cartoons of turn-of-the-century judges and politicians.

"I suppose that's because that's what it is," he mused,

setting down a tray laden with coffee and two brandy
balloons generously filled with cognac.

"Don't you get lonely?" she asked.

"From time to time," he said, pouring the coffee.

"And between times?"

"Black?" he asked, not looking at her.

"Black," she said.

"Sugar?"

"For a man who has served as a minister of the Crown and
who, it's rumoured, is about to become the youngest QC in
the country, you're still very unsure of yourself with women."

Raymond blushed, but raised his head and stared into her
eyes.

In the silence he caught Aznavour's words, "You've let
yourself go . . ."

"Would my Honourable friend care to dance?" she said
quietly.

Raymond could still remember the last occasion he had
danced. This time he was determined it would be different.
He held Stephanie so that their bodies touched and they
swayed rather than danced to the music of Marcel Stellman.
She didn't notice Raymond slipping off his glasses and
putting them into his jacket pocket. He bent over and kissed
her neck. She gave a long sigh, and when they parted, she
said, "Let's hope this is between times."

Charles studied his chart of 330 Conservatives. He felt
confident of 217, not sure about fifty-four and had almost
given up on fifty-nine. On the Labour side the best information he could glean was that fifty Socialists were expected to
defy the Whip and join the Government's ranks when the
great vote took place.

"The main fly in the ointment," Charles reported to the
Chief Whip, "is still the Trade Union Reform Bill. The left
are trying to convince those Socialists who still support the
bill that there is no cause so important for which they should
enter the same lobby as those Tory trade union bashers." He
went on to explain his fear that unless the Government were
willing to modify the Trade Union Bill they might lose

Europe on the back of it. "Alec Pimkin doesn't help matters by trying to gather the waverers in our party round him."

"There's no chance of the Prime Minister modifying one sentence of the Trade Union Bill," said the Chief Whip, draining his gin and tonic. "He promised it in his speech at the party conference, and he intends to deliver by the time he goes to Blackpool at the end of this year. I can also tell you he isn't going to like your conclusions on Pimkin, Charles. He cares almost as passionately about trade union reform as he does about Europe." Charles was about to protest. "I'm not complaining, you've done damn well so far. Just keep working on the fifty waverers. Threaten, cajole, bully, bribe. Try anything, but get them in the right lobby come the night, Pimkin included."

"How about sex?" asked Charles.

"You've been seeing too many American films," said the Chief Whip, laughing. "In any case I don't think we've got anyone other than Miss Norse to offer them."

Charles returned to his office and went over the list once again. His forefinger stopped at the letter 'P'. Charles strolled out into the corridor and looked around; his quarry wasn't there. He checked the Chamber: no sign of him. He passed the library. No need to look in there, he thought, and moved on to the smoking room where he found his man, about to order another gin.

"Alec," said Charles expansively.

The rotund figure of Pimkin looked round.

May as well try bribery first, thought Charles. "Let me get you a drink."

"That's good of you, old fellow," said Pimkin, nervously fingering his bow tie.

"Now, Alec, what's this about your voting against the European Bill?"

Simon was horrified when he read the initial document. Its implications were all too evident.

The report of the new Boundary Commission had been left in the red box for him to study over the weekend. He had agreed at a meeting of Home Office officials that he would steer it through the House as quickly as possible so that it would make the basis for the seats to be contested at the next election. As the Secretary of State reminded him: there must be no hold-ups.

Simon had read the document carefully. In essence the changes made sense and, because of the movement of families from urban to rural areas, it would undoubtedly create more winnable seats for the Conservatives overall. No wonder the party wanted no hold-ups. But what could he do about the decision the Commission had come to on his own constituency, Coventry Central? His hands were tied. If he suggested any change from the Boundary Commission's recommendations he would rightly be accused of jerrymandering.

Because of the city's dwindling population the Commission had recommended that the four constituencies of Coventry become three. Coventry Central was to be the one to disappear, its voters distributed among Coventry West, Coventry East and Coventry North. Simon realised this would leave one safe seat for his sitting colleague and two safe Labour seats. It had never been far from his mind how marginal a constituency he represented. Now he was on the verge of being without one at all. He would have to traipse around the country all over again looking for a new seat to fight at the next election, while at the same time taking care of his constituents in the moribund one; and at the stroke of a pen – *his* pen – they would pass on their loyalties to someone else. If only he had remained in Housing and Local Government he could have put up a case for keeping all four seats.

Elizabeth was sympathetic when he explained the problem but told him not to concern himself too much until he had spoken to the vice-chairman of the party, who advised candidates which constituencies were likely to become available.

"It may even work out to your advantage," she added.

"What do you mean?" said Simon.

"You could get a safer seat nearer London."

"With my luck I'll end up with a marginal in Newcastle."

Elizabeth prepared his favourite meal and spent the evening trying to keep up his spirits. After three portions of shepherd's pie Simon fell asleep almost as soon as he put his head on the pillow. But she stayed awake long into the night.

The casual conversation with the head of Gynaecology at St Mary's kept running through her mind. Although she hadn't confided in Simon, she could recall her supervisor's every word.

"I notice from the roster that you've had far more days off than you are entitled to, Dr Kerslake. You must make up your mind if you want to be a doctor or the wife of an MP."

Elizabeth stirred restlessly as she considered the problem, but came to no conclusion except not to bother Simon while he had so much on his mind.

"Do these boundary changes affect you?" Louise asked, looking up from her copy of *The Times*.

Andrew was bouncing a small rubber ball on Robert's head.

"You'll give him brain damage," said Louise.

"I know, but think of the goals he'll score – and it won't be long before I can start him on rugby."

Robert started to cry when his father stopped to answer his mother's question. "No, Edinburgh isn't affected. There's such a small movement in the population that the seven city seats will remain intact. The only real changes in Scotland will be in Glasgow and the Highlands."

"That's a relief," said Louise. "I should hate to have to look for another constituency."

"Poor old Simon Kerslake is losing his seat altogether and he daren't do anything about it."

"Why not?" asked Louise.

"Because he's the minister in charge of the bill, and if he tried anything clever we would crucify him."

"So what will he do?"

"Have to shop around for a new seat, or convince an older colleague to stand down in his favour."

"But surely ministers find it easy to pick up a plum seat?"

"Not necessarily," said Andrew. "Many constituencies don't like to have someone foisted on them and want to choose their own man. And some actually prefer a local man who will never be a minister, because they feel he can devote more time to them."

"Andrew, can you revert to being some use in Opposition?"

"What are you suggesting?" asked Andrew.

"Just keep throwing that ball at your stupid son's head or he'll be crying all day."

"Take no notice of her, Robert. She'll feel differently when you score your first goal against England."

CHAPTER
THIRTEEN

At exactly the time Raymond was ready to stop the affair Stephanie began leaving a set of court clothes in the flat. Although the two had gone their separate ways at the conclusion of the case they continued to see one another a couple of evenings a week. Raymond had had a spare key made so that Stephanie didn't have to spend her life checking when he had a three-line whip.

At first he began simply to avoid her, but she would then seek him out. When he did manage to give her the slip he would often find her back in his flat when he returned from the Commons. When he suggested they should be a little more discreet she began to make threats, subtle at first, but after a time more direct.

During the period of their affair Raymond conducted three major cases for the Crown, all of which had successful conclusions and which added to his reputation. On each occasion his clerk made certain Stephanie was not assigned to be with him. Now that his residency problem had been sorted out Raymond's only worry was how to end their relationship. He quickly discovered that getting rid of Stephanie Arnold was going to prove considerably more difficult than picking her up.

Simon was on time for his appointment at Central Office. He explained his dilemma to Sir Edward Mountjoy – vice-chairman of the party responsible for candidates – in graphic detail.

"What bloody bad luck," said Sir Edward. "But perhaps I

may be able to help," he added, opening the green folder on the desk in front of him. Simon could see that he was studying a list of names. It made him feel once again like an undergraduate who needed someone to die.

"There seem to be about a dozen safe seats that will fall vacant at the next election, caused either by retirement or redistribution."

"Anywhere in particular you could recommend?"

"I fancy Littlehampton."

"Where's that?" said Simon.

"It will be a new seat, safe as houses. It's in Sussex, on the borders of Hampshire." He studied an attached map. "Runs proud to Charles Seymour's constituency which remains unchanged. Can't think you would have many rivals there," said Sir Edward. "But why don't you have a word with Charles? He's bound to know everyone involved in taking the decision."

"Anything else that looks promising?" asked Simon, only too aware that Seymour might not prove altogether co-operative.

"Let me see. Can't afford to put all your eggs in one basket, can we? Ah, yes – Redcorn, in Northumberland." Again the vice-chairman studied the map. "Three hundred and twenty miles from London and no airport within eighty miles, and their nearest main line station is forty miles. I think that one's only worth trying for if you get desperate. My advice would be to speak to Charles Seymour about Littlehampton. He must know the lay of the land in that neck of the woods."

Two clichés in one sentence, thought Simon. Thank heavens Sir Edward would never have to make a speech from the dispatch box.

"I'm sure you're right, Sir Edward," he said.

"Selection committees are being formed already," continued Sir Edward, "so you shouldn't have to wait too long."

"I appreciate your help," said Simon. "Perhaps you could let me know if anything else comes up in the meantime."

"Of course, delighted. The problem is that if one of our side were to die during the sessions you couldn't desert your present seat because that would cause two by-elections. We

certainly don't want a by-election in Coventry Central with
you being accused of being a carpetbagger somewhere else."

"Don't remind me," said Simon.

Charles had whittled down the fifty-nine anti-Common Market members to fifty-one, but he was now dealing with the
hard kernel who seemed quite immune to future advancement or bullying. When he made his next report to the Chief
Whip Charles assured him that the Conservatives who
would vote against entry into Europe were outnumbered by
the Socialists who had declared they would support the
Government. The Chief Whip seemed pleased, but asked if
Charles had made any progress with Pimkin's disciples.

"Those twelve mad right-wingers?" said Charles sharply.
"They seem to be willing to follow Pimkin even into the
valley of death. I've tried everything but they're still determined to vote against Europe whatever the cost."

"The maddening thing is that that bloody nuisance Pimkin has nothing to lose," said the Chief Whip. "His seat
disappears at the end of this Parliament in the redistribution.
I can't imagine anyone with his extreme views would find a
constituency to select him, but by then he'll have done the
damage." The Chief Whip paused. "If his twelve would even
abstain I would feel confident of advising the PM of victory."

"The problem is to find a way of turning Pimkin into Judas
and then urging him to lead the chosen twelve into our
camp," said Charles.

"You achieve that, and we'd certainly win."

Charles returned to the Whips' office to find Simon Kerslake waiting by his desk.

"I dropped by on the off-chance, hoping you might be able
to spare me a few moments," said Simon.

"Of course," said Charles, trying to sound welcoming.
"Take a pew."

Simon sat down opposite him. "You may have heard that I
lose my constituency as a result of the Boundary Commission
report and Edward Mountjoy suggested I have a word with
you about Littlehampton, the new seat that borders your
constituency."

"It does indeed," said Charles, masking his surprise. He had not considered the problem as his own seat remained intact. He recovered quickly. "And how wise of Edward to send you to me. I'll do everything I can to help."

"Littlehampton would be ideal," said Simon. "Especially while my wife is still working in Paddington."

Charles raised his eyebrows.

"I don't think you've met Elizabeth. She's a doctor at St Mary's," Simon explained.

"Yes, I can see how convenient Littlehampton would be. Why don't I start by having a word with Alexander Dalglish, the constituency chairman, and see what I can come up with?"

"That would be extremely helpful."

"Not at all. I'll call him at home this evening and find out what stage they've reached over selection, and then I'll put you in the picture."

"I'd appreciate that."

"While I've got you, let me give you the whip for next week," said Charles, passing over a sheet of paper. Simon folded it up and put it in his pocket. "I'll call you the moment I have some news."

Simon left feeling happier and a little guilty about his past prejudice concerning Charles, whom he watched disappear into the Chamber to carry out his bench duty.

The European issue had been given six days for debate by back-benchers, the longest period of time allocated to one motion in living memory.

Charles strolled down the aisle leading to the front bench and took a seat on the end to check on another set of speeches. Usually he listened intently to see if he could spot a member wavering in his position; but on this occasion his thoughts were in Littlehampton. Andrew Fraser was on his feet, and Charles was delighted to be able to confirm the tick alongside his name before he drifted into deep thought.

"I for one shall vote for entry into Europe," Andrew was telling the House. "When my party was in power I was a pro-European, and now we are in Opposition I can see no good reason to do a volte-face. The principles that held true two years ago hold true today. Not all of us . . ."

Tom Carson leaped up and asked if his Honourable friend would give way. Andrew resumed his seat immediately.

"Would my Honourable friend really support the peasant farmers of France before the sheep farmers in New Zealand?" asked Carson.

Andrew rose and explained to his colleague that he would certainly expect safeguards for New Zealand, but the initial vote on the floor of the House was on the principle of entry. The details could and should be dealt with in committee. He went on to express the view that had his Honourable friend talked of wogs or Jews in such a context the House would have been in uproar. "Why is it therefore acceptable to the anti-marketeers to describe French farmers as peasants?"

"Perhaps it's you who is the peasant," Carson shouted back, in seven words thus ruining his case for the lamb farmers of New Zealand.

Andrew ignored the jibe and went on to tell the House that he believed in a united Europe as a further insurance against a third world war. He concluded with the words:

"Britain has for a thousand years written history, even the history of the world. Let us decide with our votes whether our children will read that history, or continue to write it." Andrew sat down to acclamation from both sides.

By the time Andrew had resumed his seat Charles had formed a plan and left the Chamber when one of his own colleagues started what promised to be a long, boring and predictable speech.

Instead of returning to the Whips' office which afforded no privacy, Charles disappeared into one of the telephone booths near the cloisters above the Members' Cloakroom. He checked the number and dialled it.

"Alexander, it's Charles. Charles Seymour."

"Good to hear from you, Charles, it's been a long time. How are you?"

"Well. And you?"

"Can't complain. What can I do for a busy man like you?"

"Wanted to chew over the new Sussex constituency with

you, Littlehampton. How's your selection of a candidate going?"

"They've left me to draw up a short list of six for final selection by the full committee in about ten days' time."

"Have you thought of standing yourself, Alexander?"

"Many times," came back the reply. "But the old lady wouldn't allow it, neither would the bank balance. Do you have any ideas?"

"Might be able to help. Why don't you come and have a quiet dinner at my place early next week?"

"That's kind of you, Charles."

"Not at all, it will be good to see you again. It's been far too long. Next Monday suit you?"

"Absolutely."

"Good, let's say eight o'clock, 27 Eaton Square."

Charles put the phone down, returned to the Whips' Office and pencilled a note in his diary.

Raymond had just finished making his contribution to the European debate when Charles returned to take a seat on a half-empty Treasury bench. Raymond had made a coherent economic case for remaining free of the other six European countries and for building stronger links with the Commonwealth and America. He doubted that Britain could take the financial burden of entering a club that had been in existence for so long. If the country had joined at its inception it might have been different, he argued, but he would have to vote against this risky, unproven venture that he suspected could only lead to higher unemployment. When Raymond sat down he did not receive the acclamation that Andrew had and, worse, what praise he did elicit came from the left wing of the party who had spent so much time in the past criticising *Full Employment at any Cost?* Charles put a cross by the name Gould.

A note was being passed along the row to Raymond from one of the House Badge messengers, dressed in white tie and black tails. It read, 'Please ring head of chambers as soon as convenient.'

Raymond left the floor of the House and went to the

nearest telephone in the corner of the Members' Lobby. He was immediately put through to Sir Nigel Hartwell.

"You wanted me to phone?"

"Yes," said Sir Nigel. "Are you free at the moment?"

"I am," said Raymond. "Why? Is it something urgent?"

"I'd rather not talk about it over the phone," said Sir Nigel ominously.

Raymond took a tube from Westminster to Temple and was in chambers fifteen minutes later. He went straight to Sir Nigel's office, sat down in the comfortable chair in the corner of the spacious club-like room, crossed his legs and watched Sir Nigel pace about in front of him. He was clearly determined to get something off his chest.

"Raymond, I have been asked by those in authority about you taking silk. I've said I think you'd make a damn good QC." A smile came over Raymond's face, but it was soon wiped off. "But I need an undertaking from you."

"An undertaking?"

"Yes," said Sir Nigel. "You must stop having this damn silly er . . . relationship with another member of chambers." He rounded on Raymond and faced him.

Raymond turned scarlet but before he could speak the head of chambers continued.

"Now I want your word on it," said Sir Nigel, "that it will end, and end immediately."

"You have my word," said Raymond quietly.

"I'm not a prig," said Sir Nigel, pulling down on his waistcoat, "but if you are going to have an affair for God's sake make it as far away from the office as possible and, if I may advise you, that should include the House of Commons and Leeds. There's still a lot of the world left over and it's full of women."

Raymond nodded his agreement: he could not fault the head of chambers' logic.

Sir Nigel continued, obviously embarrassed. "There's a nasty fraud case starting in Manchester next Monday. Our client has been accused of setting up a series of companies that specialise in life insurance but avoid paying out on the claims: I expect you remember all the publicity. Miss Arnold has been put on the case as a reserve junior. They tell me it could last several weeks."

"She'll try and get out of it," said Raymond glumly.

"She already has, but I made it quite clear that if she felt unable to take the case on she would have to find other chambers."

Raymond breathed a sigh of relief. "Thank you," he said.

"Sorry about this. I know you've earned your silk, old boy, but I can't have members of chambers going around with egg on their faces. Thank you for your co-operation: I can't pretend I enjoyed that."

"Got time for a quiet word?" asked Charles.

"You're wasting your time, dear thing, if you imagine the disciples will change their minds at this late stage," said Alec Pimkin. "All twelve of them will vote against the Government on Europe. That's final."

"I don't want to discuss Europe this time, Alec. It's far more serious, and on a personal level. Let's go and have a drink on the terrace."

Charles ordered the drinks, and the two men strolled out on to the quiet end of the terrace towards the Speaker's house. Charles stopped as soon as he was certain there was no longer anyone within earshot.

"If it's not Europe, what is it?" asked Pimkin, staring out at the Thames.

"What's this I hear about you losing your seat?"

Pimkin turned pale and touched his bow tie nervously. "It's this bloody boundary business. My constituency is swallowed up, and no one seems willing to interview me for a new one."

"What's it worth if I secure you a safe seat for the rest of your life?"

Pimkin looked suspiciously up at Charles. "Almost anything up to a pound of flesh," he added with a false laugh.

"No, I won't need to cut that deep."

The colour returned to Pimkin's cheeks. "Whatever it is, you can rely on me, old fellow."

"Can you deliver the disciples?" said Charles.

Pimkin turned pale again.

"Not on the small votes in committee," said Charles, before Pimkin could reply. "Not on the clauses even, just on the second reading, the principle itself. Standing by the party in their hour of need, no desire to cause an unnecessary general election, all that stuff – you fill in the details for the disciples. I know you can convince them, Alec."

Pimkin still didn't speak.

"I deliver a copper-bottomed seat, you deliver twelve votes. I think we can call that a fair exchange."

"What if I get them to abstain?" said Pimkin.

Charles waited, as if giving the idea considerable thought. "It's a deal," he said, never having hoped for anything more.

Alexander Dalglish arrived at Eaton Square a little after eight. Fiona met him at the door and explained that Charles had not yet returned from the Commons.

"But I expect him any moment," she added. "May I offer you a drink?"

Another thirty minutes passed before Charles hurried in.

"Sorry I'm late, Alexander," he said, grasping his guest by the hand. "Hoped I might make it just before you." He kissed his wife on the forehead.

"Not at all," said Alexander. "I couldn't have asked for more pleasant company."

"What will you have, darling?" asked Fiona.

"A strong whisky, please, and can we go straight into dinner? I've got to be back at the talkshop by ten."

Charles guided his guest towards the dining-room and seated him at the side of the table before taking his place below the Holbein portrait of the first Earl of Bridgwater, an heirloom his grandfather had left him. Fiona took a seat opposite her husband. During the meal of Beef Wellington, Charles spent a great deal of time catching up on what Alexander had been doing since they had last met. Although they had spent three years together in the Guards as brother officers they rarely saw each other outside of regimental reunions since Charles had entered the House. He made no mention of the real purpose behind the meeting until Fiona provided the opportunity when she served coffee.

"I know you two have a lot to talk about, so I'll leave you to get on with it."

"Thank you," said Alexander. He looked up at Fiona and smiled. "For a lovely dinner."

She smiled back and left them alone.

"Now, Charles," said Alexander, picking up the file he had left on the floor by his side. "I need to pick your brains."

"Go ahead, old fellow," said Charles, "only too delighted to be of assistance."

"Sir Edward Mountjoy has sent me a pretty long list for us to consider, among them a Home Office minister and one or two other Members of Parliament who'll be losing their present seats. What do you think of . . .?"

Dalglish opened the file in front of him as Charles poured him a generous glass of port and offered him a cigar from a gold case that he picked up from the sideboard.

"What a magnificent object," said Alexander, staring in awe at the crested box and the engraved C.G.S. along its top.

"A family heirloom," said Charles. "Should have been left to my brother Rupert, but I was lucky enough to have the same initials as my grandfather."

Alexander handed it back to his host before returning to his notes.

"Here's the man who impresses me," he said at last. "Kerslake, Simon Kerslake."

Charles remained silent.

"You don't have an opinion, Charles?"

"Yes."

"So what do you think of Kerslake?"

"Strictly off the record?"

Dalglish nodded, but said nothing.

Charles sipped his port. "Very good," he said.

"Kerslake?"

"No, the port. Taylor's '35. I'm afraid Kerslake is not the same vintage. Need I say more?"

"Well, no, I follow your drift but it's most disappointing. He looks so good on paper."

"On paper is one thing," said Charles, "but having him as your member for twenty years is quite another. You want a man you can rely on. And his wife – never seen in the constituency, you know." He frowned. "I'm afraid I've gone too far."

"No, no," said Alexander. "I've got the picture. Next one is Norman Lamont."

"First class but he's already been selected for Kingston, I'm afraid," said Charles.

Dalglish looked down at his file once again. "Well, what about Pimkin?"

"We were at Eton together. His looks are against him, as my grandmother used to say, but he's a sound man, and very good in the constituency, so they tell me."

"You would recommend him then?"

"I should snap him up before another constituency adopts him."

"That popular, is he?" said Alexander. "Thanks for the tip. Pity about Kerslake."

"That was strictly off the record," said Charles.

"Of course. Not a word. You can rely on me."

"Cigar to your liking?"

"Excellent," said Alexander, "but your judgement has always been so good. You only have to look at Fiona to realise that."

Charles smiled.

Most of the other names Dalglish produced were either unknown, unsuitable or easy to dismiss. When Alexander left shortly before ten Fiona asked him if the chat had been worthwhile.

"Yes, I think we've found the right man."

Raymond had the locks on his flat changed that afternoon. It turned out to be more expensive than he had bargained for, and the carpenter had insisted on cash in advance.

The carpenter grinned as he pocketed the money. "I make a fortune doing this job, Guv'nor, I can tell you. At least one gentleman a day, always cash, no receipt. Means the wife and I can spend a month in Ibiza every year, tax free."

Raymond smiled at the thought. He checked his watch; he could just catch the Thursday seven-ten from King's Cross and be in Leeds by ten o'clock for a long weekend.

Alexander Dalglish phoned Charles a week later to tell him Pimkin had made the short list, and that they hadn't considered Kerslake.

"Pimkin didn't go over very well with the committee at the first interview."

"No, he wouldn't," said Charles. "I warned you his looks were agin' him and he may come over a bit right wing at times but he's as sound as a bell and will never let you down, take my word."

"I'll have to, Charles. Because by getting rid of Kerslake we've removed his only real challenger."

Charles put the phone down and dialled the Home Office.

"Simon Kerslake, please."

"Who's calling?"

"Seymour, Whips' office." He was put straight through.

"Simon, it's Charles. I thought I ought to give you an update on Littlehampton."

"That's thoughtful of you," said Simon.

"Not good news, I'm afraid. It turns out the chairman wants the seat for himself. He's making sure the committee only interviews idiots."

"How can you be so certain?"

"I've seen the short list and Pimkin's the only sitting member they're considering."

"I can't believe it."

"No, I was pretty shocked myself. I pressed the case for you, but it fell on deaf ears. Didn't care for your views on hanging or some such words. Still, I can't believe you'll find it hard to pick up a seat."

"I hope you're right, Charles, but in any case thanks for trying."

"Any time. Let me know of any other seats you put your name in for. I have a lot of friends up and down the country."

"Thank you, Charles. Can you pair me for next Thursday?"

Two days later Alec Pimkin was invited by the Little-hampton Conservatives to attend a short-list interview for the selection of a Tory candidate for the new constituency.

"How do I begin to thank you?" he asked Charles when they met up in the bar.

"Keep your word – and I want it in writing," replied Charles.

"What do you mean?"

"A letter to the Chief Whip saying you've changed your mind on the main European vote, and you and the disciples will be abstaining on Thursday."

Pimkin looked cocky. "And if I don't play ball, dear thing?"

"You haven't got the seat yet, Alec, and I might find it necessary to phone Alexander Dalglish and tell him about that awfully nice little boy you made such a fool of yourself over when you were up at Oxford."

Three days later the Chief Whip received the letter from Pimkin. He immediately summoned his junior Whip.

"Well done, Charles. How did you manage to succeed where we've all failed – and the disciples as well?"

"Matter of loyalty," said Charles. "Pimkin saw that in the end."

On the final day of the Great Debate on 'the principle of entry' into Europe the Prime Minister delivered the winding-up speech. He rose at nine-thirty to cheers from both sides. At ten o'clock the House divided and voted in favour of 'the principle' by a majority of 112. Sixty-nine Labour MPs, led by Roy Jenkins, had helped to swell the Government's majority.

Raymond Gould voted against the motion in accordance with his long-held beliefs. Andrew Fraser joined Simon Kerslake and Charles Seymour in the Ayes lobby. Alec Pimkin and the twelve disciples remained in their places on the Commons benches while the vote took place.

When Charles heard the Speaker read out the final result he felt a moment of triumph, although he realised that he still had the committee stage to go through. Hundreds of clauses,

any of which could go wrong and turn the bill into a farce.
Nevertheless the first round belonged to him.

Ten days later Alec Pimkin defeated a keen young Conservative just down from Cambridge and a local woman councillor
to be selected as prospective candidate for Littlehampton.

CHAPTER FOURTEEN

Andrew studied the case once again and decided to make his own enquiries. Too many constituents had in the past demonstrated that they were willing to lie to him in surgery as happily as they would in the witness box to any judge.

Robert was trying to climb up on to his lap. Andrew hoisted him the remainder of the way in one tug and attempted to return to his papers. "Whose side are you on?" Andrew demanded as his son dribbled all over his freshly written notes. He stopped to pat his bottom. "Ugh," he said, putting the case file by his side on the floor. A few minutes later Robert had been changed and left with his mother.

"I'm afraid your son is not over-anxious to help me in my desire to secure the release of an innocent man," Andrew shouted over his shoulder.

He settled down to go over the papers once more, something about the case didn't ring true . . . Andrew dialled the Procurator Fiscal's number. There was one man who could cut his work in half with a sentence.

"Good morning, Mr Fraser. What can I do for you, sir?"

Andrew had to smile. Angus Sinclair was a contemporary of his father and had known Andrew all his life, but once he was in his office he treated everyone as a stranger, making no exception.

"He even calls his wife 'Mrs Sinclair' when she rings the office," Sir Duncan once told him. Andrew was willing to join in the game.

"Good morning, Mr Sinclair. I need your advice as Procurator Fiscal."

"Always happy to be of service, sir."

"I want to talk to you off the record about the Paddy O'Halloran case. Do you remember it?"

"Of course, everyone in this office remembers that case."

"Good," said Andrew. "Then you'll know what a help you can be to me in cutting through the thicket."

"Thank you, sir," the slight burr came back down the telephone.

"A group of my constituents, whom I wouldn't trust further than I could toss a caber, claim O'Halloran was framed for the Princes Street bank robbery last year. They don't deny he has criminal tendencies" – Andrew would have chuckled if he hadn't been speaking to Angus Sinclair – "but they say he never left a pub called the Sir Walter Scott the entire time the robbery was taking place. All you have to tell me, Mr Sinclair, is that you have no doubt that O'Halloran was guilty and I'll drop my enquiries. If you say nothing, I shall dig deeper."

Andrew waited, but he received no reply.

"Thank you, Mr Sinclair." Although he knew it would elicit no response, he couldn't resist adding: "No doubt I'll see you at the golf club some time over the weekend." The silence continued.

"Goodbye, Mr Sinclair."

"Good day, Mr Fraser."

Andrew settled back: it was going to be a lengthy exercise. He started by checking with all the people who had confirmed O'Halloran's alibi that night but after interviewing the first eight he came to the reluctant conclusion that none of them could be trusted as a witness. Whenever he came across another of O'Halloran's friends the expression 'anyone's for a pint' kept crossing his mind. The time had come to talk with the landlord of the Sir Walter Scott.

"I couldn't be sure, Mr Fraser, but I think he was here that evening. Trouble is, O'Halloran came almost every night. It's hard to recall."

"Do you know anyone who might remember? Someone you could trust with your cash register?"

"That'd be pushing your luck in this pub, Mr Fraser."

The landlord thought for a moment. "However, there's old Mrs Bloxham," he said at last, slapping the drying-up cloth over his shoulder. "She sits in that corner every night." He pointed to a small round table that would have been crowded had it seated more than two people. "If she says he was here, he was."

Andrew asked the landlord where Mrs Bloxham lived and then, hoping she was in, made his way to 43 Mafeking Road, neatly sidestepping a gang of young children playing football in the middle of the street. He climbed some steps that badly needed repairing and knocked on the door of number forty-three.

"Is it another general election already, Mr Fraser?" asked a disbelieving old lady as she peered through the letter-box.

"No, it's nothing to do with politics, Mrs Bloxham," said Andrew, bending down. "I came round to seek your advice on a personal matter."

"A personal matter? Better come on in out of the cold then," she said, opening the door to him. "There's a terrible draught rushes through this corridor."

Andrew followed the old lady as she shuffled down the dingy corridor in her carpet slippers to a room that he would have said was colder than it had been outside on the street. There were no ornaments in the room save a crucifix that stood on a narrow mantelpiece below a pastel print of the Virgin Mary. Mrs Bloxham beckoned Andrew to a wooden seat by a table yet unlaid. She eased her plump frame into an ancient stuffed armchair. It groaned under her weight and a strand of horsehair fell to the floor. Andrew looked more carefully at the old lady. She was wearing a black shawl over a dress she must have worn a thousand times. Once settled in her chair, she kicked off her slippers.

"Feet still giving you trouble, then?" he enquired.

"Doctor doesn't seem to be able to explain the swellings," she said, without bitterness.

Andrew leaned on the table and noticed what a fine piece of furniture it was, and how incongruous it looked in its present surroundings. He was struck by the craftsmanship of the carved Georgian legs. She noticed he was admiring it.

"My great-grandfather gave that to my great-grandmother the day they were married, Mr Fraser."

"It's magnificent," said Andrew.

She didn't seem to hear because all she said was, "What can I do for you, sir?" The second time that day he had been addressed by an elder in that way.

Andrew went over the O'Halloran story again. Mrs Bloxham listened intently, leaning forward slightly and cupping her hand round her ear to be sure she could hear every word.

"That O'Halloran's an evil one," she said, "not to be trusted. Our Blessed Lady will have to be very forgiving to allow the likes of him to enter the kingdom of heaven." Andrew smiled. "Not that I'm expecting to meet all that many politicians when I get there either," she added, giving Andrew a toothless grin.

"Could O'Halloran possibly have been there that Friday night as all his friends claim?" Andrew asked.

"He was there all right," said Mrs Bloxham. "No doubt about that – saw him with my own eyes."

"How can you be so sure?"

"Spilled his beer over my best dress, and I knew something bad would happen on the thirteenth, especially with it being a Friday. I won't forgive him for that. I still haven't been able to get the stain out despite what those washing-powder ads tell you on the telly."

"Why didn't you inform the police immediately?"

"Didn't ask," she said simply. "They've been after him for a long time for a lot of things they couldn't pin on him, but for once he was in the clear."

Andrew finished writing his notes and then rose to leave. Mrs Bloxham heaved herself out of the chair, dispensing yet more horsehair on to the floor. They walked to the door together. "I'm sorry I couldn't offer you a cup of tea but I'm right out at the moment," she said. "If you had come tomorrow it would have been all right."

Andrew paused on the doorstep.

"I get the pension tomorrow, you see," she replied to his unasked question.

It took Elizabeth some time to find a locum to cover for her so that she could travel to Redcorn for the interview. Once again the children had to be left with a baby-sitter. The local and national press had made him the hot favourite for the new seat. Elizabeth put on what she called her best Conservative outfit, a pale blue suit with a dark blue collar that hid everything on top and reached well below her knees.

The journey from King's Cross to Newcastle took three hours and twenty minutes, on what was described in the timetable as 'the express'. At least Simon was able to catch up with a great deal of the paper work that had been stuffed into his red box. Civil servants, he reflected, rarely allowed politicians time to involve themselves in politics. They wouldn't have been pleased to learn that he spent an hour of the journey reading the last four weekly copies of the *Redcorn News*.

At Newcastle they were met by the wife of the Association treasurer, who had volunteered to escort the minister and Mrs Kerslake to the constituency to be sure they were in time for the interview. "That's very thoughtful of you," said Elizabeth, as she stared at the mode of transport that had been chosen to take them the next forty miles.

The ancient Austin Mini took a further hour and a half through the winding B-roads before they reached their destination, and the treasurer's wife never drew breath once throughout the entire journey. When Simon and Elizabeth piled out of the car at the market town of Redcorn they were physically and mentally exhausted.

The treasurer's wife took them through to the constituency headquarters and introduced them both to the agent.

"Good of you to come," he said. "Hell of a journey, isn't it?"

Elizabeth felt unable to disagree with his judgement. But on this occasion she made no comment, feeling that if this was to be Simon's best chance of returning to Parliament she had already decided to give him every support possible. Nevertheless she dreaded the thought of her husband making the journey to Redcorn twice a month as she feared they would see even less of each other than they did at present, let alone the children.

"Now the form is," began the agent, "that we are interviewing six potential candidates and they'll be seeing you last." He winked knowingly.

Simon and Elizabeth smiled uncertainly.

"I'm afraid they won't be ready for you for at least another hour, so you have time for a stroll round the town."

Simon was glad of the chance to stretch his legs and take a closer look at Redcorn. He and Elizabeth walked slowly round the pretty market town, admiring the Elizabethan architecture that had somehow survived irresponsible or greedy town planners. They even climbed the hill to take a look inside the magnificent perpendicular church which dominated the surrounding area.

As he walked back past the shops in the high street Simon nodded to those locals who appeared to recognise him.

"A lot of people seem to know who you are," said Elizabeth, and then they saw the paper rack outside the local newsagent. They sat on the bench in the market square and read the lead story under a large picture of Simon.

'Redcorn's next MP?' ran the headline.

The story volunteered the fact that although Simon Kerslake had to be considered the favourite, Bill Travers, a local farmer who had been chairman of the county council the previous year, was still thought to have an outside chance.

Simon began to feel a little sick in the stomach. It reminded him of the day he had been interviewed at Coventry Central nearly eight years before. Now that he was a minister of the Crown he wasn't any less nervous.

When he and Elizabeth returned to constituency headquarters they were informed that only two more candidates had been seen and the third was still being interviewed. They walked around the town once again, even more slowly this time, watching the shopkeepers put up their coloured shutters and turn 'Open' signs to 'Closed'.

"What a pleasant market town," said Simon, trying to find out how his wife was feeling.

"And the people seem so polite after London," she added.

Simon smiled as they headed back to the party headquarters. As they passed Simon and Elizabeth they bid the strangers "Good evening," courteous people whom Simon felt he would have been proud to represent. But although they walked slowly Elizabeth and he could not make their journey last more than thirty minutes.

When they returned a third time to constituency headquarters the fourth candidate was leaving the interview room. She looked very despondent. "It shouldn't be long now," said the agent, but it was another forty minutes before they heard a ripple of applause, and a man dressed in a Harris tweed jacket and brown trousers left the room. He didn't seem happy either.

The agent ushered Simon and Elizabeth through, and as they entered everyone in the room stood. Ministers of the Crown did not visit Redcorn often.

Simon waited for Elizabeth to be seated before he took the chair in the centre of the room facing the committee. He estimated that there were about fifty people present and they were all staring at him, showing no aggression, merely curiosity. He looked around at the weather-beaten faces. Most of them, male and female, were dressed in tweed. In his dark striped London suit Simon felt out of place.

"And now," said the chairman, "we welcome the Right Honourable Simon Kerslake, MP."

Simon had to smile at the mistake so many people made in thinking that all ministers were automatically members of the Privy Council, and therefore entitled to the prefix 'Right Honourable' instead of the plain 'Honourable' accorded to all MPs – and then only when they were present in the House.

"Mr Kerslake will address us for twenty minutes, and he has kindly agreed to answer questions after that," added the chairman.

Simon felt confident he had spoken well, but even his few carefully chosen quips received no more than a smile, and his more serious comments elicited little response. This was not a group of people given to showing their emotions. When he had finished he sat down to respectful clapping and murmurs.

"Now the minister will take questions," said the chairman.

"Where do you stand on hanging?" said a scowling middle-aged woman in a grey suit seated in the front row.

Simon explained his reasons for being a convinced abolitionist. The scowl did not move from the questioner's face and Simon thought to himself how much happier she would be with Ronnie Nethercote as her member.

A man in a hacking jacket asked: "How do you feel, Mr Kerslake, about this year's farm subsidy?"

"Good on eggs, tough on beef, and disastrous for pig farmers. Or at least that's what I read on the front page of *Farmers Weekly* yesterday." Some of them laughed for the first time. "It hasn't proved necessary for me to have a great knowledge of farming in Coventry Central, but if I am lucky enough to be selected for Redcorn I shall try to learn quickly, and with your help I shall hope to master the farmers' problems." Several heads nodded their approval.

"Miss Pentecost, chairman of the Women's Advisory," announced a tall, thin spinsterish woman who had stood up to catch the chairman's eye. "May I be permitted to ask Mrs Kerslake a question? If your husband were offered this seat, would you be willing to come and live in Northumberland?"

Elizabeth had dreaded the question because she knew that if Simon was offered the constituency she would be expected to resign her post at the hospital. Simon turned and looked towards his wife.

"No," she replied directly. "I am a doctor at St Mary's Hospital, Paddington, where I practise gynaecology. I support my husband in his career but, like Margaret Thatcher, I believe a woman has the right to a good education and then the chance to use her qualifications to their best advantage."

A ripple of applause went round the room and Simon smiled at his wife.

The next question was on Europe, and Simon gave an unequivocal statement as to his reasons for backing the

Prime Minister in his desire to see Britain as part of the Common Market.

Simon continued to answer questions on subjects ranging from trade union reform to violence on television before the chairman asked, "Are there any more questions?"

There was a long silence and just as he was about to thank Simon the scowling lady in the front row, without being recognised by the chair, asked what Mr Kerslake's views were on abortion.

"Morally, I'm against it," said Simon. "At the time of the Abortion Act many of us believed it would stem the tide of divorce. We have been proved wrong: the rate of divorce has quadrupled. Nevertheless, in the cases of rape or fear of physical or mental injury arising from birth I would have to support the medical advice given at the time. Elizabeth and I have two children and my wife's job is to see that babies are safely delivered," he added.

The lips moved from a scowl to a straight line.

"Thank you," said the chairman. "It was good of you to give us so much of your time. Perhaps you and Mrs Kerslake would be kind enough to wait outside."

Simon and Elizabeth joined the other hopeful candidates, their wives and the agent in a small dingy room at the back of the building. When they saw the half-empty trestle table in front of them they both remembered they hadn't had any lunch and devoured what was left of the curling cucumber sandwiches and the cold sausage rolls.

"What happens next?" Simon asked the agent between mouthfuls.

"Nothing out of the ordinary. They'll have a discussion, allowing everyone to express their views, and then vote. It should all be over in twenty minutes."

Elizabeth checked her watch: it was seven o'clock and the last train was at nine-fifteen.

"Ought to make the train comfortably," said Simon.

An hour later when no smoke had emerged from the chimney the agent suggested to all the candidates who had a long journey ahead of them that they might like to check into the Bell Inn just over the road.

When Simon looked around the room it was clear that everyone else had done so in advance.

"You had better stay put in case you're called again," Elizabeth said. "I'll go off and book a room and at the same time call and see how the children are getting on."

"Probably eaten the poor baby-sitter by now," said Simon.

Elizabeth smiled before slipping out and making her way to the small hotel.

Simon opened his red box and tried to complete some work. The man who looked like a farmer came over and introduced himself.

"I'm Bill Travers, the chairman of the new constituency," he began. "I only wanted to say that you'll have my full support as chairman if the committee select you."

"Thank you," said Simon.

"I had hoped to represent this area, as my grandfather did. But I shall understand if Redcorn prefers to choose a man destined for the Cabinet rather than someone who would be happy to spend his life on the back benches."

Simon was touched by his opponent's goodwill, and would have liked to respond in kind but Travers quickly added, "Forgive me, I'll not waste any more of your time. I can see" – he looked down at the red box – "that you have a lot of work to catch up on."

Simon felt guilty as he watched the man walk away. A few minutes later Elizabeth returned and tried to smile. "The only room left is smaller than Peter's and it faces the main road, so it's just about as noisy."

"At least no children to say 'I'm hungry'," he said, touching her hand.

It was a little after nine when a weary chairman came out and asked all the candidates if he could have their attention. Husbands and wives all faced him. "My committee want to thank you for going through this grim procedure. It has been hard for us to decide something that we hope not to have to discuss again for twenty years." He paused. "The committee are going to invite Mr Bill Travers to fight the Redcorn seat at the next election."

In a sentence it was all over. Simon's throat went dry.

He and Elizabeth didn't get much sleep in their tiny room at the Bell Inn, and it hadn't helped that the agent told them the final vote had been twenty-five – twenty-three.

"I don't think Miss Pentecost liked me," said Elizabeth, feeling guilty. "If I had told her that I would have been willing to live in the constituency I think you'd have been offered the seat."

"I doubt it," said Simon. "In any case it's no use agreeing to their terms at the interview and then imposing your own when you have been offered the constituency. My guess is you'll find Redcorn has chosen the right man."

Elizabeth smiled at her husband, grateful for his support.

"There will be other seats," said Simon, only too aware that time was now running out. "You'll see."

Elizabeth prayed that he would prove right, and that next time the choice of a constituency would not make her have to face the dilemma she had so far managed to avoid.

When Raymond took silk, the second Tuesday after the Easter holiday, and became a Queen's Counsel, Joyce made one of her periodic trips to London. The occasion she decided warranted another visit to Harvey Nichols. She recalled her first trip to the store so many years before when she had accompanied her husband to meet the Prime Minister. Raymond had come so far since then although their relationship seemed to have progressed so little. She had given up hope of being a mother, but still wanted him to believe she was a good wife. She couldn't help thinking how much better-looking Raymond had become in middle age, and feared the same could not be said of her.

She enjoyed watching the legal ceremony as her husband was presented in court before the judges. Latin words spoken but not understood. Suddenly her husband was Raymond Gould, QC, MP.

She and Raymond arrived late in chambers for the celebration party. Everyone seemed to have turned out in her husband's honour. Raymond felt full of *bonhomie* and was chatting to the chief clerk when Sir Nigel handed him a glass

of champagne. Then he saw a familiar figure by the mantelpiece and remembered that the trial in Manchester was over.
He managed to circle the room speaking to everyone but
Stephanie Arnold. To his horror he turned to see her introducing herself to his wife. Every time he glanced towards
them they seemed deeper in conversation.

"Ladies and gentlemen," said Sir Nigel, banging a table.
He waited for silence. "We are always proud in chambers
when one of our members takes silk. It is a comment not only
on the man but also on his chambers. And when it is the
youngest silk – still under forty – it adds to that pride. All of
you, of course, know that Raymond also serves in another
place in which we expect him to rise to even greater glory.
May I add finally how pleasant it is to have his wife Joyce
among us tonight. Ladies and gentlemen," he concluded.
"The toast is Raymond Gould, QC."

"Raymond Gould, QC," said everyone in chorus. Then,
"Speech, speech."

"I would like to thank all those people who made this great
honour possible," began Raymond. "My producer, my
director, the other stars and not forgetting the criminals,
without whom I would have no profession to profess. And
finally," he said, "to those of you who want to see the back of
me, I direct you all to work tirelessly to ensure the return of a
Labour Government at the next election. Thank you."

The applause was sustained and genuine and many of his
colleagues were impressed by how relaxed Raymond had
become of late. As they came up to congratulate him
Raymond couldn't help noticing that Stephanie and Joyce
had resumed their conversation. Raymond was handed
another glass of champagne just as an earnest young pupil
called Patrick Montague who had recently joined them from
chambers in Bristol engaged him in conversation. Although
Montague had been with them for some weeks Raymond had
never spoken to him at length before. He seemed to have very
clear views on criminal law and the changes that were
necessary. For the first time in his life Raymond felt he was no
longer a young man.

Suddenly both women were at his side.

"Hello, Raymond."

"Hello, Stephanie," he said awkwardly and looked anxiously towards his wife. "Do you know Patrick Montague?" he asked, absent-mindedly.

The three of them burst out laughing.

"What's so funny?" asked Raymond.

"You do embarrass me sometimes, Raymond," said Joyce. "Surely you realise Stephanie and Patrick are engaged?"

CHAPTER
FIFTEEN

"With or without civil servants?" asked Simon as Andrew entered the minister's office.

"Without, please."

"Fine," said Simon and pressed a switch on the intercom by his desk.

"I don't want to be disturbed while I'm with Mr Fraser," he said and ushered his colleague towards a comfortable seat in the corner.

"Elizabeth was asking me this morning to find out how Robert was getting on."

"It's his second birthday next month and he's overweight for a scrum-half," replied Andrew. "And how's your search for a seat working out?"

"Not too good. The last three constituencies to come up haven't even asked to see me. I can't put a finger on why, except they all seem to have selected local men."

"It's still a long time to the next election. You're sure to find a seat before then."

"It might not be so long if the Prime Minister decides to go to the country and test his strength against the unions."

"That would be a foolish thing to do," said Andrew. "He might defeat us but he still wouldn't defeat the unions."

A young woman came into the room with two cups of coffee, put them on the low Formica table and left the two men alone.

"Have you had time to look at the file?" Andrew continued.

"Yes, I went over it last night between checking over Peter's prep and helping Michael to build a model galleon."

"And how do you feel?" Andrew asked.

"Not very good. I can't get to grips with this new maths they're now teaching, and my mast was the only one that fell off when Elizabeth launched the galleon in the bath."

Andrew laughed.

"I think you've got a case," said Simon, sounding serious.

"Good," said Andrew. "Now the reason I wanted to see you privately is because I feel there are no party political points to be made out of this case for either of us. I've no plans to try to embarrass your department, and I consider it's in the best interest of my constituents to co-operate as closely as I can with you."

"Thank you," said Simon. "So where do you want to go from here?"

"I'd like to table a planted question for your department in the hope that you would consider opening an enquiry. If the enquiry comes to the same conclusion as I have, I would expect you to order a re-trial."

Simon hesitated. "And if the enquiry goes against you will you agree to no reprisals for the Home Office?"

"You have my word on it."

"Shall I ask the civil servants to come in now?"

"Yes, please do."

Simon returned to his desk and pressed a button. A moment later three men in almost identical suits, white shirts with stiff collars and discreet ties entered the room. Between them they could have ruined any police identification parade.

"Mr Fraser," began Simon, "is asking the Home Office to consider . . ."

"Can you explain why Simon Kerslake missed a vote yesterday?"

Charles looked across the table at the Chief Whip.

"No, I can't," he said. "I've been distributing the weekly whip to him the same as every member of my group."

"What's behind it then?"

"I think the poor man has been spending a lot of his time

traipsing around the country looking for a seat to fight at the next election."

"That's no excuse," said the Chief Whip. "Duties in the House must come first, every member knows that. He missed a vote on a vital clause during the European Bill last Thursday while everyone else in your group has proved reliable. Despite our majority we seem to be in single figures for almost every clause. Perhaps I should have a word with him?"

"No, no, I'd rather you didn't," said Charles, fearing he sounded a little too insistent. "I consider it my responsibility. I'll speak to him and see that it doesn't happen again."

"All right, Charles, if that's the way you want to play it. Thank God it can't last much longer and the damn thing will soon be law, but we must remain vigilant over every clause. The Labour party know only too well that if they defeat us on certain key clauses they can still scupper the whole bill, and if I lost one of those by a single vote I would cut Kerslake's throat. Or anyone else's who was responsible."

"I'll make sure he gets the message," said Charles.

"How's Fiona reacting to all these late nights?" the Chief Whip asked, finally relaxing.

"Very well, considering. In fact now that you mention it I have never seen her looking better."

"Can't say my wife is enjoying 'the prep school antics', as she describes our continual late-night sittings. I've had to promise to take her to the West Indies this winter to make up for it. Well, I'll leave you to deal with Kerslake then. Be firm, Charles. Just remember, we can't afford to lose a vote at this late stage."

"Norman Edwards?" repeated Raymond in disbelief. "The General Secretary of the Haulage Union?"

"Yes," said Fred Padgett, getting up from behind his desk.

"But he burnt *Full Employment at any Cost?* on a public bonfire with every journalist he could lay his hands on to witness the conflagration."

"I know," said Fred, returning a letter to the filing cabinet.

"I'm only your agent, I'm not here to explain the mysteries of the universe."

"When does he want to see me?" asked Raymond.

"As soon as possible."

"Better ask him if he can come for a drink back at the house round six o'clock."

Raymond had had a heavy Saturday morning surgery and thanks to the still imminent Martians had only found time to grab a sandwich at the pub before going off to pursue his favourite pastime. This week Leeds were playing Liverpool at Elland Road. Sitting in the directors' box every other week in full view of his constituents while he supported his local football team killed 30,000 birds with one stone. Later, when talking to the lads in the dressing-room after the match, he found himself lapsing into a pronounced Yorkshire accent that bore no resemblance to the one he used to address high court judges during the week.

Leeds won three–two and after the match Raymond joined the directors for a drink in the boardroom. He became so impassioned about an off-side decision that could have lost them a point that he nearly forgot about his meeting with Norman Edwards.

Joyce was in the garden showing the union leader her early snowdrops when Raymond returned.

"Sorry I'm late," he shouted, as he hung up his yellow and blue scarf. "I've been to the match."

"Who won?" asked Edwards.

"Leeds, of course, three–two."

"Damn," said Norman, his accent leaving the other in no doubt that he had not spent many nights outside of Liverpool.

"Come on in and have a beer," said Raymond.

"I'd prefer a vodka."

The two men went into the house while Joyce continued with her gardening.

"Well," said Raymond, pouring his guest a Smirnoff. "What brings you all the way from Liverpool if it wasn't to watch the football? Perhaps you want a signed copy of my book for your next union bonfire."

"Don't give me any hassle, Ray. I came all this way because I need your help, simple as that."

"I'm all ears," said Raymond.

"We had a full meeting of the General Purposes Committee yesterday, and one of the brothers has spotted a clause in the European Bill which could put us all out of work."

Norman passed over a copy of the bill to Raymond with the relevant clause marked in red. It gave the minister power to make new haulage and lorry regulations which would come before the House as statutory instruments and thus could not be amended.

"If that gets through the House my boys are in deep trouble."

"Why?" said Raymond.

"Because those bloody Frogs know only too well that there's a Channel between us and them, and if my lads are forced by law to sleep a night each side the only people who'll end up making money on the deal will be the guest-house proprietors."

"What's behind it?" asked Raymond.

"They want us to drop the stuff our end, so they can pick it up on the other side."

"But wouldn't that also be true when they need to deliver goods to us?"

"No. Their journeys are much longer to the coast, and they have to stay overnight anyway, not to mention the fact that there are eight of them to one of us. It's diabolical. nothing less."

Raymond studied the wording in detail while Edwards helped himself to another vodka.

"The clause doesn't stop you from going over the next day."

"And how much do you think that will add to your costs?" asked Raymond.

"I'll tell you, enough to make us uncompetitive, that's how much," replied the trade-union leader.

"Point taken," said Raymond. "So what's wrong with asking your own member to put the case?"

"Don't trust him. He's pro-European at any price."

"And what about your sponsored trade union representative in the House?"

"Tom Carson? You must be joking. He's so far to the left that even his own side are suspicious when he supports a cause. We lost the 'tachograph' clause because he championed it. In any case I only put him in the House to get him off my back." Raymond laughed. "Now, all my General Purposes Committee want to know is: would you be willing to fight this clause in the House for us? Not that we can afford the sort of fees you're used to at the bar," he added.

"There would be no fee involved," said Raymond, "but I'm sure you'll be able to repay me in kind sometime in the future."

"Got the picture," said Edwards, touching the side of his nose with a forefinger. "What do I do next?"

"You go back to Liverpool and hope that I am better on an away pitch than your team."

Norman Edwards put on an old raincoat and started to button it up. He smiled at Raymond. "I may have been appalled by your book, Ray. But it doesn't mean I didn't admire it."

The Speaker looked down at the front bench. "Mr Andrew Fraser."

"Number seventeen, sir," said Andrew.

The Speaker looked down to check over the question, seeking a Home Office answer.

Simon rose to the dispatch box, opened his file and said, "Yes, sir."

"Mr Andrew Fraser," called the Speaker again.

Andrew rose from his place on the Opposition front bench to put his supplementary.

"May I thank the minister for agreeing to an enquiry so quickly, and ask him that, if he discovers an injustice has been done to my constituent Mr Paddy O'Halloran, that the Home Secretary will order a re-trial immediately?"

Simon rose again.

"Yes, sir."

"I am grateful to the Honourable Gentleman," said Andrew, half-rising from his place.

All over in less than a minute, but older members who listened to the brief exchange between Fraser and Kerslake in the House that day had no doubt that considerable preparation had gone into that minute from both sides.

"The damn man missed another three-line whip, Charles. It must be the last time. You've been protecting him for far too long."

"It won't happen again," promised Charles convincingly. "I would like to give him one more chance. Allow him that."

"You're very loyal to him," said the Chief Whip. "But next time I'm going to see Kerslake myself and get to the bottom of it."

"It won't happen again," repeated Charles.

"Hm," said the Chief Whip. "Next problem is, are there any clauses on the European Bill that we should be worried about next week?"

"Yes," replied Charles. "This haulage clause that Raymond Gould is fighting. He made a brilliant case on the floor of the House, and got all his own side and half of ours backing him."

"He's not the sponsored MP for the Haulage Union," said the Chief Whip, surprised.

"No, the unions obviously felt Tom Carson wouldn't help the cause and he's hopping mad at the slight."

"Clever of them to pick Gould. He improves as a speaker every time I hear him, and no one can fault him when it comes to a point of law."

"So we'd better face the fact that we're going to lose the clause?"

"Never. We'll redraft the damn thing so that it's acceptable and *seen* to be compassionate. It's not a bad time to be the defender of the union interests. That way we'll keep Gould from getting all the credit. I'll speak to the PM tonight – and don't forget what I said about Kerslake."

Charles returned to his office and realised that in future he would have to be more careful about telling Simon Kerslake when he was paired for the European Bill. He suspected he had carried this ploy as far as he could for now.

Simon had read the final report prepared by his department on the O'Halloran case while Elizabeth was trying to get to sleep. He only had to go over the details once to realise that he would have to order a re-trial and institute a full investigation into the past record of the police officers who had been involved in the case.

When Andrew heard the news, and that the re-trial would be held in London, he asked Raymond Gould to represent O'Halloran.

"Praise indeed," said Raymond, who still considered Andrew among the Commons' finest orators. He somehow managed to fit O'Halloran into his busy schedule.

The trial was in its third day when Mr Justice Comyns, after listening to Mrs Bloxham's evidence, stopped proceedings and instructed the jury to return a verdict of not guilty.

Andrew received praise from all quarters of the House, but he was quick to acknowledge the support given him by Simon Kerslake and the Home Office. *The Times* even wrote a leader the next day on the proper use of influence by a constituency MP.

Some months later the court awarded O'Halloran £25,000 in compensation. The only drawback Andrew's success caused was that every convict's mother north of Hadrian's wall queued to tell him about her innocent son at his fortnightly surgery. But during the year he took only one seriously and once again began to check into the details.

During the long hot summer of 1972 clause after clause of the European Bill was voted on, often through the night. On some occasions the Government managed majorities of only five or six but somehow the bill remained intact.

Charles would often arrive home at Eaton Square at three in the morning to find Fiona asleep, only to leave again before she had woken. Veterans of the House, both servants and elected, confirmed they had never experienced anything like it since the Second World War.

And, just as suddenly, the last vote was taken and the marathon was over. The European Bill was through the Commons and on its way to the Upper House to receive their lordships' approval. Charles wondered what he would do with all the hours that were suddenly left him in the day.

When the bill finally received the Royal Assent in October the Chief Whip held a celebration lunch at the Carlton Club in St James's to thank all his team. "And in particular, Charles Seymour," he said, raising his glass during an impromptu speech. When the lunch broke up the Chief Whip offered Charles a lift back to the Commons in his official car. They travelled along Piccadilly, down Haymarket, through Trafalgar Square and into Whitehall. Just as the Commons came into sight the black Rover turned into Downing Street, as Charles assumed, to drop the Chief Whip at No. 12. But as the car stopped the Chief Whip said, "The Prime Minister is expecting you in five minutes."

"What? Why?" said Charles, as he joined his colleague outside No. 10.

"Timed it rather well, didn't I?" said the Chief Whip – and headed off towards No. 12.

Charles stood alone in front of No. 10. The door was opened by a man in a long black coat. "Good afternoon, Mr Seymour."

The Prime Minister saw Charles in his study and, as ever, wasted no time on small talk.

"Thank you for all the hard work you have put in on the European Bill."

"It was a tremendous challenge," said Charles, searching for words.

"As will be your next job," said Mr Heath. "I want you to take over as one of the Ministers of State at the Department of Trade and Industry."

Charles was speechless.

"With all the problems we are going to encounter with the trade unions during the next few months, that should keep you fully occupied."

"It certainly will," said Charles.

He still hadn't been asked to sit down, but as the Prime

Minister was now rising from behind his desk it was clear
that the meeting was over.

"You and Fiona must come and have dinner at No. 10 as
soon as you've settled into your new department," said the
Prime Minister as they walked towards the door.

"Thank you," Charles said.

As he stepped back on to Downing Street a driver opened
the back door of a shiny Austin Westminster. It was several
moments before Charles realised the car was his.

"The Commons, sir?"

"No, I'd like to return to Eaton Square for a few minutes,"
he said, sitting back and enjoying the thought of tackling his
new job.

The car drove past the Commons, up Victoria Street and
on to Eaton Square. He wanted to tell Fiona that all the hard
work had been rewarded. He felt guilty about how little he
had seen of her lately, although he could not believe it would
be much better now that he was to be involved in trade union
legislation. How much he still hoped for a son, perhaps even
that would prove possible now. The car came to a halt
outside the Georgian house. Charles ran up the steps and
into the hall. He could hear his wife's voice from the first
floor. He took the wide staircase in bounds of two and three at
a time, and threw open the bedroom door.

"I'm the new Minister of State at the Department of Trade
and Industry," he announced to Fiona, who was lying in bed.

Alexander Dalglish looked up. He showed no sign of
interest in Charles's elevation.

When Andrew rang Angus Sinclair at the Procurator Fiscal's
office to find that nothing was known of Ricky Hodge and
that Sinclair was able to confirm that he had no criminal
record, Andrew felt he had stumbled on a case with international implications.

As Ricky Hodge was in a Turkish jail any enquiries had to
be made through the Foreign Office. Andrew did not have
the same relationship with the Foreign Secretary as he did
with Simon, so he felt the direct approach would be best and
put down a question to be answered in the House. He worded

it carefully: 'What action does the Foreign Secretary intend to take over the confiscation of a British passport from a constituent of the Honourable member for Edinburgh Carlton, details of which have been supplied to him?"

When the question came in front of the House on the following Wednesday the Foreign Secretary rose to answer the question himself. He stood at the dispatch box and peered over his half-moon spectacles and said:

"Her Majesty's Government are pursuing this matter through the usual diplomatic channels."

Andrew was quickly on his feet. "Does the Right Honourable Gentleman realise that my constituent has been in a Turkish prison for six months and has still not been charged?"

"Yes, sir," replied the Foreign Secretary. "I have asked the Turkish Embassy to supply the Foreign Office with more details of the case."

Andrew leaped up again. "How long will my constituent have to be forgotten in Ankara before the Foreign Secretary does more than ask for the details of his case?"

The Foreign Secretary rose again showing no sign of annoyance. "I will report those findings to the Honourable member as quickly as possible."

"When? Tomorrow, next week, next year?" Andrew shouted angrily.

"When?" joined in a chorus of Labour back-benchers, but the Speaker called for the next question above the uproar.

Within the hour Andrew received a handwritten note from the Foreign Office. It read: "If Mr Fraser would be kind enough to telephone, the Foreign Secretary would be delighted to make an appointment to see him."

Andrew phoned from the Commons and was invited to join the Foreign Secretary in Whitehall immediately.

The Foreign Office, known as 'The Palazzo' by its inmates, has an atmosphere of its own. Although Andrew had worked in a Government department as a minister he was still struck by its grandeur. He was met at the courtyard entrance and guided along yards of marble corridors before climbing a fine double staircase at the top of which he was greeted by the Foreign Secretary's Principal Private Secretary.

"Sir Alec will see you immediately, Mr Fraser," he said, and led Andrew past the magnificent pictures and tapestries which lined the way. He was taken into a beautifully proportioned room. The Foreign Secretary stood in front of an Adam fireplace over which hung a portrait of Lord Palmerston.

"Fraser, how kind of you to come at such short notice. I do hope it has not caused you any inconvenience." Platitudes, thought Andrew. Next the silly man will be mentioning my father. "I don't think we have met before, but of course I have known your father for many years. Won't you sit down?"

"I realise you are a busy man. Can we get down to the point at issue, Foreign Secretary?" Andrew demanded.

"Of course," Sir Alec said courteously. "Forgive me for taking up so much of your time." Without a further word, he handed Andrew a file marked 'Richard M. Hodge – Confidential'. "Although Members of Parliament are not subject to the Official Secrets Act I know you will respect the fact that this file is classified."

Another bluff, thought Andrew. He flicked back the cover. It was true: exactly as he had suspected, Ricky Hodge had never been arrested or charged. He turned the page. "Rome, child prostitution; Marseilles, narcotics; Paris, blackmail." Page after page, ending in Turkey, where Hodge had been found in possession of four pounds of heroin which he had been selling in small packets on the black market. In his twenty-nine years Ricky Hodge had spent eleven of the last fourteen in foreign jails.

Andrew closed the file and could feel the sweat on his forehead. It was some moments before he spoke. "I apologise, Foreign Secretary," he said. "I have made a fool of myself."

"When I was a young man," said Sir Alec, "I made a similar mistake on behalf of a constituent. Ernie Bevin was Foreign Secretary at the time. He could have crucified me in the House with the knowledge he had. Instead he revealed everything over a drink in this room. I sometimes wish the public could see members in their quiet moments as well as in their rowdy ones."

Andrew thanked Sir Alec and walked thoughtfully back to the House. The *Evening Standard* poster outside the Commons caught his eye. 'O'Halloran arrested again.' He bought a copy, stood by the railings and began reading. Paddy O'Halloran had been detained in a Glasgow police station and charged with robbing the Bank of Scotland in Sauchiehall Street. Andrew wondered if his friends would allege it was another 'frame up' by the police until he read the next paragraph. "O'Halloran was arrested leaving the bank in possession of a shotgun and £25,000 in used notes. He said when apprehended by the police, 'I've just been clearing my account.'"

At home, Louise told him that Ricky Hodge had done him a favour.

"How's that possible?" asked Andrew.

"You won't take yourself so seriously in future," she smiled.

When Andrew conducted his next surgery in Edinburgh two weeks later he was surprised to see that Mrs Bloxham had made an appointment.

As he greeted her at the door he was even more surprised. She was wearing a bright crimplene dress and a new pair of squeaky brown leather shoes. She also looked as if 'Our Blessed Lady' might have to wait a few more years to receive her after all. Andrew motioned her to a seat.

"I came to thank you, Mr Fraser," she said, once she was settled.

"What for?" asked Andrew.

"For sending that nice young man round from Christie's. They auctioned great-grandma's table for me. I couldn't believe my luck – it fetched £1,400." Andrew smiled. "So it don't matter about the stain on the dress any more." She paused. "It even made up for having to eat off the floor for three months."

Simon steered the new Boundary Commission recommendations unspectacularly through the House as an order in Council, and suddenly he had lost his own constituency. His colleagues in Coventry were understanding, and nursed those wards that would become theirs at the next election in order that he might spend more time searching for a new seat.

Seven seats became available during the year but Simon was only interviewed for two of them. Both were almost on the Scottish border and both put him in second place. He began to appreciate what it must feel like for an Olympic favourite to be awarded the silver medal.

Ronnie Nethercote's monthly board reports began to paint an increasingly sombre picture, thus reflecting in real life what the politicians were decreeing in Parliament. Ronnie had decided to postpone going public until the climate was more advantageous. Simon couldn't disagree with the judgement, but when he checked his special overdraft facility the interest on his loans had pushed the figure in red to over £90,000.

When unemployment first passed the million mark and Ted Heath ordered a pay and prices freeze strikes broke out all over the country.

The new parliamentary session in the autumn was dominated by the issue of a Prices and Incomes policy. Charles Seymour became involved in putting the case for the Government. While he didn't always win every argument, he was now so well-briefed on his subject that he no longer feared making a fool of himself at the dispatch box. Raymond Gould and Andrew Fraser both made passionate speeches on behalf of the unions, but the Conservative majority beat them again and again.

However, the Prime Minister was moving inexorably towards a head-on clash with the unions and an early general election.

When all three party conferences were over members returned to the Commons aware that it was likely to be their last session before the general election. It was openly being said in the corridors that all the Prime Minister was waiting for was a catalyst. The miners provided it. In the middle of a bleak winter they called an all-out strike for more pay in defiance of the Government's new trade union legislation.

In a television interview the Prime Minister told the nation that with unemployment at an unprecedented 2,294,448 and the country on a three-day week he had to call an election to ensure that the rule of law be maintained. The inner Cabinet advised Heath to plump for 28 February 1974.

'Who runs the country?' became the Tory theme but seemed only to emphasise class differences, rather than uniting the country as Edward Heath had hoped.

Andrew Fraser had his doubts but he faced a different threat in his own constituency, where the Scottish Nationalists were using the quarrel between the two major parties to promote their own cause. He returned to Scotland, to be warned by his father that the Scottish Nationalists were no longer a joke and that he would be facing a hard campaign against the robust local candidate, Jock McPherson.

Raymond Gould travelled back to Leeds, confident that the north-east industrial area would not tolerate Heath's high-handedness.

Charles felt sure that the people would back any party which had shown the courage to stand up to the unions, although the left wing, led vociferously by Tom Carson, made a great play of the 'two nations' issue, insisting that the Government were out to crush the Labour movement once and for all.

Charles drove down to Sussex to find his supporters glad of the chance to put those 'lazy trade unionists' in their place.

Simon, with no seat to fight, worked on in the Home Office right up to the day of the election, convinced that his career was facing only a temporary setback.

"I'll fight the first by-election that comes up," he promised Elizabeth.

"Even if it's a mining seat in South Wales?" she replied.

Many months had passed before Charles had found it possible even to sustain a conversation with Fiona for any length of time. Neither wanted a divorce, both citing the ailing Earl of Bridgwater as their reason, although inconvenience and loss of face were nearer the truth. In public it would have been hard to detect the change in their relationship since they had never been given to overt affection.

Charles gradually became aware that it was possible for marriages to have been over for years without outsiders knowing it. Certainly the old earl never found out, because even on his death bed he told Fiona to hurry up and produce an heir.

"Do you think you'll ever forgive me?" Fiona once asked her husband.

"Never," he replied, with a finality that encouraged no further discourse.

During the three-week election campaign in Sussex they both went about their duties with a professionalism that masked their true feelings.

"How is your husband bearing up?" someone would enquire.

"Much enjoying the campaign and looking forward to returning to Government," was Fiona's stock reply.

"And how is dear Lady Fiona?" Charles was continuously asked.

"Never better than when she's helping in the constituency," was his.

On Sundays, at one church after another, he read the lesson with confidence while she sang 'Fight the good fight' in a clear contralto.

The demands of a rural constituency are considerably different from those of a city. Every village, however small, expects the member to visit them and to recall the local chairmen's names. Subtle changes were taking place: Fiona no longer whispered the names in Charles's ear. Charles no longer turned to her for advice.

During the campaign Charles would ring the photographer on the local paper to discover which events his editor had instructed him to cover that day. With the list of places and times in his hand Charles would arrive on each occasion a few minutes before the photographer. The Labour candidate complained officially to the local editor that Mr Seymour's photograph was never out of the paper.

"If you were present at these functions we would be only too happy to publish your photo," said the editor.

"But they never invite me," cried the Labour candidate.

They don't invite Seymour either, the editor wanted to say, but he somehow manages to be there. It was never far from the editor's mind that his proprietor was a Tory peer so he kept his mouth shut.

All the way up to election day Charles and Fiona opened bazaars, attended dinners, drew raffles and only just stopped short of kissing babies.

Once, when Fiona asked him, Charles admitted that he hoped to be moved to the Foreign Office as a Minister of State, and perhaps to be made a Privy Councillor.

On the last day of February they dressed in silence and went off to their local polling station to vote. The photographer was there on the steps to take their picture. They stood closer together than they had for some weeks, looking like a smart register office couple. Charles knew it would be the main photograph on the front page of the *Sussex Gazette* the following day, as surely as he knew the Labour candidate would be relegated to a half-column mention on the inside page not far from the obituaries.

The count in a rural seat is always taken the following morning at a more leisurely pace than is customary for its city cousins. So Charles anticipated that by the time he arrived in the town hall the Conservative majority in the House would already be assured. But it was not to be, and the result still hung in the balance that Friday morning.

Edward Heath did not concede when the newscasters predicted he would fail to be given the overall majority he required. Charles spent the day striding around the town hall with an anxious look on his face. The little piles of votes soon became larger and it was obvious that he would hold the seat with at least his usual 21,000 – or was it 22,000? – majority. He never could remember the exact figure. But as the day progressed it became more and more difficult to assess the national verdict.

The last result came in from Northern Ireland a little after four o'clock that afternoon and a BBC commentator announced –

Labour	301
Conservative	296
Liberal	14
Ulster Unionists	11
Scottish Nationalists	7
Welsh Nationalists	2
Others	4

Ted Heath invited the Liberal leader to join him at Downing Street for talks in the hope that they could form a coalition. The Liberals demanded a firm commitment to electoral reform and, in particular, to proportional representation by the next election. Heath knew he could never get his back-benchers to deliver. On the Monday morning he told the Queen in her drawing-room at Buckingham Palace that he was unable to form a Government. She called for Harold Wilson. He accepted her commission and drove back to Downing Street to enter the front door. Heath left by the back.

By the Tuesday afternoon every member, having watched the drama unfold, had returned to London. Raymond had increased his majority and now hoped that the Prime Minister had long since forgotten his resignation and would offer him a job.

Andrew had had the hard and unpleasant fight with Jock McPherson, just as his father had predicted, and held on to his seat by only 2,229.

Charles, still unsure of the exact majority by which he had won, drove back to London, resigned to Opposition. The one compensation was that he would be reinstated on the board of Seymour's where the knowledge he had gained as a minister of Trade and Industry could only be of value.

Simon left the Home Office on 1 March 1974 with little more than an empty red box to show for nine years as a parliamentarian.

BOOK THREE
1974-1977
MINISTERS OF STATE

CHAPTER
SIXTEEN

"His diary looks rather full at the moment, Mr Charles."

"Well, as soon as it's convenient," Charles replied over the phone. He held on as he heard the pages being turned.

"12 March at ten-thirty, Mr Charles?"

"But that's nearly a fortnight away," he said, irritated.

"Mr Spencer has only just returned from the States and –"

"How about a lunch, then – at my club?" Charles interrupted.

"That couldn't be until after 19 March."

"Very well, then," said Charles. "12 March, at ten-thirty."

During the fourteen-day wait Charles had ample time to become frustrated by his seemingly aimless role in Opposition. No car came to pick him up and whisk him away to an office where real work had to be done. Worse, no one sought his opinion any longer on matters that affected the nation. He was going through a sharp bout of what is known as 'ex-ministers' blues'.

He was relieved when the day for the appointment with Derek Spencer at last came round. But although he arrived on time he was kept waiting for ten minutes before the chairman's secretary took him through.

"Good to see you after so long," said Spencer, coming round his desk to greet him. "It must be nearly six years since you've visited the bank."

"Yes, I suppose it is," said Charles. "But looking around the old place it feels like yesterday. You've been fully occupied, no doubt?"

"Like a Cabinet minister, but I hope with better results."

They both laughed.

"Of course I've kept in touch with what's been happening at the bank."

"Have you?" said Spencer.

"Yes, I've read all the reports you've sent out over the past years, not to mention the *Financial Times*'s coverage."

"I hope you feel we've progressed satisfactorily in your absence."

"Oh. Yes," said Charles, still standing. "Very impress-ive."

"Well, now what can I do for you?" asked the chairman, returning to his seat.

"Simple enough," said Charles, finally taking an un-offered chair. "I wish to be reinstated on the board."

There was a long silence.

"Well, it's not quite that easy, Charles. I've just recently appointed two new directors and . . ."

"Of course it's that easy," said Charles, his tone changing. "You have only to propose my name at the next meeting and it will go through, especially as you haven't a member of the family on the board at the present time."

"We have, as a matter of fact. Your brother the Earl of Bridgwater has become a non-executive director."

"What? Rupert never told me," said Charles. "Neither did you."

"True, but things have changed since –"

"Nothing has changed except my estimation of the value of your word," said Charles, suddenly realising that Spencer had never intended he should return to the board. "You gave me your assurance –"

"I won't be spoken to like this in my own office."

"If you're not careful, the next place I shall do it will be in your boardroom. Now, will you honour your undertaking or not?"

"I don't have to listen to threats from you, Seymour. Get out of my office before I have you removed. I can assure you that you will never sit on the board again as long as I'm chairman."

Charles turned and marched out, slamming the door as he

left. He wasn't sure with whom to discuss the problem and returned immediately to Eaton Square to consider a plan of campaign.

"What brings you home in the middle of the afternoon?" asked Fiona.

Charles hesitated, considered the question and then joined his wife in the kitchen and told her everything that had happened at the bank. Fiona continued to grate some cheese as she listened to her husband.

"Well, one thing is certain," she said, not having spoken for several minutes but delighted that Charles had confided in her. "After that fracas, you can't both be on the board."

"So what do you think I ought to do, old girl?"

Fiona smiled; it was the first time he had called her that for nearly two years. "Every man has his secrets," she said. "I wonder what Mr Spencer's are?"

"He's such a dull middle-class fellow I doubt if –"

"I've just had a letter from Seymour's Bank," interrupted Fiona.

"What about?"

"Only a shareholder's circular. It seems Margaret Trubshaw is retiring after twelve years as the board secretary. Rumour has it she wanted to do five more years, but the chairman has someone else in mind. I think I might have lunch with her."

Charles returned his wife's smile.

Andrew's appointment as Minister of State at the Home Office came as no surprise to anyone except his three-year-old son, who quickly discovered how to empty any red boxes that were left unlocked, refilling them with marbles or sweets, and even managing to fit a football into one. As Robert didn't fully understand 'For Your Eyes Only', it didn't seem to make a lot of difference that Cabinet committee papers were sometimes found glued together with old bubble-gum.

"Can you remove that latest stain in the red box?"

"Good heavens, what caused it?" asked Louise, staring down at a jelly-like blob.

"Frog spawn," said Andrew, grinning.

"He's a brain-washed Russian spy," warned Louise, "with a mental age about the same as most of your colleagues in the House. Yes, I'll remove the stain if you sit down and write that letter."

Andrew nodded his agreement.

Among the many letters of commiseration Simon received when he did not return to the House was one from Andrew Fraser. Simon could imagine him sitting in his old office and implementing the decisions he had been involved in making just a few weeks before.

There was also a letter from Ronnie Nethercote inviting him to return to the board of Nethercote and Company at £5,000 a year, which even Elizabeth acknowledged as a generous gesture.

It was not long before Ronnie Nethercote had made Simon an executive director of the company. Simon enjoyed negotiating with the trade unions at a level he had not experienced before. Ronnie made it clear how he would have dealt with the 'Commie bastards' given half a chance. "Lock them all up until they learn to do a day's work."

"You would have lasted about a week in the House of Commons," Simon told him.

"After a week with those windbags I'd have been only too happy to return to the real world."

Simon smiled. Ronnie, he felt, was like so many others – imagining all Members of Parliament were unemployable except the one they knew.

Raymond waited until the last Government appointment was announced before he finally gave up any hope of a job. Several leading political journalists pointed out that he had been left on the back benches while lesser men had been given Government posts but it was scant comfort. Reluctantly he returned to Lincoln's Inn to continue his practice at the bar.

Harold Wilson, starting his third administration, made it

clear that he would govern as long as possible before calling an election. But as he did not have an overall majority in the House few members believed that he could hold out for more than a matter of months.

Fiona returned home after her lunch with Miss Trubshaw with a large Cheshire Cat grin on her face. It remained firmly in place during the hours she had to wait for Charles to get back from the Commons after the last division.

"You look pleased with yourself," said Charles, shaking out his umbrella before closing the front door. His wife stood in the hallway, her arms crossed.

"How has your day been?" she asked.

"So-so," said Charles, wanting to hear the news. "But what about you?"

"Oh, pleasant enough. I had coffee with your mother this morning. She seems very well. A little cold in the head, otherwise –"

"To hell with my mother. How did your lunch with Miss Trubshaw go?"

"I wondered how long it would take you to get round to that."

She continued to wait just as long as it took for them to walk into the drawing-room and sit down. "After seventeen years as secretary to your father and twelve years as secretary to the board there isn't much Miss Trubshaw doesn't know about Seymour's or its present chairman," Fiona began.

"So what did you discover?"

"Which do you want to hear about first, the name of his mistress or the number of his Swiss bank account?"

Fiona revealed everything she had learned over her two-hour lunch, explaining that Miss Trubshaw usually only drank fortified wine but on this occasion she had downed most of a vintage bottle of Pommard. Charles's smile grew wider and wider as each fact came pouring out. To Fiona he looked like a boy who has been given a box of chocolates and keeps discovering another layer underneath.

"Well done, old girl," he said when she had come to the end of her tale. "But how do I get all the proof I need?"

"I've made a deal with our Miss Trubshaw."

"You've what?"

"A deal. With Miss Trubshaw. You get the proof if she remains as secretary to the board for a further five years, and no loss of benefit to her pension."

"Is that all she wants?" said Charles, guardedly.

"And the price of another lunch at the Savoy Grill when you're invited back on the board."

Unlike many of his Labour colleagues Raymond now enjoyed dressing up in white tie and tails and mixing with London society. An invitation to the annual bankers' banquet at the Guildhall was no exception. The Prime Minister was the guest of honour and Raymond wondered if he would drop a hint as to how long he expected the parliamentary session to last before he felt he had to call an election.

At the pre-dinner drinks Raymond had a quick word with the Lord Mayor before becoming involved in a conversation with a circuit court judge on the problems of the parity of sentencing.

When dinner was announced Raymond found his seat on one of the long fingers stretching away from the top table. He checked his place card. Raymond Gould QC, MP. On his right was the chairman of Chloride, Michael Edwardes, and on his left an American banker who had just taken up an appointment in the City.

Raymond found Michael Edwardes's views on how the Prime Minister should tackle the nationalised industries fascinating, but he devoted far more of his attention to the Euro Bond manager from Chase Manhattan. She must have been thirty, Raymond decided, if only because of her elevated position at the bank and her claim to have been an undergraduate at Wellesley at the time of Kennedy's death. He would have put Kate Garthwaite at far younger and was not surprised to learn she played tennis in the summer and swam every day during the winter – to keep her weight down, she confided. She had a warm, oval face, and her dark hair was cut in what Raymond thought was a Mary Quant

style. Her nose turned up slightly at the end and would have
cost a lot of money for a plastic surgeon to reproduce. There
was no chance of seeing her legs as they were covered by a
long dress, but what he could see left Raymond more than
interested.

"I see there's an 'MP' behind your name, Mr Gould. May
I ask which party you represent?" she asked, in an accent
heard more often in Boston.

"I'm a Socialist, Mrs Garthwaite. Where do your sym-
pathies lie on this occasion?"

"I would have voted Labour at the last election if I had
been qualified," she declared.

"Should I be surprised?" he teased.

"You certainly should. My ex-husband is a Republican
congressman."

He was about to ask his next question when the toastmas-
ter called for silence. For the first time Raymond turned his
eyes to the top table and the Prime Minister. Harold Wilson's speech stuck firmly to economic problems and the role
of a Labour Government in the City and gave no clue as to
the timing of the next election. Nevertheless, Raymond
considered it a worthwhile evening. He had made a useful
contact with the chairman of a large public company. And he
had acquired Kate's telephone number.

The chairman of Seymour's reluctantly agreed to see him a
second time, but it was obvious from the moment Charles
walked in when no hand was proffered that Derek Spencer
intended it to be a short interview.

"I thought I ought to see you personally," said Charles as
he settled back in the comfortable leather chair and slowly lit
a cigarette, "rather than raise my query at the AGM next
month."

The first sign of apprehension began to show on the
chairman's face, but he said nothing.

"I'm rather keen to discover why the bank should pay out
a monthly cheque of £400 to an employee called Miss Janet
Darrow, whom I have never come across, although it
appears she has been on the payroll for over five years. The

cheques, it seems, have been going to a branch of Lloyds in Kensington."

Derek Spencer's face became flushed.

"What I am at a loss to discover," continued Charles after he had inhaled deeply, "is what services Miss Darrow has been supplying to the bank. They must be quite impressive to have earned her £25,000 over the last five years. I appreciate that this is a small amount when you consider the bank's turnover of 123 million last year, but my grandfather in-stilled in me at an early age the belief that if one took care of the pennies the pounds would take care of them-selves."

Still Derek Spencer said nothing, although beads of sweat had appeared on his forehead. Suddenly Charles's tone changed. "If I find I am not a member of the board by the time of the Annual General Meeting I feel it will be my duty to point out this slight discrepancy in the bank's accounts to the other shareholders present."

"You're a bastard, Seymour," the chairman said quietly.

"Now that is not accurate. I am the second son of the former chairman of this bank and I bear a striking resem-blance to my father, although everyone says I have my mother's eyes."

"What's the deal?"

"No deal. You will merely keep to your original agreement and see that I am reinstated on the board before the AGM. You will also cease any further payments to Miss Janet Darrow immediately."

"If I agree, will you swear never to mention this matter to anyone again?"

"I will. And, unlike you, I am in the habit of keeping my word."

Charles rose from his chair, leaned over the desk and stubbed out his cigarette in the chairman's ashtray.

Andrew Fraser was surprised when he heard that Jock McPherson wanted to see him. The two men had never been on good terms since McPherson had failed to be elected to the

Scottish Labour Party Executive Committee and had then left the party to stand against him at Edinburgh Carlton. Since McPherson had switched his allegiance they had barely been on speaking terms. However, Andrew realised it would be foolish not to see him after the SNP's sweeping successes in the election.

Andrew was even more surprised when McPherson asked if all seven SNP Members of Parliament could also attend the meeting, not in Andrew's office but somewhere private. He agreed, even more mystified.

McPherson and his band of renegade Scots arrived together at Cheyne Walk, looking as though they had already held a meeting between themselves. Andrew offered them a variety of seats, including the dining-room chairs, a pouffe and even the kitchen stool, apologising that his London flat had never been intended to accommodate nine men in the drawing-room.

While the men settled themselves Andrew remained standing by the mantelpiece, facing Jock McPherson who had obviously been chosen to act as their spokesman.

"I'll get straight to the point," McPherson began. "We want you to fight under the SNP banner at the next election."

Andrew tried not to show his disbelief, and began, "I don't feel . . ."

"Hear me out," said McPherson, raising his massive palms. "We want you to contest the Edinburgh Carlton seat not just as a Scottish Nationalist candidate but as leader of the party."

Andrew still couldn't believe what he was hearing but remained silent.

"We're convinced you'll lose your seat in any case if you stand as a Socialist," McPherson continued, "but we realise that there are many people in Scotland who, whatever their political views, admire what you have achieved in the nine years you have been in the House. After all, man, you were brought up and educated in Edinburgh. With you as leader, we believe we could capture forty to fifty of the seventy-one seats in Scotland. And I may add that your own party is moving inexorably to the left, a state of affairs that I can't believe you are altogether happy about."

Andrew still made no comment. He listened as each one of the MPs put his own view, which became predictable long before the last one had spoken. Every Scottish tone from a Highland lilt to a Glasgow growl was represented in the voices. It became clear that they had given the matter considerable thought and were obviously sincere. "I am very flattered, gentlemen," he began when the last one had said his piece. "And I assure you I will give your offer my serious consideration."

"Thank you," said McPherson. They all stood up like clan leaders in the presence of a new chief.

"We'll wait to hear from you then," said McPherson. One by one they shook hands with their host before filing out.

As soon as they had left Andrew went straight into the kitchen where Robert was still waiting impatiently to play football before going to bed.

"In a moment, in a moment," he said in response to his son's noisy demands. "I'll join you in the garden."

"And what did that lot want?" enquired Louise, as she continued to peel the potatoes.

Andrew went over the details of their proposition.

"And how did you respond?"

"I didn't. I shall wait a week and then decline as gracefully as possible."

"What made you decide against the offer so quickly?"

"I don't like being told by Jock McPherson, or anyone else for that matter, that I will lose my seat at the next election if I don't fall in with their plans." He headed towards the kitchen door. "I'll be back to the red box as soon as I've scored a couple of goals against MacPele." A moment later he had joined Robert in the garden.

"Now listen, clever boots, I'm going to teach you how to feint a pass so that your opponent goes one way while you go the other."

"Sounds just like politics to me," muttered Louise, watching them out of the kitchen window.

27 Eaton Square,
London, SW1
23 April 1974

Dear Derek,

Thank you for your letter of 18 April and your kind invitation to rejoin the board of Seymour's. I am delighted to accept and look forward to working with you again.

Yours sincerely,
Charles Seymour.

Fiona checked the wording and nodded. Short and to the point. "Shall I post it?"

"Yes, please," said Charles as the phone rang.

He picked it up. "730—9712. Charles Seymour speaking."

"Oh, hello, Charles. It's Simon Kerslake."

"Hello, Simon," said Charles, trying to sound pleased to hear from his former colleague. "What's it like out there in the real world?"

"Not much fun, which is exactly why I'm phoning. I've been short-listed for Pucklebridge, Sir Michael Harbour-Baker's seat. He's nearly seventy and has decided not to stand again at the next election. As his constituency touches the south border of yours, I thought you might be able to put in a word for me again."

"Delighted," said Charles. "I'll speak to the chairman tonight. You can rely on me, and good luck. It would be nice to have you back in the House."

Simon gave him his home number which Charles repeated slowly, as if he were writing it down.

"I'll be in touch," said Charles.

"I really appreciate your help."

Simon put down the phone.

Elizabeth looked up from her copy of *The Lancet*.

"I don't trust that man," she said.

"A woman's intuition again?" said Simon smiling. "You were wrong about Ronnie Nethercote."

"That's yet to be proved."

It was several days before Kate Garthwaite agreed to see Raymond again. And when she eventually joined him for dinner at the House she was not overwhelmed or flattered and she certainly didn't hang on his every word.

She was lively, fun, intelligent and well informed and they began to see each other regularly. As the months passed Raymond found himself missing her at weekends when he was in Leeds with Joyce. Kate enjoyed her independence and made none of the demands on him that Stephanie had, never once suggesting he spend more time with her or that she might leave clothes behind in the flat.

Raymond sipped his coffee. "That was a memorable meal," he said, falling back into the sofa.

"Only by the standards of the House of Commons," replied Kate.

Raymond put an arm round her shoulder before kissing her gently on the lips.

"What! Rampant sex as well as cheap Beaujolais?" she exclaimed, stretching over and pouring herself some more coffee.

"I wish you wouldn't always make a joke of our relationship," said Raymond, stroking the back of her hair.

"I have to," said Kate quietly.

"Why?" Raymond turned to face her.

"Because I'm frightened of what might happen if I take it seriously."

Raymond leant over and kissed her again. "Don't be frightened. You're the best thing that's happened to me in my whole life."

"That's what I'm worried about," said Kate, turning away.

Charles sat through the Annual General Meeting in silence. The chairman made his report for the year ending March 1974 before welcoming two new directors to the board and the return of Charles Seymour.

There were several questions from the floor which Derek Spencer had no trouble in handling. As Charles had promised, there was not even a hint of Miss Janet Darrow. Miss Trubshaw had let Fiona know that the payment had been stopped and also mentioned that she was still worried that her contract was coming to an end on 1 July.

When the chairman brought the AGM to a close Charles asked courteously if he could spare him a moment.

"Of course," said Spencer, looking relieved that the meeting had gone through without a hitch. "What can I do for you?"

"I think it might be wiser to talk in the privacy of your office."

The chairman glanced at him sharply but led him back to his room.

Charles settled himself comfortably in the leather chair once more and removed some papers from his inside pocket. Peering down at them he asked, "What does BX41207122, Bank Rombert, Zurich, mean to you?"

"You said you would never mention —"

"Miss Darrow," said Charles. "And I shall keep my word. But now, as a director of the bank, I am trying to find out what BX41207122 means to you?"

"You know damn well what it means," said the chairman, banging his clenched fist on the desk.

"I know it's your *private*" – Charles emphasised the last word – "account in Zurich."

"You could never prove anything," said Derek Spencer defiantly.

"I agree with you, but what I am able to prove," said Charles, shuffling through the papers that were resting on his lap, "is that you have been using Seymour's money to do private deals, leaving the profit in your Zurich account without informing the board."

"I've done nothing that will harm the bank, and you know it."

"I know the money has been returned with interest, and I could never prove the bank had suffered any loss. Nevertheless, the board might take a dim view of your activities remembering they pay you £40,000 a year to make profits for the bank, not for yourself."

"When they saw all the figures they would at worst rap me over the knuckles."

"I doubt if the Director of Public Prosecutions would take the same lenient attitude if he saw these documents," said Charles, holding up the papers that had been resting on his lap.

"You'd ruin the bank's name."

"And you would probably spend the next ten years in jail. If, however, you did get away with it you would be finished in the City, and by the time your legal fees had been paid there wouldn't be much left of that nest-egg in Zurich."

"So what do you want this time?" demanded Spencer, sounding exasperated.

"Your job," said Charles.

"My job?" said Spencer in disbelief. "Do you imagine because you've been a junior minister you're capable of running a successful merchant bank?" he added scornfully.

"I didn't say I would run it. I can buy a competent chief executive to do that."

"Then what will you be doing?"

"I shall be the chairman of Seymour's which will convince City institutions that we wish to continue in the traditions of generations of my family."

"You're bluffing," stammered Spencer.

"If you are still in this building in twenty-four hours' time," said Charles, "I shall send these to the DPP."

There was a long silence.

"If I agreed," said Spencer at last, "I would expect two years' salary as compensation."

"One year," said Charles. Spencer hesitated, then nodded slowly. Charles rose to his feet and put the papers resting on his lap back into his inside pocket.

They consisted of nothing more than the morning mail from Sussex Downs.

Simon felt the interview had gone well but Elizabeth was not so sure. They sat huddled in a room with five other candidates and their wives, patiently waiting.

He thought back to his answers, and to the eight men and four women on the committee.

"You must admit it's the most ideal seat I've been considered for," said Simon.

"Yes, but the chairman kept eyeing you suspiciously."

"But Millburn mentioned that he had been at Eton with Charles Seymour."

"That's what worries me," whispered Elizabeth.

"A 15,000 majority at the last election and only forty minutes from London. We could even buy a little cottage . . ."

"If they invite you to represent them."

"At least this time you were able to tell them you would be willing to live in the constituency."

"So would anyone in their right mind," said Elizabeth.

The chairman came out and asked if Mr and Mrs Kerslake would be kind enough to return once more to see the committee.

Oh, God, thought Simon. What else can they want to know?

"It's too near London to be my fault this time," chuckled Elizabeth.

The committee sat and stared at them with long faces.

"Ladies and gentlemen," said the chairman. "After our lengthy deliberations, I formally propose that Mr Simon Kerslake be invited to contest Pucklebridge at the next election. Those in favour . . .?"

All twelve hands went up.

"Those against . . .?"

"Carried unanimously," said the chairman. He then turned to Simon. "Do you wish to address your committee?"

The prospective Conservative Member of Parliament for Pucklebridge rose. They all waited expectantly.

"I don't know what to say, except that I'm very happy and honoured and I can't wait for a general election."

They all laughed and came forward and surrounded them. Elizabeth dried her eyes before anyone reached her.

About an hour later the chairman accompanied Simon and Elizabeth back to their car and bade them goodnight. Simon wound down his window.

"I knew you were the right man," Millburn said, "as soon

as Charles Seymour phoned" – Simon smiled – "and warned me to avoid you like the plague."

"Could you tell Miss Trubshaw to come in?" Charles asked his secretary.

Margaret Trubshaw arrived a few moments later and remained standing in front of his desk. She couldn't help but notice the change of furniture in the room. The modern Conran suite had been replaced by a leather club-like sofa. Only the picture of the eleventh Earl of Bridgwater remained in place.

"Miss Trubshaw," began Charles, "since Mr Spencer has felt it necessary to resign so suddenly I think it important for the bank to keep some continuity now that I'm taking over as chairman."

Miss Trubshaw stood like a Greek statue, her hands hidden in the sleeves of her dress.

"With that in mind, the board has decided to extend your contract with the bank for a further five years. Naturally, there will be no loss in your pension rights."

"Thank you, Mr Charles."

"Thank you, Miss Trubshaw."

Miss Trubshaw almost bowed as she left the room.

"And Miss Trubshaw?"

"Yes, Mr Charles," she said, holding on to the door knob.

"I believe my wife is expecting a call from you. Something about inviting you to lunch at the Savoy Grill."

CHAPTER
SEVENTEEN

"A blue shirt," said Raymond, looking at the Turnbull and Asser label with suspicion. "A *blue* shirt," he repeated.

"A fortieth-birthday present," shouted Kate from the kitchen.

I shall never wear it, he thought, and smiled to himself.

"And what's more, you'll wear it," she said, her Boston accent carrying a slight edge.

"You even know what I'm thinking," he complained as she came in from the kitchen. He always thought how elegant she looked in her tailored office suit.

"It's because you're so predictable, Carrot Top."

"Anyway, how did you know it was my birthday?"

"A massive piece of detective work," said Kate, "with the help of an outside agent and a small payment."

"An outside agent. Who?"

"The local paper shop, my darling. In the *Sunday Times* they tell you the name of every distinguished person celebrating a birthday in the following seven days. In a week during which only the mediocre were born, you made it."

Raymond had to laugh.

"Now listen, Carrot Top."

Raymond pretended to hate his new nickname. "Do you have to call me by that revolting name?"

"Yes. I can't stand Raymond."

He scowled. "In any case, carrot tops are green."

"No comment. Try on your shirt."

"Now?"

"Now."

He took off his black coat and waistcoat, removed his white shirt and eased the stud on his stiff collar, leaving a small circle above his Adam's apple. Curly red hairs stuck up all over his chest. He quickly put on the new gift. The fabric had a pleasant soft feel about it. He started to do up the buttons, but Kate walked over and undid the top two.

"You know what? You've brought a whole new meaning to the word 'uptight'."

Raymond scowled again.

"But in the right clothes you could even pass for good looking. Now. Where shall we go to celebrate your birthday?"

"The House of Commons?" suggested Raymond.

"Good God," said Kate. "I said celebrate, not hold a wake. What about Annabel's?"

"I can't afford to be seen in Annabel's."

"With me, you mean?"

"No, no, you silly woman, because I'm a Socialist."

"If members of the Labour party are not allowed to indulge in a good meal then perhaps it's time for you to change parties. In my country one only sees the Democrats in the best restaurants."

"Oh, do be serious, Kate."

"I intend to be. Now what have you been up to in the House lately?"

"Not a lot," said Raymond sheepishly. "I've been snowed under in court and . . ."

"Precisely. It's time you did something positive before your colleagues in Parliament forget you exist."

"Have you anything particular in mind?" asked Raymond, folding his arms across his chest.

"As a matter of fact, I have," said Kate. "I read in the same Sunday paper as the one in which I discovered your best-kept secret that it is proving difficult for the Labour party to repeal the Tories' trade union legislation. It appears there are long-term legal implications which the front bench are still trying to find a way round. Why don't you set that so-called 'first class' mind of yours to working out the legal niceties?"

"Not such a stupid idea." Raymond had become used to Kate's political sense, and when he had remarked on it she had only said, "Just another bad habit I picked up from my ex-husband."

"Now, where do we celebrate?" she asked.

"Compromise," said Raymond.

"I'm all ears."

"The Dorchester."

"If you insist," said Kate, not sounding over-enthusiastic.

Raymond started to change his shirt.

"No, no, no, Carrot Top, people have been known to wear blue shirts at the Dorchester."

"But I haven't got a tie to match," said Raymond triumphantly.

Kate thrust her hand into the Turnbull and Asser bag and drew out a dark blue silk tie.

"But it's got a pattern on it," said Raymond in disgust. "What will you expect next?"

"Contact lenses," said Kate.

Raymond stared at her, and blinked.

On the way out of the door Raymond's gaze fell upon the brightly wrapped package that Joyce had posted from Leeds earlier in the week. He had completely forgotten to open it.

"Damn," said Charles, putting down *The Times* and draining his coffee.

"What's the problem?" asked Fiona as she poured out another cup.

"Kerslake's been selected for Pucklebridge, which means he's back in the House for life. Obviously my chat to Archie Millburn had no effect."

"Why have you got it in for Kerslake?" asked Fiona.

Charles folded the paper and considered the question. "It's quite simple really, old girl. I think he's the only one of my contemporaries who could stop me leading the party."

"Why him in particular?"

"I first came across him when he was President of the Union at Oxford. He was damn good then, and now he's better. He had rivals, but he brushed them aside like flies.

No, despite his background, Kerslake's the one man left who frightens me."

"It's a long race yet, my darling, and he could still stumble."

"So could I, but what he doesn't realise is that I shall be putting out some of his hurdles."

Andrew worded the letter very carefully. He assured Jock McPherson and his colleagues that he had been flattered by their approach, but explained that he had decided his loyalties were still firmly based in the Labour party.

He accepted the point Jock had made about the left trying to gain control, but felt that every democratic party was bound to have a maverick element within its ranks, which was not necessarily unhealthy. He added that he considered the offer to have been confidential on both sides.

"Why add that postscript?" asked Louise when she had read the letter through.

"It's only fair to Jock," said Andrew. "If it gets around I turned him down it will have the opposite effect to the one they were trying to create."

"I'm not so sure they will act in the same magnanimous way when the next election comes round."

"Ah, Jock will make a lot of noise, but he's all right underneath . . ."

"That isn't what your father says about him," said Louise. "He's sure they'll want revenge."

"Father always sees grubs under even the greenest leaf."

"So if we're not about to celebrate your leadership of the Scottish Nationalists we'll have to be satisfied with celebrating your fortieth birthday."

"But that's not for at least –"

"– another month, a week before Robert's fourth birthday."

"How would you like to commemorate the occasion, darling?"

"I thought we might have a week in the Algarve on our own."

"Why don't we have two weeks? Then we can celebrate your fortieth birthday as well?"

"Andrew Fraser, you just lost yourself one vote in Edinburgh Carlton."

Simon listened intently to Ronnie's report at the monthly board meeting. Two tenants had not paid their quarterly rent, and another quarter date was fast approaching. Ronnie's solicitors had sent firm reminders, followed a month later by writs but this action had also failed to elicit any money.

"It only proves what I feared most," said Ronnie.

"What's that?" asked Simon.

"They just haven't got the cash."

"So we will have to replace them with new tenants."

"Simon, when you next travel from Beaufort Street to Whitechapel start counting the 'To Let' signs on office blocks along the way. When you've passed a hundred you'll find you still haven't reached the City."

"So what do you think we should do about it?"

"Try and sell one of our larger properties to secure cash flow. We can at least be thankful that even at these prices they are still worth a lot more than our borrowings. It's the companies who are the other way around that have to call in the receiver."

Simon thought about his overdraft, now approaching £100,000, and was beginning to wish he had accepted Ronnie's generous offer to buy back his shares. He accepted reluctantly that the opportunity had now passed.

When the board meeting was over he drove to St Mary's to pick up Elizabeth. It was to be one of their three-times-a-week journeys to Pucklebridge as Simon tried to get round all the villages before Wilson called an election.

Archie Millburn was turning out to be a conscientious chairman who had accompanied them on nearly every trip.

"He's been very kind to us," said Elizabeth, on their way down.

"He certainly has," said Simon. "Remember he also has to

run Millburn Electronics. But, as he reminds us so often, once he's introduced us to every village chairman we'll be on our own."

"Have you ever discovered why he and Charles Seymour didn't see eye to eye?"

"No, he hasn't mentioned his name since that night. All I know for certain is that they were at school together."

"So what do you intend to do about Seymour?"

"Not a lot I can do," said Simon. "Except keep my eyes very wide open."

"The man who has deserted Edinburgh once too often" – Andrew read the Scottish Nationalist leaflet that had been sent to him that morning by his father. It was full of half-truths and innuendoes.

"Andrew Fraser, the man who has forgotten Edinburgh, should no longer be allowed to represent a Scottish seat." It went on to declare: "He now lives far away from the problems of his constituents in a smart apartment building in fashionable Chelsea among his Tory friends. He visits the City of Edinburgh only a few times a year to make well-publicised appearances . . . Has being a minister gone to his head?"

"How dare they?" cried Louise in a rage. Andrew had never seen his wife so angry. "How dare they come to my home, offer you the leadership of their dreadful little party and then write such a pack of lies? And did you read this?" she added, pointing to the last paragraph, " 'His wife Louise, née Forsyth'," she read out aloud, " 'comes from one of the wealthiest families in Scotland. She is a close relation of the owners of Forsyth's in Princes Street.' I'm a second cousin once removed, and they don't even give me a discount in the main store."

Andrew started to laugh.

"What's so funny?"

He took her in his arms. "I always suffered under the illusion that you would inherit the Forsyth empire and I would never have to work again," he mocked. "Now we shall have to live off Robert's earnings as a star football player."

"Don't joke, Andrew. It won't seem funny when the election comes round."

"I'm far more concerned about the extreme left trying to infiltrate my General Management Committee," he said, his voice changing, "than I am by Jock McPherson's band of mad little islanders. But at this moment of time my red box is too full to worry about either of them."

Raymond made such a penetrating speech during the second reading of the new Trade Union Bill that the Whips put him on the standing committee, the perfect medium for him to display his skills as the committee debated each clause, point by point. He was able to show his colleagues where the legal pitfalls were and how to find a way round them. The rest of the committee soon learnt from Raymond the meaning of 'mastering a brief', and it was not long before trade union leaders were calling him at the House and even at his flat to learn his views on how their members should react to a host of different legal problems. Raymond showed patience with each of them and, more important, gave them excellent professional advice for the price of a phone call. He found it ironic how quickly they chose to forget that he was the author of *Full Employment at any Cost?* Snippets began to appear in the national press, ranging from laudatory comments from those involved with the bill to a pointed suggestion in the *Guardian* that, whatever had happened in the past, it would be insupportable if Raymond Gould were not made a member of the Government in the near future.

"If they were to offer you a job, would it make any difference to our relationship?" Kate asked.

"Certainly," said Raymond. "I shall have found the perfect excuse not to wear your blue shirts."

Harold Wilson held the crumbling edifice together for a further six months before finally having to call a general election. He chose 10 October 1974.

Raymond immediately returned to his constituency to fight his fifth campaign. When he met Joyce at Leeds City station he couldn't help remembering that his dumpy wife was only four years older than Kate. He kissed her on the cheek as one might a distant relative, then she drove him back to their Chapel Allerton home.

Joyce chatted away on the journey home and it became clear that the constituency was under control and that this time Fred Padgett was well prepared for a general election. "He hasn't really stopped since the last one," she said. As for Joyce, she was undoubtedly better organised than the agent and the secretary put together. What was more, Raymond thought, she enjoyed it. He glanced over at her and couldn't help thinking she even looked prettier at election time.

Unlike his colleagues in rural seats, Raymond did not have to make speech after speech in little village halls. His votes were to be found in the high street where he addressed the midday shoppers through a megaphone, and walked around supermarkets, pubs and clubs, grasping hands before repeating the whole process a few streets away.

Joyce set her husband a schedule that allowed few people in the Leeds community to escape him. Some saw him a dozen times during the three-week campaign – most of them at the football match on the Saturday afternoon before the election.

Once the game was over Raymond was back trooping round the working men's clubs, drinking pint after pint of John Smith's bitter. He accepted it was inevitable that he would put on half a stone during any election campaign. He dreaded what Kate's comments would be when she saw him. Somehow he always found a few minutes in each day to steal away and phone her. She seemed so busy and full of news it only made Raymond feel downcast; she couldn't possibly be missing him.

The local trade unionists backed Raymond to the hilt. They may have found him stuck up and distant in the past, but they knew 'where his heart was', as they confided to anyone who would listen. They banged on doors, delivered leaflets, drove cars to polling booths. They rose before he did in the morning and could still be found preaching to the converted after the pubs had thrown them out at night.

Raymond and Joyce cast their votes in the local secondary

school on the Thursday of election day, looking forward to a large Labour victory. The Labour party duly gained a working majority in the House of forty-three over the Conservatives, but only three over all the parties combined. Nevertheless Harold Wilson looked set for another five years when the Queen invited him to form his fourth administration. The count in Leeds that night gave Raymond his biggest majority ever: 12,207 votes.

He spent the whole of Friday and Saturday thanking his constituents, then set out for London on the Sunday evening.

"He must invite you to join the Government this time," said Joyce, as she walked down the platform of Leeds City station with her husband.

"I wonder," said Raymond, kissing his wife on the other cheek. He waved at her as the train pulled out of the station. She waved back enthusiastically.

"I do like your new blue shirt, it really suits you," were the last words he heard her say.

During the election campaign Charles had had to spend a lot of time at the bank because of a run on the pound. Fiona seemed to be everywhere in the constituency at once, assuring voters that her husband was just a few yards behind.

After the little slips were counted the swing against Charles to the Labour candidate didn't amount to more than one per cent in his 22,000 majority. When he heard the overall result he returned to London resigned to a long spell in Opposition. As he began to catch up with his colleagues in the House, he found many of them already saying openly that Heath had to go after two election defeats in a row.

Charles knew then that he would have to make up his mind once again on where he stood over the election of a new party leader, and that once again he must pick the right man.

Andrew Fraser returned to London after a gruelling and unhappy campaign. The Scottish Nationalists had concentrated their attack on him, Jock McPherson sailing close to libel and slander. Sir Duncan advised his son against any legal action. "Only plays into their hands," he warned. "Small parties always benefit from the publicity."

Louise wanted him to inform the press that he had been offered the leadership of the SNP but Andrew felt it would serve no purpose, and might even rebound against him: and he also reminded her that he had given his word. In the last week of the campaign he spent most of his time trying – and failing – to stop Frank Boyle, a Communist, who had recently moved from Glasgow, from being elected to his General Management Committee. On polling day he scraped home by 1,656, Jock McPherson taking second place. At least he looked secure for another five years; but it didn't help that the Scottish Nationalists had increased their overall seats in the House to eleven.

Andrew, Louise and Robert took the plane to London on the Sunday night to find the red box awaiting them and a message that the Prime Minister wanted Andrew to continue as Minister of State at the Home Office.

Simon had a glorious campaign. He and Elizabeth had started moving into their new cottage the day the election was announced, thankful that, now she had to commute, her salary at the hospital had made it possible for them to employ a nanny. A double bed and a couple of chairs sufficed as Elizabeth cooked on an old Aga from provisions still packed in tea chests. They seemed to use the same two forks for everything. During the campaign Simon covered the 200-square-mile constituency for a second time and assured his wife that she need only take the final week off from from her duties at St Mary's.

The voters of Pucklebridge sent Simon Kerslake back to Parliament with a majority of 18,419, the largest in the constituency's history. The local people had quickly come to the conclusion that they now had a member who was destined to have a Cabinet career.

Kate kept her remarks very gentle as it became obvious by the Monday night that the Prime Minister was not going to offer Raymond a job in the new administration. She cooked his favourite meal of roast beef – overdone – and Yorkshire pudding in the flat that night, but he didn't comment on it and hardly spoke.

CHAPTER
EIGHTEEN

After Simon had been back at the Commons for a week he felt a sense of *déjà vu*, a feeling that most members returning to the House for a second or even third time often experience. The sense was heightened by finding everything unchanged, even the policeman who greeted him at the Members' Entrance. When Edward Heath announced his Shadow team Simon was not surprised that he wasn't included, as he never had been a known supporter of the Tory leader. He was, however, mystified but not displeased to discover Charles Seymour was not among the names to be found in the Shadow Cabinet.

"Do you regret turning him down now the full team has been published?" asked Fiona, looking up from her copy of the *Daily Mail*.

"It wasn't an easy decision but I think it'll prove right in the long run," replied Charles, buttering another piece of toast.

"What did he offer in the end?"

"Shadow Minister of Industry."

"That sounds rather interesting," said Fiona.

"Everything about it was interesting except the salary, which would have been nothing. Don't forget the bank pays me £40,000 a year while I'm chairman."

Fiona folded her paper. "But you've just appointed a full-time chief executive, so your responsibilities at the bank should be only part-time compared with when you took the chair over. So what's your real reason?"

Charles accepted that he could rarely fool Fiona. "The

truth is that I'm far from certain Ted will be leading the party at the next election."

"Then who will if he doesn't?" asked Fiona.

"Whoever's got the guts to oppose him."

"I'm not sure I understand," said Fiona, beginning to clear away the plates.

"Everyone accepts that he has to allow his name to go forward for re-election now that he's lost twice in a row."

"That's fair enough," agreed Fiona.

"But as he has appointed all possible contenders to the Cabinet or Shadow Cabinet over the last ten years, someone he has selected in the past will have to oppose him. No one of lesser stature would stand a chance."

"Is there a member of the Shadow Cabinet willing to stand?" asked Fiona, returning to her seat at the end of the table.

"One or two are considering it, but the problem is that if they lose it could easily end their political career," said Charles, folding his napkin.

"But if they win?"

"They will undoubtedly be the next Prime Minister."

"Interesting dilemma. And what are you going to do about it?"

"I'm not supporting anyone at the moment, but I've got my eyes wide open," said Charles, folding his copy of *The Times* and rising from the table.

"Is there a front runner?" asked Fiona, looking up at her husband.

"No, not really. Although Kerslake is trying to rally support for Margaret Thatcher, but that idea is doomed from the start."

"A woman leading the Tory party? Your lot haven't got the imagination to risk it," said Elizabeth, tasting the sauce. "The day that happens I shall eat my one and only Tory hat in full view of all the delegates at the party conference."

"Don't be so cynical, Elizabeth. She's the best bet we've got at the moment."

"But what are the chances of Ted Heath standing down? I

always thought the leader of the party stayed on until he was hit by the mythical bus. I don't know Heath very well, but I can never imagine him resigning."

"I agree," said Simon. "So the 1922 Committee will have to change the rules."

"You mean the back-benchers will put pressure on him to go?"

"No, but a lot of the committee in their present mood would be willing to volunteer as driver for that bus."

"If that's true, he must realise that his chances of holding on are slim?"

"I wonder if any leader ever knows that," said Simon.

"You ought to be in Blackpool next week," said Kate, resting her elbow on the pillow.

"Why Blackpool?" Raymond asked, staring up at the ceiling.

"Because, Carrot Top, that's where they are holding this year's Labour party conference."

"What do you imagine I could hope to accomplish there?"

"You'd be seen to be alive. At present you're just a rumour in trade union circles."

"But if you're not a minister or a trade union leader all you do at a party conference is spend four days eating foul food, sleeping in seedy guest houses, and applauding second-rate speeches."

"I've no interest in where you put your weary head at night but I do want you to revive your contacts with the unions during the day."

"Why?" said Raymond. "That lot can't influence my career."

"Not at the moment," said Kate. "But I predict that, like my fellow Americans at their conventions, the Labour party will one day select their leader at the party conference."

"Never," said Raymond. "That is and will always remain the prerogative of elected members of the House of Commons."

"That's the sort of crass, short-sighted, pompous statement I would expect a Republican to make," she said, before plonking a pillow over his head. Raymond feigned death, so she lifted up a corner and whispered in his ear, "Have you read any of the resolutions to be debated at this year's conference?"

"A few," came back Raymond's muffled reply.

"Then it might serve you well to note Mr Anthony Wedgwood Benn's contribution," she said, removing the pillow.

"What's he up to this year?"

"He's calling on 'conference', as he insists on describing your gathering of the brothers, to demand that the next leader be chosen by a full vote of the delegates, making up an electoral college from all the constituencies, the trade union movement and Parliament – I suspect in that order."

"Madness. But what do you expect? He's married to an American."

"Today's extremist is tomorrow's moderate," said Kate blithely.

"A typical American generalisation."

"Benjamin Disraeli, actually."

Raymond placed the pillow back over his head.

Andrew always attended the party conference, although he would never have voted for Tony Benn's resolution on the method of selecting a leader. He feared that if the trade unions were given that sort of power a leader who was totally unacceptable to his colleagues in the House of Commons could be selected. He was relieved when the motion was defeated but he noted that the majority against was far from overwhelming.

Despite being a minister Andrew could only get a small room at Blackpool in a guest house masquerading as a hotel, and that some two miles from the conference centre. Such were the problems created by 4,000 self-important people converging on a seaside resort for a week that many had to forgo the Presidential Suite.

Andrew still had to carry on his job as Minister of State, with red boxes being delivered and taken every morning and afternoon, while making his presence felt at the conference. He spent half his time on a phone in the hotel lobby putting through transfer-charge calls to the Home Office. No one in the Soviet Union would have believed it, especially if they had realised that the Minister of State for Defence, who had the room next to Andrew's, was pacing up and down the corridor waiting for the phone to be free.

Andrew had never addressed the 3,000 delegates at a party conference. Even Cabinet ministers are only allowed a maximum of ten minutes at the rostrum unless they are members of the National Executive. Over half the Labour Cabinet had failed to be elected to this body, which consisted mainly of the leaders of the larger trade unions.

As he left the morning session Andrew was surprised to find Raymond Gould roaming around looking lost. They fell on each other like sane men locked in an asylum and decided to lunch together at the River House, Andrew's favourite restaurant a few miles outside of Blackpool.

Although they had both been in the House for nearly ten years it was the first time they discovered how much they had in common. Andrew had never considered himself a close friend of Raymond's but he had always admired his stand on devaluation.

"You must have been disappointed when the PM didn't ask you to rejoin the Government," Andrew began.

Raymond stared down at the menu. "Very," he finally admitted, as a girl joined them in the bar to take their order.

"Nevertheless, you were wise to come to Blackpool. This is where your strength lies."

"You think so?"

"Come on. Everybody knows you're the trade unions' pin-up boy, and they still have a lot of influence as to who sits in the Cabinet."

"I haven't noticed," said Raymond mournfully.

"You will when they eventually choose the leader."

"That's funny, that's exactly what . . . Joyce said last week."

"Sensible girl, Joyce. I fear it will happen in our time as members."

Bill Scott, the proprietor, told them their table was ready and they went through to the small dining-room.

"Why fear?" asked Raymond, as he took his seat.

"Middle-of-the-road democrats like myself will end up as so many leaves on a bonfire."

"But I'm middle-of-the-road myself, practically right wing on some issues."

"Perhaps. But every party needs a man like you, and at this moment union leaders wouldn't mind if you were a card-carrying Fascist; they'd still back you."

"Then what makes you attend the conference?"

"Thank God it still gives one a chance to keep in touch with the grass roots, and I live in hope that the extreme left will never be much more than an unruly child that the grown-ups have to learn to live with."

"Let's hope you're right," said Raymond, "because they're never going to grow up." Andrew laughed as Raymond continued in a different mood. "I still envy you your job at the Home Office. I didn't go into politics to spend my life on the back benches."

"There may well come a day when I sit and envy you from those same back benches," said Andrew.

As he spoke, the chairman of the Boilermakers' Union shouted across as he passed their table, "Good to see you, Ray." He showed no recognition of Andrew. Raymond turned and smiled at the man and waved back as Caesar might have done to Cassius.

When they had both rejected the choice of date and walnut pudding or Pavlova, Andrew suggested a brandy.

Raymond hesitated.

"You'll see more double brandies drunk here than you will at the Conservative party conference next week. Ask any waitress."

"Have you decided how you're going to vote in the leadership battle?" asked Fiona over breakfast.

"Yes," said Charles, "and at this point in my career I can't afford to make the wrong choice."

"So who have you decided on?" asked Fiona.

"While there isn't a serious contender to oppose Ted Heath it remains in my best interest to continue backing him."

"Isn't there one Shadow Cabinet minister who has the guts to stand against him?"

"The rumour grows that Margaret Thatcher will act as whipping girl. If she gets close enough to force a second ballot the serious contenders will then join in."

"What if she won the first round?"

"Don't be silly, Fiona," said Charles, taking more interest in his scrambled egg. "The Tory party would never elect a woman to lead them. We're far too traditional. That's the sort of immature mistake the Labour party would make to prove how much they believe in equality."

Simon was still pushing Margaret Thatcher to throw her hat in the ring.

"She certainly has enough of them," said Elizabeth.

It amused Andrew and Raymond to watch the Tory party leadership struggle while they got on with their respective jobs. Raymond would have dismissed Thatcher's chances if Kate hadn't reminded him that the Tories had been the first party to choose a Jewish leader, and also the first to select a bachelor.

"So why shouldn't they be the first to elect a woman?" she demanded. He would have continued to argue with her but the damn woman had proved to be right so often in the past. "Let's wait and see," was all he said.

The 1922 Committee announced that the election for leader would take place on 4 February 1975.

At a press conference in early January at the House of Commons Margaret Thatcher announced she would allow her name to go forward to contest the leadership. Simon immediately spent his time exhorting his colleagues to support 'The Lady' and joined a small committee under Airey Neave that was formed for the purpose. Charles Seymour warned his friends that the party could never hope to win a general election with a woman leading them. As the days passed, nothing became clearer than the uncertainty of the outcome.

At four o'clock on a particularly wet and windy day the chairman of the 1922 Committee announced the figures:

> Margaret Thatcher 130
> Edward Heath   119
> Hugh Fraser   16

According to the 1922 Committee rules, the winner needed a fifteen per cent majority and so a second round was necessary. "It will be held in seven days' time," the Chief Whip announced. Three former Cabinet ministers immediately declared they were candidates, while Ted Heath, having been warned that he would get fewer votes a second time round, withdrew from the ballot.

They were the longest days in Simon's life. He did everything in his power to hold Thatcher's supporters together. Charles meanwhile decided to play the second round very low-key. When the time came to vote he put his cross on the ballot paper next to the former Secretary of State he had served under at Trade and Industry. "A man we can all trust," he told Fiona.

When the votes had been counted and confirmed the chairman of the 1922 Committee announced that Margaret Thatcher was the outright winner with a vote of 146 to 79 from her nearest challenger.

Simon was delighted while Elizabeth hoped he had forgotten about the promise to eat her hat. Charles was dumbfounded. They both wrote to their new leader immediately.

11 February 1975

Dear Margaret,

    Many congratulations on your victory as the first woman leader of our party. I was proud to have played a small part in your triumph and will continue to work for your success at the next election.

Yours,
Simon.

27 Eaton Square,
London, SW1
11 February 1975

Dear Margaret,

I made no secret of backing Ted Heath in the first round of the leadership contest having had the privilege of serving in his administration. I was delighted to have supported you on the second ballot. It illustrates how progressive our party is that we have chosen a woman who will undoubtedly be Britain's next Prime Minister.

Be assured of my loyalty.

Yours,
Charles.

Margaret Thatcher answered all her colleagues' letters within the week. Simon received a handwritten letter inviting him to join the new Shadow team as number two in the Education Department. Charles received a typed note thanking him for his letter of support.

CHAPTER
NINETEEN

Seymour's Bank had weathered the Great War, the thirties' crash, and then the Second World War. Charles had no intention of being the chairman who presided over its demise in the seventies. Soon after taking over from Derek Spencer – at the board's unanimous insistence – he had discovered that being chairman wasn't quite the relaxed job he expected, and while he remained confident that the bank could ride the storm he still wasn't taking any risks. The business sections of the newspapers were full of stories of the Bank of England acting as a 'lifeboat' and having to step in to assist ailing financial institutions, along with daily reports of the collapse of yet another property company. The time when property values and rents automatically increased each year had become a thing of the past.

When he had accepted the board's offer, Charles insisted that a chief executive be appointed to carry out the day to day business while he remained the man with whom other City chairmen dealt. He interviewed several people for the position but he did not find anyone suitable. Head-hunting seemed to be the next move, the expense of which was saved when he overheard a conversation at the next table at White's that the newly appointed chief executive of the 1st Bank of America was sick of having to report to the board in Chicago every time he wanted to use a first-class stamp.

Charles immediately invited the chief executive to lunch at the House of Commons. Clive Reynolds had come from a similar background to Derek Spencer: London School of Economics, followed by the Harvard Business School and a series of successful appointments which had culminated in his becoming chief executive of the 1st Bank of America. This similarity did not worry Charles, as he made it clear to Mr Reynolds that the appointee would be the chairman's man.

When Reynolds was offered the appointment he drove a hard bargain and Charles looked forward to his doing the same on behalf of Seymour's. Reynolds ended up with £50,000 a year and enough of a profit incentive to ensure that he didn't deal for himself or encourage any other head-hunters to invite him to join their particular jungle.

"He's not the sort of fellow we could invite to dinner," Charles told Fiona, "but his appointment will enable me to sleep at night knowing the bank is in safe hands."

Charles's choice was rubber-stamped by the board at their next meeting, and as the months passed it became obvious that the 1st Bank of America had lost one of its prime assets well below the market value.

Clive Reynolds was a conservative by nature, but when he did take what Charles described as a risk – and Reynolds called a 'hunch' – over fifty per cent of them paid off. While Seymour's kept its reputation for caution and good husban-dry, they managed a few quite spectacular coups thanks to their new chief executive.

Reynolds had enough sense to treat his new chairman with respect without ever showing deference while their rela-tionship remained at all times strictly professional.

One of Reynolds's first innovations had been to suggest they check on every customer account over £250,000 and Charles had approved.

"When you've handled the account of a company for many years," Reynolds pointed out, "it sometimes is not apparent when one of your traditional customers is heading for trouble as it would be to a newcomer. If there are any 'lame ducks' let's discover them before they hit the ground" – a simile that Charles repeated at several weekend parties.

Charles enjoyed his morning meetings with Clive Reynolds as he picked up a great deal about a profession to which he had previously only brought gut feeling and com-mon sense. In a very short time he learned enough from his new tutor to make him sound like David Rockefeller when he rose to speak in a finance debate on the floor of the House, an unexpected bonus.

Charles knew little of Reynolds's private life except what was on file. He was forty-one, unmarried and lived in Esher, wherever that was. All Charles cared about was that Reynolds arrived each morning at least an hour before him, and left after him every night, even when the House was in recess.

Charles had studied fourteen of the confidential reports on customers with loans over £250,000. Clive Reynolds had already picked out two companies with whom he felt the bank should revise their current position.

Charles still had three more reports to consider before he presented a full assessment to the board.

The quiet knock on the door, however, meant that it was ten o'clock and Reynolds had arrived to make his daily report. Rumours were circulating in the City that the bank rate would go up on Thursday, so Reynolds wanted to go short on dollars and long on gold. Charles nodded. As soon as the announcement had been made about the bank rate, Reynolds continued: "It will be wiser to return to dollars as the new round of pay negotiations with the unions is about to take place. This in turn will undoubtedly start a fresh run on the pound." Charles nodded again.

"I think the dollar is far too weak at two-ten," Reynolds added. "With the unions settling at around twelve per cent the dollar must strengthen, say, to nearer one-ninety." He added that he was not happy about the bank's large holding in Slater Walker and wanted to liquidate half the stock over the next month. He proposed to do so in small amounts over irregular periods. "We also have three other major accounts to consider before we make known our findings to the board. I'm concerned about the spending policy of one of the companies, but the other two appear stable. I think we should go over them together when you have time to consider my reports. Perhaps tomorrow morning, if you could manage that. The companies concerned are Speyward Laboratories, Blackies Limited and Nethercote and Company. It's Speyward I'm worried about."

"I'll take the files home tonight," said Charles, "and give you an opinion in the morning."

"Thank you, Chairman."

Charles had never suggested that Reynolds should call him by his first name.

Archie Millburn held a small dinner party to celebrate Simon's first anniversary as the member for Pucklebridge. Although these occasions had originally been to introduce the party hierarchy to their new member, Simon now knew more about the constituency and its flock than he did, as Archie was the first to admit.

Elizabeth, Peter and Michael had settled comfortably into their small cottage, while Simon, as a member of the Shadow Education team, had visited schools – nursery, primary, public and secondary: universities – red brick, plate glass and Oxbridge; technical colleges, art institutes and even borstals. He had read Butler, Robbins, and Plowden and listened to children and to professors of psychology alike. He felt that after a year he was beginning to understand the subject, and only longed for a general election so that he could once again turn rehearsal into performance.

"Opposition must be frustrating," observed Archie when the ladies had retired after dinner.

"Yes, but it's an excellent way to prepare yourself for Government and do some basic thinking about the subject. I never found time for such luxury as a minister."

"But it must be very different from holding office?" said Archie, clipping a cigar.

"True. In Government," said Simon, "you're surrounded by civil servants who don't allow you to lift a finger or give you a moment to ponder, while in Opposition you can think policy through even if you do often end up having to type your own letters."

Archie pushed the port down to Simon's end of the table. "I'm glad the girls are out," said Archie conspiratorially, "because I wanted you to know I've decided to give up being chairman at the end of the year."

"Why?" said Simon, taken aback.

"I've seen you elected and settled in. It's time for a younger man to have a go."

"But you're only my age."

"I can't deny that, but the truth is that I'm not giving enough time to my electronics company, and the board are continually reminding me of it. No one has to tell you that these are not easy times."

"It's sad," said Simon. "Just as you get to know someone in politics you or they always seem to move on."

"Fear not," said Archie. "I don't intend to leave the area, and I feel confident that you will be my member for at least another twenty years, by which time I will be happy to accept an invitation to dine with you in Downing Street."

"You may find that it's Charles Seymour who is residing at No. 10," said Simon, striking a match to light his cigar.

"Then I won't be getting an invitation," said Archie with a smile.

Charles couldn't sleep that night after his discovery, and his tossing and turning kept Fiona awake. He had opened the Nethercote file when he was waiting for dinner to be served. His first act with any company was to glance down the names of the directors to see if he knew anyone on the board. He recognised no one until his eye stopped at 'S. J. Kerslake, MP'. The cook felt sure that Mr Seymour had not enjoyed his dinner, because he hardly touched the main course.

On his arrival at Seymour's, only moments after Clive Reynolds, he called for his chief executive. He appeared a few minutes later without his usual armful of files, surprised to see the chairman so early. Once Reynolds was seated Charles opened the file in front of him. "What do you know about Nethercote and Company?"

"Private company. Net asset value approaching £10,000,000, running a current overdraft of £7,000,000 of which we service half. Efficiently managed with a good board of directors, will ride out the current problems in my view, and should be well oversubscribed when they eventually go public."

"How much of the company do we own?"

"Seven and a half per cent. As you know, the bank never take eight per cent of any company because then we would have to declare an interest under section twenty-three of the Finance Act. It has always been a policy of this bank to invest in a major client without becoming too involved with the running of the company."

"Who are their principal bankers?"

"The Midland."

"What would happen if we put our seven and a half per cent up for sale and did not renew the overdraft facility at the end of the quarter, but called it in instead?"

"They would have to seek finance elsewhere."

"And if they couldn't?"

"They would have to start selling their assets, which under that sort of forced-sale position would be very damaging for any company, if not impossible, in the present climate."

"And then?"

"I would have to check my file and . . ."

Charles passed over the file and Reynolds studied it carefully, frowning. "They already have a cash-flow problem because of bad debts. With a sudden increased demand they might go under. I would strongly advise against such a move, Chairman. Nethercote have proved a reliable risk over the years, and I think we stand to make a handsome profit when they are quoted on the Stock Exchange."

"For reasons I cannot disclose to you," said Charles, looking up from his chair, "I fear that remaining involved with this company may turn out to be a financial embarrassment for Seymour's." Reynolds looked at him, puzzled. "You will inform the Midland Bank that we will not be renewing this loan at the next quarter."

"Then they would have to look for support from another bank. The Midland would never agree to shoulder the entire amount on their own."

"And try to dispose of our seven and a half per cent immediately."

"But that could lead to a crisis of confidence in the company."

"So be it," said Charles, as he closed the file.

"But I do feel –"

"That will be all, Mr Reynolds."

"Yes, Chairman," said the mystified chief executive, who had never thought of his boss as an irrational man. He turned to leave. Had he looked back he would have been even more mystified by the smile that was spread across Charles Seymour's face.

"They've pulled the rug out from under our feet," said Ronnie Nethercote angrily.

"Who?" said Simon, who had just come into the room.

"The Midland Bank."

"Why would they do that?"

"An outside shareholder put all his stock on the market without warning, and the Midland got worried about their position. They wouldn't be prepared to continue such a large overdraft position on their own."

"Have you been to see the manager?" asked Simon, unable to disguise his anxiety.

"Yes, but he can't do anything. His hands are tied by a main board directive," said Ronnie, slumping deeper into his seat.

"How bad is it?"

"They've given me a month to find another bank. Otherwise I'll have to start selling some of our assets."

"What will happen if we don't manage to come up with another bank?" asked Simon desperately.

"The company could be bankrupt within weeks. Do you know any bankers who are looking for a good investment?"

"Only one, and I can assure you he wouldn't help."

Charles put the phone down satisfied. He wondered if there was anything that could still be regarded as secret. It had taken him less than an hour to find out the size of Kerslake's overdraft. "Banker to banker confidentiality," he had assured them. He was still smiling when Reynolds knocked on the door.

"The Midland weren't pleased," he immediately briefed Charles.

"They'll get over it," his chairman replied. "What's the latest on Nethercote?"

"Only a rumour, but everyone now knows they're in trouble and the chairman is searching around for a new backer," said Reynolds impassively. "His biggest problem is that no one is touching property companies at the moment."

"Once they've collapsed, what's to stop us picking up the pieces and making a killing?"

"A clause that was slipped through in the Finance Act which your Government passed three years ago. The penalties range from a heavy fine to having your banking licence taken away."

"Oh, yes, I remember," said Charles. "Pity. So how long do you expect them to last?"

"Once the month is up," said Reynolds stroking a clean-shaven chin, "if they fail to find a backer the creditors will swarm in like locusts."

"Aren't the shares worth anything?" asked Charles innocently.

"Not the paper they are written on at the moment," said Reynolds, watching his chairman carefully.

This time the chief executive couldn't miss the chairman's smile as Charles thought of Simon Kerslake and his overdraft of £108,000 now backed by worthless shares. Pucklebridge would soon be looking for a new member.

At the end of a month during which no bank came to his rescue Ronnie Nethercote caved in and agreed to call in the receiver and file a bankruptcy notice. He still hoped that he could pay off all his creditors even if the shares he and his fellow directors held remained worthless. He felt as worried for Simon and his career as he did for himself, but he knew there was nothing the receiver would allow him to do to help one individual.

When Simon told Elizabeth she didn't complain. She had always feared this could be the eventual outcome of her husband joining the board of Nethercotes.

"Can't Ronnie help?" she asked. "After all, you've supported him enough in the past."

"No, he can't," replied Simon, avoiding telling her where the real responsibility for his downfall lay.

"But do bankrupts automatically have to leave Parliament?" was Elizabeth's next question.

"No, but I shall because I could never be considered for further promotion – I'd always be rightly tainted with 'lack of judgement'."

"It seems so unfair when you weren't personally to blame."

"There are different rules for those who wish to live in the spotlight," Simon said simply.

"But in time, surely –" began Elizabeth.

"I'm not willing to remain on the back benches for another twenty years only to hear whispered in the corner of the smoking room – Would have made the Cabinet if it hadn't been for . . ."

"Does that mean the children will have to be taken away from school?"

"I'm afraid so," said Simon, his hands shaking. "As a bankrupt I can hardly expect the receiver to view the fees for my sons' education as a dire necessity even if I could find the money."

"So we'll have to get rid of the nanny, too?"

"Not necessarily, but we may both have to make sacrifices in order that she can be part-time."

"But my work at the hospital . . ." began Elizabeth but didn't complete the sentence. "What happens next?"

"I'll have to tell Archie Millburn tonight. I've already written my letter of resignation to hand to him. I shall make an appointment to see the Chief Whip on Monday to explain why I am going to apply for the Chiltern Hundreds."

"What does that mean?"

"It's one of the only ways of leaving the House in midsession – other than dying. Officially it's a nominal office under the Crown which therefore debars you from membership of the House."

"It all sounds rather formal to me."

"I'm afraid it will cause an embarrassing by-election in Pucklebridge," Simon admitted.

"Can nobody help?"

"There aren't a lot of people around who have a spare £108,000 for a worthless bunch of shares."

"Would you like me to come with you when you go to see Archie?" Elizabeth asked, rising from her seat.

"No, darling. It's kind of you to ask, but I'm the one who made such a fool of myself."

Elizabeth leaned over and pushed back the hair that had fallen over his forehead. She couldn't help noticing some grey strands that must have appeared in the last few weeks. "We'll just have to live off my salary while you look for a job."

Simon drove slowly down to Pucklebridge to keep his impromptu appointment with the chairman. Archie Millburn, standing hands on hips in his garden, listened to the tale with a sad face. "It's been happening to a lot of good people in the City lately, but what I can't understand is: if the company owns such prime properties, why has no one made a takeover bid? Sounds as if it's an asset-stripper's dream."

"It appears to be a matter of confidence," said Simon.

"A sacred word in the City," agreed Archie, while he continued to prune his Roosevelts and Red Mistresses.

Simon handed him the prepared letter of resignation, which Millburn read over and reluctantly accepted.

"I won't mention this to anyone until you've seen the Chief Whip on Monday. I'll call a special meeting of the full committee on Tuesday evening and inform them of your decision then. You had better be prepared for an unfriendly barrage from the press on Tuesday night."

The two men shook hands. "Your misfortune is our misfortune," said Archie. "In a very short time you've gained the respect and the affection of the local people. You'll be missed."

Simon drove back to London and, although the car radio was on low, he did not take in the news flash that they kept repeating every thirty minutes.

CHAPTER
TWENTY

Raymond was among the first to hear the announcement, and was stunned by it. Harold Wilson was going to resign less than half-way through the five-year Parliament, and for no apparent reason other than that he had just passed his sixtieth birthday. He proposed to remain Prime Minister only so long as the Labour party took to select its new leader. Raymond and Kate sat glued to the television, picking up every scrap of information they could. They discussed the implications far into the night.

"Well, Carrot Top, could this mean rehabilitation for our forgotten hero?"

"Who can say?"

"Well, if you can't, who can?"

"The next leader," said Raymond.

The fight for the leadership was a straight battle between the left and right wings of the party, James Callaghan on the right and Michael Foot on the left. Andrew and Raymond both wanted the same man and it was with some relief that they saw Callaghan, despite losing the first ballot, come through to be elected leader. The Queen duly called for Callaghan and asked him to form a new administration.

As tradition demands Andrew sent his resignation to Downing Street, as did every other member of the Government, to allow the new Prime Minister to select his own team.

Raymond was in court listening to the judge's summing up when his junior passed him a note: "Please call 10 Downing Street as soon as possible." The judge took a further thirty minutes, meticulously explaining to the jury the legal definition of manslaughter, before Raymond could escape. He ran down the corridor and stopped at one of the clerks' private boxes to make the call. The plastic dial rotating back into place after each number seemed to take forever.

After he had been passed through three people a voice said, "Good afternoon, Ray": the unmistakable gravelly tones of the new Prime Minister. "I think it's time you rejoined the Government" – Raymond held his breath – "as Minister of State at the Department of Trade." Minister of State: only one place away from the Cabinet.

"You still there, Ray?"

"Yes, Prime Minister, and I'd be delighted to accept."

He put the phone down, immediately picked it up again and dialled the City office of the Chase Manhattan Bank. They put him through to the Euro Bond manager.

Andrew had left his desk at the Home Office and returned to Cheyne Walk. He stayed away from the House of Commons where the lobby correspondents were hanging about like hyenas, scampering off to phone their papers with even the rumour of a rumour. The new Cabinet had been selected, and now it was the turn of the Ministers of State. All Andrew knew for certain was that his old job at the Home Office had been given to someone else.

"Why don't you go and play football with Robert?" Louise suggested. "And stop moping around under my feet?"

"Yes, Dad, yes, Dad, yes, Dad," demanded his son, running upstairs to reappear a few minutes later dressed in the Liverpool kit that he had bought himself from eleven weeks' hard-saved pocket money.

"Go on, Andrew. I can always call you if the phone goes."

Andrew smiled, took off his jacket and put on the pair of old gym shoes Robert was holding out for him. He followed his five-year-old son into the garden to find him already dribbling up and down the thin strip between the flower beds. The little goal he had bought for Robert – or was it for himself? – at Christmas was already set up at the far end of the grass and they took turns defending it. Andrew always had to start in goal. He rubbed his hands together to keep warm as Robert dribbled towards him. He came out of the goal ready to stifle a shot, but Robert kicked the ball to the right and ran to the left, leaving his father spreadeagled on the ground before he pushed the ball gently into the goal. "That's called a feint," he shouted triumphantly, as he ran back past his prostrate father.

Andrew picked himself up. "I know what it's called," he said, laughing. "You seem to have forgotten who taught you the feint in the first place. Let's see if you can do it twice running," he added, returning to defend the goal.

Robert dribbled away from his father until he reached the end of the garden, then turned to face him again. He had begun advancing towards the goal for a second time when there was the sound of the phone ringing. Andrew looked towards the house just as Robert kicked the ball, which rising sharply, struck him in the face. He and the ball fell back into the goal mouth.

Louise opened the kitchen window and shouted, "It's only my mother."

"Wake up, Dad," demanded Robert simultaneously.

Andrew's face was still stinging from the blow. "I'm going to get you for that," he said. "Your turn to defend the goal."

Robert rushed forward to take his place between the posts, jumping up and down trying to touch the crossbar with the tips of his fingers. Andrew took his time as he moved towards his son. When he was about a yard in front of Robert he feinted to the right and ran to the left but Robert had seen the move coming and leaped on the ball shouting, "No goal."

Once again Andrew returned to the end of the garden, thinking over what move he could try next. He suddenly ran straight at Robert and kicked the ball firmly towards the right-hand corner of the goal mouth. But again Robert anticipated the move and caught the ball above his head before pulling it to his chest and shouting, "No goal, Dad, no goal!" He tossed the ball confidently back along the ground to his father's feet.

"Right, the fooling around is over," said Andrew, not quite convinced. He kicked the ball from one foot to the other, trying to look skilful.

"Come on, Dad," Robert complained.

This time Andrew advanced with a look of determination on his face. He tried a change of pace to make his son leave the goal mouth too early. Robert duly came out of the goal; Andrew kicked the ball a little harder and higher than his previous attempt. As he did so he heard the phone ring again and turned his head towards the house. He didn't see his shot cannon against the left-hand corner of the goal post and bounce away.

"It's the Prime Minister," shouted Louise from the window. Andrew turned to walk quickly back towards the house. Out of the corner of his eye he saw the ball bounce on to the path, on its way towards the gate and into the road.

Robert was already running towards the open gate. "I'll save it, Dad, I'll save it."

"No," screamed Andrew at the top of his voice and turned back to run as fast as he could after his son.

Louise froze as she stared out of the window, still holding on to the phone with her rubber gloves. She watched as Andrew turned his back and tore towards the pavement until he was only a yard behind his son. The ball bounced on into the road and Robert dived for it a split second before his father threw himself on his son.

Louise was the only one who saw the driver of the massive Shell tanker slam on its brakes and swerve – too late – to avoid them. Andrew and Robert collided with the corner of the wide metal mudguard and were thrown back together before rolling over and over several times, ending up in the gutter.

"Are you there, Andrew?" asked the Prime Minister.

Louise dropped the phone and ran out of the kitchen towards the open gate. Her husband lay motionless beside the kerb with their son in his arms, the ball still clutched against his chest. She tried to hold on to both of them as Andrew's blood poured down over Robert's red shirt and on to her rubber gloves.

She fell on to her knees by the kerb side. "Let them live, let them live," was all she said.

Robert was crying softly as he held firmly on to the ball and stared at his unconscious father. She had to lean over to hear him repeating, "No goal, Dad, no goal."

When the complete list of ministers was published in *The Times* two days later the only unfilled post left was that of Minister of State for Defence. *The Times*'s political editor, David Wood, surmised that the position was being held open for Mr Andrew Fraser, who was expected to be out of hospital by the end of the week. Wood's final paragraph read:

> Politicians from all parties joined forces in praising Mr Fraser's remarkable courage in diving in front of a moving lorry to rescue his only son, Robert, who was chasing a football. Both father and son were rushed to St Thomas's Hospital with internal injuries, where surgeons operated through the night to save Mr Fraser's life.
> As was reported in the final edition of yesterday's paper, his five-year-old son Robert died during the night before Mr Fraser regained consciousness.

"My God," exclaimed Elizabeth, "how dreadful."

"What's dreadful?" asked Simon, as he took his seat at the breakfast table. She passed the paper to her husband and pointed to the picture of Robert.

"Poor kid," said Simon before he had finished the article. "Certainly puts our own problems into perspective. If Peter or Michael were killed we really would have something to worry about."

Neither of them spoke for several minutes. Then Elizabeth asked, "Are you dreading it?"

"Yes, I am," said Simon. "I feel like a condemned man eating his last breakfast, and the worst part of it is that I have to drive myself to the gallows."

"I wonder if we will ever laugh about today?"

"No doubt – when I collect my parliamentary pension."

"Can we live off that?"

"Hardly. I don't get the first payment until I'm sixty-five, so we have a twenty-five-year wait to find out." He got up. "Can I give you a lift to the hospital?"

"No thanks. I intend to savour the joys of being a two-car family for at least another week. Just let's hope the new Marina holds its price as well as Sir Michael Edwardes claimed it would."

Simon laughed, kissed his wife and left for his appointment with the Chief Whip at the House of Commons. As he started the car Elizabeth rushed out. "I forgot to tell you, Ronnie phoned while you were in the bath."

"I'll call him as soon as I reach the House."

Simon made his way to the Commons. He felt sick as he passed Cheyne Walk and thought of Andrew Fraser and all he must be going through. He made a mental note to write to him immediately. At the Commons the policeman on the gate saluted as he drove in. "Good morning, sir," he said.

"Good morning," said Simon. He parked his car on the second level of the new underground car park and took the escalator up to the Members' Entrance. He couldn't help reflecting that ten years ago he would have taken the stairs. He continued through the Members' Cloakroom, up the marble staircase to the Members' Lobby. Habit made him turn left into the little post office to check whether he had any mail.

"Mr Kerslake," the man behind the counter called into an intercom, and a few seconds later a parcel and a packet of letters held together by a thick elastic band thudded into an office basket. Simon left the parcel marked 'London School of Economics' and the letters on the desk in his room and checked his watch: over forty minutes before his appointment with the Chief Whip. He went to the nearest phone and dialled Nethercote and Company. Ronnie answered the phone himself.

"Sacked the telephone operator last Friday," he explained. "Only me and my secretary left."

"You called, Ronnie," a millimetre of hope in Simon's voice.

"Yes, I wanted to express how I felt. I tried to write you a letter over the weekend but I'm not very good with words." He paused. "Nor it seems with figures. I just wanted to say how desperately sorry I am. Elizabeth told me you were going to see the Chief Whip this morning. I'll be thinking of you."

"That's kind, Ronnie, but I went into it with my eyes wide open. As an advocate of free enterprise, I can hardly complain when I turn out to be one of its victims."

"A very philosophical attitude for this time of the morning."

"How are things your end?"

"The receiver's checking the books. I still believe we can get out with all our creditors fully paid. At least that way I'll avoid the stigma of bankruptcy." There was a longer pause. "Oh Christ, that was tactless."

"Don't worry about it, Ronnie, the overdraft was my decision."

Simon already wished he had been as frank with his wife.

"Let's have lunch one day next week."

"It will have to be somewhere that takes luncheon vouchers," said Simon wryly.

"Good luck, mate," said Ronnie.

Simon decided to fill up the remaining thirty minutes at the House by going to the library and glancing over the rest of the morning press. He settled himself in a corner of the 'B' Room, next to the fireplace over which hung a notice reminding members not to have overloud or prolonged conversations. He leafed through the papers, which all carried photographs of Andrew Fraser and his wife and son. The same portrait of five-year-old Robert appeared on almost every front page. Elizabeth was right: in so many respects they were lucky.

The story of the probable break-up of Nethercote and Company was detailed on the financial pages. They quoted approvingly Ronnie's view that all creditors ought to be paid in full. Not one of the articles mentioned Simon's name, but he could already anticipate the headlines in tomorrow's paper with another picture of a young MP and his happy family. 'The Rise and Fall of Simon Kerslake.' Over ten years' work quickly forgotten: he would be old news within a week.

The library clock inched towards the hour that he could no

longer put off. Simon heaved himself out of the deep leather chair like an old man and walked slowly towards the Chief Whip's office.

Miss Norse, the Chief's ancient secretary, smiled benignly as he came in.

"Good morning, Mr Kerslake," she said brightly. "I'm afraid the Chief is still with Mrs Thatcher but I did remind him of your appointment so I don't expect him to be long. Would you care to have a seat?"

"Thank you," he said.

Alec Pimkin always claimed that Miss Norse had a set patter for every occasion. His imitation of her saying, "I hope I find you in rude health, Mr Pimkin," had brought chuckles to the Members' Dining-room on many occasions. He must have exaggerated, thought Simon.

"I hope I find you in rude health, Mr Kerslake," said Miss Norse, not looking up from her typing. Simon choked back a laugh.

"Very rude, thank you," he said, wondering how many tragic stories or tales of lost opportunities Miss Norse had had to listen to over the years. She stopped suddenly and looked at her note pad.

"I should have mentioned it to you before, Mr Kerslake, a Mr Nethercote rang."

"Thank you, I've spoken to him already."

Simon was leafing through an out-of-date copy of *Punch* when the Chief Whip strode in.

"I can spare you one minute, Simon, one and a half if you are going to resign," he said, laughing, and marched off towards his office. As Simon followed him down the corridor the phone by Miss Norse's side rang. "It's for you, Mr Kerslake," she shouted to their retreating backs.

Simon turned and said, "Can you take the number?"

"He says it's urgent."

Simon stopped, hesitating. "With you in a moment," he said to the Chief Whip, who disappeared into his office. Simon walked back and took the phone from Miss Norse's outstretched hand.

"Simon Kerslake here. Who is it?"

"It's Ronnie."

"Ronnie," said Simon flatly.

"I've just had a call from Morgan Grenfell. One of their clients has made an offer of one pound twenty-five a share for the company and they're willing to take over the current liabilities."

Simon was trying to do the sums in his head.

"Don't bother working it out," Ronnie said. "At one pound twenty-five your shares would be worth £75,000."

"It won't be enough," said Simon, as he recalled his overdraft of £108,712, a figure etched in his memory.

"Don't panic. I've told them I won't settle for anything less than one pound fifty a share and it has to be within seven days, which will give them ample time to check the books. That would bring you in £90,000 but you would still be £18,000 down the Swanee, which you'll have to learn to live with. If you sell the wife as well as the second car you should just about survive."

Simon could tell by the way his friend was speaking that Ronnie already had a cigar between his lips.

"You're a genius."

"Not me – Morgan Grenfell. And I bet they'll make a handsome profit in the long run for their unnamed client who seemed to have all the inside information. If you're still on for lunch next Tuesday, don't bring your luncheon vouchers. It's on me."

Simon put the phone down and kissed Miss Norse on the forehead. She was completely taken aback by a situation for which she had no set reply. She remained silent as the Chief Whip put his head round the door. "An orgy in the Chief Whip's office? You'll be on page three of the *Sun* next, Miss Norse." Simon laughed. "I've got a crisis on over tonight's vote. The Government are reneging on our agreement for pairing, and I have to get a delegation back from Brussels in time for the ten o'clock division. Whatever it is, can it wait, Simon?"

"Yes, of course."

"Can you come to my office, Miss Norse – if I can drag you away from James Double-O-Seven Kerslake?"

Simon left and almost bounced to the nearest phone. First he called Elizabeth and then Archie Millburn at his office. Archie didn't sound all that surprised.

"Don't you think it might be wise for us to stop seeing each other?"

"Why?" said Raymond. "Palmerston had a mistress when he was seventy, and he still beat Disraeli come the election."

"Yes, but that was before the days of a dozen national newspapers *and* investigative journalism. Frankly it wouldn't take a Woodward or Bernstein more than a few hours to discover our little secret."

"We'll be all right. I've destroyed all the tapes."

"Do be serious."

"You're always telling me I'm far too serious."

"Well, I want you to be now. Very."

Raymond turned to face Kate. "I love you, Kate, and I know I always will. Why don't we stop this charade and get married?"

She sighed. "We've been over this a hundred times. I'll want to return to America eventually, and in any case I wouldn't make a very good Prime Minister's wife."

"Three American women have in the past," said Raymond sulkily.

"To hell with your historical precedents – and what's more, I hate Leeds."

"You've never been there."

"I don't need to if it's colder than London."

"Then you'll have to be satisfied with being my mistress." Raymond took Kate in his arms. "You know, I used to think being Prime Minister was worth every sacrifice, but now I'm not so sure."

"It's still worth the sacrifice," said Kate, "as you'll discover when you live at No. 10. Come on, or my dinner will be burnt to a cinder."

"You haven't noticed these," said Raymond smugly, pointing down at his feet.

Kate stared at the fashionable new slip-ons.

"I never thought the day would come," she said. "Pity you're starting to go bald."

When Simon returned home his first words were "We'll survive."

"Thank God for that," Elizabeth said. "But what have you done about your resignation letter?"

"Archie said he would return it the day I became Prime Minister."

"If that's ever to be true I want you to promise me just one thing."

"Anything," said Simon.

"You'll never speak to Ronnie Nethercote again."

For a moment Simon hesitated before saying, "That's not completely fair, Elizabeth, because I haven't been totally straight with you from the beginning." He then sat his wife down on the sofa and told her the whole truth.

It was Elizabeth's turn to remain silent.

"Oh, hell," she said, looking up at Simon. "I do hope Ronnie can forgive me."

"What are you talking about?"

"I phoned him back soon after you had left for the Commons and I spent at least ten minutes telling him why he was the biggest two-faced bastard I'd ever come across, and I didn't want to hear from him again in my life."

It was Simon's turn to collapse on to the sofa. "How did he respond?" he asked anxiously. Elizabeth faced her husband. "That's the strange thing, he didn't even protest. He just apologised."

"Do you think she will ever speak again?"

"God knows, I hope so," said his father, staring at the picture of his grandchild on the mantelpiece. "She's still young enough to have another child."

Andrew shook his head. "No, that's out of the question. The doctor warned me a long time ago that could be dangerous."

He had returned home from hospital ten days after the accident. The first thing he and Louise did was to attend

Robert's funeral. With Andrew on crutches, Sir Duncan had to support Louise during the short service. As soon as the burial was over Andrew took his wife back to Cheyne Walk and put her to bed, before returning downstairs to join his parents.

Andrew's mother bowed her head. "Whatever happens, you must move from this place as soon as possible. Every time Louise looks out of that kitchen window she'll relive the tragedy."

"I hadn't thought of that," said Andrew. "I'll start looking for a new house immediately."

"And what do you plan to do about the Prime Minister's offer?" enquired Sir Duncan.

"I haven't finally made up my mind," he said sharply. "He's given me until Monday to come to a decision."

"You must take it, Andrew. If you don't your political career will be finished. You can't sit at home and mourn Robert's death for the rest of your life."

Andrew looked up at his father. "No goal, Dad, no goal," he murmured and left them to go and sit with Louise in the bedroom. Her eyes were open but there was no expression on her face. Little white hairs had appeared at either side of her head that he had not noticed the week before. "Feeling any better, my darling?" he asked.

There was still no reply.

He undressed and climbed into bed beside her, holding her close, but she did not respond. She felt detached and distant. He watched his tears fall on her shoulder and run down on to the pillow. He fell asleep and woke again at three in the morning. No one had closed the curtains and the moon shone in through the windows, lighting the room. He looked at his wife. She had not moved.

Charles paced up and down the room angrily.

"Give me the figures again."

"Nethercote has accepted a bid of £7,500,000, which works out at one pound fifty a share," said Clive Reynolds.

Charles stopped at his desk and scribbled the figures down on a piece of paper. £90,000, leaving a shortfall of only

£18,000. It wouldn't be enough. "Damn," he said.

"I agree," said Reynolds, "I always thought we were premature to lose our position in the company in the first place."

"An opinion you will not voice outside this room," said Charles.

Clive Reynolds did not reply.

"What's happened to Nethercote himself?" asked Charles, searching for any scrap of information he could find about Simon Kerslake.

"I'm told he's starting up again in a smaller way. Morgan Grenfell were delighted by the deal and the manner in which he handled the company during the takeover. I must say we let it fall into their laps."

"Can we get any stock in the new company?" asked Charles, ignoring his comment.

"I doubt it. It's only capitalised at one million although Morgan Grenfell are giving Nethercote a large overdraft facility as part of the deal."

"Then all that remains necessary is to see the matter is never referred to again."

Andrew spent the weekend reading over the letters of condolence sent to him and Louise. There were over a thousand, many from people he didn't even know. He selected a few to take into the bedroom and read to Louise; not that he was sure she could even hear him. The doctor had told him not to disturb her unless it was really necessary. After such a severe shock she was now suffering from acute depression and must be nursed slowly back to health. Louise had walked a few paces the previous day but needed to rest today, the doctor explained to him.

He sat by the side of their bed, and quietly read the letters from the Prime Minister, from a contrite Jock McPherson, from Simon Kerslake, from Raymond Gould and from Mrs Bloxham. There was no sign that Louise had taken in anything he had said.

"What shall I do about the PM's offer?" he asked. "Shall I accept it?"

She made no response of any kind.

"He's asked me to be the Minister of State for Defence, but I need to know how you would feel." After sitting with her for a few more minutes and eliciting no response he left her to rest.

Each night he slept with her and tried to infuse her with his love, but he only felt more alone.

On the Monday morning he called his father and told him he had decided to turn down the Prime Minister's offer. He couldn't leave Louise alone for long periods while she was still in this state.

Andrew returned to the bedroom and sat by her side.

He said in a whisper, as if to himself, "Should I have taken the job?"

Louise gave such a slight nod that Andrew nearly missed it but her fingers were moving. He placed his hand between her fingers and palm and she squeezed gently and repeated the nod, then fell asleep.

Andrew phoned the Prime Minister.

Raymond dug deeper into the red box.

"You enjoying yourself, Carrot Top?"

"It's fascinating," said Raymond. "Do you know —"

"No, I don't. You haven't spoken to me in the last three hours, and when you do it's to tell me how you spend the day with your new mistress."

"My new mistress?"

"The Secretary of State for Trade."

"Oh, him."

"Yes, him."

"What sort of day did you have at the bank?" asked Raymond, not looking up from his papers.

"I had a most fascinating day," replied Kate.

"Why, what happened?"

"One of our customers required a loan," said Kate.

"A loan," repeated Raymond, still concentrating on the file in front of him. "How much?"

"'How much do you want?' I said. 'How much have you got?' they asked. 'Four hundred and seventeen billion at the last count,' I told them. 'That will do fine to start with,' they said. 'Sign here,' I said. But I couldn't close the deal because the lady concerned was only in possession of a £50 banking card."

Raymond burst out laughing and slammed down the lid of the red box. "Do you know why I love you?"

"My taste in men's clothes?" suggested Kate.

"No, no. Just your taste in men."

"I always thought that mistresses were supposed to get fur coats, trips to the Bahamas, the odd solitaire diamond, yet all I ever get is to share you with your red box."

Raymond opened the box once more, took out a small package and handed it to Kate.

"What's this?"

"Why don't you open it and find out?"

Kate slipped off the purple Asprey paper and found inside an exquisitely made miniature, a solid gold replica of a red box on a gold chain. The neat lettering on the side of the lid read, 'For Your Eyes Only'.

"Although they don't announce the birthdays of ministers' mistresses in the *Sunday Times*, I can still remember the day we met."

Andrew made a bid for the house in Pelham Crescent the day he was shown over it, and Louise's mother came down to London immediately to organise the move.

"Let's hope this does the trick," she said.

Andrew prayed for nothing more. The move from Cheyne Walk took about a fortnight, and Louise could still walk only a few paces before she had to sit down. Louise's mother rarely left the house and Andrew began to feel guilty about how much he was enjoying his new job at the Ministry of Defence. Each night and then again in the morning he would try a few words to Louise. She nodded occasionally, touched him once in a while and even began writing notes to him, but never spoke and never cried. The doctor became even more pessimistic. "The crucial time has passed," he explained.

Andrew would sit with her for hours while he worked through the red boxes. Harrier Jump jets for the RAF,

Polaris missiles for the Royal Navy, Chieftain tanks for the Army, what should Labour's attitude be to Trident when Polaris was phased out? Should we allow Cruise to be based on British soil? There was so much to learn before he could face the civil servants on their own ground or the members from the dispatch box. As the months passed Andrew was always asking questions; a year had gone by and he was beginning to know some of the answers.

He looked up at his wife once again. She was gazing at the portrait of Robert on the mantelpiece.

On the anniversary of his son's sixth birthday Andrew stayed at Pelham Crescent all day with Louise. For the first time a tear lodged in her eye. As he held her, he kept remembering the lorry. He could see it so clearly now as if in slow motion. If only the phone hadn't gone, if only the gate had been closed, if only he had turned earlier, if only he had run a little faster. 'No goal, Dad, no goal.'

If only he had scored that goal.

CHAPTER
TWENTY ONE

Raymond entered a Washington ablaze with red, white and blue as the Americans prepared for their bicentennial. He was among the three ministers chosen to represent the United Kingdom when they presented a copy of Magna Carta to the United States Congress. He was making his first trip to America on Concorde only a few weeks after its inaugural flight. Tom Carson had complained to the House about the expense of the trip but his words had fallen upon a silent Chamber.

As the plane taxied to a halt at Dulles airport three limousines drew up. The three ministers were given a car each and motorcycle outriders rushed them to the grounds of the British Embassy on Massachusetts Avenue in less than thirty minutes.

Raymond had an immediate love affair with America, perhaps because it reminded him so much of Kate with its bubbling enthusiasm, its spirit and sense of perpetual innovation. During the ten-day visit he managed to forge several useful contacts in the Senate and House, and over the weekend became an unrepentant sightseer of the beautiful Virginia countryside. He concentrated on getting to know those contemporaries whom he felt would be on the American political stage for the next twenty years, while his more senior colleagues dealt with President Ford and his immediate entourage.

Raymond enjoyed starting each day with the *Washington Post* and the *New York Times*. He quickly learned how to reject those sections that seemed full of endless advertisements for non-essentials he couldn't believe anyone really bought.

Once he had finished reading both papers he found he had to wash his hands as they were always black with newsprint. The one occasion he kept the Outlook section of the *Washington Post* was when it did profiles on the three ministers from London. He tucked the paper away as he wanted to show Kate the paragraph that read: "The two Secretaries of State are interesting men at the end of their careers, but it is Raymond Gould we should keep our eyes on because he has the look of a future Prime Minister."

As Raymond flew out of Washington on his way back to London he presumed, like any lover, that the affair with America could be continued whenever he chose to return.

Simon was in Manchester as a guest of the Business School when he received Elizabeth's message to call her. It was most unusual for Elizabeth to phone in the middle of the day and Simon assumed the worst: something must have happened to the children. The Principal of the Business School accompanied him to his private office, then left him alone.

Dr Kerslake was not at the hospital, he was told, which made him even more anxious. He dialled the Beaufort Street number.

Elizabeth picked up the receiver so quickly that she must have been sitting by the phone waiting for him to call.

"I've been sacked," she said.

"What?" said Simon, unable to comprehend.

"I've been made redundant – isn't that the modern term meant to lessen the blow? The hospital governors have been instructed by the Department of Health and Social Security to make cutbacks and three of us in gynaecology have lost our jobs. I go at the end of the month."

"Darling, I'm sorry," he said, knowing how inadequate his words must have sounded.

"I didn't meant to bother you, but I just wanted someone to talk to," she said. "Everyone else is allowed to complain to their MP, so I thought it was my turn."

"Normally what I do in these circumstances is to put the blame on the Labour party." Simon was relieved to hear Elizabeth laugh.

"Thanks for ringing me back so quickly, darling. See you tomorrow," she said and put the phone down.

Simon returned to his group and explained that he had to leave for London immediately. He took a taxi to the airport and caught the next shuttle to Heathrow. He was back at Beaufort Street within three hours.

"I didn't mean you to come home," Elizabeth said contritely when she saw him on the doorstep.

"I've come back to celebrate," Simon said. "Let's open the bottle of champagne that Ronnie gave us when he closed the deal with Morgan Grenfell."

"Why?"

"Because Ronnie taught me one thing. You should always celebrate disasters, not successes."

Simon hung up his coat and went off in search of the champagne. When he returned with the bottle and two glasses Elizabeth asked, "What's your overdraft looking like nowadays?"

"Down to £16,000, give or take a pound."

"Well, that's another problem then, I won't be giving any pounds in the future, only taking."

"Don't be silly. Someone will snap you up," he said, embracing her.

"It won't be quite that easy," said Elizabeth.

"Why not?" asked Simon, trying to sound cheerful.

"Because I had already been warned about whether I wanted to be a politician's wife or a doctor."

Simon was stunned. "I had no idea," he said. "I'm so sorry."

"It was my choice, darling, but I will have to make one or two decisions if I want to remain in medicine, especially if you're going to become a minister."

Simon remained silent: he had always wanted Elizabeth to make this decision herself and he was determined not to try to influence her.

"If only we weren't so short of money."

"Don't worry about the money," said Simon.

"I do worry, but it may just be an excuse because I worry more about becoming bored when the children have grown up. I just wasn't cut out to be a politician's wife," she added. "You should have married someone like Fiona Seymour and you'd be Prime Minister by now."

"If that's the only way I can be sure of getting the job I'll stick with you," said Simon, taking Elizabeth in his arms. Simon couldn't help thinking of all the support his wife had given him during their marriage and even more so since his financial crisis. He knew exactly what his wife must do.

"You mustn't be allowed to give up being a doctor," he said. "It's every bit as important as wanting to be a minister. Shall I have a word with Gerry Vaughan? As Shadow spokesman for Health he might –"

"Certainly not, Simon. If I am to get another job, it'll be without anyone doing you or me a favour."

Louise was now coping on her own, and had almost returned to a normal life except she still couldn't speak. She seemed to be self-sufficient within her own world and the doctor agreed that she no longer needed a full-time nurse.

The day the nurse left Andrew decided to take Louise off for a week's holiday abroad. He wanted to return to the South of France and the Colombe d'Or, but the specialist had advised against it, explaining that any past association might trigger off a memory that in itself could cause a further relapse.

"Witch doctors' mumbo jumbo," Andrew complained but nevertheless took her to Venice, not Colombe d'Or. Once there, he was delighted by the interest Louise showed in the beautiful and ancient city. Her eyes lit up at the sight of Torcello and she appeared to revel in the trip on a gondola down the twisting waterways past irreplaceable Italian architecture. Again and again she squeezed his hand. As they sat on a piazza for an evening drink, she inclined her head and listened to a quintet playing on St Mark's Square. Andrew was confident that she could now hear everything he told her. The night before they flew back to England he woke to find her reading James Morris's *Venice* which he had left by his side of the bed. It was the first time she had opened a book since the accident. When he smiled at her she grinned back. He laughed, wanting to hear her laugh.

Andrew returned to the Ministry of Defence on Monday. On his desk there was a general directive from the Chancellor of the Exchequer, requiring the budget estimates for all the big-spending Departments of State. Andrew fought hard to keep the Polaris missile after being convinced by the Joint Chiefs of its strategic importance to the nation's defence. He was, however, continually reminded by his colleagues in the House that it was party policy to rid themselves of 'the warmongers' toy'.

When the Secretary of State returned from Cabinet he told Andrew, "We've had our way: the Cabinet were impressed by the case. But I can promise you one thing – you won't be the golden boy at this year's party conference."

"It will make a change for them even to notice me," replied Andrew.

He breathed a sigh of relief while the Joint Chiefs were delighted, but a week later he lost – by default – the same argument with his own General Purposes Committee in Edinburgh. In his absence, they passed a resolution deploring the retention of the Polaris missile and demanded that all the ministers involved should reconsider their decision. They stopped short of naming Andrew, but everyone knew whose scalp they were after. His case was not helped by Tom Carson making yet another inflammatory speech in the House, claiming that Andrew had been browbeaten by the Joint Chiefs and was nothing more than a Polaris puppet.

Andrew's trips to Edinburgh had become less frequent over the past year because of his commitments to Louise and the Defence Department. During the year three members of his General Management Committee had been replaced with a new group calling themselves 'Militant Tendency' led by Frank Boyle. It wasn't just Edinburgh Carlton that was facing the problem of a left-wing insurgence – as Andrew learned from colleague after colleague who was beginning to work out why the left were pushing a resolution at the party conference proposing that members should be re-selected for each election. Some of his more right-wing colleagues had already been replaced, and it didn't take a Wrangler to work out that once a majority of the Trotskyites had secured places on his Management Committee Andrew could be removed at their whim, whatever his past experience or record.

Whenever Andrew was in Edinburgh the local people continually assured him of their support and their confidence in him, but he could not forget, despite their avowals, that it would still take only a handful of votes to remove him. Andrew feared what the outcome would be if many other members were facing the same problem as he faced in Edinburgh.

"Dad, can I have a new cricket bat, please?"

"What's wrong with the old one?" asked Simon, as they came out of the house.

"It's too small," he said, waving it around as if it was an extension to his arm.

"It will have to do, I'm afraid."

"But Martin Henderson's dad has given him a new bat to start the season."

"I'm sorry, Peter, the truth is that Martin's father is far better off than I am."

"I'll tell you one thing," said Peter with feeling. "I'm sure not going to be an MP when I grow up." Simon smiled as his son removed an old cricket ball from his trouser pocket and tossed it over to his father. "Anyway, I bet you can't get me out even though I've only got a small bat."

"Don't forget we still have the junior size stumps left over from last year," said Simon, "so it will be just as hard to hit them."

"Stop making excuses, Dad. Just admit you're past it."

Simon burst out laughing. "We'll see," he said, with more bravado than conviction. Simon always enjoyed a few overs in the garden against his elder son although at the age of thirteen Peter was already able to play his best deliveries with a confidence that was beginning to look ominous.

It was several overs before Simon removed Peter's middle stump and took his turn at the crease.

Michael ran out of the house to join them in the field and

Simon couldn't help noticing that he was wearing a pair of jeans that were far too short and had once belonged to Peter.

"Get behind the wicket, nipper," shouted Peter at his eleven-year-old brother. "Because that's where most of the balls will be going." Michael happily obeyed without comment.

A colleague in the House had recently warned Simon that by fourteen they began to beat you and by sixteen they hoped not to show they weren't trying their hardest any longer.

Simon gritted his teeth as he watched his elder son's fastest ball safely on to the middle of the bat. The way he was going Peter wouldn't have to wait much longer before he could clean bowl him.

He managed to keep his wicket intact for a further five minutes before he was rescued by Elizabeth who came out to tell them that supper was ready.

"What, hamburgers and chips again?" said Michael as his mother put a plate in front of him.

"You're lucky to get anything," Elizabeth snapped back.

Simon cursed again at the damage his own selfish greed had brought upon his family, and marvelled at how little they all complained. He said nothing, only too aware that the previous day Elizabeth had completed her last week at the hospital and was already missing St Mary's.

"How did you all get on?" she asked cheerily.

"I'll survive," said Simon, still thinking about his overdraft.

Once the Chancellor had presented his mini budget, in November 1976, the long process of the Finance Bill, confirming all the new measures proposed, fully occupied the House. Charles, although not a member of the front-bench finance team, regularly took the lead among back-benchers on clauses on which he had specialist knowledge.

He and Clive Reynolds studied the new Finance Bill meticulously and between them picked out the seven clauses that would have an adverse effect on banking.

Reynolds guided Charles through each clause, suggesting changes, rewording, and on some occasions presenting an

argument for deleting whole sections of the bill. Charles
learned quickly and was soon adding his own ideas; one or
two even made Clive Reynolds reconsider. After Charles had
put forward amendments to the House on three of the clauses
both front benches became respectfully attentive whenever
he rose to present a case. One morning, after the Government's defeat on a clause relating to banking loans, he
received a note of congratulation from Margaret Thatcher.

The clause Charles most wanted to see removed from the
bill concerned a client's right to privacy when dealing with
a merchant bank. The Shadow Chancellor was aware of
Charles's specialised knowledge on this subject and invited
him to oppose clause 110 from the front bench. Charles realised that if he could defeat the Government on this clause he
might be invited to join the Shadow finance team in the run-
up to the general election.

Judging by the chairman of Ways and Means' selection of
amendments the Whips estimated that clause 110 on banking privacy would be reached some time on Thursday afternoon.

On Thursday morning Charles rehearsed his arguments
thoroughly with Clive Reynolds, who only had one or two
minor amendments to add before Charles set off for the
House. When he arrived at the Commons there was a note on
the message board asking him to phone the Shadow Chancellor urgently.

"The Government are going to accept a Liberal amendment tabled late last night," the Shadow Chancellor told
him.

"Why?" said Charles.

"Minimum change is what they're really after, but it gets
them off the hook and at the same time keeps the Liberal vote
intact. In essence nothing of substance has changed, but
you'll need to study the wording carefully. Can I leave you to
handle the problem?"

"Certainly," said Charles, pleased with the responsibility
with which they were now entrusting him.

He walked down the long corridor to the vote office and
picked up the sheet with clause 110 on it and the proposed

Liberal amendment. He read them both through half a dozen times before he started to make notes. Parliamentary counsel, with their usual expertise, had produced an ingenious amendment. Charles ducked into a nearby phone booth and rang Clive Reynolds at the bank. Charles dictated the amendment over the phone to him and then remained silent while Reynolds considered its implications.

"Clever bunch of sharpies. It's a cosmetic job, but it won't change the power it invests in the Government one iota. Were you thinking of returning to the bank? That would give me time to work on it."

"No," said Charles. "Are you free for lunch?"

Clive Reynolds checked his diary: a Belgian banker would be lunching in the boardroom but his colleagues could handle that. "Yes, I'm free."

"Good," said Charles. "Why don't you join me at White's around one o'clock?"

"Thank you," said Reynolds. "By then I should have had enough time to come up with some credible alternatives."

Charles spent the rest of the morning rewriting his speech which he hoped would counter the Liberal argument and make them reconsider their position. If it met with Reynolds's imprimatur the day could still be his. He read through the clause once more, convinced he had found a way through the loophole the civil servants couldn't block. He placed his speech and the amended clause in his inside pocket and went down to the Members' Entrance and jumped into a waiting taxi.

As the cab drove up St James's Charles thought he saw his wife coming down the opposite side of the road. He pushed down the window to be sure but she had disappeared into Prunier's. He wondered with which of her girl friends she was lunching.

The cab travelled on up St James's and came to a halt outside White's. Charles found he was a few minutes early so he decided to walk down to Prunier's and ask Fiona if she would like to come to the House after lunch and hear him oppose the clause. Reaching the restaurant he glanced

through the pane-glass window. He froze on the spot. Fiona
was chatting at the bar with a man whose back was to
Charles but he thought he recognised his profile although he
couldn't be certain. He noticed that his wife was wearing a
dress he had never seen before. He didn't move as he watched
a waiter bow, then guide the pair towards a corner table
where they were conveniently out of sight. Charles's first
instinct was to march straight in and confront them; but he
remained outside. For what seemed an interminable time he
stood alone, uncertain what to do next. Finally he crossed
back over St James's Street and stood in the doorway of the
Economist building going over several plans. In the end he
decided to do nothing but wait. He stood there so cold and so
incensed that he did not consider returning for his lunch
appointment with Clive Reynolds a few hundred yards up
the road.

An hour and twenty minutes later the man came out of
Prunier's alone and headed up St James's. Charles felt a
sense of relief until he saw him turn into St James's Place. He
checked his watch: Reynolds would have left by now but he
would still be well in time for clause number 110. A few
minutes later Fiona stepped out of the restaurant and followed in the man's footsteps. Charles crossed the road,
causing a cab to swerve while another motorist slammed on
her brakes. He didn't notice. He shadowed his wife, careful to
keep a safe distance. When she reached the far end of the
passage he watched Fiona enter the Stafford Hotel. Once she
was through the swing doors Fiona stepped into an empty
lift.

Charles came up to the swing doors and stared at the little
numbers above the lift, watching them light up in succession
until they stopped at four.

Charles marched through the swing doors and up to the
reception desk.

"Can I help you, sir?" the hall porter asked.

"Er – is the dining-room in this hotel on the fourth floor?"
asked Charles.

"No, sir," replied the hall porter, surprised. "The dining-
room is on the ground floor to your left" – he indicated the

way with a sweep of his hand — "there are only bedrooms on the fourth floor."

"Thank you," said Charles and marched back outside.

He returned slowly to the Economist building, incensed, where he waited for nearly two hours pacing up and down St James's before the man emerged from the Stafford Hotel; Alexander Dalglish hailed a taxi and disappeared in the direction of Piccadilly.

Fiona left the hotel about twenty minutes later, and took the path through to the park before setting off towards Eaton Square. On three occasions Charles had to fall back to be certain Fiona didn't spot him; once he was so close he thought he saw a smile of satisfaction come over her face.

He had followed his wife most of the way across St James's Park when he suddenly remembered. He checked his watch, then dashed back to the roadside, hailed a taxi and shouted, "The House of Commons, as fast as you can." The cabby took seven minutes and Charles passed him two pound notes before running up the steps into the Members' Lobby and through to the Chamber out of breath. He stopped by the Serjeant-at-Arms's chair.

From the table where he sat during Committee of the whole House, the Mace lowered on its supports in front of the table, the chairman of Ways and Means faced a packed House. He read from the division list.

"The Ayes to the right 294.
The Noes to the left 293.
The Ayes have it, the Ayes have it."

The Government benches cheered and the Conservatives looked distinctly glum. "What clause were they debating?" a still out of breath Charles asked the Serjeant-at-Arms.

"Clause 110, Mr Seymour."

BOOK FOUR

1977·1989

THE CABINET

CHAPTER
TWENTY TWO

Raymond's second trip to the States was at the behest of the Secretary of State for Trade: he was asked to present the country's export and import assessment to the International Monetary Fund, following up a loan granted to Britain the previous November. His civil servants went over the prepared speech with him again and again, emphasising to their minister the responsibility that had been placed on his shoulders. Even the Governor of the Bank of England's private office had been consulted.

"A chance to impress a few people beyond the boundaries of Leeds," Kate assured him.

Raymond's speech was scheduled for the Wednesday morning. He flew into Washington on the Sunday and spent Monday and Tuesday listening to the problems of other nations' trade ministers while trying to get used to the dreadful earphones and the female interpreter.

The conference was attended by most of the leading industrial nations and the British Ambassador, Sir Peter Ramsbotham, told Raymond over dinner at the Embassy that this was a real chance to convince the hard-headed international bankers that Britain cared about economic realities and was still worth their financial backing.

Raymond soon realised that convincing such a gathering required a very different technique from shouting from a soap box on a street corner in Leeds or even addressing the House from the dispatch box. He was glad he had not been scheduled to present his case on the opening day. Over leisurely lunches he re-established his existing contacts in Congress and made some new ones.

The night before he was to deliver his speech Raymond hardly slept. He continued to rehearse each crucial phrase and repeated the salient points that needed to be emphasised until he almost knew them by heart. At three o'clock in the morning he dropped his speech on the floor beside his bed and phoned Kate to have a chat before she went to work.

"I'd enjoy hearing your speech at the conference," she told him. "Although I don't suppose it would be much different from the thirty times I've listened to it in the bedroom."

Once he had said goodbye to Kate he fell into a deep sleep. He woke early that morning and went over the speech one last time before leaving for the conference centre.

All the homework and preparation proved worthwhile. By the time he turned the last page Raymond couldn't be certain how convincing his case had been, but he knew it was the best speech he had ever delivered. When he looked up the smiles all around the oval table assured him that his contribution had been well received. As the ambassador pointed out to him as he rose to leave, any signs of emotion at these gatherings were almost unknown. He felt confident that the IMF loan would be renewed.

There followed two further speeches before they broke for lunch. At the end of the afternoon session Raymond walked out into the clear Washington air and decided to make his way back to the Embassy on foot. He was exhilarated by the experience of dominating an international conference and picked up an evening paper: an article covering the conference suggested that Raymond would be Britain's next Labor Chancellor. He smiled at the spelling. Just the closing day to go, followed by the official banquet and he would be back home by the weekend.

When he reached the Embassy the guard had to double-check: they weren't used to ministers arriving on foot and without a bodyguard. Raymond was allowed to proceed down the tree-lined drive towards the massive Lutyens building. He looked up to see the British flag was flying at half mast and wondered which distinguished American had died.

"Who has died?" he asked the tail-coated butler who opened the door for him.

"The Foreign Secretary, sir."

"Anthony Crosland? I knew he had gone into hospital, but . . ." said Raymond almost to himself. He hurried into the Embassy to find it abuzz with telexes and coded messages. Raymond sat alone in his private sitting-room for several hours and later, to the horror of the security staff, slipped out for a quiet dinner at the Mayflower Hotel with Senator Hart.

Raymond returned to the conference table at nine o'clock the next morning to listen to the French Minister of Commerce put his case for renewed funds. He was savouring the thought of the official banquet at the White House to be held that evening when he was tapped on the shoulder by Sir Peter Ramsbotham, who indicated by touching his lips with his forefinger and pointing that they must have a word in private.

"The Prime Minister wants you to return on the mid-morning Concorde," said Sir Peter. "It leaves in an hour. On arrival in Britain you're to go straight to Downing Street."

"What's this all about?"

"I have no idea, that was the only instruction I received from No. 10," confided the ambassador.

Raymond returned to the conference table and made his apologies to the chairman, left the room and was driven immediately to the waiting plane. "Your bags will follow, sir," he was assured.

He was back on English soil three hours and forty-one minutes later, a little after seven-thirty. The purser ensured that he was the first to disembark. A car waiting by the side of the plane whisked him to Downing Street. He arrived just as the Prime Minister was going to dinner, accompanied by an elderly African statesman who was waving his trademark fan back and forth.

"Welcome home, Ray," said the Prime Minister, leaving the African leader. "I'd ask you to join us, but as you can see I'm entertaining the President of Malawi. Let's have a word in my study."

Once Raymond had settled into a chair Mr Callaghan wasted no time.

"Because of Tony's tragic death I have had to make a few changes which will include moving the Secretary of State for Trade. I was hoping you would be willing to take over from him."

Raymond sat up straighter. "I should be honoured, Prime Minister."

"Good. You've earned your promotion, Raymond. I also hear you did us proud in America, very proud."

"Thank you."

"You'll be appointed to the Privy Council immediately and your first Cabinet meeting will be at ten o'clock tomorrow. Now, if you'll excuse me, I must catch up with Dr Banda."

Raymond was left standing in the hall.

He asked his driver to take him back to the flat. All he wanted to do was to tell Kate the news. When he arrived the flat was empty: then he remembered she wasn't expecting him back until the next day. He phoned her home but after twenty continuous rings he resigned himself to the fact that she was out. "Damn," he said out loud, and after pacing around phoned Joyce to let her know the news. Once again there was no reply.

He went into the kitchen and checked to see what was in the fridge: a piece of curled-up bacon, some half-eaten Brie, three eggs. He couldn't help thinking about the banquet he was missing at the White House.

The Right Honourable Raymond Gould QC, MP, Her Britannic Majesty's Principal Secretary of State for Trade, sat on the kitchen stool, opened a tin of baked beans and devoured them with a fork.

Charles closed the file. It had taken him a month to gather all the proof he needed. Albert Cruddick, the private investigator Charles had selected from the Yellow Pages, had been expensive but discreet. Dates, times, places were all fully chronicled. The only name was that of Alexander Dalglish, the same rendezvous, lunch at Prunier's followed by the

Stafford Hotel. They hadn't stretched Mr Cruddick's imagination but at least the detective had spared Charles the necessity of standing in the entrance of the Economist building once, sometimes twice a week for hours on end.

Somehow he had managed to get through that month without giving himself away. He had also made his own notes of the dates and times Fiona claimed she was going to be in the constituency. He had then called his agent in Sussex Downs and, after veiled questioning, elicited answers that corroborated Mr Cruddick's findings.

Charles saw as little of Fiona as possible during this time, explaining that the Finance Bill was occupying his every moment. His lie had at least a semblance of credibility for he had worked tirelessly on the remaining clauses left for debate, and by the time the watered-down bill had become law he had just about recovered from the disaster of the Government's successful retention of clause 110.

Charles placed the file on the table by the side of his chair and waited patiently for the call. He knew exactly where she was at that moment and just the thought of it made him sick to his stomach. The phone rang.

"The subject left five minutes ago," said a voice.

"Thank you," said Charles and replaced the receiver. He knew it would take her about twenty minutes to reach home.

"Why do you think she walks home instead of taking a taxi?" he had once asked Mr Cruddick.

"Gets rid of any smells," Mr Cruddick had replied quite matter-of-factly.

Charles shuddered. "And what about him? What does he do?" He never could refer to him as Alexander, or even Dalglish; or as anything but 'him'.

"He goes to the Lansdowne Club, swims ten lengths or plays a game of squash before returning home. Swimming and squash both solve the problem," Mr Cruddick explained cheerily.

The key turned in the lock. Charles braced himself and picked up the file. Fiona came straight into the drawing-room and was visibly shaken to discover her husband sitting in an armchair with a small suitcase by his side.

She recovered quickly, walked over and kissed him on the cheek. "What brings you home so early, darling? The Socialists taken the day off?" She laughed nervously at her joke.

"This," he said, standing up and holding the file out to her.

She took off her coat and dropped it over the sofa. Then she opened the buff folder and started to read. He watched her carefully. First the colour drained from her cheeks, then her legs gave way and she collapsed on to the sofa. Finally she started to sob.

"It's not true, none of it," she protested.

"You know very well that every detail is accurate."

"Charles, it's you I love, I don't care about him, you must believe that."

"I believe nothing of the sort," said Charles. "You're no longer someone I could live with."

"Live with? I've been living on my own since the day you entered Parliament."

"Perhaps I might have come home more often if you had showed some interest in starting a family."

"And do you imagine I am to blame for that inadequacy," she said.

Charles ignored the innuendo and continued. "In a few moments I am going to my club where I shall spend the night. I expect you to be out of this house within seven days. When I return I want there to be no sign of you or any of your goods or chattels, to quote the original agreement."

"Where will I go?" she cried.

"You could try your lover first, but no doubt his wife might object. Failing that, you can camp down at your father's place."

"What if I refuse to go?" said Fiona, turning to defiance.

"Then I shall throw you out, as one should a whore, and cite Alexander Dalglish in a very messy divorce case."

"Give me another chance. I'll never look at him again," begged Fiona, starting to cry once more.

"I seem to remember your telling me that once before, and indeed I did give you another chance. The results have been all too plain to see." He pointed to the file where it had fallen to the floor.

Fiona stopped weeping when she realised that Charles remained unmoved.

"I shall not see you again. We shall be separated for at least two years, when we will carry through as quiet a divorce as possible in the circumstances. If you cause me a moment of embarrassment I shall drag you both through the mire. Believe me."

"You'll regret your decision, Charles. I promise you. I'll not be pushed aside quite that easily."

"They've done *what*?" said Joyce.

"Two Communists have put their names forward for election to the General Purposes Committee," repeated Fred Padgett.

"Over my dead body." Joyce's voice was unusually sharp.

"I thought that would be your attitude," said Fred.

Joyce searched for the pencil and paper that were normally on the table by the phone.

"When's the meeting?" she asked.

"Next Thursday."

"Have we got reliable people to stand against them?"

"Of course," said Fred. "Councillor Reg Illingworth and Jenny Simpkins from the Co-op."

"They're both sensible enough but between them they couldn't knock the skin off a rice pudding."

"Shall I phone Raymond at the House and get him to come up for the meeting?"

"No," said Joyce. "He's got enough to worry about now that he's in the Cabinet without piling up trouble for him in Leeds. Leave it to me."

She replaced the receiver and sat down to compose her thoughts. A few minutes later she went over to her desk and rummaged about for the full list of the G.P. Committee. She checked the sixteen names carefully, realising that if two Communists were to get themselves elected this time within five years they could control the committee – and then even remove Raymond. She knew how these people worked. With any luck, if they got bloody noses now they might slink off to another constituency.

She checked the sixteen names once more before putting on a pair of sensible walking shoes. During the next four days she visited several homes in the area. "I was just passing," she explained to nine of the wives who had husbands on the committee. The four men who never listened to a word their wives said were visited by Joyce after work. The three who had never cared for Raymond were left well alone.

By Thursday afternoon thirteen people knew only too well what was expected of them. Joyce sat alone hoping he would call that evening. She cooked herself a Lancashire hotpot but only picked at it, then later fell asleep in front of the television when she tried to watch the final episode of *Roots*. The phone woke her at five past eleven.

"Raymond?"

"Hope I didn't wake you," said Fred.

"No, no," said Joyce, now impatient to learn the outcome of the meeting. "What happened?"

"Reg and Jenny walked it. Those two Communist bastards only managed three votes between them."

"Well done," said Joyce.

"I did nothing," said Fred, "except count the votes. Shall I tell Raymond what's been happening?"

"No," said Joyce. "No need to let him think we've had any trouble."

Joyce fell back into the chair by the phone, kicked off her walking shoes, and went back to sleep.

She knew she had to plan the whole operation so that her husband would never find out. She sat alone in the house considering the several alternative ways in which she could deceive him. After hours of unproductive thought the idea finally came in a flash. She went over the problems and repercussions again and again until she was convinced that nothing could go wrong. She leafed through the Yellow Pages and made an appointment for the following morning.

The sales lady helped her to try on several wigs, but only one was bearable.

"I think it makes Modom look most elegant, I must say."

She knew that it didn't – it made Modom look awful – but she hoped it would serve its purpose.

She then applied the eye make-up and lipstick she had acquired at Harrods, and pulled out from the back of her cupboard a floral dress she had never liked. She stood in front of the mirror and checked herself. Surely no one would recognise her in Sussex and she prayed that if he found out he would be forgiving.

She left and drove slowly towards the outskirts of London. How would she explain herself if she was caught? Would he remain understanding when he discovered the truth? When she reached the constituency she parked the car in a side road and walked up and down the high street. No one showed any sign of recognition which gave her the confidence to go through with it. And then she saw him.

She had hoped he'd be in the City that morning. She held her breath as he walked towards her. As he passed she said, "Good morning." He turned and smiled, replying with a casual "Good morning," as he might to any constituent. Her heartbeat returned to normal and she went back to find her car.

She drove off completely reassured she could now get away with it. She went over once again what she was going to say, then all too suddenly she had arrived. She parked the car outside the house opposite, got out and bravely walked up the path.

As Raymond stood outside the Cabinet room several of his colleagues came over to congratulate him. At exactly ten o'clock the Prime Minister walked in, bade everyone "Good morning," and took his place at the centre of the oblong table, while the other twenty-one members of the Cabinet filed in behind him and took their places. The Leader of the House, Michael Foot, sat on his left, while the Foreign Secretary and Chancellor were placed opposite him. Raymond was directed to a seat at the end of the table between the Secretary of State for Wales and the Secretary of State for Education.

"I would like to start the meeting," said the Prime Minister, "by welcoming David Owen as Foreign Secretary and Raymond Gould as Secretary of State for Trade." The other nineteen Cabinet members murmured, "Hear, hear" in a discreetly conservative way. David Owen smiled slightly while Raymond could feel himself going red.

"The first item we must discuss in detail is the proposed pact with the Liberals . . ."

Raymond sat back and decided that today he would only listen.

Andrew sat in the small office and listened carefully to the specialist's opinion. Louise was restored to almost perfect health in every way except for her speech. She was reading regularly and had even begun to write short messages in reply to Andrew's questions. The specialist now felt that she needed some other outside interest to take her mind off Robert. Over a year had passed and she could still spend hours simply staring at his photograph.

"I managed to reach Dr Kerslake at home," the specialist said, "and I must concur with her opinion that it would be unwise for your wife to contemplate another pregnancy. But Dr Kerslake does accept my judgement that you should both consider adoption."

"I've already given the idea a lot of thought, even discussed it with my father," Andrew replied. "But both of us felt that Louise would never agree to it."

"It's a calculated risk in the circumstances," said the specialist. "We mustn't forget it's been a whole year. We know to our cost that Mrs Fraser loves children, and if she is set against such a course she is now well capable of letting you know."

"If Louise shows any response I'd be only too willing to give it a try. But in the end it will all depend on her."

"Good. Find out how she feels," said the specialist, "and if you both decide to go ahead I'll arrange a meeting with the local authority." He rose from behind his desk. "I'm sure it won't be hard to find you a suitable child."

"If it were possible for him to come from a Scottish orphans' home, I would appreciate it."

The specialist nodded. "I'll be in touch with you as soon as I have any news."

When Charles returned home he knew at once Fiona had left. He felt an immediate relief. After a week at his club, he was glad the charade was over, a clean, irrevocable break. He strolled into the drawing-room and stopped: something was wrong. It took him a few moments before he realised what she had done.

Fiona had removed every one of the family paintings.

No Wellington above the fireplace, no Victoria behind the sofa. Where the two Landseers and the Constable had hung there was nothing more than thin dusty outlines indicating the size of each picture she had removed. He walked to the library: the Van Dyck, the Murillo and the two small Rembrandts were also missing. Charles ran down the hall. It couldn't be possible, he thought, as he threw open the dining-room door. It was. He stared at the blank wall where only the previous week the Holbein portrait of the first Earl of Bridgwater had hung.

Charles scrabbled in the back of his pocket diary for the number and dialled it frantically. Mr Cruddick listened to the story in silence.

"Remembering how sensitive you are about publicity, Mr Seymour, there are two avenues of approach," he began in his normal level tone and sounding unperturbed. "You can grin and bear it, or the alternative is one I have used often in the past."

Because of the demands of his new job Raymond saw less of Kate and almost nothing of Joyce apart from his fortnightly visits to Leeds. He worked from eight in the morning until he fell asleep at night.

"And you love every minute of it," Kate reminded him whenever he complained. Raymond had also become aware of the subtle changes that had taken place in his life since he had become a member of the Cabinet, the way he was treated by other people, how quickly his slightest whim was granted, how flattery fell from almost every tongue. He began to enjoy the change in status although Kate reminded him that only the Queen could afford to get used to it.

At the Labour party conference that year he allowed his name to be put forward for a place on the National Executive. Although he failed to be elected he managed to finish ahead of several other Cabinet ministers and polled only a few votes less than Neil Kinnock, the darling of the constituency section.

Andrew Fraser, who now looked upon Raymond as someone he could confide in, joined Raymond for what was becoming their traditional conference lunch together on the third day. Andrew told him of his distress at the party's continued drift to the left.

"If some of those resolutions on defence are passed my life will be made impossible," he said, trying to cut into a very tough steak.

"The hotheads always put up resolutions that are never allowed more than a token discussion."

"Token discussion be damned. Some of their mad ideas are beginning to gain credence which, translated, could become party policy."

"Any particular resolution worrying you?" asked Raymond.

"Yes, Tony Benn's latest proposal that members must be re-selected before every election. His idea of democracy and accountability."

"Why should you fear that?"

"If your management committee is taken over by half a dozen Trots they can reverse a decision 50,000 voters have previously agreed on."

"You're over-reacting, Andrew."

"Raymond, if we lose the next election I can see a split in the party that will be so great we may never recover."

"They've been saying that in the Labour party since the day it was founded."

"I hope you're right, but I fear times have changed," said Andrew. "Not so long ago it was you who envied me."

"That can change again." Raymond abandoned the steak, waved his hand and asked the waitress to bring two large brandies.

Charles picked up the phone and dialled a number he had not needed to look up. The new young Portuguese maid answered.

"Is Lady Fiona at home?"

"Lady no home, sir."

"Do you know where she is?" asked Charles, speaking slowly and clearly.

"Go down to country, expect back six o'clock. Take message please?"

"No, thank you," said Charles. "I'll call this evening." He replaced the receiver.

As always the reliable Mr Cruddick was proved right about his wife's movements. Charles called him immediately. They agreed to meet as planned in twenty minutes.

He drove into the Boltons, parked on the far side of the road a few yards from his father-in-law's house and settled down to wait.

A few minutes later a large anonymous pantechnicon van came round the corner and stopped outside No. 24. Mr Cruddick jumped out from the driver's seat. He was dressed in long brown overalls and a flat cap. He was joined by a young assistant who unlocked the back of the van. Mr Cruddick nodded to Charles before proceeding up the steps to the front door.

The Portuguese maid answered when he pressed the bell.

"We have come to collect the goods for Lady Seymour."

"No understand," said the maid.

Mr Cruddick removed from an inside pocket a long typewritten letter on Lady Seymour's personal stationery. The Portuguese maid was unable to read the words of a letter her mistress had addressed to Hurlingham Croquet Club agreeing to be their Ladies' President, but she immediately recognised the letter-head and the signature. She nodded and opened the door wider. All Mr Cruddick's carefully laid plans were falling into place.

Mr Cruddick tipped his hat, the sign for Mr Seymour to join them. Charles got out of the car cautiously, checking both ways before he crossed the road. He felt uncomfortable in brown overalls and hated the cap with which Mr Cruddick had supplied him. It was a little small and Charles was acutely conscious how strange he must look but the Portuguese maid apparently didn't notice the incongruity between his aristocratic mien and the working overalls. It did not take long to discover the whereabouts of most of the pictures. Many were just stacked up in the hall, and only one or two had already been hung.

Forty minutes later the three men had located and loaded into the van all but one of them. The Holbein of the first Earl of Bridgwater was nowhere to be found.

"We ought to be on our way," suggested Mr Cruddick a little nervously, but Charles refused to give up the search. For another thirty-five minutes Mr Cruddick sat tapping the wheel of the van before Charles finally conceded that the painting must have been taken elsewhere. Mr Cruddick tipped his hat to the maid while his partner locked up the back of the van.

"A valuable picture, Mr Seymour?" he enquired.

"A family heirloom that would fetch two million at auction," said Charles matter-of-factly before returning to his car.

"Silly question, Albert Cruddick," said Mr Cruddick to himself as he pulled out from the curb and drove towards Eaton Square. When they arrived the locksmith had replaced all three locks on the front door and was waiting on the top step impatiently.

"Strictly cash, guv'nor. No receipt. Makes it possible for the missus and me to go to Ibiza each year, tax free."

By the time Fiona had returned to the Boltons from her trip to Sussex every picture was back in its place at Eaton Square with the exception of Holbein's first Earl of Bridgwater. Mr Cruddick was left clutching a large cheque and uttering the unpalatable view that Mr Seymour would probably have to grin and bear it.

"I'm delighted," said Simon, when he heard the news. "And at Pucklebridge General Hospital?"

"Yes, I answered an advertisement in *The Lancet* for the post of general consultant in the maternity section."

"But your name must have helped there?"

"Certainly not," said Elizabeth vehemently.

"How come?"

"I didn't apply as Dr Kerslake. I filled out the application form in my maiden name of Drummond."

Simon was momentarily silenced. "But they would have recognised you," he protested.

"I had the full frontal treatment from Estée Lauder to ensure they didn't. The final effect fooled even you."

"Don't exaggerate," said Simon.

"I walked straight past you in Pucklebridge High Street, and said 'Good morning,' and you returned the greeting."

Simon stared at her in disbelief. "But what will happen when they find out?"

"They already have," replied Elizabeth sheepishly. "As soon as they offered me the post I went down to see the senior consultant and told him the truth. He hasn't stopped telling everyone since."

"He wasn't cross?"

"Far from it. In fact he said I nearly failed to be offered the post because he felt I wouldn't be safe let loose on the unmarried doctors."

Andrew held Louise's hand as they approached the door of Grunechan Children's Home on the outskirts of Edinburgh. The matron was waiting on the freshly scrubbed doorstep to greet them.

"Good morning, Minister," she said. "We are honoured that you have chosen our little home."

Andrew and Louise smiled.

"Will you be kind enough to follow me?" She led them down a dimly lit corridor to her room, her starched blue uniform crackling as she walked.

"All the children are in the playground at the moment but you will be able to see them from my window." Andrew had already gone over all the orphans' histories and photographs; he couldn't help noticing how one of them bore a striking resemblance to Robert.

They both looked out of the window for several minutes but Louise showed no interest in any of the children. When the boy who resembled Robert ran towards the window, she turned away and took a seat in the corner.

Andrew shook his head. The matron's lips turned down at the corners.

Coffee and biscuits arrived and while they were eating them Andrew tried once more. "Did you want Matron to bring anyone in to meet you, darling?" Louise shook her head. Andrew cursed himself as he feared the experience might only have done her more harm.

"Have we seen everyone?" he asked, looking for an excuse to leave quickly.

"Yes, sir," said the matron, putting down her cup of coffee. "Well," she hesitated, "there was one girl we didn't bother you with."

"Why not?" asked Andrew out of curiosity.

"Well, you see, she's black."

Andrew stiffened.

"And what's more," continued the matron, "we have absolutely no idea who her parents were. She was left on the doorstep. Not at all the sort of girl to be brought up in a minister's home."

Andrew was so incensed that he quite forgot about consulting Louise who was still resting silently in the corner.

"I should like to see her," he said.

"If you insist," said the matron, a little taken aback. "I'm afraid she hasn't got her best clothes on," she added before she left the room.

Andrew paced up and down, conscious that if Louise hadn't been there he might well have lost his temper with the woman. The matron returned a few moments later with a little girl aged four, perhaps five, and so thin that her dress hung on her like a coathanger. Andrew couldn't see her face because she kept her head bowed.

"Look up, child," commanded the matron. The girl raised

her head slowly. She had the most perfect oval face and olive skin, piercing black eyes and a smile that immediately captivated Andrew.

"What's your name?" he asked quietly.

"Clarissa," she said, and dropped her head again. He wanted to help her so much, and it made him feel guilty that he had put the poor child through such a pointless ordeal.

The matron still looked affronted and with a sniff she said, "You can leave us now, child." Clarissa turned and walked towards the door. Looking at Louise the matron added, "I am sure you agree with me, Mrs Fraser, the girl's not at all suitable."

They both turned to Louise. Her face was alight, her eyes shining in a way Andrew had not seen since Robert's death. She stood up, walked quickly towards the child before she could reach the door, and stared into her black eyes.

"I think you're beautiful," Louise said, "and I do hope you will want to come and live with us."

CHAPTER
TWENTY THREE

'Order, order' had meant nothing to the British electorate until 1978 when the House passed a resolution allowing the proceedings in the Commons to be broadcast on radio. Simon had supported the motion on broadcasting, putting forward the argument that radio was a further extension of democracy as it showed the House at work and allowed the voters to know exactly what their elected representatives were up to. Simon listened carefully to a number of his supplementaries, and realised for the first time that he spoke a little too quickly when he had a minister on the run.

Raymond, on the other hand, did not support the motion as he feared that the cries of "Hear, hear" or "Shame" and the heckling of the Prime Minister would sound to listeners like schoolchildren in a playground squabble. Overhearing the words with only one's imagination to set the scene would, he believed, create a false impression about the many aspects of a member's daily duties. When one evening Raymond heard a parliamentary debate in which he had taken part he was delighted to discover his arguments carried so much conviction.

When Andrew heard his own voice on Radio Four one morning answering questions on defence issues he was suddenly aware that what he had always considered was a faint trace of a Scottish accent was in fact – when he was angry or excited – quite pronounced.

Charles found the morning programme an excellent way of catching up with any proceedings he had missed the previous day. As he now woke each morning alone, 'Yesterday in Parliament' became his constant companion. He hadn't been aware of how upper class he sounded until the occasion on which he followed Tom Carson. He had no intention of changing his voice for the radio.

When the Queen opened the new underground extension to Heathrow airport on 16 December 1977 Raymond was the minister commanded to be present. Joyce made one of her rare trips down to London as they were invited to join the Queen for lunch after the ceremony. When Joyce selected her new dress from Harvey Nichols, she stood in the little cubicle behind a drawn curtain to make sure it was possible for her to curtsey properly. "Good morning, Your Majesty," she practised with a slight wobble, to the bemusement of the shop assistant waiting patiently outside.

By the time she had returned to the flat Joyce was confident that she could carry out her part in the proceedings as well as any courtier. As she prepared for Raymond's return from the morning Cabinet meeting she hoped he would be pleased with her efforts. She had long given up hope of being a mother, but still liked to believe she could be a good wife. Raymond had forewarned her that he would have to change as soon as he arrived at the flat to be sure of being at Green Park before the Queen arrived. After they had accompanied an entourage to Heathrow on the new extension, a journey that would take thirty minutes, they were to return to Buckingham Palace for lunch. Raymond had already come in contact with his monarch on several occasions in his official capacity as a Cabinet minister, but for Joyce it was to be the first time she had been presented.

Once she had had her bath and dressed – she knew Raymond would never forgive her if she were the reason he was late – she began to lay out his clothes. Tail coat, grey pin-striped trousers, white shirt, stiff collar and a silver-grey tie, all hired that morning from Moss Bros. All that he still needed was a clean white handkerchief for his top pocket, just showing in a straight line, as the Duke of Edinburgh always wore his.

Joyce rummaged around in Raymond's chest of drawers, admiring the new shirts as she searched for a handkerchief.

When she first saw the scribbled note peaking out underneath the collar of a pink shirt lying near the bottom of the pile, she assumed it must be an old laundry bill. Then she spotted the word 'Darling'. She felt suddenly sick as she looked more closely.

> Darling Carrot Top,
>   If you ever wear this one I might even agree to marry you.
>   Kate.

Joyce sank on the end of the bed as the tears trickled down her face. Her perfect day was shattered. She knew at once what course of action she must take. She replaced the unworn shirt and closed the drawer, after first removing the note, and then sat alone in the drawing-room waiting for Raymond to return.

He arrived back at the flat with only a few minutes to spare and was delighted to find his wife changed and ready.

"I'm running it a bit close," he said, going straight into the bedroom.

Joyce followed and watched him don his morning dress suit. When he had straightened his tie in the mirror, she faced him.

"What do you think?" he asked, not noticing the slight paleness in her cheeks.

She hesitated. "You look fantastic, Raymond. Now come along or we'll be late, and that would never do."

When Ronnie Nethercote invited him to lunch at the Ritz, Simon knew things must be looking up again. After a drink in the lounge they were ushered to a corner table overlooking the park in the most palatial dining-room in London. Scattered around the other tables were men who were household names in Ronnie's world as well as in Simon's.

When the head waiter offered them menus Ronnie waved his hand and said, "Order the country vegetable soup, followed by beef off the trolley, take my word for it."

"Sounds like a safe bet," said Simon.

"Unlike our last little venture," Ronnie grunted. "How much are you still in hock because of the collapse of Nethercote and Company?"

"Fourteen thousand three hundred pounds when I last looked but I'm making inroads slowly. It's paying the interest before you can cut down on the capital that really hurts."

"How do you imagine I felt when we were overdrawn seven mill and then the bank decided to pull the rug from under my feet without any warning?"

"As two of the buttons on your waistcoat can no longer reach the holes they were originally tailored for, Ronnie, I must assume those problems are now a thing of the past."

"You're right." He laughed. "Which is why I invited you to lunch. The only person who ended up losing money on that deal was you. If you'd stayed on as the other directors did, at five grand a year, the company would still owe you £11,100 of earned income."

Simon groaned.

The carver wheeled the trolley of beef up to their table.

"Wait a moment, my boy, I haven't even begun. Morgan Grenfell want me to change the structure of the new company and will be injecting a large amount of cash. At the moment Whitechapel Properties – I hope you approve of the name – is still a one-hundred-pound off-the-shelf company. I own sixty per cent and the bank's got forty. Now before the new agreement is signed, I'm going to offer you –"

"Would you like it well done, as usual, Mr Nethercote?"

"Yes, Sam," said Ronnie, slipping the carver a pound note.

"I am going to offer you –"

"And your guest, sir?" the carver said, glancing at Simon.

"Medium, please."

"Yes, sir."

"I am going to offer you one per cent of the new company, in other words one share."

Simon didn't comment, feeling confident Ronnie still hadn't finished.

"Aren't you going to ask?" said Ronnie.

"Ask what?" said Simon.

"You politicians get dumber by the minute. If I am going to offer you a one-pound share, how much do you think I am going to demand in return?"

"Well, I can't believe it's going to be one pound," said Simon grinning.

"Wrong," said Ronnie. "One per cent of the company is yours for one pound."

"Will that be sufficient, sir?" said the carver, putting a plate of beef in front of Simon.

"Hold it, Sam," said Ronnie before Simon could reply. "I repeat I'm offering you one per cent of the company for one pound; now ask your question again, Sam."

"Will that be sufficient, sir?" repeated the carver.

"It's most generous," said Simon.

"Did you hear that, Sam?"

"I certainly did, sir."

"Right, Simon, you owe me a pound."

Simon laughed, removed his wallet from his inside pocket, took out a pound note and handed it over.

"Now the purpose of that little exercise," said Ronnie, turning back to the carver and pocketing the note, "was to prove that Sam here isn't the only person who could make a quid for himself this afternoon." Sam smiled, having no idea what Mr Nethercote was talking about, and placed a large plate of well-done beef in front of him.

Ronnie took out an envelope from his inside pocket and passed it to Simon.

"Do I open it now?" asked Simon.

"Yes – I want to see your reaction."

Simon opened the envelope and studied its contents. A certificate for one share in the new company with a true value of over £10,000.

"Well, well, what do you say?" said Ronnie.

"I'm speechless," said Simon.

"First politician I've known who's ever suffered from that problem."

Simon laughed. "Thank you, Ronnie. It's an incredibly generous gesture."

"No it's not. You were loyal to the old company, so why shouldn't you prosper with the new one?"

"That reminds me, does the name 'Archie Millburn' mean anything to you?" asked Simon.

Ronnie hesitated. "No, no, should it?"

"Only that I thought he might be the man who convinced Morgan Grenfell that you were worth bailing out."

"No, that name doesn't ring any bells. Mind you, Morgan Grenfell have never admitted where they obtained their information from but they knew every last detail about the old company. But if I come across the name Millburn I'll let you know. Enough of business. Fill me in on what's happening in your world. How's your lady wife?"

"Deceiving me."

"Deceiving you?"

"Yes, she's been putting on wigs and dressing up in strange clothes."

Clarissa wet her bed every night for the first month at Pelham Crescent but Louise never complained. Day by day Andrew watched as mother and daughter grew in mutual confidence. Clarissa assumed from her first meeting with Louise that she could talk as normally as any grown-up and chatted away to her night and day. Half the time Louise didn't reply, only because she couldn't get a word in.

Just when Andrew felt everything was getting back on a normal footing at home trouble erupted in Edinburgh. His General Management Committee, which now included five members of Militant Tendency, tabled a motion of no confidence in their member. Their leader, Frank Boyle, had been building up a power base with the sole intention, Andrew suspected, of ousting the member and taking over himself. He didn't discuss the problem with Louise, as the specialist had advised him to avoid any undue stress while Clarissa was settling in.

The five men who wanted Andrew removed had chosen the following Thursday to hold the meeting because they knew the annual Defence Review was due for a full debate in the House that day. If Andrew was unable to attend their

meeting Frank Boyle knew they would have a better chance
of winning their motion. If he did turn up to defend himself
they were also aware that an embarrassing explanation
would have to be made for his absence during the debate.
When the Prime Minister was informed of the dilemma by
the Chief Whip he had no hesitation in telling Andrew to
forget the defence debate and go to Edinburgh.

Andrew took the shuttle up on Thursday afternoon and
was met at the airport by his chairman, Hamish Ramsey.

"I apologise about you being put through this ordeal,
Andrew," he said at once. "I can assure you it's none of my
doing, but I must also warn you it's not the same Labour
party that I joined over twenty years ago."

"How do you think the vote will go tonight?" asked
Andrew.

"You'll win this time. The votes have been decided before
the meeting takes place. There's only one waverer and he's so
gutless that your very presence will stop him siding with the
Trotskies."

When Andrew arrived at his Edinburgh headquarters he
was left alone outside the committee room in a cold corridor
for over an hour. He knew his opponents were holding things
up in the hope he would become frustrated before he eventually had to face them. At last they invited him to join them
and he immediately sensed what the Spanish Inquisition
must have felt like: question after question from sour-faced
men who had never helped him win the seat in the first place
and were now alleging that he had shown scant interest in the
constituency. Andrew stood his ground and became angry
only when Frank Boyle referred to him as 'that son of a Tory'.

"When did you last see your father?" flashed through
his mind.

"My father has done more for this city than you could ever
hope to do in your lifetime," he told Boyle.

"Then why don't you join his party?" came back Boyle's
retort.

Andrew was about to answer when Hamish Ramsey
banged the table with his gavel and said, "Enough, enough.
It's time to stop this squabbling and vote."

Andrew felt a stab of anxiety as the little slips were passed up to the chairman to be counted. The outcome was five-all and Hamish Ramsey immediately cast his vote in favour of Andrew.

"At least you'll be safe for the coming election, laddie," said Hamish as they drove to the Airport Hotel. "But I wouldn't like to account for much beyond that."

When Andrew arrived back in Pelham Crescent the next morning Louise greeted him at the door.

"Everything all right in Edinburgh?" she asked.

"Fine," said Andrew, taking her in his arms.

"Do you want to hear the good news?"

"Yes," said Andrew, smiling.

"Clarissa didn't wet her bed last night. Perhaps you should stay away more often."

Finally Charles knew he had to discuss what could be done about the stolen Holbein with his solicitor, Sir David Napley. Sir David instructed leading counsel and six weeks later Charles was told that if he sued the Holbein might eventually be returned but not before the story had been on the front page of every national paper. Charles had Albert Cruddick's opinion confirmed: "Grin and bear it."

Fiona had been out of touch for well over a year when the letter came. Charles immediately recognised her handwriting and ripped open the envelope. Only one glance at the writing was enough to make him tear up the missive and deposit the little pieces in the waste-paper basket by his desk. He left for the Commons in a rage.

All through the day he thought of the one word he had taken in from the scrawled hand. Holbein. When he returned from the Commons after the ten o'clock division Charles searched for the remains of the letter, which the daily had conscientiously deposited in the dustbin. After rummaging among potato peelings, eggshells and empty tins Charles spent over an hour Sellotaping the little pieces of paper together. Then he read the letter carefully.

24 The Boltons,
London, S W 10
11 October 1978

Dear Charles,
    Enough time has now passed for us to try and treat each other in a civilised way. Alexander and I wish to marry and Veronica Dalglish has agreed to an immediate divorce and has not insisted we wait the necessary two years to establish separation.

"You'll have to wait every day of the two years, you bitch," he said out loud. Then he came to the one sentence for which he was searching.

    I realise this might not immediately appeal to you but if you felt able to fall in with our plans I would be happy to return the Holbein immediately.
                                        Yours ever,
                                        Fiona.

He crumpled up the paper in the ball of his hand before dropping it on the fire.

Charles remained awake into the early hours considering his reply.

At a Thursday morning Cabinet meeting James Callaghan informed his colleagues that the Liberal leader, David Steel, was not willing to continue the Lib/Lab pact after the end of the current session.

"That can only mean one thing," the Prime Minister continued. "We must all be prepared for a general election at any time from now on. I am confident we can hold out until Christmas, but not for much longer after that."

Raymond was saddened by the news. He felt after two years in the Cabinet that he was just beginning to be of some use to the Department of Trade: the changes he was implementing were starting to take effect. But he knew he needed considerably more time if he hoped to leave a permanent impression on his ministry.

Kate's enthusiasm spurred him on to work even longer

hours and to push through as many of his innovations before the next election as possible.

"I'm trying my damnedest," he told her. "But do remember that the speed of the bureaucratic machine makes British Rail look like Concorde."

The Labour Government struggled on through a session dubbed by the press as 'the winter of discontent': trying to push bills through the House, losing a clause here and a clause there, Raymond was only too delighted to have reached the recess in one piece.

Raymond spent a cold Christmas in Leeds with Joyce. He returned to London early in the New Year aware it could not be long before the Conservatives felt assured enough to put down a motion of no confidence. When it eventually was tabled no one in Parliament was surprised.

The debate caused a day of intense excitement, not least because a strike had caused the Commons bars to run dry and thirsty members were huddled together in the lobbies, the tea room, the smoking room and the dining-rooms. Harassed Whips rushed hither and thither checking lists, ringing up hospitals, board rooms and even great-aunts in their efforts to track down the last few elusive members.

When Mrs Thatcher rose on 6 April to address a packed House the tension was so electric that the Speaker had considerable difficulty keeping control of the over-charged conductors. She addressed the House in firm, strident tones which brought her own side to their feet when she resumed her place. The atmosphere was no different when it was the turn of the Prime Minister to reply. Both leaders made a gallant effort to rise above the petulance of their adversaries but it was the Speaker who had the last word:

"The Ayes to the right 311,
The Noes to the left 310.
The Ayes have it, the Ayes have it."

Pandemonium broke out. Opposition members waved their order papers in triumph, knowing the Prime Minister would now have to call a general election. James Callaghan immediately announced the dissolution of Parliament and after an audience with the Queen election day was set for 3 May 1979.

At the end of that momentous week those few members left at Westminster were stunned by an explosion in the Members' Car Park. Airey Neave, the Shadow spokesman on Northern Ireland, had been blown up by Irish terrorists as he was driving up the exit ramp to leave the Commons. He died on his way to hospital.

Members hurried back to their constituencies. Both Raymond and Andrew found it hard to escape from their departments at such short notice, but Charles and Simon were out in their respective high streets shaking hands with the voters by the morning following the Queen's proclamation.

For three weeks the arguments about who was competent to govern went back and forth, but on 3 May the British people elected their first woman Prime Minister and gave her party a majority of forty-three in the Commons.

Andrew's sixth election turned out to be his most unpleasant to date and he was only glad that he had left Louise and Clarissa in London. Jock McPherson, still the SNP candidate, called him every name under the sun and added one or two new ones in the evening, while the Trotskyites who had voted against him on the committee proved no help when it came to gathering in the votes on election day. But the citizens of Edinburgh, knowing nothing of the committee's opinions, sent Andrew back to Parliament with a majority of 3,738. The Scottish Nationalist vote crumbled, leaving only two members in the House – and Jock McPherson back in Scotland.

Raymond's vote in Leeds was slightly reduced, while Joyce won the office pool for predicting most accurately what her husband's majority would be. He was beginning to accept that she knew more about the constituency than he ever would.

A few days later when Raymond returned to London Kate

had never seen him so depressed and decided to hold off telling him her own news when he said, "God knows how many years it will be before I can be of some use again."

"You can spend your time in Opposition making sure the Government doesn't dismantle all your achievements."

"With a majority of forty-three they could dismantle me if they wanted to," he told her. He placed the red leather box marked 'Secretary of State for Trade' in the corner, next to the ones marked 'Minister of State at the Department of Trade' and 'Parliamentary Under-Secretary at the Department of Employment'.

"They're only your first three," Kate tried to reassure him.

Simon increased his majority at Pucklebridge to 19,461, notching up another record after which he and Elizabeth spent the weekend in their cottage with the boys waiting for Mrs Thatcher to select her team.

Simon was surprised when the Prime Minister phoned personally and asked if he could come up to see her in Downing Street: that was an honour usually afforded only to Cabinet ministers. He tried not to anticipate what she might have in mind.

He duly travelled up from the country and spent thirty minutes alone with the new Prime Minister. When he heard what Mrs Thatcher wanted him to do he was touched that she had taken the trouble to see him in person. She knew that no member ever found it easy to accede to such a request but Simon accepted without hesitation. Mrs Thatcher added that no announcement would be made until he had had time to talk his decision over with Elizabeth.

Simon thanked her and travelled back to his cottage in Pucklebridge. Elizabeth sat in silence as she listened to Simon's account of his conversation with the Prime Minister.

"Oh, my God," she said, when he had finished. "She's offered you the chance to be a Minister of State, but in return we have no certainty of peace for the rest of our lives."

"I can still say no," Simon assured her.

"That would be the act of a coward," said Elizabeth, "and you've never been that."

"Then I'll phone the Prime Minister and tell her I accept."

"I ought to congratulate you," she said. "But it never crossed my mind for one moment . . ."

Charles's was one of the few Tory seats in which the majority went down. A missing wife is hard to explain especially when it is common knowledge that she is living with the former chairman of the adjoining constituency. Charles had faced a certain degree of embarrassment with his local committee and he made sure that the one woman who couldn't keep her mouth shut was told his version of the story 'in strictest confidence'. Any talk of removing him had died when it was rumoured that Charles would stand as an independent candidate if replaced. When the vote was counted Sussex Downs still returned Charles to Westminster with a majority of 20,176. He sat alone in Eaton Square over the weekend, but no one contacted him. He read in the Monday *Telegraph* – how he missed *The Times* – the full composition of the new Tory team.

The only surprise was Simon Kerslake's appointment as Minister of State for Northern Ireland.

CHAPTER
TWENTY FOUR

"Well, say something."

"Very flattering, Kate. What reason did you give for turning the offer down?" asked Raymond, who had been surprised to find her waiting for him at the flat.

"I didn't need a reason."

"How did they feel about that?"

"You don't seem to understand. I accepted their offer."

Raymond removed his glasses and tried to take in what Kate was saying. He steadied himself by holding on to the mantelpiece.

Kate continued. "I had to, darling."

"Because the offer was too tempting?"

"No, you silly man. It had nothing to do with the offer as such, but it gives me the chance to stop letting my life drift. Can't you see it was *because* of you?"

"Because of me you're going to leave London and go back to New York."

"To work in New York and start getting my life in perspective. Raymond, don't you realise it's been five years?"

"I know how long it is and how many times I've asked you to marry me."

"We both know that isn't the answer; Joyce can't be brushed aside that easily. And it could even end up being the single reason you fail in your career."

"We can overcome that problem, given time," Raymond reasoned.

"That sounds fine now, until the party wins the next

election and lesser men than you are offered the chance to shape future policy."

"Can't I do anything to make you change your mind?"

"Nothing, my darling. I've handed Chase my resignation and begin my new job with Chemical Bank in a month."

"Only four weeks," said Raymond.

"Yes, four weeks. I had to hold off telling you until I had severed all the bonds, had resigned and could be sure of not letting you talk me out of it."

"Do you know how much I love you?"

"I hope enough to let me go, before it's too late."

Charles would not have normally accepted the invitation. Lately he had found cocktail parties to consist of nothing but silly little bits of food, never being able to get the right drink and rarely enjoying the trivial conversation. But when he glanced on his mantelpiece and saw an 'At Home' from Lady Carrington he felt it might be an amusing break from the routine he had fallen into since Fiona had left. He was also keen to discover more about the rumoured squabbles in Cabinet over expenditure cuts. He checked his tie in the mirror, removed an umbrella from the hat stand and left Eaton Square for Ovington Square.

He and Fiona had been apart for nearly two years. Charles had heard from several sources that his wife had now moved in with Dalglish on a permanent basis despite his unwillingness to co-operate over a divorce. He had remained discreetly silent on his wife's new life except for one or two selected titbits dropped selectively in the ears of well-chosen gossips. That way he had elicited for himself sympathy from every quarter while remaining the magnanimous loyal husband.

Charles had spent most of his spare time in the Commons, and his most recent budget speech had been well received both by the House and the national press. During the committee stage of the Finance Bill he had allowed himself to be burdened with a lot of the donkey work. Clive Reynolds had been able to point out discrepancies in some clauses of the bill, which Charles passed on to a grateful Chancellor.

Thus Charles received praise for saving the Government from any unnecessary embarrassment. At the same time he disassociated himself from the 'wets' as the Prime Minister referred to those of her colleagues who did not unreservedly support her monetarist policies. If he could keep up his work output he was confident he would be preferred in the first reshuffle.

By spending his mornings at the bank and afternoons and evenings in the Commons Charles managed to combine both worlds with the minimum of interruption from his almost non-existent private life.

He arrived at Lord Carrington's front door a little after six-forty-five. A maid answered his knock, and he walked straight through to a drawing-room that could have held fifty guests and very nearly did.

He even managed to be served with the right blend of whisky before joining his colleagues from both the Upper and Lower Houses. He saw her first over the top of Alec Pimkin's balding head.

"Who is she?" asked Charles, not expecting Pimkin to know.

"Amanda Wallace," said Pimkin, glancing over his shoulder. "I could tell you a thing or two . . ." but Charles had already left his colleague in mid-sentence. The sexual aura of the woman was attested to by the fact that she spent the entire evening surrounded by attentive men, like moths around a candle. If Charles had not been one of the tallest men in the room he might never have seen the flame. It took him another ten minutes to reach her side of the room where Julian Ridsdale, a colleague of Charles's in the Commons, introduced them only to find himself dragged away moments later by his wife.

Charles was left staring at a woman who would have looked beautiful in anything from a ballgown to a towel. Her slim body was encased in a white silk dress, and her fair hair touched her bare shoulders. But what struck Charles most was the translucent texture of her skin. It had been years since he had found it so hard to make conversation.

"I expect you already have a dinner engagement?"

Charles asked her in the brief intervals before the vultures closed in again.

"No," she replied and smiled encouragingly. She agreed to meet him at Walton's in an hour's time. Charles dutifully began to circulate round the room but it was not long before he found his eyes drawn back to her. Every time she smiled he found himself responding but Amanda didn't notice because she was always being flattered by someone else. When he left an hour later he smiled directly at her, and this time did win a knowing grin.

Charles sat alone at a corner table in Walton's for another hour. He was just about to admit defeat and return home when she was ushered to the table. The anger that had developed from being kept waiting was forgotten the moment she smiled and said, "Hello, Charlie."

He was not surprised to learn that his tall, elegant companion earned her living as a model. As far as Charles could see she could have modelled anything from tooth paste to stockings.

"Shall we have coffee at my place?" Charles asked after an unhurried dinner. She nodded her assent and he called for the bill, not checking the addition for the first time in many years.

He was delighted, if somewhat surprised, when she rested her head on his shoulder in the cab on the way back to Eaton Square. By the time they had been dropped off at Eaton Square most of Amanda's lipstick had been removed. The cabbie thanked Charles for his excessive tip and couldn't resist adding, "Good luck, sir."

Charles never did get round to making the coffee. When he woke in the morning, to his surprise he found her even more captivating, and for the first time in weeks quite forgot 'Yesterday in Parliament'.

Elizabeth listened carefully as the man from Special Branch explained how the safety devices worked. She tried to make Peter and Michael concentrate on not pressing the red buttons that were in every room and would bring the police at a moment's notice. The electricians had already wired the rooms in Beaufort Street and now they had nearly finished at the cottage.

At Beaufort Street a uniformed policeman stood watch by the front door night and day. In Pucklebridge, because the cottage was so isolated, they had to be surrounded by arc lamps that could be switched on at a moment's notice.

"It must be damned inconvenient," suggested Archie Millburn during dinner. After his arrival at the cottage he had been checked by security patrols with dogs before he was able to shake hands with his host.

"Inconvenient is putting it mildly," said Elizabeth. "Last week Peter broke a window with a cricket ball and we were immediately lit up like a Christmas tree."

"Do you get any privacy?" asked Archie.

"Only when we're in bed. Even then you can wake up to find you're being licked; you sigh and it turns out to be an Alsatian."

Archie laughed. "Lucky Alsatian."

Every morning when Simon was driven to work he was accompanied by two detectives, a car in front and another to the rear. He had always thought there were only two ways from Beaufort Street to Westminster. For the first twenty-one days as minister he never travelled the same route twice.

Whenever he was due to fly to Belfast he was not informed of either his departure time or from which airport he would be leaving. While the inconvenience drove Elizabeth mad the tension had the opposite effect on Simon. Despite everything, it was the first time in his life he didn't feel it was necessary to explain to anyone why he had chosen to be a politician.

Inch by inch he worked to try to bring the Catholics and Protestants together. Often after a month of inches he would lose a yard in one day, but he never displayed any anger or prejudice except perhaps, as he told Elizabeth, "a prejudice for common sense". Given time, Simon believed, a break-through would be possible – if only he could find on both sides a handful of men of goodwill.

During the all-party meetings both factions began to treat him with respect and – privately – with affection. Even the

Opposition spokesman at Westminster openly acknow-ledged that Simon Kerslake was turning out to be an excel-lent choice for the 'dangerous and thankless ministry'.

Andrew also knew he would require a handful of men of goodwill when Hamish Ramsey resigned as chairman of Edinburgh Carlton.

"I don't need the hassle any longer," Hamish told him. "I'm not in politics for the same reason as that bunch of trouble-makers." Andrew reluctantly let him go and had to work hard to convince Hamish's deputy, David Connaught, that he should stand in his place. When David finally agreed to allow his name to go forward he was immediately opposed by Frank Boyle, who had already made his opinion of the sitting member abundantly clear. Andrew canvassed every person on the committee during the run up to election for the new chairman. He estimated the voting was going to be seven-all, which would still allow Hamish to give his casting vote in favour of Connaught.

Andrew phoned Hamish at home an hour before the meeting was due to begin. "I'll call and leave a message for you at the House when it's all over," Ramsey told him. "Don't worry, you're safe this time. At least I'll leave you with the right chairman."

Andrew left Pelham Crescent after he had tucked Clarissa up in bed and read her another chapter of *Jacob Two Two*. He told Louise he would return from Westminster straight after the ten o'clock vote. He sat in the Chamber and listened to Charles Seymour deliver a well-argued discourse on mone-tarist policy. Andrew didn't always agree with the logic of Seymour's case and he had never cared much for the man himself: but he had to admit that such talent was wasted on the back benches.

During the speech a note was passed to Andrew by an attendant. He unfolded the little white slip. Stuart Gray, the lobby correspondent for *The Scotsman*, needed to speak to him urgently. Andrew slipped from his place on the front bench, stepping over the feet of Shadow ministers still intent on

Seymour's speech. He felt like a small boy leaving a cinema in the middle of a film in pursuit of an ice lolly. He found Gray waiting for him in the Members' Lobby.

Andrew had known Stuart since he had first entered the House, when the journalist had told him, "You and I are each other's bread and butter, so we'd better make a sandwich." Andrew had laughed, and they had had few differences of opinion in the fifteen years since. Stuart suggested that they go down to Annie's Bar for a drink. They strolled along the corridor and took the stairway near the tea room to the basement bar, named after a former barlady.

Andrew settled down on a couch at the side of a pillar while Stuart went up to the bar to order two whiskies.

"Cheers," said the journalist, putting Andrew's glass down on the table in front of him.

Andrew took a long gulp. "Now, what can I do for you?" he asked. "Is my father being tiresome again?"

"I'd call him a supporter compared with your new chairman."

"What do you mean? I've always found David Connaught to be a sound fellow myself," said Andrew, a little pompously.

"I'm not interested in your views of David Connaught," said Stuart. "I want an opinion on your new chairman, Frank Boyle." The journalist sounded very much on the record.

"What?"

"He won the vote tonight seven to six."

"But . . ." Andrew fell silent.

"Come on, Andrew. We both know the bloody man's a Commie trouble-maker, and my editor is screaming for a quote."

"I can't say anything, Stuart, not until I know all the facts."

"I've just told you all the facts: now, are you going to give me a quote?"

"Yes." Andrew paused. "I am sure Mr Boyle will continue to serve in the best traditions of the Labour party, and I look forward to working in close co-operation with him."

"Balls," said Stuart. "They will only print that in Pseuds Corner in *Private Eye*."

"It's the only quote you're going to get out of me tonight," said Andrew.

Stuart looked at his friend and could see lines on his face that he had never noticed before. "I'm sorry," he said. "I went too far. Please get in touch when the time's right. With that bastard Boyle in charge you might be in need of my help."

Andrew thanked him absent-mindedly, downed his whisky in one gulp, then walked out of Annie's Bar and along the terrace corridor to the phone booths at the foot of the stairs. He dialled Ramsey's home number.

"What in heaven's name happened?" was all he could ask.

"One of our voters didn't show," said Hamish Ramsey. "Claimed he was held up in Glasgow and couldn't get back in time. I was just about to ring you."

"Bloody irresponsible of him," said Andrew. "Why didn't you postpone the vote?"

"I tried to, but Frank Boyle produced the rule book. 'Any motion proposed fourteen days before a meeting cannot be postponed without the agreement of the proposer and seconder.' I'm sorry, Andrew: my hands were tied."

"It's not your fault, Hamish. I couldn't have had a better chairman than you. I'm only sorry you didn't leave in a blaze of glory."

Hamish chuckled. "Don't you ever forget, Andrew, the voters have the last word in a democracy. In Edinburgh you're the man who has served them for more than fifteen years and they won't forget that quickly."

"You can get dressed now, Miss Wallace," said the gynaecologist returning to her desk.

Amanda started to slip back into her latest Dior outfit – a light blue denim suit bought the previous day in Conduit Street in an attempt to cheer herself up.

"It's the third time in five years," said Elizabeth Kerslake, leafing through the confidential file and trying not to sound accusing.

"I may as well book into the same clinic as before," said Amanda, matter-of-factly.

Elizabeth was determined to make her reconsider the consequences. "Is there any chance that the father would want you to have this child?"

"I can't be certain who the father is," said Amanda, looking shame-faced for the first time. "You see, it was the end of one relationship and the beginning of another."

Elizabeth made no comment other than to say, "I estimate that you are at least eight weeks pregnant, but it could be as much as twelve." She looked back down at the file. "Have you considered giving birth to the child and then bringing it up yourself?"

"Good heavens, no," said Amanda. "I make my living as a model, not as a mother."

"So be it," Elizabeth sighed, closing the file. "I'll make all the" – she avoided saying usual – "necessary arrangements. You must see your GP immediately and ask him to sign the required clearance forms. Then phone me in about a week, rather than make the trip down to Pucklebridge again."

Amanda nodded her agreement. "Could you let me know what the clinic is going to charge this time? I'm sure they are suffering from inflation like the rest of us."

"Yes, I will look into that, Miss Wallace," said Elizabeth, just managing to keep her temper as she showed Amanda to the door. Once her patient had left Elizabeth picked up the confidential file from her desk, walked over to the cabinet and flicked through S, T, U, until she found the right slot. Perhaps she should have been sterner with her but she was convinced that it would have made little difference. She paused, wondering if having the child might change the woman's cavalier attitude to life.

Charles returned home after the debate feeling pleased with himself. He had received praise for his latest speech from every wing of the party, and the Chief Whip had made it quite clear that his efforts on the Finance Bill had not gone unnoticed.

As he drove back to Eaton Square he wound down the car

window and let the fresh air rush in and the cigarette smoke
out. His smile widened at the thought of Amanda sitting at
home waiting for him. It had been a glorious couple of
months. At forty-eight he was experiencing realities he had
never even dreamed of in fantasy. As each day passed he
expected the infatuation to wear off, but instead it only grew
more intense. Even the memory the day after was better than
anything he had experienced in the past.

Once the Holbein had been restored to his dining-room
wall Charles planned to talk to Amanda about their future; if
she said "Yes" he would even be willing to grant Fiona a
divorce. He parked the car and took out his latch key, but she
was already there opening the front door to throw her arms
around him.

"Why don't we go straight to bed?" she greeted him.

Charles would have been shocked had Fiona uttered such
feelings even once in their fifteen years of married life, but
Amanda made it appear quite natural. She was already lying
naked on the bed before Charles could get his waistcoat off.
After they had made love and she was settled in his arms
Amanda told him she would have to go away for a few days.

"Why?" said Charles, puzzled.

"I'm pregnant," she said matter-of-factly. "I've already
booked myself into a clinic. Don't worry. I'll be as right as
rain in no time."

"But why don't we have the baby?" said a delighted
Charles, looking down into her grey eyes. "I've always
wanted a son."

"Don't be silly, Charlie. There's years ahead of me for
that."

"But if we were married?"

"You're already married. Besides, I'm only twenty-six."

"I can get a divorce in a moment and life wouldn't be so
bad with me, would it?"

"Of course not, Charlie. You're the first man I've ever
really cared for."

Charles smiled hopefully. "So you'll think about the
idea?"

Amanda looked into Charles's eyes anxiously. "If I *were* to have a child I do hope he'd have blue eyes like yours."

"Will you marry me?" he asked.

"I'll think about it. In any case, you may have changed your mind by morning."

Raymond drove Kate to Heathrow. He was wearing the pink shirt she had chosen for him; she was wearing the little red box. He had so much to tell her on the way to the airport that she hardly spoke at all. The last four weeks had gone by in a flash. It was the first time he had been grateful for being in Opposition.

"It's all right, Carrot Top. Don't fuss. We'll see each other whenever you come to New York."

"I've only been to America twice in my life," he said. She tried to smile.

Once she had checked her eleven bags in at the counter, a process that seemed to take forever, she was allocated a seat.

"Flight BA 107, gate number fourteen, boarding in ten minutes," she was informed.

"Thank you," she said and rejoined Raymond, who was sitting on the end of an already crowded tubular settee. He had bought two plastic cups of coffee while Kate had been checking in. They were both already cold. They sat and held hands like children who had met on a summer holiday and had now to return to separate schools.

"Promise me you won't start wearing contact lenses the moment I've gone."

"Yes, I can promise you that," said Raymond, touching the bridge of his glasses.

"I've so much I still want to tell you," she said.

He turned towards her. "Vice-presidents of banks shouldn't cry," he said, brushing a tear from her cheek. "The customers will realise you're a soft touch."

"Neither should Cabinet ministers," she replied. "All I wanted to say, is that if you really feel . . ." she began.

"Hello, Mr Gould."

They both looked up to see a broad smile spread across the face of someone whose tan proved that he had just arrived from a sunnier climate.

"I'm Bert Cox," he said, thrusting out his hand, "I don't suppose you remember me." Raymond let go of Kate's hand and shook Mr Cox's.

"We were at the same primary school in Leeds, Ray. Mind you, that was a million light years ago. You've come a long way since then."

How can I get rid of him? wondered Raymond desperately.

"This is the missus," Bert Cox continued obliviously, gesturing at the silent woman in a flowery dress by his side. She smiled but didn't speak. "She sits on some committee with Joyce, don't you, love?" he said, not waiting for her reply.

"This is the final call for Flight BA 107, now boarding at gate number fourteen."

"We always vote for you, of course," continued Bert Cox. "The missus" – he pointed to the lady in the flowered dress again – "thinks you'll be Prime Minister. I always say –"

"I must go, Raymond," said Kate, "or I'll miss my flight."

"Can you excuse me for a moment, Mr Cox?" said Raymond.

"Delighted. I'll wait. I don't often get a chance to have a word with my MP."

Raymond walked with Kate towards the barrier. "I am sorry about this. I'm afraid they're all like that in Leeds – hearts of gold, but never stop talking. What were you going to say?"

"Only that I would have been happy to live in Leeds, however cold it is. I never envied anyone in my life, but I do envy Joyce." She kissed him gently on the cheek and walked towards the barrier before he could reply. She didn't look back.

"Are you feeling all right, madam?" asked an airport official as she went through the security barrier.

"I'm fine," said Kate, brushing aside her tears. She walked slowly towards gate fourteen, happy that he had worn the pink shirt for the first time. She wondered if he had found the note she had left underneath the collar. If he had asked her just one more time . . .

Raymond stood alone and then turned to walk aimlessly towards the exit.

"An American lady, I would have guessed," said Mr Cox rejoining him. "I'm good on accents."

"Yes," said Raymond, still alone.

"A friend of yours?" he asked.

"My best friend," said Raymond.

When ten days had passed and Elizabeth had not yet heard from Miss Wallace she decided she had no choice but to contact her direct. She flicked through her personal file and noted the latest number Amanda had given.

Elizabeth picked up the phone and dialled. It was some time before anybody answered.

"730-9712. Charles Seymour speaking." There was a long silence. "Is anyone there?"

Elizabeth couldn't reply. She replaced the receiver and felt her whole body come out in a cold sweat. She closed Amanda Wallace's file and returned it to the cabinet.

CHAPTER
TWENTY FIVE

Simon had spent nearly a year preparing a White Paper entitled 'A Genuine Partnership for Ireland' for consideration by the House. The Government's aim was to bring north and south together for a period of ten years at the end of which a more permanent arrangement could be considered. During those ten years both sides would remain under the direct rule of Westminster and Dublin. Both Protestants and Catholics had contributed to 'the Charter', as the press had dubbed the complex agreement. With considerable skill, patience and fortitude Simon had convinced the political leaders of Northern Ireland to append their names to the final draft when and if it was approved by the House.

He admitted to Elizabeth that the agreement was only a piece of paper, but he felt it was a foundation stone on which the House could base an eventual settlement. On both sides of the Irish Sea politicians and journalists alike were describing the Charter as a genuine breakthrough.

The Secretary of State for Northern Ireland was to present the White Paper to the Commons when Irish business was next scheduled on the parliamentary calendar. Simon, as the architect of the Charter, had been asked to deliver the winding-up speech on behalf of the Government. He knew that if the House backed the concept of the document he might then be allowed to prepare a parliamentary bill and thus overcome a problem so many other politicians had failed to solve before him. If he succeeded Simon felt that all the sacrifices he had made in the past would prove worthwhile.

When Elizabeth sat down to read through the final draft in Simon's study that evening even she admitted for the first time that she was pleased he had accepted the Irish appointment.

"Now, embryonic statesman," she continued, "are you ready for your dinner like every normal human being at this time in the evening?"

"I certainly am." Simon moved his copy of the 129-page Charter from the dining-room table to the sideboard, planning to go over it yet again once he had finished dinner.

"Damn," he heard Elizabeth say from the kitchen.

"What is it?" he asked, not looking up from his toy, like a child studying a jigsaw and wondering where a colourless piece fitted in.

"I'm out of Bisto."

"I'll go and buy some," Simon volunteered. The two policemen on the door were chatting when the minister came out.

"Come on, my wife needs a packet of Bisto, so affairs of state must be held up for the time being."

"I'm very sorry, sir," said the sergeant. "When I was told you would be in for the rest of the evening I allowed the official car to go off duty. But Constable Barker can accompany you."

"That's no problem," said Simon. "We can take my wife's car. I'll just find out where she's parked the damn thing."

He slipped back into the house but returned a moment later. "Been in the force long?" he asked Constable Barker as they walked down the road together.

"Not that long, sir. Started on the beat just over a year ago."

"Are you married, Constable?"

"Fine chance on my salary, sir."

"Then you won't have encountered the problem of being Bisto-less."

"They've never heard of gravy in the police canteen, sir."

"You should try the House of Commons sometime," said Simon. "I don't think you'd find it any better – the food, that is, not to mention the salary."

The two men laughed as they headed off towards the car.

"What does your wife think of the Mini Metro?" the constable asked as Simon put the key in the door.

Like everyone else in Beaufort Street, Elizabeth heard the explosion, but she was the first to realise what it had to be. She ran out of the front door in search of the duty policeman. She saw him running down the road and quickly followed.

The little red Metro was scattered all over the side street, the glass from its windows making the pavement look as though there had been a sudden hailstorm.

When the sergeant saw the severed head he pulled Elizabeth back. Two other bodies lay motionless in the road, one of them an old lady with the contents of her shopping bag spread around her.

Within minutes, six police cars had arrived and Special Branch officers had cordoned off the area with white ribbon. An ambulance rushed the bodies to Westminster Hospital. The job of picking up the remains of the police constable needed a very resolute man.

Elizabeth was taken to the hospital in a police car, where she learned that the old lady had died before arrival while her husband was on the critical list. When she told the surgeon in charge that she was a doctor he was more forthcoming and answered her questions candidly. Simon was suffering from multiple fractures, a dislocated hip and a severe loss of blood. The only question he was not willing to be drawn on was when she asked about his chances.

She sat alone outside the operating theatre waiting for any scrap of news. Hour after hour went by, and Elizabeth kept recalling Simon's words: "Be tolerant. Always remember there are still men of goodwill in Northern Ireland." She found it almost impossible not to scream, to think of the whole lot of them as evil murderers. Her husband had worked tirelessly on their behalf. He wasn't a Catholic or a Protestant, just a man trying to do an impossible task. Although she couldn't help thinking that it was she who had been the intended target.

Another hour passed.

A tired, grey-faced man came out into the corridor through

the flapping rubber doors. "He's still hanging on, Dr Kerslake. Your husband has the constitution of an ox; most people would have let go by now." He smiled. "Can I find you a room so that you can get some sleep?"

"No, thank you," Elizabeth replied. "I'd prefer to be near him."

She rang home to check the children were coping and her mother answered the phone. She had rushed over the moment she had heard the news and was keeping them away from the radio and television.

"How is he?" she asked.

Elizabeth told her mother all she knew, then spoke to the children.

"We're taking care of Grandmother," Peter told her.

Elizabeth couldn't hold back the tears. "Thank you, darling," she said, and quickly replaced the receiver. She returned to the bench outside the operating theatre, kicked off her shoes, curled her legs under her body and tried to snatch some sleep.

She woke with a start in the early morning. Her back hurt and her neck was stiff. She walked slowly up and down the corridor in her bare feet stretching her aching limbs, searching for anyone who could tell her some news. Finally a nurse brought her a cup of tea and assured her that her husband was still alive. But what did 'still alive' mean? She stood and watched the grim faces coming out of the operating theatre and tried not to recognise the tell-tale signs of despair. The surgeon told her she ought to go home and rest: they would have nothing to tell her for several hours. A policeman kept all journalists – who were arriving by the minute – in an ante-room off the main corridor.

Elizabeth didn't move from the corridor for another day and another night, and she didn't return home until the surgeon told her it was all over.

When she heard the news she fell on her knees and wept.

"God must want the Irish problem solved as well," he added. "Your husband will live, Dr Kerslake, but it's a miracle."

"Got time for a quick one?" asked Alexander Dalglish.

"If you press me," said Pimkin.

"Fiona," shouted Alexander. "It's Alec Pimkin, he's dropped in for a drink."

She came through to join them. She was dressed in a bright yellow frock and had allowed her hair to grow down past her shoulders.

"It suits you," said Pimkin, tapping his bald head.

"Thank you," said Fiona. "Why don't we all go through to the drawing-room?"

Pimkin happily obeyed and had soon settled himself into Alexander's favourite chair.

"What will you have?" asked Fiona, as she stood by the drinks cabinet.

"A large gin with just a rumour of tonic."

"Well, how's the constituency faring since my resignation?"

"It ticks along, trying hard to survive the biggest sex scandal since Profumo," chuckled Pimkin.

"I only hope it hasn't harmed your election chances," said Alexander.

"Not a bit of it, old fellow," said Pimkin, accepting the large Beefeaters and tonic Fiona handed him. "On the contrary, it's taken their minds off me for a change."

Alexander laughed.

"In fact," continued Pimkin, "interest in the date of your wedding has only been eclipsed by Charles and Lady Di. Gossips tell me," he continued, clearly enjoying himself, "that my Honourable friend, the member for Sussex Downs, made you wait the full two years before you could place an announcement in *The Times*."

"Yes, that's true," said Fiona. "Charles didn't even answer my letters during that period, but lately when any problem's arisen he's been almost friendly."

"Could that be because he also wants to place an announcement in *The Times*?" said Pimkin, downing his gin quickly in the hope of being offered a second.

"What do you mean?"

"The fact that he has lost his heart to another."

"Another?" said Alexander Dalglish.

"No less –" Pimkin paused as he sipped pointedly at his empty glass "– than Miss Amanda Wallace, only daughter of the late and little lamented Brigadier Boozer Wallace."

"Amanda Wallace?" said Fiona in disbelief. "Surely he's got more sense than that."

"I don't think it has a lot to do with sense," said Pimkin holding out his glass. "More to do with sex."

"But he's old enough to be her father."

"If that is the case," said Pimkin, "Charles can always adopt her."

Alexander laughed.

"But I am informed by a reliable source," continued Pimkin, "that marriage is being proposed."

"You can't be serious," said Fiona flatly.

"The subject has most certainly been broached for she is undoubtedly pregnant and Charles is hoping for a son," said Pimkin in triumph as he accepted his second double gin.

"That's not possible," said Fiona under her breath.

"And I am also informed," continued Pimkin, "that some of the more ungenerous of our brethren are already suggesting the name of several candidates for the role of father."

"Alec, you're incorrigible."

"My dear, it is common knowledge that Amanda has slept with half the Cabinet and a considerable cross section of back-benchers."

"Stop exaggerating," said Fiona.

"And what's more," continued Pimkin as if he hadn't heard her, "she has only stopped short of the Labour front bench because her mother told her they were common and she might catch something from them."

Alexander laughed again. "But surely Charles hasn't fallen for the pregnancy trick?"

"Hook, line and sinker. He's like an Irishman who's been locked into a Guinness brewery over the weekend. Dear Amanda has my Honourable friend uncorking her at every opportunity."

"But she's plain stupid," said Alexander. "The only time I

met her she assured me that Michael Parkinson was turning out to be an excellent chairman of the party."

"Stupid she may well be," said Pimkin, "but plain she is not and together, I'm told, they are updating the *Kama Sutra*."

"Enough, Alec, enough," said Fiona laughing.

"You're right," said Pimkin, aware that his glass was nearly empty once again. "A man of my impeccable reputation cannot afford to be seen associating with people living in sin. I must leave immediately, darlings," he said, rising to his feet. Pimkin put his glass down and Alexander accompanied him to the front door.

As it closed Alexander turned to Fiona. "Never short of useful information, our former member," he said.

"I agree," said Fiona. "So much gleaned for such a small investment in Beefeaters."

As Alexander walked back into the drawing-room he added, "Does it change your plans for the return of the Holbein?"

"Not in any way," said Fiona.

"So you'll still be at Sotheby's next week for their Old Masters sale?"

Fiona smiled. "Certainly. And if the price is right we won't have to worry about what we give Charles for a wedding present."

Three weeks after the bombing Simon left the Westminster Hospital on crutches, Elizabeth by his side. His right leg had been so shattered that he had been told he would never walk properly again. As he stepped out on to Horseferry Road a hundred cameras flashed to meet their editors' demand to capture the instant hero. He smiled as if there were no pain. "Don't let those murderers think they got to you," he was warned by both sides. Elizabeth's smile showed only relief that her husband was still alive.

After three weeks of complete rest Simon returned to his Irish Charter against doctor's orders, knowing the document was still due to be debated in the House in less than a fortnight. The Secretary of State and the other Minister of

State for Northern Ireland visited him at home on several occasions and it was agreed that the Minister of State would take over Simon's responsibilities temporarily and deliver the winding-up speech. During his absence the whole Northern Ireland office grew to realise just how much work Simon had put into the Charter, and no one was at all complacent about taking his place.

The attempt on Simon's life and the build up to the special debate on the Charter became of such national interest that the BBC decided to broadcast the entire proceedings on Radio Four from three-thirty to the vote at ten o'clock.

On the afternoon of the debate Simon sat up in bed listening to every word on the radio as if it were the final episode in his favourite serial and he was desperate to know the outcome. The speeches opened with a clear and concise presentation of the Charter by the Secretary of State for Northern Ireland, which left Simon feeling confident that the whole House would support him. The Opposition spokesman followed with a fair-minded speech, raising one or two queries he had over the controversial Patriots' Clause with its special rights for Protestants in the south and Catholics in the north, and also how it would affect the Catholics unwilling to register in Northern Ireland. Otherwise he reassured the House that the Opposition supported the Charter and would not be calling for a division.

Simon began to relax for the first time as the debate continued, but his mood changed as some back-bench members started to express more and more anxiety over the Patriots' Provision. One or two back-benchers were even insisting that the Charter should not be sanctioned by the House until the need for the Patriots' Provision was fully explained by the Government. Simon realised that a few narrow-minded men were simply playing for time in the hope the Charter would be held up and later forgotten. For generations such men had succeeded in stifling the hopes and aspirations of the Irish people while they allowed bigotry to undermine any real desire for peace.

Elizabeth came in and sat on the end of the bed. "How's it going?" she asked.

"Not well," said Simon, "it will all depend on the Opposition spokesman."

They both sat and listened. But no sooner had the Opposition spokesman risen than Simon realised that he too had misunderstood the real purpose of the Patriots' Provision and that what Simon had agreed to with both sides in Dublin and Belfast was not being accurately explained to the House. There was no malice in the speech and he was clearly following what had been agreed through the usual channels but Simon could sense that his lack of conviction was sowing doubts in the minds of his fellow members. He feared a division might be called after all.

After one or two members had interrupted to voice further doubts about the Patriots' Clause the Shadow minister suggested: "Perhaps we should wait until the Minister of State is fully recovered and able to report to the House himself." A few 'hear, hears' could be heard around the Chamber.

Simon felt sick. He was going to lose the Charter if it didn't get through the House tonight. All the hard work and goodwill would count for nothing. He made a decision.

"I'd love a hot cup of cocoa," he said, trying to sound casual.

"Of course, darling. I'll just go and turn the kettle on. Would you like a biscuit while I'm up?"

Simon nodded. Once the bedroom door was closed, he slipped quietly out of bed and dressed as quickly as possible. He picked up his blackthorn stick, a gift from Dr Fitzgerald, the Irish Prime Minister, which had been among the dozens of presents awaiting his return from hospital. Then he hobbled silently down the stairs and across the hall, hoping Elizabeth would not hear him. He eased the front door open. When the policeman on duty saw him Simon put a finger to his lips and closed the door very slowly behind him. He made his way laboriously up to the police car, lurched into the back and said, "Switch on the radio, please, and drive me to the House as quickly as possible."

Simon continued to listen to the Opposition spokesman as the police car weaved in and out of the traffic on a route he hadn't travelled before. They arrived at the St Stephen's entrance to the Commons at nine-twenty-five.

Visitors stood to one side as they might for royalty but Simon didn't notice. He hobbled on through the Central Lobby, oblivious to the awkwardness of his gait, turning left past the policeman and on towards the entrance of the House. He prayed he would reach the Chamber before the Government spokesman rose to deliver his winding-up speech. Simon passed an astonished chief doorkeeper and arrived at the bar of the House as the new digital clock showed nine-twenty-nine.

The Opposition spokesman was resuming his place on the front bench to muffled cries of "Hear, hear." The Speaker rose but before he had time to call upon the Minister of State to reply Simon stepped slowly forward on to the green carpet of the Commons. For a moment there was a stunned silence; then the cheering began. It had reached a crescendo by the time Simon arrived at the front bench. His blackthorn stick fell to the floor as he clutched the dispatch box. The Speaker called out his name *sotto voce*.

Simon waited for the House to come to complete silence.

"Mr Speaker, I must thank the House for its generous welcome. I return this evening because having listened to every word of the debate on the radio I feel it necessary to explain to Honourable members what was behind my thinking with the Patriots' Provision. This was not some superficial formula for solving an intractable problem, but an act of good faith to which the representatives from all sides felt able to put their names. It may not be perfect, since words can mean different things to different people – as lawyers continually demonstrate to us."

The laughter broke the tension that had been building up in the House.

"But if we allow this opportunity to pass today it will be another victory for those who revel in the mayhem of Northern Ireland whatever their reason, and a defeat for all men of goodwill."

The House was silent as Simon went on to explain in detail the thinking behind the Patriots' Provision and the effect it would have on both Protestants and Catholics in north and south. He also covered the other salient clauses in the Charter, answering the points that had been raised during the debate until, in glancing up at the clock above the Speaker's chair, he realised he had less than a minute left.

"Mr Speaker, we in this great House, who have in the past decided the fate of nations, are now given an opportunity to succeed today where our predecessors have failed. I ask you to support this Charter – not unreservedly, but to show the bombers and the murderers that here in Westminster we can cast a vote for the children of tomorrow's Ireland. Let the twenty-first century be one in which the Irish problem is only a part of history. Mr Speaker, I seek the support of the whole House."

The motion on the Charter was agreed without division.

Simon immediately returned home and on arrival silently crept upstairs. He closed the bedroom door behind him and fumbled for the switch. The light by the side of the bed went on and Elizabeth sat up.

"Your cocoa's gone cold and I've eaten all the biscuits," she said, grinning, "but thank you for leaving the radio on, at least I knew where you were."

CHAPTER
TWENTY SIX

Charles and Amanda were married at the most inconspi-
cuous register office in Hammersmith. They then departed
for a long weekend in Paris. Charles had told his bride that he
preferred her not to let anyone learn of the marriage for at
least another week. He didn't want Fiona to find yet a further
excuse for not returning the Holbein. Amanda readily
agreed, and then remembered – but surely Alec Pimkin
didn't count.

Paris turned out to be fun, even though Charles was
sensitive about Amanda's obvious pregnancy – never more
so than when they arrived on the Friday night at the Plaza
Athenée and were escorted to a suite overlooking the courtyard. Later, over dinner, Amanda astonished the waiters
with her appetite as well as the cut of her dress.

Over breakfast in bed the next day Charles read in the
Herald Tribune that Mrs Thatcher was considering a reshuffle
that very weekend. He cut the honeymoon short and returned to London on the Saturday, two days earlier than
planned. Amanda was not overjoyed. Her husband spent the
whole of Sunday at Eaton Square alongside a phone that
never rang.

That same Sunday evening the Prime Minister called for
Simon Kerslake and told him that he was to be made a Privy
Councillor and would be moved from the Northern Ireland
Office to Defence as Minister of State.

He had started to protest, but Mrs Thatcher forestalled
any discussion. "I don't want any more dead heroes,
Simon," she said sharply.

Elizabeth was relieved when she heard the news, although

it took her some time to get used to her husband being referred to as 'the Right Honourable Simon Kerslake'. For some weeks the old joke of 'rarely right and never honourable' had to be suffered by both of them from countless well-meaning constituents who imagined they were the only people who had thought of the quip.

Mrs Thatcher called Charles Seymour on the Monday morning while he was waiting in Eaton Square for the return of the Holbein. Both sides' solicitors had agreed that the first Earl of Bridgwater should be back at Charles's home by eleven that morning. Only the Queen or Mrs Thatcher could have kept Charles from being there to receive it.

The Prime Minister's call came long after he thought the reshuffle was over, but then Mrs Thatcher had been informed that Charles was in Paris on his honeymoon and wouldn't be back until the Monday morning.

Charles took a taxi to Downing Street and was quickly ushered into the Prime Minister's study. Mrs Thatcher began by complimenting him on the work he had carried out on successive Finance Bills in Opposition and in Government. She then invited him to join the front-bench team as the Financial Secretary to the Treasury.

Charles accepted gracefully, and after a short policy discussion with the Prime Minister drove back to Eaton Square to celebrate both his triumphs. Amanda met him at the door to tell him the Holbein had been returned. Fiona had kept her part of the bargain: the painting had been delivered at eleven o'clock sharp.

Charles strode confidently into his drawing-room and was delighted to find the bulky package awaiting him. He was by no means so pleased to be followed by Amanda, a cigarette in one hand and a glass of gin in the other; but this was not a day for quarrels, he decided. He told her of his appointment, but she didn't seem to take in its significance until her husband opened a bottle of champagne.

Charles poured out two glasses and handed one to his bride.

"A double celebration. What fun," she said, first draining the gin.

Charles took a quick sip of the champagne before he began to untie the knots and tear away the smart red wrapping paper that covered his masterpiece. Once the paper had been removed he pulled back the final cardboard covers. Charles stared with delight at the portrait.

The first Earl of Bridgwater was back home. Charles picked up the gold frame he knew so well to return it to its place in his study but he noticed that the picture had come a little loose. "Damn," he said.

"What's the matter?" asked Amanda still leaning against the door.

"Nothing important, only I shall have to get the frame fixed. I'll drop it into Oliver Swann on the way to the bank. I've waited nearly three years; another couple of days won't make any difference."

Now that Charles had accepted the post of Financial Secretary to the Treasury he knew there was one little arrangement he had to clear up before the appointment became public knowledge. With that in mind, he left Eaton Square and dropped the Holbein off at the framer. He then went on to the bank and summoned Clive Reynolds to his office. It was clear from Reynolds's manner that the news of Charles's ministerial appointment had not yet leaked out.

"Clive," Charles called him for the first time. "I have a proposition to put to you."

Clive Reynolds remained silent.

"The Prime Minister has offered me a post in the Government."

"Congratulations," said Reynolds, "and well deserved, if I may say so."

"Thank you," said Charles. "Now: I'm considering offering you the chance to stand in for me as chairman during my absence."

Clive Reynolds looked surprised.

"On the clear understanding that if the Conservatives were to return to Opposition or I were to lose my appointment in Government I would be reinstated as chairman immediately."

"Naturally," said Reynolds. "I should be delighted to fill the appointment for the interim period."

"Good man," said Charles. "It can't have escaped your notice what happened to the last chairman in the same situation."

"I shall make certain that will not happen again."

"Thank you," said Charles. "I shall not forget your loyalty when I return."

"And I shall also endeavour to carry on the traditions of the bank in your absence," said Reynolds, his head slightly bowed.

"I feel sure you will," said Charles.

The board accepted the recommendation that Clive Reynolds be appointed as temporary chairman and Charles vacated his office happily to take up his new post at the Treasury.

Charles considered it had been the most successful week of his life and on the Friday evening on the way back to Eaton Square he dropped into Oliver Swann's gallery to pick up the Holbein.

"I'm afraid the picture didn't quite fit the frame," said Mr Swann.

"Oh, I expect it's worked loose over the years," Charles said non-committally.

"No, Mr Seymour, this frame was put on the portrait quite recently," said Swann.

"That's not possible," said Charles. "I remember the frame as well as I remember the picture. The portrait of the first Earl of Bridgwater has been in my family for over 400 years."

"Not this picture," said Swann.

"What do you mean?" said Charles, beginning to sound anxious.

"This picture came up for sale at Sotheby's about three weeks ago."

Charles went cold as Swann continued.

"It's the school of Holbein, of course," he said, "probably painted by one of his pupils around the time of his death. I should think there are a dozen or so in existence."

"A dozen or so," repeated Charles, the blood drained from his face.

"Yes, perhaps even more. At least it's solved one mystery for me," said Swann, chuckling.

"What's that?" asked Charles, choking out the words.

"I couldn't work out why Lady Fiona was bidding for the picture, and then I remembered that your family name is Bridgwater."

"At least *this* wedding has some style," Pimkin assured Fiona between mouthfuls of sandwich at the reception after her marriage to Alexander Dalglish. Pimkin always accepted wedding invitations as it allowed him to devour mounds of smoked salmon sandwiches and consume unlimited quantities of champagne. "I particularly enjoyed that *short* service of blessing in the Guards' Chapel; and Claridges can always be relied on to understand my little proclivities." He peered round the vast room and only stopped to stare at his reflection in a chandelier.

Fiona laughed. "Did you go to Charles's wedding?"

"My darling, the only Etonians who have ever been seen in Hammersmith pass through it as quickly as possible on a boat, representing either Oxford or Cambridge."

"So you weren't invited," said Fiona.

"I'm told that only Amanda was invited, and even she nearly found she had another engagement. With her doctor, I believe."

"Well, Charles certainly can't afford another divorce."

"No, not in his present position as Her Majesty's Financial Secretary. One divorce might go unnoticed but two would be considered habit-forming, and all diligent readers of Nigel Dempster have been able to observe that consummation has taken place."

"But how long will Charles be able to tolerate her behaviour?"

"As long as he still believes she has given him a son who will inherit the family title. Not that a marriage ceremony will necessarily prove legitimacy," added Pimkin.

"Perhaps Amanda won't produce a son."

"Perhaps whatever she produces it will be obvious that it's not Charles's offspring," said Pimkin, falling into a chair that had been momentarily left by a large buxom lady.

"Even if it was I can't see Amanda as a housewife."

"No, but it suits Amanda's current circumstances to be thought of as the loving spouse."

"Time may change that too," said Fiona.

"I doubt it," said Pimkin. "Amanda is stupid, that has been proved beyond reasonable doubt, but she has a survival instinct second only to a mongoose. So while Charles is spending all the hours of the day advancing his glittering career she would be foolish to search publicly for greener pastures. Especially when she can always lie in them privately."

"You're a wicked old gossip," said Fiona.

"I cannot deny it," said Pimkin, "for it is an art at which women have never been as accomplished as men."

"Thank you for such a sensible wedding present," said Alexander, joining his wife of two hours. "You selected my favourite claret."

"Giving a dozen bottles of the finest claret serves two purposes," said Pimkin, his hands resting lightly on his stomach. "First, you can always be assured of a decent wine when you invite yourself to dine."

"And second?" asked Alexander.

"When the happy couple split up you can feel relieved that they will no longer have your present to quarrel over."

"Did you give Charles and Amanda a present?" asked Fiona.

"No," said Pimkin, deftly removing another glass of champagne from a passing waiter. "I felt your return of the bogus Earl of Bridgwater was quite enough for both of us."

"I wonder where he is now?" said Alexander.

"He no longer resides in Eaton Square," said Pimkin with the air of one who has divulged a piece of information which can only guarantee further rapt attention.

"Who would want the phoney earl?"

"We are not aware of the provenance of the buyer, as he

emanates from one of Her Majesty's former colonies, but the seller . . ."

"Stop teasing, Alec. Who?"

"None other than Mrs Amanda Seymour."

"Amanda?"

"Yes. Amanda, no less. The dear, silly creature retrieved the false earl from the cellar where Charles had buried him with full military honours."

"But she must have realised it was a fake."

"My dear Amanda wouldn't know the difference between a Holbein and an Andy Warhol but she still happily accepted £10,000 for the impersonation. I am assured that the dealer who purchased this fabricated masterpiece made what I think vulgar people in the City describe as 'a quick turn'."

"Good God," said Alexander. "I only paid £8,000 for it myself."

"Perhaps you should get Amanda to advise you on these matters in future," said Pimkin. "In exchange for my invaluable piece of information I'm bound to enquire if the real Earl of Bridgwater is to remain in hiding."

"Certainly not, Alec. He is merely awaiting the right moment to make a public appearance," said Fiona, unable to hide a smile.

"And where is Amanda now?" asked Alexander, obviously wanting to change the subject.

"In Switzerland producing a baby, which we can but hope will bear sufficient resemblance to a white Caucasian to convince one of Charles's limited imagination that he is the father."

"Where *do* you get all your information from?" asked Alexander.

Pimkin sighed dramatically. "Women have a habit of pouring their hearts out to me, Amanda included."

"Why should she do that?" asked Alexander.

"She lives safe in the knowledge that I am the one man she knows who has no interest in her body." Pimkin drew breath, but only to devour another smoked salmon sandwich.

Charles phoned Amanda every day while she was in Geneva.
She kept assuring him all was well, and that the baby was
expected on time. He had considered it prudent for Amanda
not to remain in England advertising her pregnancy, a less
than recent occurrence to even the most casual observer. She
for her part did not complain. With £10,000 safely tucked
away in a private Swiss account there were few little necessi-
ties she could not have brought to her, even in Geneva.

It had taken a few weeks for Charles to become accustomed to Government after such a long break. He enjoyed
the challenge of the Treasury and quickly fell in with its
strange traditions. He was constantly reminded that his was
the department on which the Prime Minister kept the closest
eye, making the challenge even greater. The civil servants,
when asked their opinion of the new Financial Secretary,
would reply variously: able, competent, efficient, hard-
working – but without any hint of affection in their voices.
When someone asked his driver, whose name Charles could
never remember, the same question he proffered the view,
"He's the sort of minister who always sits in the back of a car.
But I'd still put a week's wages on Mr Seymour becoming
Prime Minister."

Amanda produced her child in the middle of the ninth
month. After a week's recuperation she was allowed to return
to England. She discovered travelling with her offspring was
a nuisance and by the time she arrived at Heathrow she was
more than happy to turn the child over to the nanny Charles
had selected.

Charles had sent a car to pick her up from the airport. He
had an unavoidable conference with a delegation of Japanese
businessmen, he explained, all of them busy complaining
about the new Government tariffs on imports. At the first
opportunity to be rid of his oriental guests he bolted back to
Eaton Square.

Amanda was there to meet him at the door. Charles had
almost forgotten how beautiful his wife was, and how long
she had been away.

"Where's my child?" he asked, after he had given her a
long kiss.

"In a nursery that's more expensively furnished than our bedroom," she replied a little sharply.

Charles ran up the wide staircase and along the passage. Amanda followed. He entered the nursery and stopped in his tracks as he stared at the future Earl of Bridgwater. The little black curls and deep brown eyes came as something of a shock.

"Good heavens," said Charles, stepping forward for a closer examination. Amanda remained by the door, her hand clutching its handle.

She had a hundred answers ready for his question.

"He's the spitting image of my great-grandfather. You skipped a couple of generations, Harry," said Charles, lifting the boy high into the air, "but there's no doubt you're a real Seymour."

Amanda sighed with inaudible relief. The hundred answers she could now keep to herself.

"It's more than a couple of generations the little bastard has skipped," said Pimkin. "It's an entire continent." He took another sip of christening champagne before continuing. "This poor creature, on the other hand," he said, staring at Fiona's firstborn, "bears a striking resemblance to Alexander. Dear little girl should have been given a kinder legacy with which to start her life."

"She's beautiful," said Fiona, picking Lucy up from the cradle to check her nappy.

"Now we know why you needed to be married so quickly," added Pimkin between gulps. "At least this child made wedlock, even if it was a close-run thing."

Fiona continued as if she had not heard his remark. "Have you actually seen Charles's son?"

"I think we should refer to young Harry as Amanda's child," said Pimkin. "We don't want to be had up under the Trade Descriptions Act."

"Come on, Alec, have you seen Harry?" she asked, refusing to fill his empty glass.

"Yes, I have. And I am afraid he also bears too striking a resemblance to his father for it to go unnoticed in later life."

"Anyone we know?" asked Fiona, probing.

"I am not a scandalmonger," said Pimkin, removing a crumb from his waistcoat. "As you well know. But a certain Brazilian *fazendeiro* who frequents Cowdray Park and Ascot during the summer months has obviously maintained his interest in English fillies."

Pimkin confidently held out his glass.

CHAPTER
TWENTY SEVEN

James Callaghan's resignation as Labour party leader in October 1980 took none of the political analysts by surprise. Unlike his predecessor he was over sixty-five, the age at which his party had recommended retirement.

Those same analysts were surprised, however, when Michael Foot, the veteran left-winger, defeated Denis Healey by 139 votes to 129 to become the new leader of the Labour party. The analysts immediately predicted a long spell of opposition for the socialists.

The Conservatives took much pleasure in watching a leadership struggle from the sidelines for a change. When Charles Seymour heard the result it amused him that the Labour party had ended up replacing a sixty-year-old with a sixty-four-year-old, who in turn was being replaced by a sixty-seven-year-old. Lord Shinwell, who at the age of ninety-six was the oldest living former Labour Cabinet minister, declared that he would be a candidate for party leadership when Foot retired.

When the election for the Shadow Cabinet came a week later Andrew decided not to submit his name. Like many of his colleagues he liked the new leader personally but had rarely been able to agree with him on domestic issues and was totally opposed to his defence and European policies. Instead he took on the chairmanship of the Select Committee on Scottish Affairs. Raymond for his part considered that Foot was destined to be no more than an interim leader and was therefore quite happy to serve under him. When the election to the Shadow Cabinet was announced Raymond came eighth. Michael Foot invited him to continue shadowing the Trade portfolio.

When Andrew entered the Commons Chamber the day after the election he walked up the gangway and took a seat on the back benches for the first time in fourteen years. He looked down at Raymond lounging on the front bench and recalled his own words: "There may well come a day when I sit and envy you from the same back benches."

Andrew was not surprised when he heard from his local committee in Edinburgh that he would once again have to submit himself to re-selection as their candidate some time during 1981. When the Labour conference the previous October had approved the mandatory re-selection of Labour MPs he had realised his biggest battle would be internal. Frank Boyle had even managed to replace another of Andrew's supporters with one of his own henchmen.

Roy Jenkins, the former deputy leader of the Labour party, was returning from Brussels as soon as his term as President of the European Commission came to an end. After delivering the Dimbleby lecture on television Jenkins made no secret of the fact that he was considering founding a new party that would take in those moderate radicals who felt the Labour party had swung too far to the left. The party conference had removed the power of selection of the leaders from Members of Parliament; for many this was the final straw, and several Labour MPs told Jenkins they were ready to defect. Andrew would have preferred to remain loyal to the party and try to change it from the inside, but he was fast coming to the conclusion that that hour had passed.

In his morning mail was a curt note from the constituency secretary informing him that Frank Boyle was going to oppose him for the nomination. Andrew flew up to Edinburgh on the day of the meeting, fearing the worst. No one met him at the airport, and at party headquarters David Connaught greeted him with a glum face.

Andrew stood in front of the committee in a cold, cheerless room and answered the same questions that had been put to him only three years before. He gave exactly the same answers: where he stood on nuclear disarmament, why he was in favour of a close association with the United States, his attitude to a wealth tax – on and on, predictable question after predictable question, but he never once allowed them to exasperate him.

He ended with the words: "I have been proud to serve the people of Edinburgh Carlton for almost twenty years as the Labour member and hope to do so for at least another twenty. If you now feel unable to re-select me I would have to consider standing as an independent candidate." For the first time, one or two members of the committee looked anxious.

"We are not intimidated by your threats, Mr Fraser," said Frank Boyle. "The Labour party has always been bigger than any individual. Now we know where Mr Fraser's real interests lie I suggest we move to a vote."

Twelve little slips of paper were passed out. 'Fraser' or 'Boyle' were scribbled on them before they were sent back to the chairman.

Frank Boyle slowly gathered up the slips, clearly relishing Andrew's discomfort. He unfolded the first slip of paper. "Boyle," he said, glancing at the others round the table.

He opened a second – "Fraser" – then a third, "Boyle", followed by "Fraser, Fraser, Fraser."

Andrew kept count in his head: four-two in his favour.

"Fraser," followed by "Boyle, Boyle, Fraser."

Six-four in Andrew's favour, with two still unopened: he only needed one more vote. "Boyle." Six-five. The chairman took some considerable time opening the last slip.

"Boyle," he announced in triumph.

He paused for effect. "Six votes all," he declared. "Under standing order forty-two of the Party Constitution," he said, as if he had learnt the words off by heart before the meeting, "in the result of a tie the chairman shall have the casting vote." He paused once again.

"Boyle," he said, lingering for a moment. "I therefore declare that Frank Boyle is selected as the official Labour party candidate for the constituency of Edinburgh Carlton at the next general election." He turned to Andrew and said,

"We shall no longer be requiring your services, Mr Fraser."

"I would like to thank those of you who supported me," Andrew said quietly and left without another word.

The next day the *Scotsman* came out with a lengthy article on the dangers of a small group of wilful people having the power to remove a member who had served his constituents honourably over a long period of time. Andrew phoned Stuart Gray to thank him. "I only wish the article had come out the day before," he said.

"It was set up for yesterday," Stuart told him, "but the announcement from Buckingham Palace of Prince Charles's engagement to Lady Diana Spencer moved everything else out – even the Rangers–Celtic report. By the way, doesn't Boyle's nomination have to be confirmed by his General Management Committee?"

"Yes, but they are putty in his hands. That would be like trying to explain to your mother-in-law about your wife's nagging."

"Then why don't you appeal to the National Executive and ask for the decision to be put to a full meeting of the constituency party?"

"Because it would take weeks to get the decision over-turned and more importantly I'm no longer certain that I want to fight the seat as a Labour candidate."

Andrew listened to the reporter's question and said, "Yes, you may quote me."

As the date for an election drew nearer Charles decided it might be wise to introduce Amanda to the constituency. He had explained to those who inquired that his wife had had rather a bad time of it after the birth, and had been told by her doctors not to participate in anything that might raise her blood pressure – though one or two constituents considered that the Sussex Downs' Conservatives would find it hard to raise the blood pressure of a ninety-year-old with a pace-maker. Charles had also decided to leave Harry at home, explaining that it was he who had chosen a public life, not his son.

The annual Garden Party held in the grounds of Lord

Cuckfield's country home seemed to Charles to be the ideal opportunity to show off Amanda and he asked her to be certain to wear something appropriate.

He was aware that designer jeans had come into fashion, and that his clothes-conscious wife never seemed to dress in the same thing twice. He also knew that liberated women didn't wear bras. But he was nevertheless shocked when he saw Amanda in a near see-through blouse and jeans so tight it looked as if she had been poured into them. Charles was genuinely horrified.

"Can't you find something a little more . . . conservative?" he suggested.

"Like the things that old frump Fiona used to wear?"

Charles couldn't think of a suitable reply. "The Garden Party will be frightfully dull," said Charles desperately. "Perhaps I should go on my own."

Amanda turned and looked him in the eye. "Are you ashamed of me, Charlie?"

He drove his wife silently down to the constituency and every time he glanced over at her he wanted to make an excuse to turn back. When they arrived at Lord Cuckfield's home his worst fears were confirmed. Neither the men nor the women could take their eyes off Amanda as she strolled around the lawns devouring strawberries. Many of them would have used the word 'hussy' if she hadn't been the member's wife.

Charles might have escaped lightly had it only been the one *risqué* joke Amanda told – to the bishop's wife – or even her curt refusals to judge the baby contest or to draw the raffle; but he was not to be so lucky. The chairman of the Women's Advisory Committee had met her match when she was introduced to the member's wife.

"Darling," said Charles. "I don't think you've met Mrs Blenkinsop."

"No, I haven't," said Amanda, ignoring Mrs Blenkinsop's outstretched hand.

"Mrs Blenkinsop," continued Charles, "was awarded the OBE for her services to the constituency."

"OBE?" Amanda asked innocently.

Mrs Blenkinsop drew herself up to her full height.

"Order of the British Empire," she said.

"I've always wondered," said Amanda, smiling. "My dad used to tell me it stood for 'other buggers' efforts'."

"Seen the Persil anywhere?" asked Louise.

"No, I stopped washing my own pants some time ago," replied Andrew.

"Ha, ha," said Louise. "But if you haven't taken them who has – two giant packets are missing?"

"The phantom Persil thief strikes again. Whatever next?" said Andrew. "The Bovril perhaps?"

"Stop making a fool of yourself and go and fish Clarissa out of the bath."

Andrew pulled himself out of the armchair, dropped *The Economist* on the carpet and ran upstairs. "Time to get out, young lady," he said even before he reached the bathroom door. First he heard the sobbing then when he opened the door he found Clarissa covered from head to toe in soap flakes. Her thick black curly hair was matted with them. Andrew burst out laughing but he stopped when he saw Clarissa's knees and shins were bleeding. She held a large scrubbing brush in one hand which was covered in a mixture of soap powder and blood.

"What's the matter, darling?" asked Andrew, kneeling on the bath mat.

"It isn't true," said Clarissa, not looking at him.

"What isn't true?" asked Andrew gently.

"Look on the box," she said pointing at the two empty packets which were standing on the end of the bath. Andrew glanced at the familiar picture on the box of a little fair-haired girl in a white party dress.

"What isn't true?" he repeated, still uncertain what Clarissa meant.

"It isn't true that Persil washes whiter and can remove even the blackest spots. Two large packets and I'm still black," she said.

Andrew had to smile which only made Clarissa cry even more. After he had washed off all the suds and gently dried her he put antiseptic ointment on the cuts and bruises.

"Why am I so black?" she asked.

"Because your mother and father were black," replied Andrew, guiding his daughter through to her bedroom.

"Why can't you be my father? Then I'd be white."

"I am your father now so you don't need to be."

"Yes, I do."

"Why?"

"Because the children at school laugh at me," Clarissa said, clutching firmly on to Andrew's hand.

"When I was at school they used to laugh at me because I was small," said Andrew. "They called me puny."

"What did you do about it?" asked Clarissa.

"I trained hard and ended up as captain of the school rugby team and that made them stop laughing."

"But by then you were big. I can't train to be white."

"No, I was still small, and you won't need to train."

"Why?" asked Clarissa, still not letting go of his hand.

"Because you're going to be beautiful, and then all those ugly white girls will be oh so jealous."

Clarissa was silent for some time before she spoke again. "Promise, Daddy?"

"I promise," he said, remaining on the edge of the bed.

"Like Frank Boyle is jealous of you?"

Andrew was startled. "What do you know about him?"

"Only what I heard Mummy say, that he's going to be the Labour man for Edinburgh, but you'll still beat him."

Andrew was speechless.

"Is he going to be the Labour man, Daddy?" she asked.

"Yes, he is."

"And will you beat him?"

"I'll try."

"Can I help?" Clarissa asked, a tiny smile appearing on her face.

"Of course. Now off you go to sleep," said Andrew, getting up and drawing the curtains.

"Is he black?"

"Who?" asked Andrew.

"The nasty Frank Boyle."

"No," said Andrew laughing, "he's white."

"Then he ought to be made to have my skin then I could have his."

Andrew turned off the light, relieved Clarissa could no longer see his face.

Harry's second birthday party was attended by all those two-year-olds in the vicinity of Eaton Square whom his nanny considered acceptable. Charles managed to escape from a departmental meeting accompanied by a large paint board and a red tricycle. As he parked his car in Eaton Square he spotted Fiona's old Volvo driving away towards Sloane Square. He dismissed the coincidence although he still had plans for regaining the priceless Holbein. Harry naturally wanted to ride the tricycle round and round the dining-room table. Charles sat watching his son and couldn't help noticing that he was smaller than most of his friends. Then he remembered that great-grandfather had only been five feet eight inches tall.

It was the moment after the candles had been blown out, and nanny switched the light back on, that Charles was first aware that something was missing. It was like the game children play with objects on a tray: everyone shuts his eyes, nanny takes one away and then you all have to guess which piece it was.

It took Charles some time to realise that the missing object was his gold cigar box. He walked over to the sideboard and studied the empty space. He continued to stare at the spot where the small gold box left to him by his great-grandfather had been the previous night. Now all that was left in its place was the matching lighter.

He immediately asked Amanda if she knew where the heirloom was, but his wife seemed totally absorbed in lining up the children for a game of musical chairs. After checking carefully in the other rooms Charles went into his study and phoned the Chelsea police.

An inspector from the Crime Squad came round immediately and took down all the details. Charles was able to supply the police officer with a photograph of the box which carried the initials C.G.S. He stopped just short of mentioning Fiona by name. The inspector assured Charles that he would deal with the investigation personally. Charles returned to the party to find nannies arriving to gather their wards.

When the Edinburgh Carlton Labour party issued a press statement after their AGM announcing that Frank Boyle had been selected to fight the seat as their candidate, Andrew was surprised and touched by the flood of letters and calls of goodwill he received, many from people he didn't even know. Most of the messages begged him to stand at the next general election as an Independent.

Twenty Labour MPs and one Conservative had joined the newly formed Social Democratic Party and many others were expected to follow. Andrew knew he would have to make an announcement soon if he didn't want his supporters to drift away. He spent agonising hours discussing with Louise the problem of severing the final bonds with the party.

"What shall I do?" he asked, yet again.

"I can't tell you that; I just hope you make up your mind fairly quickly."

"Why quickly?"

"Because I'm going to vote for the Social Democrats at the next election, so you had better be my local candidate."

A few days later Roy Jenkins, Andrew's old chief at the Home Office, phoned to say he was fighting a by-election in Glasgow as the SDP candidate.

"I do hope you will feel able to join us," said Jenkins.

Andrew had always admired Jenkins's firm stand against the left and felt he was the one man who might break the two-party system.

"I need a little more time," he replied.

A week later Andrew made up his mind and informed the Chief Whip that he was leaving the party and would be joining the SDP. Then he packed a bag and travelled to Glasgow.

Roy Jenkins won the seat at Glasgow Hillhead with a large enough swing to worry both main parties. By Easter, a total of twenty-nine Members of Parliament had broken away to join him, while the alliance of SDP and Liberal MPs together could muster more than forty votes on the floor of the House.

With opinion polls putting them in second place, it began to look possible that the Social Democrats might hold the balance of power after the next election. The Conservatives were now running a poor third in all the national opinion polls.

Charles heard nothing for three weeks about the missing gold box and was beginning to despair when the inspector phoned to say that the family heirloom had been found.

"Excellent news," said Charles. "Are you able to bring the box round to Eaton Square?"

"It's not quite as simple as that, sir," said the policeman.

"What do you mean?"

"I would prefer not to discuss the matter over the phone. May I come and see you, sir?"

"By all means," said Charles, slightly mystified.

He waited impatiently for the inspector to arrive, although the policeman was at the front door barely ten minutes later. His first question took Charles by surprise.

"Are we alone, sir?"

"Yes," said Charles. "My wife and son are away visiting my mother-in-law in Wales. You say you've found the gold box," he continued, impatient to hear the inspector's news.

"Yes, sir."

"Well done, Inspector. I shall speak to the Commissioner personally," he added, guiding the officer towards the drawing-room.

"I'm afraid there's a complication, sir."

"How can there be when you've found the box?"

"We cannot be sure there was anything illegal about its disappearance in the first place."

"What do you mean, Inspector?"

"The gold case was offered to a dealer in Grafton Street for £2,500."

"And who was doing the selling?" asked Charles impatiently.

"That's the problem, sir. The cheque was made out to Amanda Seymour and the description fits your wife," said the inspector. Charles was speechless. "And the dealer has a receipt to prove the transaction." The inspector passed over a copy of the receipt. Charles was unable to steady his shaking hand as he recognised Amanda's signature.

"Now, as this matter has already been referred to the Director of Public Prosecutions I thought I ought to have a word with you in private, as I am sure you would not want us to prefer charges."

"Yes, no, of course, thank you for your consideration, Inspector," said Charles flatly.

"Not at all, sir. The dealer has made his position clear: he would be only too happy to return the cigar box for the exact sum he paid for it. I don't think that could be fairer."

Charles made no comment other than to thank the inspector again before showing him out.

He returned to his study, phoned Amanda at her mother's house and told her to return immediately. She started to protest, but he had already hung up.

Charles remained at home until they all arrived back at Eaton Square late that night. The nanny and Harry were immediately sent upstairs.

It took Charles about five minutes to discover that only a few hundred pounds of the money was left. When his wife burst into tears he struck her across the face with such force that she fell to the ground. "If anything else goes missing from this house," he said, "you will go with it and I will also make sure you spend a very long time in jail." Amanda ran out of the room sobbing uncontrollably.

The next day Charles advertised for a full-time governess. He also moved his own bedroom to the top floor so that he could be close to his son. Amanda made no protest.

Once the governess had settled in Amanda quickly became bored with the child and began disappearing for long periods. Charles couldn't be sure where she was most of the time, and didn't care.

After Pimkin had recounted the latest state of affairs to Alexander Dalglish in well-embroidered detail Fiona

remarked to her husband, "I never thought the day would
come when I would feel sorry for Charles."

On a sleepy Thursday in April 1982 Argentina attacked and
occupied two small islands whose 1,800 British citizens were
forced to lower the Union Jack for the first time in over a
hundred years. Few members returned to their constituency
that Friday and the House met unusually on a Saturday
morning to debate the crisis while the nation followed every
word on the radio.

The same day Mrs Thatcher immediately despatched a
task force halfway around the globe to recapture the islands.
Her fellow countrymen followed every scrap of news so
intently that the London theatres found themselves empty at
the height of the season.

Simon felt exhilarated to be a member of the Defence team
at such an historic moment, and Elizabeth didn't begrudge
him those days when he left before she had woken and
arrived home after she had fallen asleep.

Under less public scrutiny but almost equal pressure,
Charles beavered away at the Treasury addressing the economic problems that had been presented. He spent day after
day in the House helping to put the Government's case. Like
Simon he found he could only snatch moments to be at home
but, unlike Elizabeth, his wife remained in bed until midday.
When Charles did manage to slip away from the department
he spent all his spare time with Harry, whose progress he
followed with delighted concern.

At the time when the Union Jack was raised once again in
the Falklands, the budget became an Act.

CHAPTER
TWENTY EIGHT

'PM to go in Nov' and 'Will Maggie wait till June?' were two of the headlines Andrew read on the first day of the new Parliamentary session.

Anyone who is defending a marginal seat is always on edge as the statutory five years draws to a close, and the new SDP members all treated their seats as marginal. Andrew was no exception.

He had worked hard to prove he was worth his place in the group the leader of the Social Democrats was beginning to form in the Commons. When Roy Jenkins had announced the make-up of his Shadow team Andrew was appointed Defence spokesman and enjoyed the challenge of pitting himself against the two main parties in the Commons in the run-up to the election. But once the Falklands crisis was over he knew his real problems were not going to be in Westminster but in Edinburgh, where he spent an increasing amount of his time. Hamish Ramsey phoned to ask him if there was anything he could do to help.

"Be my chairman for the election campaign," said Andrew simply.

Ramsey agreed without hesitation and within a fortnight four members of Andrew's old Labour party committee had defected to join him. Support for Andrew came from the most surprising quarters, including Jock McPherson, who pledged that the Scottish Nationalists would not be contesting the Edinburgh Carlton seat as they had no desire to see Frank Boyle in Parliament. Sir Duncan Fraser kept very quiet about what the Conservatives were up to until they announced that Jamie Lomax would be their standard-bearer.

"Lomax. Lomax," repeated Andrew. "He and I were at school together," he told his father. "He was known as Loopy Lomax. You've selected the biggest idiot of his generation."

"That's a disgraceful slur on an able man," said Sir Duncan, trying to keep a straight face. "I can assure you it took a lot of convincing the committee to make certain Lomax was selected."

"How did you fix it?"

"I must admit it wasn't easy. We had some very good applicants, but I managed to undermine every one of them and point out how blemish-free Lomax's political past was," said Sir Duncan, winking.

"Non-existent careers make for the best blemish-free pasts," said Andrew, and burst out laughing.

"Yes, I'm afraid one or two of the committee noticed that. But you must admit Lomax is a fine figure of a man," added his father.

"What's that got to do with it?" asked Andrew. "You weren't looking for a male model as candidate."

"I know, but it did help me to swing the ladies on the Women's Advisory Committee round to my way of thinking."

"You're a rogue, Father."

"No, I'm not. There isn't a Conservative in Scotland who would rather see Frank Boyle in the House than you, and as we have no chance of winning the seat, why let *him* in?"

Louise and Clarissa spent the Christmas recess in Edinburgh. Sir Duncan warned Louise that if Andrew lost this election he could never hope to return to the House of Commons again.

During 1983 Margaret Thatcher stuck firm to her monetarist policies and brought inflation below four per cent, while in parts of Scotland unemployment rose to fifteen per cent. She had gradually stifled any opposition from the 'wets' and by the end of her first administration they were totally outmanoeuvred. But it was the outcome of the Falklands crisis that had kept her ahead in the opinion polls for over a year. The press speculated on the date of the general election all through the month of April, and after the Conservatives' success in the local elections on 5 May the Prime Minister sought an audience with the Queen. Shortly afterwards Margaret Thatcher told the nation that she needed another five years to continue her policies and prove that they worked. The election date was set for 9 June.

Once the election campaign had begun in earnest Stuart Gray interviewed all three candidates on behalf of the *Scotsman* and told Andrew he had a plan to help him.

"You can't," said Andrew. "You're bound to remain neutral and give all three candidates equal column inches during the campaign."

"Agreed," said Stuart. "But on the one hand we know Frank Boyle is sharp and has the looks of an escaped convict, while Jamie Lomax looks like a film star but makes crass statements every time he opens his mouth."

"So?" said Andrew.

"So I'm going to cover the political pages with the worst shots I can find of Boyle and fill up inch after inch with the sayings of Lomax. They'll both get equal coverage while at the same time they'll lose votes."

"They'll suss it out and complain to the editor."

"I doubt it," said Stuart. "I have yet to meet a politician who complained about having his photo in the paper, or one who was angered by seeing his mad views aired to a larger audience than he could have hoped to influence in the past."

"And what do you propose to do about me?"

"That's a problem," admitted Stuart, laughing. "Perhaps I'll leave the columns blank. That's one way you can't lose votes."

Whenever Andrew carried out a door-to-door canvass he found a clear division between those who still backed him and those who thought he had been disloyal to the Labour party. As the canvass returns came in and the colours were put out on the trestle tables in the new party headquarters it became clear from even a cursory glance that it was going to be his toughest election yet.

Andrew had experienced some dirty campaigns over the years, especially when he had been up against the Scottish Nationalists, but after only a few days he had sweet memories of Jock McPherson who was Little Red Riding Hood compared with Boyle. Andrew could just about tolerate hearing that he had been thrown out of the Labour party because he was such a lazy member, even that he had left them in the lurch because he had been told he could never hope to be a minister again, but when it was repeated to him that the Boyle camp were spreading a rumour that Louise had lost her voice because, when she had her baby, it turned out to be black he was furious.

If Andrew had seen Boyle that day he would undoubtedly have hit him. Sir Duncan counselled restraint, pointing out that any other action could only harm Louise and Clarissa. Andrew took a deep breath and said nothing.

With a week to go a local opinion poll in the *Scotsman* showed Boyle leading by thirty-five per cent to Andrew's thirty-two. The Conservatives had nineteen per cent but fourteen per cent remained undecided. Jock McPherson had kept his word: no Scottish Nationalist candidate had entered the lists.

On the Friday before the election McPherson went one better by issuing a statement advising his supporters to back Andrew Fraser.

When Andrew phoned to thank him, he said, "I'm returning a favour."

"I don't remember ever doing you a favour," said Andrew.

"You certainly did, remembering you're an Edinburgh man. One mention to the press of my offer of the leadership of the Scottish Nationalists and I'd have been sunk down the nearest pothole."

With five days to go Alliance supporters from the two Edinburgh constituencies which were not fielding an SDP candidate swarmed in to help Andrew, and he began to believe the canvass returns that were now showing he could win. With two days to go the *Scotsman* proclaimed it was thirty-nine per cent to thirty-eight per cent in Boyle's favour, but also went on to point out that the Labour party would have a better-oiled machine to depend on when it came to polling day.

In his eve-of-poll message Andrew issued a clear statement on why his views differed from those of his opponent in the Labour party, and how he saw the future of Britain if the Alliance gained enough seats to hold the balance of power. He reminded voters that without exception the national opinion polls showed the SDP now running neck and neck with Labour.

Frank Boyle also put out an eve-of-poll message, delivered to every house in the constituency, showing a picture of Andrew holding Clarissa in his arms under the caption 'Does your member tell you the whole truth?' There was no mention of Louise or Clarissa in the text but the innuendo could not have been clearer. Andrew didn't see the sheet until the morning of polling day by which time he knew there was nothing effective he could do to refute Boyle's implied slur. Issuing a writ that could not be dealt with until weeks after the election was over could only prove impotent. He either won the day or he lost it.

To that end, he and Louise never stopped working from seven that morning until ten at night. Helpers arrived from the most unexpected places, as if to prove the *Scotsman* wrong about the Labour party machine, but Andrew couldn't help noticing that there were red rosettes everywhere he went.

Towards the end of the day even Sir Duncan joined him and began chauffeuring SDP voters to the polls in his Rolls Royce.

"We've faced the fact that our candidate has lost so now I've come to help you," he told Andrew bluntly.

As the city hall clock struck ten Andrew sat down on the steps of the last polling station. He knew there was nothing he could do now. He had done everything possible, only avoiding members of the House of Lords and lunatics – neither of which group was entitled to vote.

An old lady was coming out of the polling station with a smile on her face.

"Hello, Mrs Bloxham," said Andrew. "How are you?"

"I'm fine, Andrew," she smiled. "I nearly forgot to vote and that would never have done."

He raised his tired head.

"Now don't fret yourself, laddie," she continued, "I never failed to vote for the winner in fifty-two years and that's longer than you've lived." She chuckled and left him sitting on the steps.

Andrew somehow picked himself up and made his way through the dark cobbled streets to his election head-quarters. They cheered him as he entered the room, and the chairman offered him a 'wee dram of whisky'.

"To hell with a wee dram," said Andrew. "Just keep pouring."

He tried to get round the room to thank everyone before Hamish Ramsey told him it was time to go over to the city hall for the count. A small band of supporters accompanied the Frasers to the city hall to witness the proceedings. As he entered the hall the first person he saw was Boyle, who had a big smile on his face. Andrew was not discouraged by the smile as he watched the little slips of paper pour out of the boxes. Boyle had yet to learn that the first boxes to be counted were always from the inner wards, where most of the committed Socialists lived.

As both men walked round the tables, the little piles began to be checked – first in tens, then hundreds, until they were finally placed in thousands and handed over to the Sheriff. As the night drew on Boyle's smile turned to a grin, from a grin to a poker face, and finally to a look of anxiety as the piles grew closer and closer in size.

For over three hours the process of emptying the boxes continued and the scrutineers checked each little white slip before handing in their own records. At one twenty-two in the morning the Sheriff added up the list of numbers in front of him and asked the three candidates to join him.

He told them the result.

Frank Boyle smiled once again. Andrew showed no emo-tion, but called for a recount.

For over an hour, he paced nervously around the room as

the scrutineers checked and double-checked each pile: a change here, a mistake there, a lost vote discovered and, on one occasion, the name on the top of a pile of one hundred votes was not the same as the ninety-nine beneath it. At last the scrutineers handed back their figures. Once again the Sheriff added up the columns of numbers and asked the candidates to join him.

This time Andrew smiled while Boyle looked surprised and demanded another recount. The Sheriff acquiesced, but said it must be the last time. Both candidates agreed in the absence of their Conservative rival, who was sleeping soundly in a corner, secure in the knowledge that no amount of recounting would alter his position in the contest.

Once again the piles were checked and double-checked and five mistakes were discovered in the 42,588 votes cast. At three-twenty a.m., with counters and checkers falling asleep at their tables, the Sheriff once more asked the two candidates to join him. They were both stunned when they heard the result and the Sheriff informed them that there would be a further recount in the morning after his staff had managed to get some sleep.

All the voting papers were then placed carefully back in the black boxes, locked and left in the safe-keeping of the local constabulary while the candidates crept away to their beds.

Andrew slept in fits and starts through the remainder of the night. Louise, pale with exhaustion but still grinning, brought him a cup of tea at eight in the morning. He took a cold shower, shaved slowly and was back at the city hall a few minutes before the count was due to recommence. As he walked up the steps he was greeted by a battery of television cameras and journalists who had heard rumours as to why the count had been held up overnight and knew they couldn't afford to be absent as the final drama unfolded.

The counters looked eager and ready when the Sheriff checked his watch and nodded. The boxes were unlocked and placed in front of the staff for the fourth time. Once again the little piles grew from tens into hundreds and then into thousands. Andrew paced around the tables, more to burn up his nervous energy than out of a desire to keep checking. He had thirty witnesses registered as his counting agents to make sure he didn't lose by sleight of hand or genuine mistake.

Once the counters and scrutineers had finished they sat in front of their piles and waited for the slips to be collected and taken to the Sheriff. When the Sheriff had added up his little columns of figures for the final time he found that no votes had changed hands.

He explained to Andrew and Frank Boyle the procedure he intended to adopt in view of the outcome. He told both candidates that he had spoken to Lord Wylie at nine that morning and the Lord Advocate had read out the relevant statute in election law that was to be followed in such circumstances. Both candidates agreed on which of the two choices they preferred.

The Sheriff walked up on to the stage with Andrew Fraser and Frank Boyle in his wake, both looking anxious.

Everyone in the room stood to be sure of a better view of the proceedings. When the pushing back of chairs, the coughing and the nervous chattering had stopped, the Sheriff began. First he tapped the microphone that stood in front of him to be sure it was working. The metallic scratch was audible throughout the silent room. Satisfied, he began to speak.

"I, the returning officer for the district of Edinburgh Carlton, hereby declare the total number of votes cast for each candidate to be as follows:

Frank Boyle	18,437
Jamie Lomax	5,714
Andrew Fraser	18,437."

The supporters of both the leading candidates erupted into a noisy frenzy. It was several minutes before the Sheriff's voice could be heard above the babble of Scottish burrs.

"In accordance with section sixteen of the Representation of the People Act 1949 and rule fifty of the Parliamentary Election Rules in the second schedule to that Act, I am

obliged to decide between tied candidates by lot," he announced. "I have spoken with the Lord Advocate of Scotland, and have confirmed that the drawing of straws or the toss of a coin may constitute decision by lot for this purpose. Both candidates have agreed to the latter course of action."

Pandemonium broke out again as Andrew and Boyle stood motionless on each side of the Sheriff waiting for their fate to be determined.

"I have borrowed from the Royal Bank of Scotland," continued the Sheriff, aware that twenty million people were watching him on television for the first and probably the last time in his life, "a golden sovereign. On one side is the head of King George III, on the other Britannia. I shall invite the sitting member, Mr Fraser, to call his preference." Boyle curtly nodded his agreement. Both men inspected the coin.

The Sheriff rested the golden sovereign on his thumb, Andrew and Boyle still standing on either side of him. He turned to Andrew and said, "You will call, Mr Fraser, while the coin is in the air."

The silence was such that they might have been the only three people in the room. Andrew could feel his heart thumping in his chest as the Sheriff spun the coin high above him.

"Tails," he said clearly when the coin was at its zenith. The sovereign hit the floor and bounced, turning over several times before settling at the feet of the Sheriff.

Andrew stared down at the lady and sighed audibly. The Sheriff cleared his throat before declaring, "Following the decision by lot, I declare the aforementioned Mr Andrew Fraser to be the duly elected Member of Parliament for Edinburgh Carlton."

Andrew's supporters charged forward and on to the stage and carried him on their shoulders out of the city hall and through the streets of Edinburgh. Andrew searched for Louise and Clarissa, but they were lost in the crush.

The Royal Bank of Scotland presented the golden sovereign to the member the next day, and the editor of the

Scotsman rang to ask if there had been any particular reason why he had selected tails.

"Naturally," Andrew replied. "George III lost America for us. I wasn't going to let him lose Edinburgh for me."

CHAPTER
TWENTY NINE

Raymond read the *Daily Mail* caption again and smiled: 'On the toss of a coin'.

It saddened Raymond that Andrew had felt it necessary to leave the Labour party, although he was delighted that he had been returned to the Commons. Raymond was only thankful that there had been no Frank Boyles in his constituency. He often wondered if it was because Joyce kept such a watchful eye on all the committees.

Margaret Thatcher's second victory had come as a bitter blow to him although he couldn't have pretended it was a surprise. Her overall majority of 144 was even larger than had been predicted, while the SDP managed only six seats – although the Alliance were only two percentage points behind Labour in actual votes cast. Raymond was enough of a realist to know that now nothing was going to stop the Tories from governing for another five-year term.

Once again Raymond returned to his practice at the bar and a new round of time-consuming briefs. When the Lord Chancellor, Lord Hailsham, offered him the chance to become a High Court judge, with a place in the House of Lords, Raymond gave the matter considerable thought before finally asking Joyce for her opinion.

"You'd be bored to tears in a week," she told him.

"No more bored than I am now."

"Your turn will come."

"Joyce, I'm nearly fifty, and all I have to show for it is the chairmanship of the Select Committee on Trade and Industry. If the party fails to win next time I may never hold office again. Don't forget that the last occasion we lost this badly we were in Opposition for thirteen years."

"Once Michael Foot has been replaced the party will take on a new look, and I bet you'll be offered one of the senior Shadow jobs."

"That'll depend on who's our next leader," said Raymond. "And I can't see a great deal of difference between Neil Kinnock who looks unbeatable, and Michael Foot – except that Kinnock's ten years younger than I am."

"Then why not stand yourself?" asked Joyce.

"It's too early for me," said Raymond.

"Then why don't you at least wait until we know who's going to be the leader of the party," said Joyce. "You can be a judge at any time – they die off just as quickly as Cabinet ministers."

When Raymond returned to his chambers the following Monday he followed Joyce's advice and let Lord Hailsham know that he was not interested in being a judge in the foreseeable future, and settled down to keep a watchful eye on Cecil Parkinson, the new Secretary of State for Trade and Industry.

Only a few days later Michael Foot announced that he would not be standing for leader when the party's annual conference took place. When he informed the Shadow Cabinet several faces lit up at the thought of the forthcoming battle at Brighton in October. Neil Kinnock and Roy Hattersley became the front runners, while during the weeks leading up to the conference several trade unionists and MPs approached Raymond and asked him to stand; but he told them all "next time".

The vote for the new leader took place on the Sunday before the conference began: as Raymond predicted Kinnock won easily and Hattersley, his closest rival, was elected as his deputy.

After the conference Raymond returned to Leeds for the weekend, still confident that he would be offered a major post in the Shadow Cabinet despite the fact he hadn't supported the winner. Having completed his morning surgery he hung around the house waiting for the new leader to call him, even missing the match against Chelsea. He didn't like being in the second division.

When Neil Kinnock eventually phoned late that evening Raymond was shocked by his offer and replied without hesitation that he was not interested. It was a short conversation.

Joyce came into the drawing-room as he sank back into his favourite armchair.

"Well, what did he offer you?" she asked, facing him.

"Transport. Virtually a demotion."

"What did you say?"

"I turned him down, of course."

"Who has he given the main jobs to?"

"I didn't ask and he didn't volunteer, but I suspect we'll only have to wait for the morning papers to find out. Not that I'm that interested," he continued, staring at the floor, "as I intend to take the first place that comes free on the bench. I've wasted too many years already."

"So have I," said Joyce quietly.

"What do you mean?" asked Raymond, looking up at his wife for the first time since she had come into the room.

"If you're going to make a complete break, I think it's time for me to do so as well."

"I don't understand," said Raymond.

"We haven't been close for a long time, Ray," said Joyce, looking straight into her husband's eyes. "If you're thinking of giving up the constituency and spending even more time in London I think we should part." She turned away.

"Is there someone else?" asked Raymond, his voice cracking.

"No one special."

"But someone?"

"There is a man who wants to marry me," said Joyce, "if that's what you mean. We were at school in Bradford together. He's an accountant now and has never married."

"But do you love him?"

Joyce considered the question. "No, I can't pretend I do. But we're good friends, he's very kind and understanding and, more important, he's there."

Raymond couldn't move.

"And the break would at least give you the chance to ask Kate Garthwaite to give up her job in New York and return to London." Raymond gasped. "Think about it and let me know what you decide." She left the room quickly so that he could not see her tears.

Raymond sat alone in the room and thought back over his years with Joyce – and Kate – and knew exactly what he wanted to do now that the whole affair was out in the open.

He caught the last train to London the same evening because he had to be in court by ten o'clock the next morning to attend a judge's summing up. In the flat that night he slept intermittently as he thought about how he would spend the rest of his new life. Before he went into court the next morning he ordered a dozen red roses via Interflora. He phoned the Attorney General. If he was going to change his life he must change it in every way.

When the summing up was over and the judge had passed sentence Raymond checked the plane schedules. Nowadays you could be there in such a short time. He booked his flight and took a taxi to Heathrow. He sat on the plane praying it wasn't too late and that too much time hadn't passed. The flight seemed endless and he took another taxi from the airport.

When he arrived at her front door she was astonished. "What are you doing here on a Monday afternoon?"

"I've come to try and win you back," said Raymond. "Christ, that sounds corny," he added.

"It's the nicest thing you've said in years," she said as he held her in his arms; over Joyce's shoulder Raymond could see the roses brightening up the drawing-room.

"Let's go and have a quiet dinner."

Over dinner Raymond told Joyce of his plans to accept the Attorney General's offer to join the bench, but only if she would agree to live in London. After a second bottle of champagne which Joyce had been reluctant to open they finally returned home.

When they arrived back a little after one the phone was

ringing. Raymond opened the door and stumbled towards it while Joyce groped for the light switch.

"Ray, I've been trying to get you all night," a lilting Welsh voice said.

"Have you now?" Raymond said thickly, trying to keep his eyes open.

"You sound as if you've been to a good party."

"I've been celebrating with my wife."

"Celebrating before you've heard the news?"

"What news?" said Raymond, collapsing into the armchair.

"I've been juggling the new team around all day and I was hoping you would agree to join the Shadow Cabinet as . . ."

Raymond sobered up very quickly and listened carefully to the new leader. "Can you hold the line?"

"Of course," said the surprised voice the other end.

"Joyce," said Raymond, as she came out of the kitchen clutching two mugs of very black coffee. "Would you agree to live with me in London if I don't become a judge?"

A broad smile spread across Joyce's face with the realisation that he was seeking her approval.

She nodded several times.

"I'd be delighted to accept," he said.

"Thank you, Raymond. Perhaps we could meet at my room in the Commons tomorrow and talk over policy in your new field."

"Yes, of course," said Raymond. "See you tomorrow." He dropped the phone on the floor and fell asleep in the chair.

Joyce replaced the phone and didn't discover until the following morning that her husband was the new Shadow Secretary of State for Social Services.

Raymond sold his flat in the Barbican, and he and Joyce moved into a small Georgian house in Cowley Street, only a few hundred yards from the House of Commons.

Raymond watched Joyce decorate his study first, then she set about the rest of the house with the energy and enthusiasm of a newly-wed. Once she had completed the guest bedroom Raymond's parents came down to spend the weekend. He burst out laughing when he greeted his father at the door clutching on to a bag, marked 'Gould, the family butcher'.

"They do have meat in London, you know," said Raymond.

"Not like mine, son," his father replied.

Over the finest beef Raymond could remember he watched Joyce and his mother chatting away. "Thank God I woke up in time," he said out loud.

"What did you say?" asked Joyce.

"Nothing, my dear, nothing."

Although Raymond spent most of his time on the overall strategy for a future Labour Government, like all politicians he had pet anomalies that particularly upset him. His had always been war widows' pensions, a preoccupation which dated back to his living with his grandmother in Leeds. He remembered the shock when he first realised shortly after leaving university that his grandmother had eked out an existence for thirty years on a weekly widow's pension that wouldn't have covered the cost of a decent meal in a London restaurant.

From the back benches, he had always pressed for the redeeming of war bonds and higher pensions for war widows. His weekly mail showed unequivocally just how major a problem war widows' pensions had become. During his years in Opposition he had worked doggedly to achieve ever-increasing, smaller rises, but he vowed that were he to become Secretary of State he would enact something more radical.

Joyce left a cutting from the *Standard* for him to read when he returned from the Commons that night. She had scribbled across it: "This could end up on the front page of every national paper."

Raymond agreed with her, and the following day he tried to press his view on to a reluctant Shadow Cabinet who seemed more concerned with the planned series of picketing by the Yorkshire miners' union than the case of Mrs Dora Benson.

Raymond researched the story carefully and discovered that the case didn't differ greatly from the many others he had looked into over the years, except for the added ingredient of a Victoria Cross. By any standards, Mrs Dora Benson highlighted Raymond's cause. She was one of the handful of surviving widows of the First World War and her husband, Private Albert Benson, had been killed at the Somme leading an attack on a German trench. Nine Germans had been killed before Albert Benson died, which was why he had been awarded the VC. His widow had continued working as a cleaner in the King's Head at Barking for over fifty years. Her only possessions of any value were her war bonds, but with no redemption date they were still passing hands at twenty-five pounds each. Mrs Benson's case might have gone unnoticed if in desperation she had not asked Sotheby's to auction her husband's medal.

Once Raymond had armed himself with all the facts he put down a question to the minister concerned asking if he would at last honour the Government's long-promised pledges in such cases. A sleepy but packed House heard Simon Kerslake, as Minister of State for Defence, reply that his department was once again considering the problem and he would make known their findings in the near future. Simon settled back on to the green benches satisfied that would pacify Gould. But Raymond's supplementary stunned him and woke up the House.

"Does the Right Honourable Gentleman realise that this eighty-four-year-old widow, whose husband was killed in action and won the Victoria Cross, has a lower income than a sixteen-year-old cadet on his first day in the armed forces?"

Simon rose once more, determined to put a stop to the issue until he had had more time to study the details of this particular case.

"I was not aware of this fact, Mr Speaker, and I can assure the Right Honourable Gentleman that I shall take into consideration all the points he has mentioned."

Simon felt confident the Speaker would now move on to the next question. But Raymond rose again, the Opposition benches spurring him on.

"Is the Right Honourable Gentleman also aware that an admiral, on an index-linked income, can hope to end his career with a pension of over £500 a week while Mrs Dora Benson's weekly income remains fixed at £47.32?"

There was a gasp even from the Conservative benches as Raymond sat down.

Simon rose again, painfully aware that he was unprepared for Gould's attack and that he had to stifle it as quickly as he could. "I was not aware of that particular comparison either, but once again I can assure the Right Honourable Gentleman I will give the case my immediate consideration."

To Simon's horror Raymond rose from the benches for yet a third time. He could see that Labour members opposite were enjoying the rare spectacle of watching him up against the ropes. "Is the Right Honourable Gentleman also aware that the annuity for a Victoria Cross is £100 with no extra pension benefits? We pay our fourth-division footballers more, while keeping Mrs Benson in the bottom league of the national income bracket."

Simon looked distinctly harassed when he in turn rose for a fourth time and made an uncharacteristic remark that he regretted the moment he said it.

"I take the Right Honourable Gentleman's point," he began, his words coming out a little too quickly. "And I am fascinated by his sudden interest in Mrs Benson. Would it be cynical of me to suggest that it has been prompted by the wide publicity this case has enjoyed in the national press?"

Raymond made no attempt to answer but sat motionless with his arms folded and his feet up on the table in front of him while his own back-benchers screamed their abuse at Simon.

The national papers the next day were covered with pictures of the arthritic Dora Benson with her bucket and mop alongside photos of her handsome young husband in private's uniform. Many of the papers went on to describe how Albert Benson had won his VC, and some of the tabloids used considerable licence. But all of them picked up Raymond's point that Mrs Benson was in the bottom one per

cent of the income bracket and that the annuity for a Victoria
Cross was a pathetic £100.

It was an enterprising and unusually thorough journalist
from the *Guardian* who led her story on a different angle which
the rest of the national press had to turn to in their second
edition. It transpired that Raymond Gould had put down
forty-seven questions concerning war widows' pension rights
during his time in the House and spoken on the subject in
three budgets and five social service debates from the back
benches. He had also made the subject the thrust of his
maiden speech over twenty years before. But when the
journalist revealed that Raymond gave £500 a year to the
Erskine Hospital for wounded soldiers every member knew
that Simon Kerslake would have to retract his attack and
make an apology to the House.

At three-thirty the Speaker rose from his chair and told a
packed house that the Minister of State for Defence wished to
make a personal statement.

Simon Kerslake rose warily from the front bench and stood
nervously at the dispatch box.

"Mr Speaker," he began. "With your permission and that
of the House I would like to make a personal statement.
During a question put to me yesterday I impugned the
integrity of the Right Honourable Gentleman, the member
for Leeds North. It has since been brought to my attention
that I did him a gross injustice and I offer the House my
sincere apologies, and the Right Honourable Gentleman
the assurances that I will not question his integrity a third
time."

While younger members were puzzled by the reference,
Raymond smiled to himself.

Aware of how rare personal statements were in anyone's
parliamentary career, members looked on eagerly to see how
he would respond.

He moved slowly to the dispatch box.

"Mr Speaker, I accept the gracious manner in which the
Right Honourable Gentleman has apologised and hope that
he will not lose sight of the greater issue, namely that of war

widows' benefits, and in particular the plight of Mrs Dora Benson."

Simon looked relieved and nodded courteously.

Many Opposition members told Raymond he should have gone for Simon when he had him on the run, while Tom Carson continued shouting at Simon long after the House had proceeded to the next business. *The Times* leader writer proved them wrong when he wrote the next morning: "In an age of militant demands from the left, Parliament and the Labour party have found a new Clement Attlee on their front bench. Britain need have no fear for human dignity or the rights of man should Raymond Gould ever accede to the high office which that gentleman held."

When Raymond returned home from the Commons that night he found Joyce had cut out all the press comments for him to study and had also somehow managed to make inroads into his overflowing correspondence.

Joyce turned out to have a better feel for gut politics than the entire Shadow Cabinet put together.

Alec Pimkin threw a party for all his Tory colleagues who had entered the House in 1964, "To celebrate the first twenty years in the Commons," as he described the occasion in an impromptu after-dinner speech.

Over brandy and cigars the corpulent, balding figure sat back and surveyed his fellow members. Many had fallen by the wayside over the years, but of those that were left, he believed only two men now dominated the intake.

Pimkin's eyes first settled on his old friend Charles Seymour. Despite studying him closely he was still unable to spot a grey hair on the Treasury minister's head. From time to time Pimkin still saw Amanda, who had returned to being a full-time model and was rarely to be found in England nowadays. Charles, he suspected, saw more of her on the covers of magazines than he ever did in his home at Eaton Square. Pimkin had been surprised by how much time Charles was willing to put aside for little Harry. Charles was the last man he would have suspected of ending up a doting father. Certainly there was no sign of his ambitions diminishing, and Pimkin suspected that only one man remained a worthy rival for the party leadership.

His eyes moved on to someone for whom in 1984 Orwell's big brother seemed to hold no fears. Simon Kerslake was deep in animated conversation about his work on the proposed disarmament talks between Thatcher, Gorbachov and Reagan. Pimkin studied the Defence minister intently. He considered that had *he* been graced with such looks he would not have had to fear for his dwindling majority. Rumours of some financial crisis had long since died away, and Kerslake now seemed well set for a formidable future.

The party began to break up, as one by one his contemporaries came over to thank him for such a 'splendid', 'memorable', 'worthwhile' evening. When the last one had departed and Pimkin found himself alone he drained the drop of brandy that remained in his balloon and stubbed out the dying cigar. He sighed as he speculated on the fact that he could now never hope to be made a minister. He therefore determined to become a kingmaker, for in another twenty years there would be nothing left on which to speculate.

Raymond celebrated his twenty years in the House by taking Joyce to the Guinea Restaurant off Berkeley Square for dinner. He admired the long burgundy dress his wife had chosen for the occasion and even noticed that one or two women gave it more than a casual glance throughout their meal.

He too reflected on his twenty years in the Commons, and he told Joyce over a brandy that he hoped he would spend more of the next twenty years in Government. 1984 had not turned out to be a good year for the Conservatives, and Raymond was already forming plans to make 1985 as uncomfortable for the Government as possible.

A few weeks later Tony Benn, who had lost his seat at the general election, returned to the House of Commons as the member for Chesterfield. The Conservatives came a poor third and went on to lose two more by-elections early in 1985. Even the press began to acknowledge that the Labour party was once again looking like a serious alternative Government.

The winter of 1985 brought a further rise in the unemployment figures which only increased the Labour party's lead in the polls. And then after the resignation of two cabinet ministers over a small helicopter company in the West Country and the loss of two further by-elections, the Conservatives fell into third place for the first time in five years.

A drop in the price of oil from $22 to $10 a barrel in the space of six weeks did not help the Chancellor's budget judgement. After a long, hot summer Mrs Thatcher decided on a further cabinet reshuffle bringing in those who would be formulating policy in the run-up to the general election. The average age of the cabinet fell by seven years and the press dubbed it, 'Mrs Thatcher's new lamps for old reshuffle'.

CHAPTER
THIRTY

Andrew was on his way to the House of Commons when he heard the first reports on his car radio. There had been no mention of the news in the morning papers so it must have happened overnight. It began with a news flash: just the bare details. HMS *Broadsword*, one of the Navy's destroyers, had been passing through the Gulf of Surt between Tunis and Benghazi when she was boarded by a group of mercenaries, posing as coastguard officials, who took over the ship in the name of Colonel Gaddafi. The newscaster went on to say that there would be a more detailed report in their ten o'clock bulletin.

Andrew had reached his room in the House of Commons by nine-thirty, and he immediately phoned the SDP leader David Owen to discuss the political implications of the news. Once a course of action had been agreed on Andrew took a handwritten letter round to the Speaker's office before the noon deadline, requesting an emergency debate following question time that afternoon. He also sent a copy of the letter by messenger to the Foreign Secretary and the Secretary of State for Defence.

By staying near a radio most of the morning Andrew was able to learn that HMS *Broadsword* was now in the hands of over a hundred guerillas. They were demanding the freedom of all Libyan prisoners in British jails in exchange for the 217-strong crew of the *Broadsword*, who were being held hostage in the engine room.

By twelve o'clock the ticker-tape machine in the Members' Corridor was hovered over by craning necks, and the dining-rooms were so full that many members had to go without lunch.

Question time that day had been allocated to Welsh Affairs, so the Chamber itself did not start filling up until nearly three-fifteen although the Palace of Westminster was already packed and buzzing with each new snippet of information. Political correspondents waited hawk-like in the Members' Lobby seeking opinions on the crisis from any senior politicians as they passed to and from the Chamber. Few were rash enough to say anything that might be reinterpreted the next day.

When Andrew came into the Chamber he took his seat next to David Owen on the Opposition front bench below the gangway. Since Andrew had the overall responsibility for the Alliance Defence portfolio he was expected to represent the other twenty-two Alliance members. At three-twenty-seven the Prime Minister, followed by the Foreign Secretary and the Secretary of State for Defence, filed into the House and took their places on the Treasury bench. All three looked suitably sombre. The last two questions on Welsh Affairs had the largest audience of members since the Aberfan disaster of 1966.

At three-thirty Mr Speaker Weatherill rose and called for order.

"Statements to the House," he announced in his crisp, military style. "There will be two statements on HMS *Broadsword* before the House debates Welsh Affairs." The Speaker then called the Secretary of State for Defence.

Simon Kerslake rose from the front bench and placed a prepared statement on the dispatch box in front of him.

"Mr Speaker, with your permission and that of the House, I would like to make a statement concerning Her Majesty's frigate *Broadsword*. At seven-forty GMT this morning HMS *Broadsword* was passing through the Gulf of Surt between Tunis and Benghazi when a group of guerillas, posing as official coastguards, boarded the ship and seized the officer in command, Captain Lawrence Packard, and placed the crew under arrest. The captain and his company did everything possible to resist but were outnumbered three to one. The guerillas, claiming to represent the People's Liberation Army, have since placed Captain Packard and the crew in the engine room of the ship. As far as it is possible to ascertain from our Embassy in Tripoli no lives have been lost, although Captain Packard sustained severe injuries during the battle, and we cannot be certain of his fate. There is no suggestion that *Broadsword* was doing anything other than going about her lawful business. This barbaric act must be looked upon as piracy under the 1958 Geneva Convention on the High Seas. The guerillas are demanding the release of all Libyan prisoners in British prisons in exchange for the return of HMS *Broadsword* and her crew. My Right Honourable friend, the Home Secretary, informs me there are only nine known Libyans in British jails at the present time, two of whom have been sentenced to three months for persistent shoplifting, two who were convicted on more serious drug charges, and the five who tried to hijack a British Airways 747 last year. Her Majesty's Government cannot and will not interfere with the due process of law and has no intention of releasing any of these men."

Loud "Hear, hears," came from all sections of the House.

"My Right Honourable friend, the Foreign Secretary, has made Her Majesty's Government's position clear to the Libyan Ambassador, in particular that Her Majesty's Government cannot be expected to tolerate this sort of treatment of British subjects or of British property. We have demanded and expect immediate action from the Libyan Government."

Simon sat down to loud and prolonged cheers before the leader of the Opposition rose from his place to say that he would wish it to be known that the Opposition gave the Government their full backing. He asked if any plans had been formulated at this early stage for the recovery of *Broadsword*.

Simon rose again. "We are, Mr Speaker, at present seeking a diplomatic solution, but I have already chaired a meeting of the Joint Chiefs and I anticipate making a further statement to the House tomorrow."

"Mr Andrew Fraser," said the Speaker.

Andrew rose from his place. "May I inform the Right

Honourable Gentleman that we in the Alliance also concur with his views that this is an act of piracy. But can he tell the House how long he will allow negotiations to continue when it is well known throughout the diplomatic world that Gaddafi is a master of procrastination, especially if we were to rely on the United Nations to adjudicate on this issue?" From the noise that greeted Andrew's question it seemed that his views were shared by the majority of the House.

Simon rose to answer the question. "I accept the point the Honourable Gentleman is making but he will know, having been a Minister of State for Defence himself, that I am not in a position to divulge any information which might imperil the safety of *Broadsword*."

Question after question came at Simon. He handled them with such confidence that visitors to the Strangers' Gallery would have found it hard to believe that he had been invited to join the Cabinet only five weeks before.

At four-fifteen, after Simon had answered the last question the Speaker was going to allow, he sank back on the front bench to listen to the statement from the Foreign Office. The House fell silent once again as the Foreign Secretary rose from his place and checked the large double-spaced sheets in front of him. All eyes were now on the tall, elegant man who was making his first official statement since his appointment.

"Mr Speaker, with your permission and that of the House, I too would like to make a statement concerning HMS *Broadsword*. Once news had reached the Foreign Office this morning of the plight of Her Majesty's ship *Broadsword* my office immediately issued a strongly worded statement to the Government of Libya. The Libyan Ambassador has been called to the Foreign Office and I shall be seeing him again immediately this statement and the questions arising from it has been completed."

Raymond looked up at the Strangers' Gallery from his place on the Opposition front bench. It was one of the ironies of modern diplomacy that the Libyan Ambassador was sitting in the gallery making notes while the Foreign Secretary delivered his statement. He couldn't imagine Colonel Gaddafi inviting the British Ambassador to take notes while he sat in his tent addressing his followers. Raymond was pleased to see an attendant ask the ambassador to stop writing; the prohibition dated from the time when the House had jealously guarded its privacy. Raymond's eyes dropped back to the front bench, and he continued to listen to Charles Seymour.

"Our ambassador to the United Nations has tabled a resolution to be debated by the General Assembly this afternoon, asking representatives to back Britain against this flagrant violation of the 1958 Geneva Convention on the High Seas. I confidently expect the support of the free world over this act of piracy against Her Majesty's ship *Broadsword*. Her Majesty's Government will do everything in its power to ensure a diplomatic solution bearing in mind that the lives of 217 British servicemen are still at risk."

The leader of the Opposition rose for a second time and asked at what point the Foreign Secretary would consider once again breaking off diplomatic relations with Libya.

"I naturally hope it will not come to that, Mr Speaker, and I expect the Libyan Government to deal quickly with their own mercenaries."

Charles continued to answer questions from all sections of the House but could only repeat that there was little new intelligence to offer the House at the present time. Raymond watched his two contemporaries as they displayed over twenty years of parliamentary skill in presenting their case. He wondered if this episode would make one of them Mrs Thatcher's obvious successor.

At four-thirty, the Speaker, realising nothing original had been said for some time, announced that he would allow one further question from each side before returning to the business of the day. He shrewdly called Alec Pimkin who sounded to Raymond like 'the very model of a modern major-general' and then Tom Carson who suggested that Colonel Gaddafi was often grossly misrepresented by the British press. Once Carson had sat down, Mr Speaker found it easy to move on to other business.

The Speaker rose again and thanked the Honourable Gentleman, the member for Edinburgh Carlton, for his courtesy in informing him that he would be making an application under standing order number ten for an emergency debate. The Speaker said he had given the matter careful thought but he reminded the House that, under the terms of the standing order, he did not need to divulge the reasons for his decision, merely decide whether the matter should have precedence over the orders of the day. He ruled that the matter was not proper for discussion within the terms of standing order number ten.

Andrew rose to protest but as the Speaker remained standing he had to resume his seat.

"This does not mean, however," continued Mr Speaker, "that I would not reconsider such a request at a later date."

Andrew realised that Charles Seymour and Simon Kerslake must have pleaded for more time, but he was only going to allow them twenty-four hours. The clerk at the table rose and bellowed above the noise of members leaving the Chamber, "Adjournment." The Speaker called the Secretary of State for Wales to move the adjournment motion on the problems facing the Welsh mining industry. The Chamber emptied of all but the thirty-eight Welsh MPs who had been waiting weeks for a full debate on the Principality's affairs.

Andrew went straight to his office and tried to piece together the latest information from news bulletins before preparing himself for a full debate the following day. Simon made his way back to the Ministry of Defence to continue discussions with the Joint Chiefs of Staff, while Charles was driven quickly to the Foreign Office.

When Charles reached his room, he was told by the Permanent Under-Secretary that the Libyan Ambassador awaited him.

"Does he have anything new to tell us?" asked Charles.

"Frankly, nothing; it seems that we're not the only people who are unable to make any contact with Colonel Gaddafi."

"Send him in then."

Charles stubbed out his cigarette and stood by the mantelpiece below a portrait of Palmerston. Charles had never met the ambassador before, largely because he had taken over at the Foreign Office only five weeks previously.

When Mr Kadir, the five-foot-one, dark-haired, immaculately dressed Ambassador for Libya entered the room, the office resembled nothing so much as a study in which a headmaster was about to tick off an unruly boy from the lower fifth.

Charles was momentarily taken aback when he noticed the ambassador's old Etonian tie. He recovered quickly.

"Foreign Secretary?" began Mr Kadir.

"Her Majesty's Government wishes to make it abundantly clear to your Government," began Charles, not allowing the ambassador to complete his sentiments, "that we consider the act of boarding and holding Her Majesty's ship *Broadsword* against her will as one of piracy on the high seas."

"May I say –?" began Mr Kadir.

"No, you may not," said Charles, "and until our ship has been released, we shall do everything in our power to bring pressure, both diplomatic and economic, on your Government."

"But may I just say –?" Mr Kadir tried again.

"My Prime Minister also wants you to know that she wishes to speak to your Head of State at the soonest possible opportunity, so I shall expect to hear back from you within the hour."

"Yes, Foreign Secretary, but may I –"

"And you may further report that we will reserve our right to take any action we deem appropriate if you fail to secure the release into safe custody of HMS *Broadsword* and her crew by twelve noon tomorrow, GMT. Do I make myself clear?"

"Yes, Foreign Secretary, but I would like to ask –"

"Good day, Mr Kadir."

After the Libyan Ambassador was shown out Charles couldn't help wondering what it was he had wanted to know.

"What do we do now?" he asked when the Permanent Under-Secretary returned, having deposited Mr Kadir in the lift.

"We act out the oldest diplomatic game in the world."

"What do you mean?" said Charles.

"Our sit-and-wait policy. We're awfully good at it," said

the Permanent Under-Secretary, "but then we've been at it for nearly a thousand years."

"Well, while we sit let's at least make some phone calls. I'll start with Secretary of State Kirkpatrick in Washington and then I'd like to speak to Gromyko in Moscow."

When Simon arrived back at the Ministry of Defence from the Commons he was told that the Joint Chiefs were assembled in his office waiting for him to chair the next strategy meeting. As he entered the room to take his place at the head of the table the Joint Chiefs rose.

"Good afternoon, gentlemen," Simon said. "Please be seated. Can you bring me up to date on the latest situation, Sir John?"

Admiral Sir John Fieldhouse, Chief of the Defence Staff, pushed up the half-moon glasses from the end of his nose and checked the notes in front of him.

"Very little has changed in the last hour, sir," he began. "The Prime Minister's office has still had no success in contacting Colonel Gaddafi. I fear we must now treat the capture of *Broadsword* as a blatant act of terrorism, rather similar to the occupation seven years ago of the American Embassy in Iran by students who backed the late Ayatollah Khomeini. In such circumstances we can either 'jaw-jaw or war-war', to quote Churchill. With that in mind, this committee will have formed a detailed plan by the early evening for the recapture of HMS *Broadsword*, as we assume the Foreign Office are better qualified to prepare for jaw-jaw." Sir John replaced his glasses and looked towards his minister.

"Are you in a position to give me a provisional plan which I could place in front of the Cabinet for their consideration?"

"Certainly, Minister," said Sir John, removing his glasses again before opening a large blue file in front of him.

Simon listened intently as Sir John went over his provisional strategy. Around the table sat eight of the senior-ranking staff officers of the Army, Navy and Air Force, and even the first draft plan bore the stamp of their 300 years of military experience. He couldn't help remembering that his call-up status was still that of a Second Lieutenant. For an hour he asked the Joint Chiefs questions that ranged from the elementary to ones that demonstrated a clear insight into their problems. By the time Simon left the room to attend the Cabinet meeting at No. 10 the Joint Chiefs were already up-dating their plan.

Simon walked slowly across Whitehall from the Department of Defence to Downing Street, his private detective by his side. Downing Street was thronged with people curious to see the comings and goings of ministers involved in the crisis. Simon was touched that the crowd applauded him all the way to the front door of No. 10, where the journalists and TV crews awaited each arrival. The great television arc lights were switched on as he reached the door and a microphone was thrust in front of him, but he made no comment. Simon was surprised by how many of the normally cynical journalists called out, "Good luck" and "Bring our boys home."

The front door opened and he went straight through to the corridor outside the Cabinet room, where twenty-two of his colleagues were already waiting. A moment later the Prime Minister walked into the Cabinet room and took her seat in the centre of the table with Charles and Simon opposite her.

Mrs Thatcher began by telling her colleagues that she had been unable to make any contact with Colonel Gaddafi and that they must therefore decide on a course of action that did not involve his acquiescence. She invited the Foreign Secretary to brief the Cabinet first.

Charles went over the actions in which the Foreign Office was involved at the diplomatic level. He reported his meeting with Ambassador Kadir, and the resolution which had been tabled at the UN and was already being debated at an emergency session of the General Assembly. The purpose of asking the United Nations to back Britain on Resolution 12/40, he said, was to gain the diplomatic initiative and virtually guarantee international sympathy. Charles went on to tell the Cabinet that he expected a vote to take place in the General Assembly in New York that evening which would demonstrate overwhelming support for the United Kingdom's resolution, and which would be regarded as a moral victory by the whole world. He was delighted to be able to report to the Cabinet that the Foreign Ministers of both the United States and Russia had agreed to back the UK in her diplomatic endeavours as long as she launched no retaliatory action. Charles ended by reminding his colleagues of the importance of treating the whole affair as an act of piracy, rather than an injury at the hands of the Libyan Government itself.

A legal nicety, thought Simon as he watched the faces of his colleagues round the table. They were obviously impressed that Charles had brought the two super powers together in support of Britain. The Prime Minister's face remained inscrutable. She called upon Simon to air his views.

He was able to report that *Broadsword* had, since the last meeting of the Cabinet, been towed into the Bay of Surt and moored; there was no hope of boarding her except by sea. Captain Packard and his crew of 216 remained under close arrest in the engine room on the lower deck of the ship. From confirmed reports Simon had received in the last hour it appeared that the ship's company were bound, gagged and that the ventilation systems had been turned off. "Captain Packard," he informed the House, "had refused to co-operate with the guerillas in any way, and we remain unsure of his fate." He paused. "I therefore suggest," Simon continued, "that we have no choice but to mount a rescue operation in order to avoid a protracted negotiation that can only end in grave loss of morale for the entire armed forces. The longer we put off such a decision the harder our task will become. The Joint Chiefs are putting the final touches to a plan code-named 'Shoplifter' which they feel must be carried out in the next forty-eight hours, if the men and the ship are to be saved." Simon added that he hoped diplomatic channels would be kept open while the operation was being worked out, in order that the rescue team could be assured of the greatest element of surprise.

"But what if your plan fails?" interrupted Charles. "We would risk losing not only *Broadsword* and her crew but also the goodwill of the free world."

"There is no serving officer in the British Navy who will

thank us for leaving *Broadsword* in Libyan waters while we negotiate a settlement in which, at best, our ship will be returned when it suits the guerillas – to say nothing of the humiliation of our Navy. Gaddafi can laugh at the United Nations while he has captured not only one of our most modern frigates but also the headlines of the world's press. As Ayatollah Khomeini did, he will want to keep them both for as long as he can. These headlines can only demoralise our countrymen and invite the sort of election defeat Carter suffered at the hands of the American people after the Iranian Embassy débâcle."

"We would be foolish to take such an unnecessary risk while we have world opinion on our side," protested Charles. "Let us at least wait a few more days."

"I fear that if we wait," said Simon, "the crew will be transferred from the ship to a military prison, which would only result in our having two targets to concentrate on, and then Gaddafi can sit around in the desert taking whatever amount of time suits him."

Simon and Charles weighed argument against counter-argument while the Prime Minister listened, taking note of the views of her other colleagues round the table to see if she had a majority for one course or the other. Three hours later, when everyone had given his opinion, she had 'fourteen-nine' written on the pad in front of her.

"I think we have exhausted the arguments, gentlemen," she said, "and having listened to the collective views around this table I feel we must on balance allow the Secretary of State for Defence to proceed with Operation Shoplifter. I therefore propose that the Foreign Secretary, the Defence Secretary, the Attorney General and myself make up a sub-committee, backed up by a professional staff, to consider the Joint Chiefs' plan. The utmost secrecy will be required from us at all times, so the subject will not be raised again until the plan is ready for presentation to a full meeting of the Cabinet. Therefore, with the exception of the sub-committee, all ministers will return to their departments and carry on with their normal duties. We must not lose sight of the fact that the country still has to be governed. Thank you, gentlemen." The Prime Minister asked Charles and Simon to join her in the study.

As soon as the door was closed she said to Charles, "Please let me know the moment you hear the result of the vote in the General Assembly. Now that the Cabinet has favoured a military initiative, it is important that you are seen to be pressing for a diplomatic solution."

"Yes, Prime Minister," said Charles without emotion.

Mrs Thatcher then turned to Simon. "When can I have a run-down on the details of the Joint Chiefs' plan?"

"We anticipate working on the strategy through the night, Prime Minister, and I should be able to make a full presentation to you by ten tomorrow."

"No later, Simon," said the Prime Minister. "Now our next problem is tomorrow's proposed emergency debate. Andrew Fraser will undoubtedly put in a second request for a full debate under standing order number ten and the Speaker gave a clear hint today he will allow it. Anyway, we can't avoid making a policy statement without an outcry from the Opposition benches – and I suspect our own – so I've de-cided that we will grasp the nettle and no doubt get stung."

The two men looked at each other, exasperated at the thought of having to waste precious hours in the Commons.

"Charles, you must be prepared to open the debate for the Government, and Simon, you will wind up. At least the debate will be on Thursday afternoon; that way some of our colleagues may have gone home for the weekend, though frankly I doubt it. But with any luck we will have secured a moral victory at the United Nations, and we can keep the Opposition minds concentrating on that. When you sum up, Simon, just answer the questions put during the debate without offering any new initiative."

She then added, "Report any news you hear direct to me. I shan't be sleeping tonight."

Charles walked back to the Foreign Office, at least thank-ful that Amanda was somewhere in South America.

Simon returned to the Joint Chiefs to find a large map of Libyan territorial waters pinned to a blackboard. Generals, admirals and air marshals were studying the contours and ocean depths like children preparing for a geography test.

They all stood again when Simon entered the room. They looked at him in anticipation, men of action who were suspicious of talk. When Simon told them the Cabinet's decision was to back the Ministry of Defence the suggestion of a smile came over the face of Sir John. "Perhaps that battle will turn out to be our hardest," he said, just loud enough for everyone to hear.

"Take me through the plan again," said Simon, ignoring Sir John's comment. "I have to present it to the Prime Minister by ten o'clock tomorrow."

Sir John placed the tip of a long wooden pointer on a model of HMS *Broadsword* in the middle of a stretch of water in a well-protected bay.

When Charles reached his office the international telegrams and telexes of support for a diplomatic solution were piled high on his desk. The Permanent Under-Secretary reported that the debate in the United Nations had been so one-sided that he anticipated an overwhelming majority when they came to vote. Charles feared his hands were tied; he had to be seen to go through the motions, even by his own staff, although he had not yet given up hopes of undermining Simon's plan. He intended the whole episode to end up as a triumph for the Foreign Office and not for 'those war-mongers' at the Ministry of Defence. After consulting the Permanent Under-Secretary Charles appointed a small Libyan task force consisting of some older Foreign Office mandarins with experience of Gaddafi and four of the department's most promising high fliers.

Mr Oliver Miles, the former Ambassador to Libya, had his leave cancelled and was deposited in a tiny room in the upper reaches of the Foreign Office so that Charles could call on his local knowledge at any time, day or night, throughout the crisis.

Charles asked the Permanent Under-Secretary to link him up with Britain's ambassador at the United Nations.

"And keep trying to raise Gaddafi."

Simon listened to Sir John go over the latest version of
Operation Shoplifter. Thirty-seven men from the crack
Special Boat Service, the Marine equivalent of the SAS
regiment which had been involved in the St James's Square
siege in April 1984, were now in Rosyth on the Scottish coast,
preparing to board HMS *Brilliant*, the sister ship to *Broadsword*.

The men were to be dropped from a submarine a mile
outside Rosyth harbour and to swim the last mile and a half
under water until they reached the ship. They would then
board *Brilliant* and expect to recapture her from a mock
Libyan crew in an estimated twelve minutes. *Brilliant* would
then be sailed to a distance of one nautical mile off the
Scottish coast. The operation was to be completed in sixty-
five minutes. The SBS planned to rehearse the procedure on
Brilliant three times before first light the following morning,
when they hoped to have the entire exercise down to one
hour.

Simon had already confirmed the order to send two submarines from the Mediterranean full steam in the direction of
the Libyan coast. The rest of the fleet was to be seen to be
conspicuously going about its normal business while the
Foreign Office appeared to be searching for a diplomatic
solution.

Simon's request to the Joint Chiefs came as no surprise
and was granted immediately. He phoned Elizabeth to
explain why he wouldn't be home that night. An hour later
the Secretary of State for Defence was strapped into a
helicopter and on his way to Rosyth.

Charles followed the proceedings at the United Nations live
in his office on a satellite link-up. At the end of a brief debate
a vote was called for. The Secretary General announced
147–3 in Great Britain's favour, with twenty-two absten-
tions. Charles wondered if such an overwhelming vote would
be enough to get the Prime Minister to change her mind over
Kerslake's plan. He checked over the voting list carefully.
The Russians, along with the Warsaw Pact countries and the
Americans, had kept their word and voted with the UK.

Only Libya, South Yemen and Djibouti had voted against. Charles was put through to Downing Street and passed on the news. The Prime Minister, although delighted with the diplomatic triumph, refused to change course until she had heard from Gaddafi. Charles put the phone down and asked his Permanent Under-Secretary to call Ambassador Kadir to the Foreign Office once more.

"But it's two o'clock in the morning, Foreign Secretary."

"I am quite aware what time it is but I can see no reason why, when we are all awake, he should be having a peaceful night's sleep."

When Mr Kadir was shown into his room it annoyed Charles to see the little man still looking fresh and dapper. It was obvious that he had just shaved and put on a clean shirt.

"You called for me, Foreign Secretary?" asked Mr Kadir politely, as if he had been invited to afternoon tea.

"Yes," said Charles. "We wished to be certain that you are aware of the vote taken at the United Nations an hour ago supporting the United Kingdom's Resolution 12/40."

"Yes, Foreign Secretary."

"In which your Government was condemned by the leaders of ninety per cent of the people on the globe" – a fact the Permanent Under-Secretary had fed to Charles a few minutes before Mr Kadir had arrived.

"Yes, Foreign Secretary."

"My Prime Minister is still waiting to hear from your Head of State."

"Yes, Foreign Secretary."

"Have you yet made contact with Colonel Gaddafi?"

"No, Foreign Secretary."

"But you have a direct telephone link to his head-quarters."

"Then you will be only too aware, Foreign Secretary, that I have been unable to speak to him," said Mr Kadir with a wry smile.

Charles saw the Permanent Under-Secretary lower his eyes. "I shall speak to you on the hour every hour, Mr Kadir, but do not press my country's hospitality too far."

"No, Foreign Secretary."

"Good night, Ambassador," said Charles.

"Good night, Foreign Secretary."

Kadir turned and left the Foreign Office to be driven back to his Embassy. He cursed the Right Honourable Charles Seymour. Didn't the man realise that he hadn't been back to Libya, except to visit his mother, since the age of four? Colonel Gaddafi was ignoring his ambassador every bit as much as he was the British Prime Minister. He checked his watch: it was two forty-four.

Simon's helicopter landed in Scotland at two forty-five. He and Sir John were immediately driven to the dockside, then ferried out to HMS *Brilliant* through the misty night.

"The first Secretary of State not to be piped on board in living memory," said Sir John as Simon made his way with difficulty, his blackthorn stick tapping up the gangplank. The captain of the *Brilliant* couldn't disguise his surprise when he saw his uninvited guests and took them quickly to the bridge. Sir John whispered something in the captain's ear which Simon missed.

"When is the next raid due?" asked Simon, staring out from the bridge but unable to see more than a few yards in front of him.

"They leave the sub at 0300, sir," said the captain, "and should reach *Brilliant* at approximately three-twenty. They hope to have taken command of the ship in eleven minutes and be a mile beyond territorial waters in under the hour."

Simon checked his watch: it was five to three. He thought of the SBS preparing for their task, unaware that the Secretary of State and the Chief of the Defence Staff were on board *Brilliant* waiting for them. He pulled his coat collar up.

Suddenly he was thrown to the deck, a black and oily hand clamped over his mouth before he could protest. He felt his arms whipped up and tied behind his back as his eyes were blindfolded and he was gagged. He tried to retaliate and received a sharp elbow in the ribs. Then he was dragged down a narrow staircase and dumped on to a wooden floor. He lay trussed up like a chicken for what he thought was about ten minutes before he heard the ship's engines revving up and felt the movement of the ship below him. The Secretary of State could not move for another fifteen minutes.

"Release them," Simon heard a voice say in distinctly Oxford English. The rope around his arms was untied and the blindfold and gag removed. Standing over the Secretary of State was an SBS frogman, black from head to toe, his white teeth gleaming. Simon was still slightly stunned as he turned to see the Services Chief also being untied.

"I must apologise, Minister," said Sir John, as soon as his gag was removed, "but I told the captain not to inform the submarine commander we were on board. If I am going to risk 217 of my men's lives I wanted to be sure this rabble from the SBS knew what they were up to." Simon backed away from the six-foot-two giant who towered over him, still grinning.

"Good thing we didn't bring the Prime Minister along for the ride," said Sir John.

"I agree," said Simon, looking up at the SBS commando. "She would have broken his neck." Everyone laughed except the frogman who pursed his lips.

"What's wrong with him?" said Simon.

"If he utters the slightest sound during the first sixty minutes he has no hope of being selected for the final team."

"The Conservative party could do with some back-bench Members of Parliament like that," said Simon, "especially when I have to address the House tomorrow and explain why I'm doing nothing."

By three-forty-nine *Brilliant* was a mile beyond territorial waters. The newspaper headlines that morning ranged from 'Diplomatic Victory' in *The Times* to 'Gaddafi the Pirate' in the *Mirror*.

At a meeting of the inner Cabinet held at ten in the morning Simon reported his first-hand experience of Shop-lifter to the Prime Minister. Charles was quick to follow him. "But after the overwhelming vote in our favour at the UN it must be sensible for us to postpone anything that might be construed as an outright act of aggression."

"If the SBS don't go tomorrow morning we will have to

wait another month, Prime Minister," said Simon, interrupting him. All eyes at the meeting of the inner Cabinet turned to Kerslake.

"Why?" asked Mrs Thatcher.

"Because Ramadan, when Moslems fast and cannot take drink during daylight hours, will be coming to an end tomorrow. Traditionally the heaviest eating and drinking takes place the following day, which means tomorrow night will be our best chance to catch the guerillas off guard. I have been over the entire operation in Rosyth and by now the SBS are well on their way to the submarines and preparing for the assault. It's all so finely tuned, Prime Minister, that obviously we can't throw away such a strategic advantage."

"That's good reasoning," she concurred. "With the weekend ahead of us we must pray that this mess will be all over by Monday morning. Let's put on our negotiating faces for the Commons this afternoon. I expect a very convincing performance from you, Charles."

When Andrew rose at three-thirty that Thursday afternoon to ask for a second time for an emergency debate under standing order number ten the Speaker granted his request, directing that the urgency of the matter warranted a debate to commence at seven o'clock that evening.

The Chamber emptied quickly as the members scuttled off to prepare their speeches, although they all knew that less than two per cent of them could hope to be called. The Speaker departed the Chamber and did not return until five to seven when he took over the chair from his deputy.

By seven o'clock, when Charles and Simon had entered the House, all thirty-seven SBS men were aboard Her Majesty's submarine *Conqueror*, lying on the ocean bed about sixty nautical miles off the Libyan coast. A second submarine, *Courageous*, was ten miles to her rear. Neither had broken radio silence for the past twelve hours.

The Prime Minister had still not heard from Colonel Gaddafi and they were now only eight hours away from Operation Shoplifter. Simon looked around him. The atmosphere resembled Budget Day and an eerie silence fell as the Speaker called Andrew Fraser to address the House.

He began by explaining, under standing order number ten, why the matter he had raised was specific, important and needed urgent consideration. He quickly moved on to demand that the Foreign Secretary confirm that if negotiations with Gaddafi failed or dragged on the Secretary of State for Defence would not hesitate to take the necessary action to recover HMS *Broadsword*. Simon sat on the front bench looking glum and shaking his head.

"Gaddafi's nothing more than a pirate," said Andrew. "Why talk of diplomatic solutions?"

The House cheered as each well-rehearsed phrase rolled off Andrew's tongue. When he sat down the cheers came from all parts of the Chamber and it was several minutes before the Speaker could bring the House back to order. Mr Kadir sat in the distinguished Strangers' Gallery staring impassively down, trying to memorise the salient points that had been made and the House's reaction to them, so that – if he were ever given the chance – he could pass them on to Colonel Gaddafi.

"The Foreign Secretary," called the Speaker and Charles rose from his place on the Treasury bench. He placed his speech on the dispatch box in front of him and waited. Once again the House fell silent.

Charles opened his case by emphasising the significance of the United Nations' vote as the foundation for a genuine negotiated settlement. He went on to say that his first priority was to secure the lives of the 217 men on board HMS *Broadsword* and that he intended to work tirelessly to that end. The Secretary General was hoping to contact Gaddafi personally and brief him on the strong feelings of his colleagues in the General Assembly. Charles stressed that taking any other course at the present time could only lose the support and goodwill of the free world. When Charles sat down he realised that the rowdy House was not convinced.

The contribution from the back benches confirmed the Prime Minister's and Simon's beliefs that they had gauged the feelings of the nation correctly, but neither of them allowed the slightest show of emotion to cross their faces and give hope to those who were demanding military action.

By the time Simon rose to wind up for the Government at nine-thirty that night he had spent two and a half hours in the Chamber listening to men and women tell him to get on with exactly what he was already doing. Blandly, he backed the Foreign Secretary in his pursuit of a diplomatic solution. The House became restive, and when the clock reached ten Simon sat down to cries of "Resign" from some of his own colleagues and the more right-wing of the Labour benches.

Andrew watched carefully as Kerslake and Seymour left the Chamber. He wondered what was really going on in his old department.

He arrived home after the debate. Louise congratulated him on his speech and added, "But it didn't evoke much of a response from Simon Kerslake."

"He's up to something," said Andrew. "I only wish I was sitting in his office tonight and could find out what it is."

When Simon arrived in that office he phoned Elizabeth and explained that he would be spending another night at the ministry.

"Some women do lose their men to the strangest mistresses," said Elizabeth. "By the way, your younger son wants to know if you will have time to watch him play hockey in his cuppers' match at Oxford on Saturday."

"What's today?"

"It's still Thursday," she said, "and you're the one in charge of the nation's defences."

Simon knew the rescue attempt would be all over one way or the other by lunchtime the next day. Why shouldn't he watch his son play hockey?

"Tell him I'll be there," he said.

Although nothing could be achieved between midnight and six o'clock now the submarines were in place, none of the Joint Chiefs left the operations room. Radio silence was not broken once through the night as Simon tried to occupy himself with the bulging red boxes containing other pressing matters which still demanded his attention. He took advantage of the presence of the Joint Chiefs and had a hundred queries answered in minutes that would normally have taken him a month.

At midnight the first editions of the morning papers were brought to him. Simon pinned up the *Telegraph*'s headline on the operations board. 'Kerslake's in his Hammock till the great Armada comes.' The article demanded to know how the hero of Northern Ireland could be so indecisive while our sailors lay bound and gagged in foreign waters, and ended with the words 'Captain, art thou sleeping there below?' "Not a wink," muttered Simon. 'Resign' was the single-word headline in the *Daily Express*. Sir John looked over the minister's shoulder and read the opening paragraph.

"I shall never understand why anyone wants to be a politician," he said before reporting: "We have just heard from reconnaissance in the area that both submarines *Conqueror* and *Courageous* have moved up into place."

Simon picked up his stick from the side of his desk and left the Joint Chiefs to go to Downing Street. He took the private lift to the basement and then walked through the tunnel which runs under Whitehall direct to the Cabinet room, thus avoiding the press and any curious onlookers.

He found the Prime Minister sitting alone in the Cabinet room.

Simon went over the final plan with her in great detail, explaining that everything was ready and would be over by the time most people were having their breakfasts.

"Let me know the moment you hear anything, however trivial," she concluded, before returning to the latest gloomy study of the economy from the Wynne Godley team, who were suggesting the pound and the dollar would be on an equal parity by 1988. "One day you may have all these problems on *your* shoulders," she said.

Simon smiled and left her to walk back through the private tunnel to his office on the other side of Whitehall.

He took the lift back up to his room on the sixth floor and joined the Joint Chiefs. Although it was past midnight none of them looked tired despite their all having shared the lonely vigil with their comrades 2,000 miles away. They told stories

of Suez and the Falklands, and there was frequently laughter. But it was never long before their eyes returned to the clock.

As Big Ben struck two chimes, Simon thought: four o'clock in Libya. He could visualise the men falling backwards over the side of the boat and deep into the water before starting the long, slow swim towards *Broadsword*.

When the phone rang, breaking the eerie silence like a fire alarm, Simon picked it up to hear Charles Seymour's voice.

"Simon," he began, "I've finally got through to Gaddafi and he wants to negotiate." Simon looked at his watch; the SBS men could only be a few hundred yards from *Broadsword*.

"It's too late," he said. "I can't stop them now."

"Don't be such a bloody fool — order them to turn back. Don't you understand we've won a diplomatic coup?"

"Gaddafi could negotiate for months and still end up humiliating us. No, I won't turn back."

"We shall see how the Prime Minister reacts to your arrogance," said Charles and slammed down the receiver.

Simon sat at his desk and waited for the telephone to ring. He wondered if he could get away with taking the damn thing off the hook — the modern equivalent of Nelson placing the telescope to his blind eye, he considered. He needed a few minutes, but the phone rang again only seconds later. He picked it up and heard Margaret Thatcher's unmistakable voice.

"Can you stop them if I order you to, Simon?"

He considered lying. "Yes, Prime Minister," he said.

"But you would still like to carry it through, wouldn't you?"

"I only need a few minutes, Prime Minister."

"Do you understand the consequences if you fail, with Charles already claiming a diplomatic victory?"

"You would have my resignation within the hour."

"I suspect mine would have to go with it," she said. "In which case Charles would undoubtedly be Prime Minister by this time tomorrow." There was a moment's pause before she continued. "Gaddafi is on the other line and I am going to tell him that I *am* willing to negotiate." Simon felt defeated.

"Perhaps that will give you enough time, and let's hope it's Gaddafi who has to worry about resignations at breakfast."

Simon nearly cheered.

"Do you know the hardest thing I have had to do in this entire operation?"

"No, Prime Minister."

"When Gaddafi rang in the middle of the night, I had to pretend to be asleep so that he didn't know I was sitting by the phone."

He laughed.

"Good luck, Simon. I'll phone and explain my decision to Charles."

The clock read three-thirty.

On his return the bevy of admirals were variously clenching their fists, tapping the table or walking around it, and Simon began to sense what the Israelis must have felt like as they waited for news from Entebbe.

The phone rang again. He knew it couldn't be the Prime Minister this time as she was the one woman in England who never changed her mind. It was Charles Seymour.

"I want it clearly understood, Simon, that I gave you the news concerning Gaddafi's desire to negotiate at three-twenty. That is on the record, so there will be only one minister handing in his resignation later this morning."

"I know exactly where you stand, Charles, and I feel confident that whatever happens you'll come through your own mound of manure smelling of roses." He slammed down the phone just as four o'clock struck. For no fathomable reason everyone in the room stood up, but as the minutes passed again one by one they sat back down.

At seven minutes past four radio silence was broken with the five words, "Shoplifter apprehended, repeat Shoplifter apprehended."

Simon watched the Joint Chiefs cheer like schoolchildren reacting to the winning goal at a football match. *Broadsword* was on the high seas in neutral waters. He sat down at his desk and asked to be put through to No. 10. The Prime Minister came on the line. "Shoplifter apprehended," he told her.

"Congratulations, continue as agreed," was all she said.

The next move was to be sure that all the Libyan prisoners who had been taken aboard *Broadsword* would be discharged at Malta and sent home unharmed. Simon waited impatiently for radio silence to be broken again, as agreed, at five o'clock.

Captain Lawrence Packard came on the line as Big Ben struck five. He gave Simon a full report on the operation: one Libyan guerilla had been killed and eleven injured. There had been no, repeat no, British deaths and only a few minor injuries sustained. The thirty-seven SBS men were back on board the submarines *Conqueror* and *Courageous*. HMS *Broadsword* had two engines out of action and currently resembled an Arab bazaar, but was sailing the high seas on her way home. God Save the Queen.

"Congratulations, Captain," said Simon. He returned to Downing Street, no longer bothering to use the secret tunnel. As he limped up the road journalists with no idea of the news that was about to be announced were already gathering outside No. 10. Once again he answered none of their shouted questions. When he was shown into the Cabinet room he found Charles already there with the Prime Minister. He told them both the latest news.

"Well done, Simon," said Mrs Thatcher.

Charles made no comment.

It was agreed that the Prime Minister would make a statement to the House at three-thirty that afternoon.

"I must admit that my opinion of Charles Seymour has gone up," said Elizabeth in the car on the way to Oxford to watch Peter play in his hockey match.

"What do you mean?" asked Simon.

"He's just been interviewed on television. He said he had backed your judgement all along while having to pretend to carry out pointless negotiations. He had a very good line to the effect that it was the first time in his life that he had felt honourable about lying."

"Smelling like roses," Simon said sharply. Elizabeth didn't understand her husband's response.

He went on to tell his wife everything that had gone on between them during the last few hours.

"Why didn't you say something?"

"And admit that the Foreign Secretary and I were quarrelling throughout the entire operation? It would only show up the Government in a bad light and give the Opposition something to latch on to."

"I'll never understand politics," said Elizabeth resignedly.

It amused Simon to watch his son massacred in the mud while he stood on the touchline in the rain only hours after he had feared Gaddafi might have done the same to him. "It's a walkover," he told the Principal when Peter's college were four goals down by half-time.

"Perhaps he'll be like you and surprise us all in the second half," came back the reply.

At eight o'clock on the following Saturday morning Simon sat in his office and heard the news that *Broadsword* had all engines on full speed and was expected to reach Portsmouth by three o'clock, exactly one week after his son had lost his college match eight—nil: they hadn't had a good second half. Simon had tried to console his downcast son but it didn't help that he had been the goalkeeper.

He was smiling when his secretary interrupted his thoughts to remind him that he was due in Portsmouth in an hour. As Simon reached the door the phone rang. "Explain to whoever it is I'm already late," he said.

His secretary replied, "I don't think I can, sir."

Simon turned round, puzzled. "Who is it?" he asked.

"Her Majesty the Queen."

Simon returned to his desk, picked up the receiver and listened to the sovereign. When she had finished Simon thanked her and said he would pass on her message to Captain Packard as soon as he reached Portsmouth. During the flight down Simon looked out of the helicopter and stared at a traffic jam that stretched from the coast to London with people who were going to welcome *Broadsword* home. The helicopter landed an hour later.

The Secretary of State for Defence stood on the pier and was able to pick out the destroyer through a pair of binoculars. She was about an hour away but was already so surrounded by a flotilla of small craft that it was hard to identify her.

Sir John told him that Captain Packard had signalled to ask if the Secretary of State wished to join him on the bridge as they sailed into port. "No, thank you," said Simon. "It's his day, not mine."

"Good thing the Foreign Secretary isn't with us," said Sir John. A squad of Tornadoes flew over, drowning Simon's reply. As *Broadsword* sailed into port, the ship's company were all on deck standing to attention in full dress uniform. The ship itself shone like a Rolls-Royce that had just come off the production line.

By the time the captain descended the gangplank a crowd of some 500,000 were cheering so loudly that Simon could not hear himself speak. Captain Packard saluted as the Secretary of State leaned forward and whispered the Queen's message in his ear:

"Welcome home, Rear-Admiral Sir Lawrence Packard."

CHAPTER
THIRTY ONE

The *Broadsword* factor remained in the memories of the electorate for a far shorter time than had the Falklands victory and the Conservative cause was not helped by the breakdown in Geneva of the disarmament talks between Reagan, Gorbachov and Thatcher.

The Russians put the blame for the breakdown on Mrs Thatcher's 'aggressive stance' over *Broadsword* after they had backed her for a diplomatic solution at the UN. Within six months the Conservative lead in the opinion polls had dropped to three per cent.

"The truth is," noted Raymond at a Shadow Cabinet meeting, "Mrs Thatcher has had nearly eight years at No. 10 and no Prime Minister has served two full terms in succession – let alone three – since Lord Liverpool in 1812."

At that time of the year when referees leave the field to be replaced by umpires Raymond watched his predictions become history. Once the Christmas recess had ended he felt sure the Prime Minister would go to the country in late May or some time in June rather than face another winter. When the Conservatives held on to the marginal seat in Birmingham and fared better than expected at the local elections in May no one believed the Prime Minister would delay the announcement much longer.

Margaret Thatcher seemed to care nothing for Lord Liverpool or historical precedent, because she called an election for late June, believing that the month that had been a winner for her in the past would prove to be good for her again.

"It's time to let the nation choose who is to govern for the next five years," she declared on *Panorama*.

"Of course, it's got nothing to do with the fact she's regained a slight lead in the opinion polls," said Joyce tartly.

"A lead that could well disappear during the next few weeks," Raymond added.

He returned to Yorkshire for only three days of the campaign. As one of the party's leading spokesmen he had to travel around the country addressing meeting after meeting in marginal seats. Many journalists went as far as to suggest that were Raymond leading the party they would be in a far stronger position to win the election. On the few occasions he was back in Leeds he enjoyed the electioneering and felt completely relaxed with his constituents for the first time in his life. He also felt his age when he discovered that the new Tory candidate for Leeds North had been born in 1964, the year he had first entered Parliament. When they met the only insult Raymond suffered at his young rival's hands was being called 'sir'.

"Please call me by my Christian name," said Raymond.

"Raymond –" began the young man.

"No, Ray will do just fine."

Charles and Simon also saw little of their constituencies as they too toured the marginal seats, adding more and more to their schedules as the polling day became closer. Half-way through the campaign the Conservatives mounted a massive attack on the Alliance, as opinion polls were continuing to show that they were making considerable inroads into the Conservative vote, while traditional Labour supporters were returning to their old allegiance.

Andrew had to remain in Edinburgh for the entire campaign, to face Frank Boyle once again. But this time, as Stuart Gray informed the constituents of Edinburgh Carlton through his columns in the *Scotsman*, it was a Frank Boyle without teeth. Andrew felt what was left of those teeth a few times during the final three weeks but at least the Royal Bank of Scotland did not find it necessary to part with a second golden sovereign in their 300-year history. Andrew retained his seat by over 2,000 votes, to be returned to Parliament for the eighth time. Louise claimed that her husband's majority were the 2,000 people who had fallen in love with the thirteen-year-old coltish Clarissa, who was already fulfilling her father's prophecy as gauche fifteen-year-old Scots blushed in her presence.

The final result of the election did not become clear until four o'clock on the Friday afternoon as several recounts took place up and down the country.

"It will be a hung Parliament," David Dimbleby told the viewers tuned into the BBC 'Election Special' programme that afternoon. He repeated the detailed figures for those people still returning from work:

Conservative	313
Labour	285
Liberal/SDP Alliance	31
Irish/Ulster Unionist	17
Speaker and others	4

Dimbleby went on to point out that there was no necessity for Mrs Thatcher to resign as she was still the leader of the largest party in the Commons. But one thing was apparent, the SDP might well hold the balance at the next election.

The Prime Minister made very few changes to her front-bench team as she clearly wished to leave an impression of unity despite her small majority. The press dubbed it 'The cosmetic Cabinet'. Charles moved to the Home Office while Simon became Foreign Secretary.

Everyone at Westminster was thankful when a few weeks later Parliament broke up for the summer recess and politicians returned home for a rest.

That rest was to last a complete week before Tony Benn rolled a thundercloud across the clear blue summer sky by announcing he would contest the leadership of the Labour party at the October conference.

Benn claimed that Kinnock's naivety and gauche approach as leader had been the single reason that the Labour party had not been returned to power. There were many Socialists who agreed with this judgement, but they also felt they would have fared considerably worse under Benn.

What his announcement did, however, was to make respectable the claim of any other candidates who wished their names to be put forward. Roy Hattersley and John Smith joined Benn and Kinnock for the first ballot. Many Members of Parliament, trade-union leaders and constituency activists pressed Raymond to stand for the leadership.

"If you don't stand now," Joyce told him, "you'll have no chance in the future."

"It's the future I'm thinking about," replied Raymond.

"What do you mean?" she asked.

"I want to stand for deputy leader against Michael Meacher and John Cunningham, and that will secure me a power base in the party which would afford me a better chance next time."

Raymond waited another week before he launched his candidacy. On the following Monday, at a packed press conference, he announced he would be standing for deputy leader.

With four candidates in the field for the leadership no clear favourite emerged although most prophets accepted Benn would lead after the first ballot. Hattersley came to an agreement with Smith that whichever one of them captured the most votes in the first round the other would drop out and support the leader of the right in the final ballot.

When the vote had been counted Benn, as predicted, topped the first ballot, with Kinnock in third place. To everyone's surprise when Kinnock dropped out he advised his supporters not to back Benn as he felt it could only spell a further prolonged period of Opposition for the Labour party.

A few hours later the party chairman announced that Tony Benn had been soundly beaten. The Labour party had a new moderate leader.

The vote then took place for the deputy leadership and although the new leader made clear his preference for Raymond everyone still expected it to be close. Joyce spent the last hour running from delegate to delegate while

Raymond tried to appear calm. At eleven o'clock that Sunday night the chairman of the Labour party's National Executive announced that by a mere three per cent Raymond Gould was the newly elected deputy leader of the Labour party.

The new leader immediately appointed Raymond Shadow Chancellor of the Exchequer.

Among the many letters and telegrams Raymond received was one from Kate, which read: Congratulations. But have you read standing order no. 5(4) of the party constitution? Raymond replied: Hadn't. Have now. Let's hope it's an omen.

In their first twelve months the new Labour team looked fresh and innovative as Mrs Thatcher began to look tired and out of touch. She was not helped in her cause by the election of Gary Hart to the White House in November 1988. President Hart's avowed intention to lower unemployment and spend more of the nation's wealth to help 'genuine Democrats' left Britain with a handful of new problems. The pound strengthened against the dollar overnight, and large export orders sat gathering dust in dockside warehouses.

But what threw her economic forecasts into total disarray was the decision of the recently elected Governments of Brazil and Argentina to refuse to repay any of the loans negotiated by their former military rulers leaving the Bank of England with what could only be described as an overdraft.

During the long cold winter of 1988 the Conservatives lost several votes on the floor of the House and many more upstairs in committee. The Prime Minister seemed somewhat relieved to find herself spending Christmas at Chequers.

The relief did not last long as two elderly Conservative members died before the House convened in January. The press dubbed the Government the 'lame drake' administration.

Both of the pending by-elections were held in May: the Conservatives fared far better than might have been expected, holding on to one and just losing the other. For a third time Mrs Thatcher plumped for a June election.

After a decade of the lady from Grantham Raymond sensed the mood was for change. The monthly unemployment, inflation and import/export figures announced at regular intervals during the campaign all augured badly for the Conservatives.

The Prime Minister's reiterated plea that a Government shouldn't be judged on one month's figures now sounded unconvincing, and by the final week the only point of contention was whether the Labour party would end up with a decent working majority.

Raymond woke up on the Friday morning after the election to be told by Joyce that the computer predictions indicated an overall majority of four seats. Together they toured the constituency that morning before joining Raymond's parents for a late lunch. When they left the little butcher's shop that afternoon there was a crowd of well-wishers awaiting them on the pavement who cheered them all the way to their car. Raymond and Joyce travelled down to London and were back in Cowley Street in time to watch the first Labour Prime Minister since 1979 emerge from Buckingham Palace with the television cameras following him all the way back until he took up residence at 10 Downing Street.

This time Raymond did not have long to wait for a telephone call because the first appointment the new Prime Minister confirmed was his Chancellor. Raymond and Joyce travelled to No. 11 later that afternoon, instructing estate agents to lease their Cowley Street house on a six-month let that might or might not be renewable. Joyce spent hours checking over her new home and replacing some of the objects she had inherited from Diana Brittan while Raymond called his team over from Transport House to prepare the Labour party's first budget, and replace even more of what Leon Brittan had left behind.

After Raymond's advisers returned to Transport House that night he started to go over the hundreds of letters and telegrams of congratulations that had been flooding in throughout the day. One from America made him particularly happy, and he returned his own best wishes to Mrs Kate Wilberhoff.

Andrew had defeated Frank Boyle for a third time and the left-winger announced that he would not be standing again.

Andrew had also spent a weekend thanking all his helpers. When he returned to the Commons on the Monday morning he found a note awaiting him on the Members' Letter-board.

Over lunch in the Members' Dining-room David Owen informed him privately that he would not be seeking re-election as leader of the SDP: seven years had been quite enough. Although the party had slightly improved their position in the House he accepted that they now faced a five-year Parliament, and he wanted Andrew to take over.

As soon as Owen had issued an official press statement Geoffrey Parkhouse of the *Glasgow Herald* was the first to phone and ask Andrew, "When will you be announcing your bid for the SDP leadership?"

Leaving the Home Office came as a great blow to Charles. His period of time there had been so short that he felt he had achieved very little. The civil servants had procrastinated over all major decisions as they waited for another general election and a clear mandate. He informed Amanda over breakfast on the Monday after the election that he would be returning to Seymour's Bank and that his salary would once again be sufficient for her allowance to remain constant – so long as she kept to her part of the bargain. Amanda nodded and left the breakfast table without comment just as Harry came in.

It was an important morning for Harry as he was to be taken to his first day of prep school at Hill House to begin the academic course mapped out for him by his father. Charles tried to convince him that it would be the start of a wonderful future, but Harry looked apprehensive. Once he had deposited a tearful eight-year-old with his first headmaster Charles continued on to the City, cheerful at the prospect of returning to the world of banking.

When he arrived at Seymour's, he was met by Clive Reynolds's secretary who immediately took him through to the boardroom and asked him if he would like a coffee.

"Thank you," said Charles, taking off his gloves, placing

his umbrella in the stand and settling himself in the chairman's seat at the head of the table. "And would you tell Mr Reynolds I'm in?"

"Certainly," said the secretary.

Clive Reynolds joined him a few moments later.

"Good morning, Mr Seymour. How nice to see you again after such a long time," he said, shaking Charles by the hand.

"Good morning, Clive. It's nice to see you too. First I must congratulate you on the manner in which you have conducted the bank's affairs in my absence."

"It's kind of you to say so, Mr Seymour."

"I was particularly impressed by the Distillers takeover; that certainly took the City by surprise."

"Yes, quite a coup, wasn't it?" said Reynolds, smiling. "And there's another one in the pipeline."

"I shall look forward to hearing the details."

"Well, I'm afraid it remains confidential at the moment," said Clive, taking the seat beside him.

"Of course, but now I have returned I had better be briefed fairly soon."

"I'm afraid shareholders cannot be briefed until we are certain the deals have been concluded. We can't afford any rumours harming our chances, can we?"

"But I'm not an ordinary shareholder," said Charles sharply. "I am returning as chairman of the bank."

"No, Mr Seymour," said Reynolds quietly. "I am chairman of this bank."

"Do you realise whom you are addressing?" said Charles.

"Yes, I think so. A former Foreign Secretary, a former Home Secretary, a former chairman of the bank and a two per cent shareholder."

"But you are fully aware that the board agreed to have me back as chairman when the Conservatives went into Opposition," Charles reminded him.

"The composition of the board has changed considerably since those days," said Reynolds. "Perhaps you've been too busy running the rest of the world to notice minor comings and goings in Cheapside."

"I shall call a board meeting."

"You don't have the authority."

"Then I shall demand an Extraordinary General Meeting," said Charles.

"And tell the shareholders what? That you had a standing order to return as Chairman when you felt like it? That won't sound like a former Foreign Secretary."

"I'll have you out of this office in twenty-four hours," Charles continued, his voice suddenly rising.

"I don't think so, Mr Seymour. Miss Trubshaw has completed her five years and left us on a full pension, and it won't take you long to discover that I don't possess a Swiss bank account or a well-compensated mistress."

Charles went red in the face. "I'll get you removed. You don't begin to understand how far my influence stretches."

"I hope I'm not removed, for your sake," said Reynolds calmly.

"Are you threatening me?"

"Certainly not, Mr Seymour, but I would hate to have to explain how Seymour's lost over £500,000 on the Nethercote account because of your personal wish to ruin Simon Kerslake's career. It may interest you to know that the only thing the bank gained from that fiasco was goodwill, and we only managed that because I recommended that Morgan Grenfell pick up the pieces."

Charles couldn't resist a smile. "When I make that public it will finish you," he said triumphantly.

"Perhaps," said Reynolds calmly, "but it would also stop you from becoming Prime Minister."

Charles turned, picked up his umbrella, put on his gloves and walked away. As he reached the door, a secretary walked in holding two cups of coffee. Charles passed her without a word and slammed the door.

"I'll only be needing one, Miss Bristow."

During the first week after the Queen's Speech Andrew was pleased to discover that a majority of his colleagues wrote to say that they would support him if he put his name forward for the leadership of the SDP.

At their weekly parliamentary meeting the party Whip asked that names for the post of party leader be submitted to his office within seven days. Each candidate had to be proposed and seconded by Members of Parliament.

For the next week the popular press tried to suggest, conjure up or even invent a rival for Andrew. Louise, who believed almost everything she read in the papers, took to perusing the *Morning Star*, the only paper which showed no interest in the outcome. But by five o'clock on the seventh day it had become obvious that Andrew was to be the sole nomination.

At the next parliamentary meeting of the SDP he was not so much elected as anointed. On the following Saturday, having been made a Privy Councillor the day before, Andrew addressed the party faithful at a packed Albert Hall. After a well-received speech, the press unanimously predicted – yet again – an SDP-Liberal revival. One or two journalists were quick to point out that if the balance of power did ever rest in his hands the Right Honourable Andrew Fraser might not know which way to jump: with on the one hand a father who was a distinguished Tory, while on the other having been a member of the Labour party himself for twenty years, which party would he consider the lesser of the two evils? Andrew always told the press that he would worry about that when the problem arose, because the SDP might not even be able to come to an agreement with the Liberals.

Numerous articles on the new SDP leader appeared in newspapers and magazines across the country. They all reported the stories of his attempt to save his son's life, the gradual recovery of his wife after Robert's death, the successful adoption of Clarissa and his re-election to Parliament on the toss of a golden sovereign.

All the publicity made Clarissa feel like a film star, she told her father. She was the most popular girl in school, she added, so he had better become Prime Minister. He laughed but proceeded to lead his party with a determination and energy that caused him to be talked of in the same breath as the leaders of the two main parties.

No sooner had the publicity over Andrew's election died

down than the press started speculating as to whether Mrs Thatcher would now make way for a younger man.

"Don't you know any other restaurant?"

"Yes, but they don't know me," replied Ronnie Nethercote, as the two men strolled into the Ritz for the first time in a couple of years. Heads turned as people leaned forward and whispered Simon's name to their guests.

"What are you up to nowadays? I can't believe Opposition fully occupies you," Ronnie said as they took their seats.

"Not really. I might also be described as one of the four million unemployed," replied Simon.

"That's what we're here to talk about," said Ronnie, "but first I recommend the country vegetable soup and the . . ."

"Beef off the trolley," interjected Simon.

"You remembered."

"It's the one thing you've always been right about."

Ronnie laughed more loudly than people normally did in the Ritz before saying, "Now you no longer have the entire armed forces at your disposal or ambassadors to call you Your Eminence or whatever they call you now, why don't you join the board of my new company?"

"It's kind of you to ask, Ronnie, but the answer has to be no."

They both broke off their conversation to allow the head waiter to take their orders.

"There's a salary of £20,000 a year that goes with it."

"I can't deny that Elizabeth and I could do with the money. With Peter staying up at Oxford to do a D.Phil. and Michael bent on being an actor I wonder if my bank account will ever be in credit."

"Then why not come in with us?" asked Ronnie.

"Because I'm a committed politician," said Simon, "and I no longer want to involve myself in any commercial activities."

"That might stop you becoming Prime Minister?"

Simon hesitated at the bluntness of Ronnie's question then said, "Frankly, yes. I've got a better than outside chance and

I'd be foolish to lengthen the odds by becoming involved in anything else right now."

"But everyone knows that as soon as Margaret announces she's going to pack up you'll be the next leader. It's as simple as that."

"No, Ronnie, it's never as simple as that."

"Then tell me, who could beat you?"

"Charles Seymour, for one."

"Seymour? He's a toffee-nosed git," said Ronnie.

"He has a lot of friends in the party, and his patrician background still counts for something with the Tories. Sir Alec remains the best loved of our most recent Prime Ministers."

"Yes, but he was given the leadership by the magic circle," said Ronnie. "You'd kill Seymour with every elected member of the party having a vote."

"Time will tell," said Simon, bored with a conversation he had had with so many people lately. "But what have you been up to?" he asked, deliberately changing the subject.

"I've been working my backside off in preparation for going public in about a year's time, which is why I wanted you on the board."

"You never give up."

"No, and I hope you haven't given up your one per cent of the company."

"Elizabeth has it locked away somewhere."

"Then you had better find the key."

"Why?" asked Simon.

"Because when I put out ten million shares on the market at three quid a time, your one original share will be exchanged for 100,000 shares of common stock. I know you weren't ever Chancellor but that's £300,000 of anyone's money."

Simon was speechless.

"Well, say something," said Ronnie.

"Frankly I'd forgotten the share existed," Simon finally managed.

"Well, I think I can safely say," said Ronnie, parodying

one of Mrs Thatcher's favourite phrases, "that's not a bad investment for a pound, and one you will never regret."

As the budget debate drew nearer Raymond found twenty-four hours each day were not enough, even without sleep. He discussed the changes he required with the Treasury mandarins, but it became more obvious as each week passed that he would have to make sacrifices. He was sick of being told that there would always be next year, feeling he had waited far too long already. He often went over to Transport House to discuss with his party researchers those promises in the manifesto which they considered the top priorities. Raymond had been pleased by the party's decision to leave Walworth Road and return to Transport House as the party head-quarters soon after their victory at the polls.

As the weeks passed, compromises were reached and cut-backs agreed but Raymond managed to cling to the changes about which he felt most passionate. By the Friday morning before the budget the mandarins had handed him his speech. It ran to 143 pages and they estimated it would keep him at the dispatch box for two and a half hours.

On the Tuesday morning of Budget Day he spelt out his tax changes to the Cabinet, who traditionally did not hear the full details until a few hours before the budget was presented to the House.

Budget Day in the House of Commons is a traditional affair. Ambassadors, diplomats, bankers and members of the House of Lords rub shoulders with the general public in the tiny Strangers' Gallery. The queue for seats often stretches for a quarter of a mile from St Stephen's to Westminster Bridge, but only half a dozen people at the front of the line actually hear the Chancellor's speech, because every other place has been allocated even before the queue has begun to form. The Chamber itself is usually packed by two-thirty although the Chancellor does not rise until an hour later. The Press Gallery is equally overcrowded with correspondents ready to run to the nearest phone as soon as any change in taxation is announced. Back-benchers, who because of the size of the Chamber cannot be guaranteed their normal places, are mostly seated by two-twenty-five. Conservatives can reserve their seats by filling in a small prayer card during the morning and leaving it on the place they wish to occupy. Socialists, who consider the system undemocratic, refuse to use the prayer cards and make a mad rush for places at two-thirty. The atheists on both sides wait for the chaplain to finish prayers before they charge in, hoping to find their usual places free.

Budget Day is also traditionally one for eccentric dress. A few top hats can be observed on the Conservative benches and the odd miner's helmet rests on a Labour head. Tom Carson arrived in a boiler suit with a Liverpool scarf around his neck, while Alec Pimkin satisfied himself with a red silk waistcoat and a white carnation in the buttonhole of his morning coat.

The green leather of the two front benches begins to disappear long before three o'clock, and by then any straggling back-bencher will be relegated to the floor or to the upstairs galleries, known as the 'Members' Side Galleries', which lack the atmosphere of the House and from which members traditionally do not rise to interrupt or make a speech.

At ten past three Raymond stepped out of No. 11 and held the famous battered budget box, first used by Gladstone, high above his head, so that the press photographers could take the traditional picture before he was driven off to the Commons.

By three-fifteen, when the Prime Minister rose to answer questions, the Chamber had taken on the look of an opening night in the West End, for what members were about to experience was pure theatre.

At three-twenty-five Raymond entered the Chamber to be greeted by cheers from his own side. Every place in the Commons except his had been filled. He looked up to see Joyce in the Strangers' Gallery, and smiled. At three-thirty, when the Prime Minister had finished answering questions, the chairman of Ways and Means – who traditionally takes the Speaker's place for a budget debate as the Speaker, being 'the King's man', does not preside over money matters – rose from his chair and called:

"Budget statement, Mr Chancellor of the Exchequer."

Raymond rose and placed his speech in front of him. He began with a review of the world economic position and went on to inform the House of the philosophy behind his first budget, namely to bring down unemployment without driving up inflation. He spoke for the first hour and a half without divulging to the House any of the fiscal changes that he would be making, so abiding by the tradition that no irreversible decisions could be considered until the Stock Exchange had closed, but also giving him the opportunity to tease the House with the odd hint or suggestion.

Raymond took a sip from the glass of water by his side when he had turned page seventy-eight. He had finished with the theory and was now ready to start on the practice.

"Old-age pensions will be raised to a record level," he declared, "as will allowances for single-parent families and disablement grants." Raymond paused and taking a faded sheet from his inside pocket read from the first speech he had ever delivered in public. "No woman whose husband has sacrificed his life for his country shall be allowed to suffer because of an ungrateful nation. War widows' pensions will go up by fifty per cent and war bonds will be honoured at their full face value." The cheering after this statement lasted for some considerable time. Once the House had settled again he continued. "The tax on beer, cigarettes, petrol and perfume will go up by five per cent. Taxes on salaries of more than £30,000 a year will be raised to eighty-five per cent and capital gains tax to fifty per cent." Several Conservatives looked glum. The Chancellor went on to announce an expansion programme in the regions to stimulate employment. He detailed his plan region by region, to cheers from different sections of the House.

He ended his speech by saying, "My purpose as the first Labour Chancellor for ten years is not to rob the rich and give to the poor, but rather to make those who live in comparative ease pay taxes that will alleviate the plight of those in genuine need. Let me tell those Honourable members who sit on the benches opposite that this is only a fifth of what I intend to achieve in the lifetime of this Parliament, and by then Britain can hope to be a more equal and just society. We intend to create a generation in which class is as outdated as the debtors' prison, in which talent, hard work and honesty are their own reward, a Socialist society that is the envy of the East as well as the West. This budget, Mr Speaker, is nothing more than the architect's plan for that dream. I look forward to being given enough time to build the reality."

When Raymond resumed his seat after two hours and twenty minutes, the length of time it takes to run a world-class marathon, he was greeted by cheers and the waving of order papers from the benches behind him.

The leader of the Opposition was faced with the almost impossible task of an immediate response, and couldn't hope to do more than pick up one or two weaknesses in the Chancellor's philosophy. The House did not hang on her every word.

BOOK FIVE
1989-1991
PARTY LEADERS

CHAPTER
THIRTY TWO

After the success of Raymond's first budget the leader of the Opposition made changes to her Shadow Cabinet as quickly as was diplomatic. She moved the former Chancellor to cover the Foreign Office, Simon to tackle Home Affairs and Charles to counter the formidable problems now raised by Raymond Gould at the Treasury.

Raymond soon discovered his task of pushing legislation through became that much harder when Charles had added the enthusiasm of his new young team to his own considerable experience of financial matters.

Raymond's success continued, however, even if it was at a slower pace than that for which he would have hoped. Labour won the first two by-elections occasioned by members' deaths, which in itself was remarkable in Government. The by-election results only started a fresh round of rumours that Denis Thatcher was pressing his wife to retire.

Charles Seymour knew that when such moves were finally made they could happen so suddenly that everyone seemed unprepared and uncertain what to do next. By the time Mrs Thatcher announced her resignation he had been building up a loyal team around him for several months.

The former Prime Minister sent a letter to Sir Cranley Onslow, the new chairman of the 1922 Committee, letting him know that she would not be putting her name forward for re-election. She explained that she would be over sixty-five at the next election and had already led the party for fourteen years, the longest period for any Conservative since Churchill, and that she now felt she was ready to pass the leadership on to new blood.

The moment everyone in the party had said the usual phrases about the retiring leader being the greatest Prime Minister since Churchill, they proceeded to look for the new Churchill.

Within hours of Mrs Thatcher's resignation both Charles Seymour and Simon Kerslake had received calls and messages from about fifty or sixty supporters, and been contacted by all the leading political journalists. Charles went about his campaign in the thorough manner in which he approached everything, appointing lieutenants to cover each intake of new members since 1964. Simon had invited Bill Travers to organise his back-up team. Travers, like any farmer, rose early each morning to gather in his harvest.

Both Simon and Charles were nominated within twenty-four hours of the necessary seven days, and by the weekend none of the rumoured third candidates had appeared in the lists which convinced the press it would be a two-horse race.

The *Financial Times* went one better than its rivals. Its political editor, Peter Riddell, spent the whole week trying to contact the 289 Tory members. He succeeded in reaching 228 of them and was able to report to his readers that 101 had said they would vote for Simon Kerslake, ninety-eight for Charles Seymour, while twenty-nine had refused to give any opinion. The article's headline read 'Narrow lead for Kerslake', and went on to point out that although the two men were polite about each other in public no one pretended they were friends.

'King Kerslake' ran the banner headline in the Monday editions of the *Sun*, and its political editor predicted Simon would win by 116 to 112: Simon suspected that they had done little more than divide the *Financial Times*'s don't-knows down the middle. With eight days to go he was being quoted at two–one on with Charles eleven–eight against by the veteran ex-Labour MP Lord Mikardo, who had run a book on the last fourteen leadership contests irrespective of party. When Elizabeth told him the odds Simon remained sceptical, as he knew from bitter experience that it never paid to underestimate the Right Honourable member for Sussex

Downs. Elizabeth agreed and then pointed to a small paragraph in the paper which he had overlooked. Ronnie's new company was going public, and the shares looked certain to be well over-subscribed.

"That's one prediction that's turned out to be accurate," said Simon, smiling.

With twelve hours to go to the close of nominations a new candidate appeared in the lists, which came as a shock to everyone because until that moment the general public were entirely unaware of Alec Pimkin. Some of his colleagues even expressed surprise that he had been able to find a proposer and a seconder. As it had been assumed that Pimkin's supporters were all men who would have backed Charles it was considered a blow to his cause, although most political pundits doubted if Pimkin could scrape together more than seven or eight out of the 289 votes to be cast.

Charles pleaded with Pimkin to withdraw but he stubbornly refused, admitting to Fiona that he was thoroughly enjoying his brief moment of glory. He held a press conference in the Commons, gave endless interviews to television, radio and the national press, and found he was receiving considerable political attention for the first time in his life since the Common Market debate. He even enjoyed the cartoon that appeared in the *Daily Telegraph* of the three candidates in the 100 metres which had Charles portrayed as a string bean, Simon as a jumping bean and Alec as a has-bean waddling in a long way behind the other two. But Alexander Dalglish remained puzzled as to what had made Pimkin place his name in the lists in the first place.

"My majority in Littlehampton had plummeted from over 12,000 to 3,200 since I was first elected, and frankly the Social Democrats have been getting a little too close for comfort. That tiresome fellow Andrew Fraser is in Sussex once a month making speeches on behalf of his candidate and there are still over four years to go until the election."

"But how many votes can you hope to pick up?" asked Fiona.

"Many more than those drunken scribblers realise. I have

nine votes already pledged, not including my own, and I could well end up with as many as fifteen."

"Why so many?" asked Fiona, immediately realising how tactless the question must have sounded.

"Dear, simple creature," Pimkin replied. "There are some members of our party who do not care to be led either by a middle-class pushy minor public schoolboy or an aristocratic, arrogant snob. By voting for me they can lodge their protest very clearly."

"But isn't that irresponsible of you?" asked Fiona, annoyed by the 'simple' quip.

"Irresponsible it may be, but you can't begin to imagine the invitations I have been receiving during the last few days. They should continue for at least a year after the election is over."

Bombshells occur in the House of Commons only on rare occasions, mainly because the elements of bad luck and timing have to come together. Something that will create a headline one week may be hardly worthy of a mention the next. On the Thursday before the leadership election the House was packed for questions to the Chancellor. Raymond and Charles were having their usual verbal battles across the dispatch box, Charles coming out slightly on top. As the Treasury wasn't his portfolio, all Simon could do was sit with his legs up on the table and listen while his rival scored points.

Tom Carson seemed extremely anxious to get in a supplementary on almost any question that was down on the order paper. Between two-thirty and five past three he had leaped up from his place no less than a dozen times. The digital clock above the Speaker's chair had reached three-twelve when, out of exasperation, the Speaker called him on a seemingly innocuous question on windfall profits.

With Prime Minister's questions just about to begin Carson faced a packed House and a full press gallery. He paused for a moment before putting his question.

"What would be my Right Honourable friend's attitude to a man who invests one pound in a company and, five years later, receives a cheque for £300,000 despite not being on the board or appearing to be involved in any way with that company?"

Raymond was puzzled as he had no idea what Carson was talking about. He did not notice that Simon Kerslake had turned white.

Raymond rose to the dispatch box. "I would remind my Honourable friend that I put capital gains tax up to fifty per cent which might dampen his ardour a little," he said. It was about the only attempt at humour Raymond had made at the dispatch box that year, which may have been the reason so few members laughed. As Carson rose a second time Simon slipped a note across to Raymond which he hurriedly skimmed.

"But does the Chancellor consider that such a person would be fit to be Prime Minister or even leader of the Opposition?"

Members started talking amongst themselves, trying to work out at whom the question was directed while the Speaker stirred restlessly in his seat, anxious to bring a halt to such disorderly supplementaries. Raymond returned to the dispatch box and told Carson that the question was not worthy of an answer. There the matter might have rested had Charles not risen to the dispatch box.

"Mr Speaker, is the Chancellor aware that this personal attack is aimed at my Right Honourable friend, the member for Pucklebridge, and is a disgraceful slur on his character and reputation? The Honourable member for Liverpool Dockside should withdraw his allegation immediately."

The Conservatives cheered their colleague's magnanimity while Simon remained silent, knowing that Charles had successfully put the story on the front page of every national paper.

Simon read the papers over breakfast on the Friday morning, and was not surprised by the coverage of Charles's bogus supplementary. The details of his transaction with Ronnie Nethercote were chronicled in the fullest extent, and it did not read well that he had received £300,000 from a 'property speculator' for a one pound investment. Some of the papers felt 'bound to ask' what Nethercote hoped to gain out of the transaction. No one seemed to realise that Simon had been on the previous company's board for five years, had invested £60,000 of his own money in that company and had only recently finished paying off the overdraft.

By the Sunday Simon had made a full press statement to put the record straight, and most of the papers had given him a fair hearing. However, Sir Peter McKay, the editor of the *Sunday Express*, didn't help matters with a comment in his widely-read PM column on the centre page.

> I would not suggest for one moment that Simon Kerslake has done anything that might be described as dishonest, but with the spotlight turned so fiercely on him there may be some Members of Parliament who feel they cannot risk going into a general election with an accident-prone leader. Mr Seymour, on the other hand, has made his position abundantly clear. He did not seek to return to his family bank in Opposition while he was still hoping to hold public office.

The Monday papers were reassessing the outcome of the ballot to take place the next day and were predicting that Seymour now had the edge. Some journalists went so far as to suggest that Alec Pimkin might profit from the incident as members waited to see if there would be a second chance to give their final verdict.

Simon had received several letters of sympathy during the week, including one from Raymond Gould. Raymond assured Simon that he had not been prepared for the Carson supplementary and apologised for any embarrassment his first answer might have caused.

"It never crossed my mind that he had," said Simon, as he passed Raymond's letter over to Elizabeth.

"*The Times* was right," she said a few moments later. "He is a very fair man."

A moment later Simon passed his wife another letter.

Seymour's Bank,   15 May 1989
202 Cheapside,
London, EC1

Dear Mr Kerslake,
    I write to correct one fact to which the press have
continually referred. Mr Charles Seymour, the former
chairman of this bank, did seek to return to Seymour's
after the Conservatives went into Opposition. He hoped
to continue as chairman on a salary of £40,000 a year.
    The board of Seymour's did not fall in with his wishes.
Yours sincerely,
Clive Reynolds.

"Will you use it?" asked Elizabeth, when she had finished
reading the letter through.

"No. It will only draw more attention to the issue."

Elizabeth looked at her husband as he continued to read
the letters, and remembered the file that she still possessed on
Amanda Wallace. She would never reveal its contents to
Simon; but perhaps the time had come to make Charles
Seymour sweat a little.

On the Monday evening Simon sat on the front bench
listening to the Financial Secretary moving those clauses of
the short Finance Bill which were being taken in committee
on the floor of the House. Charles never let any of Raymond
Gould's team get away with a phrase or even a comma if he
could see a weakness in their case, and the Opposition were
enjoying every moment. Simon sat and watched the votes
slipping away, knowing he could do nothing to stop the
process.

Of the three candidates only Pimkin slept well the night
before the election.

Voting began promptly at nine o'clock the next day in the
Grand Committee room of the House of Commons, the party
Whips acting as tellers. By three-ten all but one of those
entitled to vote had done so. John Cope, the Chief Whip,
stood guard over the large black tin box until Big Ben struck
four, when it became apparent that Mrs Thatcher had
decided to remain neutral.

At four o'clock the box was removed to the Chief Whip's

office and the little slips were tipped out and checked twice in less than fifteen minutes. As John Cope left his room he was followed, Pied Piper-like, by lobby correspondents hoping to learn the result, but he had no intention of divulging anything before he reached the 1922 Committee who were keenly awaiting him.

Committee room fourteen was filled to overflowing, with some 280 of the 289 Conservative Members of Parliament present. Their chairman, Sir Cranley Onslow, welcomed the Chief Whip and asked him to join him on the small raised platform. He did so and passed over a folded piece of paper. The chairman of the 1922 Committee rose, faced the committee, unfolded the piece of paper and pushed up his glasses. He hesitated as he took in the figures.

"The result of the ballot carried out to select the leader of the parliamentary party is as follows:

>   Charles Seymour   138
>   Simon Kerslake   135
>   Alec Pimkin   15"

There was a gasp followed by prolonged chatter, which lasted until members noticed that the chairman remained standing as he waited for some semblance of order to return among his colleagues.

"There being no outright winner," Sir Cranley continued, "a second ballot will take place next Tuesday without Mr Pimkin."

The national press surrounded Pimkin as he left the Commons that afternoon, wanting to know whom he would advise his supporters to vote for in the second ballot. Pimkin, obviously relishing every moment, declared a little pompously that he intended to interview both candidates in the near future and ask them one or two apposite questions. He was at once dubbed 'Kingmaker' by the press, and the phones at his home and office never stopped ringing. Whatever their private thoughts, both Simon and Charles agreed to see Pimkin before he told his supporters how he intended to cast his vote.

Elizabeth sat alone at her desk willing herself to go through with it. She glanced down at the faded file that she had not looked at for so many years. She sipped the brandy from the tumbler by her side, both of which she had discovered in the medicine cabinet a few minutes before. All her years of training and commitment to the Hippocratic oath went against what she felt she must now do. While Simon had slept soundly she had lain awake considering the consequences, then made the final decision. Simon's career came first. She picked up the receiver, dialled the number and waited. She nearly replaced it at once when she heard his voice.

"730–9712. Charles Seymour speaking."

"It's Elizabeth Kerslake," she said, trying to sound confident. There was a long silence in which neither of them spoke.

Once Elizabeth had taken another sip of brandy she added, "Don't hang up, Mr Seymour, because I feel confident you'll be interested in what I have to say."

Charles still didn't speak.

"Having watched you from a distance over the years I am sure that your reaction to Carson's question in the Commons last week was not spontaneous."

Charles cleared his throat but still didn't speak.

"And if anything else happens this week that could cause my husband to lose the election, be assured I shall not sit by and watch."

There was still no reply.

"I have a file in front of me marked 'Miss Amanda Wallace', and if you wish all its contents to remain confidential I would advise you to avoid any repercussion of your antics. It's packed with names *Private Eye* would wallow in for months."

Charles said nothing.

Elizabeth's confidence was growing. "You needn't bother to inform me that such an action would get me struck off the medical register. That would be a small penalty for watching you have to suffer the way my husband has this week." She paused. "Good day, Mr Seymour."

Charles still didn't speak.

Elizabeth put the phone down and swallowed the remainder of the brandy. She prayed that she had sounded convincing because she knew she could never carry out such a threat.

Charles took Pimkin to dinner at White's – where Alec had always wanted to be a member – and was escorted to a private room on the first floor.

Charles didn't wait long to ask, "Why are you going through with this charade? Don't you realise I would have won it in the first round, if you hadn't stood?"

Pimkin bridled. "No doubt, but I haven't had so much fun in years."

"Who the hell got you your seat in the first place?"

"I well remember," said Pimkin. "And I also remember the price you exacted for it. But now it's my turn to call the tune, and this time I require something quite different."

"What are you hoping for? Chancellor of the Exchequer in my first administration?" said Charles, barely able to keep the sarcasm from his voice.

"No, no," said Pimkin, "I know my worth; I am not a complete fool."

"So what do you want? Membership of White's? Perhaps I could fix that."

"Nothing as mundane. In return for putting you into Downing Street I expect to be translated to the House of Lords."

Charles hesitated. He could always give Pimkin his word; and who other than Pimkin would notice if in three years' time he didn't carry it through?

"If you and your fifteen men vote for me next Tuesday I'll put you in the Lords," said Charles. "You have my word on it."

"Good," said Pimkin. "But one small thing, old chum," he added as he closely folded his napkin.

"Christ – what do you want now?" asked Charles, exasperated.

"Like you, I want the agreement in writing."

Charles hesitated again, but this time he knew he was beaten. "I agree," he said.

"Good, then it's a deal," said Pimkin. Looking round for a waiter he added, "I rather think champagne is called for."

When Pimkin put the same proposition two days later Simon Kerslake took some time before he answered. Then he said, "That's a question I would have to consider on its merits at the time, if and when I became Prime Minister."

"So bourgeois," said Pimkin as he left Simon's room. "I offer him the keys to No. 10 and he treats me like a locksmith."

Charles left the Commons that night having spent his time going round a large cross-section of his supporters, and he was reassured to discover they were standing firm. Wherever he went in the long Gothic corridors members singly or in groups came up to pledge their support. It was true that Kerslake's windfall of £300,000 was fast becoming yesterday's news, but Charles still felt enough blood had been let from that wound to ensure his final victory, even though he still cursed Pimkin for holding up the result. One anonymous note, with all the necessary details, sent to the right Labour member, had certainly proved most effective. Charles cursed as he realised Elizabeth Kerslake had successfully stopped any further covert attacks on his rival.

When he arrived home he was appalled to find Amanda waiting for him in the drawing-room.

"I thought I told you to stay away until the middle of next week?"

"I changed my mind, Charlie," said Amanda.

"Why?" he asked suspiciously.

"I think I've earned a little reward for being such a good girl."

"What do you have in mind?" he asked as he stood by the mantelpiece.

"Fair exchange."

"For what?"

"For the world rights to my life story."

"Your *what*?" said Charles in disbelief. "Who is going to be the slightest bit interested in you?"

"It's not me they're interested in, Charlie, it's you. The *News of the World* have offered me £100,000 for the unexpurgated story of life with Charles Seymour." She added dramatically, "Or what it's like to live with the second son of an earl who will go to any lengths to become Prime Minister."

"You can't be serious," said Charles.

"Deadly serious. I've made quite a few notes over the years. How you got rid of Derek Spencer but failed to pull the same trick on Clive Reynolds. The extremes you went to trying to keep Simon Kerslake out of the House. How your first wife swapped the famous Holbein picture of the first Earl of Bridgwater. But the story which will cause the most interest is the one in which the real father of young Harry Seymour is revealed because his dad's life story was serialised in the *People* a couple of years ago, and that seems to be one episode they missed out."

"You bitch. You know Harry is my son," said Charles, advancing towards her. But Amanda stood her ground.

"And perhaps I should include a chapter on how you assault your wife behind the closed doors of your peaceful Eaton Square mansion."

Charles came to a halt. "What's the deal?"

"I keep quiet for the rest of my life and you present me with £50,000 now and a further £50,000 when you become leader."

"You've gone mad."

"Not me, Charlie, I've always been sane. You see, I don't have a paranoia to work out on dear harmless brother Rupert. The *News of the World* will love that part now that he's the fifteenth Earl. I can just see the picture of him wearing his coronet and decked out in his ermine robes."

"They wouldn't print it."

"They would when they learn that he's as queer as a two-pound note, and therefore our only son will collect the earldom when he's not entitled to it."

"No one would believe it, and by the time they print the story it will be too late," said Charles.

"Not a bit," said Amanda. "I am assured by my agent that the true reason behind the resignation of the leader of the

Conservative party would be an even bigger scoop than that of a one-time contestant."

Charles sank down in the nearest armchair.

"Twenty-five thousand," he said.

"Fifty thousand," replied his wife. "It's only fair. After all, it's a double deal: no story to the press and you become leader of the Conservative party."

"All right," whispered Charles, rising to leave the room.

"Wait a minute, Charlie. Don't forget I've dealt with you in the past."

"What else are you hoping for?" said Charles, swinging round.

"Just the autograph of the next Tory leader," she replied producing a cheque.

"Where the hell did you get hold of that?" asked Charles, pointing to the slip of paper.

"From your cheque book," said Amanda innocently.

"Don't play games with me."

"From the top drawer of your desk."

Charles snatched it from her and nearly changed his mind. Then he thought of his brother in the House of Lords, his only son not inheriting the title and having to give up the leadership. He took out his pen and scribbled his name on the cheque before leaving his wife in the drawing-room holding £50,000. She was checking the date and the signature carefully.

Simon and Elizabeth spent a quiet weekend in their country cottage while the photographers pitched camp in Eaton Square. They had received a leak from an 'authoritative' source that Pimkin would come out in support of his old school chum.

"A brilliant move," said Elizabeth over breakfast on the Sunday morning admiring the picture on the front page of the *Observer*.

"Another photo of Seymour telling us what he will do when he's Prime Minister?" said Simon, not looking up from the *Sunday Times*.

"No," said Elizabeth, and passed her paper across the

table. Simon stared at the Holbein portrait of the first Earl of Bridgwater under the headline 'A gift to the nation'.

"Good God," said Simon. Are there no depths he will not sink to, to win this election?"

"My dear, by any standards you have delivered the *coup de grâce*," said Pimkin to Fiona over lunch that Sunday.

"I thought you would appreciate it," said Fiona, pouring him another glass of his own wine.

"I certainly did and I particularly enjoyed the director of the National Gallery's comments – 'that Charles's gesture of presenting the priceless painting to the nation was the act of a selfless man'."

"Of course, once the story had been leaked to the press Charles was left with no choice," said Alexander Dalglish.

"I realise that," said Pimkin, leaning back, "and I would have given a dozen bottles of my finest claret to have seen Charles's face the moment he realised the first Earl of Bridgwater had escaped his clutches for ever. If he had denied giving the earl to the nation the publicity that would have followed would have certainly ensured defeat in the election on Tuesday."

"Win or lose next week, he daren't then suggest it was all done without his approval," said Alexander.

"I love it, I love it," said Pimkin. "I am told that Princess Diana will be unveiling the portrait on behalf of the nation – and rest assured that when she performs the official ceremony, I shall be there to bear witness."

"Ah, but will Charles?" asked Fiona.

On Monday morning Charles's brother phoned from Somerset to ask why he had not been consulted about donating the Holbein to the nation.

"It was my picture to dispose of as I pleased," Charles reminded him and slammed down the phone.

By nine o'clock on Tuesday morning, when the voting took place for the last time, the two contestants had spoken to nearly every member twice. Charles joined his colleagues in

the Members' Dining-room for lunch while Simon took
Elizabeth to Locketts in Marsham Street. She showed him
some coloured brochures of a holiday on the Orient Express
which would be the most perfect way to see Venice. She
hoped that they wouldn't have time to go on the trip. Simon
hardly mentioned the vote that was simultaneously taking
place in the Commons but it never was far from either of their
minds.

The voting ended at three-fifty but once again the Chief
Whip did not remove the black box until four o'clock. By
four-fifteen he knew the winner but did not reveal his name
until the 1922 Committee had assembled at five o'clock. He
informed their chairman at one minute to five.

Once again, Sir Cranley Onslow stood on the small raised
platform in the committee room fourteen to declare the
result. There was no need to ask if the people at the back
could hear.

"Ladies and gentlemen," he said, his words echoing round
the room, "the result of the second ballot for the leadership of
the Tory Party is as follows:

> Charles Seymour   130
> Simon Kerslake   158."

Just over half the members present rose and cheered while
Bill Travers ran all the way to Simon's room to be the first to
report the news. When he arrived Simon swung round and
faced the open door.

"You look and sound as though you'd run a marathon."

"Like Pheidippides, I bring great news of victory."

"I hope that doesn't mean you're going to drop down
dead," said Simon, grinning.

The new leader of the Conservative party said nothing
more for a few moments. It was obvious that Pimkin had
come out in favour of him. Later that night, one or two other
members also admitted that they had changed their minds
during the second week because they hadn't liked the blatant
opportunism of Charles presenting a priceless portrait to the
nation only a few days before the final vote.

The following morning Fiona phoned Pimkin to ask him

why he had acted as he did. "My dear Fiona," he replied, "like Sidney Carton I considered it would be good to go to my grave knowing I had done one honourable thing in my life."

It took only a week for Simon's little house in Beaufort Street to be transformed. He could not as much as turn his head without facing a camera. Everywhere he went he was followed by a platoon of press men. He was surprised how quickly the experience became part of his daily routine, although Elizabeth never found it an edifying experience. She was, however, as booked up as Simon and once again they seemed only to meet in the evenings. He spent his first two weeks selecting the Shadow Cabinet he wanted to take into the next general election. He was able to announce the composition of his new team to the press fourteen days after his election as leader of the Conservative party. He made one sentimental appointment: that of Bill Travers as Shadow Minister of Agriculture.

When asked at a press conference why his defeated rival would not be serving in the team Simon explained that he had offered Charles Seymour the deputy leadership and any portfolio of his choice, but Charles had turned the offer down, saying he preferred to return to the back benches for the present time.

Charles had left for Scotland the same morning for a few days' rest by the river Spey, taking his son with him. Although he spent much of their short holiday feeling depressed about the final outcome of the leadership struggle, Harry's original efforts at fishing helped deaden some of the pain. Harry even ended up with the biggest fish.

Amanda, on the other hand, realising how slim her chances were of coaxing any more cash out of her husband, re-opened negotiations over her life story with the *News of the World*.

When Nick Lloyd, the editor, read through Amanda's notes he decided on two things. She would require a ghost writer and the paper would have to halve their original offer.

"Why?" demanded Amanda.

"Because we daren't print the better half of your story."

"Why not?"

"No one would believe it."

"But every word is true," she insisted.

"I'm not doubting the veracity of the facts," said Lloyd, "only readers' ability to swallow them."

"They accepted that a man climbed the walls of Buckingham Palace and found his way into the Queen's bedroom."

"Agreed," replied Lloyd, "but only after the Queen had confirmed the story. I'm not so sure that Charles Seymour will be quite as co-operative."

Amanda remained silent long enough for her agent to close the deal.

The watered-down version of 'My Life with Charles Seymour' appeared a few months later to coincide with Charles's much-publicised divorce, but it made no more than a faint ripple in political circles. Now that Charles had no prospect of leading his party it was very much yesterday's news.

Amanda came out of the divorce settlement with another £50,000 but lost custody of Harry, which was all Charles really cared about. He prayed her irresponsible remarks reported in the papers concerning the boy's claim to the title had been quickly forgotten.

Then Rupert phoned from Somerset and asked to see him privately.

A week later they sat facing each other in Charles's drawing-room at Eaton Square.

"I am sorry to broach such an embarrassing subject," said Rupert, "but I feel it is my duty to do so."

"Duty, poppycock," said Charles, stubbing out his cigarette. "I tell you Harry is my son, and as such will inherit the title. He's the spitting image of great-grandfather and that ought to be enough proof for anyone."

"In normal circumstances I would agree with you, but the recent publicity in the *News of the World* has been brought to my notice and I feel . . ."

"That sensationalist tabloid," said Charles sarcastically, his voice rising. "Surely you don't take their word before mine?"

"Certainly not," said Rupert, "but if Amanda is to be believed Harry is not your son."

"How am I meant to prove he is?" asked Charles, trying to control his temper. "I didn't keep a diary of the dates when I slept with my wife."

"But it seems Amanda did so I have had to take legal advice on the matter," continued Rupert, "and am informed that a blood test is all that will prove necessary to verify Harry's claim to the title. We both share a rare blood group as did our father and grandfather, and if Harry is of that group I shall never mention the subject again. If not, then the title will eventually be inherited by our second cousin in Australia."

"And if I don't agree to put my son through this ridiculous test?"

"Then the matter must be placed in the hands of our family solicitors," said Rupert, sounding unusually in control. "And they must take whatever course they consider fit."

CHAPTER
THIRTY THREE

Simon's first year as leader was one of unbounded energy and ideas which bore fruit as the Conservatives picked up three seats at by-elections and whittled away the Government's majority. The press were already predicting that the Socialists wouldn't be able to complete their full five-year term, which moved Simon to goad Central Office into a perpetual state of readiness for an election.

Raymond continued to gain respect at the Treasury as his policies began to show results. He had to cut back on some of the more ambitious projects as his gloomy predictions about American interest rates and the drop in the production of North Sea oil proved daily more accurate. After his second budget the financial press felt he had done all that was possible, given the world situation. When unemployment fell below two million and strikes to their lowest level since the Second World War some members hailed Raymond as the unions' Messiah, while others noted that he had been shrewd enough to steal some of the Opposition's co-inflation clothes in the absence of Charles Seymour.

As Raymond entered his third year as Chancellor the opinion polls showed the two main parties neck and neck again, with a surprising proportion of people saying that they would vote for the Alliance for the first time.

The Liberals still held sixteen seats in the Commons but, as in the past three elections, they had decided to fight under the collective banner as the Social Democrats during the general election campaign.

As the time for election drew near both small parties knew they would have to declare their choice for overall leader if a combination of Liberals and Social Democrats ever held the balance of power in Parliament. When the pollsters dug a little deeper it transpired that Andrew Fraser had become the most popular political leader in the country despite the fact he only led forty-two members in the Commons.

Andrew spent a lot of his time addressing meetings all over the country trying to convince the voters that at the next election the political balance would change. He said it so often he began to believe it himself, and two good by-election victories early in 1990 helped his supporters feel it was possible too. The press began to take such claims seriously when at the local election in May the Alliance captured 102 council seats at the expense of both the major parties.

"Daddy, Daddy, open my school report."

Charles left the morning mail unopened as he held Harry in his arms. He knew nothing could ever part them now but he dreaded Harry finding out that he might not be his real father.

"Please open it," pleaded Harry, wriggling free.

The school doctor had been asked to take a sample of Harry's blood along with six other boys from his form so that he would not consider the request unusual. Even the doctor hadn't been told the full significance of the action.

Harry extracted the envelope from the pile by Charles's side – the one with the school crest in the top left-hand corner – and held it out for his father to open. He looked excited and seemed hardly able to contain himself. Charles had promised he would phone his brother as soon as the result of the blood test was confirmed. He had wanted to phone the doctor a hundred times during the past week but had always stopped himself, knowing it would only add to the man's curiosity.

"Come on, Dad, read the report and you'll see it's true."

Charles tore open the letter and removed the little book which would reveal the result of all Harry's efforts during the term. He flicked through the pages – Latin, English, History, Geography, Art, Divinity, Games, Form master, Head-master. He reached the last page, a small yellow sheet headed: 'Term medical report'. It started: Harry Seymour, age eleven, height four feet nine inches – he's suddenly sprung up, thought Charles – weight five stone four pounds. He glanced up at Harry who looked as if he was about to burst.

"It is true, Dad, isn't it?"

Charles read on without answering the boy's question. At the foot of the page was a typewritten note signed by the school doctor. Charles read it twice before he understood its full significance and then a third time. "As requested I took a sample of Harry's blood and analysed it. The result shows that Harry shares a rare blood group . . ."

"Is it true, Dad?" asked Harry yet again.

"Yes, my son, it's true."

"I told you, Dad – I knew I'd be top in the class. That means I'll be captain of the school next term. Just like you."

"Just like me," said his father, as he picked up the phone by his side and began to dial his brother's number in Somerset.

When the Prime Minister went into hospital for a minor operation the press immediately started to speculate on his resignation. Ten days later when he walked out looking better than ever the rumours ceased immediately. In the Prime Minister's absence as deputy leader Raymond chaired Cabinet meetings and stood in for him during questions in the Commons. This gave the lobby correspondents a chance to proclaim, like Caesarian soothsayers plucking at entrails, that Raymond was *primus inter pares*.

Raymond enjoyed presiding over the Cabinet, but was surprised that the civil servants expected him to spend his entire Tuesday and Thursday mornings preparing for Prime Minister's questions.

Both Simon Kerslake and Andrew Fraser had gained formidable reputations during Prime Minister's questions, and Raymond found the fifteen-minute encounter more demanding than a full winding-up speech in a major debate;

in retrospect, he was relieved that he had prepared so thoroughly. The lobby correspondents seemed to be in agreement that Raymond had held his own on both occasions and that, if anything, Simon Kerslake had underestimated him.

The Prime Minister returned to Downing Street the following week and assured Raymond that the operation had been a success and the likelihood of any recurrence of the trouble was, in the surgeon's opinion, minimal. He admitted to Raymond that he hoped to lead the party to a second victory at the polls, by which time he would be within a few years of his seventieth birthday and ready to bow out quietly. He told Raymond bluntly that he hoped he would be his successor. But Raymond couldn't help remembering that Neil Kinnock was eight years younger than he was.

Raymond returned to the Treasury to prepare for what looked like his final budget before the general election. His stewardship had made it possible to loosen the reins slightly with an election in mind. He described the loosening to the Cabinet as no more than a percentage point or two; he had no intention, he assured them, of letting three years' hard work be sacrificed at the altar of vote-catching. Some of his colleagues round the Cabinet table wished he were not quite so unbending at times.

Whenever Raymond spoke around the country more and more people approached him about standing for the leadership. He always thanked them courteously but maintained his loyalty to the Prime Minister, which loyalty, he added, would remain constant until he chose to resign.

Simon and Andrew also spent every weekend in planes, cars or trains fulfilling speaking engagements right up until the party conferences in October.

Andrew, in his summing-up speech to the SDP conference at Weston-super-Mare, told the delegates that they should expect to hold the balance of power between the two major parties after the next election. For the first time, he told them, they would have the chance to participate in a national Government. He sent the delegates home warning them to prepare for an election within the coming twelve months, by which time they would be able to welcome SDP Members of

Parliament who would already be playing a major role in the running of the nation. Andrew's supporters left the West Country keyed up for battle.

The Labour party conference followed a week later at Brighton and Raymond delivered a keynote speech on the state of the nation's finances. He pressed the unions to continue supporting their Government by keeping the twin evils of inflation and unemployment at acceptable levels. "Let us not pass on three years of achievement to be squandered by a Conservative Government," he told the cheering delegates. "Brothers, I look forward to presenting five more Labour budgets that will make it impossible for the Tories to imagine a future victory at the polls."

Raymond received one of the rare standing ovations to be given to any Cabinet minister at a Labour party conference. The delegates had never doubted his ability, but over the years they had grown to respect his sincerity as well as his judgement.

Seven more days passed before Simon addressed the Tory faithful at the Conservative party conference in Blackpool. By tradition, the leader always receives a four-to-six-minute standing ovation after he completes his speech on the final day. "He'd still get four minutes," said Pimkin to a colleague, "if he read them *Das Kapital*."

Simon had spent six weeks preparing for the occasion since, like Andrew, he was convinced this would be the last conference before the election. He was pleasantly surprised to find Charles Seymour coming forward with new ideas on tax reform which he hoped might be considered for inclusion in the leader's speech to the conference.

Charles had recently been making useful contributions in the House during finance debates, and Simon hoped that it would not be long before he would be willing to return to the front bench. His main preoccupation in the House had been as a member of the Chairmen's Panel from which committee chairmen were recruited for each bill. Charles had mellowed considerably during his time on the back benches and many of his friends feared he had lost his ambition for high office and might not even stand at the next election. Simon hoped this wasn't the case as he desperately needed someone of Charles's ability to counter Raymond Gould at the Treasury. Simon included Charles's suggestions in the final draft of his speech and dropped him a handwritten note of thanks.

On that Friday morning in Blackpool, in front of 2,000 delegates and millions more watching on television, Simon presented a complete and detailed plan of what he hoped to achieve when the Conservatives were returned to Government.

"Power is what we want and *power* is what we seek," he told a mesmerised audience. "For without *power* we cannot serve."

After the peroration the delegates duly rose for a genuine six-minute ovation. When the noise had died down Pimkin was heard to remark, "I think I made the right decision."

The conference season over, members made their way back from the three seasides to Westminster. Sadness overcame the House in their first week back when the ageing Mr Speaker Weatherill suffered a minor heart attack and retired to the Lords. The Government's overall majority was only two at the time and the Labour party Chief Whip feared that if they supplied the new Speaker from their own ranks and the Conservatives were to retain the old Speaker's safe seat the Government majority would cease to exist.

Simon reluctantly agreed that the Speaker should come from his own benches and asked his Chief Whip to suggest a suitable candidate.

When Charles Seymour asked to be granted a private interview with the leader Simon agreed immediately.

Charles arrived at the Opposition leader's office the following morning. It was the first time they had talked alone since the leadership battle. A head of white hair had grown from the roots of Charles's once Odyssean locks, and the deeper lines in Charles's face gave him a more gentle look. Simon couldn't help noticing a slight stoop had replaced his ramrod bearing. Looking at them now no one would have suggested they were contemporaries. Charles's request came as a shock to Simon for he had never once considered his great rival as a candidate for that particular job.

"But I want you to return to the front bench and be my Chancellor," said Simon. "You must know I would be delighted to have you back in the team."

"That's considerate of you," said Charles. "But I would prefer the more restful life of being an arbitrator rather than an antagonist. I've lost that desire always to be on the attack. For over twenty years you've had the advantage of Elizabeth and two sons to keep your feet on the ground. It's only quite recently that Harry has done the same for me."

All men are thought to have one great moment in their careers in the House, and for Alec Pimkin it was to be that day. The election of a Speaker in the Commons is a quaint affair. By ancient tradition no one must appear to want the honour, and it is rare for more than one person to be proposed for the post. During Henry VI's reign three Speakers were beheaded within a year, although in modern times it has been more the heavy burden of duties that has often led to an early grave. This tradition of reluctance has carried on through the ages, and for that reason a future Speaker frequently does not know who has sponsored him. Dressed in a smart blue suit, sporting a red carnation and his favourite pink-spotted bow tie, Alec Pimkin rose from his seat on the back benches to move that 'the Right Honourable Charles Seymour does take the chair of this House as Speaker'. His speech was serious yet witty, informed but personal. Pimkin held the House in his grasp for nine minutes and never once let it go. "He's done his old friend proud," one member muttered to another across the gangway when Pimkin sat down, and indeed the look on Charles's face left no doubt that he felt the same way, whatever had taken place in the past.

After Charles had been seconded the tradition of dragging the Speaker-elect to the chair was observed. This normally humorous affair, usually greeted with hoots of laughter and cheering, became even more of a farce with the sight of the small, portly Pimkin and his Labour seconder dragging the six-foot-four former Guards' officer from the third row of the back benches all the way to the chair.

Charles surveyed the Commons from his new vantage point. He began by expressing his grateful thanks for the high honour the House had bestowed on him. From the moment he rose and stood his full height, every member knew they had selected the right man to guide them through the parliamentary calendar. The sharpness of his tongue may have gone but there remained a firm delivery and natural authority that left none of his colleagues in any doubt that Mr Speaker Seymour intended to keep 'order' for many years to come.

The Conservatives held the Croydon North-East seat comfortably at the by-election, and captured a marginal six weeks later. The press pointed out that it only needed the Tories and the SDP/Liberal Alliance to join together for the Government and Opposition to be in equal numbers, leaving the seventeen Irish members to decide the fate of the Parliament. Raymond was determined that the Government should hold on for another few weeks so that he could deliver his third budget, which he was convinced would act as a launching pad on which to fight the election.

Andrew had realised that Raymond's next budget might help Labour's chances at the polls, and he sought an official meeting with the leader of the Opposition to discuss the possibility of a 'no confidence' motion.

Simon agreed with Andrew's suggestion and thought that they should time the debate for the end of March. If they won that would ensure an election before the budget.

Raymond had accepted an invitation to address a large Labour rally in Cardiff the weekend before the vote of 'no confidence'. He boarded the train at Paddington, settled into his compartment and began to check over his speech. As the train pulled into Swindon a railway official stepped on board and, having discovered where the Chancellor of the Exchequer was seated, asked if he could speak to him privately for a few minutes. Raymond listened carefully to what the man had to say, replaced the speech in his brief case, got off the train, crossed the platform and returned by the first available train to London.

On the journey back he tried to work out all the consequences of the news he had just been told. As soon as he arrived at Paddington he made his way through the waiting photographers and journalists, answering no questions. A car took him straight to Westminster Hospital. Raymond was shown into a private room, to find the Prime Minister sitting upright in bed.

"Now don't panic," he said before Raymond could speak. "I'm in fine shape considering I'm over sixty and with all the pressure we've been under this last year."

"What's wrong with you?" asked Raymond, taking a chair next to the bed.

"Recurrence of the old trouble, only this time they say it will take major surgery. I'll be out of this place in a month, six weeks at the most, and then I'll live as long as Harold Macmillan, they tell me. Now, to more important matters. I want you to take over for me again, which will mean you will have to speak in my place during the 'no confidence' debate on Wednesday. If we lose the vote, I shall resign as leader."

Raymond tried to protest as he had already worked out the implications the moment he had heard his leader was ill again. The Prime Minister held up his hand and continued talking. "No party can fight an election with its leader laid up in bed for six weeks, however well he might be when they release him. If there is to be an election, the voters have the right to know who is going to lead the party in Parliament, and of course in such an emergency under standing order number five (four) of the Labour party's constitution," continued the Prime Minister, "the National Executive would meet and automatically select you to take over as party leader."

Raymond raised his head. "Yes. The importance of that particular standing order has already been pointed out to me."

The Prime Minister smiled. "Joyce, no doubt."

"Her name was Kate, actually."

The Prime Minister looked puzzled and then continued. "I think you must get used to the idea, Raymond, that you may well be running for Prime Minister in three weeks' time. Because if we lose the 'no confidence' vote on Wednesday I am given no choice but to advise the Queen to call an immediate general election."

Raymond remained silent.

"I can assure you," continued the Prime Minister, "the National Executive will not want an internal blood bath three weeks before a general election. Nothing could be more certain to guarantee a Tory victory. If, however, we do win the 'no confidence' vote then it's a different matter altogether because I'll be back and running the ship long before the Easter recess is over. That will give us enough time to call the election after you've delivered your third budget. So make sure you win on Wednesday."

"I am unable to express how much we will all miss your leadership," said Raymond, without guile.

"As every member of the House except the Irish will know which lobby they'll be voting in long before the debate begins, my leadership may turn out to be less important than any single vote. And don't forget it will be the first occasion at which they've allowed television on the floor of the Commons, so make sure Joyce picks out one of those smart shirts you sometimes wear."

Raymond spent the final few days before the 'no confidence' vote preparing his speech. He cancelled all the engagements in his diary except for the Speaker's dinner to celebrate the Queen's sixty-fifth birthday, at which he would be standing in for the Prime Minister.

The Government and Opposition Whips spent Monday and Tuesday checking that every member would be present in the House by ten o'clock on Wednesday night. The political journalists pointed out that, if the vote were a tie, Mr Speaker Seymour had already made it clear that he would abide by the ancient tradition of giving his casting vote to the Government of the day. Charles was armed with precedents from Speaker Addington in the eighteenth century to Speaker Denison in the nineteenth. Charles pointed out that, in line with the principle, he must vote in such a manner as not to make the decision of the chair final.

Simon was to open the debate for the Opposition while Andrew was being allowed to wind up, the only concession Simon had granted the SDP/Liberal Alliance for ensuring their support in the lobbies. Neil Kinnock was to open for the Government with Raymond winding up.

When Raymond read his speech out to Joyce on the Tuesday night the entire rehearsal took only twenty-four minutes, but he explained to her that with the noise and interruptions that would occur in the Chamber he would be on his feet the full thirty minutes. In fact he might have to cut short some lines on the night.

The following day members began arriving hours before the debate was due to begin. The Strangers' Gallery had been booked days in advance, with many senior ambassadors and even some Privy Councillors unable to be guaranteed a seat. The Press Gallery was filled and editors were sitting at the feet of their political journalists' desks. The Commons itself was like a stand at a cup final where twice as many tickets had been sold as there were seats. The only difference from a Budget Day was that the House was taken up with lighting equipment that had been tested a dozen times that morning.

Between two-thirty and three-thirty Mr Speaker Seymour had been unable to stop members chattering during questions to Mr Meacher, the Secretary of State for Education, but at three-thirty he duly shouted for "Order" and did not have to wait long for silence before calling: "The leader of the Opposition."

Simon rose from his place on the front bench to be greeted with cheers from his own side. He was momentarily surprised by the brightness of the arc lights which he had been assured he would hardly notice, but soon he was into his stride. Without a note in front of him he addressed the House for fifty minutes, tearing into the Government one moment, then switching to the policies he would implement the next. He ended his peroration by describing the Labour party as "the party of wasted opportunity" then added – jabbing his finger at Raymond – "but you will be replaced by a party of ideas and ideals."

He sat down to the cheers of his back-benchers who thought they had already won the vote – if not the next election as well. The noise continued for some time before Charles could bring the House back to order and call the next speaker.

Neil Kinnock had always revelled in his Welsh ancestry and had often been compared by older members to Aneurin Bevan. The *bête noire* of the Tories set in to the Opposition leader with a vengeance, expounding his beliefs and rousing his own side to cheers when he said that the Tories would be routed and would regret this no confidence 'trick' for a decade. "The Right Honourable Gentleman," he said, pointing at Simon, "has the nerve to call us the party of wasted opportunities. For the past two years it is he who has led the party of opportunists, and who will be the leader of the Opposition until it is time for him to be replaced." When Kinnock sat down the television producers couldn't be blamed for thinking that they were covering a lions *v* Christians slaughter. Again it took the Speaker several minutes to bring the House back to order.

The back-benchers also rose to the occasion with speeches from past ministers quoting precedent and from young turks demanding change, which helped confirm old and established new reputations. The House remained packed that night right up until nine o'clock when the Speaker called Andrew Fraser to wind up for the Opposition.

Andrew delivered a 'plague on both your houses' speech and shouted above the protests from the two main parties. "When the time comes you will both need to call on an honest broker." At nine-thirty when he resumed his seat Andrew was cheered as loudly as forty-two members in unison could manage.

When it came to Raymond's turn to wind up, members wondered how he would make himself heard above the noise that greeted him. He rose to the dispatch box and, looking grave, with head bowed, almost whispered his first words, "Mr Speaker, I know the whole House would wish me to open my speech by saying how sad we all are that the Prime Minister is unable to be present tonight. I am sure all Honourable members will want to join me in sending him, his wife and family our best wishes as he prepares for his operation."

Suddenly the House was silent and, having caught its mood Raymond raised his head and delivered for the eleventh time the speech he had prepared so assiduously. When he had seen Simon give his apparently impromptu speech Raymond had torn up his notes. He spelt out the achievements of the Government during the past two and a half years and assured the House that he was only half-way through his time as Chancellor. "I have not been able to achieve equality in three years, but of one thing I am certain: I look forward to delivering my next budget whatever the outcome of the vote tonight. We shall not see the opportunist Government of the Conservatives or the Alliance's so-called 'honest broker'. Indeed, looking at the Alliance I can say there is no one less honest and no one more broke. We, Mr Speaker, will see the return of a Labour Government for another full Parliament." Raymond sat down as the clock reached ten. He found, like the speakers before him, that he was drenched in sweat from the heat sent out by the powerful arc lights.

The Speaker rose and his first words were lost as he put the question:

"This House has no confidence in Her Majesty's Government. As many as are of that opinion say Aye, to the contrary, No. I think the Ayes have it."

"No," hollered back the voices from the Government benches.

"Clear the lobbies," called the Speaker above the cheers for Raymond Gould. Members departed to the lobbies to cast their votes. The Irish members surprised no one by dividing among themselves. Fourteen minutes later the tellers returned to a noisy Chamber to give the result of the division to the clerk at the table who then entered the figures on a division paper. The four tellers lined up and advanced towards the table from the bar of the House. They came to a halt and bowed for a third time. One of the Opposition Whips read out: "Ayes to the right 323, Noes to the left 322" and passed the piece of paper to the Speaker who tried to repeat it above the bedlam. Few members heard him say:

"The Ayes have it, the Ayes have it."

Raymond sat on the front bench and watched the delighted Tories bobbing up and down like children on a carousel. He reflected that if the Prime Minister had been present to register his vote the Government would have saved the day.

Her Majesty the Queen visited her Prime Minister in hospital twenty-four hours after his successful operation. He advised the monarch to dissolve Parliament immediately and asked that the general election be set for 9 May. He explained to the Queen that he intended to resign as leader of his party that morning and would relinquish the office of Prime Minister as soon as the outcome of the election was clear.

Before she left the Westminster Hospital the Queen spent some time discussing a private constitutional issue with the Prime Minister. He suggested that when the Labour party had confirmed their new leader he must be the man to offer her advice on such a personal matter.

The National Executive of the Labour party met behind the closed doors of Transport House in Smith Square at ten o'clock the following morning to select their new leader.

Three hours and twenty minutes later the committee issued a one-line press statement: "Mr Raymond Gould has been invited to lead the party at the forthcoming general election."

Although no one was in any doubt about the fierce arguments that must have taken place during the meeting the press were met by a unified voice once the committee finally broke up.

As Lord Broadstairs, the former Prime Minister, wrote in the centre page of the *Sunday Express* that weekend, "The Labour party in selecting their leader resembled nothing less than the old-fashioned magic circle of Lord Rosebery in their

determination to prove unity." The only leak he had managed to gather from the meeting was that Raymond Gould's acceptance speech had impressed every one present.

But Lord Broadstairs went on to point out that if the Labour party should lose the general election Raymond Gould could be the shortest serving leader in the Labour party's history, as under standing order five (four) of the constitution his appointment had to be confirmed by the delegates at the next party conference in October.

It had been two hours before Raymond was able to leave Transport House and escape the press. When he eventually got away he went straight to Westminster Hospital to visit the Prime Minister. The operation had visibly aged him. He was in good spirits, but admitted that he was glad not to be facing a gruelling election campaign. After he had congratulated Raymond on his new post he went on to say: "You're dining with the Queen tonight?"

"Yes, to celebrate her sixty-fifth birthday," said Raymond.

"There's more to it than that," said the Prime Minister gravely and he then revealed the private conversation that he had had with the monarch the previous day.

"And will her decision depend on the four people in that room?"

"I suspect it will."

"And what's your attitude?"

"That's no longer relevant because I shall resign as Prime Minister the day after the election, so it's more important the new Prime Minister considers what is best for the country."

For the first time Raymond felt like the leader of the party.

CHAPTER
THIRTY FOUR

Elizabeth straightened Simon's white tie and took a pace back to look at him.

"Well, at least you *look* like a Prime Minister," she said, smiling.

Her husband checked his watch. Still a few minutes to spare before he needed to be at the Speaker's private apartments – not that he was willing to risk being late for this particular birthday celebration. Elizabeth helped him on with his overcoat and after a search realised he had lost another pair of gloves.

"I do hope you can take care of the nation's belongings a little better than you do your own," she sighed.

"I'm sure I'll find it hard to lose a whole country," said Simon.

"Do remember that Raymond Gould will be trying to help you," said Elizabeth.

"Yes, that's true. I only wish I was fighting Kinnock."

"Why?" she asked.

"Because Gould was born into the wrong party," said Simon as he kissed his wife and walked towards the front door, "and a lot of the electorate have already reached the same conclusion."

The policeman on the gates of New Palace Yard saluted as Simon was driven into the courtyard and dropped at the Members' Entrance. He glanced at his watch again: ten minutes to spare. He never could resist checking how many people were in the Chamber or what the latest news was on the ticker-tape machine.

He put his head round the door of the smoking room. A few members were scattered around, mainly from safe seats they felt did not need nursing. Pimkin, surrounded by his usual cronies, hailed him. His face lit up when he saw Simon formally dressed. "I say, waiter, mine's a double gin and tonic." His companions duly laughed. Simon responded by asking the barman to give Mr Pimkin a large gin and tonic and to charge it to his account.

He spent a few minutes moving from group to group chatting to members about how the election might go in their constituencies. Pimkin assured Simon that the Tories would return in triumph. "I wish everyone was as confident as you are," Simon told him before leaving for the Speaker's private apartments as Pimkin ordered another gin.

He strolled along the library corridor, lined from floor to ceiling with venerable old journals of the House, until he reached the Speaker's office, which is the route members take to the Speaker's private rooms. When Simon reached the Grand Stairway dominated by Speaker Addington's portrait he was met by the Speaker's train-bearer clad in white tie and black tails.

"Good evening, Mr Kerslake," he said and led Simon down the corridor into the antechamber where a relaxed Charles Seymour stood ready to receive his guests. Charles shook Simon's hand warmly. Simon thought how well his colleague looked compared with their meeting of a few months before.

Andrew Fraser had already arrived and soon the three men were deep into a discussion about the course the election would take when another guest walked in.

"The Right Honourable Raymond Gould," announced the train-bearer. Charles went over to greet his guest.

"Many congratulations on your election as leader," were his first words. "You've had one hell of a week; you must be exhausted."

"Exhilarated, to be honest," replied Raymond.

He moved towards Simon, who in turn offered his congratulations. The two men shook hands and for a moment resembled medieval knights who had lowered their visors before the final joust. The unnatural silence that followed was broken by Andrew.

"Well, I hope it's going to be a clean fight," he said. Both men laughed.

The train-bearer came to the Speaker's side to inform him that Her Majesty had left Buckingham Palace a few moments earlier.

Charles excused himself while the three leaders continued their conversation.

"Has either of you been told the real reason why we are bidden here this evening?" asked Raymond.

"Isn't the Queen's sixty-fifth birthday enough?" said Simon.

"No, that's just an excuse for us to meet without suspicion. I think it might be helpful for you both to know that Her Majesty has a highly sensitive question to put to us."

Simon and Andrew listened as Raymond revealed the substance of his discussion with the Prime Minister.

Charles waited in the entrance of the courtyard of the Speaker's House to welcome the Queen.

It was only a few minutes before he spotted two police outriders entering the gates of New Palace Yard followed by the familiar maroon Rolls Royce, which displayed no numberplate. A tiny white light on the centre of the roof blinked in the evening dusk. As soon as the car had come to a halt a footman leaped down and opened the back door.

The Queen stepped out, to be greeted by the commoner history had judged to be the monarch's man. She was dressed in a simple cocktail dress. The only jewellery she wore was a string of pearls and a small diamond brooch. Charles bowed before shaking hands and taking his guest up the carpeted staircase to his private apartments. Her three party leaders stood in line waiting to greet her. She shook hands first with the new leader of the Labour party and congratulated him on his election that afternoon before enquiring how the Prime Minister was faring. Then she shook hands with her leader of the Opposition and asked how his wife was coping at Pucklebridge General Hospital after the new National

Health cutbacks. Simon was always amazed by how much
the Queen could recall from her past conversations, few of
which could ever last more than a few moments. She then
moved on to Andrew whom she teased about his father's
recent speech in Edinburgh on the Social Democrats' greatest
weakness being their lack of leadership.

"He's very old, ma'am," insisted Andrew.

"Not as old as Gladstone when he formed his last administration," she replied.

She removed the gin and tonic offered to her on a silver
tray and looked around the magnificent room. "My husband
and I are great admirers of the Gothic revival in architecture,
though being infrequent visitors to Westminster we are,
however, usually forced to view the better examples from
the outside of railway stations or from the inside of
cathedrals."

The four men smiled and a few minutes later Charles
suggested they adjourn to the State dining-room where five
places were set out round an oval table covered with silver
which glittered in the candlelight. The four men waited until
the Queen was seated at the head of the table.

Charles had placed Raymond on the Queen's right and
Simon on her left while he and Andrew filled the other two
places.

When the champagne was served Charles and his colleagues rose and toasted the Queen's health. She reminded
them that her birthday was not for another two weeks and
remarked that she had twenty-four official birthday engagements during the month, which didn't include the family's
private celebrations. "I would happily weaken but the
Queen Mother attended more functions for her ninetieth
birthday last year than I have planned for my sixty-fifth. I
can't imagine where she gets the energy."

"Perhaps she would like to take my place in the election
campaign," said Raymond.

"Don't suggest it," the Queen replied. "She would leap at
the opportunity without a second thought."

The chef had prepared a simple dinner of smoked salmon
followed by lamb in red wine and aspic. His only flamboyant

gesture was a birthday cake in the shape of a crown resting on a portcullis of sponge. No candles were evident.

After the meal had been cleared away and the cognac served the servants left them alone. The four men remained in a light mood until the Queen without warning put to them a delicate question that surprised only Charles. She waited for an answer.

No one spoke.

"Perhaps I should ask you first," said the Queen, turning to Raymond, "as you are standing in for the Prime Minister."

Raymond didn't hesitate. "I am in favour, ma'am," he said quietly.

She next turned to Simon.

"I would also support such a decision, Your Majesty," he replied.

"Thank you," said the Queen, and turned to Andrew.

"At heart I am a traditionalist, Your Majesty, but I confess to having given the subject a great deal of thought over the last few years and I have come round to supporting what I think is described as the 'modern approach'."

"Thank you," she repeated, her eyes finally resting on Charles Seymour.

"Against, ma'am," he said without hesitation, "but then I have never been a modern man."

"That is no bad thing in Mr Speaker," she said, and paused before adding: "Some years ago I asked a former Lord Chancellor to draw up the necessary papers. He assured me then that if none of my parliamentary leaders was against the principle the legislation could be carried through while both Houses were still in session."

"That is correct, ma'am," said Charles. "It would require two or three days at most if all the preparations have already been completed. It's only a matter of proclamation to both Houses of Parliament: your decision requires no vote."

"Excellent, Mr Speaker. Then the matter is settled."

BOOK SIX

1991

PRIME MINISTER

CHAPTER
THIRTY FIVE

Her Majesty's proclamation passed through the Lords and Commons without a division.

Once the initial shock had been absorbed by the nation the election campaign took over. The first polls gave the Tories a two-point lead. The press attributed this to the public's unfamiliarity with the new Labour leader, but by the end of the first week the Tories had slipped a point while the press had decided that Raymond Gould had begun his stewardship well.

"A week is a long time in politics," he quoted.

"And there are still two to go," Joyce reminded him.

The pundits put forward the theory that Raymond had increased his popularity during the first week because of the extra coverage he had received as the new leader of the Labour party. He warned the press department at Transport House that it might well be the shortest honeymoon on record, and they certainly couldn't expect him to be treated like a bridegroom for the entire three weeks. The first signs of a broken marriage came when the Department of Employment announced that inflation had taken an upturn for the first time in nine months.

"And who has been Chancellor for the last three years?" demanded Simon in that night's speech in Manchester.

Raymond tried to dismiss the figures as a one-off monthly hiccup but the next day Simon was insistent that there was more bad news just around the corner.

When the Department of Trade announced the worst deficit in the balance of payments for fourteen months Simon took on the mantle of a prophet and the Tories edged back into a healthy lead, but with the Social Democrats stealing a point from both of them.

"Honeymoon, broken marriage and divorce, all in a period of fourteen days," said Raymond wryly. "What can happen in the last seven?"

"Reconciliation, perhaps?" suggested Joyce.

During the campaign all three leaders managed to visit most of the one hundred marginal seats in which the outcome of any general election is decided. None of them could afford to spend too much time worrying about those 550 of the 650 seats that could not change hands without a swing of at least eight per cent.

Andrew was willing to make one exception to the eight per cent rule in the case of Alec Pimkin's seat in Littlehampton, which he had considered vulnerable for some time. The Social Democrats had selected an able young candidate who had nursed the constituency assiduously over the past three years and couldn't wait to take on Pimkin.

Alec Pimkin eventually made an appearance in Littlehampton – only after the local chairman had tracked him down to his London flat to say they were becoming desperate. The Alliance yellow lines were almost as abundant on the canvass returns as the Conservative blue ones, he warned.

"Don't you realise that I have had grave responsibilities in the Commons?" Pimkin declared. "No one could have anticipated that members would have been called back for a special declaration by the monarch."

"Everyone knows about that," said the chairman. "But the bill commanded by the Queen went through all its three readings last week without a division."

Pimkin inwardly cursed the day they allowed television into the House. "Don't fuss," he soothed. "Come the hour, cometh the man and the voters will remember that I have had a long and distinguished parliamentary career. Damn it, old thing, have you forgotten that I was a candidate for the leadership of the Tory party?"

No, and how many votes did you receive on that occasion, the chairman wanted to say, but he took a deep breath and repeated his urgent request that the member visit the constituency as soon as possible.

Pimkin arrived seven days before the election and, as in past campaigns, settled himself in the private bar of the Swan Arms – the only decent pub in the constituency, he assured those people who took the trouble to come over and seek his opinion.

"But the Alliance candidate has visited every pub in the division," wailed the chairman.

"More fool he. We can say that he's looking for any excuse for a pub crawl," said Pimkin, roaring with laughter.

From time to time Pimkin did stroll over to his local committee headquarters to find a few loyal workers, licking envelopes and folding election messages. On the one occasion on which he ventured into the high street he was appalled to discover Andrew Fraser standing on an upturned box extolling the virtues of the Alliance candidate to a large crowd. Pimkin wandered over to listen to what Andrew had to say and was not pleased to find that hardly anyone in the crowd recognised him.

"Humbug," said Pimkin at the top of his voice. Andrew waved back. "Littlehampton needs a member who lives in the constituency," declared Andrew genially, and went on with his speech. Pimkin turned to retreat to the warmth of the fireside at the Swan Arms. After all, as the landlord had assured him, put up a donkey with a blue ribbon as the Conservative candidate in Littlehampton and they would elect it. Pimkin had not been overwhelmed by the analogy.

With six days to go Andrew held a meeting with the Liberals to discuss tactics. The Alliance began to record over twenty-two per cent in some polls while the Labour and Conservative vote remained neck and neck with thirty-eight per cent each. Andrew's continual claim that he would hold the balance of power in the next Parliament was analysed seriously by the *Observer* and *Sunday Times* over the last weekend of the campaign, and few political pundits were now disagreeing with him. Both the BBC and ITV were already trying to book him for the first interview after the election. Andrew made no commitment.

He travelled up from Liverpool to Glasgow on the Monday before the election and then trekked across Scotland, pursued by a pack of journalists, until he reached Edinburgh on the Wednesday night.

The same evening Simon returned to Pucklebridge to deliver his last speech of the campaign in the local village hall. Four hundred and eighteen sat inside to hear his speech. Four thousand more stood outside in the cold listening to his words being relayed by loudspeaker. Simon's final message to his supporters all over the country was, "Be sure you go to the polls tomorrow. Every vote will be vital."

The statement turned out to be the most accurate any of the three leaders had made during the entire three-week campaign.

Raymond had returned to Leeds on the evening and was met on the platform of Leeds City station by the Lord Mayor and over half the Corporation. He was driven to the town hall to deliver his last appeal to the electorate before an audience of 2,000 people. Somehow he raised himself to give one more speech, and the cheers that greeted his arrival at the town hall made him forget he hadn't had more than four hours' sleep a night during the last month. Introducing the Labour leader the Mayor said, "Ray has come home."

Raymond stood up and delivered his speech as vigorously as if it were the opening day of the campaign. When he sat down forty minutes later he felt his legs give way. As soon as the hall was cleared Joyce and Fred Padgett took the exhausted candidate home. He fell asleep in the car on the way back so the two of them helped him upstairs, undressed him and let him sleep on until six the next morning.

All three leaders were up by six preparing for interviews on both breakfast television channels followed by the obligatory photo of each arriving at a polling station accompanied by his wife to cast their votes.

Andrew enjoyed being back in Edinburgh where for a few hours he was allowed to recall the days of recounts and catch up with the many old friends who had made it possible for him to remain in Parliament. Once again he ended up on the steps of the final polling station as the city hall clock struck ten. No Mrs Bloxham was there to remind him that she only voted for winners; she had died the previous year. Andrew, Louise and Clarissa walked back to the local SDP head-quarters arm in arm to join their supporters and watch the results as they came in on television.

Raymond and Joyce remained in Leeds overnight while Simon and Elizabeth returned to London to follow the outcome at Central Office in Smith Square. Raymond couldn't remember when he had last watched television for three hours without a break. The first result came from Guildford at eleven-twenty-one, and showed a two per cent swing to the Conservatives.

"Not enough," said Simon from the party chairman's room at Central Office.

"It may not be enough," said Raymond when the next two seats delivered their verdict, and the swing remained the same. The first shock came a few minutes after midnight when the Social Democrats captured the Labour seat of Rugby, and less than thirty minutes later followed it by taking Billericay from the Conservatives. When the first hundred seats had been declared the pundits were certain of only one thing: they were uncertain what the final outcome would be. Opinions, expert and amateur, were still fluid at one o'clock that morning, by which time 200 results were in, and remained so at two o'clock when over 300 constituencies had selected their member.

Raymond went to bed with a lead of 236–191 over Simon, knowing it would be offset by the county shires the next day. Andrew had gained four seats and lost one, to give the Alliance thirty-two seats overnight.

The next morning pundits were back on radio and televi-sion by six o'clock, all agreeing with the *Daily Mail*'s headline 'Stalemate'. Raymond and Joyce returned to London on the early morning train while the rural seats were proving their traditional loyalty to the Conservatives. Simon travelled down to Pucklebridge to acknowledge a record majority. He wished he could have sacrificed a couple of thousand for the marginals that weren't going his way. By twelve-thirty-three when Raymond had reached No. 11 Downing Street, the

Labour lead had fallen to 287–276 while the Alliance had captured forty-four seats.

At twelve o'clock that Friday morning, the cameras from all four channels swung over to Edinburgh where the Sheriff was declaring that Andrew Fraser had been returned to the House with a majority of over 7,000. The cameras moved on to show the victor, hands high above his head. The number on the SDP chart flicked up to forty-five. By one o'clock the Social Democrats had notched up their forty-sixth victory by a mere seventy-two votes, a result which saddened Simon.

"The House won't be quite the same without Alec Pimkin," he told Elizabeth.

At two-twenty-three that Friday afternoon both the major parties had 292 seats with only two safe Tory-held seats still to be declared. Simon retained the first but Andrew picked up the last after three re-counts.

At four o'clock Lord Day of Langham announced from the BBC studios the final result of the 1991 election:

Conservative	293
Labour	292
SDP/Liberal	47
Irish	17
Speaker	1

Lord Day went on to point out that the popular vote made the outcome even more finely balanced with Labour taking 12,246,341 (35.2 per cent), Conservatives 12,211,907 (35.1 per cent) and the Alliance 8,649,881 (25.4 per cent). He told viewers that he had never experienced a result like it in his thirty-six years as a political journalist. He apologised for his failure to get an interview with Andrew Fraser who now held the key as to who would form the next Government.

Andrew phoned Simon first, then Raymond. He listened intently to both men and what they were willing to offer before telling them that he intended to hold a meeting of his members in London on Sunday and relay their comments. He would report back with their decision in the hope that a Government could be formed by Monday.

Andrew and Louise flew down from Edinburgh on the

Saturday morning together with a planeload of journalists but by the time Andrew disappeared outside Terminal One into a waiting car the press had nothing new to report.

Sir Duncan had already told the *Scotsman* that his son would naturally back the Conservatives, while the former Prime Minister announced from his bedside that Andrew had always been a good Socialist at heart and would have nothing to do with the capitalist cause.

On the Saturday Andrew held several informal meetings in Pelham Crescent with senior members of the Alliance to ascertain the views of his colleagues, old and new. By the time he went to bed he still had no clear mandate and when a newscaster said no one was sure how the SDP/Liberal Alliance would vote the following day in their private meeting Andrew added out loud, "Me included." Even so he had decided after much deliberation on the qualities of the two men and what they stood for and that helped him make up his mind which party he thought should form the next Government.

At the Commons the next morning he and every other SDP and Liberal member had to run the gauntlet of journalists and photographers on the way to a closely guarded committee room on the third floor. The Whip had deliberately selected one of the less accessible rooms and had asked the Serjeant-at-Arms to be certain the recording machines were disconnected.

Andrew opened the meeting by congratulating his colleagues on their election to the House of Commons. "But it is important to remember," he continued, "that the nation will never forgive us if we are irresponsible with our new power. We cannot afford to say we will support one party, then change our minds after only a few weeks, causing another general election. We must be seen to be responsible. Or you can be sure that when the next election comes every one of us will forfeit our seats."

He went on to describe in detail how both the major party leaders had accepted the general direction in which he felt the new Government should be moving. He reported that they had both accepted that two members of the Alliance should have seats in the Cabinet. Both had also agreed to back a motion in the Commons for a referendum on proportional representation. For three hours the SDP/Liberal members gave their views, but by the end of that time Andrew was still unable to steer them to a consensus and had to call for a ballot. Andrew did not vote himself and left the SDP Liberal and Chief Whips to count the votes and announce the result.

Twenty-three votes each was the decision of his members.

The Chief Whip informed the parliamentary party that they would have to allow their elected leader to make the final decision. He, after all, was the biggest single reason they had been returned to the House in such relatively large numbers. After twenty-seven years in the Commons he must have the clearest view of which man and which party was most capable of governing the country.

When the Chief Whip sat down, the word "Agreed" came over clearly from the lips of the members sitting round the long table, and the meeting broke up.

Andrew returned to Pelham Crescent and told Louise which man he had decided to support. She seemed surprised. Later that night he left for a quiet dinner at the Atheneum with the sovereign's private secretary. The equerry returned to Buckingham Palace a little after eleven o'clock and briefed the monarch on the salient points of their discussion.

"Mr Fraser," the private secretary said, "is not in favour of another quick election and has made it quite clear which party the Social Democrats are willing to support in the Commons."

The monarch nodded thoughtfully, thanked his private secretary and retired to bed.

CHAPTER
THIRTY SIX

King Charles III made the final decision.

As Big Ben struck ten o'clock on that Saturday morning, a private secretary to the Royal household phoned the Right Honourable Simon Kerslake and asked if he would be kind enough to attend His Majesty at the palace.

Simon stepped out of the Conservative party headquarters on the corner of Smith Square and into the clear morning sunlight to be greeted by crowds of wellwishers, television cameras and journalists. He only smiled and waved as this was not the occasion to make a statement. He slipped quickly through the police cordon and into the back of his black Rover. Motor cycle outriders guided the chauffeur-driven car through the dense crowds slowly past Transport House. Simon wondered what would be going through Raymond Gould's mind at that moment as he considered the decision Andrew Fraser must have made.

The chauffeur drove on to Millbank past the House of Commons, round Parliament Square and left into Birdcage Walk before reaching the Mall.

Scotland Yard had been briefed as to which party leader had been called to see the King and the car never stopped once on its journey to the palace.

The chauffeur then swung into the Mall and Buckingham Palace loomed in front of Simon's eyes. At every junction a policeman held up the traffic and then saluted. Suddenly it was all worthwhile: Simon went back over the years and then considered the future. His first thoughts were of Elizabeth and the children. How he wished they could be with him now. He recalled his selection at Coventry, the loss of his seat and the continual rejections before Pucklebridge. The financial crisis, the resignation letter that Archie Millburn had promised to return the day he became Prime Minister. The Irish Charter, *Broadsword*, and his final battle with Charles Seymour.

The Rover reached the end of the Mall and circled the statue of Queen Victoria before arriving at the vast wrought-iron gates outside Buckingham Palace. A sentry in the scarlet uniform of the Grenadier Guards presented arms. The huge crowds that had been waiting round the gates from the early hours craned their necks in an effort to see who had been chosen to lead them. Simon smiled and waved. In response some of them waved back and cheered more loudly while others looked sulky and downcast.

The Rover continued on its way past the sentry and across the courtyard through the archway and into the quadrangle before coming to a halt on the gravel by a side entrance. Simon stepped out of the car to be met by the King's private secretary. The silent equerry led Simon up a semicircular staircase, past the Alan Ramsey portrait of George III and down a long corridor before entering the audience chamber. He bowed and left Simon alone with his new sovereign.

Simon could feel his pulse quicken as he took three paces forward, bowed and waited for the King to speak.

The forty-three-year-old monarch showed no sign of nervousness in carrying out his first official duty, despite its unusual delicacy.

"Mr Kerslake," he began, "I wanted to see you first as I thought it would be courteous to explain to you in detail why I shall be inviting Mr Raymond Gould to be my first Prime Minister."

The End